THE FURYCK SAGA

WINTER'S FURY

THE BURNING SEA

NIGHT OF THE SHADOW MOON

HALLOW WOOD

THE RAVEN'S WARNING

VALE OF THE GODS

KINGS OF FATE
A Prequel Novella

THE LORDS OF ALEKKA

EYE OF THE WOLF

MARK OF THE HUNTER

BLOOD OF THE RAVEN

HEART OF THE KING

Sign up to my newsletter, so you don't miss out
on new release information!

http://www.aerayne.com/sign-up

MARK

· OF THE

HUNTER

THE LORDS OF ALEKKA : BOOK TWO

A.E. RAYNE

For more information about A.E. Rayne
and her upcoming books visit:

www.aerayne.com

www.facebook.com/aerayne

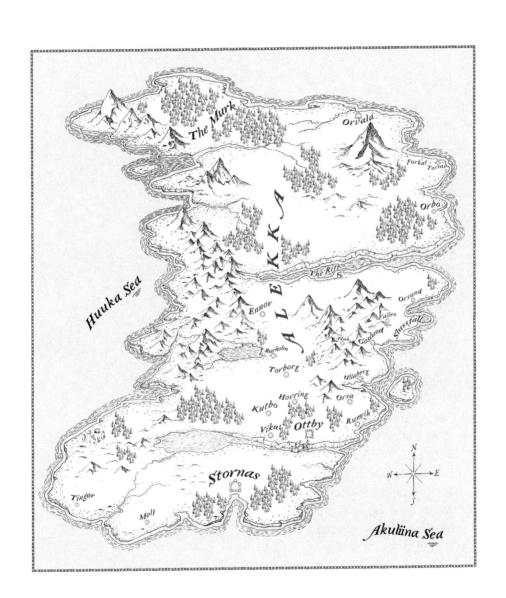

The Murk

Orvala

Furkat
Torsa

Orbo

Huuka Sea

A L E K K A

The Rift

Orsund

Ennor

Vallen

Arnon

Goslung

Slassfall

L. Burholm

Torborg

Ullaberg

Hovring

Orsa

Kutbo

Rumvik

Vikat

Ottby

Stornas

N

W   E

S

Tingor

Moll

Akulüna Sea

CHARACTERS

In the Forest
Alys de Sant, 28, (pronounced Alice)
Stina Arnborg, 38, *Alys' best friend*
Eddeth Nagel, 57, *healer*
Lotta de Sant, 8, *Alys' daughter*
Ulrick Dyre, 53, *Hakon's scout*

In Ottby
Lord Reinar Vilander, 32, (pronounced Ray-nar)
Sigurd Vilander, 29, *his brother*
Stellan Vilander, 63, *their father*
Gerda Vilander, 57, *their mother*
King Ake Bluefinn, 57, (pronounced Ak-ee)
Algeir Tarkel, 48, *head of Stornas' garrison*
Agnette Sansgard, 29, *Reinar & Sigurd's cousin*
Bjarni Sansgard, *Agnette's husband/Reinar's best friend*
Ludo Moller, 25, *fostered to the Vilanders/Sigurd's best friend*
Berger Eivin, 31, *warrior*
Ilene Gislar, 25, *the husband thief*
Bolli Ollsfar, 65, *helmsman*
Holgar Agmund, 62, *helmsman*
Torfinn Bellig, 28, *Sigurd & Ludo's friend*
Rilda, *the cook*
Martyn, *Stellan's steward*
Rienne and Matti, *Gerda's servants*

CHARACTERS

Escaping Ottby
Lord Hakon Vettel, 23 (pronounced Hay-kon)
Ivan Vettel, 23, *Hakon's cousin*
Lief Gundersen, 44, *Falla's husband/Hakon's champion*
Falla Gundersen, 34, *Lief's wife*
Rikkard Varnass, 17, *Hakon's steward*
Jerrick and Njall, *Hakon's men*
Lord Erlan Stari, 27, *formerly of Hovring*
Lord Alef Olstein, 31, *formerly of Vika*

In Slussfall
Jonas Bergstrom, 69, *Alys' grandfather*
Vik Lofgren, 59, *Jonas' best friend*
Magnus de Sant, 10, *Alys' son*
Karolina Vettel, 22, *Hakon's wife*
Bergit Dyre, 46, *Ulrick's wife*
Leonid Grubert, 19, *silversmith*
Ollo Narp, 55, *master of the square*
Haegel Hedvik, 51, *Ollo's loyal off-sider*
Baldur Skoggi, 50, *head of the garrison*
Aldo Varnass, 15, *kitchen helper*
Anders Vettel, infant, *Hakon & Karolina's son*
Borg Arnesson, 2, *Falla's son with her second husband*

PROLOGUE

'And you won't raise her? Bring her back?'

They stood in the tent, eyes on the frozen body of the dead dreamer.

'You think I should reward *failure*?' Alari spat, turning to her sister, Vasa, who towered over her like a tall tree. 'She's dead for a reason.'

'She's dead because of Valera!' Vasa was angry. 'That bitch is always interfering, and now the Vettels are running away like frightened children from a fight they were destined to win. A dead dreamer can't help them or us!'

'You think I had just the *one* dreamer, Sister?' Alari laughed. 'That the Goddess of Magic had only one old woman to assist her?' She was just as angry as Vasa, but her fury smouldered like embers. 'Though after what happened, why should I trust any of them to do what needs to be done? We must fight against Thenor himself now. Thenor and his pet dog, Ake Bluefinn.' She turned, slipping out of the tent, black cloak sweeping behind her, long white braid hanging down her back. Alari had been beautiful in her youth, until her father, Thenor, had punished her insolence, taking her right eye, hoping to dilute her power. Though the loss of her eye had done nothing to diminish Alari's anger, nor her desire for vengeance.

Vasa followed her sister, an angular, gaunt figure with sunken eyes and skin as dark as the depths of her famous cave. She had no hair, just a shining ebony head. Her cloak was made of raven's wings, and it shimmered darkly as she walked.

The sisters emerged into the abandoned campsite, littered with snow-covered corpses, weapons, supplies; all of it abandoned in the Vettel army's retreat.

'We must fight against Thenor,' Vasa agreed, stroking one the two ravens that perched on her shoulders, both of them cawing loudly, seeking her attention. 'So it is time to choose whether to keep seeking victory here or abandon the field altogether.'

'Meaning?'

'There are other contenders, Sister. Others who may stand a far greater chance of taking Stornas, of claiming Alekka.'

Alari's eye sparked with indignation. 'You think I would abandon the Vettels? But they are my blood! I gave birth to their line. They may choose to claim Thenor if it makes them feel like mighty warriors, but I know the truth, and so does he. I cannot abandon that which is mine. I won't.'

Vasa was bored. Impatient to leave the revolting place.

It reeked of failure.

'No, we have a clear path ahead of us now.' Alari could see it in her mind; dark with night, shot with moonbeams. 'A path back to power, here, in the South. And once the Vettels rule in Stornas again, there'll be nothing to stand in my way.' She felt Vasa stiffen. '*Our* way.' And smiling now, she headed for their horses, one white, one black, both of them shadow spirits. 'Mother Arnesson was a greedy, self-centred witch. I should never have relied on her to do what I'm perfectly capable of doing myself.'

Vasa smiled, knowing exactly what Alari was capable of. 'Well, then, Sister, let us begin.'

PART ONE

The Forest

CHAPTER ONE

Some things were undeniable.

The feel of Reinar's lips.

The look in his eyes as he bent his head, leaning in close, his cold hand brushing hair away from her face...

Alys rolled over, sensing movement, but not wanting to let go of her dream.

It wasn't the dream she needed to be having. It didn't tell her where her grandfather was. It didn't show her how to find Magnus and Lotta. It wasn't a dream that warned of danger lurking.

It was a dream of longing.

Pointless, hopeless, soul-crushing longing.

Eddeth sneezed, and Alys opened her eyes, blinking, clouds of breath smoke hovering above her face. She stared up at the trees, gnarled branches fighting each other in the chill breeze. The ground was thick with snow, wet, soaking into her back.

She hadn't felt her toes since they'd left Ottby two days ago.

Stina was talking to Eddeth as they wrapped bed furs around their shoulders and set about organising breakfast. The horses shuffled around, nickering softly in the distance, looking for something to eat, and soon they would be on the road again, trying to find Jonas and the children.

Alys closed her eyes, seeing Reinar's face, feeling his lips pressing against hers, then stopping, lingering, waiting.

Why hadn't she kissed him back?

Eddeth shook her shoulder. 'Are you unwell, Alys? Is something wrong? You have a very odd look on your face. Could be that stew. My belly's been griping all night long. Oh, the smell! Reminded me of my second husband. I had to make him sleep outside many a night, snow or not!'

Alys opened her eyes, surprised once again, to find Eddeth leaning over her, noses almost touching. 'I...' She edged away, wanting to get up, out of the snow. Stina had worked quickly to bring their fire back to life, and Alys could hear the flames crackling invitingly nearby. 'No, I feel fine.'

Eddeth continued to peer at her, picking her wart as Alys slid away, wrapping her frosty fur around her shoulders, heading for the fire. 'Fine?' she muttered. 'I don't think so, dreamer.' Alys was too far away to hear her, Eddeth was sure, but in the next breath, she spun around, staring at her, a sad look in her eyes.

And after holding Eddeth's gaze for a moment, Alys turned away.

***

Reinar sat on the bed, ready to head outside. There was so much to do, so much waiting for him beyond his chamber door. He could hear the murmur of activity in the hall growing louder, knowing that his mother was likely rushing around, fussing over Ake, struggling without Agnette.

Sighing, he stared down at the scrap of vellum in his hand.

Alys had left it for him, with the green dress.

He'd slept with it for two nights, slipped under his pillow, trying to decide what to do. But what could he do? The fort was broken, devastated by Hakon Vettel's attack. The king was still in Ottby, making plans for what would come next. More pyres needed to be built. His brother was still missing, grieving Tulia.

What could he do?

'Reinar?'

Agnette popped her head around the door, smiling.

He was surprised to see her, but pleased, for she carried her newborn daughter in her arms. Liara. A pretty name for a squawking baby, he thought with a sigh. 'I'm coming. Just needed a moment.'

Agnette sat down beside him, wincing, still uncomfortable after Liara's birth, which had been both terrifying and draining. 'Gerda's already high-pitched out there.' She leaned the baby towards her cousin. 'This one doesn't seem to mind it, though.'

Reinar peered at the baby, her eyes closed, lying so peacefully in Agnette's arms. He tried not to think of his own sons, though it was impossible not to. Looking away, he rubbed his eyes. 'Well, I expect she'll only get worse. It's still early.'

'What's that?' Agnette wondered, inclining her head to the vellum.

'Alys...' It felt strange to say her name out loud. 'Alys left it.' And opening up the note, Reinar showed Agnette.

'Oh.' She stared at her cousin, seeing the pain in his tired eyes. 'What will you do?'

Reinar turned to her. 'What should I do?' He looked back down at the vellum, which read: *Reinar, I dreamed of your wife. She is alive and well in Lundvik.*

Agnette sensed that her daughter was growing restless. Liara's little face had turned from pink to red, her forehead furrowed as she started wriggling, trying to escape her swaddling cloths. 'You have a lot to do here. I'm not sure you can leave Ottby. Not now. And there's Sigurd. We need to know if he's alright.' She shook her head, tears in her eyes. 'Poor Sigurd, of course he's not alright. He loved Tulia. I know he loved her, no matter how many problems they had.'

Reinar nodded.

'And Ake wants the fort repaired, and he has plans for Hovring and Vika, that's what Bjarni said. He won't stomach their treachery for long.'

Reinar nodded.

'Not to mention Hakon Vettel. He's still out there somewhere, isn't he? So, I don't know what to advise. Elin wasn't right before she left. Though in truth, I don't think she was right for a long time.' Agnette's voice faded away, knowing Reinar didn't like to hear that sort of talk about his wife.

'I need to tell her about Torvig.'

Agnette could see it in his eyes: that desperation to know the truth; to hear from Elin herself why she'd left him. He would never be able to move on until he heard it from her lips. And feeling decisive, Agnette stood. 'You should go, then. Go to Lundvik. Ake will be gone tomorrow. Leave Bjarni in charge of the fort, and go. Find Elin. Talk to her. Tell her about her brother. Things will be clearer for you then.'

Liara burst into tears, mouth open, and Agnette lifted her up to her shoulder, kissing her head. 'I think someone's hungry. Someone besides Bjarni!' She grinned at her cousin. 'You'll know what to do, Reinar. When you see Elin, you'll know what to do.'

Reinar watched her go, eyes drifting to the green dress, still draped over the end of the bed. He reached out a hand, touching it, knowing he should pack it away.

Elin's dress.

But when he saw it now, he no longer thought of Elin.

***

'Did you hear those wolves last night?' Eddeth called from the trees. She was on her hands and knees, collecting mushrooms.

Stina was packing her saddlebags. 'Wolves?' Her eyes darted to Alys, who shrugged as she wrapped Tulia's swordbelt around the waist of her faded green dress. 'I didn't hear any wolves, Eddeth. Perhaps you were having a dream?' Though she was quickly scanning the forest, ears open. She could hear the soothing babble of the mist-touched stream, the industrious chirping of the birds out searching for breakfast.

No wolves.

'Or perhaps it was that old dreamer you killed, wanting her revenge?' Eddeth emerged from behind a tree, carrying a mound of mushrooms in the hem of her tunic. She wiped a dirty hand down her dead husband's trousers, grinning.

'Do you think that's possible?' Alys wondered, feeding Eddeth's horse, Wilf, a half-frozen carrot. He was an old muddy-brown stallion, small in stature and flighty in temperament, though always in a much calmer state when he was well fed. There wasn't much for the horses to eat in their snow-blanketed campsite, and she wanted to give them all a little energy for the day. They had brought along small sacks of barley and oats to supplement what the horses could dig up themselves, though if Wilf had his way, it wouldn't last long.

'Oh yes, evil spirits are always lurking in the shadows, especially in the dark depths of the forest!' Eddeth announced gleefully, pleased to see that the water was boiling in the tiny cauldron she'd brought along. Depositing her mushrooms onto the ground, she set about organising cups. 'Who knows what we might meet on our travels? Or who!'

'Who?' Alys joined her by the fire, crouching down, warming her hands over the flames.

'Well, after what you did in Ottby? Killing the old bat like that? With Valera's help? I imagine the gods are watching. Following us, even. Valera knew you!' Using the cloth tucked into her trousers, Eddeth lifted the cauldron off its hook, pouring boiling water into three wooden cups. 'She was waiting for you to come to her, that's what she said, so those gods are certainly watching us now, waiting to see what will happen next! Or perhaps, not waiting at all...'

Stina's eyes were heavy. The night had been cold, and her dreams had tortured her. She couldn't escape the nightmares of Torvig and Tulia and what had happened in the shed. The relief of knowing that Torvig was dead could not erase the pain of what he had done to her. It was a wound that burned and stung, and Stina knew that no salve or tea would give her any relief.

There was no cure, but time.

'Don't drink yet!' Eddeth warned, handing Stina a cup of licorice and lavender tea. 'But do inhale! The aroma is powerful. Oh yes, just smell those ancient herbs! They will calm your mind and soothe your ragged spirit!'

Stina eyed her doubtfully, watching as Eddeth twitched, hopping around the fire, the least calm person she'd ever met, despite the amount of herbs she brewed in her teas.

Alys turned her head, Eddeth's voice disappearing in the distance. She stared into the trees, trying to remember if she'd seen anything else in her dreams.

It was unhelpful to dream of Reinar.

Pointless.

Dreaming of Reinar and Ottby would not help them decide where to go next.

Alys' heart ached, knowing that Magnus and Lotta were so far away. She needed to feel them against her, holding them close, smelling their hair, knowing they were safe with her.

'Alys?'

Blinking, Alys turned around, eyes on Eddeth, who had shoved her fur hat over her wild grey hair and was back on her hands and knees, sorting out her mushrooms. 'Where will we be heading this morning, then? What did you see for us?'

Alys' eyes skipped to Stina, who was braiding her long dark hair, looking her way. She didn't know what to say. She'd seen nothing.

Nothing of her children at all. Not since leaving Ottby behind.

Not since her last glimpse of Lotta riding through the forest with that man.

Everything she so desperately sought to know was shrouded in darkness.

'I...' Alys stood with a shrug. 'We must continue on to Slussfall, I...' She stopped, spinning around. 'Did you hear that?'

Eddeth froze, mushrooms in hand, eyes jumping. She'd heard something too.

Alys' right hand flexed above the hilt of Tulia's sword, poking out of its scabbard as she glanced around. Shivers ran up her spine, down her arms as she edged towards Eddeth, whose body remained oddly still, eyes fixed on the trees on the opposite side of the stream. Stripped of their leaves by the coming winter, they were a maze of spindly grey trunks and branches snarled together. It was almost impossible to see through them, but Alys thought she saw something move.

'What is it?' Stina hissed, abandoning her braid and creeping around the fire towards Eddeth. 'A bear?'

Eddeth didn't answer. Her eyes were on the dreamer, knowing that she'd felt it too.

Something was out there.

Watching them.

***

Ake Bluefinn was the King of Alekka.

The southern half.

Two thousand years ago, the gods had broken Alekka in two, wrenching the North from the South, determined that no one man or woman would ever wield ultimate power over the land again.

There had been high kings for thousands of years before that. High kings of malice and cruelty, who wielded their power as soulless tyrants, crushing those who displeased them, who did not bend and break and give their lives in service of them and their allies. They were vengeful and capricious men, motivated by greed, indulgent of every whim and vanity.

Murderous.

Ruling from their great towers in Orvala in the North, they had worshipped Eutresia, Goddess of the Sun, sacrificing their people and their livestock to their golden patron. And she had bestowed upon them her favour, granting them fertile land of bounteous wealth, warmed by the sun. The winters were cold, the summers bright. The land was rich and moist and nurturing of its crops.

In her eyes, the kings were righteous and worthy of her loyalty. They adored her, and their sacrifices pleased her, so she was happy to watch them rule with iron fists and empty hearts.

The rest of the gods were not...

Ake smiled at Reinar, who was scowling as he stomped across the square in his black bear-fur cloak, barking orders. Snow was falling again, and Reinar's hands were red with cold, pointing his men and women to work. The snow didn't matter. What mattered was that they had gates off their hinges, ramparts in need of repair, cottages burned, pyres to build, weapons' stores to replenish, and a king who had warned them of a coming war greater than any they'd faced in their lifetimes.

And yet, despite all of that, Ake smiled, because it was good to have loyal men on his side. Men like Reinar and Sigurd Vilander, who had kept Ottby safe until he arrived, stopping Hakon Vettel before he could claim the valuable fortress. Ake frowned, realising that if he had dealt with the Vettels before now, they wouldn't have been roaming the Eastern Shore causing problems for them all.

A king always had problems, his dreamer liked to remind him, but none greater than the ones he made for himself.

'Any sign of that brother of yours?' Ake wondered as Reinar approached. He glanced up at the sky, conscious of the snow clouds, which appeared to be dropping lower, thickening with intent. 'Not the sort of weather to be lost out in the wild.'

'No, it's not. I've sent Ludo after him, though I doubt he's gone far.' Reinar felt worried. It wasn't like Sigurd to just disappear, though the shock of Tulia's death had tipped his life upside down, and Reinar didn't blame him for wanting to run away. 'He just needs some time.'

Ake nodded. 'Well, while the snow blows and the Vettels make their way back to Slussfall, there'll be time. Time for us to start again. If we can't keep Ottby safe, Stornas may as well open its gates and welcome all our enemies in.' It was only partly true. The bridge Ottby guarded led to Alekka's capital, but it was not the only way into the walled city. Though anyone attempting to scale the mountain ranges that led from the North into Ennor was going to have a terrible time of it, especially in winter. And the Huuka Sea was freezing fast, making any attack by ships less likely.

And yet...

Reinar stared at his king, who, despite his increasing troubles and the weight of the crown upon his head, still had a twinkle in his dark-blue eyes. He felt both affection for him and fear of him, and most of all, the worry that he would let him down. 'We'll secure Ottby as quickly as we can, though the damage to the walls was extensive in places. And the gates...' He saw Bjarni out of the corner of his eye, arguing with Bolli. They were almost the same height and shape, arms flailing, faces red with irritation, and Reinar smiled, pleased that they'd both survived the battle.

'Mmmm, so I saw. Though once the gates are back on, the walls will hold. I have some ideas about how we can reinforce the new gates further. More beams will help. And eventually, perhaps another wall too?'

'Another wall?'

'Why not? We can make our enemies go through three sets of gates. Give them some climbing practice! Exhaust them before they get anywhere near the square!'

Reinar laughed. 'I'm going to need a lot more men if you want another wall, my lord.'

'You are, Reinar, and you'll find them. Once they hear about the curse being lifted, about your luck changing, men will return. They will, and quickly too. They'll want to fight for the Lord of Ottby when he defeats the Vettels.' Ake clapped him on the shoulder, remembering too late that Reinar had dislocated it. 'I must be getting old,' he cringed, 'forgetting about that.'

'It's fine,' Reinar lied, shutting away the throbbing pain.

Ake glanced around, eyes on the singed branches of Valera's Tree, which stood to one side of the square, snow-dusted now, and he walked Reinar towards it, wanting some privacy. 'We need to end Hakon Vettel and his idiot cousin quickly. Once you're secure here, I want you to go North and finish them.'

Reinar nodded; there were few things he wanted more.

'You'll have the men you need, I assure you of that. Algeir will take care of Hovring and Vika before he returns to Stornas. He'll install new lords, and once you've taken Slussfall, we'll find someone to command that fort too.'

'I still can't believe Alef and Erlan went in with the Vettels. They're not the men their fathers were. To have broken that quickly?' Reinar shook his head, having known both men since they were boys. They had never been close friends, but their arrogance and stupidity had surprised him.

'No, though greed has a way of corrupting a man's soul. Or perhaps, it merely reveals it? But in any case, Reinar, we need to talk about the Vettels.' Ake stepped closer, watching flurries twirling down around the tree, feeling enclosed beneath its ponderous branches. 'About what you'll need to do.'

'Do?'

'I want you to kill Hakon and his cousin. But once that's done, you'll have to kill Hakon's son too.'

'What?' Reinar looked horrified.

Ake knew how he felt. He'd been faced with the same decision twenty years ago, yet he hadn't been able to go through with it. Another mistake coming back to bite him, he thought, scratching his stubbly cheek. 'We can't leave any Vettels alive. Not one. If you can't stomach it, find someone who can, someone you trust. The boy is young, not a year old, from what I hear. It won't be easy, doing a thing like that.'

Reinar was speechless, never having imagined those words coming from his king's mouth.

'It's not something I wish to order, trust me, but while there is Vettel blood in Alekka, our land stands no chance of being free. We must remove every threat to peace if we wish to protect our people. And for now, the Vettels are the most immediate threat we face. We have to eradicate them once and for all. Every last one of them.' Ake felt odd, staring at Reinar. 'I know what Ragnahild foretold about your destiny. Perhaps one day that will come to pass, and you'll become the high king somehow? Perhaps my end is near, and you will rule in Stornas...' He ran a hand over his hair, brushing off traces of snow. 'If that ever happens, then take this lesson from me, please, Reinar. Kill your enemies. Crush them. End them. Never leave a loose thread, not a single one, for there is nothing more motivating to a man than a desire for vengeance.'

Reinar waited, certain there was more Ake wanted to say, but the king merely grunted, turning away, uncomfortable with the conversation.

He walked to the edge of the tree's branches, stopping, glancing over his shoulder. 'Don't run from this, Reinar. I demand it of you, as I would demand it of your father if he still commanded this old fortress. I trusted him, put my faith in him, and now, I put it in you.' And turning back around, Ake headed into the square, slipping his hands inside his cloak.

Reinar watched him go, shivering.

***

They muttered in a corner, talking about him.

Sometimes their voices were as intrusive as thunder, other times as gentle as a purring cat curled up by the fire.

Hakon couldn't make out what they were saying.

He drifted in and out of consciousness, the pain in his belly like a burning poker, spearing him in agony. Writhing around, he cried out, and they hurried back to him, peering down at their lord.

Falla stooped low, placing a hand on Hakon's forehead. 'He's hotter. Much hotter.'

Ivan looked worried, eyes on his cousin's chattering teeth. 'But he's cold.'

'The fever will do that.'

'And what can be done about it? How can we stop it?' Ivan wanted to know, tension gripping him like claws. His body ached, bandages swathed around his chest. His wounds stung, and his head pounded, thoughts swirling around it like the smoke from

Ottby's field. He was frozen with cold, unable to think. He stared at Falla, who looked pale and tired and ready to bolt out of the makeshift tent and run away from their mounting problems.

'I...' Falla stepped away from Hakon's bed of furs as he groaned, reaching a hand to her, trying to grab her cloak. 'I don't know how to help him. We have to find a healer. There must be someone who knows herbs? Some servant?' Her eyes were frantic as they sought her husband's advice.

Lief looked reliably calm and emotionless despite his frustration that their journey back to Slussfall had been halted by Hakon's injury; despite the snow threatening to bury them in a frozen grave; despite their humiliating defeat and the fear of what would come next. 'Go and ask again, my love. Ask the servants. There'll be someone who knows what to do.' He wished Falla knew. He wished she'd learned something from all her time spent with that horrible old crone, Mother Arnesson. He wished they hadn't run away from Ottby in such a disorganised mess, not caring to check what or who they'd left behind. It was only now becoming apparent just how many people and supplies they were without – none of greater importance than their healers.

Ivan watched Falla leave the tent without even a hint of interest in his eyes. He pushed his braids away from his face, scratching his head. 'We can't stay here for long. We need to keep moving. Ake's army might be right behind us. We can't trap ourselves in the forest.'

Lief nodded. It was an odd series of events that had led him and Ivan to the unexpected place where they were of the same mind. Without Hakon standing in between them, everything suddenly seemed so much clearer.

Ivan could hear snow pattering on the tent roof, getting heavier. He dreaded to think how much worse it would become, his thoughts returning to their dead dreamer and their sudden lack of insight. Though had Mother ever really had true insight, he wondered absentmindedly? Or was she merely trying to further her own interests? He sighed, needing to focus. 'We can't travel while Hakon is like this, though. We have to hunker down. Get everything secure. Wait out the snowstorm. He may be better by then.'

Hakon didn't appear to even recognise them as he stared somewhere past Lief's shoulder with glassy eyes, hand out.

'Mother...' And hand dropping down, brushing the ground, Hakon's eyes closed.

Ivan lifted up his cousin's hand, gently placing it on the furs, horrified by how cold it was. Hakon's body was on fire, but his hands were like ice. 'I'll stay with him for now,' he said, turning to Lief. 'Hopefully, Falla will find someone with healing skills. If you see Rikkard, send him back in.'

Lief nodded, heading for the tent flap, lifting the hood of his cloak over his dark hair.

Ivan watched him go before turning back to his cousin, sighing.

'Mother,' Hakon whimpered, shivering violently, eyes still closed. 'Please, Mother!'

***

Sigurd stared at the body of the old woman.

She stunk.

Blue-faced and rigid, her corpse lay in the middle of a snow-heavy tent, abandoned by Hakon Vettel and his men as they'd run out of their campsite, no doubt heading straight back to Slussfall.

Alys had killed her, Sigurd remembered; stopped her from torturing them with illusions of wolves, screeching ravens, and smoke; saved them from whatever the old dreamer had been planning next.

Alys had killed Torvig too.

He swallowed, pain searing through his chest.

Torvig, who'd killed Tulia.

Turning away from the bloated corpse, Sigurd ducked his head, slipping out of the tent. He heard a horse blowing, snow crunching, and turning, sword drawn, he saw the familiar figure of Ludo Moller sitting astride his white horse.

And he sighed.

Ludo dismounted quickly, hood hanging over his face, guiding his horse through the abandoned campsite, littered with firepits and tents, a few bodies too. 'Didn't think I was going to find you!' he called, feeling relieved, though Sigurd didn't look pleased to see him. 'Reinar's worried about you. He sent me to bring you home.'

Sigurd stared at his friend, blue eyes dull, frown digging a deep rift between his eyebrows. 'Surely he's got enough worries without thinking about me?' It was hard to speak. He wanted to cry. Or scream. He'd done both in the two days he'd been trekking through the forest, and he wanted to do more.

It didn't feel real.

He could almost see Tulia, sitting naked in the chair by the fire, cup of wine in her hand, scowling at him, the flames burnishing her skin with a deep bronze glow.

She was beautiful.

She *had* been beautiful.

Soon she would be ash, and he would never see that scowl again.

Dropping his head, Sigurd burst into tears, his body heaving, his heart breaking.

And then he felt Ludo's arms around him, pulling him close.

CHAPTER TWO

They rode in silence throughout the morning, which was odd, Alys realised, knowing how Eddeth struggled to remain quiet for long. It wasn't that she was always talking; she made other noises as well: muttering and mumbling, whispering under her breath. She was rarely still, or silent, and Alys turned around, staring at her. 'Are you alright, Eddeth?'

They were following the winding path of the stream, still misted with fog. There was barely a breeze, and the mist hung motionless, as though it was frozen in place. The ground was boggy where the sun shone through leafless birch trees, icy when they entered the shadows thrown by thick spruces, and they were slow, keeping the horses to a gentle walk, not wanting to risk them.

Eddeth looked up in surprise, frowning at Alys, fur hat sitting low like a big, furry eyebrow. She didn't speak, but her frown intensified and eventually, she took one gloved hand off the reins, curling a finger in Alys' direction.

Stina, who was riding behind Eddeth, distracted and silent herself, almost ran her horse headlong into Wilf's rump. 'Oh! What is it?'

Eddeth turned, glaring at Stina, finger to her lips as Alys tugged her horse around, riding back to them both.

'What's wrong?' Alys wondered, feeling odd herself.

'I think we're being followed,' Eddeth rasped, head twisting this way and that. 'Someone's out there, watching us. I'm sure of it.'

Stina felt worried. She hadn't noticed anything odd, but both Alys and Eddeth looked so disturbed that she started peering between the trees, searching for signs of what might be out there. 'Can you see anything, Alys?' Stina edged her bay mare closer to Alys' snorting grey stallion. 'Anything?'

Alys couldn't, and that worried her. She couldn't see anything at all.

Slipping one hand inside her black cloak, she touched the cold hilt of Tulia's sword. It needed a name, she thought distractedly, wondering what Tulia had called it.

'We keep going,' Eddeth sniffed, wiping her nose on the back of her thick blue glove. 'If we stay here much longer, we'll freeze to the spot! But make sure to let your mind wander now. Set it free, into the forest! We need you, dreamer. We need you to find the danger before it finds us!'

Panic tightened Alys' chest, but thinking of Magnus and Lotta, she nodded, turning her horse, Haski, back around, listening to his hooves lifting out of the sucking mud. It was dark on the sloping bank, littered with leaves, sloppy and slippery. She wanted to get out of the shadows quickly, conscious of how easily someone hiding amongst the trees could pounce on them. Patting Haski's grey head, she watched his ears, hoping he would give her some warning about what was coming.

And nudging her heels against his flanks, she urged him on, deeper into the forest.

***

Sigurd didn't want to go back to the fort. He was frozen solid, shivering, but not even the thought of a hot fire and a cup of ale could tempt him to follow Ludo.

Ludo stood before him, squirming, shoulders hunched around his ears. 'Reinar won't be pleased if I come back without you.'

'I know, but I won't stay away long, I just...' Sigurd wanted to cry again. His head hurt from how much he'd cried already. His ribs ached too. He was tortured by regrets, wishing he'd forced Tulia to get those arrows out of her arm, knowing that if he had, she might still be alive. She could have beaten Torvig. She was a far better warrior than Torvig Aleksen in every way; with a sword, a spear, a bow. She'd been breathtakingly good at all of it.

He swallowed, wanting Ludo to go.

And sensing how much Sigurd wanted him to go, Ludo nodded. 'I'll tell Reinar you're alive. That you're not going to do anything silly.' He peered at Sigurd, trying to see his eyes. 'That's right, isn't it? Nothing silly?'

Sigurd looked up, deciding. His heart was broken, shattered like glass. He wanted to lie in the snow until he froze. Until he felt nothing. Until he drifted away from all the pain to be with Tulia.

It wouldn't take long in this weather...

But blinking, he saw his brother's face. 'I'll be back for supper.' He didn't want food. He didn't want to be in the hall, see his mother, hear Agnette and Bjarni's baby cry, talk to the king, endure the looks and whispers, suffer the sympathy. But he couldn't run from Reinar. His brother needed him. The fort was a mess, and he had to help Reinar put it back together. 'Supper.' And turning, Sigurd walked away from a worried-looking Ludo, who forced himself to keep his freezing hands by his sides and his boots in the snow, letting Sigurd leave, knowing that Reinar wouldn't be happy at all.

**

And he wasn't.

'You *left* him there?' Reinar's eyes were wide, angry, disappointed. 'You should have brought him back, Ludo!' He glanced at Bjarni, who stood beside him, jiggling on the spot, needing a piss.

Bjarni shrugged. 'Doubt Ludo could have done any more. If Sigurd doesn't want to come back, he won't. Leave him be, Reinar. You know how it feels to lose the woman you love, but for Sigurd, it's worse, knowing Tulia's dead. He'll never see her again.' And gritting his teeth, he hurried away to the latrines.

'He was so sad,' Ludo almost whispered when Bjarni had gone. 'He just wanted to be alone. I couldn't drag him back.'

Reinar sighed, feeling his shoulder ache. 'I know.' And he did. More than anything, Reinar felt the demanding need to be alone. He ran a hand over his face, cupping his bearded chin. 'Well, let's just hope he doesn't fall asleep somewhere and freeze to death.' Trying to smile, he failed, and hearing his mother's raised voice, calling for him from the hall steps, Reinar ignored her, heading towards the broken inner gates.

Ludo remained behind, turning to a red-cheeked Gerda, who pulled up with a yelp. 'Are you alright?'

Gerda shook her head dismissively. 'Just my hip, aching in the cold. I feel like an old woman today!' She searched Ludo's face, trying to see what he knew. 'You found Sigurd?'

He nodded.

Gerda couldn't express her worry as anything more than irritation. She frowned at Ludo. 'Is he leaving?'

'Leaving? Ottby? No, I don't imagine so.' Looking up, Ludo saw Bolli shuffling towards them through the snow; bandaged head, still half-deaf from the battle. 'He just needs time. It was a shock.'

'It was,' Gerda agreed, still reeling herself. 'And a relief, in the end, that Ake came.' She gripped her throat, feeling anything but relieved. 'Though, that will not be the end of it, will it? There's always some new threat. Some danger lurking just out of reach. Another enemy approaching on the horizon like a dark storm!'

Ludo nodded, knowing what Ake had warned. 'Though we're in no position to do much about it right now. We need some time to recover, to prepare for what comes next.'

'But will we get it?' Gerda wondered, spying Agnette talking to Rienne, showing the servant the fur-wrapped bundle that was her newborn daughter. 'Will we get any time before the next attack comes?'

'I hope so,' Ludo said sadly, wondering about Alys and Eddeth and Stina. 'I hope so, Gerda. We need it.'

***

The silence was becoming oppressive.

They could all feel it.

It was as though every creature had hidden away, the sounds of the forest so oddly deadened now.

Frozen hands squeezed reins tightly, heads swivelling.

Alys blinked at Stina, who had ridden up beside her.

Eddeth urged her horse up to Alys' other side. 'What's out there?' she hissed impatiently. 'Surely something?'

'*Something*?' Stina looked terrified.

Eddeth blinked, her stomach growling loudly. She took one hand off the reins, placing it over her cloak, seeking to quieten her complaining belly.

'We're not alone,' Alys said with certainty. 'We're being followed.'

'Maybe evil spirits? Maybe the gods didn't like what you did, Alys? Killing that dreamer like that? Maybe they've sent them after us!'

'Evil spirits?' Stina turned in the saddle, checking behind them.

Eddeth dropped Wilf's reins entirely, digging beneath her thick cloak, opening up the leather purse which hung from her belt. 'I have stones!' she called loudly, her booming voice bouncing off the trees around them.

They all cringed then, even Eddeth.

Hunching up her shoulders, she handed Stina a grey river stone painted with symbols. She took another stone out of her pouch, giving it to Alys. 'I made these before we left. Forgot all about them!' She was whispering now, her breath a steady stream of frosty smoke. 'They'll help keep the evil spirits away.'

'Will they?' Stina looked doubtful as she flipped over the smooth stone. There didn't appear to be anything special about it.

Alys nodded. 'They will. Eddeth's stone saved my life in Ottby. When that dreamer was trying to kill me, I grabbed the stone, and I could breathe again.'

Eddeth tucked her purse back beneath her cloak, readjusting herself in the saddle. 'Oh yes, these symbols are more powerful than anything you –' She froze, staring at Alys' face, which had suddenly gone paler than snow. 'What?'

'Ride!' Alys screamed, spinning around in the saddle, fumbling with Haski's reins, kicking his flanks with urgency, eyes quickly on the path. They were still following the stream, and the muddy bank wasn't amenable to fast travel. 'Hurry!' she yelled, head down, avoiding the low branches threatening her head. 'Duck!'

Stina was slow to get going, her horse slipping in the mud. 'Come on, Eddeth!' she called, sensing that Eddeth hadn't even grabbed her reins yet. Stina didn't know what Alys had seen, but images of Ullaberg's beach flashed before her eyes, and kicking her flustered horse, Stina spurred her on.

***

Ake was impatient to head back to Stornas. It had been over a month since he'd seen his wife and children, and the memory of their sweet faces tugged at his heart. He hated being away from them, especially now, when every enemy was descending upon Stornas.

He'd never felt such great peril for himself and his family.

For the whole of Alekka.

Leaning over the map table, he gnawed a long toothpick, muttering.

Reinar watched him, unsure whether to speak. Sigurd wasn't there, and he felt conscious of that. Bjarni, Bolli, and Ludo were, though. Ake's man, Algeir, too. They were all as quiet as Reinar, waiting to be called on.

'We don't have enough men!' That was the truth of it, and Ake straightened up with a sigh, eyes on Stellan Vilander, who slumped in his wheelchair, in between Reinar and Bolli. Ake felt the loss of his wisdom and advice, still expecting his old friend to jump up and start barking at them all, though Stellan didn't even appear to be listening.

There were few loyal men left that he could trust anymore.

Hector was gone. Stellan too.

His faithful warriors had scattered across Alekka after his victory. They came back occasionally, when there was a new threat, but never all of them. Never his entire brotherhood of experienced men who had helped him rip that old bastard Jorek Vettel from Alekka's throne.

If only he'd finished the job...

Excuses bubbled up into Ake's throat. Old and tired excuses that he'd used to justify his failure, but in truth there were none. He had failed, and now he was left with the nagging problem of the Vettels at just the wrong moment.

They all were.

Reinar stepped closer to the table. 'In Ottby, we certainly don't have enough men, but you have thousands, my lord. More scattered around the South. More who can help. They will come, as you said.'

Ake smiled wearily, grateful for the cup of ale Stellan's old steward, Martyn, brought him on a tray. He took a long drink, wiping a hand over his short beard, now shot with so much grey that he was starting to feel old. Yet there was so much to do. And it was all on him to decide the how, when, and why of it all. 'You're right, and I'll send word to gather them all in. Every man who can fight, who has fought. Even those whose only experience is to wield a pitchfork at a bale of hay. We need them all!' He frowned, staring back at the map, placing his cup on the edge of the table.

'We've got enough men to attack Slussfall, and sort out Hovring and Vika, but here...' And he moved his hand up the map, further north and west. 'In Ennor, I heard stories about what's happening in The Murk.' Ake swallowed, feeling odd. Another problem that could be laid squarely at his door. Another loose end he'd failed to tie up. 'I had to return, to save Ottby, to keep Stornas safe, but my dreamer sees bigger problems coming.' And leaning forward, he pointed to Orvala, a large territory east of The Murk.

'Who's up there now?' Bolli wondered, adjusting his bandage. He was struggling to hear with it wrapped around his head, though he wondered if he needed it at all. 'Thought it was just a bunch of half-frozen tribes and polar bears. All of them fighting each other!'

Ake grinned. 'Once, old friend. Now, it's a beacon. A light in the darkness. Many are flocking there.'

'To Orvala?' Bjarni looked surprised. He remembered his journey to the North with Stellan and Ake when he was twelve-years-old. They had sailed to Orvala to visit the man who'd claimed kingship of the North; the self-proclaimed ruler of the northernmost tribes. Ake had sought to make peace and forge an alliance, and the new king had been amenable, as desirous of peace as Ake.

Bjarni remembered their time as one of feasts and games, wild beasts and rabid boys, all of whom had wanted to fight him and Reinar to the death. He smiled, then frowned, remembering how that king had been killed as soon as they'd departed for Ottby, replaced by an angry, blood-thirsty man who had simply wanted to murder every rival until he stood alone, the King of the North.

Orvala had been a brutal, untamed sort of place.

'Thousands of years ago, a great city perched here,' Ake said, pointing to what was now just a shadow of its former self. 'When the gods broke Alekka in two, the North was crushed. Punished. But memories of what existed here remain. Memories of what Orvala was and what it stood for. Some have not forgotten.'

'And they're rising up,' Algeir put in. He was a sour-faced man, with hooded eyes, and a flattened nose. His straight chestnut hair hung lankly to his shoulders, his beard kept short, turning grey. But despite his dour appearance and sharp tone, he was extremely loyal to Ake and effective at managing his lord's men. And his lord. 'They aim to take the South.'

Reinar looked surprised. '*Take* the South?'

Ake nodded. 'It's their belief that they will. And these men here.' His hand moved back to Ennor, and up to The Murk. 'These men want to crush us too.' His hand lingered for a moment, feeling another tremor of regret, before moving east to Slussfall. 'Not to mention our good friend Hakon Vettel and his cousin. So...' And standing back, he opened up his arms, stretching them from one side of the map table to the other. 'We're threatened from both sides. From above too. And we don't have the men to simply divide our forces and crush them all at once. To staunch every inevitable break in our wall.' His eyes were on Reinar. 'Many want my crown.'

Reinar held his king's gaze, not wanting to be lumped in with their Northern enemies. 'We need allies.'

Ake smiled, pleased that Stellan's son was smart like his father. 'We do. And we have some. But first, I want us to push up North. We can't expose Stornas, so we need to strengthen Ottby. Algeir, you'll take six hundred men to sort out Hovring and Vika. After what those idiots tried, I doubt they went back to their forts. I imagine they remained with Hakon, hoping he'd keep them safe.' Everything was always a hope, Ake knew, shoulders aching with the lumberous weight of responsibility. 'So quell any unrest, then install new lords. Give me your proposals for those men before you leave. Send half your men with Emil. Attack both forts at once. Give them no time to warn each other about what's coming. Likely there won't even be a fight. Most people want peace. They want a lord who keeps them safe. I hardly think they'll go against us without Erlan and Alef there to twist the truth of their betrayal into something more palatable.'

Algeir nodded, lifting his chin, enjoying the prospect of restoring order around Ottby.

'I'll take the rest of our men back to Stornas, for that is where we must be strongest. I'll ensure we have everything in place there. Messengers will be sent through the North and the South, and beyond. And you, Reinar...' Ake lifted his eyes to the hall doors as they opened, wondering if it was Sigurd, but it was two men he didn't know; swarthy-looking types, who quickly made themselves at home by the fire. 'I'll leave you eight hundred men, and you and your brother will take Slussfall.'

Now it was Reinar's turn to look pleased. He nodded. 'After what Hakon Vettel did to Ottby, I'd be happy to.'

'Good!' Ake was ready for something to eat. Whatever was roasting in the kitchen had his stomach growling in anticipation. 'And Sigurd? Will he return?'

Reinar blinked, jaw working. 'He will. He just needs time. Tulia was his woman. Her loss...' He shivered, remembering the image of Sigurd throwing himself onto Tulia's body. The ship nail she'd fallen onto had gone through her neck. She'd stood no chance. 'She was one of my finest warriors. There were few better. When Sigurd returns, we'll honour her. And then we'll begin.'

'Good.' It was what Ake needed to hear. He saw Stellan raise his head, and he smiled. 'You get back to work, then. I'll sit here with Stellan for a while before I join you.' And dismissing them all with a barely discernible nod of his head, Ake took a seat beside Stellan, patting his friend's hand.

Reinar turned after Bjarni, who was following Ludo out of the hall. His mind started whirring, knowing that there was so much to think about, so much to organise and plan. He was worried about Sigurd, wondering what to do about Elin.

Unable to stop thinking about Alys.

***

Alys had been taught to ride by her grandfather, Jonas.

His best friend, Vik, lived a day's ride from their cottage, and they were always heading north to visit him. The road from

Torborg to Burholm cut through the forest, with the odd stream to cross, and it gave Jonas an opportunity to teach Alys how to ride. Fast. They would often leave as dawn whispered its first breath, hoping to arrive at Vik's in time for supper.

Over the years, they became increasingly competitive, for the loser would be lumped with cooking duties for the next month.

Alys hated cooking, so she could ride fast. And she did.

She could hear men shouting, horses crashing through the trees to her right, snow crunching, flung into the air by pounding hooves, flashes of armour glinting in the odd burst of sunshine.

There was at least a handful of them.

And they could ride too.

Glancing around, Alys felt panic threatening to freeze her. Stina was not an experienced rider, but terror had her clinging on as her nimble horse raced through the slushy mud. Eddeth, though, was another story. Alys could see her big eyes bulging as she yelped, banging up and down in the saddle, struggling to control Wilf with little command of the reins at all.

Turning back around, she could feel Tulia's sword slapping against her hip, knowing she had no chance to use it. Her bow and quiver banged against her back, but she could barely stretch out her arms as she twisted Haski away from the stream, into the trees. There was nowhere to stop and regroup. Nowhere to hide. They just had to try and get away.

The men were gaining.

'Alys!' Stina screamed.

Alys turned, catching a glimpse of a dirty-white horse jumping over a fallen tree into Stina's path. The helmeted warrior grabbed for Stina, who swung away from him, yelping. He reached for her long braid, and snatching it, he used it like a rope, pulling himself closer to her.

'No!' Stina tried to fight him off, but the warrior banged his horse into hers, nearly sending her flying, fighting for control of the reins.

Alys wheeled her horse around, charging back for Stina, heart racing, eyes up as Eddeth was yanked backwards, a shaven-headed man grabbing her cloak. Eddeth barked at him, anger in her voice. Too afraid to take her hands off Wilf's reins, she leaned forward, trying to wrench her cloak out of the man's grasp, urging her horse onwards. But the man clung on, tugging Eddeth straight out of the saddle, dropping her onto the ground; Wilf ploughing on, oblivious.

More men came out of the trees, horses blowing.

Five of them.

Alys tugged on the reins, Haski pawing the ground, panting as she tried to think, eyes darting left and right, body humming.

The men had Stina and Eddeth, but she could still escape. She was far enough away from them, and Haski was young and spritely, with an appetite for speed. Her body shook with cold and fear, indecision enclosing her like fog.

'Go!' Eddeth bellowed, elbowing the shaven-headed man, who had wrapped an arm around her chest. 'Ride, Alys! Ride!'

Stina joined in as her captor snatched the reins from her grasp, pulling her mare to a stop. 'Ride, Alys!' Her grey eyes were pleading, urging her friend to get away.

But Alys dropped her shoulders in defeat, loosening her hold on the reins, watching as the men dismounted, running towards her.

CHAPTER THREE

Slussfall.

Jonas sighed, tension creeping up his back, squeezing his shoulder blades.

It wasn't going to be easy, he thought, staring up at the towering wooden gates of the old fortress. It had been years since they'd last visited the place. Years since Sirrus Ahlmann had been overthrown, and the Vettels had taken control. And though it was a dull day, and his eyesight had deteriorated, he wondered if the round shapes hanging from the gates were heads.

Knowing the Vettels' reputation, likely they were.

'What do we think?' Vik grinned beside him. His fur cloak was white with snow, hood pulled low. He felt tired and cold, but up for the challenge.

Jonas didn't. 'I think we need to think.'

Magnus was impatient, jiggling on his pony. 'But why don't we just go in?' His nose had stopped dripping some time ago. Now it was completely frozen. As much as he was desperate to find his sister, he was also eager to get to a fire. The fortress looked enormous. He could see smoke rising from its old stone walls, bleeding into one big murky cloud, sinking low.

'They might recognise us, Magnus.' As much as Vik wanted to thaw his frozen toes by some crackling flames, he knew what had Jonas feeling oddly anxious. 'We fought beside the Slussfall men for years. Their old lord was one of our friends. Hakon Vettel took his fort and killed him. And he had some help. Men betrayed Sirrus. Likely they're still in there. And those men will know our faces.'

Magnus shivered. 'But how will we get inside, then?' Daisy seemed as impatient as he felt, prancing forward, wanting something more to eat than snowy dirt. She lifted her nose, sniffing, as Magnus gathered the reins, pulling her to a stop.

'Good question,' Jonas mumbled. He was thinking about Lotta, wondering if she was inside those walls. They hadn't seen any sign of her or her captors on their long and slow journey from Akaby to Slussfall – not a single hint of the men – though the weather had continued to deteriorate as they climbed north, hiding any signs they might have left behind beneath fresh piles of snow.

'Let's duck back into the forest,' Vik suggested. 'Think it through. I'll get a fire going, warm us up a bit.' He turned his horse, nudging him towards the rows of dark-green spruce trees that marked the entrance to the forest, not waiting for an answer. Both his companions were shivering, cold and wet, and he knew there wouldn't be any arguments.

Magnus encouraged Daisy after Vik's horse, and Jonas turned after them both, still frowning. They had spent so much time trying to find Lotta that they'd not thought through what would happen if they ended up in Slussfall. They couldn't risk making a mistake now. Not with Magnus to care for and Lotta to find.

'I could go into the fort!' Magnus called, turning back to Jonas. 'They wouldn't know me.'

'The people of Slussfall wouldn't, that's true. But those men who took Lotta would. I imagine they'd be quite surprised to see you again. Not happy either.'

It was Magnus' turn to frown, worrying about his sister; still wracked with guilt that he'd let them both be captured. He hoped she was in the fort, that Silver Tooth and Long Beard had lived long enough to get her there.

He wanted to see what Jonas and Vik would do to them.

***

Lotta's mind wandered like a river, a very long, winding river. She struggled to keep her thoughts in any one place for long. Her worries were overwhelming and dark. She feared what the old dreamer would do with the clump of hair she'd sawn off. She saw images of her mother in danger, and Magnus trying to find her. And more. More she couldn't understand, but it frightened her so much that she often woke in the night crying.

Ulrick had let her ride Clover. It made her happy, and he liked to see her happy, so, while the terrain was not too challenging, and the worst of the weather was yet to arrive, they rode side by side in silence, eyes on the clouds, watching as they gradually deepened to a dark grey.

Lotta could tell that Ulrick had a lot on his mind. Previously, he'd worked hard to try and draw conversation out of her. Now, he was more withdrawn, barely speaking. She wondered why, finding herself thinking about that too.

'You'll need to give your pony a break soon,' Ulrick called down to her. 'We've been on the rise for some time. Those stumpy legs aren't made for so much hard work!'

Lotta scowled up at him, not wanting to get off Clover. Not wanting to share his saddle again.

Ulrick laughed, reading her expression. 'Think of your poor pony! Snow's coming, and I'm sure she'd like a break from your heavy lump!'

Lotta scowled some more, doubting she was very heavy at all, but she'd felt Clover slowing down herself. 'Alright,' she admitted with some reluctance. And tugging on the reins, she brought her plump pony to a gradual stop.

'Good girl.' Ulrick swung his legs over his fleece-covered saddle, jumping down into the snow with a yelp. His lower back ached from near-constant riding, and his right leg burned with discomfort, a pain shooting all the way from his calf to his numb arse.

Lotta peered up at him as he shook and shuffled around, trying to stretch out his body. 'How much longer will it take?'

Ulrick froze, blinking, before his smile came rushing back. 'A good question, little princess. A good question indeed.'

'What's wrong? Something's wrong. Are you in trouble?' Lotta's eyes were wide with curiosity, her mind open, trying to read Ulrick's, but nothing came to her, just an overwhelming sense of fear.

'Well, I wouldn't say trouble...' He looked away from her, opening a saddlebag, hunting for something to eat. And finding a squashed lump of cheese, he pulled off a small chunk, handing it to Lotta. 'Though we may have to rethink our plans for Slussfall.'

Lotta blinked. 'But we must go to Slussfall. Your wife is in Slussfall!' she reminded him. 'We must go!'

Ulrick was surprised. 'You *want* to go to Slussfall?'

'I want to stop travelling. I want a house with a bed and a roof. It's so cold!' Lotta shivered for effect, though it wasn't much of an effort.

'True, but Slussfall might be a problem for us now, after leaving like we did. The battle. Hakon. I don't think he'll be pleased with me. And as for that old woman... if she were to find you.'

Lotta shivered some more, unable to stop.

'I couldn't let her keep you, take you from me. I couldn't.' Ulrick didn't regret his decision to take Lotta from Ottby, but it certainly had the potential to cause him problems. Him and Bergit both. 'Hakon will understand, I know the boy well, but that dreamer?' He shuddered, wondering what the woman could see. Wondering what she had the power to do.

'But what about your wife?'

Ulrick's face brightened just thinking of Bergit. 'She'll be happy for an adventure, I'm sure. She's always wanted to see a polar bear!'

'A polar bear?'

'I've got friends up North. In Orbo. The sort of friends more than capable of dealing with an old witch and a young lord, if that young lord has a mind to take revenge upon me. '

'But...'

'Eat up, and then we'll tie Clover onto Skuld. Don't worry, princess, I'll keep you safe. You've nothing to fear from that dreamer anymore.'

***

Hakon saw Mother standing at the foot of his bed.

She kept shaking her head at him, and though she didn't speak, her head never stopped moving. Grey curls bounced, jowls jiggled, eyes bulged.

But not one word escaped her mean mouth.

Hakon tried to get away from her. He wanted to roll over, to crawl out of bed, to run out of the tent, but he was a prisoner. His body wouldn't move. He couldn't lift an arm or a leg. He couldn't even turn his head.

His belly burned, his throat as dry as sand.

Closing his eyes, he sought some respite, but in the darkness, he heard his father's cold voice. 'Is this the end, my son? Of you? Of our hopes? Of our long and noble line? For if you do not get out of that bed, Ake will come for you. And then where will our hopes rest? With your pointless cousin?'

Silence.

Hakon listened, wondering if there was more.

'Ake will *come* for you!' Jesper Vettel roared, voice like a whetstone scraping down a blade. 'My failed son! My embarrassment! My greatest regret! I married a weak woman and look at what that cheating bitch gave me! A pathetic lump of nothing, lying there like a baby. Wrapped up like a fucking baby, waiting for his mother to come and save him!'

Hakon started shivering. He wanted to wrap his arms around his legs and roll into a ball. He wanted to feel safe.

And then Mother finally spoke.

'He's not wrong. You needed me to save you, didn't you, Hakon? And now I am dead, just a useless corpse abandoned in the forest. And who will save you now? Trapped in the snow, dying from Reinar Vilander's cut. Who will save you now?'

***

Alys didn't have time for regrets. She couldn't have left Stina and Eddeth behind with the men. They were skilled warriors and horsemen who seemed intent on capturing them. Scouts. Men who had tracked them all morning, watching, waiting, biding their time, and then pouncing. They quickly plonked Stina and Eddeth back on their horses, and grabbing all three sets of reins, they led them back to their camp.

They had a camp.

Alys' throat tightened, chest aching, quickly realising whose camp it was.

There must have been over a thousand men milling around the campsite. Warriors. Armed. Most dressed in mail. They sat and stood around, talking, working. There were scores of horses tied up amongst the trees looking for something to eat. Servants crouched over cooking fires wafting thick smoke.

And injuries.

Alys could smell the injuries. She could hear those who were injured too, crying out, groaning, pleading for help.

Slussfall men.

'Slussfall men,' Eddeth whispered as she was pulled off her horse and dropped onto the ground next to Alys and Stina.

Alys turned to glare at her. They had to be smart now.

They had to be quiet.

Two men strode towards them, and one of their captors stepped forward to meet them. Alys watched, shuffling away from Eddeth, wanting to hear what they were saying, but the camp was loud, too many people shouting and calling out to make out much.

The two men looked their way, pointing. Both were dressed in mail. One was older, with straight dark hair that just touched his broad shoulders, and a heavily scarred, long face, dominated by a wide mouth. The other man was young, with a mischievous air about him; brown hair braided at the sides, pulled back from a handsome face. His tunic was wrapped in bandages, patches of dried blood showing through. His eyes jumped around like fleas, lingering on Alys' breasts, while the other man was listening intently, interested in what their captor was saying.

Alys edged back to Eddeth, pulling her close. 'Be quiet,' she warned, eyes widening nervously as the three men walked towards them. 'Please.'

'What were you doing in the forest?' Lief's attention was drawn to Alys, who had quickly moved forward, wanting to prevent anyone from asking Eddeth any questions. He glanced at Eddeth and Stina before returning his ruined eyes to Alys. 'Running, according to my man.'

Alys tried to look insulted or surprised, but mostly she just felt scared. 'We *were* running. Of course we were running.' She coughed, clearing her throat, nerves almost paralysing her voice. 'Your men stalked us. They started chasing us. We didn't know who they were or what they wanted. What woman wouldn't run?' She blinked, lifting her chin.

'Where were you headed?' Lief asked.

'East.' Alys felt Eddeth step towards her, and she tried to quell her panic, wanting to edge further away from her. 'To Ullaberg.'

Lief turned to Ivan, who shrugged.

'It's a small village on the coast.'

'Are any of you healers?' Lief wondered, head swinging from side to side, considering the women. 'Do you know herbs? How to heal the sick?' He fixed his attention on Eddeth, who looked ready to burst. She was jiggling about with such energy, almost hopping, that Lief couldn't tell if she was nodding her head. 'We are without healers here, and we've many sick and injured men, as you can see.'

Alys swallowed, trying to think. She doubted the men would let them go if she said no. But if she said yes? 'We... know how to use herbs, yes. Some of us more than others.' She said it reluctantly, turning to Stina and Eddeth. Stina looked pale, blinking nervously at Eddeth. Eddeth looked as though she was about to tell the men everything they wanted to know. Turning back in a hurry, Alys rushed ahead of her. 'We'll help with your injured, but please, let us go on our way when we're done. We must get home, to Ullaberg.'

Lief glanced at Ivan, who nodded. 'Of course, though we will decide when that is to be. Until then, we will make use of you as we see fit.' He peered at Eddeth, who had a wild look in her eye, as though her bladder was full and she was trying to hold it in. 'I take it you're the most experienced healer?'

Eddeth nodded with speed, glancing at Alys. 'I am! Yes, indeed, I most certainly am!' She wanted to prove herself useful. Useful enough to get them out of this mess and back on the road again with haste. 'I have supplies in my saddlebags.'

'Good.' Lief turned to Stina. 'And you?'

'I... do,' Stina said, though that wasn't entirely true, but someone had to keep an eye on Eddeth, and it was better to leave Alys out of things.

If anyone found out that she was a dreamer...

'You two will come with me. Ivan, I'll leave this one to you.' And sighing, Lief walked Eddeth to her horse, waiting while she twitched and sneezed, unstrapping her saddlebags.

Stina stood next to him, trying not to stare at Alys, who had been left behind with the leery-looking young man. She thought back to Ottby and Ludo, remembering how kind he'd been to her. How respectful. She doubted they would receive the same treatment from anyone here.

Ivan inclined his head for Alys to follow him, and reluctantly, eyes still on Eddeth and Stina, she did. 'And what are your... skills?' he wondered, his voice full of amusement, his eyes considering her with intent. 'You appear to have a sword. Perhaps you are a famed warrior like Jael Furyck?' She didn't look as though she could knock down a straw man, he thought, seeing how the long black cloak swamped her slight figure. 'What is your name?'

Alys walked beside Ivan, heading further into the camp where the smell of festering wounds and smoke, latrines and roasting meat assaulted her. And then she saw the men lying on the ground, groaning, wet-looking burns disfiguring faces; seeping wounds on half-naked bodies; some wrapped in filthy bandages in need of changing. There were few helping, Alys could see. Few tending to them at all.

She blinked, remembering the question, debating whether to lie. 'Alys.'

'And why do you have a sword, Alys? Were you anticipating trouble?' Ivan wondered, walking close to her, head cocked to one side. She smelled of lavender, he thought, inhaling her; it was the most pleasant thing he'd smelled in days.

Alys tried to step away from him, but a hedge of blackthorn bushes had her trapped, and she was forced to remain near him, arm bumping against his. 'I... thought it wise, travelling alone as we were, though it appears to have done me no good.'

'Is it your husband's sword?' Ivan smiled, slipping an arm behind Alys' back, ushering her into the clearing, moving her around the various stone circles, bright with flames.

Alys tried to move ahead of Ivan and his eager arm, glancing over her shoulder, wondering where the stern man was taking Eddeth and Stina. 'My husband has no need of a sword, he's dead.' That didn't answer his question, but Alys didn't care. She was more concerned with where the young man was leading her; worried too about what Eddeth might reveal.

'Oh, I'm sorry.' Ivan's smile grew as he pushed Alys forward, into a lean-to shelter that appeared to have been made out of bedsheets. 'This is Falla, Lief's wife. You met him earlier. The miserable-looking man? Ugly, with screwed-up eyes? Doesn't know how to smile?' He winked at Falla, who glowered at him, insulted on her husband's behalf. 'She will show you what to do.' Ivan's eyes jumped from the luscious Falla to the lovely Alys, realising that he needed to leave before he found it impossible to concentrate. 'I will...' His eyes drifted back to Alys, 'come and see you later!' And with one, final, predatory smile, Ivan spun away.

Falla frowned at Alys, taking in her long black cloak. The sword. 'Who are you?'

Alys sighed. 'I'm Alys. Captured by your men. I am... here to help.'

***

No matter how many times they thought it through, there was a real risk of getting captured. Discovered. Their identities revealed. Whether it was Vik or Jonas who went into Slussfall's fortress. Or Magnus. There were likely men in there who would recognise them.

But it had to be one of them. If only they could decide who.

Magnus voted for himself. 'There are only two men who'd recognise me, if they're in there,' he insisted. 'And I'm small. I could hide. Disguise myself.'

'With what?' Jonas snorted. 'A bedroll? A few leaves?'

'We could cut off his hair,' Vik said thoughtfully, studying the boy.

'You're not seriously considering sending Magnus in!' Jonas leaned forward, glaring at Vik.

Vik ignored him, returning his attention to his smallest knife which glinted in the flames. The day was darkening rapidly, promising another dump of snow, and they were grateful for the warmth of the fire. 'He could buy a hat inside the fort. They always had a busy market in Slussfall. Or a new cloak with a hood. He certainly needs one.' Magnus was rugged up beneath their bed furs, teeth chattering. 'He'd be harder to spot than us.'

Jonas sat back with a growl, knowing they were both right.

'Besides, it's easier for us to rescue Magnus if he gets in trouble, than him having to save our sorry arses!'

That was a fair point, Jonas thought, and sighing, he stretched out his legs until his damp boots were almost touching the flames. 'Alright. Alright. We'll have to cut off your hair, Magnus. I'll give you some coins, and you can buy yourself something warm to wear when you get inside. But you won't be able to take Daisy. You'll need to go in on foot.'

Vik smiled at his friend, who was usually much more difficult to work around. 'And we need to try and think of why a small boy wants to get into a big fort on his own. In case you're stopped and asked.' He peered at Magnus, sensing him freeze. 'You any good at lying? Lying to save your own skin? That of your sister's too?'

Magnus nodded vigorously. 'I can. I will.'

Jonas swallowed. Magnus was a brave boy, with a fire burning in his belly. He reminded him of himself at that age: ten-years-old and ready to be a man.

Sometimes...

'Well then, let's eat, and we can decide on a plan for tomorrow.' Jonas looked over to where they'd erected Vik's old striped tent, looking forward to resting his aching body. 'Who feels like doing a little hunting?'

***

Lief had brought a constantly moving Eddeth and an increasingly frozen Stina into Hakon's shelter. The smell of his pustulating wound was overpowering.

Eddeth sneezed.

Stina held a hand up to her nose.

'My lord has a... vicious wound.'

Eddeth nodded, surprised by the shabby shelter, which looked as though it could be knocked over by a child. The lord himself appeared to be sleeping on a mound of furs, which was lucky for him, though he may as well have been sleeping outside. 'I can smell it, that I can. But see it? I would need to be the Goddess of the

Sun herself!' She twisted around, eyes on Lief's morose face. 'More light would be useful. And water.' Eddeth peered at the sloppy mess of bowls and bandages on the ground by the furs. 'Fresh bandages too!'

Lief nodded, motioning to Hakon's steward, who slouched nervously by the end of his lord's bed. He was a shy boy of seventeen, of average height and build, with short red hair, and a face covered in spots. He turned his eyes to the ground, as though he didn't want to be seen. 'This is Rikkard. He'll find what you need. What is your name?' Lief wondered, eyeing Eddeth with no interest in his voice.

'I am Eddeth, that is Stina, and we shall care for your lord now, never fear!' The wound smelled foul. It had gripped hold of Hakon Vettel, threatening his life, and Eddeth knew that if he were to die, his men would not look kindly upon them. She smiled broadly, ignoring Stina, who appeared ready to cry, though she could hardly blame her after what she'd been through lately.

'I'm glad to hear it, Eddeth, for we need our lord back on his feet quickly. As soon as he is able to travel, you will let me know. Send Rikkard for me. He will return shortly with your supplies.' And nodding briefly at Stina, and mostly ignoring the strange Eddeth, Lief followed Hakon's steward outside.

Stina waited a few heartbeats before letting out a long, terrified breath. 'Eddeth!' she hissed, eyes on the bed where a pale-faced man lay beneath a heavy fur, brown hair pulled back from his face, a cloth draped over his forehead. He looked ghostly. Possibly dead. 'What are we going to do? That's Hakon Vettel! We can't help him live, but we can't let him die!' Stina froze, afraid that she'd spoken too loudly, eyes jerking towards the tent flap.

Eddeth smiled, rubbing her hands together, too excited by the challenge to feel fearful. 'We will save him, Stina! I have all manner of herbs in my saddlebags, and we can forage for more besides. Honey too! We will save him, and they will set us free. Perhaps even reward us for our kind deed!'

Stina looked at Eddeth as though she was mad, watching as she hopped away from her towards the bed, one hand on Hakon

Vettel's head, stooping over, muttering to herself.
'Oh, yes, oh, yes, but we have work to do!'

CHAPTER FOUR

Reinar paced up and down the low wall, running through the things they had to organise before they left for Slussfall – of which there were already far too many – when he saw a lone rider emerge from the forest.

He watched the horse walk down the path towards the fort, remembering the pain of being hit in the shoulder; the surprise of hearing Ake's horn, his hopes rising, knowing that the king was coming to save them all from certain death.

He remembered laughing with Torvig.

They had shared the low wall, keeping each other company on many a cold night, talking about women, the Vettels, the Sun Torc. Torvig had been his friend since they were boys, and the idea that he'd always been such a twisted bastard made Reinar feel ill.

He didn't know how he was going to tell Elin.

The memory of the note Alys had left behind was on his mind as well.

But he put all of it to one side, recognising the slumped figure riding the familiar horse, and leaving the wall behind, he hurried to the guard tower, heading down the stairs.

Sigurd was off Tulia's horse by the time Reinar made it into the courtyard, and he threw back his hood with a weary sigh. The horse looked sad, Reinar thought, though not as sad as his brother. He stopped, waiting, as Sigurd looked up at him, dropping the reins, tears falling, body curling forward.

Reinar strode towards him, forgetting all about his injured shoulder as he took Sigurd in his arms. 'I'm so sorry.' He could feel his brother's body heaving against his, pain and grief like a flood, washing over him, and he held on tightly. 'So sorry.'

'Your shoulder,' Sigurd sniffed, pulling back, rubbing his eyes. 'Your shoulder.'

'It's not going anywhere,' Reinar smiled sadly. 'Don't worry about it. Come on, let's get Velos inside. Orm can rub him down. You're frozen solid.'

Sigurd shivered to prove that that was true, but he didn't want to go to the hall. He didn't want to face anyone yet. 'I...' Keeping his boots where they were, he resisted his brother's efforts to lead him through the inner gates. 'I might go to a barn. Somewhere else. Not the hall.' The hall was where he'd lived with Tulia. Where they'd slept together, her ebony body curled up beside his.

'You can go to Alys' cottage. She's... gone.'

'What?' Sigurd looked up in surprise, wiping his nose on the back of his sleeve. 'Gone where?'

Reinar ducked his head, Alys' words still echoing inside it. Guilt made him embarrassed, unable to meet his brother's eye. 'To look for her children. She has two of them, ten and eight. A boy and a girl. Magnus and Lotta.' He'd remembered everything Alys had said. Every word a wound.

Sigurd blinked. '*Children?*' He flinched, feeling a sharp pain in his leg; not caring. 'She had children? On the beach? In Ullaberg?'

Reinar nodded.

'Where are they?'

'I'm not sure, but she didn't want my help, just her freedom.' Reinar grabbed Velos' reins, pulling him towards the gates, pleased when Sigurd walked with them, his attention away from Tulia for a moment. 'She took Eddeth with her, though. Eddeth and her friend, Stina.'

'The one Torvig...'

Reinar nodded.

They walked silently through the gates, Sigurd ducking his head, avoiding the eyes of everyone he passed, not wanting sympathy. Tears came again, every step bringing up another memory. 'We should have women fighting with us, don't you think?' he said, eyes up. 'Tulia showed what they could do, so why not?'

Reinar smiled. 'Volunteering to train them, are you? Maybe we'll get Agnette up on the wall!'

Sigurd shook his head. 'She wouldn't be able to see over it.' He grinned, and it felt odd. And then, glancing around, he frowned. 'Where are the rest of the Ullaberg women?'

'I had Holgar take them home. All but one. I sent a full crew with him, in case there's any trouble. Gave them silver too. I didn't want them waiting on me. There's so much to do here.'

'And Ake?' Sigurd stopped, eyes on Valera's Tree, remembering Alys crouched near it with Eddeth, drawing symbols. Seeing the wolves. The smoke and the screams. Amir.

'He'll be leaving in the morning, though he's given us a lot to be getting on with, that's for sure.'

Sigurd could see the door to Alys' cottage, more memories surging back. 'I like the sound of that.' And he did. The more there was to do, the less time there was to think about Tulia and all he wished he'd said to her. All he wished he'd done differently. 'I hope it involves crushing the living shit out of Hakon Vettel.'

'Oh, it does,' Reinar promised. 'It does.'

***

Lief popped his head around the tent pole, smiling at Falla, who had one hand over her mouth, ready to vomit. 'I came to check on the other woman,' he said, unable to see her anywhere.

'I sent her away. Someone needs to stop all that wailing, though she doesn't look like much use to me. Where did you get her?'

'Scouts found three women in the forest. One of them appears to be a real healer, so she might be able to save Hakon.' He stepped into the shelter, reaching for his wife, who looked unsteady on her feet. 'Here, sit down. You've been doing too much.'

Falla sighed, flopping down onto the tree stump he pulled towards her. 'I'm not a healer. I'm not a servant. This is not the life you promised me, Lief! A lady, you said. You would make me a lady! A queen! You and Mother both! And now, she's gone, and we're stuck in this forest. Burned and stinking. All that smoke!' She was sobbing and angry. Her throat hurt, her breasts ached, the taste of sick was in her mouth, and she wanted to cry until it all went away. Lief was quickly by her side, and Falla grabbed his arm tightly. 'Why do you care if Hakon dies?' she hissed. 'Why? Those men out there don't care. They'll follow anyone who wants to lead them. They'll follow you, my love. You don't need Hakon, you don't need Ivan. *You* can lead!'

Lief rushed a hand over her mouth, bringing his lips to her ear. 'You mustn't speak of such things, Falla. The gods are always listening. They will not reward me for trying to claim a throne meant for the Vettels. For letting my lord die of sickness. They will not reward a coward.'

'No?' Falla snorted. 'You think all gods are like Thenor? Like Valera?' Her eyes were sharp as she leaned back, considering him. 'Those are not the gods Mother spoke to. Not the ones who helped her. Not every god wants men like Ake Bluefinn on the throne. Some want those prepared to do whatever it takes. Those who aren't afraid to take what they want, by whatever means necessary.'

Lief stared at his wife, surprised by her ambition. Though, after what had happened in Ottby, he'd begun to question what sort of king Hakon would make himself. He was a vengeful boy, who made reckless decisions with little thought for how they affected those around him.

But to simply abandon him?

'Alekka was broken because it was ruled by men who didn't care for their people. I won't pretend to care for Hakon personally, but I won't leave him to die. Whatever gods Mother worshipped, they aren't mine. And they shouldn't be yours either, Falla. We will get where we want to be by doing things my way. The right way.'

His voice was deep and reassuring, hard as stone.

And despite her jumping nerves, exhaustion and terror, Falla didn't mind it, and she leaned into his chest, encouraging his arms around her. 'I don't care about Hakon, or who is king, I just want to go home, and forget everything that's happened. I want to see Borg, to all be together again. To be in our cottage! To have a roof and a bed!'

Lief smiled, feeling the same, though he'd never admit it. 'And you will, soon, I promise. Once the healers help Hakon, we'll head back to Slussfall. Back home. It will be like it never even happened.' He closed his eyes, wishing that were true, but the cries of his dying men still rang in his ears; the smell of smoke was still strong in his nostrils. And he knew that it would be a long time before he forgot what had happened in Ottby.

***

Agnette and Bjarni's daughter cried so loudly that no one could hear themselves think, which was saying something as the hall was ringing with loud voices and urgent conversations. They were making plans to repair the walls and the gates, and trying to decide on a strategy for the attack they would need to mount on Slussfall. But little Liara Sansgard was determined to be heard over all of them.

Bjarni looked tired as he picked up his cup of ale, considering it with a yawn.

'Sure you want to be here?' Reinar wondered with a grin.

'You think I want to be in there? I can assure you that my daughter is even louder in person!' Bjarni took a long drink of ale, shoulders aching.

Reinar laughed, trying to keep his smile going. It was hard, though. Liara's crying was a constant reminder of the children he didn't have. 'I expect she's always hungry, much like her father.'

'That's what Agnette keeps saying,' Bjarni groaned. 'She's blaming me already!'

Gerda bustled forward, forcing her way in between Bjarni and Reinar. 'Do go and see that wife of yours, Bjarni. Must we listen to that baby all night long? I'm sure the king would like to enjoy his last night here, not have his ears ringing all the way back to Stornas!' Gerda was on edge, uncomfortable with Ake's presence. Once she would have enjoyed the occasion, but Ottby was a smoky wreck overflowing with problems and injuries, and she was struggling without Agnette's help. Stellan had been Agnette's to care for, and now he was just a lifeless lump in his wheelchair that she needed to worry about constantly. Every time she turned her head, he'd spilled his drink, or dropped food down his tunic, or his nose needed wiping. She was exhausted, running from one end of the hall to the other, frazzled and fed up. 'Why don't you go and look after the baby for a while? Send Agnette out for a break? I'm sure she'd appreciate it.' And abruptly removing the cup from Bjarni's hand, Gerda hurried him away before he could protest.

Ludo took his place, worry in his eyes. 'I saw Sigurd at Alys' cottage.'

It was strange, Reinar realised, that Salma's cottage was now Alys'.

He wondered whose it would be next, and whether another dreamer would arrive in Ottby. And though he couldn't imagine replacing Alys, he worried what he'd do without one.

'How was he?'

'Tired, mostly. I brought him wood, some food and ale, though he looked ready for sleep.'

'It might help. I think we could all do with some of that.' Reinar glanced at Ake, who was slapping Bolli on the back, the two men playing a game of dice that appeared to be going Ake's way. 'It's going to be a busy time when the king leaves.'

Ludo nodded. He felt odd, worrying about Alys and Stina. About Eddeth too. 'Do you think they're alright? On their own?'

'What? You mean Alys?' Reinar turned back to him with a frown. 'I hope so. I should have sent someone with them, but

Alys just wanted to leave. I wasn't thinking clearly at all. It was a shock... what happened. What she did. Tulia.'

'It was,' Ludo began delicately, 'but perhaps not entirely. Torvig was a real arsehole.' And ending much less delicately than he'd planned, he shrugged. 'He was your brother-in-law, so it was hard to say anything.'

'He was my friend too,' Reinar admitted with regret. 'And only mine. Still, at least he's dead, or I would've had to kill him myself.'

'Tulia always wanted to kill him,' Ludo said sadly. 'She should've been the one to end him. He was never nice to her.'

'She would have, from what Alys said, if everything hadn't gone against her. She didn't have any luck in the end.'

'No, well, I hope Alys has some on her journey. Stina too. I hope they find the children quickly. It's too cold for anyone to be outside for long.' Ludo poured himself a cup of ale, nearly dropping it as Liara erupted into a loud wail. 'Think I might go and sleep in Alys' cottage. I'm sure Sigurd wouldn't mind if I slept on the floor!'

***

Ivan found Alys gently dabbing one of Eddeth's salves onto a man's cheek. The man was one of his, young, and once popular with the women of Slussfall, but now, with extensive burns melting his face, he would be disfigured for life. Ivan felt sorry for him, doubting any woman would want to share his bed now.

Alys spun around with a frown, almost blurting out a sharp rebuke, quickly grabbing hold of her tongue. 'Did you need me?' she asked, wanting to shoo Ivan away. There were many men with wounds that needed her attention, and the afternoon was darkening rapidly. She was sure to run out of light before she ran out of salve.

'Your strange friend wants you.'

'My strange friend? You mean Eddeth?'

Ivan smiled. 'Yes, Eddeth. A strange name for a strange woman, though it doesn't matter how odd she is if she can save my cousin.'

Wiping her hands on a cloth, Alys followed Ivan out of the shelter, into the busy camp where he walked quickly, head up, eyes alert. They had been forced to stop when Hakon fell off his horse, unconscious, his belly wound a pustulating mess, though they were lucky to have found a stream and enough of a clearing where their men were put to work setting up shelters. After their frantic escape from Ottby, it had given them all a chance to take stock, and they'd quickly discovered how much they'd left behind: servants and horses, weapons and supplies, their dead and wounded. It wasn't ideal, and most were struggling to rise above the defeated gloom. 'The lord is your cousin?'

Ivan appeared to puff out his injured chest ever so slightly, one eye on the ground, wet with muddy slush. 'He is. We are like brothers, raised together since we were boys. Hakon's father won the right to claim the Alekkan throne after he'd killed mine, so I was sent to live with them.' There was only a hint of resentment souring Ivan's voice, for his father had been so cruel and soulless that even he had despised him in the end.

'Oh.'

Ivan laughed at the look on Alys' face. 'We Vettels are an unusual family, I think, born of Thenor himself. Always trying to kill and outdo each other.'

'Though not you and your cousin?' Ivan seemed happy to talk, keen for her company, and Alys wanted to pry as much information out of him as possible.

'No, not us. I don't have any desire to kill Hakon.' Ivan stared into Alys' eyes as she turned to him, surprised to see how blue they looked. Earlier, he'd sworn they were green, but whatever the colour, she was exquisite. 'And, as far as I'm aware, Hakon doesn't wish to kill me. Though,' he realised, ushering her around the harried servants with flushed faces and red hands, 'perhaps it won't matter anyway, if your friends can't save him?'

He sounded worried, Alys thought as she ducked her head,

entering Hakon Vettel's tent. It was brighter than outside, filled now with a handful of candles and lamps, and a beaming Eddeth, who swung around with a smile.

'There you are, and just in time! Stina had to leave.'

Alys looked concerned. 'Leave?' She glanced back at the tent flap.

'She felt ill. Perhaps it's the smell? It's a vile beast of a wound! Oh, so vile!'

Ivan looked disturbed, not wanting another glimpse of it himself. 'I'll leave you to it, then,' he decided, lifting a hand to his nose. 'Unless you require anything else?'

'No, no.' Eddeth rushed him out of the tent. 'I shall send Alys to find you if I do. Though I don't even know who you are!' She cocked her head to one side, studying him closely.

'I'm Ivan. Ivan Vettel.'

Eddeth's eyes rounded. 'Oh, well, I shall send someone to find you, Ivan Vettel, if I need you. Your cousin is resting comfortably, and I am hard at work, never fear!'

Ivan sighed, relieved that his men had found the healers. Their time in Ottby had been a disaster, led by their reckless lord, who now lay in bed, lifeless, possibly dying. Ivan didn't want him to. For all that he was tired of Hakon's constant need to be at the centre of everything, he was his best friend, and he couldn't imagine what he'd do without him. 'Night is falling,' he mumbled. 'I'll have a servant bring you some bedding. You can all sleep in here.'

Eddeth nodded, barely listening.

Alys froze, not wanting to sleep near Hakon Vettel, but Ivan wasn't looking her way for once, and he disappeared before she could protest. She waited until his footsteps were far enough away before turning back to the bed. 'Will he live?' she asked in a hushed voice, eyes on the ashen-faced lord. 'Can you save him?'

'Well, there's no choice, is there?' Eddeth whispered back. 'If he doesn't live, I fear we'll be trapped here. Or worse.'

'Worse?'

'Perhaps they'll kill us?' Eddeth mouthed. 'You need to see what will happen. You need to have a dream!'

'Ssshhh!' Alys stepped towards her. 'Eddeth, please, you can't say anything about me. Nothing. Please.'

Eddeth was shaking her head and her arms, cross with herself and her flapping tongue, which, more often than not, had a mind of its own. 'No, no, of course I won't. I won't! I know what it's like to be in danger, I do.'

'You do?'

'Well, we're here, aren't we? In danger. Right now! Not to mention what happened in Ottby.'

'Eddeth!' Alys hissed. 'You can't say anything about Ottby either.'

'No, no, of course, you're quite right. I may need to eat something. I fear that I'm a jumbled mess. Or a tea! Oh, to have some tea!'

'I can make you one,' Alys suggested.

'I don't think so!' Eddeth huffed, snatching one of her saddlebags from the ground. 'My teas are not something that can be pulled out of thin air. I must percolate what is needed before I ever choose a herb. It isn't something you can just throw together!' And she headed out of the tent, looking over her shoulder with a toothy grin. 'I shall think of what to make and bring us back something delightful. Something for poor Stina too!' And turning back around, she disappeared with a sneeze.

Leaving Alys alone with Hakon Vettel.

The man who had tried so desperately to kill Reinar and Sigurd, and take Ottby. The man whose dreamer she had killed, and who, if he found out, would likely try to kill her.

Placing a tentative hand on his head, she closed her eyes, wanting to see whether he would live, hoping to find something about the future. And gasping, Alys opened her eyes, unable to catch her breath.

***

He hadn't wanted to come.

And yet he had.

Sigurd ran a hand over Velos' muzzle, feeling his sadness. Sharing it.

Tulia had loved her horse, bringing him all the way from Kalmera with her.

And now?

Flames flickered from the torch he'd shoved into a sconce, and leaning forward, Sigurd rested his head against Velos' cheek, tears coming. 'We'll look after each other,' he decided, sniffing. 'I promise. I won't let anything happen to you. You'll stay here with me.'

Velos dropped his head, and Sigurd stepped away, out of his stall, closing the gate. He shivered, crying more now. He didn't want to go and see Tulia's body, because that would remind him that she was dead. That she wasn't in the hall, waiting for him with a scowl on her face and a cup of wine in her hand.

He didn't want to see her.

Rubbing tears out of his eyes, trying to see, Sigurd turned around, heading for the door. He would go back to the cottage. Sleep. He needed sleep first, he tried to convince himself.

Velos whinnied loudly, and he stopped, almost hearing Tulia shouting at him.

He should never have walked away from her. She'd been upset, grieving for Amir, broken-hearted. He should never have left her. He should have stayed with her until he broke through her anger, until she softened and let him in.

She would have, he knew.

If he hadn't walked away.

So, taking a breath, and trying to stop crying long enough to see where he was going, Sigurd walked slowly back to the stall. Opening the gate, he saw Tulia's body lying in the straw, wrapped in a shroud, and everything inside him shattered.

Dropping to his knees, he reached out, touching the pale linen. Touching her.

So empty and cold.

Gone.

And throwing himself forward, he wrapped his arms around her body, wanting to feel some sign of life, some sense that she was still there; to know that part of her remained, with him. 'I'm so sorry! I should have... I... Tulia... I love you! Please come back to me. Please... I'm so sorry.'

CHAPTER FIVE

Magnus yawned, eyes on his great-grandfather. 'Will you tell me a scary story?'

'Scary?' Jonas chuckled. They had built the fire up high, and he could see how tired Magnus looked, how nervous about going into the fort in the morning. Their tent fluttered noisily behind them, and Jonas almost felt like heading for bed too, though it was barely dark. 'Not sure a scary story will give you the sort of sleep you need tonight.'

'But I like scary stories,' Magnus insisted. 'Not something boring about the gods.'

Now it was Vik's turn to chuckle. 'You think stories about the gods are boring? What has your mother been telling you, then?' He'd spent the afternoon cutting Magnus' hair, and it had inspired him to trim his beard. He looked up, shaking tiny bits of hair off his cloak. 'There's nothing more interesting than a story about the gods.'

Magnus tried not to roll his eyes. 'But the gods do nothing! If something bad happens, everyone thinks the gods are angry with them. And if something goes well, they think they've pleased them. But how does anyone know? What has luck got to do with the gods at all?'

Vik sat up straight, frowning at Jonas. 'Seems to me your great-grandson might need a nudge back on the right track. Who's been telling you that, then? Your father?'

Vik sounded cross, Jonas thought, which didn't surprise him, knowing how superstitious his friend was.

'I suppose. He hated the gods. He blamed them for the sickness and the rain. He blamed them for the raids that went badly. I imagine he's blaming them for getting killed too.' He bent forward, resting his elbows on his knees, feeling strange all over.

Jonas moved towards Magnus, arm around his back. 'It must have been hard having a father like that,' he said softly. 'Such an angry man.'

Magnus' lips quivered, but he didn't cry. He didn't want to cry for his father.

'Though, I suppose, some children are unlucky enough to have two terrible parents.'

Magnus nodded, thinking back to the farmer and his wife, and their unfortunate daughter.

'So, you could either see yourself as unlucky that your father was a cruel man or lucky that your mother is such a good woman,' Jonas smiled. 'I know which I'd rather focus on.'

Magnus lifted his head, almost smiling. He liked to hear Jonas talk about his mother. There was such warmth in his voice. And love. It always made him feel better.

'You're very much like her, you know,' Jonas went on. 'She loved to hear scary stories before bed too.' And pulling Magnus close, he lowered his voice. 'Why don't you pop into the tent, burrow under the furs, and I'll come and tell you a story. I'll just finish my ale with Vik first.'

Magnus nodded, glancing at Vik, feeling awkward, but Vik smiled at him as he headed away. 'Goodnight.'

'Sleep well, Magnus. And don't worry, I'll come and save you if evil spirits try to steal you away!' Vik finished trimming his beard and looked up at Jonas. 'What do you think?'

'You look younger,' Jonas decided, squinting. 'Perhaps you can trim me next? I wouldn't mind looking younger. Or feeling it, at least!'

'I will, but in the morning, before we take Magnus to the fort. I think my back will give out if I sit like this any longer.'

Jonas burst out laughing. 'If Ake were here, he'd send us on our way! What use would he have for a couple of decomposing farts like us?'

Vik grinned. 'True. Think we need to get in a little practice tomorrow, then. Forget your beard, old man, let's see if we can loosen up those creaking arms of yours. Sharpen you up a bit!'

'Old man, is it?' And Jonas struggled to his feet, feeling stiff and sore all over, laughing some more. 'I think you've got the right of it there! Practice it is, first thing in the morning. But first, I must terrify my great-grandson!' And winking at Vik, he ducked his head, disappearing into the tent, hoping that wherever Alys was, she knew that Magnus was safe with him.

***

Lief eyed Hakon's tent with a frown. He stamped his foot, trying to shake off whatever he'd stepped in. It was dark, and they were away from any fires. He couldn't see, but whatever it was stunk. 'Are you sure about letting those women stay in there with Hakon?'

Ivan laughed, draining his cup of ale. He wanted more, more ale to numb his body and his mind, but their stores were perilously low, and he was smart enough to foresee the problems that was going to cause. Better that he wasn't seen having more than his fair share. 'What do you think they're going to do to him? I think it's more of a punishment than some reward. Staying in there with that stink?' He shuddered. 'Whatever that odd woman put on Hakon, it smells even worse than his wound.'

Lief's frown was like a canyon, carved in between two thick black eyebrows. It wouldn't budge. 'I just don't have a good feeling.' And flicking the dung off his boot, he looked for some snow to wipe it on.

'About the women?' Ivan laughed again, enjoying Lief's irritation. 'I think they could probably say the same about us!'

'Not the women, not really. It's everything. Where's Ake? Why hasn't he followed us?' Tiredness had Lief doubting their strategy to head back to Slussfall, questioning whether they should have stayed to face Ake's army. They took the word of a handful of scouts that Ake was bringing thousands of men to swallow them whole. But had that been true? He glanced at Ivan. 'For all that she was a difficult woman, I miss Mother.'

Ivan couldn't say the same, though insight would have been useful. They were stuck in a forest, waiting for their lord to die, or the Alekkan king to come and kill them all. He spun, hearing a noise, worrying that someone was creeping through the underbrush, listening. Stepping towards Lief, he lowered his voice. 'We don't need a dreamer to tell us how bad things are. What we need is a plan. Two plans. One for if Hakon lives, and one for if he dies.'

Lief stiffened, wondering where this was going. They were not allies, and he wasn't prepared to play games. He stepped away from Ivan. 'Agreed. But let's see what the morning brings. The healers need time to use whatever skills they have. And it gives us the night to think things over.'

Ivan nodded, teeth clenched in irritation, wanting to slam his fist into Lief's ribs. The man had to try and control everything. Everything! He stepped back himself, smiling again. 'We can talk in the morning after we've seen Hakon, then. And in the meantime, you needn't worry about those women. Rikkard's in there, and Njall's keeping watch outside. Hakon has nothing to fear from three harmless women!'

***

Stina rolled towards Alys. They had been allowed to use their own furs and told to sleep in turns, ensuring that one of them was watching over the Lord of Slussfall all night long. 'How can we sleep with that smell?' She glanced at Eddeth, who was hovering over Hakon, fingers slick with honey

'You don't like garlic?' Eddeth sounded offended. So many people disliked the pungent aroma, but it had always been one of her favourite healing tools. There was something so powerful about garlic. So magical. She felt indignant when people took up against it.

'I don't mind garlic, but Eddeth, it smells as though you've slathered his entire body in the stuff!'

Alys wasn't listening, nor was she bothered by the smell. She was thinking about Reinar's offer to send men with them; warriors with weapons who could have protected them. Or could they? Had she simply made the mistake of riding too close to where the retreating Slussfall army was marching? Sighing, Alys stared up at the roof of the shelter, watching its linen sheet rippling like waves, and she remembered Ottby and the wind and the smoke. Her weary mind started wandering, Stina and Eddeth's argument becoming a hum in the distance.

The fur over her felt almost warm, though she couldn't feel her nose or her toes. But she felt her body sink into the hard ground, thoughts of Ottby dragging her towards a dream.

And how desperately she needed a dream.

She needed to see what to do.

***

Reinar had struggled to sleep since Elin had disappeared, since Hakon Vettel had broken his walls and Torvig had killed Tulia.

Since Alys had left.

His thoughts tormented and teased him. He couldn't quiet them long enough to relax. They jumped around like sparks of lighting, a new one exploding every few moments, trying to drag him away from any hope of sleep.

Torvig was dead, and he needed to tell Elin.

And the fort was broken.

The baby started crying through the wall, and Reinar realised that he'd been struggling to sleep for longer than he'd ever acknowledged. He ran his hands over his face, rubbing his eyes, wanting to rub everything away; every ache and pain, every mournful feeling. He wanted to feel something joyful. Some warmth and light.

Some happiness.

And then he saw Alys' face. Alys with her bruises.

He remembered the feel of her skin, her freckles scattered over her nose. It wrinkled when she smiled. He remembered the feel of her lips too. Soft and gentle and delicate. Just like Alys.

Kissing her was the single nicest experience he could remember in such a long time, though even that was tainted with guilt.

Sighing, Reinar closed his eyes, pulling the furs up over his shoulder, trying to forget it all. He focused on the sound of the wind whistling angrily around the hall, ignoring the howling of Liara Sansgard through the wall, trying to fall asleep.

**

'*Almasa.*'

Alys turned in surprise, recognising the sharp voice.

'My sword. Its name is *Almasa.*' Tulia Saari stood in the moonlight watching her, silken hair shimmering like raven's wings, voice as hard as ever.

Alys shivered, seeing the bloody hole in her neck.

Tulia shook her head, full of regret. 'I should have listened to you, dreamer. If I had, I wouldn't be here, and Sigurd wouldn't be...' She frowned, turning away.

She was dead, but not empty of pain.

Alys followed her, seeing clearly now that Tulia was in Ottby's square, standing outside the hall. She could see the glow of light seeping beneath the closed doors; hear the boom of laughter and murmur of conversation from within.

Smoke filled her nostrils; the smell of roasting meat; the tang of ale in the air.

'What about Sigurd?' Alys felt worried.

Tulia didn't turn around. She'd remained in Ottby since her death.

Her body lay wrapped in a shroud, awaiting her pyre.

And when that was done?

'Sigurd can look after himself,' she sighed, stopping, letting Alys catch up to her. 'But you?'

'I killed Torvig.'

Tulia smiled. 'You did, though you shouldn't have had to. It was my fault... all of it. All my fault.'

Regret was the heaviest weight of all; an unshakeable burden.

Alys heard other noises now: the scraping of blades, the rustling of trees; horses, becoming disturbed, were pulling against their ropes.

She looked up at Valera's Tree, though there was no wind. Its branches were entirely motionless.

'*Almasa*,' Tulia repeated, gripping Alys' arm. 'Find her before it's too late, for danger is all around you. Can't you feel it? Danger is coming for you now!'

***

Unsettled by his conversation with Lief, Ivan had roamed the camp, yawning, shivering, eyes up on the trees, seeking any hint of moon or stars. His feet were frozen, his wounds stinging and he wanted a bed, but Lief's words rang in his ears, and he kept moving. He'd always suspected that Lief was ambitious. That his unfailingly calm face was merely a mask he hid behind. That eventually, the real Lief Gundersen would be revealed.

Was that going to be now?

Was now the moment he would pull off the mask and try to seize control?

Ivan stepped around a tiny pit of embers, wishing there were flames. He heard a couple humping in a nearby tent, feeling envious. It was certainly one way to stay warm. He hadn't seen his pretty servant in days, worrying suddenly that he'd mistakenly left her behind.

The crunch of snapping twigs had Ivan's head twisting left and right. He froze, shivers racing up his spine. It wasn't the first time he'd felt as though he was being followed.

The camp was walled by trees: spruce, birch, and pine.

Mostly evergreen. Tightly packed together.

Nudging open his cloak with his right hand, Ivan exposed the iron hilt of his sword. And stepping away from the tent and the humping sounds as they reached a crescendo, he headed into the trees.

***

Alys woke with a yelp. She was lying on her arm, and it had gone to sleep. Moving it was painful, and as she sat up, Eddeth jerked awake. She was curled up on the ground beside Hakon, wanting to keep a close eye on him, though sleep had overwhelmed her quickly and she woke up confused.

'What? What?'

Rikkard scrambled to his feet, having fallen asleep sitting in a corner. He panicked, knowing that it was his responsibility to keep an eye on the women.

And that woke up Stina.

'What's happening?' she croaked, trying to swallow, eyes still closed.

'Nothing. Sorry.' Alys got to her feet, aware of how much

colder it was than when she'd gone to sleep. The tent was frosty, white smoke swirling around blue-lipped faces.

'It's so c-c-cold,' Stina shivered, trying to gather her fur around her.

'I'll light a fire,' Rikkard mumbled nervously.

'Good boy, good boy!' Eddeth said, creaking to her feet, blowing on her hands. She wondered where she'd last seen her gloves, though the tent was dark, and she couldn't see more than shadows and lumps all around her, the biggest one being Hakon Vettel. Leaning over him, she felt his forehead, surprised by the icy chill of his skin. It was like touching a frozen lake.

Frowning, she looked up at Alys, who stood by the entrance of the tent. 'Something's happening.'

Alys nodded; she could feel it too, remembering her dream. 'I have to go.'

'Go?' Stina sat up. 'Where?'

***

Vik had decided to keep watch. It made sense. They were close to Slussfall, and he didn't know who might be hiding in the bushes, creeping through the forest. With the Vettels in charge of that old fort now, the likelihood of unsavoury types in the area was high.

Hearing a shout from inside the tent, he was quickly off his feet, turning, tripping over his saddlebag. And picking himself up with a grumble, he headed into the tent.

***

Ivan walked through the trees, cringing at every snapping twig beneath his boots, trying to hear what was going on. The odd noises shifted around him, moving constantly. Someone was out there, he was sure.

More than someone.

He swung around, sword out now, squinting in the darkness, trying to make out anything more than trees and bushes. He saw occasional moonbeams, and in those moments of pale light, Ivan swore he saw something moving. They had men guarding the perimeter, but those men were not this close to camp. They were watching for signs of Ake Bluefinn's army, but Ivan wasn't sure that's what was lurking in the trees.

If something was.

He paused, shivers tingling his body with renewed vigour, his attention snapping to his right. He'd seen a flash of something, as though a tree was moving; thoughts jumping around, trying to explain it. Spinning left and right, he couldn't see anything more, and deciding that it was time to get back to camp, Ivan turned around. He could smell the smoke from those fires still burning, see the enticing glow of flames. As much as he wanted to know what was out there, he was well aware that he was only one man. It was better to be back in the camp, able to warn everyone if danger was approaching.

And so, taking one slow step at a time, Ivan edged towards the sparse rows of birch trees. He felt a rush, like a gust of wind, blow past him, and swallowing now, he twisted around, eyes scouring the trees. He saw another huge shadow, wondering for the first time if it was a bear.

It was big enough.

He moved quickly now, not caring how much noise he was making, convincing himself that it was definitely a bear.

Or perhaps, a wolf?

And then he was out of the dark trees, panting, sword arm shaking, breath smoke clouding his face. He saw someone striding towards him, just a shadow in a hooded cloak, and he held out his sword, thoughts of Mother flashing before his eyes; Mother and her gleeful prediction that he would meet an embarrassing end, murdered by someone he knew. 'Who's there?' Ivan shouted, voice trembling.

Alys froze. 'I... Alys.' It hadn't been hard to find her swordbelt. Everything had been left in a heap by their horses, who were restless, wide awake, desperate to escape their confinement amongst the trees.

Something was disturbing them, Alys could feel it.

Ivan hurried forward, sheathing his sword. 'What are you doing here? Is it my cousin?' He couldn't see her face, but he heard the worry in her voice. 'Is he alright?'

Alys nodded. 'He is, yes. I... heard something. I came to see what it was.'

Ivan glanced down at her swordbelt, seeing the flash of a hilt. 'Where did you...?' He shook his head, hearing more noises. 'What did you hear?'

'It sounded like... something is coming.' It was hard to describe for there was nothing to see, just a feeling of growing terror.

'I heard it too.'

'Did you?' The hairs on Alys' neck lifted as Ivan dragged his sword out of its scabbard again. 'Best you go back to Hakon's tent. It might be a bear.'

Alys gripped his arm as he walked away from her. 'Wait. Please.' She turned her head, listening. 'Can you hear that?' She hoped it wasn't just something in her mind. 'It sounds like –'

'Drumming.'

Alys nodded.

'Go! Go now!' Ivan ordered, one hand on her elbow, pushing her away. And turning towards the centre of the camp, he ran, leaving Alys behind.

CHAPTER SIX

Jonas encouraged Magnus back to bed, shaking his head. 'That's the last time I listen to you,' he grinned. 'Tomorrow, we'll have a story about Thenor and Eskvir, and how those two brothers fell out.' And tucking his fur around Magnus' shoulders, he watched him, waiting. Magnus didn't move, and reassured that the boy was already sound asleep, Jonas crept out of the tent, to where Vik was stoking the fire.

'How is he? Scarred forever? Never to sleep soundly again?'

Jonas snorted. 'Well, yes, serves me right, though Alys always loved scary stories. They never gave her nightmares that I know of.' He frowned, suddenly wondering why that was.

'Stories about evil spirits who attack in the dark would give anyone nightmares,' Vik said, sitting back down, moving his saddlebag behind him, not wanting to make a fool of himself twice. 'Especially a ten-year-old boy who's missing his mother, camping out in the woods with two old has-beens, about to head into a fortress all on his own to rescue his sister, who was stolen by strange men. The same men who recently sold him off as a slave!'

'Well, you might have a point there,' Jonas chuckled, taking a seat beside Vik, wide awake now. He stared into the flames, thinking back to the story. 'You think they're real?'

'Evil spirits? Oh, they're real,' Vik said darkly. 'The gods want to be entertained, so we must please them. And if we don't?' Now Vik grinned, pulling out an iron spearhead which hung from a leather cord around his neck. 'Well, Thenor has ways of bringing us back into line.'

Jonas shivered, glancing back at the tent. 'Mmmm, I say we try hard not to get on his bad side.'

Vik nodded, feeling the chill of the amulet in his hand.

He knew all about Thenor.

He knew how vengeful that god could be.

***

Falla sat bolt upright, her fur falling away from her, quickly shivering.

Lief was jiggling on the spot as he tightened his swordbelt around his waist, grabbing his cloak.

'Something's coming!' Falla shrieked, jumping up, naked and shaking. 'That's a dreamer's sound!'

'What do you mean?' Lief dragged the fur off the ground, covering up his wife. Wrapping her up tightly, he gripped her arms, peering at her. 'Sounds like war drums to me.' He needed to leave quickly and find Ivan.

'No! That's the sound Mother made when she was casting spells. I used to drum for her. That's the sound!'

It didn't make sense to a groggy Lief, but hearing the terror in his wife's voice, he nodded patiently. 'Stay here, keep warm. I'll see what's happening.' It was so bitterly cold that his thoughts were as frozen as his body. His mind had quickly gone to Ake and his army on the attack, but now...

Then he heard Ivan shouting, calling their men together.

***

'The drumming!' Eddeth was beside herself, picking her wart, eyes darting around the tent, a sudden gust of wind trying to tear off the roof. 'What does it mean? What could it possibly mean?' Her thoughts had blown away from her like storm clouds, lingering out of reach. She wanted to open up her grandmother's book and search for an answer, but that boy was there, peering at her and Stina, and she didn't dare. 'You should go!' she suggested loudly, pointing at Rikkard. 'See what you can do to help! Something is coming! Quick, hurry outside!'

Stina stared at Rikkard, who looked indecisive. 'Yes, you must go and see what's happening. We may need to move your lord quickly. We'll protect him until you come back, don't worry.' She said it gently, quietly, though her heart was pounding, frosty breath streaming from her nose and mouth.

Rikkard nodded, running out of the tent without looking back, almost banging into Njall, a shaven-headed giant, who stood guard outside, peering back at the women, axe in both hands.

***

The trees shook with urgency, the wind sweeping through the camp like an army of horses had flown by.

But no one was there.

Everyone was on their feet, heads spinning, running to find weapons, blinking in the darkness.

Lief ran out of his shelter, Falla following after him, still wrapped in a fur, eyes on Ivan. 'What is it? Ake?'

Ivan turned to Alys, who had frozen. She could hear something rattling, though she didn't dare say anything, worried that she was the only one who could hear it.

Screams.

Everyone turned, eyes on the dark void in the distance.

Silence.

'What do we do?' Falla whispered, sensing that neither man was moving. She glanced at Alys, who appeared to have a sword in her hand, and she frowned, confused by that. 'We must run! *Leave!*' Clutching Lief's arm, she urged him to act.

'We need to see what's there,' Ivan decided, though he didn't want to volunteer. 'Might just be a bear?'

'A bear? Drumming?' Lief was dismissive. 'I'll go.'

'What? No, you won't!' Falla was furious, glaring at Ivan. 'You have a family. Besides, you're not the head of the army, are you? It's not your job.'

Jerrick ran up to them, a group of men trailing behind him. 'Can you hear the drumming? It must be Ake. He's found us!'

'Let's go!' Ivan's guts twisted painfully as he turned to Alys. 'Go back to my cousin, get him ready to move. Njall is there. He'll protect you.' He peered up at Lief, freezing as more screams pierced the veil of silence that had descended over the camp, this time from the east. 'Gather everyone together. Prepare the horses. If we have to go, we'll need to move fast.'

Lief nodded, feeling the pressure of his wife's cold hands on his arm, finding it difficult not to charge after Ivan and Jerrick. 'Shield men!' he called, spinning away from Falla. 'We'll form a wall here! Archers too!' Ivan had already disappeared into the night, bellowing for men to join him. Lief turned to Alys, who had stayed to stare after Ivan, worried that she should have stopped him. She shook all over. 'Go!' he ordered. 'Back to Hakon. Now!'

Ivan ran away from them, passing through the centre of the camp quickly, senses alert, raising his voice occasionally, encouraging more men to join him; others he sent to look after the horses, wanting them ready. He hoped he wasn't overreacting, though the knots in his stomach told him that something was definitely out there. And now it was his job to find out what. 'Lenn! Take your men to the south. I want a shield wall. Spears and archers! Go!' He pointed in the opposite direction as Erlan Stari stumbled towards him, swordbelt in hand.

'What's that noise? Is it Ake?' Erlan scanned the trees, panicking.

It was a good question, and one Ivan urgently needed an answer to.

He saw Alef Olstein, struggling towards him with only one boot on.

'Alef! Take your men west! We need to surround the camp! Erlan! Follow him!' Ivan's voice was lost amongst the sudden panic that had exploded in the darkness. He heard growling, deep grunting noises, and turning around, he tried to see.

Another blood-curling scream.

Ivan shivered, seeing nothing but dark trees shaking in the distance.

Voices like whispers flowed around him, and he kept turning, hoping it was his men, but their mouths were closed, clamped shut, eyes bulging in terror.

Swinging back around, Ivan squeezed his hand around his sword. 'Jerold! Ekki!' And the two men who'd wrapped cloth around long sticks to make torches rushed up to the front. 'Lead the way. We need to see what's out there! The rest of you, shields up!'

The two men, eyes blinking in the flames, hurried up to the front of their ragged column.

Leading their men into the darkness.

***

Njall pushed Alys into the tent. The whole camp was in chaos, panicked noises sounding from every direction now, and he was conscious of the need to keep Hakon safe. 'Stay inside!' he bellowed, surprised to see that she had a sword. Lifting a hand, he considered taking it, but hearing a crunching noise in the bushes behind the tent, he disappeared quickly, forgetting all about Alys.

Stina nearly threw herself at her friend as she slipped inside. 'What's happening out there?'

Eddeth would have thrown herself at Alys too, but she couldn't get off the ground quickly enough. 'Ouch!' And finally untangling herself, she was at Alys' side. 'The vatyr!'

'What?' Both women turned to Eddeth, who was panting.

'Well, what else could it be? I don't hear an army. I don't hear bears or wolves, and I certainly don't hear dragons!' Eddeth chuckled, though the terror rushing through her body was making her dizzy with fear. Or perhaps she'd simply stood up too quickly? Shaking her head, she tried to concentrate. 'We're trapped in the depths of the forest. What else could it be but evil spirits? I can't imagine the gods are happy with Hakon Vettel and his army! They will have sent the vatyr after them!'

All three of them turned to Hakon, who lay perfectly still on his mound of furs, fire blazing away in a tiny circle of stones nearby.

'I've got some flying powder in my saddlebag,' Eddeth whispered loudly, teeth bared, eyes aflame.

'Flying powder?' Stina looked confused as Eddeth and Alys crept even closer to her, not wanting to be heard.

Alys' attention was on the strange noises coming from behind the tent, heart racing now. She remembered the waking nightmare and the wolf, and she tried to calm down. 'Get the powder, Eddeth. I need to see what's out there.' Something had been blocking her visions since she'd left Ottby, but maybe Eddeth's powder would help?

***

Falla was deposited into a tent with the servants; eleven women who sobbed and clung to each other in fear. Falla didn't want to be one of them, though she worried that she might vomit. 'Be quiet!' she grumbled, pushing away from the women as the wind strengthened, threatening to topple the ramshackle tent down on their heads. 'How can we hear what's happening if you're mewling like goats!'

The servants quietened down, knowing Falla Gundersen's temper as they did. It was dark; there was nothing for them to do but shelter and wait.

And listen.

'The gods will protect us!' wailed the youngest servant, barely sixteen. 'They will!'

Falla snorted. 'Depends whose side they're on, doesn't it?' She felt a twinge in her stomach, and concerned, she slipped a hand beneath her cloak, wishing Mother was with her. Mother would know what to do. She would have spoken to Alari, asked for her help.

Asked her to protect them all.

***

'My lord, my lord, my precious little lord. Do you know who I am? Why I have come?'

She was ugly. Or beautiful.

Hakon couldn't decide.

The woman's skin was oddly pale, her one eye blue like a bright sapphire. The space where her other eye had been was a sunken hole, puckered with pink skin. Hair like snow wrapped around her head, twisting to form a long braid that hung to her waist. A necklace of tattooed symbols circled her throat; long earrings of bones dangling from her ears, touching her narrow shoulders. She appeared middle-aged, though there was nothing motherly about her, and as she leaned towards him, Hakon felt afraid.

He nodded, for though he'd never met a goddess in his life, he had seen her image carved onto many a saga stone; embroidered on gold-threaded tapestries hung in fine halls. 'Yes.'

Alari smiled, though her eye remained cold. 'I had such high hopes for you, Hakon, yet here you are, a wounded failure, approaching death. It is only fitting, I suppose. I handed you everything, including my most precious dreamer, my beloved Mother. Yet what did you do to protect her? To honour her?' Alari spat in anger as she straightened up. 'What did you do to live up to your name at all?'

She was the Goddess of Magic, a dreamweaver of such power and menace that she could kill with a look.

Alari smiled. That was a rumour she had ensured was spread from the North to the South; a rumour Hakon Vettel appeared to have heard, for he shrank away from her, trembling.

'I am dying?'

'Do you wish to die, Hakon, my little lord, for I could kill you right now!' Alari was irritated by his weakness. By his fear.

He stunk of failure.

This was who her hopes rested on? This trembling wreck of a boy?

She snarled, turning around until the back of her shimmering black cloak was the only thing Hakon could see. Her temper was like a violent storm, at times hard to control. Yet, she knew, as her father had always reminded her, anger was more effective when it remained tightly bound. 'You are a Vettel, Hakon. Have you forgotten? Yet you failed at Ottby. Failed to defeat the Vilanders. Failed to take that fort!' And turning around, she pointed a pale finger at him, edging closer, eye glowing. 'And now? Listen to what is happening now!'

Hakon heard screaming. His belly felt hot, burning hot. He held a hand to it, desperate for a drink of water. His heart pounded, and his legs shook.

He felt in danger.

'I've tried to protect you. I've always had someone watching over you, for I knew that one day you would take the throne. It was my greatest wish. Your grandfather was a powerful man until the end, a loyal servant until he weakened and bowed to the sanctimonious fool, Ake Bluefinn. Your father... he was always distracted, and eventually, I saw how that would go, but you? Oh, I had such plans for you!' Alari's hands were in the air, and she inhaled slowly, blowing out a great white breath, watching as the smoke consumed Hakon, masking him from her. 'And now? How can I possibly keep you safe now?'

***

Alys sat in the corner of the tent, trying to concentrate, Eddeth's voice a deep hum before her. She felt herself panicking, worried that the powder wouldn't work.

Nothing was coming to her – just darkness.

Eddeth tried to calm her down, sensing that Alys wasn't even breathing. 'Deep breaths now. Just let everything fade, let it all soften, like clouds. Everything before you is just clouds, soft and round and floating.' She frowned, realising that Alys had not slipped away at all. She saw the way her hands were gripping her legs, the tension in her jaw.

Stina stood by the entrance, one hand on the tent flap, not wanting anyone to come in. She saw flashes of lightning, felt the icy wind trying to tear the sheet out of her hand, but she held on, willing Alys to find an answer to what was out there.

Alys heard the odd rattling as though someone was standing behind her, shaking a stick strung with bones. She tipped forward suddenly, tumbling into the darkness, trying to brace herself, seeing the shadows shifting before her.

Men were dying, and though they were Slussfall men and Hovring and Vika men, she wanted to help them, because whatever was out there would shortly be trying to kill her and her friends too.

Landing on her forearms, hands slipping on icy pine needles, towering trees all around her, Alys lifted her head, trying to see. Cool shards of moonlight lit a path, and then they were gone, storm clouds rushing to mask the light.

Alys thought she saw creatures, though she couldn't make out their features. They had flashed past with such speed, as though they were riding horses. She heard a deep-throated growl behind her, and turning, trembling, Alys tried to push on, to see more.

And then a hand on her shoulder, and she jerked awake.

CHAPTER SEVEN

Lief swept into Hakon's shelter, Njall and Rikkard on either side of him. He peered down at the women, two of whom were crouching in a corner, one who appeared to be chattering with nerves. 'What's going on? What are you doing? You were told to get the lord ready!'

Stina couldn't speak.

Eddeth scrambled to her feet, bones clicking. 'Alys was unwell. She... fainted!'

Lief had no time for it. 'We need to get him up. We need to move.'

'What? Now? *No!*' Eddeth rushed ahead of him as Lief strode to Hakon's bed of furs. 'You can't take him out there! Can't you hear what's happening?'

'We need to be prepared to leave. Ake's army –'

'You think that's an *army*?' Eddeth snorted, sensing Alys rising behind her. 'But that's not men out there!'

Lief peered down at her, impatient to return to his men. 'Why do you say that?'

'Because I have ears, of course, and they're telling me that we're under attack from other forces! Dark, mysterious forces. The drumming, the rattling, the cold? Oh, but that is not of our making!' Eddeth narrowed her eyes, creeping towards Lief, who was holding his breath, Njall and Rikkard not even blinking beside him. And then she sneezed. 'Other forces, I tell you!' Lief wasn't convinced, and sensing it, Eddeth grabbed his arm. 'You move your lord now, and you'll risk his life. His destiny hangs in the balance! *Now*! The gods are deciding whether he'll live or die! Will you be the one to tip the scales?' Lifting a finger, she stuck it near Lief's face. 'Or you?' And she turned her finger on Rikkard, who looked petrified, blinking rapidly.

'Perhaps we should wait?' Njall grunted at Lief. 'Find Ivan? He'll be able to tell you what's happening. He must have seen who's out there by now.' He ran a filthy hand down his long coppery beard, braided into one thick rope. His guts griped, and he needed to head for the latrines, though he knew he had to stay, keeping watch. He'd found nothing in the bushes behind the tent, though he was certain something was out there, if the odd sounds were anything to go by.

But what?

Lief nodded reluctantly, not wanting to be responsible for killing his lord. 'I'll find Ivan. Njall, keep an eye on the tent. Rikkard, you get out there too. Call out if you see anything.'

The three women held their breaths, waiting, and eventually, with some mumbling and grunting, the men left, dropping the tent flap after them.

Eddeth slumped forward. 'I thought they'd never leave!'

'What happened?' Stina rushed to Alys, who looked half asleep. 'What did you see?'

'I, I think Eddeth's right... I think it's the vatyr.' Alys sought out Eddeth, who spun around, smug face glowing above the flames of their tiny fire. 'They're like shadows, moving quickly. It was so dark, but I swore I saw a glimpse of eyes. And teeth.'

'Oh, well, well, well! What shall we do about that then, Alys the dreamer?' Eddeth clamped both hands over her mouth, all three of them glancing at the bed.

'Eddeth!' Stina hissed.

Eddeth kept her hands where they were, eyes jumping above her fingers.

Alys didn't say anything. There was no time. She could hear screams, the drumming, every sound exploding inside her head as the threat drew closer. 'What can we do?' Her eyes were on Eddeth, her mind a black hole.

Eddeth was blinking rapidly. 'You're the one who can see, Alys. Shut us all out now. Go into the forest and find the answers!'

Alys turned towards the tent flap. 'But I...'

'Not the *actual* forest! Sit down! Here.' And Eddeth drew her back towards the corner. 'Close your eyes now. You need to breathe this time, really breathe. Listen to that drumming out there. Feel it inside you, like your beating heart.' She squatted down beside Alys, gripping her arm. 'The beat will take you where you need to go. There's always an answer, Alys, so go and find it!'

***

Ivan wheeled around in circles, screaming at his men to hold their shield wall, though the grunting, screaming noises moved constantly, and he felt disoriented, not sure where to defend from. They hadn't seen anyone. Running north, through the trees, they hadn't seen any sign of their enemy at all, just bodies of the men Ivan had left guarding the perimeter, hacked to pieces.

'Ivan!'

The drumming had become louder, throbbing inside his head, and Ivan hadn't heard Lief approach. He turned, eyes bursting open in surprise. 'Is it Hakon?'

Lief blinked, certain he'd just seen something fly through the air. Moonbeams, momentarily bright and helpful, were quickly gone again, and they were plunged into darkness. The men with torches had struggled to keep them alight as the wind roared through the camp, abandoning them for axes.

He heard a crash, trees moving before him like waves, everything blurring as though he was dreaming. He remembered what Eddeth had said, but dismissing her words, Lief tried to clear his vision, wanting to see what was truly before him, not just a trick of the mind. He thought of Mother, knowing that magic was real, but if magical creatures had ambushed them, trying to kill them, what could they do to stop them? 'Hakon's safe. The healer doesn't want to move him unless we need to. It's too risky!' He kept turning, trying to find an answer, a logical explanation, though the odd growling noises and shrill cries of pain simply amplified everything Eddeth had said.

Ivan felt trapped. He didn't know how to defend themselves against an enemy they couldn't see. 'It's too risky!' he agreed. 'We can't see anyone. Can't see a way out either. I've got men dead up there!' And he pointed north. 'We can't run!'

Lief nodded. 'We need more shield walls!'

Ivan agreed. 'We'll draw in close, surround the camp on every side! Get me every archer we have, every arrow! I want fires blazing. We need to see!'

Their siege engines were lost, left behind in Ottby, their arrow supply almost non-existent, but they had men and those men had shields, and if they brought them all together, they might be able to keep safe till dawn.

Erlan came running up to them, blood pouring down his face from a deep cut in his scalp. He'd lost his sword in the dark, unable to find another weapon. Rubbing blood out of his eyes, he tried to see. 'Alef's dead! He's dead! They're everywhere! My men... we need help!'

***

Alys shook with fear as the man slipped through the trees.

He was just a shadow, hints of moonlight glowing around him, though she couldn't see his face. He was tall, hooded, his cloak flapping behind him like wings.

He was everywhere. All around her.

Always moving.

Not a man, she realised, swallowing.

'You are in the wrong place, Alys de Sant, and yet you are exactly where you need to be.'

Alys shivered; the voice, hard as granite, was so unnerving.

And sensing how scared she was, he sought to reassure her. 'I do not seek to harm you, know that. I did not come for you, Alys, though nor do I wish you to try and stop me.'

'Stop you?'

The shadow man stopped moving, lingering by a tree. 'It's why you've come, isn't it? To find a way to help? To stop the killing?'

Alys could hear the killing. She nodded.

'And you're that powerful, are you?' He smirked now, edging closer. 'Powerful enough to stop a god?'

'I... no.' Alys was certain that was true. 'But why are you killing them?'

'They are oathbreakers. Oathbreakers and failures. Weak men vying for power. And now they will die. It's a beginning. Something I should have done years ago. And yet, everything must happen in its own time, for life is a puzzle, even for my kind. A puzzle where every piece must wait for the perfect moment to take its place.'

Alys didn't understand. She heard a raven cawing somewhere in the distance, and she wanted to know more, but everything started to blur around her, and she held out a hand, trying to keep her balance. Peering at the shadow god, she blinked, ears ringing. 'But who are you?'

And then she heard a terrifying roar.

***

Thunder rumbled in the distance.

Or was it the drums?

Ivan didn't know, but he felt rain misting his face, hoping it was just a storm. 'Fall back! Fall back to me!' He stood on the left side of a long shield wall, struggling to see, though he could hear the terrified screams of the Hovring and Vika men as they were attacked, ripped to pieces.

He saw glimpses of bodies thrown against trees, heard bones snapping, necks breaking, but he couldn't see what was out there.

The stink of death permeated the air as Ivan's archers shot into the darkness, each one of them wishing they had flaming arrows, but the fires were still being set. In the dark, it was proving impossible for anyone to see much.

Dull thuds, bodies dropping.

Men crying for help.

'Stop!' Lief held up a hand, trying to get Ivan's attention. 'We're just killing our own men!' And those men were trying to escape, running for the shield wall, desperate to get behind it. Eyes peeled open, they tried to see with only occasional flashes of moonlight to aid them. Some fell into firepits, others tripped over tree roots as they ran, shunted by their fellow warriors, who were injured, fearful, panicking.

'Aim!' Ivan ignored Lief. They couldn't let whatever was out there into the camp. They had to hold them here, no matter how many of their men had to die. 'Loose!'

Arrows whipped over the heads of his retreating men, arcing through the frosty darkness, digging into the earth behind them.

Ivan straightened up, mouth falling open. Fear wrenched his guts, robbing him of his voice as streaks of lightning shot through the sky, exploding the campfires into life, revealing the dark bodies of the towering vatyr, long white fangs snapping together, claws gleaming.

Charging straight for them.

***

Alys' eyes sprang open as she jerked back from Eddeth, who was peering at her, mouth ajar.

'Eddeth, let her catch her breath,' Stina insisted, hand on Eddeth's arm, pulling her back.

Eddeth closed her mouth, waiting, shuffling on the spot.

'What's happening?' Alys panted, scrambling to her feet.

Stina frowned, listening. 'Sounds like a storm now.' She crept towards the tent flap, pulling it open, popping her head outside.

'Stay inside till it's safe to come out!' Njall growled, legs like tree trunks, standing astride the entrance.

'I'm not sure,' Stina frowned, turning back inside, 'but I can hear screaming.' She shook as a clap of thunder boomed overhead.

'I didn't see anything,' Alys said. 'Just a man, though I doubt he was a man. It was too dark. He was just a shadow, moving around.'

'Was he a god?' Eddeth edged towards her, grabbing her arm. 'Did you see a god?' She was gleeful, eyes popping open.

'I didn't see him. Not really,' Alys insisted, stepping back, away from Eddeth, trying to think, 'but he spoke to me. He warned me not to get involved, said that it was his... punishment. He was punishing oathbreakers, he said.'

'It was most definitely a god!' Eddeth announced loudly. 'Oooh, I wonder who? Perhaps Eskvir, though, he doesn't seem to have a problem with oathbreakers. A man, you say?' She barely paused for breath, tapping her head now. 'Maybe Godi?' And then she stopped, turning to Alys. 'Thenor! It was Thenor! He's the God of the Forest, you know. The god of many things, of course, but he is wont to walk through a forest on a dark night, punishing his enemies!'

Alys froze, looking past Hakon's motionless figure to the back of the tent, hand slipping inside her cloak, touching the hilt of Tulia's sword.

Almasa.

She drew the sword from its scabbard, body tingling with certainty. 'Get behind me,' she ordered creeping towards the bed of furs where Hakon lay. 'Njall! Rikkard!'

Neither Stina nor Eddeth spoke as they hurried behind the

dreamer.

And then the back of the tent was ripped open, a dark creature standing amongst the trees, white fangs dripping, eyes glowing.

And growling, it swung its long arms forward, lunging inside.

***

Ivan had been picked up and thrown away as though he was a stone. He'd hit the back of his head on something hard when he'd landed, and now his ears were ringing. He lay on his back, eyes on the storm-tossed trees, trying to move. He heard thunder crashing above him, something rattling in the distance, the screams of his men echoing around him. And then a grunting vatyr lurched into view, looming over him, mouth open, fangs exposed, black body masked by the night. Ivan tried to pick up his sword, but the creature slammed a leg down on his arm, lashing his claws at Ivan's face.

Rolling quickly to his right, arm still pinned, Ivan heard the vatyr hissing in annoyance as its claws scraped dirt. He tried to sit up, to move, but the strength in that leg was stonelike, and Ivan panicked, visions of Hakon flashing before his eyes; of Alys too. He drew out his knife, stabbing it at the vatyr's leg, *through* the vatyr's leg, not feeling anything at all.

Yet how was that possible?

His arm felt as though it was being crushed by a giant.

Kicking and wriggling, Ivan tried to move as the hand swung at him again. He swayed left and right, back scuffing dirt, screaming as the sharp tip of a claw caught his cheek. The vatyr moved, shifting its weight onto its right leg and Ivan felt a release, quickly freeing his arm, back on his feet, ducking another blow to the head.

Turning, he started running, legs trembling, almost giving way.

Eyes up, Ivan aimed for the trees, hoping to find somewhere to hide.

And then he was jerked backwards, the growling vatyr swinging him by the cloak.

***

Eddeth screamed, clinging to Stina, who was too frightened to even breathe.

'Stay behind me!' Alys cried, unleashing Tulia's sword as the vatyr lunged at Hakon. She felt her blade slice through nothing, and stumbling, she righted herself quickly as the creature turned to grab her. Alys ducked, Eddeth tumbling to the ground behind her. Stina rushed to pick her up, shrieking in terror as the vatyr turned its glowing eyes on her.

Njall burst into the tent, Rikkard behind him. Rikkard had picked up a spear, though he was not skilled with it, and Njall charged ahead of him, aiming for the dark creature.

'We can't kill them!' Alys shouted as more of the tent was ripped open, another angry vatyr looking to kill the Lord of Slussfall. The tent poles started tumbling down, unbalancing everything.

'Aarrghh!' Eddeth yelped, hit on the head, falling to the ground again.

'Give me the spear!' Njall yelled, brushing off the branches and sheets that had dropped on his head. And grabbing Rikkard's spear, he stabbed to his left, keeping his right axe hand just as busy, head swivelling, trying to see.

Thunder crashed overhead, and Alys saw a glimpse of something from Salma's book. For a moment, she was back in Ottby, inside her cottage, Winter curled up beside her, purring, while a storm raged outside. She'd read that book without taking much of it in, but a few things had stuck. So stepping back, Alys let Njall take on both creatures alone, slipping behind Rikkard. She sheathed *Almasa*, dragging out her small knife, and quickly nicking her palm, she threw the knife to the ground and unsheathed the sword again, gently pressing its tip against her bleeding hand.

'Aarrghh!' Njall was knocked to the ground, the bigger of the two vatyr looming over him, hissing.

'Alys!' Stina panicked, the other creature aiming straight for her, roaring with intent, fangs gleaming in the firelight.

Jumping back in front of her two friends and a frozen Rikkard, Alys ducked a clawed hand, grunting. She backhanded her sword, trying to drag it across the vatyr's leg. It lurched away, screeching, leaving its friend to knock Alys off her feet.

'Alys!' Eddeth dragged Stina back to what was once the tent flap. 'Help! Help!'

***

The vatyr had surrounded them.

There were flashes of lightning; just enough to see eyes and teeth, shapes moving.

Lief couldn't breathe. He could hear them coming closer, their growling sounds rumbling deeply, rippling all around them. He felt nauseous, thoughts scattered. He needed to hold the shield wall, but he could sense that his men were ready to run. Bowels turning to liquid, they wanted to flee.

But they had to protect the camp.

Falla. The servants. The men and women behind them, relying on them.

They had to protect them all.

'Hold!' he yelled, voice breaking. 'Hold the wall!'

***

Ivan could hear the desperation in Lief's voice as he ripped his cloak out of the vatyr's claws, charging away from the creature again. He blinked, trying to see, thoughts skipping ahead to how he would find a weapon, to where he could go.

Eyeing the trees, he aimed for them again.

And then he pulled up, two vatyr leaping over the bushes towards him, bodies hunched over, claws out.

Snarling.

***

Lief could hear the creatures behind him now, and he twisted his head, looking over his shoulder, eyes bursting open.

They'd been outflanked.

The vatyr were in the camp.

'Hold!' he yelled, heart thumping, trying to see the tent he'd left Falla in. 'Hold here!' He pulled out of the shield wall, arms trembling now. The archers behind him were having no luck, their arrows flying straight through the vatyr, stabbing into the ground.

But still, he called for half of them to follow him. 'Kurt! Eino! Bring your men. With me!' And not waiting to see if they were behind him, Lief ran towards the centre of the camp, eyes on the giant shadows looming over the tents.

***

Njall couldn't move. The vatyr had him pinned to the ground, lightning streaking through the sky above his head, revealing a face devoid of any features; just eyes and teeth; long, sharp fangs dripping saliva, coming straight for him.

A.E. RAYNE

Alys was trying to get back to her feet as the other creature growled, lunging at her. But seeing that Njall was about to be killed, she rolled, lashing out with her sword, stabbing Njall's attacker through its side.

The vatyr's shriek of pain was like a thousand ravens taking to the sky, and Stina, Eddeth, and Rikkard threw their hands over their ears, crying out. Alys staggered back to her feet, both hands around her sword, panting, one eye on Njall, who wasn't moving, her other eye on the two vatyr, who were howling before her now.

Large, dark bodies curled over, masking glowing teeth and fangs, until they resembled storm clouds, twisting and turning and bleeding into one another.

And then, like smoke, vanishing up a hole in the roof, they were gone.

***

'Aarrghh!' Ivan rolled quickly, feeling the scrape of claws down the side of his neck. He scrambled to his feet, panting, no memory of where his sword was, but he held a knife in his hand, and, hair in his eyes, he stabbed it forward.

Blinking.

Suddenly aware that the vatyr had gone.

***

Alys and Stina helped Njall to sit up, all three of them trembling.

Njall shook his head, trying to hear. 'What? What happened? Where did they go?' He grimaced, feeling around his wounded throat, already bleeding down his tunic. And then, eyes up, he glanced at the mound of furs, rain falling into the broken tent. 'My lord!' Up on his feet quickly, he peered at Hakon.

Stina and Alys followed him, but Hakon hadn't even stirred, and then they were all shrieking as Ivan ran inside.

'Are you alright?' He was breathless, heart thumping.

'Well, until you gave me a heart attack, yes, perfectly fine, thank you,' Eddeth muttered, stepping quickly towards the bed, checking on Hakon.

'Has it stopped?' Stina wondered as Ivan looked towards his cousin.

'I think so, yes.' He was breathless, still in shock. 'Vatyr. They... killed many, then vanished.' Ivan shook his head, thinking how close he'd come to having it removed from his body. 'I don't know what happened, but my cousin, is he alright?'

Eddeth nodded. 'Sleeping like a baby! Lucky man. I think tonight's taken years off my life. Oh, what I wouldn't give for a sip of chamomile tea!' She glanced at Ivan, who was staring at Alys, rolling her eyes.

Every man with a pulse was always staring at Alys.

Ivan finally drew his attention away from Alys, glancing around at the mess of the broken tent. 'Njall, help Rikkard put everything back together, then send him to me. There'll be a lot of injured.' He ignored Eddeth, whose mouth was open, hanging on his every word, instead turning back to Alys. 'Once we ensure it's safe, I'll send him back for you. We'll need your help.'

Alys nodded, chest heaving.

She just wanted to leave the Vettels and their army behind. She needed to escape and find Magnus and Lotta, but even the gods seemed to be conspiring to draw her further and further away from her children now.

***

Lief held Falla in his arms outside the servant's tent, feeling her trembling against his chest. 'They're gone. All of them.'

'But what's to stop them coming back?' Falla felt ill. Exhausted. The gaping hole Mother had left behind was becoming a great chasm they were all about to tip into. She'd resented the dreamer, constantly irritated by her, but she hadn't realised how much she'd relied upon the old woman. Mother had been stronger than any of Hakon's warriors. Wiser, braver, more dangerous and much more useful.

And now, without her?

She panicked, seeking Lief's reassurance. 'We have to get back to Slussfall! We have to get to safety!'

'We will, as soon as Hakon is recovered we can start moving again.'

'Hakon? He's not the king Alekka needs,' Falla hissed. 'You know that. Nor is Ivan. Can you imagine either of those fools in charge? Look at what happened in Ottby! Mother tried her best to help Hakon, and look at what happened to her!'

'You need sleep, my love,' Lief soothed, wanting to stop Falla there, knowing that a door, once opened, could never be truly shut again. 'I must go back, see to the injured. Don't think about Hakon anymore, please.' Falla was his weakness, he knew, but he could not become consumed by ambition, lost in a haze of greed and desire.

He couldn't.

CHAPTER EIGHT

Ake looked sad as he took his leave of Stellan. 'You must come to Stornas, visit Estrella and the children. My daughters are growing tall! Both of them!' His grin was wide, but his eyes stung with tears. His son had died four months ago. Stellan didn't know that. A sickness had taken him, as it had taken many children in Stornas over the summer. It was part of the reason he'd left, wanting to head west, to put down any hint of rebellion, hoping that the time away from Stornas and its many problems would give him the chance to grieve. He bent down to hug Stellan, feeling as terrible as ever, the grief eating him up inside. 'You keep holding the fort, old friend, and I'll see you soon.' Standing, he nodded at Gerda. 'I thank you for your hospitality as always, Gerda. The memory of those spiced sausages will keep me hungry all the way back to Stornas!'

Gerda was pleased with the compliment, smiling broadly. 'I shall send some to you when we make another batch. They're Reinar's favourite too.' She glanced at Reinar, who looked distracted, not paying attention to the king at all. He had dark circles under his eyes, as though he hadn't slept in days. She frowned, hoping to get his attention, wanting him to look Ake's way.

Reinar could sense her displeasure, and he smiled at the king, eyes brighter now, though just as tired and grainy. 'I wish you a quick journey home, my lord.'

Ake laughed. The snow was coming down in thicker and thicker flakes, clumping together, and he was ready to head back into the hall and sit by the fire for the day. 'Yes, well, it's a good wish to have! I wish you luck finishing off the Vettels. And once I've made my plans, and Algeir has seen to Hovring and Vika, we'll meet. Head north. I must assemble an army big enough to withstand all our enemies. It will take some time, and a lot of talking!' Ake felt the tension in his body tighten a notch, not looking forward to that. 'And, in the meantime, I'll await news from the Eastern Shore and my loyal men doing all my hard work for me!' Turning, he headed for his mighty horse, Frey, who kept flicking his head, not enjoying the snow in his eyes. Ake grabbed the reins in one hand, wrapping them around the pommel, and sticking a boot into a stirrup, he threw himself up into his fleece-covered saddle. His steward hurried towards him, handing up his polished helmet, ringed with a thin band of gold. And shoving it on his head, Ake grinned down at Reinar, who'd been joined by Bjarni and Sigurd now. 'Keep me informed. I want to hear everything you hear. Everything that's happening with our pesky neighbours. All your progress.'

Reinar nodded, happy to see Sigurd, who looked as though he'd spent the night crying. Or drinking. Likely both. They would put Tulia's body on her pyre in the afternoon, and he knew Sigurd would be dreading that. 'I will. Of course.'

Raising a hand to Stellan, and Bolli, who stood behind Stellan's chair, looking just as bleary-eyed as everyone else, Ake nudged Frey towards the bridge gates, thoughts immediately turning to his wife, eager to be home.

Reinar glanced at his miserable brother, then up at the sinking snow clouds. 'Well, that's not going to make the day any easier, but we need to get those gates back on.'

Sigurd nodded, almost looking forward to it. He wanted to use his hands. He wanted to do, not feel. And avoiding looking up at the inner wall, which just reminded him of Tulia and her archers, he headed after Bjarni, who was walking towards the broken gates.

Reinar hurried to catch up with them. 'We need to think about training, getting ourselves ready to leave. Ake's left us eight hundred men. They won't want to camp out on the field for long.

And we've got all those Slussfall prisoners to see to as well. Best we get moving as soon as we can. Ludo! You head out to the field. Take Berger and Svenn with you! Let's see how many of those catapults can be repaired easily. Bring them all into line. I'll inspect them this afternoon. If we can still see by then!' He clapped Sigurd on the back, feeling him flinch. 'Sorry! I keep forgetting how many holes you have in you now!'

Sigurd shook his head, not caring. The pain in his shoulder didn't bother him; the pain in his back or his leg either. That pain would recede. That pain would not break him. But grief... the finality of loss...

He dropped his aching eyes, wanting to disappear.

Then sensing his brother's worry, he lifted his head, attempting a smile. 'Not sure either of us are going to be much use, but we can still yell orders, I suppose.'

Reinar nodded. 'That we can.' And he headed through the gates, forcing his mind away from Alys and Elin and especially Tulia and the pyre to come, trying to convince himself that there was no time for any other thought in his head now but defeating the Vettels.

***

The camp was a mess.

The morning had dawned bright and clear, and Alys, Stina, and Eddeth walked around the fires in silence, still shocked by the damage the vatyr had wrought in the night. They had been helping the injured, using what supplies they could find. Most of those men had been taken care of now, though many had lost limbs, some scarred for life.

Ivan's men had been working since dawn to bring the bodies out of the trees, into the clearing, where a long pit was being dug. The Lords of Hovring and Vika had been laid out separately, and their remaining men stood over their lords' headless bodies, trying to understand what had happened.

Stina turned away. 'I never imagined anything like that was real,' she breathed, worried eyes on Alys. 'I... how did you know what to do?'

The smell of death and blood was overpowering.

Alys felt sick, reluctant to speak. She could still hear the voice of the god who had come to her, and she wondered who he was. Eddeth kept whispering that it was Thenor, and that made Alys even more unsettled. She blinked, trying to bring herself back into the moment, listening to the cries of the injured, many still writhing in pain, begging for help. 'Something I read in Salma's book. About using dreamer's blood as a weapon. A way to defeat evil. I didn't think it would work, though.'

'Well, I'm glad it did,' Stina sighed. 'So glad.'

They were not alone.

Njall walked behind them, eyes on the women, his neck expertly stitched by Stina, his ears still ringing.

Eddeth's lips were clamped together, trying to resist the urge to speak. Even she was aware of how dangerous her twitchy lips could make things for them.

Alys was pleased, slipping her arm through Eddeth's. 'Are you hungry?' She saw Falla Gundersen crouched over a fire, hood back, beautiful red cloak lying in the slush. 'Smells like porridge.'

Stina looked ill at the thought of food, but Eddeth's eyes brightened. She almost thought about speaking but nodded instead.

Alys turned to Njall. 'Can we stop here? Find something to eat?'

Njall tugged on his long beard, looking for all the world as though he would say no, but he nodded. 'But then we must go back to the lord's tent. He will need you.'

Stina looked away from Njall, feeling self-conscious. After what Torvig had done to her, she felt under threat from every man who came near her. She stepped closer to Alys, who was smiling at Falla.

'May we join you?' Alys asked, catching a hint of irritation in Falla's eyes, sensing that she didn't appear to enjoy helping others. And then she froze, seeing a glimpse of Falla with Lotta, holding her daughter's hand, feeding her, trying to keep her warm.

'Is something wrong?' Falla wondered, struggling back to her feet.

Alys shook her head. 'No, I think we're just tired. It was a strange night.' She shivered, deciding that strange was not quite the right word for it, still seeing those gleaming white fangs snapping at her.

Falla turned to one of the servants. 'You may serve the women some porridge, if there's enough?' She swallowed, feeling ill. The waves of nausea sometimes disappeared quickly. Other times, they lingered for hours, and she didn't want to even move.

The servant nodded, ducking her head, looking for more bowls, doubting she'd find any.

'Are you unwell?' Alys asked, eyes on an ashen-faced Falla.

She shook her head dismissively. 'I am with child. The mornings can be... difficult.'

No one spoke.

Lief arrived, pleased to see Njall with the three women. 'And how is the lord this morning?' He addressed Eddeth, whose eyes popped open, not trusting herself to say one word.

Stina rushed ahead of her. 'We've only just finished helping the wounded, but he was resting comfortably when we last saw him.'

'And will he recover?' Again Lief addressed Eddeth, who was trying to avoid his dark eyes. 'Is there something you're not telling us?' He was tired, impatient and suspicious.

'Eddeth is just nervous,' Alys said. 'We... you captured us. Forced us to care for your lord, and then last night...' She blinked rapidly, feeling just as scared as she was trying to sound. 'I'm not sure we slept after that.'

Lief sighed, eyes moving to Falla, who dashed away from them all, hand over her mouth, wanting some privacy. 'My wife is pregnant,' he said by way of an explanation. 'Perhaps you have something for that?'

And this time, Eddeth answered. 'A tea! I can make her a tea! Though, whether I have everything I need, I don't know.' She scratched the tip of her nose, thinking. 'Perhaps!' Thinking about teas made Eddeth happy, forgetting all about trying to remain quiet. 'There's peppermint, of course. I remember packing peppermint, or do I?'

Alys watched her twitching, eyes bulging, and she realised that getting Eddeth away from Lief was suddenly a matter of urgency. 'Why don't you take Eddeth to get what she needs?' she suggested to Njall, who glared at her, not moving.

Lief nodded. 'Yes, do that, Njall. My wife would enjoy some relief, I'm sure, especially after last night.'

Njall remained unimpressed with the thought of accompanying Eddeth anywhere, but he turned, heading off after the healer as she scampered away.

Alys and Stina watched her go, faces tense with worry.

'Once you've eaten, I'll return you to the tent,' Lief said, eyes on the servant, who had made two bowls and one cup of porridge, leaving them on the ground.

'No need for that, Lief!' Ivan called, striding towards them. He glanced at the porridge and grimaced, certain that the encounter with the vatyr had removed his appetite for life. 'I'm heading there next to talk to Jerrick, so you can get on, see how Erlan's men are doing. They were debating a pyre. I think we just throw them in the pit with everyone else.'

Lief stiffened, always surprised when Ivan chose to impose his authority on him. It grated, though he barely blinked. 'I will, of course.' And turning, he kept his head high, striding across the camp, aiming for the western corner.

Ivan couldn't help but smile. Everything had fallen apart. Everything was worse than he'd imagined possible, but the thought of irritating the sullen beast that was Lief Gundersen still made him happy. He turned to Alys, who stood alone, Stina having sat down on a log to eat her porridge out of a cup. He glanced around. 'Do you think my cousin is in danger? That the vatyr knew who he was? That they wanted to kill him?' His eyes kept moving, searching the trees.

Alys was tired, and she felt worried that she too would say the wrong thing. 'I... it's hard to say. They certainly tried to kill us, though they killed many, didn't they? But I don't think they were after your cousin.'

Ivan nodded, agreeing, his attention drawn to Falla as she returned to the fire, her face pale, her eyes swollen, but still the most desirable woman he'd ever seen. Ignoring him, she headed after Lief. 'Though perhaps that was just the beginning?' Ivan was tired, his fears becoming more pronounced. He saw dark omens everywhere now, and trying to drag himself away from that gloomy place, he turned to Alys, who radiated like sunshine before him. 'You must stay alert to danger, and keep my cousin safe. Rikkard is a good boy but slightly dim, as boys usually are! He won't see everything that's coming, every sign of trouble. And I need my cousin to stay safe, to return to me. We have plans, so many plans, and I need him. We all do.'

Alys wanted to ask Ivan what his plans were, but she didn't need to. She could hear Ivan's thoughts, and they were loud, screaming at her. The Vettels wanted Stornas, Stornas, only Stornas. To rule Alekka as they believed they were born to do.

She shook her head, not wanting to think about any of it, desperate to escape to find her children.

***

Magnus was surprisingly well rested after a disturbed sleep, interrupted by nightmares of his father and Long Beard, though he felt too anxious to eat, and he returned his trencher of cold trout and berries to Vik with a shrug.

Vik smiled. 'I can give you something to stick in your pouch, in case you get hungry.' Caring for Magnus was something he'd taken on naturally. He had little experience with children, apart from Alys, who was like a daughter to him, but he found himself enjoying taking care of Magnus.

Jonas was as anxious as his great-grandson, fussing around their tent as he started dismantling it.

'Makes no sense to take the tent down!' Vik grumbled, glancing over his shoulder. 'What are you doing that for?'

Jonas had woken up unsettled. He didn't feel at all comfortable sending Magnus into the fort. But, at the same time, he hadn't been able to think of an alternative that made sense. Still, it left him worrying. He kept seeing Alys' face, wondering what she would think. He closed his eyes, already knowing the answer. 'Alright, calm down! I thought we'd move closer to the fort. We're far away, and it's hardly the best spot we could have chosen. It's a long walk to that stream!'

Vik smiled at Magnus. 'That's when you know you're old,' he whispered. 'When walking a few paces is an inconvenience!' He turned around to Jonas, who was glaring at him.

Magnus ignored both of them, jiggling on the spot, just wanting to make a start. 'How will I get out? Will they keep the gates open all day? What if I can't get out?'

That worried Jonas too, but he smiled broadly, walking towards his panicking great-grandson. 'They'll shut them come dark, I imagine. It's usually the way. We'll find someone to go in with you, don't worry. It may be that we can get them to take you out too, if they want to earn a few coins.'

Magnus swallowed, not really listening. His mind was on Lotta.

It didn't matter how scared he was if he could just find his little sister.

'Well, if you don't want any more to eat, we may as well head to the fort. Morning is when you'll find the traders going in. The farmers and the craftsmen too.' Vik paused, eyes on Jonas. 'That's if things are still working the same with Hakon Vettel in charge.' It was a worry, not knowing the lay of the land anymore, and having no ability to determine it for themselves. It was just too risky. If either of them got captured, Magnus would be left on his own.

'I'm sure it is,' Jonas said. 'Most forts work the same. Can't think he wouldn't want to keep that market alive. It'll be making him a lot of coins, which is surely what the Vettels are all about.'

Magnus was nodding without listening, eyes on Daisy, who was pawing through the snow trying to find something edible. He felt anxious about leaving her behind. 'We should go,' he said, shutting his fears away, trying not to feel anything at all. 'Before it's too late.'

***

Having checked on his cousin, Ivan headed back into the camp with some reluctance. Their problems were mounting at such a pace now that he was struggling to keep them all in his mind. He had the worry of what was behind them, the worry of Hakon and what would come when they reached Slussfall, and now, the worry of what was lurking in the forest. Then there was Lief, who always appeared to be biting his tongue, never saying what he really thought. And what he really thought was what Ivan wanted to know most of all.

He watched as Lief approached, sensing that the miserable man was already tying his big lips in knots.

'How are the Hovring and Vika men?' Ivan wondered.

'Those who are left? Scared. They're worried about what it meant. About what will come next.'

'Next?' Ivan didn't want to imagine that. 'You think they'll come again?'

Lief had a full skin of water in one hand, and he took a long drink. It was another icy morning, but after a long, sleepless night, he welcomed the cold water. He offered the skin to Ivan, who shook his head. 'I've no idea. Perhaps they've made their point? Perhaps there's more to say?'

'But who sent them? The gods?'

Lief was reluctant to reveal what he thought.

Ivan could tell, and he clenched a fist, trying to calm himself down. 'We don't help each other by keeping our thoughts to ourselves. Not now. Not with Hakon so ill. Not with us in danger, trapped here, at Ake's mercy. We must help each other. Surely?'

Lief sighed, glancing around. 'I think Thenor sent the vatyr. My father told me that he especially despised oathbreakers. Men who turned against their lords, their kings. Perhaps it was a warning of his displeasure?'

Ivan forgot his irritation. 'A warning? And what does that mean for us?'

'I don't know, but I don't want to stay in this forest a moment longer than we have to.' Lief swallowed, listening to a wail of pain in the distance. 'We must get out of here, back to Slussfall, back to safety.'

Ivan nodded, hoping his cousin would recover quickly.

Wondering what they were going to do if he didn't.

***

Saliva flooded Magnus' mouth, and he swallowed with every blink of his sea-green eyes, too nervous to speak.

Jonas stood on one side of him, Vik on the other, and Magnus tried to focus, listening to their instructions, of which there were many.

'You shouldn't make eye contact with anyone,' Jonas insisted, hand on his great-grandson's shoulder.

'Well, if you avoid everyone's eyes, you'll look suspicious,' Vik argued. 'You need to act like a child. Children are curious.'

'What do you know about children?' Jonas frowned, hand off Magnus' shoulder now, peering at Vik.

'Well, I was one, wasn't I? I remember how to act like a child.

I'm not so old that I can't remember that!'

'Well, Magnus,' Jonas went on, turning back to the boy, 'I think we're in agreement, then.'

'We are?' Magnus was confused, swallowing some more.

'Yes, you'll just act like yourself. Be curious, if that's your nature, which, I think it is,' Jonas said, smiling again. 'So, take a look around. And if anyone stops you, or wants to know what you're doing, say you've lost your sister. You're looking for your sister who ran away.'

Vik nodded. 'It's a big fortress, so you might struggle to get into every nook and cranny in a day. But come out anyway. You can go back in the morning if you have no luck today.'

'And remember, if you see them, get straight out of that fort. All we need to know is if they're in there. If not, we're going to have to think of another plan.' Jonas didn't want to imagine that Lotta wouldn't be in there. He'd hoped to have another dream, but there had been no sign of Alys in his dreams for days.

He felt worried, hoping she was safe.

Vik smiled. 'There'll be other children, likely some beggary types. You can pay them for information. Here.' And he handed Magnus three silver coins.

Magnus took them with a shaking hand, shoving them into his pouch. He needed a new cloak, and he shivered, cold in his dark-grey tunic which was torn and filthy and not as warm as it needed to be.

Jonas gave him more coins. 'And if you see a cloak, buy it. One with a hood!' He winked at Magnus, before lifting his eyes to the train of farmers and merchants who were trekking towards the fort with carts and cattle and all number of baskets and buckets filled with their precious goods. 'I'll go see if I can find someone to go in with you. It's lucky I brought so many coins with me!' And winking at Magnus, he started walking towards the gates.

Vik put a hand on Magnus' shoulder, holding him back. 'Promise me you'll come out when you spot those men. Promise me you won't try to save Lotta.' Magnus reminded him of Jonas, who had a stubborn streak, prone to recklessness. Jonas would do anything for Alys, he knew. For Lotta and Magnus too. But Magnus wasn't an experienced warrior, and Vik didn't want him making a mistake he couldn't undo.

Magnus nodded. 'I will. I promise, Vik, I'll come out as soon as I see them.'

Vik hoped he was right, and seeing Jonas with his hand in the air, motioning them over, he gently pushed Magnus forward, towards Slussfall's open gates.

***

Agnette had left her daughter with Rienne, who loved children and enjoyed watching the tiny baby for a few moments in between her own tasks. Gerda scowled but didn't say a word as Agnette slipped out of the hall, wanting to see Bjarni. She had put together a tray of warm flatbreads and cheese, knowing how hungry he always was, especially when he was working in the cold. Her hood blew backwards, hair swept around by the blustery wind, boots buried beneath the snow as she made her way towards the wall, wishing she'd thought to drape a napkin over the flatbreads which were likely no longer warm at all.

'You've been sent by the gods!' Bjarni called when he saw her. One of the outer gates had been hoisted back onto its repaired hinges, and Bjarni had been wondering how much longer he could stand the blizzard before heading to a fire. Hurrying away from Reinar and Sigurd, he rubbed his hands together, wanting to help himself to the food before it was all gone.

Agnette frowned at him. 'You can't even see out here! Come and eat this inside!'

Bjarni shook his head as Reinar, Sigurd, and Ludo came to join them. 'We have to secure the fort, Agnette.' He ran a hand over his beard, wiping snowflakes out of his mouth. 'Even if we're frozen solid by the end of it!' And taking the tray from her, he handed it around. 'Next time, maybe bring some hot milk!'

Agnette grinned, her attention drifting away from the repaired gate to the field that led to the forest. She squinted, certain she could see something coming in the snow. Blinking, she tried to clear her eyes. 'There's someone out there. Or am I seeing things?'

Reinar and Sigurd turned around. Ludo was too busy helping himself to the last flatbread, much to Bjarni's annoyance.

There was definitely someone coming.

'You watching up there?' Reinar called to Torfinn, who was supervising the repair of the low wall. 'Who is it?'

Torfinn leaned over the ramparts, calling down to him. 'No idea! Just the one rider!'

Reinar left them behind, rubbing his eyes, trying to see, blinking as the rider fell off the horse, into the snow. 'Come on!' Reinar called. And leaving Bjarni and Sigurd behind, he ran into the descending blizzard, Ludo loping after him.

Agnette gripped Bjarni's arm, watching as Reinar and Ludo reached the fallen rider. And leaving Ludo to grab the horse, Reinar turned the cloaked figure over, mouth falling open in surprise, unable to speak.

Ludo peered over Reinar's shoulder, his own mouth dropping open. 'Elin?' He shook his head, not believing what he was seeing, but there was no denying that familiar face. 'Elin?'

CHAPTER NINE

Jonas and Vik stayed watching Magnus as he shuffled along with the men and women heading into Slussfall's fortress. It had a popular market, where farmers and traders from the neighbouring villages, and from Orbo in the North came in droves to sell their goods. Those few lucky enough to have coins to spare in these perilous times of endless rain and illness, came along to spend them, hoping to find warm furs, candles, wool, and food for the coming winter.

Magnus turned as he neared the gates, resisting the urge to wave to Jonas and Vik, who had retreated back to the forest, not wanting to draw anyone's attention to their presence.

Armoured men flanked the entrance, running their eyes, and sometimes their hands over the men and women entering the fort. There were few children, though Jonas had paid a young silversmith to take Magnus in as his assistant. Magnus peered up at the slight man who limped awkwardly beside him, muttering beneath his breath. He had big green eyes and a nervous manner, cleanly-shaven with short blonde hair and a raggedy woollen cloak. Jonas hadn't been convinced that he was the best choice, though he seemed eager to help, and even more eager for the two silver coins Jonas had paid him.

'What are you selling?' one of the guards growled, peering at Magnus, then seeing Leonid, he rolled his eyes. 'You again? The best silversmith in all of Alekka, isn't that right?'

'Indeed, it is! I have silver of the highest quality!' Leonid declared boldly, opening the flap of the weighty satchel slung across his body. 'As you can see!' And reaching into the satchel, he pulled out a coiled arm ring, a brooch, and a buckle.

The guard ignored Leonid and his silverware, turning his attention to Magnus. 'And you, boy?' He nudged Magnus, who had Leonid's smaller satchel slung over his back. 'You're with him?'

'Oh, yes!' Leonid puffed up his chest, eager to feel heroic, though butterflies flittered around his belly as he stared up at the guard's calculating eyes. 'I've taken on an assistant. That's how popular my work is becoming. I'd get in quickly if I were you!' And one arm around Magnus' back, he ushered the boy into the fort.

Magnus tripped, slightly unbalanced by Leonid's satchel, but he hurried along, eager not to lose the man, who had charged away from him suddenly, desperate to get a good table.

'We must hurry now! Hurry!' Leonid urged, calling over his shoulder. 'That one, there!' And he ran towards a long table nearest the hall. A rosy-cheeked weaver had spied it too, and there was a tussle for a moment, before her husband called her away, deciding that he would rather set up closer to the gates.

Magnus' mouth dropped open as he stared around the busy square, ringed by a high stone wall that reached up to a sky of dull-grey clouds. The square was long and deep, with stalls draped in colourful cloth awnings, and tables full of things he had never seen before. The smell was overpowering, both good and bad, and Magnus struggled to get his bearings, unable to decide what he wanted to do first.

Lifting his eyes, he could see the enormous stone hall in the distance, and the ramparts which led to guard towers, where warriors came and went, some talking as they trained their attention on the forest in the distance. Others remained quiet, eyes on the square.

Magnus had never seen anything so impressive in his life, so big and loud and busy. Leonid nudged him, and he spun around.

'Unpack my bag onto the table, and then you can go,' he whispered, lowering his voice. 'But return often, just to show your face. Since they killed poor Lord Sirrus, this place isn't safe. Not as it once was. Your grandfather promised me more coins if I returned you safely, so I want you in one piece!' And lifting the satchel over Magnus' head, he handed it to him. 'Put it out nicely, mind. We want to encourage the right sort of customer.'

Magnus nodded, eyes peeled open.

Wondering where his sister could be.

***

Lotta had lost another tooth that morning, and it made her so sad that she didn't speak at all. Ulrick watched her as they rode, side by side, along a flat path that cut through a wooded area. Snow had fallen in the night, though it was melting as the sun rose high above the tree canopy, and he could almost feel its warmth as he lifted his head. 'You can't keep your baby teeth forever,' he joked, knowing that she was still holding the tooth in her hand.

Lotta didn't look around. Holding the tooth reminded her of Ullaberg, and of the moment her mother had been wrenched away from her. It made her think of Magnus too, remembering how they had hidden in the barn; how they'd been kidnapped themselves. And she sighed, wanting to be a proper dreamer.

A proper dreamer would have useful dreams.

Lotta didn't think she saw anything useful.

She had seen Stina. Stina had been crying and scared, riding through a forest all by herself. It worried Lotta because she loved Stina with all her heart. She didn't want to think that she was scared, but had it even been a real dream?

She turned back to Ulrick, seeing the smile in his eyes, though it didn't cheer her. 'I don't want to grow up.'

'No?' Ulrick looked amused. 'Why is that, then?'

'Because grown-ups are always sad. They are mad and mean and scared. And they have no fun!'

Ulrick burst out laughing. 'What grown-ups are these, then? These miserable grown-ups you know?'

Lotta didn't want to say.

Ulrick nudged his horse closer to her pony. 'Your parents, maybe?'

Now Lotta hunched over, hiding beneath her hair.

'Well, it's not easy growing up, I suppose. Though, you've not much choice in the matter.' He remembered little of his childhood, though images of his brothers flashed before his eyes, and he felt the loss of them. 'Best thing about growing up is freedom. Freedom to be whoever you want!'

Lotta looked up at him, sun in her eyes, and she frowned. 'I'm your prisoner, Ulrick, so that's not the best thing to say!' She looked back down at Clover, who appeared to be enjoying the slow pace of their morning ride.

Ulrick laughed, ignoring the nagging sensation that told him he was doing the wrong thing. It was the right thing, he insisted, shoving the dark thoughts away again. Lotta's mother was gone, captured by slavers. She needed a new home. A new life. 'Well, you won't be for long, not once you see how happy you can be.'

'But what about Hakon Vettel's dreamer? What about Mother? She won't be so happy, knowing you took me from her, will she?'

That had Ulrick swallowing. He'd known old crone dreamers and temptress dreamers and every ugly duckling witch in between, but never had he encountered one who scared him as much as Mother Arnesson. 'Well, we'll deal with her when the time comes. If it does. And if we can get back to Slussfall quickly enough, pack our things and get Bergit, we'll be on our way in no time.'

Lotta panicked. 'To where?' She squeezed her tooth tightly, wanting to hear her mother's voice, wanting her mother to hear what Ulrick said. 'Where will you take me?'

But Ulrick just grinned, eyes on the path. 'Move ahead of me now, little princess,' he urged. 'That's not wide enough for us both.'

***

Agnette fussed around Reinar, who leaned over Elin. He had laid her on their bed, and with Agnette's help, they had taken off her wet clothes, found her some dry ones and wrapped her in furs. The bedchamber had been cold, though Bjarni had quickly set a new fire. Now, he returned with an armload of logs, freshly chopped.

'Maybe you should come out, Agnette?' he hissed, sensing that Reinar was getting frustrated with his cousin.

'But...'

'Rienne can't watch Liara forever. She needs you. Can't you hear her crying out there?'

Agnette looked annoyed, torn, but she could hear her daughter, and she sighed. 'Alright. Reinar, you will come and tell me if she wakes, won't you?'

Elin hadn't opened her eyes yet. She was frozen solid. Unconscious.

Reinar nodded, returning to his chair by the bed.

Gerda stood in the doorway with Ludo and Sigurd. 'What's happening?' she muttered as Agnette and Bjarni came out, closing the door after them.

'She hasn't woken up,' Agnette said. 'I don't know what's happened to her, but she hasn't woken up.' She felt worried, confused by Elin's return, desperate to know what had happened. Gerda made to open the door, but Agnette stuck out an arm. 'Reinar wants to keep her resting. And she is. Come away, Aunty. We should go and tidy things up, have them ready for the Lady of Ottby's return!' She said it with a forced smile, barely thinking, seeing the sadness in her aunt's eyes as she turned away with a nod.

Reinar could hear them outside the door, whispering as loud as children who didn't know how to whisper at all. He frowned, increasing his pressure on Elin's cold hand, willing her to wake up.

And then she did.

Blinking, Reinar leaned forward, watching her eyes flutter

open. Hazel. Like Torvig's. Exactly like Torvig's.

Reinar blinked some more. 'Hello.'

Elin gasped, turning her head in surprise. 'What? What happened? Where am I?' She tried to sit up, but her arms were weak and wouldn't lift her body, and she slumped back with a groan. 'I... my horse! What happened?'

Reinar held up a hand. 'Ssshhh, it's alright. You fell off your horse. She's in the stables getting warm. She was as frozen as you. Well, maybe not quite as frozen as you.'

'Torvig!' Now Elin did manage to push herself up. 'I came for Torvig!'

Reinar sat back slightly, mouth ajar.

'I saw a dreamer. There was one where I've been...staying.' Elin felt more aware of where she was now, of who she was with. It made her uncomfortable, and she backed away, feeling weak. Shivering, she grabbed a fur, pulling it around her shoulders, noticing for the first time that she was wearing one of her old nightdresses.

'A dreamer?' Reinar didn't know what to say about that. He saw a green dress; golden hair blowing in the wind.

'She warned me that Torvig was in danger. That he was going to die!' Elin shuffled to the edge of the bed, ears buzzing. 'I had to come back. I bought a horse. I left as soon as she told me. I...' She saw the odd look in Reinar's eyes. She knew him better than anyone. Except Torvig. 'I...'

Reinar took her hand. 'I'm sorry, Elin.'

'No!' Elin jumped out of bed, fur dropping to the floor, nightdress swirling. 'No! No! No!' Hands to her head, she screamed, auburn hair tangled around her. 'Why? What happened? What happened to him?'

She was quickly hysterical but also weak, and Reinar leaped up from his chair just in time to catch her as she collapsed. 'Here, you must sit down. Stay on the bed. Rest.'

Sobs wracked Elin's exhausted body, her chest aching as she reached for her husband. 'What happened? Please, tell me! *Please!*'

The pain in her eyes was familiar, Reinar thought. Her words too. He squeezed Elin's hand, bringing himself back into the chamber. 'There was a battle. Hakon Vettel brought an army to Ottby. They breached the gates.' He considered lying, but it wasn't a lie he could protect. Everyone knew what Torvig had done, so it wouldn't be long before Elin heard a whisper.

She needed to know the truth.

Her head was in her hands, sobbing, her nose blocking, quickly unable to breathe. Reinar looked around for a napkin. 'I'll get you something to blow your nose.'

'No!' Elin wiped her nose on her sleeve, eyes full of madness. 'No, Reinar! I don't care about my nose. Tell me what happened to my brother, please!' She was shouting, though he stood an arm's length from her, and gripping his hand, she demanded an answer.

'Alright, alright. I...' He didn't know how to say it. 'He tried to kill Tulia. She did die. She fell. They had a fight, with swords. Tulia was injured from the battle, and weak. They were fighting in a shed. Tulia slipped in the straw, fell on a ship nail.' Reinar saw Sigurd's face when he'd told him. Sigurd weeping over his dead woman. And here he was, breaking another heart.

'Why?' Elin stopped crying, stunned. 'Why were they fighting?'

'We... took some women to sell as slaves, but we couldn't get to Goslund, we were ambushed, so they stayed here, with us. Tulia trained them to fight.' He stopped, trying to focus. 'Torvig had been taking one of them at night... raping her. Tulia saved her.' Reinar didn't mention Alys.

Elin didn't understand. 'No, not my brother. No! Who said that? *Who*? The woman? Why would you believe her? Some slave? Someone you don't know? You know Torvig! You know he's not like that!'

She had a round face, with full cheeks. They were blotchy, pink and tear-stained. Her hazel eyes were swollen, full of confusion and anger; her chin pointed, jaw clenched. She listened, but she wanted to scream some more.

Reinar knew her. He knew everything about that face.

He wanted to touch it, to comfort her, but Elin looked ready to spit at him.

'Why did you believe this woman?'

'Tulia found him raping her, Elin! I wasn't there. It was nothing to do with me. Tulia died to save the women!'

Elin froze. *'Women*? There was more than one?'

Reinar stared at her, unblinking, his heartbeat like a drum, pounding in his chest. 'There was another woman in the shed, yes. She's the one who killed Torvig after Tulia died. He... threatened to kill them all. She had no choice.'

Elin stared into his eyes, narrowing hers. 'And this woman, she was a warrior, like Tulia?'

'No. No.' Reinar shook his head. 'She was a dreamer.'

Elin's eyes flared with anger, furious now. 'A dreamer killed my brother? A *dreamer*?' None of it made sense. Arms flapping by her sides, she glanced around in panic. 'I have to go! I have to leave!' She needed clothes. A cloak. Some boots. 'I can't stay here! I won't!' Her eyes rested on the chests at the end of the bed, and she hurried to them, brushing away Reinar's hands as he tried to grab hold of her.

'Elin! Please. You're not well. You were unconscious. Please!'

The door burst open, and in came Agnette, Liara in her arms, Gerda behind her with a tray. 'We've brought you something warm to drink, dear Elin!' Agnette said, smiling. She'd been listening outside the door – they all had – and it was obvious that Reinar was going to need some help, though he didn't look happy to receive it.

'Now, why don't you hop back into bed and drink this warm milk? Just what you need to calm you down.' Gerda bustled past Reinar, hand quickly around Elin's back, steering her towards the bed.

Reinar stumbled, moving out of the way, catching the firm look in Agnette's eyes that told him to leave it to them. And needing to take a breath, he nodded, turning around, heading through the door.

***

Eddeth became so self-conscious around Falla that she almost stopped breathing. And sensing everything going dark, she gripped the table, stumbling.

Falla peered at her in the dull light of the tent. 'What is wrong with you?'

'Food!' Eddeth announced loudly, almost tipping over as she turned around. 'I've barely eaten since we were kidnapped. I am faint with hunger!' And she gripped the table again, eyes on the two cups steaming before her. She had made Falla a tea of peppermint and chamomile, with some dandelion root too. She'd eagerly made a second cup for herself, fleeting thoughts of her cottage and her cat making her homesick.

'I have nothing in here,' Falla said, almost apologetically as Eddeth brought the cup to her. She felt terrible. The journey and the smoke and the shock over Mother's death, not to mention the terror of the vatyr, had drained her. She took the cup, enjoying the warmth of it in her cold hands.

Eddeth took a seat opposite her, blinking rapidly.

'You're not a dreamer, are you?' Falla wondered, eyeing the woman.

Eddeth's eyes bulged, and she looked away, not wanting to even touch the edges of that topic. She snorted dismissively. 'You think I look like a dreamer? Ha!'

'You do, yes,' Falla insisted. 'And you know herbs, as many dreamers do. As Hakon's last dreamer did.' She felt odd speaking about Mother, who had been cruel, and manipulative, and a general nuisance, but more skilled than any woman she'd ever met.

'What happened to her, then?' Eddeth asked, knowing the answer, but wondering if Falla did. She dropped her head forward, inhaling the tea, not wanting to show her face.

'She died.'

Falla didn't elaborate, and Eddeth couldn't keep inhaling the tea forever, so she took a quick sip, lifting her eyes. 'That's a shame.

Useful, was she?'

'Of course, aren't all dreamers useful?' Falla didn't trust the odd woman, though she was enjoying the tea, which had warmed her frozen lips. 'What lord doesn't need a dreamer's guidance? The loss of Mother's sight is sorely missed already. We're stuck here in this forest with no idea what's coming.'

'Mmmm,' Eddeth murmured. 'And will your lord find a new dreamer, then? I imagine he'd want to, wouldn't he? Though where does one go to get a dreamer? There's hardly a dreamer market!' Eddeth took an enormous gulp of tea, sensing that her mouth was running away with her.

'Well, if he lives.' Falla leaned forward, aware of the sound of Lief's voice in the distance. 'Do you think he'll live?'

'He is improving,' Eddeth decided after considering the question for some time. 'Yes, he is, but I'm no dreamer. I can't see the future! Though I can make a delicious cup of tea, don't you think?' She finished off hers with a slurp, standing in a hurry. 'I must get back to the lord and check his wounds. Oh yes, indeed! Enjoy your tea. I shall make you more tomorrow if you like!' And swinging around, Eddeth almost tripped over her boots as she hurried outside.

Falla watched her go, head cocked to one side, thinking.

***

'She didn't take it well, then?' The distraction of Elin's dramatic return had stopped Sigurd from dwelling on his own heartbreak for a moment. He lifted a cup of ale to his lips, waiting for Reinar's reply.

'No.' Reinar stared at his own cup, then turned his head, looking towards the back of the hall, wondering if he should return to the bedchamber. 'Hard to tell someone their brother died. Harder still to tell them he was a rapist.'

Sigurd bit his teeth together, hand clenching around his cup.

The thought of what Torvig had done to Tulia, what he did to Stina, and would've likely tried to do to Alys if she hadn't killed him, made him wild. He left the cup on the table, pushing it away, dropping his head to his hands.

'I'm sorry,' Reinar said with a sigh. 'Sorry I ever brought the bastard back.'

'It's not your fault, Reinar.' Sigurd didn't know what to say, but he knew that only Torvig could be blamed for what Torvig had done. 'You're no dreamer. You couldn't see into his twisted heart. Not even Alys saw what he was doing.'

Reinar blinked, face changing. He felt trapped between two worlds and two women, more confused than ever. 'No, she didn't, did she? Though I imagine she had a lot on her mind, what with worrying about her children and trying to protect the fort.'

Sigurd lifted his head, still horrified to think that Alys had children. 'Do you think she's found them?'

'I hope so. She deserves to after what she did for us.'

'Though is anything ever that easy?' Sigurd wondered sadly, reaching for his cup again. 'Life has a way of complicating everything.' He saw Reinar's eyes shift to the back of the hall again. 'You should go. She's your wife. If you want to see her, Agnette and Gerda can't stop you.'

Reinar nodded. 'I know.' But he stayed where he was, returning his eyes to his cup, trying not to think at all.

***

Stina stared at the sheet flapping over the entrance to the tent, which looked as though it was trying to fly away. She felt much the same, and sighing, she turned around to Alys.

Alys had embraced the silence of the tent, sitting in the corner on a tree stump, shutting out the noise of the camp. She wanted to see images of her children, but when she closed her eyes, she saw the vatyr sweeping through the forest. She heard the deep voice of the god rolling over her like thunder.

'You.'

Alys jumped off the tree stump with a yelp, eyes on the ground where Hakon Vettel had started stirring on his pile of furs. One eye was open, blinking at her.

'Who... are... you?'

Stina rushed to Alys, clutching her arm, both of them peering down at the pale-faced lord.

'I... we are healers,' Alys croaked.

'I don't know you.' Hakon's eyes were fully open now, curious about these two women, both attractive, one of them mesmerisingly beautiful. He swallowed, his throat so parched that he struggled to form a word. 'Water.'

Stina hurried away to the table.

'Where have you come from?' Hakon grimaced, suddenly aware of the searing pain rippling across his belly. 'Where are we?' He couldn't remember anything for a moment, then bright images flashed before his eyes: Ottby, Reinar Vilander's sword, the horn, Mother's dead body. The pain. 'What happened to me?' He tried to sit up, but Alys leaned forward, gently pushing him back down.

'Your wound became infected. Your men stopped so you could recover. I don't know where we are. Your cousin's scouts, they... captured us.'

Hakon frowned. 'Why? Who are you?'

'You left many of your servants behind, certainly your healers. They thought we could help you.'

'And did you?' Stina had returned with the cup, and Hakon took it in an unsteady hand, spilling water everywhere. She helped to prop him up so he could take a drink, and gasping in discomfort, Hakon tipped most of the water out of the side of his dry mouth, over his chest, wetting his beard. 'Did you heal me?' He sank back against the furs, exhausted.

Stina took the cup to the table, shaking all over.

'Not us, but our friend, Eddeth, did,' Alys said. 'She's an

experienced healer.'

'Eddeth?' Hakon closed his eyes, images of Karolina swirling before him. He saw her smiling, her soothing hands smoothing hair away from his face.

And then another hand, on his forehead.

Eyes springing open, he stared up at Alys, who smelled like honey, he thought, reminded of his step-mother.

'You're not feverish, which is good.'

'I will live?'

Alys hesitated, images rushing before her eyes. She felt confused, lost in them. After days without any insight, now she was being drowned in visions.

'Alys?' Stina squeezed her arm.

'Sorry, yes, it was a strange night. I... I'm not the healer. We'll find Eddeth... I will. Stina can stay with you.' She smiled apologetically at her friend, hurrying out of the tent, not sure what she had seen at all.

***

Elin had cried herself to sleep, and Agnette tried to sneak out of the bedchamber. Gerda had reluctantly taken Liara, who had fallen asleep and needed to be put in her crib, leaving Agnette to fuss around the fire, wanting to keep Elin warm.

'Don't go.'

Agnette turned around with a smile. 'I thought you were asleep.'

'No, though perhaps I should be? Although, I'm not sure I'd want to wake up again. I...' Tears came quickly, and Elin shook her head which throbbed painfully. 'It was too much to hear. Torvig's my brother. It was too much to hear.'

Agnette sat on the bed, taking her hand. 'I'm so sorry for you, dear Elin. You've had a hard time. Such a hard time.'

Elin nodded, tears leaking into the creases around her eyes. 'I wasn't going to come back,' she whispered. 'I wasn't. You know that.'

Agnette leaned in. 'I know, so why did you?'

'A dreamer. I saw a dreamer. She sold her visions for coins, but everyone in Lundvik swore by her.' Elin sighed, rolling over to face Agnette, sniffing. 'I was trying to decide what to do. I kept thinking I would write to Reinar, or perhaps, come back, and explain things myself. Other times, I felt like sailing away to Osterland or the Fire Lands. Somewhere exciting. Somewhere new. I thought I could begin again...'

Agnette could see the same turmoil in Elin's eyes that she'd had before she ran away; the same wide-eyed pain and confusion. She patted her hand, trying to soothe her. 'So you talked to this dreamer?'

'Yes, and she told me about Torvig, that he was in danger. She told me other things, of course, but I had to come. When I thought Torvig might die, I had to come right away!'

'Poor Elin. Torvig did it to himself, he did. No one can understand it. It doesn't make any sense.' Agnette smiled through the lie, knowing how they all felt about Torvig. It was only Reinar who'd allowed his love for Elin to cloud his judgement. Only Reinar who hadn't seen the truth.

'And you're sure it's real? That it happened that way, Agnette? You're sure?'

Agnette nodded. 'I am. It's lucky it did, or he would have killed two more women.'

Elin couldn't believe it. She closed her eyes, wanting to escape Agnette's words. 'And this woman? The one who killed him? Where is she? I want to see her. I need to talk to her. I need to...'

Agnette froze, staring at Elin's closed eyes, sensing her body relax, exhausted, as though she was falling asleep. And she waited, hoping she would, not wanting to answer the question.

Eventually, Elin did fall asleep, and Agnette crept towards the door, hurrying out before her friend could utter another word.

CHAPTER TEN

Alys found Ivan with his tunic off, Eddeth bent over, slathering a salve over his tattooed back. 'Oh!'

Ivan was pleased to see her, but catching the concern in her eyes, he frowned. 'Is something wrong? Is it my cousin?'

'Your cousin is awake.'

Ivan jerked forward, away from Eddeth's sticky fingers. 'Awake?' He grabbed his tunic, grimacing, for though his wounds were not infected like Hakon's, they still stung. 'Come on, then!' he grinned at Eddeth, feeling a wash of relief calm his tense body. 'You need to come and check your patient!'

Alys grabbed hold of Eddeth as they turned after Ivan, trying to read her mind, wondering what she'd been up to, but all she could see was a jumbled mess of half-finished thoughts, and it left her feeling even more uncertain about what Eddeth might have said and done.

Ivan almost skipped around the fires, encouraging his men to keep working, finishing the big pit already piled high with bodies. They were digging individual graves for Erlan and Alef, Lief insisting that this was no time to breed resentment amongst their remaining allies by disrespecting their fallen lords.

Ivan tried to keep his smile going, masking his anxiety about what had happened, and the sinking feeling he had that was not at all alleviated by the news of Hakon's recovery. He slipped into the tent with a wink at Njall, pleased to see his cousin awake. 'You took your time! Having a nice rest while we freeze our arses off out there, were you? We should have stripped away the furs! That would have had you out of bed right away!'

Stina and Rikkard had propped Hakon up, leaning him against a pile of rolled-up furs so he could see and drink, though there was no smile in his eyes at the sight of Ivan. Everything had come back. He'd remembered every moment of their failed attack on Ottby. Of his interrupted fight with Reinar Vilander. Of Mother's death and their hasty retreat. 'Hello, Cousin.'

Ivan felt relieved that Hakon looked so alert, ignoring his miserable tone. 'Eddeth is a miracle worker!'

'Where is this Eddeth I keep hearing about?' Hakon rasped irritably, and then his eyes popped open as Eddeth burst into the tent, rushing past Ivan to his cousin.

'You look well, my lord! I am surprised! That wound was deadly. Too much for most healers, but not for me, it seems!' She grinned at Ivan, her eyes skipping past him to Alys and Stina, who looked awkward and nervous. And taking a deep breath, Eddeth dropped her shoulders, and leaned forward, gently pulling the bandages away from Hakon's belly, peering at his wound. The bandages were still mostly clean, and she didn't want to change them yet. 'Much better!'

Ivan leaned over her shoulder, squinting. 'What's that?'

'What?' Hakon started to wriggle, but Eddeth placed a hand on his shoulder, keeping him still.

'Maggots?'

'*What?*' Now Hakon did wriggle, jerking away from Eddeth, wanting to see for himself. And catching a glimpse of the tiny creatures wriggling inside his wound, he panicked. 'Get them out! Get them out of me now!' He grabbed Eddeth by the throat, dragging her towards him. 'What have you done to me?'

Ivan quickly pulled Eddeth back, out of Hakon's arms. 'Stop! She's healed you! Cured you! Look.' And pushing the bandage down, he showed Hakon how clean his wound was looking, despite the maggots and the honey and the garlic paste Eddeth had painted all around it. 'She's a healer, so if she thinks maggots help, perhaps they do?'

Eddeth nodded, hands around her aching throat, trembling now. 'They do, my lord. You can see, they do!'

Hakon lay back on the furs, not wanting to catch another glimpse of his stomach. Not wanting to imagine the creatures crawling inside him. 'How long must they be in there?' He glared at Eddeth, noticing her properly for the first time. She looked odd, and she smelled terrible, though he was struck by an immediate thought. 'You're not a dreamer, are you?'

Eddeth peered at Alys, who blinked, willing her to stop staring. And realising it, Eddeth swung back to Hakon. 'The number of people who ask me that! I'm beginning to wonder if I am!' She sniggered, amusing herself, though she could sense Alys and Stina growing worried behind her, and Ivan and Hakon staring at her curiously. 'No! The right answer, of course, is no, I'm not. Sadly, my only skills lie with herbs and maggots!'

Hakon didn't appreciate a reminder of the maggots, and he started squirming again, unable to remain still while those creatures crawled inside him. 'I'm not sure I can stand the thought of knowing they're in there. How will I sleep?'

'Keep them, Cousin, keep them,' Ivan urged with a grin. 'Listen to Eddeth. She'll take them out when we get back on the road, won't you?'

Eddeth nodded vigorously. 'Oh yes, I will. If you can keep them in there tonight, you'll be jumping out of bed come tomorrow!'

Hakon didn't take his eyes off her. 'You may go. All of you. I must speak to my cousin now.'

Eddeth breathed out a loud sigh of relief, creeping back towards Alys and Stina, who were quickly heading out of the tent, not wanting to be stopped.

Hakon didn't notice. Ivan, however, turned his head, eyes on Alys' rear end, head cocked to one side.

'So, you've forgotten Falla, Cousin? Finally? I was unconscious that long?'

Ivan laughed. 'Not that long, but no, Alys is hard to miss. Worth a look, I'd say, unlike Eddeth!'

Hakon grimaced, reminded of the maggots again. 'What's been happening? Any sign of Ake?'

'No sign of Ake. He hasn't followed us that I can see.'

Hakon felt relieved, though slightly disappointed. He didn't want to return to Slussfall a failure, though that looked likely now. 'Where are we?'

'Somewhere between Solstad and Reppa, I'd guess. In the snow. Stuck in the forest.'

Hakon yawned. 'Feels like I've been asleep for weeks. I had so many dreams. Such strange dreams!' He closed his eyes, working hard to ignore the maggots.

Ivan poured himself a cup of water, sitting down on a tree stump. 'About?'

Hakon frowned, bringing the memory of Alari back to his mind. 'Nothing that makes any sense.' He peered at his cousin, wanting to change the subject. 'You don't look like you've slept at all.'

'I... we had an interesting night while you were sleeping with your maggots. An army of vatyr attacked the camp.' Ivan started shaking his head and couldn't stop. 'I've never seen anything like it.' Reaching up, he touched the back of his head, still throbbing. 'The damage they left behind was real enough. We're still cleaning it up.'

'What?' Hakon sat up abruptly, almost screaming in pain, explosions of light bursting before his eyes. He slumped back, taking a breath, teeth gritted. 'What do you mean?'

'They killed Alef and Erlan, many of their men too. Just ripped them to pieces. Some of our men were killed as well. We lost a few hundred altogether by last count. They were in here too, according to Njall. Pulled the tent down. Luckily he was here to stop them.' Ivan saw the horror in his cousin's eyes, and he kept going. 'I don't know why they came, what they wanted, what it all means, but we have to leave. As soon as you're able, Cousin, we have to get out of here.'

Hakon just stared at him, Alari's voice screeching in his ears.

Neither of them spoke.

***

Alys, Stina, and Eddeth had edged away from Njall, whose sharp eyes followed them, ensuring that they remained nearby. He'd taken Alys' swordbelt off her, leaving it with their horses, still trying to piece together what had happened in the tent.

'What now?' Stina wondered, gripping Eddeth's arm. 'Will Hakon be well enough to travel soon?'

Eddeth nodded. 'Yes! It's just what we wanted. They will leave us behind.'

Alys didn't look so sure. She saw Lief and Falla coming towards them, and smiling, she turned away from Eddeth. 'Your lord is awake. He's with his cousin.' Alys watched disappointment flash across Falla's face, resignation on Lief's. Neither of them looked especially pleased.

She saw a sudden image of Reinar, and irritated, she blinked it away.

Lief eyed the tent. 'That's good. Good news,' he said dully. He was too exhausted to summon much enthusiasm, though it was surely better to have a path to follow now.

'I'll tell Hakon you're here,' Njall said, disappearing inside.

Lief turned to Falla. 'I won't be long. Perhaps you can show the women where they can be of most use? After last night, there's still a lot to do.'

Falla wanted to go to bed for the rest of the day and be left in peace. Though quickly remembering that her bed was a meagre mound of furs inside a shelter of branches and leaves, covered by cloaks, she thought better of it. 'Well, the sooner you get everyone back on their feet, the sooner we can all get out of here and go home.'

Eddeth looked thrilled. Though the night had terrified her, and the sight of the bodies was horrifying, she also felt exhilarated, for they were now walking amongst the gods; the gods who were watching, deciding which threads of fate to pull next. She winked at Alys, knowing for certain that the dreamer was going to be at the centre of it all.

***

Too upset and restless to stay in bed for long, Elin had dressed, heading to the stables to check on both her new horse and her old horse, and she was busy brushing Milka when Reinar found her.

'Are you sure you're well enough to be up?' He remembered the crumpled figure he'd picked out of the snow only hours earlier. 'It's not warmed up all day.'

Elin's swollen eyes briefly met his before returning to her gentle grey mare. 'What happened to Milka? She's injured.'

Reinar dropped his head, eyes on his hands which he'd clasped in front of his cloak, feeling awkward. Elin was his wife, but so much had happened since they'd last seen each other. It was as though they were strangers, meeting for the first time. 'She fell in a hole.'

'*You* were riding her?' Elin was surprised.

Reinar looked up, staring into her curious eyes. He remembered those big eyes, and he smiled. 'No, not me. I don't think she would have appreciated that.' He held out his hand for Milka to snuffle. Her leg had not broken, though keeping her in the stables while the snow was terrorising the fort would aid her recovery.

'Who was riding her, then?' Elin's voice was sharp.

Reinar froze, though denying the truth would only get him in trouble eventually. 'One of the women we took as slaves. The dreamer.'

It was Elin's turn to freeze. 'Oh?'

Reinar quickly changed the subject. 'How are you feeling? Agnette said you'd rushed out of the hall without a word. You need some food inside you. That journey could have killed you.'

Elin was dismissive. 'I'm not hungry. Ask Sigurd if he feels like eating. Grief makes you ill, not hungry, Reinar, though perhaps you've forgotten?' She wanted to hurt him because she felt hurt. Because she was in pain.

'I haven't forgotten.'

Silence.

Reinar stepped closer to his wife. 'Will you stay? Here? Do you... want to stay?' His eyes sought hers, though Elin would not look at him. Her brother was dead, and she felt broken-hearted and sad. Exhausted too.

She sighed. 'I don't know.' And then she turned her face to his, hands remaining by her sides. 'You are poison, Reinar Vilander. You kill what you touch. Your luck is gone. I'm not sure what I –'

'No!' Reinar grabbed her hand, wanting her to hear the truth, to see the change in him. 'No, it was a curse! Eddeth discovered that it was all a curse!'

'What?'

'All of it, everything that happened, there were symbols carved into trees in the forest. It was a curse.'

Elin's mouth hung open. She couldn't close it.

'It was Hakon Vettel's dreamer. She cursed me. The entire fort. Everyone!'

'You're sure?' Elin was stunned. 'All of it?'

Reinar nodded. 'All of it. She cursed us, but now she's dead. And the curse is lifted. We burned all the trees. It's gone, I promise.'

'The dreamer killed our babies?'

Reinar blinked. 'I think so... yes. She was trying to weaken us, destroy us. Destroy me.'

Elin burst into tears, the pain of the last year rushing out of her like a waterfall. 'I didn't want to leave, I didn't. Reinar!' And she fell into his arms, a sense of relief rendering her limp. 'I never wanted to leave you, but I was so scared about what would happen next! I couldn't... I couldn't go through that again!'

Reinar pulled her close, feeling the familiar contours of her body as she shuddered against him. It was everything he wanted. To know that she was safe. Home. With him.

Yet he felt empty. As though he wasn't there at all.

***

Hakon was just as eager to get to Slussfall as Ivan, already talking about how they would regroup once they were safely inside the fortress; how they would plot another attack on Ottby in the spring.

Ivan left him resting, with Eddeth working hard to convince Hakon to leave the maggots where they were, and he headed across the camp, eager to check on the wounded. He quickly found Alys and Stina working on their hands and knees, bent over a trembling man, who lay on his stomach as they tried to stitch up the great slashes down his back. The man was in shock, shaking so much that Alys was having trouble keeping him still. 'You've been busy.'

Stina tied the last piece of thread, snipping off the end with a knife, and she started trying to make the man more comfortable. They were exposed out in the forest, with little more than rudimentary shelters for some, and none at all for most. She grabbed a cloak, draping it over the man's legs.

Alys stood, wiping hair out of her eyes with the back of a bloody hand. 'We've dealt with everyone now, I think. They only just found this poor man in the forest.'

Ivan encouraged her to walk with him, away from Stina. 'Now that Hakon is on the mend, I expect you'll want to leave? Especially after last night.'

Alys nodded, trying not to appear as desperate as she felt. 'We want to go home, yes, of course. It wasn't our intention to be here.' She smiled, sensing how eager Ivan was to please her. Though, would he try to keep her? His thoughts were messy, much like Ivan himself, and Alys couldn't find the answer.

Ivan continued walking, hand in the air, motioning for Jerrick to come to him. 'Well, I couldn't blame you. We're not the most attractive proposition. A defeated army crawling home, hounded by vengeful spirits? We're hardly the heroes of this saga!' He grinned at Alys before turning to Jerrick. 'Hakon is better, much better, thanks to a handful of hungry maggots! So prepare the men to leave in the morning. He's impatient to get back to Slussfall.' Ivan sighed, not keen to head back to Slussfall at all. He missed his childhood home in Orbo, with its magnificent views of the sea. Their trip to Ottby had been a disappointing waste of time and men, and once he was fully recovered, Hakon would be unbearable. And that meant that life would quickly become unbearable for all of them, especially Ivan, who would be forced to placate and calm his cousin as he raced towards his next plans for attacking the Vilanders.

Ivan knew Hakon.

He would never rest until every last one of them was dead.

***

After spending some time with Leonid, Magnus had slipped away to explore the fort. With Jonas' coins, he'd purchased a hooded cloak that was far too big for him, but it was warm, made with thick wool, dyed a dark blue, and his teeth almost stopped chattering long enough for him to think. Flurries of snow swept through the wintry air, and he lifted his head, eyes on the towering figures that crowded around tables and braziers, talking and trying to keep warm.

Magnus hoped that Jonas and Vik would stay safe. That he would too.

And glancing around, he tried to think of what to do.

There were so many men and women hurrying past him that he felt small and unseen, and though he could weave his way through them without being noticed, that wouldn't help him find Lotta. And he certainly couldn't stand and stare, peering at faces, trying to find Long Beard or Silver Tooth, or Long Beard's wife, though he remembered Silver Tooth's vividly terrifying description of her.

And he barely knew their names...

Magnus froze, listening to someone calling out.

'Bergit Dyre, I haven't seen you in days!'

Stumbling around, mouth hanging open, Magnus realised that he did know one name.

That of Long Beard's wife.

***

Alys watched Ivan and Lief in the distance. They looked like two stags butting antlers. She had a sense that there were many men in the camp who wanted to be the lord, who thought they knew how things should run. Alys supposed that was always the way. She thought back to Ottby and Reinar. And Torvig.

A good lord listened to those men he trusted to give him sound advice. Though a good lord could still be blinded by loyalty and not see the truth.

'You are dreaming?'

Alys spun around, horror in her eyes. 'I'm sorry?'

'I was talking to you, but you didn't answer,' Falla smiled coldly. 'I thought perhaps you were dreaming?'

Alys relaxed her face. 'I think I was. Last night was so terrifying. It has... not been easy being here.'

'No?' Falla stepped closer, wanting to know more.

And sensing it, Alys held her ground, wishing she could hold her tongue too. 'We are prisoners. It's impossible to know our fate when we're not the ones deciding it.'

Falla almost sneered. 'You're helpers, not prisoners. You helped the lord, and soon you will leave.'

'I hope so, we would like to go home.'

'And you will, as I'm sure my husband will tell you now.' Falla eyed Lief, who was walking their way. 'You have news of our departure?' She gripped his hand with some urgency, desperate to leave the stench of death and defeat behind.

'Yes, it's decided, we'll leave tomorrow morning. Hakon insists he will be well enough to ride, and Ivan agrees.'

Alys felt a lift that was quickly crushed by a growing certainty that their time with the Vettels was not over yet. She tried not to think about Magnus and Lotta, knowing that she couldn't do anything about finding them while they were trapped with the army. 'I'll tell my friends, thank you.' And spying Stina and Eddeth talking to Njall, she hurried away.

***

The urge to run was strong.

Sigurd fought it as he stood before the pyre, imagining Tulia standing on the opposite side of it, sneering at the ceremony. He didn't know what her people did, or what was the best way to honour her. He just wanted to curl up next to her and feel her warm skin beneath his cold hands.

Reinar nudged him, offering him the torch.

It was his last moment seeing her body, and though it was wrapped in a shroud, she was still there with him.

Reinar had spoken warmly of her, and Sigurd had cried, listening.

Snow was falling, wet on his face, melting like tears.

He saw images of Torvig, rage mingling with sorrow until he wanted to roar in agony.

And sighing, he blinked Torvig away.

His last moment.

Tears ran down Sigurd's cheeks as he took the flaming torch and edged forward to the tightly stacked tower of wood, eyes on the gifts they had brought to honour Tulia. The weapons and jewellery. The food and coins. She would be comfortable on her journey to the Underworld, he thought.

Though would she like being so comfortable?

He smiled sadly, pushing the torch in between two pieces of wood.

And closing his eyes, he saw her sitting on top of him, black hair covering her breasts, hands on his shoulders as she leaned forward, staring into his eyes. 'I love you,' she whispered, her voice hoarse. 'Whatever else you remember about me, Sigurd Vilander, remember that.'

And stepping back from the pyre, Sigurd watched it spark into life for a moment, before dropping his head, and turning away.

CHAPTER ELEVEN

Hakon had dozed on and off throughout the day, dreaming of his wife. In his dreams, she was usually naked, her hair wild about her face, lying in their comfortable bed, surrounded by furs.

He liked to see her that way.

But he'd also seen her sitting beside him in Stornas' grand hall, a golden crown on her head, coloured jewels at her throat, her eyes sparkling in the glow of a thousand candles.

Hakon woke slowly, smiling, and then Eddeth leaned over him, and he yelped. 'What are you doing?' He spoke with a rasp, and coughing, he tried to find his old voice, desperate to feel more like himself again. He was the Lord of Slussfall, the rightful King of Alekka. He didn't want anyone forgetting that, especially not him. 'Stop it!'

'I'm going to take out my little friends,' Eddeth grinned, though she did not feel happy. Her maggots had worked hard, and if the lord wanted to get out of bed and spend all day on a horse come morning, he was likely to undo all their good work. She felt offended on their behalf. 'I must rub more honey on you now, then I shall strap you up!'

Hakon squirmed as Eddeth's cold, rough hands started exploring his exposed belly. He wanted to push her away, but he was also well aware that Eddeth and her maggots had likely saved his life. Eyes up as Ivan entered the tent, he smiled, happy for the distraction. 'You've spoken to Lief?' He tried to wriggle upwards, wanting to sit, but Eddeth pushed him down.

'I have. The man's an old woman! I'm surprised he left his bed to come here in the first place. He thinks we should stay longer. And after last night? We'd be mad to stay here a moment longer than we need to. We need to head back to Slussfall. We need to get somewhere we're not so exposed!'

Eddeth froze, maggots crawling over her fingers. She forced her eyes to remain on Hakon's wound, desperately trying not to ask questions.

But she had so many!

Lips quivering, she picked each maggot up, placing it back into her little jar.

Hakon peered at Eddeth, sensing her interest in their conversation, though that was hardly surprising. He glared at his cousin, shuddering. The sensation of those maggots inside him, crawling over his flesh, was something he'd been unable to get used to, and he tried to distract himself further, which was easy as Ivan was a constant distraction. 'Any sign of Ulrick?'

'Ulrick? No, no sign at all. He wanted that little girl, and, in the end, he got her. Ha! I thought for certain Mother would have won that battle, though now he's had the last laugh. He's got the girl, and his life!'

Hakon wasn't happy. 'He left. Me. His lord. In the middle of a battle! Perhaps Mother needed that girl? Perhaps she died because she didn't have her?' Hakon doubted that was true, but he wasn't inclined to wish Ulrick Dyre the best for betraying him. And worrying that Alari was watching and listening, he felt inclined to defend Mother.

Loudly.

Eddeth left her maggot jar on the table and started applying more honey, twitching, struggling to stay quiet.

'And you would've felt good about that, would you?' Ivan stepped closer, wanting to see what Eddeth was doing. He peered over her shoulder, impressed by how clean the wound looked, though the smell of garlic was overpowering. Trying not to inhale, he turned his attention back to his cousin. 'If that old dreamer witch had killed her? You're surely not happy about killing a child?'

Hakon shrugged, wanting to change the subject. 'Well, whatever the case, when we get back to Slussfall, Ulrick and I will need to have a word.'

Ivan laughed, turning around. 'Leave him alone, and little Lotta. Let him be happy. Him and Bergit both.' He headed out of the tent. 'You're doing a masterful job, Eddeth!' he grinned, grabbing a handful of the flapping sheet. 'I'm not sure how we'll cope without you!' And disappearing outside, he wondered where Alys had gotten to.

***

Magnus didn't know if Bergit was a common name, though he'd never met one. But there were surely more Bergits in Slussfall, because the woman who'd answered to that name and was now deep in conversation with the weaver who'd let Leonid have the table he so desired, was no old crone.

Silver Tooth had described her in such a way that Magnus was afraid of finding her, but this woman was attractive. She looked older than his mother – perhaps Stina's age, Magnus thought – and Stina was thirty-eight, he remembered. She had orange hair, which rippled like flames, hanging loose down her back as she laughed with the weaver. Her face was pale, her lips full and pronounced, her cheeks rounded. She appeared healthy and happy, not at all like Silver Tooth's description. Not like Long Beard either, who was a filthy barnacle of a man, all rough edges and foul smells.

Magnus shook his head, deciding that she was not the right Bergit. But something nagged at him when he looked at her, and he knew that he needed to know for sure. Perhaps Silver Tooth had just been teasing him? Perhaps this Bergit was blind and didn't notice how mean and ugly Long Beard was?

Magnus saw Leonid out of the corner of his eye, and he

crept forward, ignoring him, edging towards the table next to the weaver's where an old woman was selling a paltry selection of vegetables. She looked half-starved, and Magnus wondered why she didn't just eat them herself. His eyes snapped to the parsnips, reminded of Urna Kraki, and blinking, he tried to focus, pretending to browse as he moved closer to the chatting women.

Their gossip was dull and uninteresting, and there weren't enough vegetables on the old woman's table to keep him busy for long. She shooed him away with a toothless bark, unhappy with his loitering. Magnus stumbled, turning to leave, ears open to the last snatches of conversation. The women had moaned about the weather, gossiped about their friends, and complained about the price of wine, before progressing to talk about their husbands.

'Ulrick might be home before the rest of them,' Bergit smiled. 'He's been scouting for Hakon Vettel. He's one of his most valued men, you know. He's been gone for weeks. All I can hope is that he misses the battle and just comes home to me. Like my child, he is! My husband and child rolled into one!' She glanced at Magnus, who had stopped to stare. 'What do you want, then? A boy your age? Have you nothing better to do?' She peered down at Magnus, hands on hips, pouting lips curled into a snarl.

And then Leonid was there, all smiles and bows, pulling Magnus away. 'Ahhh, lady, I do apologise. It's what happens when you employ a boy, I'm afraid. Averse to hard work, the lot of them!'

Bergit turned away, ignoring Magnus' gaping mouth, and Leonid's pandering, eager to continue her conversation. Magnus watched her, though, barely noticing that Leonid had dragged him back to his table.

He could feel his heart banging in his chest, realising that he knew another name.

Ulrick.

***

Eddeth burst open like a ripe plum, talking so quickly that neither Alys nor Stina could understand her.

Then one word stuck out.

In all the mumbling, spluttering, one word stuck out.

'Lotta? What do you mean, Lotta?' Alys hissed, grabbing Eddeth's arm. They were walking through the centre of the camp, within view of their guardian, Njall, struggling to find anywhere to be alone.

Eddeth couldn't breathe. She stopped, collapsing forward, hands on her knees. 'Oh... oh!' And standing up, she sucked in an enormous breath, shoulders heaving. 'So hard that was, trying not to say anything! Not able to ask questions, to know more! For surely there is more to know! Who is this Ulrick? Where is he taking Lotta? To Slussfall? Well... now that looks unlikely, wouldn't you say?'

Stina hurried to Eddeth's other side, wanting to stick a hand over her mouth. There was no sign of Falla or Lief Gundersen, or Ivan Vettel, though who knew how many of the warriors and servants milling around were loyal to Hakon. Likely all of them. 'Eddeth, ssshhh,' she warned. 'You shouldn't mention names. Please.'

Eddeth nodded. 'A man named Ulrick took Lotta away from the old dreamer. The one you...' Eddeth peered around, lowering her voice to a whisper, 'killed.'

Alys glared at her. 'Alright, alright, I think we know what you mean.' She glanced over her shoulder, seeing Njall stomping their way. 'And he's taking her to his wife? Is that what you said?' It sounded similar to something she remembered from her dreams.

'Yes, but he may not stay in Slussfall, or go there at all if he thinks the old dreamer will try to steal Lotta away,' Eddeth warned, weary mind whirring. She sneezed, immediately feeling better.

Alys felt terrible.

Stina grabbed her hand, sensing it. 'We just need to know more. Perhaps you can find information in... other ways?' She didn't want anyone discovering that Alys was a dreamer. They would never be free if they did.

Alys squinted, the sun in her eyes as it headed for its bed. She remembered standing on Ullaberg's beach, watching the sun set, and she could almost feel Lotta's cold little hand in hers, trying to pull her along, wanting her to see the shell she'd found. She blinked, turning as Njall stopped before them.

'Ivan wishes to see you,' he mumbled, eyeing the women in turn. They looked suspicious to him, always whispering to each other, especially that odd Eddeth. He was certain they couldn't be trusted, though it was hard to say why.

'He wants to see all of us?' Stina wondered, hoping to keep Eddeth far away from the Vettels.

'No, just you,' Njall said, inclining his head to Alys. 'He's waiting in his tent.'

Alys nodded, wrapping her cloak around her chest as she hurried after him.

'What do we do?' Eddeth fretted, stomach rumbling. 'We must do something. A plan! We should work on a plan!'

'A plan for what?' Stina asked quietly, drawing Eddeth close.

'A plan for when everything goes wrong, for surely it's about to!'

***

Supper was plentiful, which made Bjarni happy. He was ravenous, delighting in the fare Gerda had instructed Rilda to cook. It was a special occasion, after all, welcoming back the true Lady of Ottby.

Bjarni thought Gerda looked slightly put out that Elin had come back, though he was sitting between her and Agnette, and there was no opportunity to gossip about her. He would save that for later, when he was tucked up in bed with his wife, who would surely have something to say about it.

Agnette was distracted. Liara was asleep in their chamber, and though she had left the door open, she kept turning around, listening.

'Perhaps you should take your plate to your chamber?' Gerda grumbled, fed up with Agnette's wriggling. She spoke quietly, still smiling, conscious that Elin was sitting in her place.

'I'm nearly finished,' Agnette said sharply. She saw Gerda recoil, not used to being the one on the end of a tongue lashing. Agnette didn't have time to feel guilty, though, she had far too much on her mind, worrying about her baby, and the fort, Bjarni, and now Elin. She glanced down the table, seeing Elin sitting next to Reinar, smiling and laughing as though she'd never left.

It confused her.

Ludo caught Agnette's eye, almost reading her mind, which reminded him of Alys and Stina. The Ullaberg women had fitted into the fort effortlessly, especially Alys. It was strange not to see her near Reinar or Sigurd; strange not to see her with Eddeth, Winter bounding after her. He frowned, realising that he hadn't seen Winter all day. Rigfuss was no trouble to look after. He ignored Ludo, just happy to have a bowl of milk, and some fishy scraps left out for him. Winter, however, was aloof, barely present.

They were all missing Alys, it seemed.

Ludo turned, staring down the table at Reinar, whose face was almost unreadable. Sometimes, he looked happy, but perhaps it was just his lips curling into a smile, he thought, staring more closely, wanting to see his eyes.

'Ludo!' Bjarni nudged him, having gotten no response. 'Pass the ale jug!'

Reinar blinked, realising that he'd been holding an empty cup for some time. He put the cup down on the table, turning to face Elin, trying to focus.

'I hope Sigurd's not hiding from me,' Elin said, feeling upset. Her head ached from crying. Her eyes too. It was hard to believe that Torvig had hurt anyone. Impossible, even. Though it was what everyone seemed to have decided had happened. It was what Sigurd obviously believed as he'd barely met her eyes since she'd returned.

'No.' Reinar shook his head. 'After the pyre? He just wants to be alone. He's gone to the dreamer's cottage.' That felt odd to say, and Reinar had to work hard to suppress the feelings of guilt that bubbled up inside his chest when he thought of Alys.

'Salma was a dear woman. So kind. And now you're without a dreamer...' Elin's eyes narrowed, searching Reinar's.

Reinar turned away from her as the doors opened, checking on the latest arrivals. Some of his warriors had returned to the fort, hearing the news of their victory over the Vettels; those without wives, who weren't too proud to show their faces again. Reinar wasn't about to judge. He needed every man he could get his hands on, and it was encouraging to feel the fort filling up again. Now he had his reputation back. His wife too. And smiling at Elin, he reached down to hold her hand. 'I'm not that interested in dreams anymore. Not when I have you back. What do I need to dream of?' He leaned in to kiss her, surprised when Elin recoiled, her smile slipping for a moment.

'Well, it's always useful to know what's out there. To have a warning of what's coming, don't you think? For how can we save ourselves if we don't know the danger we face?'

She sounded odd, Reinar thought, not like herself at all. He smiled, though, nodding, trying to convince himself that what she needed was time. She was grieving, exhausted, displaced. It would just take some time for everything to fall back into place again.

But it would, Reinar told himself.

It would.

***

'He hasn't found anything,' Jonas muttered, eyes on the fort in the distance. There'd barely been a hint of sun throughout the day, but it was certainly on its way down. Rain was falling steadily now, like tiny shards of ice as it hit their faces. 'They'll close the gates soon.'

Vik nodded, frozen body tense. 'No, he hasn't found anything, but that's to be expected, isn't it? Hard to find someone who's not out in the open, and not everyone's strutting around a fort all day, showing off the little girl they kidnapped.'

Jonas turned to him. 'We should have gone in. Why didn't we go in?' Lifting his hands to his wet face, he scratched his beard.

'Because we made a decision. We had a plan. We want to get them both out alive. And this is the best way.' Though doubts had ripped great holes in Vik's confidence too, and he was left wondering what their next plan was going to be.

The traders and farmers were leaving the fort, most without their goods. Some were still lumbered with theirs, and those men and women had slumped shoulders, walking slowly, weighed down by their problems and the failure of their day to turn things around.

'He might still come,' Vik decided. 'You told that silversmith to find us, so we wait. He might still come.'

Jonas edged closer, until he was almost out of the forest entirely, hoping and wishing and praying to the gods that Magnus would get out of the fort safely.

***

Magnus had hovered around the busy square all day, wanting to hear more information about Ulrick. Bergit was a popular woman in Slussfall, it appeared, and wealthy enough to have spent much of the day conversing with the stallholders, parting with many coins.

Information too.

She liked to talk about herself and how valuable her husband was to Hakon Vettel. She seemed at her happiest when people were telling her how lucky and beautiful she was, and how great her prospects would be once Hakon reached Stornas and rewarded his most loyal men.

Though realising that there was little else to discover, and no point in remaining in the fort, Magnus had returned to Leonid, who had spent the afternoon embroiled in an argument with his neighbour, a rival silversmith. Leonid was not an argumentative man, but his desperation to sell his goods had led to him becoming increasingly vocal in his attempts to attract customers to his table. Insults had flown back and forth throughout the afternoon as each man vied to secure a purchase.

Magnus stood behind Leonid's table, smiling awkwardly at prospective customers, trying to ignore the arguing, sniping men before him as they became even angrier.

Leonid Grubert was a slight, nervous man, inexperienced in all matters of weaponry, raised by an equally nervous silversmith who had never shown him how to fight. His rival had four brothers, two of them warriors, and all of them as thick-necked and bone-headed as he was, so when the insults had become too galling to ignore, the thick-necked silversmith had whipped out a knife, ordering Leonid to shut his yapping mouth before he cut out his tongue.

Leonid panicked, not even having an eating knife to hand. Looking around quickly, he swooped up a water jug from a neighbouring table. His remaining goods were already packed into his satchels, and he was eager to be gone. He'd meant to simply throw the water from the jug at the man, grab Magnus' hand and run, but a sudden downpour of sleety rain had his hands both numb and wet, and he slipped, throwing the heavy jug at his rival's head instead.

And the rival silversmith, Malick Valborg, was a sturdy man, who would've normally stood his ground and ended up with a lump on his head and an urgent need to beat Leonid black-and-blue. But the rain had soaked the boards they stood on, and he slipped, losing his balance, falling to the ground with a thump, hitting his head on a rock.

Magnus froze, staring down at the man.

Leonid looked ready to faint, holding his breath, willing Malick to stand up.

MARK OF THE HUNTER

The neighbouring stallholders rushed over, including one of Malick's brothers, who dropped to his knees, feeling for a pulse.

Looking up, blood on his hands, he called out in horror. 'He's dead! He's dead! Look at his head. You killed him!' And pointing a finger at Leonid, he raised his voice, screaming louder. 'He killed him! He murdered my brother!'

Magnus wondered if it was all a joke, a dream. He started to step away. As much as he wanted to help Leonid, he didn't see what he could do. He was conscious of the rain-soaked sky darkening above his head, worried that he would not be able to escape the fort before the gates were closed for the night.

And then a hand on his shoulder, and Magnus turned around as a helmeted guard grabbed him, dragging both him and Leonid across the square, through the pouring rain.

CHAPTER TWELVE

Alys didn't know what Ivan was up to.

He had invited her into his small tent, where boulders and tree stumps had been rolled in to make a table and two chairs. The table had been laid out with a selection of fish and cheese, bowls of soup that smelled strongly of dill and onions, and two cups of ale. A fire blazed away in a ring of stones in the corner, a few candles guttering scant light across the table.

Alys had remained by the entrance initially, hoping to leave quickly, concerned that Ivan appeared to have tidied himself up. He had combed and rebraided his hair and changed into a light-coloured tunic, mostly washed clean of any blood and dirt. Alys had swallowed, sensing that she needed to make a quick escape, but Ivan had encouraged her to sit down, and they had eaten supper together. As worried as she felt about her children, she had rediscovered her appetite, almost enjoying the roasted perch, despite the abundance of bones. She took a few sips of ale, surprised to discover that it tasted stronger than anything she'd drunk in Ottby.

And blinking quickly, she tried not to think about Ottby.

'We'll depart for Slussfall at dawn,' Ivan said, wiping soup out of his beard.

'You must be in a hurry to get home if you want to leave that quickly. Your cousin shouldn't be riding yet. Eddeth's not happy.'

'Mmmm, well, my cousin has other ideas. He wants to get

home as soon as possible,' Ivan said, struggling to keep his eyes on Alys' face. He'd been helping himself to ale all day and was slightly drunk, his attention wandering to her lips, dropping suddenly to her breasts.

'But not you?' Alys' voice was sharp, trying to focus him.

Ivan blinked, lifting his eyes. 'Slussfall's a base. A stepping stone.'

'But not home?'

'Not home,' Ivan agreed, wanting to change the subject. He hadn't invited her into his tent to talk about him. 'And you, do you like your home? I forget its name.'

'Ullaberg.' Alys forced herself to smile because now when she thought of Ullaberg, she thought of her cruel, dead husband. 'It's barely a village, but it's my home. Where I must return.'

'Must you, though?' Ivan leaned across the table, reaching for her hand. 'Must you go, Alys? To... Ullaberg? It sounds like a nothing sort of place if I don't even know its name.'

Alys squirmed, slipping her hands off the table, into her lap. Ivan's intentions had become abundantly clear, and she needed to find a way to leave quickly. 'Ullaberg has the most beautiful beach,' she mumbled. 'There are many coves and beaches down the coast with nothing but stones, but Ullaberg's beach is all sand. It doesn't have to be known by you, or anyone else to be my home.'

Ivan moved his tree stump closer to Alys, and sitting back down, he lifted his cup in one hand, placing his other hand on Alys' knee.

Alys froze. 'I...' Ivan was their best chance of being freed quickly, and she didn't want to risk offending him. Then, remembering what had happened to Stina, she jumped to her feet with a scowl. 'Are you planning to rape me?'

Ivan rocked back in surprise, almost falling off his stump. 'What?' He staggered to his feet, legs wobbling. '*Rape* you?' He snorted. 'You think that's why you're here?'

Alys glared at him. 'What else do you want with me?'

Ivan stepped towards her. Just the one step. He swayed, trying hard to stay still, to sound like a man. 'I'm a lord. A Vettel. A famed warrior!' He frowned, doubting the last was true. 'I've no need to rape anyone. No desire to, either.' And slamming one hand down on the table, he tried to steady himself, eyes on Alys.

'Why did you bring me here, then?'

Ivan smiled, his face lighting up. 'Because you are the most beautiful woman I've ever seen. You have a face like a goddess. I wanted to feed you, talk to you. Most women I know don't have much to say. Or perhaps, I'm too busy trying to get their clothes off to listen!' He laughed, not feeling embarrassed. 'You, though... you're different, I think. Perhaps because you're older?'

'Older?'

'Older than me, I'd guess, for I am merely a boy. Not even twenty-four!'

'Well, then, compared to you, I'm an old crone,' Alys smiled, not revealing anything further. She froze suddenly, seeing an image of Magnus, feeling his terror. And shivering, she turned away from Ivan, hoping to see more.

'Are you alright? Alys?' Ivan hurried to her, hand on her arm.

Alys stayed where she was, desperately trying to see Magnus, but now there was only darkness. Darkness and Ivan Vettel's hand touching her. She turned around quickly, wanting to shake it off, but it didn't budge. 'I think it was the ale. Or the fish. I feel a little full.'

'Well, come, sit back down. I want to talk to you, about tomorrow. About what we will do with you.'

'*Do* with us?'

Ivan started rambling about things that were important, about things Alys very much needed to listen to, but her mind was flashing with worrying images of Magnus.

Of her grandfather. Of Vik.

She kept frowning, blinking, looking around.

And then Ivan finally got to what he was trying to say.

'...so, we both think it best if you come with us to Slussfall.'

Alys stared at him, trying to focus, though that only seemed to encourage Ivan to come closer, and she stepped back. 'What? Why?' She had an urgent need to tip some more of his potent ale down her throat, sensing everything tangling up into the most impossible mess; reminded again of Reinar's offer to send warriors with her. 'Slussfall? But we're going to Ullaberg, Ivan, we're not going to Slussfall.'

Ivan was surprised by her resistance. He had thought they were getting along so well. 'Once Hakon has fully recovered, you'll be free to go on your way.'

Alys narrowed her eyes, completely focused on him now.

'You will, I swear it. I do. I just don't want Hakon falling ill again, and he's bone-headed enough to push himself too hard just to prove that he's the lord who will be king. It would do our hopes no good if something were to happen to him now.'

Alys sighed, shoulders tight, impatient to leave. 'Slussfall?'

Ivan smiled at her, nodding. 'Slussfall.'

***

The rain turned to sleet, and then snow, and both men knew that they had to seek the shelter of their tent, which Jonas quickly regretted pulling apart in a burst of nervous energy. But there was no point standing out in the foul weather, watching the dark silhouette of the fortress, its gates long closed.

'We might have missed him,' Vik mumbled, frozen solid. He didn't move, though. He barely blinked, looking at the old fort, trying to remember how it looked inside, and where Magnus might have hidden away to get some sleep.

'That Leonid looked very keen for more silver,' Jonas sighed. 'He wanted the rest of it, I saw that in his eyes. Half-starved he was, so why didn't he come to us? Even if we missed Magnus, why didn't Leonid find us? We haven't moved all day. Where is the man?' He ran a wet hand over his beard, shoulder blades tight with tension. 'We have to get in there!'

Vik nodded. 'We do, I know. And we will. First thing come

morning. So that's what we need to do now. Not stand out here like two old fools trying to undo something that can't be undone tonight. We can go and plan. Get warm, get some food. We can't help Magnus if we don't help ourselves first.'

Jonas didn't even blink, but he took one last look at the fort, before turning around to follow Vik back into the trees, hoping that wherever he was, Magnus was safe and warm.

***

They had been taken to the prison hole. That's what Leonid called it, and Magnus was too scared to ask anything further. It was a long, dark hole that smelled of shit. Rats too. Magnus could hear them squeaking and scurrying around. It was too dark to see much, but occasionally, he felt something furry brush past his leg. There was one small barred window that looked out onto the square, one iron-strong door with a flap where the guards would bark at the prisoners or throw some slop inside when it was time for supper.

It was a miserable place, promising a miserable death.

Leonid had sobbed for the first few hours, uncontrollably, and loudly.

They were not alone in the hole, though, and eventually, some of the other prisoners, who looked bigger, harder, and meaner than Leonid, had threatened him with fists and broken teeth if he didn't shut up, and after that he'd slumped down beside Magnus under the window, mostly silent.

Magnus didn't know what to say. He was in shock; unsure why he'd been blamed for what Leonid had done; wondering how he was going to escape and get word to Jonas and Vik about what had happened.

Leonid didn't appear to care. He hadn't said a word to Magnus. He hadn't even looked his way.

Magnus dropped his head to his knees, feeling the icy snow

blowing through the barred window, trying to see his mother's face.

***

Reinar felt awkward being in the bedchamber with Elin, which was ridiculous, he knew. They had slept in the bed together for nearly a year before she'd disappeared.

Before she had left him.

After supper, they'd escaped the hall and Gerda's company, taking wine into their chamber, where they sat around the fire, talking, reminiscing about Torvig. Reinar had indulged Elin because she had lost her only brother, and she was in pain. He hadn't wanted to talk about Torvig at all, because Torvig had killed Tulia and tried to kill Alys. Torvig had raped Stina, and likely more. And Reinar hated himself for not seeing who he really was before it was too late.

He blinked, realising that he was going over what had already happened, trying to distract himself from what would come next. 'Should I go?' he mumbled, staring at Elin, who stood on the opposite side of the bed.

'Go where?' she wondered with a yawn, pulling back the furs. 'You don't want to sleep?'

'Sleep?'

'In the bed. It's what you do in here most nights, I imagine,' Elin smiled, heading for her chests. She pulled out a nightdress, and draping it over the bed, she started unpinning her dress.

Reinar looked away, still feeling strange. He sat on the bed, tugging off his boots, thoughts scattered.

Elin slipped her nightdress on quickly, for, despite the heat from the fire, the stone chamber was drafty and cold. And jumping into bed, she pulled the furs up to her chin, nestling down, enjoying the familiar feel of the mattress. It felt soft and welcoming after days on the road, and weeks before that in an uncomfortable cottage with a straw-stuffed mattress. Turning to Reinar, she held out a hand. 'You aren't tired? It's a little early, I know, but I could sleep till spring!'

Reinar stood, pulling down his trousers, leaving them in a heap on the floor. Sliding into bed beside her, he frowned. 'I'm nothing but tired these days, though it's been hard to sleep.' He rolled onto his side, eyes searching hers. It was all he'd wanted: Elin back in bed with him, lying by his side. It was all he'd thought about for weeks as he lay there feeling so alone. But now she was here, and he felt uncomfortable. The distance between them was barely the width of a pillow, but to Reinar, it felt as though they were standing on opposite sides of The Rift.

Liara started crying through the wall, and Reinar could see the tension in Elin's face. 'It must be strange, being here again?'

Elin murmured, yawning. 'It is, but I'm glad I came back. I never wanted to leave, but I didn't know what else to do, Reinar. You wouldn't talk to me. I didn't think you even wanted to listen to me anymore. No one understood. Not even Agnette, as much as she tried. I had to go.'

'And now... do you want to stay?'

Elin smiled, lifting a hand to his face. 'I do. Running away is never the answer.' And edging closer, she kissed Reinar's cheek, smelling the familiar smoky scent of him, her lips brushing his bristles. She brought her other hand up, holding his face, bringing it towards hers, kissing him deeply. 'I'm back, where I belong. With you.'

***

Ivan's words rang in Alys' ears as she lay on the hard ground between Stina and Eddeth. Now that Hakon no longer needed such intensive care, they had been moved out of his tent, left to sleep outside. It was a relief, despite the fact that they were not alone. Three servants slept on the ground behind them, though they were young and timid, wary of the strangers.

Stina was worried that Eddeth would start blurting out everything she shouldn't blurt out, but Eddeth had fallen asleep almost immediately, exhausted by the stress of the day, snoring loudly. Stina had doubted that she could fall asleep at all. Eddeth's snoring was horrific, and she was terrorised by memories of Torvig, his hand over her mouth, suffocating her. Though, within moments of Eddeth snoring, she too had drifted off.

Leaving Alys to lie in the dark, on the uneven ground, listening to all the breathing, sleeping noises around her, wanting to slip away into a dream. She tried to hear voices – Magnus', Lotta's, her grandfather's – but all she heard was snoring.

Magnus was in danger, though. Something had happened to him.

She'd seen glimpses of him with Jonas while she was in Ottby, and it had comforted her. He was safe, she'd felt it.

But now?

Now Alys knew he wasn't safe at all.

So taking a deep breath, she closed her eyes, squeezing her grandfather's arm ring in one hand, wanting to find a dream.

***

Vik knew that his body's need for renewal was important. He'd spent years forcing himself to sleep when the horrors of what he'd done had threatened to keep him tossing and turning all night long.

But Magnus?

They'd sent him into that fort, and now Vik couldn't sleep at all.

Jonas lay opposite him, just as tired, just as awake. 'We can figure it all out in the morning,' he tried convincing them both.

'And how are we going to get in? What do we have for trading?'

That was a good point.

'I've got my silver, plenty of silver still. That will get us inside the fort. Silver can open a lot of doors, you know that.'

He sounded worried, Vik thought, feeling worried himself. 'Weather doesn't sound too good out there.'

They both looked up at the tent, which appeared to be sinking under the weight of snow. It sounded as though it was swirling around them, likely settling. 'No, but hopefully, Magnus found himself a bed somewhere warm.' Jonas was so cross with himself, so unsettled that he wanted to scream. It had been his job to look after Magnus, just as it had been his job to look after Alys.

And look at what had happened to the both of them.

He thought of Eida, wanting to hear his wife's voice, telling him what to do.

Though he heard nothing but the storm.

***

Hakon couldn't sleep, tossing and turning, uncomfortable and restless. He'd been sleeping for days. His body needed it, and the sleep had helped him recover, according to Eddeth. He grimaced, reminded of the strange woman and her jar of wriggling maggots. Lifting a hand to his tender belly, he shifted it towards the bandage Eddeth had secured around him. Touching the edge of the cloth, he could almost feel the searing pain as Reinar Vilander's blade pierced his skin. He wondered if the blade had been poisoned. Perhaps Reinar's dreamer had thought of that? Why else had he become so ill? Had so many strange nightmares?

The wind was picking up.

Hakon watched the tent bluster like dark waves, reminding him of Mother, and he could almost hear her familiar cackle in his ears. It was strange to be so affected by her loss, but he felt vulnerable without her.

Uncertain about the future.

Closing his eyes, Hakon tried to find a different, more comforting image, but he saw Alari glaring at him, and opening his eyes, he stared into the darkness. He had let her pet dreamer die, and the goddess was angry with him. She was watching him now, he knew, but was she trying to hurt him or keep him safe?

He wasn't sure.

He wanted to leave his shelter and run away from all those men who slept outside, waiting for him to lead them again. He heard his father's harsh voice mocking him; his uncle, laughing as he hacked off his thumbs; Mother again, chanting, bellowing, scolding.

Hakon clamped his hands over his ears, trying to shut them all out.

He couldn't think. Couldn't breathe.

And closing his eyes, he tried to find the image of his wife in his mind.

Wishing he was home.

**

Reinar stood on the inner wall ramparts alone.

Not entirely alone.

Those men on watch were there, wandering back and forth down the ramparts, talking to each other in murmurs, rubbing cold hands over braziers, checking the field, covered in tents now. The forest too. But they didn't stray near their lord, for he kept his eyes down, not inviting their company.

Snow was falling, and Reinar tipped back his head, letting the flakes settle on his face, wetting his lips. Hearing a noise, he turned, seeing the familiar figure of his brother limping towards him. 'Couldn't sleep?'

Sigurd shivered, nodding. 'Didn't expect to find you up here with Elin back.' He peered at his brother, eager to take his mind off his own problems. 'Is she alright?'

Reinar stared at the forest, shoulders tense. 'She is.' He wasn't reluctant to talk to Sigurd, he just didn't know what to say. He didn't know how he felt, except odd.

Sigurd could sense it. 'It's not always easy being with someone, loving them. Sometimes you don't realise how much you want to be with that person until they're gone. But then it's too late. You can't go back, undo all your mistakes, change your mind, make it all different.' Tears welled in Sigurd's eyes again, and he dropped his head, resting his hands on the wall, remembering the noise of the battle: boulders shattering the ramparts, arrows flying, Tulia screaming at her archers.

Reinar leaned over beside him. 'Doesn't make it any easier, though, getting this right.' And he tapped his head, annoyed with himself.

'No, it doesn't.' It was so quiet on the wall. Perfectly so. Snow had a way of doing that, Sigurd knew; blocking out every noise, as though you were under a fur, the harshness of the world dulled so you could hear your own thoughts.

The beat of your broken heart.

Tulia hated the snow, he remembered. She hated the cold and the wind and the rain. Though, had she really ever hated anything? She'd grumbled and moaned, but she'd never backed away. And she'd never given up.

And she'd never left.

More tears.

Reinar edged towards him, slipping an arm around Sigurd's shoulder. 'There'll never be anyone like Tulia Saari,' he grinned. 'I imagine those Ullaberg women will never forget what she taught them. Their husbands won't recognise them!' Images of Alys in the green dress shooting arrows flashed before Reinar's eyes, and he blinked them away, disappointed in himself.

Elin was here. Everything he wanted.

He needed to stop thinking about what had happened and

move forward.

Sigurd wiped his eyes, just as keen for a distraction as Reinar. 'I've been thinking about Slussfall. About how to get the Vettels and finish them off.'

Reinar turned to him, eyebrow raised.

'Ships.'

'Ships?' And just like that, Reinar's mind was right back on Alys.

***

The shadow was small, hunched over in a corner.

Alys didn't know where she was, but it was dark. Dripping. She turned, hearing scurrying noises. Rats. The smell was bad, like an overflowing latrine. She looked around, not sure what she was doing here, wanting to leave.

More shadows. All of them bigger. Slumped against a wall.

Snoring.

Beams of moonlight shone through the narrow window to her right, and she saw a glimmer of her son. Gasping in horror, Alys tried to run to him. She couldn't move, and as she stood there, Magnus looked up, terror in his eyes, shaking with cold and fear. She turned around, hoping to see Jonas or Vik, but everyone else was just shadows. Dark. Not moving.

'Magnus!' she called, turning back, trying to get his attention. 'Magnus!'

The moon hurried behind thick clouds, hiding its light, and Alys spun around and around, trying to find her son, needing to see him. Wanting him to see her.

Now she couldn't see at all.

'You can never tell her, Jonas. We must keep it from her. We have to protect her. If the truth gets out, they will take her from us!'

Alys was confused. A woman's voice.

It was still mostly dark, but the foul smell was gone now, replaced with sweeter aromas that stirred old memories. And then a burst of flame, glowing from a lamp, and Alys stepped forward, floorboards beneath her feet.

In a cottage now.

A man and a woman were talking across a table.

Alys stopped, recognising her grandfather. She couldn't see the woman's face, though it must have been her grandmother, for they were holding hands.

Jonas looked so young.

She stared, smiling.

The cottage...

Alys glanced around, remembering every corner, every hole in the walls. She smelled cinnamon. And lavender. Her grandmother had used lavender for everything, from teas to honey, to healing salves. She'd made the moistest apple cake, spiced with cinnamon. Jonas would always steal a piece when it was far too hot, the cake crumbling in his fingers as he shared it with Alys.

Alys turned back to her grandfather, realising that he was crying.

'How do I lie about everything, Eida? To everyone? About who she is? About where she came from? How?' Jonas was bereft, dark hair falling over his face.

Eida released his hands, brushing it out of his eyes, tucking it behind his ears. She cupped his face in her hands, wanting him to hear her. 'You have gone to war for less important things than this, Jonas Bergstrom,' she reminded him firmly. 'You would happily pick up a sword to defend your lord, so why not a little fibbing to save your family? Hmmm? It won't be so hard, I promise you, for the alternative is far, far worse. We must keep this secret. All of it. We can. We can keep the secret to save her life.'

Alys stared at them, confused, wondering who they were talking about.

'You.'

She spun around, noticing a figure lurking in the shadows now, and narrowing her eyes, Alys squinted, trying to see who was there. She didn't recognise the voice. It was a woman's voice. Not old. Not young either. 'Who are you?'

Laughter.

'What do you want from me?'

'From you? Nothing at all. I just wanted to open the door. After all these years, don't you think it's time, Alys? Time you discovered the truth they were so desperate to hide?'

Silence for a moment.

'And soon you will, my precious little Alys. The gods are stirring, the threads of fate being woven... and soon you'll know everything.'

Alys shivered, hearing the hate in that voice. The cold, dark, malevolence.

She turned away, looking for her grandparents, but they were gone. And she stood in that familiar cottage in the darkness, all alone.

Shivering.

PART TWO

Hunted

CHAPTER THIRTEEN

Ivan cupped red hands around his mouth, blowing vigorously. It was so cold that his breath smoke consumed his entire face. His head pounded, his back ached, and he was struggling to be interested in anything but his desire to head back to bed.

Though bed made him think of Alys and he sighed, frustrated.

She had slipped and slithered away from him like a beautiful snake, trying to keep out of his grasp. He didn't understand it. Women flocked to him, encouraging his attention. All but the two he was so desperate to bed. And not just bed, but love.

He laughed, head splitting, feeling idiotic.

Seeing Lief striding towards him, Ivan straightened up, turning around. 'We are leaving!' he bellowed to his shivering men, eyes on the servants who were kicking dirt over fires, emptying cauldrons filled with nothing he wanted to eat. He blew out a breath, trying not to retch. 'It's time to go home! See our families! Make a new plan and start again!' His enthusiasm had gone by the time he'd uttered his last words, and even he felt miserable. The thought of starting again, of rebuilding and rethinking and enduring Hakon's rages of impatience that it was all happening too slowly was not appealing in the slightest.

Hakon's desire to be on that throne would burn like the sun, blazing above them all. They would have to build ships, steal them if necessary, Ivan decided. He wasn't going to trek over those mountains again.

His mood lightened when he saw Alys, Stina, and Eddeth heading towards him wrapped in their cloaks, not one of them able to raise a smile. 'Ready for our journey?' he grinned.

Even Eddeth looked miserable at the thought of being dragged to Slussfall in the company of the Vettels. Stina was silent, on edge. She trusted Alys not to reveal their secrets, but Eddeth? Surely it was only a matter of time before she blurted out who they were and where they'd come from?

'We are,' Alys said, noting the spark of interest in Ivan's bleary eyes as he stepped closer. She edged away. 'Though, it's not where we wish to go, as I told you last night.'

'No,' Ivan acknowledged, following her, trying to look sympathetic, but secretly he was thrilled. He saw Falla out of the corner of his eye and barely felt a twinge, all his attention on the freckle-nosed Alys now. 'It's not, I know, and I am sympathetic to that. But think of the service you'll be providing, helping the future King of Alekka himself! He'll reward you mightily, enough to make your sacrifice worthwhile, I'm sure. And once we're at Slussfall, you can be on your way again.' Ivan flashed his brightest smile. 'Though, by then you might have decided that Slussfall is a much more desirous place to be than your sandy beach.'

Alys turned away from him, walking towards Eddeth, who had frozen, eyes on Hakon, being helped towards them by Njall.

'It's a bad idea!' Eddeth announced, loudly enough to be heard some distance away, and Hakon pulled up in surprise, yelping. 'You need more rest! And jerking about on a horse all day is not restful, my lord!'

Hakon felt like collapsing into a heap, his stomach burning intensely, his head a buzzing storm. But everyone had stopped, staring at him, thanks to Eddeth and her booming voice, and he couldn't let them see a weak lord who had failed.

A man ready for his bed.

They had to follow him. Again. He had to show them the way.

Lief peered at him, dark eyes full of concern, noting the sheen of sweat on Hakon's sallow face. 'Perhaps it would be better, my lord, if we waited another day?'

'Another day away from Slussfall? Leaving it vulnerable? Leaving us at the mercy of whoever seeks to corner us here, in this forest?' Hakon attempted to snort, though it hurt. Everything hurt. He clamped his lips together, trying to keep upright. He wanted Lief to be wrong, but every blink of his mangled eyes had him doubting his own bravado. Still, he couldn't stay in bed. His dreams taunted him, warning him of what would come if he failed to act; of what would happen if he didn't take charge of his army and return to his fortress.

Nodding, Lief left Hakon with Njall and headed for Falla, who was already mounted beside his horse, her face pale, her brow furrowed. 'You are unwell?'

Falla couldn't speak, couldn't move. She just blinked.

'You should have had some of Eddeth's tea before we left.'

Falla took a deep breath, the wave of nausea finally passing. 'It will be better when we're moving. All that smoke... it reminds me of what happened in Ottby.'

Lief agreed, mounting his horse with one last look at his lord, trying to ignore the voices in his head warning him that they weren't out of danger yet.

***

Reinar was so engrossed in his thoughts as he bent over the map table, moving the wooden ships and men around, that he didn't hear Elin come up behind him.

Then the baby cried, and he jumped, turning around.

Elin held Liara in her arms, the tiny baby squirming, mouth open, eyes screwed up in annoyance. 'Agnette's having a wash,' she explained, peering down at Liara.

Reinar blinked, heart aching. 'She sounds hungry.'

'Well, she's Bjarni's daughter,' Elin smiled, 'so that would be right.'

Leaning forward, Reinar kissed his wife's cheek. There was colour on her face, he noticed. She looked much better than the ghostly figure he'd carried into the hall covered in snow.

Elin glanced over her shoulder, wondering how long Agnette would be. Liara's crying was becoming explosive, and she was growing uncomfortable. She turned back to Reinar, frowning. 'I was looking for a dress this morning. In my chest. My favourite dress. I couldn't find it.'

Reinar froze, eyes jumping around the hall, looking anywhere but at Elin. 'No?'

'My green one. I couldn't see it anywhere.'

'They'll be listening to my daughter in Stornas!' a fresh-faced Agnette announced, bustling into the hall, taking Liara from Elin. 'I'm sorry, I thought she'd be able to go longer.' She lifted the baby up to her shoulder, gently rubbing her back, eyes on Reinar. 'Is something wrong?'

Elin turned to her. 'I've lost a dress. I was just asking Reinar about it. My green one.'

Agnette quickly looked as uncomfortable as her cousin. 'Well, we had those women from Ullaberg here, and they were so cold, poor things. We gave them what we could, including some of your clothes, I'm afraid.'

'Oh.'

Reinar nodded, grateful for Agnette's quick thinking. 'We didn't know if you were coming back.'

'I have to feed her,' Agnette said, looking at Reinar with some sympathy, jiggling Liara, who was howling now. 'Sorry! I'll talk to you later, Elin.'

'Slussfall!' Bjarni announced as he stomped his boots by the hall doors, shaking snow off his cloak. 'Let's talk about Slussfall!'

Reinar was pleased for the interruption.

Bolli, Ludo, and Sigurd hurried in after Bjarni, all of them making for the map table. Berger Eivin, yawning and scratching his long beard, pulled himself up from a bench and made to join them, not wanting to be left out when it came to deciding how to attack Slussfall by sea. With his brother, Rutger, dead on their raid to Ullaberg, he'd assumed command of their small band of men, still debating whether he wanted to serve the Lord of Ottby at all.

Elin watched the men gather around the map table, surprised by how easily Reinar had drawn his attention away from her. She was barely home, their reunion new, and yet he seemed eager to get away from her at every opportunity.

She stared at him with a frown before turning away.

The fires spat, the doors shook, and Liara cried in the distance.

Reinar didn't notice any of it. 'Thought you might want to stay behind,' he said quietly to Bjarni, not wanting Agnette to hear. 'What with the baby.'

Bjarni chewed his lip, working hard to get his thoughts in order. Eventually, he shook his head. 'Can't say I didn't think about it, but I'm not the only husband and father in Ottby. We can't all stay home to keep our families safe, can we? Odd Forsten should stay. He always used to. Before Tulia.' He felt uncomfortable even saying her name, not wanting to upset Sigurd.

Who looked upset, but nodded anyway. 'Odd's the best choice, and you'd be more use to us at Slussfall than getting under Agnette's feet, driving her mad.' He dropped his head quickly, feelings bubbling intensely. He was looking forward to getting away from the fort; away from the concerned looks and the awkward sympathy too. He longed to ride the waves with nothing but the sound of a roaring wind in his ears.

He wanted to go to Slussfall.

***

Vik peered up at Slussfall's old walls, memories stirring. He'd defended those walls more than once. He'd climbed them too. The fortress had changed hands many times over the years. Its location near The Rift had always made it a popular target for Northerners seeking a foothold in the South. Sirrus Ahlmann, made Lord of Slussfall by Ake, had been besieged countless times, finally overthrown by the Vettels.

And now?

Now enemies resided behind those walls. Enemies who'd be more than happy to see their return, eager for a hefty helping of revenge.

Jonas nudged Vik forward to where two guards waited to inspect their cart. They'd paid three fur traders a couple of coins to let them accompany them into the fort. The burly men were keen to help, friendly, and pleased for the company. Snow swirled around them all, and Jonas felt grateful for it, hiding beneath his hood, one hand on the cart, cloak flapping behind him.

'Not really the weather for it!' one of the guards called over the howling wind, fingering through the furs. 'Though I'm sure you'll be popular in there!'

Jonas nodded, letting the traders do all the talking. He sensed that the guards were more inclined to head back into their tower than stand out in the bone-chilling cold. They looked over the cart with little interest, making a note, taking payment, quickly stepping back to usher them inside.

Vik kept his hood low, shoulders hunched. It was easy to look as though you were trying to hide from the weather, though it would get harder inside the fort if conditions improved. But, looking up as the dark-grey clouds descended upon them, Vik doubted that would be any time soon.

***

Now that they'd decided to take ships, and had worked through who would stay and who would go, they needed a plan, a way into Slussfall without losing too many men.

The arguments rang throughout the hall, voices rising and falling as Reinar battled them all, deciding how they would approach the fort.

At least initially.

He didn't feel convinced by anything he'd proposed, nor especially confident. He felt preoccupied, and irritable because of it.

Gerda had pushed her way into the conversation. Having put Liara down for a sleep, Agnette had joined them. Elin too. They were curious about what would happen; anxious about being left behind with a damaged fort and few men to protect it.

Agnette peered at Sigurd, who looked so lost. She doubted many would notice, but she did. His tired eyes barely stayed in one place for long, not wishing to attract anyone's attention. 'But what if the Vettels return to attack us?'

It was what Gerda was thinking too, and she blinked at Reinar, feeling anxious.

'They won't,' Bjarni assured her. 'They'll be limping back to Slussfall, worrying that Ake's on their tail. It will take time to plan what to do next. Their first thought won't be to attack us, it will be to protect themselves.'

Sigurd lifted an eyebrow. 'You sure about that? They seemed to have no idea what they were doing out on the field, except to go round in smoky circles!'

'Nothing's certain,' Reinar said, smiling at Elin, who watched him from the other side of the map table. 'But Ake will be in Stornas soon, and Algeir's tidying up Hovring and Vika. There are men to call on. Only a few days marching will get them here. Odd can send a note. He'll have scouts out. I know Torfinn wants to come with us, but Beggi will remain. He'll get more men to help him.'

Berger nodded, combing his bushy auburn beard. He was less uptight than his brother had been; laid back in a way Reinar found irritating.

Overly concerned with his appearance.

'No chance they'll come back,' Berger decided with a sleepy grin. 'Not till spring. But by spring we'll have killed them all!' He winked at Gerda, who didn't feel reassured in the slightest.

She touched Agnette's shoulder, thinking about Stellan.

'How long will Liara be asleep, do you think? Stellan needs to be changed.'

'I can help you, Gerda,' Elin offered. 'I'm sure Agnette has many things to do before the baby wakes. I can help you with Stellan.'

Gerda looked pleased, and so did Agnette, who smiled at Elin. It had been strange without her. And then strange with her back. But, she realised, glancing at Reinar, it would just take some time. Time for them all to remember how it used to be.

Time to forget about Alys.

***

Alys hadn't spoken since they'd left their camp, and Stina was growing concerned. They were packed in tightly on their horses as they trekked down a narrow path between rows of snow-heavy trees, and trying to ask her what was wrong was impossible. Likely it was something they couldn't discuss in front of Falla, who had joined them, leaving her husband to ride with Hakon and Ivan.

Eddeth was mostly silent beside them. She wriggled in the saddle, unable to keep still, but her mouth remained closed, aware of how important it was to keep their identities hidden.

So Stina was left to talk to Falla. 'Are you from Slussfall, then?'

'No. I come from the Slave Islands.'

'Oh?' Stina was intrigued. 'I've never been anywhere but Alekka. How did you end up in Slussfall?'

Falla watched snow flurries twirling before her, settling on her horse's chestnut head. 'My second husband was from Alekka. When he died, I came to find his mother. I was... carrying my son. I wanted him born here.' She kept her eyes ahead, not offering anything further, lost in the memory of her arrival, and Mother's welcome. The old dreamer had been waiting for her, promising a revenge that now seemed impossible to attain.

Unless Lief had more power.

Falla narrowed her eyes, watching her husband riding ahead of her.

If Lief commanded an army and a fleet mighty enough to take to the seas and defeat the Slave Islands, then anything was possible.

Stina realised that Falla wasn't listening anymore, and she turned to Eddeth, who appeared to be falling asleep. 'Eddeth!' And leaning out, Stina prodded her arm.

'What!' Eddeth jerked up, frightening Wilf, who threw up his head, skittering in a bluster. He was old and deaf and prone to nervous outbursts, and Eddeth couldn't control him as he lurched forward, barging past Lief and Ivan, his yelping rider clinging on for dear life.

Falla covered her mouth, trying not to laugh, listening to Eddeth's yelps of terror.

Alys called out. 'Ivan! Help her!'

Ivan, eager to please, spurred his horse on, hurrying after Eddeth, who bounced wildly ahead of him, threatening to tip out of the saddle. Eventually, Ivan caught up with her as the urgency for Wilf's escape diminished. And tired now, he allowed himself to be turned around and led back to their column, Eddeth slumped over him, nose dripping, unable to catch her breath. 'That... I... well...' She didn't know what to say, too relieved to make any sense. 'Thank you.' And nodding at Ivan, Eddeth made her way back to Alys and Stina, ignoring Falla, who was wiping tears of laughter from her eyes. She turned Wilf around, nudging him in between the horses, still panting. 'And I thought Rigfuss was difficult!' Falla looked confused, and Eddeth turned to her. 'Rigfuss is my cat, back in –'

'Ullaberg!' Stina exclaimed. 'Eddeth has a cat in Ullaberg, don't you?'

Eddeth nodded, lips pressed together.

'Well, I hope someone is caring for him,' Falla purred, leaning in, 'for I don't imagine you'll be seeing him for some time. Not now Hakon has you.'

Alys peered at Falla, sensing problems. The woman was

ambitious and manipulative, and solely interested in what served her best. Falla turned, staring at her, and Alys saw a glimpse of the old dreamer. They had been close, she realised. She saw Falla's hand on a drum, the dreamer creeping around a fire, smoke wafting, consuming them both.

'Are you alright?' Falla wondered sharply, for Alys appeared to be staring right through her.

Alys nodded, blinking herself out of the vision. 'Yes, just tired. It can be a little monotonous, can't it?' And moving her eyes away from Falla, she stared straight ahead as Ivan twisted around, winking at her.

Falla laughed. 'I'm grateful to you for taking Ivan's attention away from me. I think Lief was ready to kill him.'

Alys wasn't surprised. Ivan was like a big child, unable to control his impulses, though she no longer felt threatened by him, not as she did by his cousin. Hakon was pale and weak, barely able to ride, but wide awake, and Alys' fears were growing, worrying that soon, he would discover the truth.

***

Reinar and Elin left the hall behind, braving the blizzard. Elin wanted to take Milka a few carrots, and Reinar needed to see how the wall repairs were going. Now that they'd chosen a departure date, he felt an even greater urgency to have the fort back in order, and he needed to get those walls right quickly.

'I want to come.'

'What?'

'To Slussfall. I don't want to stay here, Reinar. Take me with you. I can help care for the men, and you. I have healing skills. Not as good as Eddeth's, but better than most. I want to come.'

Reinar had one hand on Milka, who was happily munching her carrots. He froze. 'I...'

'I've only just returned. To you. Don't leave me here, please.' Elin was insistent, eyes blinking, full of urgency.

Reinar frowned, wanting to talk her out of it. 'You don't like ships, remember?'

'No, but I like you, and I want to be with you. I want to come.' Elin rose up onto her tiptoes, kissing him. 'I want to make everything right before it's too late.'

'Too late?' Reinar peered into her frantic eyes. They skipped about like Eddeth under a full moon. 'What do you mean?'

Elin slipped her arms around his waist, holding him close. 'Look at what happened to Torvig,' she mumbled into his chest, tears stinging her aching eyes. 'I don't want to be apart from you, Reinar. I made a mistake running away. I don't want to be apart again!'

Reinar held onto her, feeling her desperation, though his reluctance to take her with him was strong. 'It's best if you stay here with Agnette. With Gerda. You're the Lady of Ottby. You should be here, looking after things. The attack on Slussfall... we'll be on ships. I won't be able to protect you. There won't be anywhere to take shelter.' He ran through every reason he could think of, watching tears flood her eyes, remembering how it was for them once.

He'd always hated leaving her behind.

And sighing, Reinar nodded. 'Alright, if you want to come, then come. Come with us to Slussfall.'

CHAPTER FOURTEEN

Slussfall's square was not quite as they'd remembered.

Jonas eyed Vik, both of them holding their hoods low, fighting the swirling wind's best efforts to reveal their faces. Their cloaks billowed like full sails, and Jonas felt himself becoming irritated with the snow and the wind and himself most of all for sending Magnus into the fort on his own.

He could tell Vik felt the same. His frown was deep, eyes scouring the busy fortress, lips set in a straight line. They needed to find that silversmith, and then Magnus. And they needed to do it all without being discovered.

They had spent decades fighting Vettels.

First King Jorek's men, then his two sons, Jesper and Gunnar. And though neither of them had fought against Hakon's army, Slussfall was likely commanded by old hands loyal to both his father and grandfather. And those men were certain to be lurking around somewhere. Though, at first glance, the fort seemed light on warriors.

'Is Hakon Vettel here?' Vik asked one of the fur traders.

The big man shook his head, pushing down his fur hat as it threatened to blow away. 'He's in Ottby, from what I hear. At least, he's hoping to be! On his way to claim Stornas!' They were Northerners. Men who roamed the wild frozen land above The Rift. Men who were enjoying access to Slussfall's market and the prospect of more Southern customers to come.

Vik glanced at Jonas, eyes wide, body twitching. Once that was a fight they would have been in. Helping Stellan. Helping Ake. They'd both heard what had happened to Stellan Vilander, and Vik frowned again, hoping his sons would be up to the task of beating back the Vettel cousins before they took any more of Alekka for themselves.

Relieved to hear that Slussfall's lord was far away from his fort.

***

Hakon hadn't spoken since they'd left their camp, and Lief was growing uncomfortable with the silence. He'd even made conversation with Ivan, who rode on Hakon's left, both of them becoming concerned.

Ivan had made Njall ride just behind them in case Hakon fell off his horse, or needed to be lifted down. His cousin's skin was ashen, the colour of snow clouds, and his silence was worrying.

Hakon didn't care about their discomfort, though he could sense it. He was just trying to stay upright. The pain in his belly made him want to hunch over and grip it till he felt better. He thought of Eddeth and her maggots, wondering if he should have listened to her. And blinking, he could hear his father roaring his disappointment; disappointment tinged with hate and regret. He heard his uncle too – a man even crueller than his father had been - screaming that Ivan should have been the one chosen to rule. Not Hakon. What was the point of Hakon?

Hakon swallowed, turning to his cousin, who smiled at him.

'We should stop. Rest the horses,' Ivan suggested.

'What? No!' Hakon was annoyed, his voice breathless, the pain blinding. 'We've only just begun. The weather is holding, the path ahead looks clear enough. We can make real progress today, don't you...' He sucked in a long breath, and squeezed his gloved hands around the reins, closing his eyes, waiting for the pain to pass. Eventually, he opened them, turning to Lief. 'Don't you agree?'

Lief nodded. 'We can, lord, and we're nowhere suitable for stopping anyway. Best we carry on, if you think you're able?' He glanced over his shoulder at Njall, who rode alongside Jerrick, both men staring at Lief, wondering if their help was required.

'Of course!' Hakon insisted loudly. 'More than able!' He forced a smile, ignoring the voices in his head and his growing fear that the gods had abandoned him, nudging his horse forward. 'We'll never reach Slussfall at this rate if we spend all our time sitting around drinking and moaning!'

***

Leonid was miserable, groaning in discomfort. Before he'd accidentally killed the rival silversmith, the man had punched him in the face and broken his nose, and all his crying had blocked it, and now he was struggling to breathe, which made him panic and want to cry some more.

They stood before the prison hole window, Magnus on top of an overturned bucket, gripping its rusty bars, peering out onto the square, hoping to see a sign of Jonas and Vik. He'd told Leonid that his great-grandfather and his friend would come looking for them, certain that they'd have to once he failed to return. Leonid felt guilty about that too, worried what the two old warriors would do to him for getting the boy locked up. It was hardly what they'd paid him for, and it wouldn't get him any more of the silver he so desperately needed.

They saw a lot of legs, some wrapped in thick wool, boots packed in snow. The weather was disintegrating, though Leonid could see that the traders and farmers were setting up their stalls, hunched over against the wild wind, frozen solid, but still in need of coins.

'Looks cold,' Magnus said, teeth chattering.

'It does,' Leonid agreed, feeling around his nose. 'Which won't be good for business. Unless you're selling furs.' And his eyes snapped to two strapping men who had dragged their cart of pelts and furs towards an empty table. 'If I were out there, that's where I'd go first. Buy myself a hat. Those men will do a great trade today!' His attention shifted to Magnus, who had gripped his arm.

'There!' Magnus hissed, pointing to the two men whose faces were almost entirely covered by their hoods, though Magnus recognised the shape of his tall great-grandfather, and his not quite as tall, but just as powerful looking friend. 'That's them!'

Leonid blinked, following Magnus' arm, deciding that he would have to take the boy's word for it. 'I hope you're right, my friend. But what good it does us in here, I don't know. I killed that man. Killed!' And then he was sobbing again, nose throbbing, blocking immediately, making him panic.

'Ssshhh,' Magnus soothed. 'They'll help us, I know, if they can find us.' And turning around, he peered into the darkness, needing to find something to throw.

***

Karolina Vettel had been walking the ramparts with the head of the garrison, a self-important man called Baldur Skoggi. She didn't want to remain in the hall and hide until her husband returned. If Hakon was determined to become the King of Alekka, then one day, her son would likely assume that role. And so, despite Hakon insisting that she think about hairstyles and dresses while he was gone, Karolina had spent some time learning about the fort. About their enemies and their allies. About their strengths and weaknesses.

Baldur was a patient, if disapproving teacher, though she hadn't been put off by his gruff replies to her questions. He thought women should sit in chairs and embroider things while fussing over their children, and Karolina didn't mind doing either. Though, without Hakon to terrify her, she found herself becoming interested in learning how the fort ran, and how safe they were. She had a child to protect and another on the way, and a husband who might not return at all.

Karolina was not prepared to sit in the hall and wait to receive that news.

She wanted to prepare for it.

Having spied the fur traders setting up their table, though, she left Baldur behind, eager to find something warm for Anders. This would be his first winter, and she was conscious of how cold the hall already was. So, hood up, she hurried into the guard tower, and out into the busy market square, where she immediately bumped into Bergit Dyre.

'You have the same idea as me, my lady!' Bergit laughed, orange hair dusted with snow. The hood of her cloak had blown back, though she was far more interested in fingering through the furs and pelts than keeping her hair dry. The best ones always went first, and Bergit was not prepared to settle for anything but the best. 'They say this winter will be worse than any in living memory!'

Karolina frowned, not having heard that. 'They do? Who? Who says that, Bergit?' She was curious, and though Karolina had never warmed to the woman, there was no more reliable source of information in all of Slussfall.

'The old gossips! I'm not sure who they hear it from? Maybe Mother? Though that old dreamer never talked to anyone when she was here, only your husband and Falla Gundersen.' Bergit scowled, her attention on the pure-white fur she had grabbed at the same time as another woman. Her neighbour. A sour-faced girl, newly married, setting up a home while her husband was away with the army. The girl glared at Bergit, yanking the fur towards her.

Bergit yanked it back, jaw clenched, and a tussle began.

Jonas and Vik watched from behind the fur traders. They

had wandered around the square, seeing no sign of Magnus or Leonid, quickly realising that they were going to have to start asking around. And they were more likely to escape notice if they enquired with the women.

If they could stop them fighting.

'I'm sure I have another one of those in here!' the big fur trader called out, half amused, half irritated. The two screeching women were scaring away the Lady of Slussfall, who stepped back, not wanting an elbow in her pregnant belly.

Karolina turned away, yelping suddenly, losing her balance, reaching out a hand. 'Bergit!'

And releasing the fur, Bergit grabbed Karolina before she could fall. 'What happened?'

Jonas and Vik were alert, dashing around the tables.

'Are you alright, lady?' Jonas asked, still holding down his hood.

Bergit looked annoyed, shooing him away. 'You leave her alone, old man!' she grumbled, eyes sharp.

Karolina bent down, grabbing her ankle, feeling the sting. 'Something hit me.'

Vik picked up a rock, shielding it in his hand, glancing across the square, head swivelling through the snow, trying to see where it had come from. 'The wind's bad!' he called to Karolina. 'Likely it blew something at you. Best you get inside!' And he headed away from the arguing women and the fur traders, slipping through the snow-blown crowds, eyes open.

If the stone had hit the woman on the ankle...

He dropped his eyes and then blinked, coming face to face with Magnus.

Magnus, who was gripping the bars of a window.

In the prison hole.

***

Alys was struggling to focus.

They were riding up a narrow path into the mountains, and she needed to concentrate. Haski was prone to skittering sideways, not inclined to bend to her will. She thought of Ludo, who had chosen him for her, almost smiling. And then Sigurd, whose heart was broken. She could feel that. Then feeling cross for letting her mind wander, Alys frowned, bringing her focus back to her dream. She didn't want to even tiptoe towards the threatening woman's voice and the odd things she had said. Alys wanted to see more of Magnus. He was imprisoned. Those bars, that smell, the hunched shadows and the rats... Alys was certain he was imprisoned.

But where?

Slussfall?

Her body shivered explosively, answering that question.

And though the thought was terrifying, her hopes lifted, for if Jonas and Vik had taken Magnus to Slussfall, then she stood a chance of finding them all. And Lotta. Wherever she was.

Eddeth nudged her. 'You should talk to your friend, Ivan!'

Stina hissed for Eddeth to be quiet as her booming voice would soon have everyone turning their way.

Alys just looked confused. 'About what?'

'The lord up there. Can't you see him, swaying like a sapling in a storm? He'll be face down in the snow before long!'

Alys leaned out, trying to see past Njall, who was like a bear in front of her in his thick fur cloak. And finally, catching a glimpse of Hakon, she could see that he did appear to be heeling to starboard. She smiled sadly, reminded of sailing on *Dagger* with an injured Sigurd at her feet, Ludo beside her for company, Reinar riding onboard *Fury*, turning to stare at her often.

She'd always sensed that.

'Ivan doesn't need me telling him how to look after his cousin,' she whispered to Eddeth. 'They can all see him. Surely?'

But it appeared that they couldn't, for in the very next breath, Hakon tipped out of his saddle, falling into the snow with a thump, boot stuck in a stirrup. His horse took fright, skipping sideways, legs flicking. Hakon's boot slid free, and his horse bolted away, down their snowy path. Lief turned, inclining his head for Jerrick to go after him, while he swung down off his own horse.

Eddeth turned to Alys with a shrug.

'Eddeth!' came the shout from Ivan, who was quickly on the ground, leaning over his cousin.

'I'll go with you,' Alys said, leaving Stina with Falla Gundersen. And dismounting, handing their reins to Stina, they both hurried up the line to where Hakon was picking himself out of the snow.

'I was just tired!' he insisted grumpily, fighting against Lief and Ivan, who were trying to keep him down.

'Let me see! Let me see!' Eddeth demanded loudly. 'Stay where you are and let me see!'

Alys stood behind her, glancing over Eddeth's shoulder, ignoring Ivan's smile. Dense trees fenced them in on both sides. The snow was thick beneath her feet, encasing her boots, and Alys thought wistfully about flames, hot and bright. She turned her head, staring through the trees, listening. The snow made everything quieter, though voices rose as their column came to a creaking halt, none louder than Hakon's as he fought off Eddeth and her cold hands.

'You should have stayed in Ottby, Alys Bergstrom.'

Alys froze, shivers racing up her spine, hairs on her arms rising.

She turned, searching the trees.

'North is not where you belong.'

The memory of that voice was like a blade, and Alys knew it was the woman from her dream.

She felt in danger.

Stepping away from Eddeth, eyes narrowed, she peered into the trees again. And then Ivan was beside her.

'Is something wrong?' he whispered, slipping an arm around her waist, lips near her ear. He had noticed an odd look on her face.

Alys slid away from Ivan and his eager hands. 'I heard a noise.' She turned back to him, legs shaking. 'Just a strange noise, though after the vatyr, who knows what's out there?'

Ivan looked concerned, his head still pounding from the vatyr attack.

'Come on!' Hakon bellowed, helped to his feet by Lief and Njall. The pain of his wound was unbearable, though he was working hard not to show it. 'Come on, Ivan!'

And dragging himself away from Alys, who was far better company than his festering and feeble cousin, Ivan headed back to his horse.

Alys remained where she was, searching the trees again before dropping her shoulders, and turning back to Haski.

***

After leaving the limping Lady of Slussfall behind, Vik had scouted the square, heading down alleys, slipping around the back of the hall, wanting to keep away from as many people as possible. Eventually, he'd stopped, eyes on the covered entrance to the hole where a handful of well-armed warriors sheltered from the snow, warming their hands over a brazier. One of them he'd recognised: a middle-aged, big-bellied man, with thick coppery braids, swathed in furs. Turning away, Vik had kept walking, hood low, trying to think as he made his way back to Jonas, who was hiding in an alley, sheltering under the porch of a tiny cottage, though the wind was blowing the snow horizontally now, and there was little respite from it. 'I saw Ollo Narp,' he muttered when he arrived. 'Traitorous shit. Dressed like he's the King of Alekka.'

'I saw Haegel Hedvik,' Jonas said. 'A couple of other faces I recognised too. The Vettel boys have taken their youngest warriors, leaving the old farts behind. Just our luck.'

Vik still couldn't understand it. 'How did Magnus wind up in the hole?'

'Doesn't matter. We just have to get him out of there fast.'

Tension gripped Vik's shoulders like a vice; that and the bone-chilling cold, which wouldn't let up. 'We have to find somewhere to hide. Somewhere out of sight.'

'Sounds like that place isn't going to have a fire and a jug of ale.'

'I'd say not.' Vik saw a flash of orange, and the rude woman with the bright hair swept towards them, full basket in her arms, struggling with two new furs which were heavier than she'd anticipated, both of them trying to blow away from her. 'Would you like some help?' he offered, leaping into her path, leaving Jonas behind. He pushed back his hood for a moment, smiling.

Vik had a handsome face, barely troubled by a scar, and he knew women responded to him, and this woman was no exception, though there was a wary look in her eyes. Still, he'd watched her as she gossiped her way around the square, and she seemed like the sort of woman who would know everyone's comings and goings.

'What are you doing skulking around? Following me?'

Vik grinned, his smile friendly and open. 'We were here first, lady, so no. We're fur traders, but they're mostly sold now, so we're on our way to the tavern, but I thought you might need some help.'

Bergit wasn't sure she believed him, though he had a nice face and she did need the help. 'You can carry those furs for me, up there and around the corner. And that's all. I have no coins to pay you!'

'And nor will you need to, for we made enough today thanks to the weather gods!' Vik sounded confident, cheerful even. He helped himself to the furs, and without even a glance at Jonas, he headed down the alley.

Bergit was grateful for the help, though she didn't show it.

'I'm sure your husband will be warm tonight,' Vik smiled.

Bergit scowled, hurrying along. 'My husband is none of your business, but be assured that he is more than a match for you if you intend me harm.'

She was feisty, Vik thought, not sure how to charm such an abrasive woman. 'I intend no harm, and it's a long time since I used my sword, so your husband has nothing to fear from me.'

Bergit eyed him, relaxing slightly. 'Of course he hasn't. My husband is one of Hakon Vettel's most valued men. He's been a loyal servant to the Vettels since King Jorek was on the throne. Likely you've heard of him. Ulrick Dyre? A famous scout and warrior?'

Vik blinked.

Men were approaching. Young boys, he realised, barely men at all, and he didn't reach for his hood, keeping his wind-whipped face uncovered. 'I hear the army has gone to Ottby to try and take back the throne.'

'And they will! They'll rip Ake Bluefinn's head off too. That snivelling usurper, keeping us prisoner all these years. Forcing us to endure his illegitimate reign!' She reached the doorstep of her cottage, and dropping her basket, she snatched the furs from Vik's hands. 'Be on your way now! There's nothing for you in here!' And she lurched forward angrily, hand flapping, shooing Vik away.

Vik bobbed his head, still smiling despite the snarling woman's rudeness. And hood up now, he turned back into the alley, certain that Ulrick had not made it back to Slussfall with Lotta.

***

The weather disintegrated so much that Ulrick made them stop, pulling Lotta's pony off what he assumed was the path, into the trees where the snow dropped off branches, falling on them in clumps. Amongst the trees, the wind did not bite as much, so securing the horses with great care, Ulrick grabbed his furs, draping them around both him and Lotta as they sat against a broad tree trunk in the snow.

Lotta shivered against him, teeth chattering as he held her close, and eventually, he felt one of her little arms edge around his belly. Ducking his head down to her, Ulrick held the furs tightly, dreaming of the warmth of a fire and his wife's sweet face. 'Tomorrow,' he whispered in Lotta's ear. 'We'll be at Slussfall tomorrow.'

CHAPTER FIFTEEN

Agnette was surprised to find Elin in her bedchamber, leaning over the baby's crib.

Elin swung around, flustered.

'I didn't expect to find you here,' Agnette frowned.

'I, I... thought I heard her crying, but she's sound asleep.'

Agnette's shoulders relaxed. 'I'm sure she is, though come a few hours from now she won't be!' She peered into the crib, pleased to see Liara looking so perfectly content. Her heart swelled with love, and she felt terrible for thinking badly of Elin at all. It would be so impossibly hard being around babies, knowing that her sons had never even taken a breath.

'Well, if you ever need some rest, Agnette, I can take her,' Elin offered. 'I'd be happy to. Until we go, of course, though I don't know when that will be. Likely soon. Everyone seems quite impatient about it, especially Reinar.'

'Go? To Slussfall? *You're* going?' Agnette took a seat on the bed, not worried about waking her daughter, knowing that she was due for another feed soon.

Elin nodded, sitting down beside her. 'I don't want to be left behind. After being apart all those weeks, I don't want Reinar to leave me here.'

Agnette always struggled not to say what was on her mind. She didn't want to upset Elin, who looked swollen-eyed and exhausted, but she'd felt troubled from the first moment she'd seen her friend again. 'I never thought you'd return, Elin. You swore you wouldn't. You said you...' Her eyes raced to the open door, and she lowered her voice. 'You said you didn't love Reinar anymore. I thought you came back because of Torvig, wanting to save him, not for Reinar.'

Elin clenched her hands in her lap. They were chapped, red and dry; cold too. 'I...' She looked up at Agnette, who had once been her best friend, though they had drifted apart over the years. 'I saw a dreamer in Lundvik. She warned me about Torvig. I tried to save him, but I couldn't get back in time.'

Agnette nodded encouragingly, knowing that, but sensing there was more.

'She told me many things about my future. About what was... happening here.'

Agnette's eyes opened wider, limbs twitching. 'Oh?'

'About the dreamer and Reinar.'

Agnette tried to remain perfectly still. 'Dreamer?' Her voice sounded oddly high-pitched, and she coughed, trying to cover her awkwardness.

'She told me everything, you needn't worry, Agnette. I know everything that happened.'

'Happened?' Just repeating whatever Elin said would not get her out of trouble, Agnette knew. 'There was a dreamer in the group of women they stole from Ullaberg, but she's gone now. They're almost all gone now, just that Ilene stayed behind.' Agnette felt sad, thinking about Tulia again, remembering how she'd trained Ilene.

'So you never saw the dreamer with Reinar? Never saw them together?'

Agnette felt as though her toes were being dragged towards a burning fire. The desperate look in Elin's big eyes told her that there was no escape now. She swallowed. 'They were often together, of course. He needed her help. Salma was gone, and Reinar needed her help. We had a terrible time, terrorised by a wolf nightmare, and then the fort was under attack from Hakon Vettel and his evil dreamer.' Agnette grabbed Elin's hand, needing to turn her away from the path she seemed so determined to go down. 'Whatever the dreamer told you, it sounds as though she misunderstood. Reinar was with Alys because she was helping him. That's all.' Agnette felt the need to lie. It would break Elin's heart to know that Reinar had become besotted with a pretty dreamer while she was gone. She appeared more fragile than ever; Agnette could see that when she looked into Elin's frantic eyes. 'Reinar loves you. He was broken-hearted without you. Beside himself with worry!'

Elin nodded, remembering what a terrible liar Agnette was, and squeezing her hand, she smiled. 'Well, that's good, then. I didn't imagine it could be true. That's not like Reinar, is it? He was always so loyal to me.'

Liara started whimpering, and Agnette stood, heading for the crib, eager to end the conversation, not noticing the hardened expression on Elin's face as she watched her.

***

Sigurd was confused as he topped up Reinar's ale. Leaving the jug on the table behind them, he turned around, catching a glimpse of Ilene Gislar, who stood amongst Berger's men, ignoring their attention. She smiled sadly at him, and Sigurd stared at her, feeling a shared sense of loss. It was never easy to lose someone, whether you'd been with them for days or years. And sighing, he turned back to Reinar, asking his question again. 'I thought Elin hated the sea?'

Reinar knew there would be more than a few raised eyebrows at Elin wanting to come along – his included – but she wanted to, and part of him felt happy about that. It had been a shock to see her again, but everything would feel right within days, he was certain. He would regret it if he left her behind knowing how much she wanted to come.

'She doesn't know how to use a weapon,' Bjarni added. 'What's she going to do?'

'We're taking servants, aren't we? They don't know how to use weapons either. Elin will manage them. We've agreed. She's going to help with any wounded as well. Likely you,' Reinar winked at his brother, 'knowing how slow you've become lately.'

Sigurd ignored him. He didn't care either way. He just wanted to be gone.

Ludo felt just as impatient to leave the fort. It was hard to live under the constant threat of war, and while the Vettels remained in the wind, that threat would continue to grow. Though he felt concerned, remembering what Agnette had said. 'But what if we miss them? If we sail up here,' Ludo said, leaning over the map, pointing to the Eastern Shore. 'To Slussfall. What if Hakon Vettel comes straight down on foot, over the mountains, back to Ottby?'

It was a risk.

Reinar tried not to let his fear of that happening show on his face.

Bjarni said what they were all thinking. 'Without Alys, we have no one to see what's coming.'

'No,' Reinar agreed quietly, eyes up, searching the back of the hall where Elin had gone. 'But unless he's got another dreamer locked away in his fort, nor has Hakon Vettel.' He watched his mother combing Stellan's hair. She looked up, meeting his eyes, and he saw her concern. But they were never going to be safe until they ended the Vettels. There was no choice.

They had to leave Ottby.

***

Alys had been disturbed since Hakon had fallen from his horse. The rest of the afternoon had passed without incident, though she kept listening, glancing around, worried that someone was out there.

Watching her.

Eddeth held out a hand, not looking around, and Alys handed her another bandage. 'Best thing you can do is nothing!' she declared crossly, wrapping the cloth around Hakon's stomach. 'Riding in the snow after being bedridden, with a wound like this?' She muttered and mumbled, growing angrier by the moment. 'And my maggots were doing such a fine job! Only a few days more and you would have skipped back to Slussfall, yes indeed!' And tying the ends of the bandage into a knot, she stepped back to look her patient over. 'Alys, can you go and see if the water's ready? I've got my herbs waiting in that cup. Over there, on the tree stump. Take it outside and fill it up. That's just what you need, my lord. A hot tea!'

Hakon was reminded of Mother's tonic. It had helped him get right again after the smoke had threatened to ruin everything, and he turned to Eddeth, peering up at her. 'You look like a dreamer, Eddeth. Perhaps you are, and you won't reveal the truth? You seem to have a lot of knowledge about a lot of things.'

'You must want a dreamer badly if you're trying to make me into one!' Eddeth snorted loudly, not answering the question. But sensing that Hakon was waiting for an answer, she sighed. 'My grandmother was a dreamer. She spoke to the gods themselves! But not me. I always wanted to be one, but no dreams ever came my way, so I learned all about herbs instead. Which is just as well for you!'

Hakon lurched up. 'The gods spoke to your grandmother? Which gods?'

Eddeth almost fell over, suddenly aware that she'd revealed too much. She glanced at the tent flap, knowing that Stina and Alys would be cross with her. 'Well... that I don't know. But all of the good ones, I imagine.' She sneezed, feeling flustered. 'Now, you stay there, and I'll see where Alys is with that tea.' She reached for Hakon's tunic, lying on his bed of furs, though he grabbed her wrist, forcing her attention back to him.

Eddeth cried out, eyes bulging.

'Which gods did she speak to, Eddeth? I'm not a fool. Not a

boy. Not the half-dead wreck they all think I am. I don't need a dreamer to hear and see all that's happening around me. And what I know is that you're not telling me everything!' He kept squeezing her wrist until Eddeth bent towards him, face contorted in pain.

'Valera!' Eddeth blurted out. 'Mostly Valera. Sometimes Vesti, I think. I don't know!' She was quickly hot all over, panicking, her mind oddly blank.

'What's happening?' Alys was horrified as she hurried into the tent, having heard Eddeth's shout. 'What are you doing?'

'Whatever I want!' Hakon snarled. 'Leave the tea there. Eddeth and I haven't finished our conversation yet, have we?' He glared at Alys until she turned to the table. And leaving the cup, she glanced over her shoulder at Eddeth before slipping out of the tent.

'Are you alright?' Ivan asked as she emerged into the campsite.

'It's your cousin. He's hurting Eddeth! I don't know why. She's only trying to help him! Please, do something!' Alys grabbed Ivan's arm, imploring him to act.

And nodding, Ivan hurried into the tent.

***

'We have to do something! But what?' Jonas wanted to pull out his hair. The fur traders had taken to the tavern to spend some of their hard-earned coins, and though the thought of warmth and ale and something hot to eat had them both shaking with need, they couldn't risk being seen up close, so they'd chosen to remain outside, in the snow. Eventually, they'd found their way to a barn, sharing it with a few noisy goats. It wasn't going to be the most comfortable night, but they were grateful for the roof and the walls and the almost dry straw beneath their sodden boots.

Vik didn't know. He rubbed his hands together, shuddering. 'We need an informant. Someone to tell us what's happening. Someone to help us.'

Jonas frowned. 'And you think we're going to find one of those around here? Someone who wants to help the likes of us?'

'They're not all Slussfall men.'

Jonas nodded. 'But they're all loyal to the Vettels now, aren't they? Whoever remains?'

'Maybe. But there's always one who's got a foot in both camps. The sort of man who's happy to go where the silver leads. I think we both know who I've got in mind.'

'It's a good thing I brought so much silver with me!'

'And why is that?' Vik wondered, tugging off a wet boot, wanting to shake out a pebble that had been bothering him all day. 'You've been doling out coins like it's Solsta.'

Jonas laughed. 'I dug up my hoard when I went back to Torborg. After what Alys said about the children being taken, about Magnus being sold as a slave, I thought I might have to pay for his release.'

'Well, lucky for us you're such a rich man!'

'Ha! If I was a rich man, you think I'd be living in that old cottage with you?'

Vik shook his pebble into the straw. 'I do. Yes, you would.'

'You're right about that,' Jonas admitted, rummaging in his pouch for something to eat. He had a few furry nuts, but that was all. 'I'm not a man who needs a hall.'

'Not like Hakon Vettel. Though that boy seems to want a kingdom rather than just a hall.'

'He does. I only hope the Vilanders can stop him. After all we did, all Ake did, I'd hate to see a Vettel on the throne again in my lifetime. There's just something wrong with that bloodline. Cursed by the gods it is.'

'Or not,' Vik said darkly. 'Perhaps they're favoured by those gods who wish us all harm? Those who don't want to see a good man on the throne. A man who cares for his people.'

Jonas handed him a couple of nuts. 'I made you supper! Don't say I never do my share of the cooking.'

And taking the unappealing looking nuts, Vik popped them into his mouth. 'Not quite a nice fillet of smoked trout.'

'No, not quite,' Jonas agreed, listening to the wind howling around the old barn, shaking the doors, disturbing the goats, who started mewling loudly.

***

Ivan yanked Eddeth away from Hakon, who looked ready to take a sword to them both. 'Stop it! Hakon!' And pushing Eddeth behind him, he shoved his cousin back down onto the stool. 'What are you doing? Eddeth's only trying to help you!' He glanced at Hakon's freshly wrapped belly, seeing the old bandages lying on the ground.

'She knows more than she's saying! I know she does!' Hakon spluttered angrily, eyes on Eddeth. 'Ask her!'

Ivan felt embarrassed. Hakon hadn't been the same since their attack on Ottby. He worried that he was losing his mind. 'What's he talking about?' he asked Eddeth.

She twitched nervously, edging towards the tent flap. 'My grandmother was a dreamer. She spoke to the gods. There's little I know beyond that! Little! I swear it on my life!'

Ivan spun back to his cousin. 'Why are you worried about the gods all of a sudden?'

'Because –' Hakon didn't want to say. 'Go!' he screamed at Eddeth. 'Just go!' And slumping over on the tree stump, he yelped, pointing a thumbless hand at Ivan. 'You too! Get out!'

Ivan opened the tent flap for Eddeth to scamper through, turning back to Hakon. His cousin was disturbed in ways that were starting to worry him. 'Hakon, what is it? Tell me.' And grabbing another tree stump, he sat down. He was starving, impatient to get moving, but most of all, he needed to know what was wrong with his cousin.

Hakon turned his head, watching the rippling wall of the tent, thinking of his stone fortress. 'It doesn't matter.' He felt Ivan grip his arm.

'You want to convince those men out there to fight for you? Then it matters, because they need to see you as their future king. They need to believe in you again!' Ivan hissed. 'So tell me. I can't help you if you don't tell me what's wrong, Hakon. And something is. I know you.'

Hakon was watching the flames in the small circle of stones at their feet, beaten by the wind, fighting a furious battle that surely the wind would win eventually. Like Ottby. He should have won that battle. He'd fought his way into the fortress, armed men supporting him, overwhelming any defense the Vilanders could mount. Their walls were breached, their gates broken. They were outnumbered.

That was a battle a lucky man would have won.

Hakon couldn't get comfortable. He wanted to straighten out his stomach, so he leaned to one side, irritated. 'When I was ill, Alari came to me. She was angry with me for Ottby. For Mother.' He grimaced, pain blazing across his belly. 'Perhaps she's abandoned me? Perhaps all the gods have?'

'The gods? Why would you think that?' Ivan had started to wonder the same thing himself, though it would hardly help his cousin recover if that thought took hold.

'I feel it. Here.' Hakon pointed to his belly. 'Here! I feel cursed by ill-luck!'

'And what should we do about that, then? Out here, in the middle of nowhere? Stuck in the freezing snow? Trapped!' Ivan jumped to his feet, glaring down at his cousin, patience worn out.

Standing outside the tent, hand on the flap, ready to find out what was happening, Lief froze, listening.

Alys watched him out of the corner of her eye as she dragged Eddeth away to find Stina. Snow was falling, blown across the campsite by a determined wind, and she pulled her cloak tightly around her shivering body. 'What happened? Why was Hakon yelling at you?'

Eddeth couldn't speak. Her wrist hurt where Hakon had squeezed it, though she wasn't bothered by a little pain. She was far more worried about what she might have revealed to cause them all problems. 'He... oh dear... he wanted to know whether I was a dreamer. He thought I was, which, I don't blame him for, of course! With my knowledge?'

'Eddeth!' Alys hissed. 'Focus!'

'Alright. Yes, alright.' Eddeth blinked, attention drifting to the stew Stina was stirring, stomach rumbling. 'I... might have told him about my grandmother.'

'Your grandmother, the dreamer? The one who spoke to the gods?'

Eddeth nodded, nose twitching.

'Oh.'

'He wanted me to tell him about the gods. He was very insistent.' She gripped her wrist, feeling the burn.

'Why?'

Eddeth shrugged. 'Perhaps he wants their help? I would if I were him. Poor wretch. After what he's been through?'

Alys thought of the vatyr, listening to Eddeth's belly rumble. 'Go and eat,' she smiled, though her body was tense, watching Lief standing outside Hakon's tent, trying not to look as though he was doing the very thing he was so obviously doing.

Sensing that he was being watched, Lief ducked his head, deciding to go and check on Falla. He felt disturbed by what he'd heard. Unsettled. Like his father before him, he'd grown up believing that the Vettels were destined to be the rulers of Alekka, chosen by the gods themselves.

Lief had given Jesper Vettel his oath, and then his son.

But if the gods had abandoned the Vettels, what was he going to do now?

***

Reinar was sick of talking about the Vettels. Sick of thinking about them too. The day had been long and cold, but the fort was finally starting to look like its old self. A few familiar faces had returned, which had raised all their spirits. Word was spreading about Reinar's luck changing. About Ake's arrival. About the betrayal of their neighbours too. He nudged Bjarni, who looked half asleep beside him, ale cup tilting in his hand. 'Not sure that's going to end well.'

Bjarni muttered loudly, sitting up with a jerk. 'What?' He blinked at Reinar, following his gaze to where Sigurd and Ilene sat, heads together, both of them more than a little drunk.

'Mmmm, but who could blame either of them?'

Reinar supposed that was true, and Sigurd did seem to like a strong woman. He smiled sadly, memories of Tulia haunting him again.

If only he'd seen the truth about Torvig earlier...

'You couldn't have done anything,' Bjarni yawned, reading his mind. 'Torvig was always a snake, but even I didn't suspect what he was doing. Steffan told me he tried to rape his sister. Who knew that?' Bjarni shook his head, incensed. 'The bastard was going around threatening all these women. Raping them, hurting them, making them too afraid to say anything.'

Reinar was furious at the thought of it. If Alys hadn't stopped Torvig, he would have raped her too. Likely killed her.

'Reinar?'

'Sorry?'

'You didn't answer.'

'No, I think you're right, but I never looked hard enough at Torvig. I befriended him because I wanted to spend time with Elin. Even back then. I thought if I could get her brother to like me, become friends with me, that she might talk to me.'

Bjarni smiled. 'She did more than talk to you, so that worked!' Reinar didn't look happy, though, and glancing around, Bjarni edged closer. 'Is it strange having her back? Knowing she ran away? That she left you?'

'I... don't know what's real. Agnette thought she was done with me, but now she's here again. I want her to be, I do. I missed her, but...' His voice drifted into silence, and he stared at his cup of ale.

'You mean Alys?'

Reinar's head snapped up. He glared at Bjarni, who was well used to his friend's temper.

'We're not blind, Reinar, especially not me. I saw how it was.'

'It was nothing.' And barely acknowledging Bjarni, Reinar stood, deciding it was time for bed. 'Goodnight, Brother!' he called to Sigurd, who didn't even look his way. Shaking his head, he turned it towards Bjarni. 'It was nothing. Elin's back where she belongs and only now matters. Elin and I are meant to be, you know that.'

Bjarni nodded, sensing how hard Reinar was working to convince them both, and he sought to help him. 'Of course I do. Sleep well, Reinar. Hopefully, my daughter will behave herself tonight!'

Reinar smiled now, relaxing slightly. 'I hope so, or Gerda might throw you all out. Make you sleep with the goats!' He clapped Bjarni on the shoulder, yawning as he headed away to the bedchambers, his smile gone in a heartbeat.

***

Magnus was miserable, staring out at the square, bathed in moonglow and shadows. He saw cats chasing each other, an old drunk stumbling about singing, a crippled man crawling around, searching for food. But he didn't see his great-grandfather and Vik.

'Maybe they left,' Leonid said mournfully. 'It would make sense, wouldn't it?'

'No, it wouldn't,' Magnus disagreed. 'Vik saw me. They would have stayed behind, trying to find a way to get us out of here.'

Leonid's mood rose and fell quickly. 'But how could they? How? Look at that door! Look at this place! One way in, one way out. And those men guarding the door look ready for war!'

Magnus wished that Leonid was slightly less dramatic. He grabbed his arm, leaning towards his ear. 'They might have good hearing, Leonid. You should whisper.' He remembered Lotta, who couldn't whisper either, and he felt sad. 'I found the woman, you know. The one Long Beard was taking my sister to.'

'Oh?' Leonid was eager to take his mind off his aching nose and his empty belly, and the looming promise of certain death. 'Did you see your sister, then?'

'No. They're not here yet, but she hoped they would be soon. He's one of Hakon Vettel's men, she said. One of his most valued warriors.'

Leonid swallowed. 'Well, that can't be good, Magnus, for he's a cruel lord. A cruel lord indeed.' Tears welled in his eyes, and he dropped his head forward, not wanting to cry, knowing how badly it would block his nose again.

'What happened? Leonid? What did he do?'

'To me? Nothing,' Leonid sighed, lifting his head. 'But he... killed my father. Him and his men. Raped my mother, then killed her too. They tore through our village like wildfire when they came down from Orbo.' Now Leonid couldn't stop his tears. 'I was in the forest with my younger brothers. My mother, she...' He started sobbing, just thinking about it. 'She sent us berry picking. She was going to make a cake for my father's birthday. It would have been a surprise. He liked cake.' And then his nose blocked and he couldn't breathe.

'I'm sorry.' Magnus felt like crying himself. 'I'm very sorry for you, Leonid. What happened to your brothers?'

Leonid lifted his head. 'They're still there. We made a pyre, tidied things up, got back to work. My father was the village silversmith. A very skilled man indeed. He taught me everything he knew, so I carried on. This was a few years ago now. But my brothers are young, only eleven and thirteen. They'll be on their own, wondering why I haven't returned. I look after them, you see. Feed them, keep them clothed and warm.' He became anxious again, shuffling around fretfully. 'What was I thinking, getting into an argument with that man? What was I thinking!'

'Shut your fucking mouth!' came a grumbling voice. 'Or you won't be doing any thinking soon!'

Leonid clamped his lips together, grateful for Magnus' sympathy.

Wondering if he was ever going to see his brothers again.

CHAPTER SIXTEEN

Darkness had fallen rapidly, and not waiting to find anywhere more suitable, they had camped amongst the trees. It wasn't really a clearing, and shelters and fires had been erected haphazardly in clumps where they could find enough space amongst the tangled tree roots. It was snowing again, and even Ivan was losing his smile.

He turned to Alys, who shivered behind him in the dark. He had taken her away into the trees, wanting to talk privately. And though he could sense her desire to leave, he hurried on. 'My cousin is... not feeling himself, I think. Since the battle. Since his wound. He thinks Eddeth's a dreamer.' Ivan peered at Alys. 'Is she a dreamer?' He wasn't sure what he wanted to be true.

Alys shook her head. 'No, I'm sorry, she's not, but she has good instincts, and a way with herbs, as you've seen. And maggots,' she grinned. It helped to have Ivan on their side, Alys knew. Hakon wasn't right, and she could sense a darkness around him, as though it was trying to consume him.

There was no one for Ivan to talk to. He couldn't share his concerns with Lief, and despite his closeness to his men, he would not speak to them about Hakon.

He couldn't.

But Alys?

Ivan sighed, shoulders tense. He turned, hearing a shout as a shelter fell down, two men arguing over whose fault it was. 'Hakon thinks the gods have abandoned him. Us. The Vettels.'

'Abandoned you?'

'The gods choose the Kings of Alekka, and if they no longer want my family on the throne?' Ivan shuddered, feeling oddly lost. 'It's all we've known. All we heard about from our fathers. All we've fought for since we were boys.' He lowered his voice. 'And if those men hear about it, what will happen then?' He blinked, realising what he'd just revealed to a complete stranger. Grabbing her arm, Ivan pulled Alys close. 'You can't tell anyone. Not a soul.'

'I... I wouldn't.' Alys could sense the change in him. She could hear his thoughts stampeding around his head. He was afraid. Afraid he'd done the wrong thing, trusting her. 'But, Ivan, I...' Alys didn't want to help the Vettels, but she needed to find a way to extract herself from this mess before anyone found out that she was a dreamer.

And then an explosion of noise as a flock of birds took off all at once, shattering the silence, a flurry of dark feathers flapping into the dusk sky.

'What was that?' Ivan shoved Alys behind him, hand slipping inside his cloak, head swivelling. 'Where are they going?'

The echo of the birds' grating cries reverberated around the forest, and Alys turned, trying to hear anything else, hoping to sense what was out there. The tree canopy above their heads, dark with shadows, shook angrily as though disrupted by a furious storm.

And then nothing.

Ivan's breath smoked around his face as he turned back to Alys, trying to smile. 'At least it's not the vatyr!' he laughed, though his eyes blinked rapidly, full of fear. 'What were you going to say before?'

'Just that your cousin has been through a lot. When something happens to our body, it can also affect our mind.' She smiled, wanting to encourage him to take her back to the camp. 'He needs time to feel like himself again.'

Ivan sighed, knowing that was true. 'And in the meantime? What if the gods send more evil spirits after us?'

Alys was worried about that too, but she kept her smile going. 'We can only cope with what's before us, not try to imagine the future, for that is in the hands of the gods.'

***

Sigurd saw Tulia's face as Ilene bent to kiss him.

He had no idea why Ilene was kissing him, except that she'd wanted to kiss him, and he was too drunk to see that it was a bad idea.

Was it a bad idea?

Ilene was lonely and sad, he was broken-hearted and rudderless, and she had a way about her that made it almost impossible to resist doing what she wanted. So he hadn't resisted, and now he lay beneath her, in his bed, seeing Tulia's face. He felt confused and sad, his attention wandering to Alys, wondering why she hadn't seen what would happen to Tulia.

Wondering why she hadn't warned her...

Ilene appeared to be enjoying herself, Sigurd thought groggily, feeling like a horse being ridden at pace. She was not like Tulia, though Tulia had very much liked to sit on top of him too. She'd been like a sleek cat, wild and exotic, leaving him breathless. Ilene was like a bear, angry and aggressive, and Sigurd found himself becoming more distracted by the moment.

'Sigurd?' Bending forward, Ilene kissed him again, finally sensing his unease. 'What is it?' He was handsome, she thought. The lord's brother. And with all the trouble brewing in Alekka, there was always a good chance that a lord's brother would one day become the lord himself.

And every lord most certainly needed a wife.

'I...' Sigurd didn't want to talk. He didn't want to think, so, gripping the back of Ilene's head, he pulled her to him, kissing her roughly, wanting respite from all the faces and the voices and the soul-crushing regrets most of all.

And closing his eyes, he flipped Ilene over, desperate to make the pain go away.

***

Reinar heard them through the wall.

He glanced at Elin, who sat before him, sipping her wine, eyes on the flames.

She looked sad.

Sensing her husband watching her, Elin lifted her head. 'Sigurd's moved on rather quickly.'

'Not moved on. He's trying to feel better.'

'Sounds like he's feeling rather good right now.'

Reinar grinned as the rhythmic noises became impossible to ignore, the headboard banging against the wall now. 'Not sure Gerda will be. No doubt she'll be lying in bed with a pillow over her head. Just her luck that Liara's finally quiet.'

Elin laughed. 'Poor Gerda!' Her laugh faded quickly, though, her sadness returning. 'It's so strange without Tulia. Without Torvig. Ottby doesn't feel the same anymore.'

'No, it doesn't. And more missing besides.'

Leaving her cup on the table, Elin clasped Reinar's hand. 'When will we leave? For Slussfall?'

'Seven days, I hope, depending on how quickly we can organise ourselves. We can't give the Vettels time to settle in. We want to hit them hard before they've had time to recover.'

'Did they lose a lot of men?'

'They did. We had a pile of bodies to burn. But not just men. They left behind siege towers and catapults. Oxen. Weapons. Tents. Horses. Even servants. They ran out of here like Thenor himself was chasing them.' Reinar pulled Elin to her feet, not wanting to talk about the Vettels anymore. 'Perhaps we should head for bed?'

'You think we can sleep through that?'

'They sound almost finished to me, and no, I wasn't planning on sleeping at all.'

Elin smiled, wrapping her arms around Reinar's waist, tipping back her head as he bent down to kiss her. He was like hugging a tree, a fur-covered tree, with the tenderest lips. And feeling them on hers, Elin closed her eyes, smiling.

***

Ivan had hurried away to talk to his men, and Alys had headed back into the trees, wanting to escape, but not from the camp – she couldn't leave Eddeth and Stina behind – just from the noise and distractions. Someone was out there, hiding in the darkness, taunting her. She trembled as she walked, one hand out, trying not to lose her balance.

Someone was out there, watching her, and she needed to know who it was.

Stopping, Alys placed her hands on a tree trunk, trying to calm her mind. She thought of the trees in Ottby's forest, symbols hidden by their roots. She thought too of Valera's Tree, and Valera herself.

That goddess had helped her kill an evil dreamer.

But could she help her now?

Closing her eyes, Alys listened, thoughts blurring into crashing waves of terror, her heart beating faster. She saw horses stampeding through the forest, heard the urgent cries of birds above her head, the screams of men in pain, the tall figure of that god turning away from her, chuckling.

And eyes bursting open, Alys couldn't catch her breath.

***

Rikkard had been in and out of the tent so many times that Hakon finally bellowed at him to go away. The boy had left him a cup of ale, a plate of berries, a selection of nuts, and pieces of what might have been venison. Some cheese too.

Though he wasn't hungry.

He thought of Mother, looking at the empty tree stump before him, almost seeing her sitting there, growling at him. Scolding him.

Helping him.

She had always been helping herself, he knew, but as long as it got him where he wanted to be, he hadn't cared.

And now, without her?

He felt blind, worried about the attack on the camp, unable to see what was coming next, thinking about Slussfall.

In pain.

***

'Alys!' Stina exclaimed, squeezing her hand. 'You're frozen solid! Come to the fire!' She tugged Alys along, quickly realising that their fire was almost out, assaulted by snow. Eddeth didn't appear to notice as she hopped about, stirring the stew. She had added some ale and herbs from her saddlebag, a few of the mushrooms she'd foraged for too. And despite Stina feeling slightly put out that Eddeth had elbowed her out of the way and taken over, she had to admit that it smelled more enticing now. 'Sit,' she ordered. 'Stay there, and I'll get you a bowl.'

Alys wasn't hungry.

She was still hearing voices.

Women's voices. More than one.

It was as though they were hiding from her, sneaking behind one tree, rushing to the next. Playing. Alys blinked, remembering what Eddeth had said about the gods being like children.

Stina was talking to her, but she sounded so far away.

Eddeth turned her face up to the blizzard, mouth open, letting the snow settle on her tongue. She spun around, swallowing it, eyes bright above the dying flames.

And Alys heard Valera's voice, as though it was coming from Eddeth herself. 'The wolf did not kill you, Alys, but the boar might. Watch yourself now, for you are in danger, and here, I cannot protect you. I cannot protect you from Hakon Vettel and what he might do if he finds out the truth...'

'Eat!' Eddeth ordered, sounding like herself again, shoving a bowl of steaming stew at a shivering Alys. 'After that day, we all need something hot in our bellies!' She didn't even wait before hurrying back for her own bowl.

The boar.

Alys slowly turned her head, seeking out Hakon's tent, his red banners fluttering from spears dug into the frozen ground, threatening to fly away; the angry boar's jaw open, teeth exposed.

She thought of Magnus and Lotta, trying to picture their faces.

She could feel her heartbeat slow, the warmth of the bowl thawing her frozen fingers, the shout from Eddeth as she burned her tongue.

And swallowing, Alys dug her spoon into the thick stew, still looking at Hakon's tent, knowing that more than anything, she needed to find a dream.

***

The baby cried so often that Agnette was sure she was only sleeping for moments at a time. There was no chance to feel rested, no chance to dream. She peered at Bjarni, who was staring at the rafters, listening to his daughter's ear-piercing wail.

'I need her to cry herself to sleep,' Agnette whispered in his ear.

'Do you, though?' Bjarni wasn't convinced it was a strategy that would result in him getting much sleep before dawn came to start another day. 'She's upset. Hungry.'

'She's tired, can't you hear?' Agnette had been looking after children since she was a child herself. She had good instincts, though being so tired, she was beginning to doubt herself.

Bjarni didn't need to know that, though.

'Well, I'm tired, so perhaps I should cry too?' he grumbled, feeling cross.

Agnette snuggled up to him, enjoying how much closer she could get to her husband without her enormous belly getting in the way. 'You can cry, I wouldn't blame you.' She smiled, closing her eyes, trying to imagine that Liara was a bird flying above the hall. A raven. A tired raven, just wanting to find shelter, somewhere to sleep undisturbed.

'How are you sleeping through that?' Bjarni wondered, peering at Agnette.

She kept her eyes closed, certain that she could sleep through a battle. 'Well, in a few hours she'll be hungry again, so I have to at least pretend. Wouldn't hurt you to try.'

Bjarni was surprised that she remained so perfectly still, her eyes closed. 'You're sure we shouldn't pick her up?' he whispered as the wailing intensified, tugging at his heartstrings. 'Something might be wrong.'

'You do remember training your old dogs, don't you? Babies are no different.'

'You think we should put her out in the barn too?'

Agnette smiled. 'Go to sleep, Bjarni Sansgard. That Ilene looks like the sort of woman who might wake Sigurd up and have another go at him. This might be our only chance!'

Bjarni wriggled down in the bed, shuffling closer to Agnette, clasping her hand in his. And, weary body sinking into the mattress, he closed his eyes.

'Soon, you'll miss this. When Liara is too busy to even look at us, or talk to us. Don't wish it all away just yet...'

Bjarni smiled, squeezing her hand, letting the not-at-all-soothing cries of his daughter lull him to sleep.

***

'When you were a baby, I used to rub your back,' came the familiar voice. 'It was the only way you'd fall asleep. I tried to get you to suck your thumb. Your mother liked to suck her thumb, but not you, Alys, you liked to scream.' The woman chuckled softly.

Alys crept closer, into the bedchamber.

Her bedchamber.

The shadowy figure stood over the crib. Alys could see the glow of a lamp behind her.

'You were always mine. Mine to love and care for. Mine to keep safe. But, in the end, I couldn't. I tried so hard, my darling girl, but I couldn't. And now you're lost. Trapped. And they're all coming for you.'

Alys stepped closer, reaching out a hand, wanting to touch the woman, to turn her around.

And then Eddeth shoved a hand over her mouth, waking her up, lifting a finger to her lips. Alys nodded, still half asleep, heart racing as Eddeth took her hand away, motioning for Alys to follow her. They were sleeping near the servants, and they had to shuffle around the maze of women, trying not to topple over, which was challenging for Eddeth, who had terrible balance. Eventually, they made it into some space. And blowing on her hands, trying to warm them up, Eddeth headed for the trees, Alys following after her.

The snow had stopped, though it had settled deeply, and Alys was quickly conscious that her boots were submerged in it. 'What is it?' she asked, shuddering with cold.

'You tell me!' Eddeth hissed. 'You're the one calling out in your sleep. You're the one saying something's coming!'

'Did I?'

They froze, eyes on each other, hearing that familiar drumming again.

Not drumming, Alys realised, quickly blinking herself awake.

It wasn't drumming this time.

It sounded like hooves...

CHAPTER SEVENTEEN

Hakon groaned, his sleep disturbed by unbearable pain and nightmares so dark that he was desperate to wake up. And then the mournful call of a horn echoed in the distance, and he jerked awake, gripping his fur, conscious that Rikkard was moving around, trying to light a lamp.

Njall burst into the tent, breath smoke pumping. 'Get up, my lord! Hurry! Something's coming!'

***

It sounded as though all the trees in the forest were breaking, hooves pounding the earth, shaking it beneath their feet.

Eddeth's eyes sprung open, and wheeling away from Alys, she disappeared into the darkness.

'Eddeth!'

Another long call of a horn and Alys ran back to the servants. 'Wake up! Quickly!' She didn't need to try and wake anyone up, though, everyone was already hurrying to their feet, huddling together, sleep-dazed and scared.

Stina stumbled towards her, hand out in the darkness. 'What is it? What's happening?'

'I don't know,' Alys admitted, wondering where Eddeth had gone.

'The Hunter is coming! The Hunter is coming!' came a bellow.

And then the baying of dogs in the distance.

'Move! Now! Into the trees!' Alys ordered, dragging Stina towards her. 'Go with them! Stay safe! I have to find Eddeth!' And squeezing Stina's hand, she took one last look at her friend before disappearing after Eddeth.

Eddeth was working hard, trying to calm Wilf as she dug a hand into her saddlebag. She had one more packet of flying powder tucked away somewhere, though perhaps Alys didn't need to see anything at all? It appeared quite obvious was what coming. She could hear the hooves, the hounds, the rattling, creaking trees brushed aside like blades of grass as the forest opened itself to the hunt.

Alys tapped Eddeth on the shoulder, and she swung around, screaming, packet flying out of her hand. 'What are you doing?'

'I... wanted to see if you were alright!' Alys called over the thunderous noise.

'Well, not now!' Eddeth called. 'I've lost the powder!'

'What?' The noise became louder. It was impossible to hear. 'Come on! We have to leave the horses! We have to clear everyone out of their path!'

And then screaming.

Alys and Eddeth left their horses behind, secure to the rope that ran between the trees, hurrying back to the camp as quickly as the snowy darkness would allow. There was a hint of moon occasionally as it popped its head above the swirling clouds; just enough to reveal the chaos unfolding before them.

'Get back!' Lief yelled, dark cloak nearly torn from his broad shoulders in the roaring wind. 'Clear a path! Hurry!' And sweeping his arms around, he pointed everyone into the trees.

There was no path to clear, or so it had seemed when they'd made camp, but now the trees were crashing in the distance.

A path was certainly being made.

The horn sounded again, and Hakon was there now, slumped

between Njall and Rikkard. 'What is it?' he called to Lief.

'My lord!' Lief turned around in surprise. 'Njall, take him into the trees! Hurry!'

Hooves sounded louder now, getting closer. Hounds barking viciously.

Ivan stumbled towards them, boots sinking into the snow, tripping often. 'Hakon, come with me! Njall, help Lief!' And taking over from Njall, he helped Rikkard guide Hakon into the trees. 'Move! Move!' The howls from those hounds rose the hairs on his arms, and Ivan stumbled again, biting his lip, head swivelling, trying to see what was coming.

Screams from somewhere. Thunder cracking overhead.

The earth vibrating beneath their feet.

Alys and Eddeth hurried back to Stina, Eddeth limping, having fallen over some snow-buried roots, tearing her trousers. Stina grabbed Eddeth's arm to steady her. 'What can we do?'

'It's the hunt!' Eddeth cried, yelping. 'There's nothing we can do now!'

The dogs' barking intensified. Bridles jangling.

Voices shrieked in warning, echoing all around them.

'Move back!' Ivan yelled, hands out, having left Hakon with Rikkard, wanting to guide more of their people to safety. He froze, mouth open, glimpsing The Hunter sitting astride his two-headed shadow horse, charging towards them, antlers rising out of his head like an enormous stag. He was as dark as a moonless night, eyes glowing like embers as he led his army of shadow spirits forward, tearing through the camp.

The story of the hunt was one of Alys' favourites, and she thought of her grandfather and how much he'd liked to tell it. Though this was no story, and this was no dream, and Alys froze as The Hunter spurred his horse towards them.

The terrifying sounds blurred around her, Jonas' voice rising out of the noise. 'The Hunter comes for Thenor's enemies, for the weak and corrupt, the feckless and disloyal. For those who have displeased the Father of the Gods himself. And if you're unlucky to be caught by The Hunter in the dark depths of a forest, he will mark you with Thenor's symbol. A powerful mark that will eat your soul. And if you do not redeem yourself, Alys, that mark will take your life! For The Hunter needs riders for his shadow army. Will you be one?' Jonas' voice was deep and gravelly as he leaned over, chuckling, kissing her goodnight.

Alys saw herself gripping his arm, wanting to know one thing before he left. 'But how do you save yourself from The Hunter, Grandfather? How?'

But Jonas was gone, and Alys couldn't remember his answer.

Hakon stumbled towards them, having batted away a fussing Rikkard, who'd remained hidden in the trees, frantic eyes seeking Eddeth. 'What do we do?'

Njall was running towards Lief, who had bent down in the middle of the camp, helping one of the servants, who'd tripped into a buried fire pit, breaking her ankle.

And then he was gone.

Hakon blinked. 'Njall!' He saw the horses, the hounds, all of them as though they were shadows, bleeding into the darkness, just memories of shapes.

Teeth bared. Eyes blazing.

Guttural noises that tore strips of terror off them all.

And then blades, shining and scything through the bitter night air.

Lief threw himself into the snow, hand on the whimpering servant's back, screams of panic echoing around him, horses thundering past, Njall's headless body falling into the snow with an almighty thud beside him.

Alys turned, slamming her hand over Stina's mouth, sensing that she was about to scream. She lifted a finger to her lips, and together they slipped away from the tents, moving further into the trees. Eddeth, watching them, put her own finger to her lips, urging the servants to follow them.

Hakon was unsteady on his feet, unable to move. There was no Njall, no Rikkard to support him. He couldn't see Ivan anywhere.

He couldn't move.

Dark horses and their shadow riders sped through the camp,

blades swinging, hacking down any who stood in their way, scavenging hounds tearing the flesh of those who had fallen.

The Hunter blew his horn, spinning his horse around in a circle, eyes bright, searching the darkness. And dropping the horn, which hung from his neck, he unsheathed his long sabre, inlaid with symbols that glowed like stars, urging his horse forward. The hounds and horses flew by after their prey, The Hunter oblivious to it all, his own horse stepping through the snow almost delicately now, eyes on Hakon.

***

'How do you know so much, Grandfather?'

Alys was eleven. They sat at their table, shelling peas.

'Me? Oh, well I'm old, you see. The old know many things, though the young are usually too busy to ask.'

'You're not *that* old.'

Jonas smiled. 'I'm old enough to know some things. Your grandmother taught me a lot. She was a wise woman.'

Alys peered at him, seeing the sadness lurking behind his smile. They didn't talk about her grandmother. They didn't talk about her mother either.

She knew that.

Dropping her head, she stared at the tiny green peas, glistening in their pod. And lifting it up, she scraped her finger under the peas, watching them slide into the bowl.

Jonas reached across the table, hand on her arm. 'What use is knowledge if we never share it? That's what Eida always said. Though some things make you unsafe. It's better never to know about them. The darkness is not frightening if you don't know what's lurking in it...'

Frowning, Alys stared at him. 'But what is lurking in it, Grandfather?'

***

The Hunter pointed his sabre at Hakon, his two-headed horse rearing up angrily; big teeth bared, flicking saliva, impatient to rejoin the shadow riders. The Hunter leaned forward, antlers towering above his head. 'Soon!' he bellowed, jerking the sabre at Hakon's chest, beams of moonlight glinting from its sharp blade. 'Soon!' And yanking his horse away, he charged off into the night, thunder shaking the forest all around them.

Alys blinked, the stench of blood and death wafting towards her like smoke; screams ringing in her ears, loud now. She gripped Eddeth, who was hopping on one foot, glancing around, eyes on Stina.

They stood like that for a heartbeat, maybe more, and then Alys woke up, sensing a change. The terrifying noises had retreated; the rattling and howling and sounds of killing too. And squeezing Eddeth's arm, she let her go. 'We need to help the injured! We need fires. We have to see!'

Ivan ran up to them, sword drooping in his hand, mouth hanging open. He turned slowly towards Hakon, who leaned on a tree nearby, shivering uncontrollably. 'Cousin?'

Hakon was stunned, and then quickly panicking. 'We have to get to Slussfall. We need to be back in the fortress! Now!'

Ivan turned back to Alys. 'I have to go. I have to... see who needs help. I have to... help Hakon.' He thought of Njall, wondering what had happened to Rikkard.

And then Falla's screams rang through the night as she ran towards her fallen husband, snow twirling gently now, sprinkling her dark hair. 'Lief! Lief!' Throwing herself onto his body, she tried to turn him over, relief surging through her as he groaned, eyes flickering open, rolling over himself.

His head was bleeding, having fallen onto the stones of the fire pit, knocking himself out. He blinked, confused for a moment, then, grabbing his wife, he held her to him. 'What happened?' Struggling back to his feet, Lief pulled Falla up with him, blood pouring from his head. He lifted a hand, wiping it away, eyes meeting Ivan's.

Bodies littered the campsite.

Many of them headless.

'The hunt.' Ivan saw Njall, lying beside his giant head. He felt sick. 'The hunt.'

Lief's eyes went to Hakon, who was shouting now.

'Double the men on the perimeter!' Hakon called, his voice cracking. Coughing, he tried to clear his throat. 'Jerrick!' He was relieved to see him still alive. 'Double the watch! We need to...' Head swimming with terror, memories of The Hunter staring him down flashing before his eyes, he lost the ability to speak.

Ivan took charge. 'We need to gather the men together! Bring the injured here. We'll make fires!'

Alys ushered a hobbling servant towards the centre of the camp, and leaving her on a log, she turned back for Eddeth and Stina.

'You need to help!' Ivan's head was swimming, too unsettled to feel any relief that it was over. 'Help my men. Please!'

And nodding, the women moved past him, past the bodies of the headless, who were not in need of help, aiming for those who had been wounded by The Hunter and his shadow riders; chewed on by his hounds.

Eddeth slipped her hand through Alys' arm. 'The gods have taken up against him for sure.'

Alys swallowed. 'And what will that mean for us?'

'Nothing good,' Eddeth warned. 'Nothing good that I can think of.'

***

Sigurd felt ill. Ale and Ilene were no cure for heartbreak.

He rolled out of bed, looking for his trousers.

His and Tulia's bed.

He shook his head, not wanting to see the shape of Ilene lying there.

He hated himself.

Wriggling on his trousers, he raced to grab his tunic, tugging it over his head. And with one, long, regretful glance back at Ilene, he eased open the door, slipping out into the corridor where Agnette was pacing up and down with Liara, trying to get her to sleep.

Sigurd blinked in surprise.

'Running away?' his cousin whispered with a weary smile. She wasn't sure if she'd slept yet, but at least Bjarni was, she thought, listening to him snoring through the wall. 'Running away from your own bed?'

Sigurd stood beneath a flaming sconce, not wanting to be seen, especially not by Agnette, who was far too insightful for her own good. He shrugged, moving away from her, towards the hall.

Agnette followed him.

'Where are you going, Sigurd? It's hours till dawn, I'd say.'

'Going to check the wall. See what's happening.' He didn't turn around, but then, sensing that his tired, baby-carrying cousin was still following him, he stopped. 'Agnette, go back to bed. Please. Get some sleep.'

'Oh, you don't think I'd like to do that? But look at this little ball of trouble. Does she look tired to you?' And she held the swaddled baby towards Sigurd, who stared at her.

'I wouldn't know,' he mumbled, not wanting to think about babies. They all looked and sounded the same to him.

'Well, she doesn't, I promise, and the moment I put her down she'll be bleating like Bolli's goat, waking up the entire hall. And Gerda's already going to be in a foul mood after you and Ilene, so I don't want to make it worse.'

Sigurd's head hurt, and Agnette's words made him cringe with embarrassment. 'Don't remind me.'

'No? You weren't enjoying yourself, then? Sounded like you were having a wonderful time!' Agnette jiggled Liara, smiling at her miserable cousin.

'I don't know what I was thinking. What I was doing.' Sigurd's shoulders slumped, and he flopped down onto a bench, sighing.

'You were trying to feel better,' Agnette smiled, sitting beside him. 'Nothing wrong with that. You don't think Tulia would have done the same?'

Sigurd leaned towards her. 'I don't want Ilene.'

'I know.'

Tears came as he dropped his head to his hands, feeling desperately alone. 'Fucking Torvig. If he wasn't dead, if Alys hadn't killed him...' He lifted his head, rubbing his eyes, staring at Agnette. 'You remember his father?'

'Who could forget Tor Aleksen? Like father, like son, I suppose. He was a terrible man. Stellan never liked him.'

'He was. No one ever spoke about him, though. After Stellan killed him, no one ever spoke about him again.'

'Well, Reinar was betrothed to Elin. Torvig was his best friend. They felt sorry for them both, I suppose, orphaned as they were.'

Torvig and Elin's father, Tor, had been a highly skilled warrior, fearless in battle, but an argumentative man, unable to hold his ale. Merciless and vengeful, he had maimed and killed more than one of Stellan's men without cause. In the end, Stellan had been forced to kill him, and after his death, rumours had continued to swirl that Tor had even killed his own wife.

'But didn't anyone think that his blood ran thickly in his children's veins? Or, at least, his son's?'

'He was a horrible man, I know, but Elin was always so lovely. *Is* so lovely,' Agnette corrected herself with a yawn. 'She takes after her mother, I'd say, not that we ever met the woman. But Torvig... he was definitely his father's son in the end.'

'I wish Tulia had killed him. She was only here because of me. It's all my fault! And Amir. It's all my fault, Agnette!' Sigurd tried to rub away the tears before they fell from his eyes. He wanted to rub away the pain too, and the memory of what he'd done with Ilene.

Everything was broken. Ruined forever.

Nothing felt right without Tulia.

***

'And you thought that wolf was t-t-terrifying!' Eddeth spluttered, unable to stop her teeth chattering. They were standing in a tent, tending to the injured, and though its makeshift walls were shaking violently, it was almost keeping the worst of the weather at bay.

Though it was colder than ever.

Alys glared at Eddeth, and Stina froze, needle in hand, stitching Lief's wound. He gripped the sides of a tree stump, trying not to wobble, though the ground was uneven and the stump tilted occasionally, causing Stina to jab Lief in the head.

'What wolf?' he asked, wanting to take his mind off the pain. He felt impatient, exhausted, and desperate to find Falla. She had left the tent, unable to stand all the blood. He was worried about her and the baby. About how they were going to get back to Slussfall now.

'We saw a wolf!' Eddeth announced loudly. 'On our travels, before you kidnapped us. Seemed to be following us, though it did not linger long.' She tried to wake herself up, not wanting to ramble on, tangling them all up in an even bigger mess.

Stina was eager for Lief to be gone. He had such strange eyes: black and slightly twisted with scars. He didn't smile, but he always appeared to be listening, and she wanted him far away from Eddeth before she said anything else. 'Well, rather a wolf than what we saw out there. I'm not even sure I'm awake. Surely that was a nightmare?' She smiled nervously at Lief, but he looked past her to Eddeth.

'Do you have knowledge about these things, Eddeth?'

Eddeth looked excited to have been asked, but glimpsing the warning in Alys' eyes, she tried to grab the reins of her enthusiasm. 'I have... some, yes indeed. The Hunter!' She pulled up a stool, wishing she was holding a cup of steaming elderflower tea in her numb hands. 'He is sent by the gods. They have many willing servants, and The Hunter is but one.'

Lief remained silent, encouraging Eddeth to continue.

'They say he belongs to Thenor. That he marks those doomed to die, those Thenor wants punished. He gives them a mark, and that mark is a promise of a miserable death to come.'

Lief shivered. If the gods had forsaken Hakon, they weren't safe. The Hunter would come again. Or worse.

Was there worse?

Ivan hurried into the tent, eager to escape the wind. 'The fires keep blowing out! It's going to be impossible to get your hot water going, Eddeth.'

She looked disappointed. 'Well, what else could we expect, cursed as we are!'

Ivan frowned, glancing at Lief, who was looking on with sharp eyes. 'You think we're cursed?'

'With this weather? Your lord's wound? The vatyr and The Hunter? Oh yes, I would say so! It's only a matter of time before something else goes wrong, mark my words. Only a matter of time!'

Ivan wanted to scream. He wanted to run out of the camp and leave them all behind. He longed to be back in Orbo, standing on the wall, eyes on the vast expanse of glittering sea. He didn't want to claim thrones that no longer belonged to them. He didn't want to trek up and down Alekka seeking vengeance.

He wanted to go home.

Stina tied a knot in the thread, stepping back, checking Lief's stitches, which was mostly impossible in the near-darkness. Soapstone lamps burned on the table beside her, but their glow was dim, flames disturbed by the wind, and she could only assume that she'd done a passable job. 'You need to be careful,' she warned. 'Don't touch your head. I'll wrap a bandage around it. It's still bleeding.'

'Thank you,' Lief muttered, impatient to be gone. 'Well, cursed or not, we need to get on the road come first light. We won't get to Slussfall waiting and hiding in the forest.'

Ivan peered at him. 'No, we won't. Hakon's already making plans for a quick departure.'

'Is he?'

Ivan could hear it then: the first hint of a problem.

Not the first hint, he knew, but he could sense a worrying change in Lief. 'He is, of course. He's our lord. Our leader. He's making plans for how to keep us all safe.' None of it was true, and Ivan was struggling to even say the words. A lord could be defeated by a rumour. By the merest tremor of distrust.

One sign of weakness...

CHAPTER EIGHTEEN

Morning tried to dawn through a wall of clouds that promised another grim day. Vik and Jonas had been woken early by the goats, and a rooster they hadn't realised was sleeping in the barn, though both men doubted they'd slept much at all.

Jonas dragged a hand down his face, wanting a splash of cold water, a sip of something to moisten his throat, which was so dry he almost had to peel his tongue off the roof of his mouth. Vik looked eager to be gone, tightening his swordbelts, wrapping his cloak around his shoulders, eyes on the faint light seeping in through holes in the barn door. 'Better be going before someone comes to milk those goats.'

Jonas nodded, standing, thinking of Magnus, hoping he'd had more than a few nuts for his supper. His own stomach growled endlessly, irritating him. They could hardly sneak around the fort with his belly making such a ruckus.

'Ready?' Vik asked as Jonas pulled up the hood of his cloak, dropping it over his face.

And nodding, Jonas followed him out of the barn into the blustery morning.

***

Hakon wasn't ready to leave his tent.

After The Hunter?

Before last night he'd let his imagination do all the work, making up explanations for what was happening, weaving it into a story he'd almost convinced himself was true.

But now, it was plain to everyone.

The gods had turned against him.

And what would they do next?

What would he do?

Ivan poked his head inside the tent; tired eyes, forced grin, braids almost entirely undone by the vicious wind. 'Hungry?'

Hakon could smell the cooking fires. He could hear the scrape and slop of porridge being lumped into bowls, and he thought of his hall and his high table and his cook who made him venison sausages for breakfast. If she hadn't been such a frail old woman, he would've brought her along. 'Not hungry at all. You?'

Ivan slipped inside, pleased to see Hakon looking better, which was surprising after the terrifying night they'd endured. 'No, it's colder than Vasa's tits out there! I just want to get on the road. Standing around here won't put anyone in a good mood.'

'And what about the bodies?' Hakon wondered.

'All seen to.'

'And Lief?'

'He's getting the servants sorted, those women too.'

'Well, it was worth keeping them after all,' Hakon decided. 'They'll be busy for days.'

Ivan nodded, staring at Hakon's belly. 'And you? How's the pain?'

'Gone,' Hakon lied, not wanting to appear weak, not even to his cousin. The pain was like bolts of lightning shooting through him. Sometimes, he couldn't speak. He wanted to curl up on his bed and close his eyes. 'Eddeth's maggots worked their magic, and now I am healed!' He tried to push back his shoulders, setting his jaw firmly, heading towards Ivan. 'Come on, Cousin, let's get outside. I'm sure there's a drop of ale to find, perhaps even some wine!' He hadn't seen Rikkard in some time, though he knew Ivan had put him to work, helping to move the dead and injured. He felt annoyed, wanting the boy with him, tending to his every need.

Ivan knew Hakon well enough to sense how uptight he was, how worried he was too, but he felt a lift. His cousin had not retreated. He was not hiding from what was coming for them. That was something, at least.

But only something.

He smiled as Hakon peered at him, trying to ignore the tension in his shoulders that warned him that everything was falling apart. 'Alright, I'll go and see what I can do about some breakfast.'

***

Vik made his way across Slussfall's square to buy two hot sausages for breakfast. Jonas took his guiltily, thinking of poor Magnus, who would surely not be eating anything that resembled food in that prison hole. He tried not to look his way as they stood between two old sheds, watching.

The tables were being dragged out in the hopes that some hardy folks still wanted to part with their hard-earned coins. And those selling lamps or candles or furs would surely do a good trade – those selling hot food too.

'We need to get him out tonight, just before the gates close,' Jonas decided.

Vik nodded, unable to stop yawning. It felt as though he hadn't slept in days, and his thoughts were slow to form, yet they had to be decisive and sharp. It would do none of them any good to make a mistake now.

'Ollo Narp,' Jonas murmured, eyes on the stout man striding across the square, barking at a group of small children who were throwing snowballs at each other. Hands flapping imperiously, he tried to move them away from the tables and those men who were out with their shovels working to clear the snow. 'Never has a man been more in love with the sound of his own voice than Ollo Narp. Snively little shit.'

'You think we can trust him?'

Jonas narrowed his eyes, considering things. Ollo Narp had been one of Sirrus Ahlmann's men, but rumours had drifted down the Eastern Shore that Ollo had turned on Sirrus in return for a powerful new position and a chest full of silver. Jonas didn't doubt it. Sirrus had always been too loyal, keeping men like Ollo around when he should have cut them loose.

'I think we couldn't trust him to keep his own mother safe, but we've little choice now. He's devious. Greedy. Might work in our favour.'

Vik nodded, eyes on Ollo, who had grabbed a little boy by the collar, threatening him with a heavily ringed finger. 'Let's hope so.' He looked over his shoulder, shivering. 'Gates are open.'

'Then you should go. Get out while you can. I'll stay. Bring Magnus.'

Lifting an unimpressed eyebrow at his old friend, Vik turned into the alley. 'Not likely. And not today. Let's tuck ourselves away awhile. We can go find Ollo when things warm up. We don't want to give him too much time to betray us now, do we?'

***

Everyone's eyes were on Hakon.

Including Lief's.

They had finally left their camp as the sun was reaching its peak, eager to leave behind the reminder of what had happened in the night.

Hakon rode at the head of their long column, thinking of Ulrick, who had abandoned him for the little girl; Mother, who had died; and Njall, who had saved his life then lost his own. He turned to Lief, who rode alongside him, feeling the need to reassure him that he was still a lord worth following. 'The weather appears to have improved.'

Lief nodded. 'It does, my lord. We'll make good progress today, though there are many wounded, including yourself. It wouldn't be wise to push you too hard.'

Hakon flinched, not wanting to be lumped in with the injured, though he couldn't deny that he was barely able to tolerate the pain in his belly. 'Makes sense,' he grunted, trying to think of something else to say. 'Though nothing will make them feel as good as seeing Slussfall's walls in the distance. I would rather we made progress than sat around feeling sorry for ourselves. I'd happily ride through the night if it weren't for all of them!' And turning in the saddle, he glared at the slow-moving train of warriors and servants.

Lief doubted that was true. He could see the pain in Hakon's eyes.

The fear too.

Lief was forty-four. Old enough to be Hakon's father.

He remembered how loyal his own father had been to Jorek Vettel; to his son, Jesper. He had given his oath to protect them all, as had Lief as a young man.

Lief frowned, knowing that Falla was riding behind him with the women.

His pregnant wife.

His oath to Hakon mattered, but he'd also taken an oath to Falla before the gods, and that oath was carved into his heart.

He would do whatever it took to keep her safe.

***

'What we need is someone on the inside. Inside Slussfall. One of Sirrus' men, if there's any left. Someone to open the gates and let us in!'

Reinar laughed, clapping Bolli on the back. 'I like the sound of that. We can send a note, ask them to help us out!'

They were moving through the ships, checking for problems. Once it had been reassuring to know that a fleet of twenty expertly crafted warships waited down in the harbour, though over the past year, Reinar had lost many of his helmsmen, and then many of his oarsmen too. They'd struggled to put crews together.

But now?

Now they had eight hundred Stornas men and those captured Slussfall warriors who had wisely chosen to live and give their oath to Reinar. And with word being sent to the settlements around Ottby, soon they would have even more men. Enough hands to launch the entire fleet.

And more.

Ake had promised to send ten ships of his own, wanting to ensure the success of their attack on the Vettels.

Reinar puffed out a cold breath, eyes on the gloomy bank of clouds hanging above the fort. 'Feels like winter's already here. Those clouds aren't going to shift till spring, are they?'

Bolli frowned, following his gaze. He wore his favourite old blue gloves; fingerless, and repaired so often that they were a ratty mess, but he was rarely without them. 'I'd say not. You know the rumours. They say this winter will crush us.' He looked up at Reinar, who stood taller than every man in Ottby, apart from Ludo, who'd come down to the piers with Elin.

Reinar frowned at his wife, Bolli's words ringing in his ears.

'What is it?' Elin wondered, waiting by *Fury* as Reinar hopped over the gunwale, boots banging on the pier. 'Is something wrong?'

'Just worried about the weather. You don't launch a fleet in winter. Makes no sense.'

Elin laughed. 'It's not winter yet, Reinar.' She held out her arms, turning around, eyes on the dark water. 'There's no ice! We can still sail.'

Ludo looked worried beside her. 'But for how long? We don't want to get up the coast and be stopped, trapped in ice.'

'No, we don't,' Reinar agreed, looking back to Bolli, who had crouched down, muttering to himself.

'This is getting very long,' Elin said, tugging on the end of her husband's blonde beard. 'Why don't I give it a trim before you turn into an old helmsman?'

Reinar stared into her twinkling eyes, and he smiled. 'Thought I might grow it. It'll keep me warm over winter.' He winked at his wife before turning to Ludo. 'How's Sigurd?'

'Keeping busy this morning, staying away from Ilene.' Ludo tried not to smile because he felt so sorry for Sigurd, but it was almost pleasant to have a distraction from all the grief and misery and worry.

Reinar laughed. 'Imagine what Tulia would do to Ilene if she came back. That's a fight I'd like to see.'

Ludo nodded, glancing around as more men lumbered down the stairs, heading for the piers, arms loaded with barrels of ale. 'I'd better go, see how Sigurd's doing. Don't want him running away again.'

'Do that. We're going to need him. And Ludo, send Ilene to me when you find her. I think we'd better have a little talk, she and I.'

Elin was staring at her husband, sensing his desire to keep his mind on everything else but the woman standing right in front of him. She put a gloved hand on his chest, pressing, wanting to claim all of his attention. 'Why don't you show me where we'll be. Which ship. Where I'll be sitting. What I'll be doing.'

And dropping his head, staring into those familiar eyes again, Reinar smiled, trying to give it to her.

***

Ivan had forced Hakon to stop. His cousin hadn't wanted to appear weak and in need of a rest, though he certainly felt weak and in need of a rest. But Ivan had insisted that they take a break. Since leaving their camp in a hurry, they'd pushed the horses and men hard, and that sort of pace would wear on anyone after a while.

So Hakon stood by his horse as he drank from the stream which rushed past them in an icy babble.

'Your cousin asked me to check your wound, my lord,' Alys said nervously. She hadn't wanted to. Eddeth had been caring for Hakon, though, according to Ivan, he no longer wanted her near him.

Hakon flapped a gloved hand at Alys, irritated by her interruption. He didn't want company. Nor did he wish to be fussed over like an ill child. 'See to someone who needs your help. I don't.'

Alys was relieved, stepping away from the stream, head bowed.

'Wait.' Hakon peered at her. 'Why are you here? Who sent you?' He saw enemies everywhere now, as though the gods were following him, planning another attack, determined to rip off any last vestiges of favour.

Alys looked confused. 'Sent me? I was captured by your men.'

Hakon lunged at her, belly stinging, grabbing her wrist with his riveted glove. Alys yelped, feeling those rivets dig into her, but Hakon didn't care. 'So you say, but why should I believe that three healers were riding through the forest just when we had such great need of them?'

His breath was rancid, and Alys let it wash over her, trying not to screw up her nose or gag. He smelled of ale and fear, his thoughts cantering around his head like a pack of horses. 'We are not three healers, my lord. Eddeth is a healer, she has skills, but Stina and I are just her friends. We were on our way home. No one sent us to you, unless you think the gods are watching. Perhaps they brought us together? Eddeth did save your life. Perhaps it was the gods who sent us to help you?' Alys watched him, her wrist burning beneath his grip, which finally weakened, all energy leaving Hakon's trembling body in a rush.

He stumbled away, snarling. 'You think the gods wanted to save me?' Leaning against his horse, he tried to catch his breath, wanting to collapse to the ground; the pain had his ears ringing. 'Saved me so I could be killed by The Hunter or the vatyr or whatever is coming for us next? That makes no sense!'

Alys saw the fear in Hakon's strange eyes as he turned them on her; flashes of images that confused her once more.

'What? What is it?' Hakon watched her face change. She was a beautiful woman, he thought, studying her closely for the first time. Changeable and lovely.

He felt his tension release, ever so slightly.

'I... I feel worried,' Alys said, dropping her eyes, not wanting to reveal anything further. 'If the gods are in such a vengeful mood, what will that mean for tonight and the night after? It's very troubling.'

Hakon swallowed, not wanting to agree with her, though he did. Sighing, he peered over her shoulder, watching Eddeth hop around the stream, filling up water skins. 'You'd better send that Eddeth woman to me, then. She can ride with me today, tell me everything she knows about the gods.'

Alys froze. 'Eddeth?'

But Hakon was already turning away from her, wishing Njall was there to give him a boost onto his horse, though it would hardly dispel the notion that he was weak and helpless if he needed to be coddled like a baby. So grabbing a handful of reins, and gritting his teeth, Hakon shoved a wet boot into the stirrup, pulling himself up into the saddle. 'Yes,' he breathed, pain in his eyes as he stared down into hers. 'Eddeth.'

***

Reinar had never imagined that he would miss Eddeth, but he walked past her cottage with a wistful feeling, eyes on the boots stuffed onto her bench, hoping she was safe, wherever she was.

Ilene Gislar walked beside him. She wore a grey woollen cloak over her grey woollen dress, a pair of half-decent boots on her feet too. Yet she shivered, cheeks and nose red, shoulders hunched around her ears. She was a handsome woman, he supposed, with generous hips, an ample bosom, and unblemished skin, though her tiny eyes were calculating and she smirked rather than smiled.

As though she was always playing games.

'It gets cold in Ullaberg, then? At this time of year?'

Ilene wondered what the lord wanted with her. He didn't look at her as other men did, and she sensed that he had no interest in her body, and that worried her. She wanted to stay, to make a new home in Ottby. Ullaberg was a heap of crumbling cottages she didn't wish to return to, and no men worthy of her time now that Arnon de Sant was dead. 'It is. The wind blows from the sea, freezing us solid, though Ottby is just as cold, I'd say.'

'And you wish to stay here?' Reinar asked, nodding at his old scout, Beggi, who walked past with his lanky son, Torfinn. 'You wish to stay in the fort?'

Ilene nodded. 'I can be useful. You've seen that... my lord.'

Reinar smiled. 'I have, Ilene.' He stopped, turning to her. 'You have skill with a bow, with a sword too. I saw how Tulia helped you, what she started to turn you into. I watched you, and I'd be happy to have you stay, though I'm worried too.'

Ilene peered up at him, anger flickering in her eyes.

'I'm worried about your reputation. I don't want anyone causing trouble amongst my men. We're about to head to Slussfall, to take the fortress, kill the Vettels. We're taking ships, all of us crammed in together. There's no time for jealousies and rivalries on ships. Nor in battle. We must be one, working together, not whispering and gossiping, tearing each other apart.'

Ilene looked insulted. 'I don't know what you're saying.' She glanced around, lowering her voice. 'Or what Alys told you about me. She was always jealous. Her husband had no real love for her.'

Reinar leaned in close, grabbing her arm, eyes sharp. 'What Alys told me was the truth, I've no doubt about that. And I saw what Alys' husband did to her. You should think more of yourself than wanting to pursue a man like that. A man who would beat a woman? The woman he loved? Alys was trapped, trying to get out, but you?'

Ilene was unused to being spoken to so harshly. Men usually just wanted to bed her, not care to talk to her or help her. She tried to pull away from him, but Reinar wouldn't let her go.

'You can fight, Ilene, so I will let you come and fight for me. But not if you continue to play games, not if you try to turn my men against each other. And especially not if you try to tangle Sigurd up in something he doesn't want or need.'

There it was.

Ilene froze, everything making perfect sense now.

'Your brother –'

'My brother is grieving for the woman he loved. Leave him alone. Let him mourn. He needs time. If he wants you, he'll come to you, I'm sure. But you will leave him alone to make up his own mind now. Understood?'

Ilene glared at Reinar, deciding, and lips twisting into a furious pout, she nodded, forcing out the word. 'Understood.'

CHAPTER NINETEEN

Ollo Narp liked to eat, and being the master of the market, he had no need to dip into his pouch to pay for anything he chose to sample. His pouch bulged with coins he collected but had no need to spend. He smiled, hearing the coins clinking together, and sweeping his cloak around his ample belly, he bobbed his head at Bergit Dyre, who stood in line, basket over one arm, eyes on the glowing lumps of amber arrayed before her. 'Making the most of the weather?' he grinned, nibbling a chestnut.

Bergit eyed him coldly. He was a leering sort of man, slithering around the fort and into Hakon Vettel's confidence. She wondered how a lord could trust a man who'd once been an enemy, though Ulrick had told her that the wisest lords always kept their enemies close. Even slimy ones like Ollo Narp. 'I am, yes. I imagine the snow will soon be too high to even open my door. I aim to have such an abundance of stores that I won't need to come out till spring!' Polite conversation strained Bergit's patience, though it did no harm to keep the little worm on her side, for a little worm would always come in handy.

And though his eyes were constantly moving, Ollo suddenly fixed them on Bergit, hearing her warm tone, noting how full her lips were, his eyes dropping to her bosom, hidden beneath a thick cloak and a fur wrap. He grinned, gulping down the warm chestnut. 'Well, Ulrick will be a lucky man... if he returns. Otherwise, you'll need to look for other companions. I'm sure there'll be plenty of contenders.'

Bergit shuddered, trying to ignore Ollo's roaming eyes. 'Not if I don't increase my stores. A man might wish for a woman's company in his bed, but he also needs feeding, that I do know. And I'd like some wine too, though I'm not sure what's happened to all the wine merchants. Those who are here are charging such exorbitant prices!'

Ollo lifted an eyebrow. 'I may be able to find you a cask of wine, Bergit, my dear. For a price, of course. Hakon has his wine from Varis. In great demand, it is, though I can certainly get my hands on a cask for you.'

Bergit turned her entire body towards Ollo now, knowing how much Ulrick liked Hakon's wine. 'You could?' And already reaching into her cloak for her purse, she smiled.

Vik watched them, tucked around the corner of the shoemaker's cottage. It wasn't the most pleasant place to stand, as a swirling breeze wafted the great stink of the tannery towards him, though Vik was desperate not to be seen. Not by Ollo. And not by that sharp-tongued witch. His eyes skipped to the opposite side of the square, where he saw Jonas trying to look just as inconspicuous.

The fort was not full, which was a relief, but there were still too many eyes, too much bright sunshine for either man to feel comfortable.

Vik looked up, praying for snow.

Wanting the day to hurry away.

***

Ulrick was vibrating with excitement, Lotta could feel it. She could hear his thoughts jumping around his head like a little boy at Solsta. He was impatient to see his wife, and as the tops of Slussfall's guard towers appeared in the distance, Lotta knew that soon, he would.

She rode Clover beside his giant horse, Skuld, trying to think.

Ulrick cared for her, and she needed to stay with him until her mother came. For the first time in days, Lotta had felt her getting closer. It was a strange feeling, like a warmth she couldn't explain. The cold clung to her, numbing her face, aching her legs, but inside her heart, she felt warm, as though soon she would be happy again.

And smiling as the sun headed down, Lotta spurred Clover on.

***

Alys felt sick, watching Hakon and Eddeth riding at the very tip of their column.

Alone.

Ivan and Lief rode behind them with Jerrick and another man Alys didn't know. She rode further back with a sullen Falla, and Stina, who looked just as petrified as Alys felt.

Eddeth alone with Hakon was too terrifying for words.

Eddeth felt just as anxious as her friends as she tried to navigate the perilous path between helping the lord with what he needed to know, and trying not to reveal anything that would catch Alys in a trap. For if Hakon found out that Alys was a dreamer, he would never let her go. Eddeth feared that, and for the first time in days, she thought of her own lord, Reinar Vilander, hearing his booming 'Eddeth!' in her ears, making her jolt upright.

'You were saying?' Hakon was growing impatient. Eddeth would start speaking then abruptly stop, leaving a gaping silence, before resuming the conversation on an entirely different path. He was losing track of where they were going. Eyes on the mountains in the distance, peeking through the clouds, he felt a lift, desperate to get back to Slussfall, though the thought of climbing over more mountains made his belly ache.

'The gods' favour once granted, can be quickly taken away.'

Hakon glanced over his shoulder, pleased that there was still some distance between him and those men following with curious eyes and twitching ears, no doubt wondering what they were talking about. 'Though, perhaps they're inclined to return that favour when it's warranted?' he suggested, hoping to strip his voice of the desperation he felt twisting his guts. He peered at Eddeth, sensing her hesitation. 'You and your friends wish to leave and resume your journey, I know, so be honest with me, Eddeth. Tell me all you know about the gods, then you can leave. I give you my word. Tell me the truth, and you'll be free to go.' He thought quickly, wanting to tempt the healer into revealing everything she was hiding from him. 'Tomorrow. You can be on your way tomorrow!'

Eddeth's eyes bulged. 'Well, I... that would... yes, alright, of course, yes!' Her thoughts raced ahead, skipping left and right, words fighting to come out her mouth all at once. 'The gods are always at war, always arguing over some slight, so they seek out warriors of great value to have on their side. Thenor and Eskvir, the two brothers, have not seen eye to eye in centuries. Some say that one day there will be a great war. A war to end all wars...'

Hakon looked intrigued, leaning towards her.

Eddeth blinked, feeling muddled, losing focus. 'The gods are proud! Some might say vain. Their reputations mean everything to them. They do not wish to champion those who fail, for that would be a stain on their reputation. A great, hideous blight!' She eyed Hakon closely, quickly regretting the use of that particular word, though it was too late to grab it and stuff it back inside her mouth.

'Fail?' Hakon almost whispered. He hadn't revealed his fears to Eddeth. What she thought was influenced only by her own knowledge, and what she'd seen. As much as he wanted to grab her by the throat and squeeze, he also knew that he needed to listen. If he was to change the arc of his destiny, he had to listen carefully. Hands squeezing around his horse's reins instead, Hakon waited to hear more.

'Well, fail to impress, perhaps?' Eddeth suggested, trying to remake her words into something more palatable. 'If the gods see themselves as rivals and us mortals as their playthings, then they will only grant their favour to those they believe will succeed. For the success of their favourites will burnish their own reputations.'

Hakon's eyes were bright with hope for the first time since leaving Ottby. The pain of his wound was demanding, but he turned his head, peering at Eddeth. 'So how do I convince them that I will succeed? How do I right my ship, for it must be righted quickly, mustn't it?'

Eddeth froze. She didn't want to help Hakon Vettel succeed at anything. He was a man her lord wanted dead. But perhaps, she thought, pragmatically, perhaps it was better to let Reinar worry about Hakon? She just needed to get Alys to safety before she was discovered. Reinar would certainly advise her to do that. 'You must show them victory! Victory over your fiercest enemy and theirs! If the gods that favour you want to see the throne torn from Ake Bluefinn's hands, then you must show them that you're the man capable of doing it!' She waited, watching as Hakon turned away from her, eyes fixed ahead, wide with possibilities now.

And inhaling an enormous breath of relief, Eddeth sneezed.

***

Sigurd didn't know how he felt about Ilene coming with them to Slussfall.

But mostly not good.

'She can sail with me, I'll keep an eye on her,' Reinar promised, trying not to grin.

Sigurd sighed, turning away from his brother, eyes on the forest. It was hard to stand on the wall. The low wall had been Reinar's and Torvig's, and that made him feel sick. He looked back to the inner wall that had been his and Tulia's, and that made him feel sad. 'She'll cause problems whichever ship she's on.'

'I hope not. It would be a shame for her if she did. But maybe she'll stop being so interested in causing problems if she has a purpose?' Reinar knew that Sigurd was right to be concerned, and not just for his own discomfort. Ilene was attractive and seductive, and she played games. Alys had implied as much.

Would Alys have suggested he take her along?

Reinar smiled, imagining the answer.

'What?' Sigurd was watching him.

'Just thinking about...' Reinar stopped himself. 'About what else we have to do. We're leaving in six days. There's so much to do. More things I probably haven't even thought of yet.'

Sigurd frowned, hearing the lie, but letting it go. 'Likely there is, though it'll be nice to leave. Nice to get away from here for a while. I think we both need that.' He turned away from the inner wall, eyes on the guard tower, the crash of boulders still ringing in his ears. 'Maybe we should leave earlier?'

Reinar laughed. 'You can't run away that quickly, Brother. And besides, we need to leave ready. Getting into Slussfall won't be easy. Ships and men won't be enough. We need more arrows. More shields. If only we had a dreamer to tell us what's coming.'

Now it was Sigurd's turn to laugh, thinking of Alys, hoping she'd found her children. 'Well, dreamer or not, we have to follow the king's orders. Take Slussfall, end the Vettels. I'm sure the gods will be smiling on you then.'

Reinar nodded, hoping his brother was right.

***

Ollo Narp yawned his way towards the tavern, frozen solid. He wanted a fire with flames not blowing in every direction, eager to thaw out his feet before he needed to go back to the square again.

'Ollo!'

He turned, hearing the shout, almost recognising the voice. He hesitated, not wanting to be delayed from his bench and his flames, though he was curious about that voice. And dropping his hood over his head, he turned away from the tavern door, eyes on the alley.

Jonas waited in the middle of it, hands by his sides, hood over his face.

Ollo frowned, skin tingling in anticipation. Stepping closer, his eyes bulged as the man lifted up his hood. 'Jonas?' He looked over his shoulder, scratching his head, thoughts skipping to his sword which hadn't been drawn from its scabbard in months. He'd grown fat and lazy. Not nearly as sharp as he'd once been. 'What are you doing here?' Lowering his voice, Ollo crept closer, curiosity giving way to reason. 'You shouldn't be here, Jonas.' He stepped forward with caution, one frozen boot at a time. The snow had been cleared from the alley in a long path, though it was already icy underfoot, and he moved slowly.

Jonas waited for him to come, wanting Ollo away from that tavern; away from anyone at all. 'I have a proposal for you, old friend.' They had never once been friends, though Sirrus had always found use for the treacherous turd. 'A lot of silver too, if you're interested?'

Ollo lifted a wild eyebrow, glancing around again. Stopping, he waited, not wanting to go any further, not wanting it to be some sort of trap. Though, he realised, Jonas Bergstrom was the chicken in a fort of foxes. He had nothing to fear, not from this old man. 'Well, you know me, Jonas, silver always appeals, though I've more than I know what to do with these days. Hakon Vettel pays better than Sirrus ever did,' he lied. 'Sirrus was a stingy old prick! All the years I gave to that man? Self-serving bastard!'

That was rich, Jonas thought, trying to remain focused. 'Well, there's nothing more to say about Sirrus, seeing as how his head's hanging from the gates.'

'It is, and more besides. But not mine.' Ollo had a big head, and a lot of hair; flaxen coloured braids framing a bloated face. 'No, I saw how things would go, and quickly too. I didn't intend to become just a head. For what? Ake Bluefinn? And what did he ever do for us?'

Jonas needed to get him onside quickly. 'Let's not talk about kings who'll soon be dead. From what I hear, your new lord has plans for him.'

'He does indeed.' Ollo puffed out his chest, wanting to appear content with his choice. 'And soon I'll be in Stornas, master of that famous market, or more, so perhaps I have no need of your silver, Jonas Bergstrom?'

Jonas smiled, hearing the interest in Ollo's voice. 'I understand. I didn't mean to trouble you. I've seen other familiar faces. Men I can ask for help. Men more in need of my silver.' He turned, making to leave.

'Help for what?' Ollo called, hand out. 'Why are you here?'

And tucking away his smile, Jonas turned back around.

***

'When we're in Stornas,' Hakon began, eyes on the mountains that loomed before them now. He was feeling better after his talk with Eddeth, and he carried his head high, his voice strong. 'I'll need to install my most trusted men around me in ways that will protect the kingdom. Ulrick spoke of the Northern threat, and I've no doubt it will come, knowing the ambitious men up there. So Stornas must be kept safe. I shall send you to Ottby, Lief. That's where Ake put his most trusted man, and once I'm on the throne, it's where I'll place you.'

Ivan's eyebrows sharpened in surprise, wondering if his cousin had forgotten that he was riding right beside him.

Lief looked just as confused. 'Ottby?' It wasn't what he'd imagined at all, though such an appointment would not be without honour. His mind had been drifting away from his lord, trying to envision a future where Hakon, cast out by the gods, was no longer the right man for the Alekkan throne, and he blinked, feelings of guilt making him uncomfortable.

'Yes, Ottby. You would like that, I think. And Falla.'

Lief nodded. 'She would, of course.'

Ivan's annoyance sparked, and sensing it, Hakon turned to him with a grin. 'Do you think I could be without you, Ivan? That I would send you away from Stornas? I could install you in Asberg or Blixo, both of them worthy lordships for you, Cousin, but I want you in Slussfall with me. I will be the King of Alekka, and you will be my Lord of Stornas.'

Ivan's frown eased, liking the sound of that.

'I will have a kingdom to protect, to fight for and rule. And to protect my greatest jewel? Well, there could be no one but my greatest friend for that prestigious role.'

Ivan was speechless. His cousin, who had nearly ruined everything in Ottby, who had then almost died, and then lurched around in a state of madness and terror, had returned to him, as bold and decisive and ambitious as ever. 'Your talk with Eddeth went well, then?' he laughed, shaking his head.

'It did, it did,' Hakon smiled. 'Her advice was surprisingly succinct for such a strange creature, but it was gratefully received. The gods brought those women to me, I'm certain of it now. To save me, to show me the path to victory. And now I see it so clearly, as though it is bathed in the glow of Solla herself!'

Lief eyed his lord, wondering if he was feverish. But no, Hakon appeared clear-eyed and full of intent. It was as though the hunt had never happened, as though The Hunter had not aimed his giant sabre at him, threatening his life. He tried not to shake his head, though he very much wanted to. 'And where does that path lead to, my lord?' he wondered with some trepidation.

'Slussfall!' Hakon announced, eyes up, as though he was seeing the fortress before him. 'Everything waits for us in Slussfall!'

***

Jonas had kept Vik away from Ollo Narp, not wanting to frighten him off. Vik intimidated Ollo, always had. It was better that he kept an eye on the rest of the fort, watching the prison hole, making sure that nothing happened to Magnus.

Those thrown into the hole were left to await their punishment. Some lingered there over time, but eventually, they were called before the lord, and his judgement was delivered. Jonas hoped that judgement would be delayed while Hakon Vettel remained further south.

The sky was darkening, wind rushing into the fort, sweeping around its walls, lifting cloaks, whipping hair around frozen faces. Vik pulled his hood down low, wanting to escape the worst of it, eyes on the prison hole.

'Who *are* you?' came the shrill voice. And there was that orange-haired shrew again, peering at him as though she wanted to skin him and cook him for supper. 'Where have you come from?'

'I'm with the fur traders, lady,' Vik smiled. She had certainly taken up against him, though he wasn't sure why. 'Remember?'

Bergit scowled at him. 'Why are you still here, then?' She eyed him closely. He was a well-dressed man; strong-looking too. The wind flapped his cloak open, and her eyes went to his many belts, stuffed full of knives.

All of them gleaming.

'My companions had too much ale last night. They're sleeping it off. I'm just trying to pass the time before we leave. Thought I might find something tasty to take with me. We'll be heading up to The Murk. Not much tasty in that black hole.' Vik spoke from experience, and he could see Bergit's interest spark. Her shoulders dropped as she peered at him.

'You're from The Murk?'

Vik shook his head. 'No, from a small village further south, but The Murk's where you want to go for pelts and furs. If you can stand the cold and the dark. And the beasts.'

'I've heard there's no sun.'

'Well, not no sun, but you barely catch a glimpse of it before it's snatched away by night again. All year round. It's a wonder anything lives in that frozen land. So you'll forgive me for being so curious about your fort. I haven't seen life like this in some time. I have to soak it in before I leave.'

He really was a handsome man, Bergit thought, staring closely. He reminded her of Ulrick, and she stared at the gates, wondering if she would ever see her husband again. 'Well, I wish you luck soaking it in. If I were you, I'd purchase a jar of that honey. Herta Karsson has the sweetest honey I've ever tasted. She makes it with lavender. Drizzle some of that over your porridge, and you won't mind The Murk so much.'

Vik nodded, still smiling. 'I will, thank you.' And bobbing his head, he headed towards the honey seller, resetting his hood low over his eyes, polite smile vanishing, hoping Jonas was having some luck with Ollo Narp.

Magnus watched him, hands around the window bars. He hadn't said a word to Leonid, not wanting to get his hopes up; not wanting to dash them either. Vik and Jonas were still in the fort, as he knew they would be. It was dangerous, though. Men knew them, and if those men spotted them, soon they'd have more company in their miserable hole. Magnus' stomach ached with hunger, but the smell of the dark pit had him gagging as he watched Vik slip down an alley, wondering what he was planning.

***

Ollo wasn't sure what he thought. The crevices between his wild eyebrows deepened considerably. 'Well, to do that I'd need to pay Elmar. He watches the hole during the day. Takes turns with Pakki Hallen, you remember him?'

Jonas nodded, irritated with Ollo's farting around. 'I'd pay extra for that, of course.'

'And how are you so rich?' Ollo wondered. 'To pay for this boy?'

'He's my blood, and I want him out of here. You wouldn't pay to save someone you cared about?'

Ollo had had a wife once. A son too. A long time ago now. Memories of love were so long gone they barely rippled in his heart. 'Perhaps,' he considered, scratching his beard.

'All you need to do is organise it. Get Elmar to let the boy out, and get us out of the fort before the gates close. You'll have the rest of your coins then.'

Ollo was busy calculating the risk. 'And you say you've got twice as much as this waiting?' He'd always known Jonas Bergstrom as an honest man, but still, they were on opposite sides now. 'You're not trying to fleece me, are you?'

Jonas laughed. 'I have it, Ollo, and you'll have it too, I swear it to you. On Thenor himself. Let him take my sword and send me into Vasa's arms if I'm lying. I have it waiting, though I won't tell you where. Not till that boy is outside the gates.'

'Alright.' Ollo could see a way to make it work. 'I'll do it.' And spitting on his dirty palm, he held out his hand to Jonas, who did the same, clasping Ollo's arm. 'We have a deal then, old friend. One to make us both smile, I hope. Now go, make yourself scarce. After I get myself thawed out in the tavern, I'll have a word with Elmar. He'll see us right.'

Jonas nodded, preparing to leave, but Ollo kept a hand on his arm.

'Though, I'll be needing those coins now.'

Nodding some more, Jonas dug into his cloak, opening his pouch, pulling out a big lump of silver coins. He handed them to Ollo, who took them with shining eyes, slipping them into his own pouch, quickly realising that he didn't have enough room. 'That's enough for now. We'll meet again later. Don't worry, I'll find you.' And with that, he turned around, boots slipping on the cleared path, heading back to the tavern.

Jonas watched him go, shivering, knowing that he couldn't trust Ollo Narp.

Not for even one moment could he trust Ollo Narp.

CHAPTER TWENTY

Reinar stopped outside the cottage door.

It was a horrible old hovel. He didn't know why he'd made Salma stay in it. And then, Alys. He sighed, shoulders dropping. There was no time to think of dreamers, especially dreamers in green dresses.

No time at all, he tried to convince himself, not moving.

'Looking for someone?' came a voice behind him, and Reinar jerked around to Ludo. Mouth open, he just stared, no words popping into his head.

Ludo edged closer, and seeing the confusion in Reinar's eyes, he lowered his voice. 'I hope they're safe, wherever they are. I keep thinking about Stina, and what Torvig did to her. I failed to protect her. He could have killed her. And Alys.' Twisting around, Ludo checked behind them, but no one was there. The sun was heading for its bed, and those who'd been rushing around the square or working up a sweat in the training ring were turning their minds to fires and furs and food.

Reinar frowned, both pleased and irritated that Ludo had read his mind. 'They're both lucky that Alys knew more about weapons than any of us realised.'

'Mmmm, makes you wonder why she let Ilene punch her. Or her husband. Not even Tulia could defeat Torvig, but Alys did. So why did she let her husband hurt her for all those years?'

Reinar had wondered the same thing, though love was

complicated, he knew.

And Alys had a lot of secrets.

Perhaps more than even she realised...

***

They made camp near sheer-faced cliffs. The mountains had been rising steadily throughout the afternoon, and as dusk came to turn the sky a deep lilac colour, the army got to work. There was little wind, though the snow was still deep and they built shelters and fires far away from the edge of the cliffs, nearer the trees.

Alys stood watching the sun sink over the valley, taking any hint of warmth with it. Shivering, she wrapped her cloak around her chest, trying to stop it flapping away from her. She felt lost in a blizzard of thoughts and images, trying to find anything useful; anything to aid their journey. Thanks to Eddeth, they were going to be freed in the morning, and Alys needed to know more about where they were going.

She saw Magnus in that dark hole, but was he in Slussfall?

She'd seen nothing of Lotta at all.

It worried her.

'Alys?'

Jerking forward, Alys almost tripped over. She'd been standing far too close to the cliff edge, and she hurried to move back, heart thumping.

'I didn't mean to frighten you,' Stina smiled wearily. 'I thought we should make sure everything's ready for the morning. We want to leave at dawn, don't we? Before they change their minds.'

'We do,' Alys agreed, eyes on the camp in the distance, sensing the speed with which everyone was working to prepare fires before the sky deepened to black. 'We really do.' She could see Ivan talking to his cousin, who, not wanting to appear as an invalid anymore, was keen to see them go.

'As long as Eddeth can keep quiet a little longer,' Stina whispered, watching Eddeth hand Falla a cup of tea. They had spent the afternoon riding with Falla, and Stina hadn't been able to shake her fear that Eddeth would ruin everything.

'She will,' Alys promised her. 'Eddeth can control herself when she needs to.' And smiling, she led Stina back to the camp. 'I'll see what food I can find to take with us. It would be helpful to have a few things. It doesn't look like the easiest journey.' She lifted her head to those mountains whose tips were lost in the darkening clouds.

'Good. I'll check on the horses. I don't want anything to delay us.' Stina hated being in the camp around all those men. She hated them watching her, leering at her, whispering about her. She felt like a dreamer, almost able to read their thoughts; watching their eyes move from her lips to her breasts, and beyond. Those eyes followed her wherever she walked, lingering long enough for her to shudder. She would feel better, she knew, safer, once they were out of the Vettels' grip. Glancing over her shoulder, she saw Ivan making a beeline for Alys, and smiling sympathetically at her friend, Stina slipped away into the trees to find their horses.

Alys sighed, forcing a smile as Ivan approached. And not wanting to be alone with him, she quickened her pace. 'I thought you'd be sitting around a fire already, warming up?'

Ivan looked irritated as he turned to follow her. 'There's a lot to do yet. I can't sit around while my men do it all for me. Even I know that wouldn't be a good idea right now.' He frowned, his mood sinking further. 'Hakon tells me he's letting you go. Tomorrow.'

Alys nodded, trying not to look as happy as she felt. 'He is, which is good news for all of us. We can be on our way home, and your cousin is feeling better. You must be pleased about that?'

Ivan didn't look pleased in the slightest. 'Hakon's trying to pretend that he's not injured.' He slipped an arm around Alys' waist, ushering her towards the back of a shelter, away from Hakon's view. 'He's trying to pretend last night didn't happen.'

'Well, you can't blame him for that. Leaders have to inspire confidence, don't they? They have to show strength.'

'Of course, but after The Hunter?'

Alys didn't want to be trapped counselling Ivan, but he didn't appear to be going anywhere in a hurry. 'Perhaps he's in shock? He was very ill, and the pain must be intense. I imagine he doesn't know what else to do but wish it all away. You can help him, I'm sure, just by giving him some time.'

Ivan nodded, thinking how wise she was. How wise and beautiful. 'You can come and eat in my tent again,' he grinned, leaning in close. 'Though I've no idea what food there'll be tonight. Not sure anyone has much appetite for hunting.'

Alys backed away. 'No, and I've no appetite for eating. You go, Ivan. I need to find Eddeth, make sure she hasn't wandered off somewhere.'

And nodding his head with some regret, Ivan turned to leave. Stopping, he glanced over his shoulder with a wink. 'But if you change your mind, you know where to find me!'

***

It was getting late.

Soon darkness would swallow up the fort, and the main gates would close. The traders were packing their unsold goods into baskets, and onto carts and horses, ready for the cold trudge home to villages and back to ships moored in the harbour. They moved slowly, half-frozen after a day spent outside trying to encourage equally frozen villagers to part with their coins.

Jonas' pouch felt much lighter now as he waited in the mouth of the alley, eyes darting around. Ollo Narp had disappeared towards the prison hole some time ago, and Jonas couldn't stop muttering to himself, certain the greedy turd had betrayed him. He squinted into the distance, eyes on the gates as the guards roused themselves out of their frigid state, making moves towards those traders who were funnelling out of the square.

Vik was with them.

They didn't want to spook Ollo, who had always been nervous around Vik, so Vik had rejoined the fur traders who had left the tavern behind. And happy to see him, they chatted away to a hooded Vik as he slipped out with them.

He looked cross, Jonas thought, seeing that familiar sharp jawline poking out beneath his friend's hood. And grinning, Jonas turned his attention back to the prison hole, wanting to catch a glimpse of Magnus, though the window was in deep shadow, and he saw nothing but darkness. Shoulders tensing, Jonas blew out a smoky breath, hoping Ollo would hurry.

Those guards would shut the gates.

Soon.

***

Hakon had no appetite, yet he made a great pretence of being hungry. He was loud and smiling as he sat with Lief and Ivan, Jerrick, and two of Ivan's men. He wanted word to spread through the camp of how improved their lord was. Of how unaffected by his wound and their strange journey. Those wary of the gods' wrath needed to know that their lord was not concerned at all.

He was not ill. He was not marked. He was just fine.

Rikkard had managed to find enough ale to keep Hakon happy, and he was hard at work, refilling cups, offering bowls of nuts while the men waited for their meal to arrive.

'Your recovery has been swift, my lord,' Lief noted, no smile on his serious face. He felt uneasy. Jaw clenched, he held out his cup for a nervous-looking Rikkard to fill. 'We were lucky to have come across those healers.'

Hakon's eyes brightened. 'We were lucky, indeed! If Mother were here, she would tell us that the gods wanted me to live, to see the throne return to the Vettels after all this time.'

'And The Hunter?' Jerrick wondered, shaking his head at Rikkard, not wanting any ale. He felt nauseous, unsettled, and more superstitious than any of them; more concerned about what would come next too. Shadows lengthened around them like dark giants, and he couldn't stop shivering, remembering the vatyr. 'That wasn't lucky, my lord. Only the doomed see The Hunter.'

Ivan laughed, the least superstitious of them all. He tucked his worries far away from his eyes, throwing back his last drop of ale. 'Do we look doomed, Jerrick?' They all turned to stare at Ivan, whose broad smile was at odds with his twitching jaw. 'The gods challenge us every day, we all know that. They seek the best to be the rulers of this land. Only the bravest warriors, the quickest minds. They must challenge us by rewarding those who rise and punishing those who fall. We're not doomed, for Hakon has no mark! We're being tested by Thenor himself!'

Hakon felt the comfort of having his cousin nearby, and his confidence surged. 'Ivan's right. The gods wish to challenge us, to see us prove to every Alekkan why the Vettels are the rightful rulers of this land.' He wanted to fall to the ground and curl into a ball, wrapping his arms around his aching belly. Eyes on Rikkard, he stuck out his cup, needing more ale, though he doubted there was enough ale in all of Alekka to drown his terror and his fear that every word he uttered was a lie. But turning to Ivan with a full cup, he banged it into his cousin's. 'I welcome whatever tests Thenor has in mind, for he will not find me wanting!' And lifting his cup high, he forced his smile even wider.

Lief raised his own cup, though not his lips. There was no smile in him at all. Ivan and Hakon were doing a masterful job of trying to convince them that what they saw with their eyes and heard with their ears was not the truth they knew in their hearts. He saw Jerrick and Ivan's men nod and smile with some enthusiasm, almost convinced. But the truth left Lief cold, and no amount of expertly woven words would convince him that Hakon was not doomed.

For doomed, he most certainly was.

***

Men were talking outside the iron door.

Night was falling in the fort and Magnus couldn't stop shaking. Shoulders hunched up to his ears, he turned to Leonid, who had spent much of the afternoon sobbing.

There were no tears in Magnus. He was too scared to cry.

Scared and hopeful, for he had seen Jonas and Vik, and he knew they'd be working to try and get him out. Yet another day was ending and another night in the dank darkness with the smell and the sound of squeaking rats beckoned.

But men were talking outside the prison door.

And what did that mean?

***

Alys knew Stina had already checked on the horses, but she wanted a moment to herself. A moment away from the nervous chatter around the fire, and the sharp-eyed Falla Gundersen, who peered at her as though she could see right through her. So Alys had made her way to Haski, who appeared happy for her company. She hadn't had her own horse since she'd run away from Torborg all those years ago, and smiling sadly, she ran a hand over his grey coat, images of her grandfather drifting into her mind.

Closing her eyes, Alys breathed deeply, letting the camp noises disperse. She inhaled the wafting smoke, remembering Ottby and her disastrous idea to launch Eddeth's herbs into Hakon's army. That old dreamer had blown the smoke straight back at them.

Alys shivered, eyes open now, glancing around, but they were alone.

She placed a cold hand on Haski's cheek, pleased when he leaned into it, and then she remembered the apple she'd secreted away for him, and pulling it from her pouch, she held it out, watching as he gobbled it up. And in a flash, she was back in Ullaberg, and Magnus stood before her, hand curled like he was holding an apple. 'No,' she laughed, shaking her head. 'Flat, Magnus, you must keep your hand flat. She won't bite you, she just wants to nuzzle you.' Magnus had been terrified of horses as a child, and she'd convinced Arnon to buy him a pony so he could grow his confidence. 'Don't give her any fingers to nibble!' Magnus had looked at her in horror then, and Alys had laughed some more as she showed her six-year-old son what to do; holding her own hand out, letting Daisy snort and snuffle it. Magnus' hair had been lighter then, she realised. Not like Lotta's, but a deep gold like hers.

And hand frozen against Haski's cheek, Alys saw an image of Jonas, hood over his face, hiding in a dark street. Terror gripping her body, she closed her eyes, trying to see more.

***

Ollo Narp's pouch was heavy, banging against his thigh, a reminder of how much more silver awaited him when he delivered the boy to his grandfather. One of the prison guards was Elmar Soti, an old friend whose wife he often humped. She was just as hungry for Ollo's coins as her husband. A couple of very useful mercenaries, he thought to himself, whispering in Elmar's ear.

And nodding, Elmar slipped the coins Ollo had pressed into his sweaty palm into his pouch, turning back to the prison door.

Jonas Bergstrom had been a famed warrior in his time. The gods had favoured him highly, Ollo knew. They would not wish to see a man like that betrayed. Jonas had survived the worst battles in Alekka's history with all his limbs intact. There was barely a scar on the man. And Ollo knew that to betray him now would be to spit in the eyes of the gods themselves.

And yet...

***

Vik didn't feel good as he headed away from the main gates. The fur traders had walked down to the harbour, and Vik was certain they'd have a more comfortable night sleeping on their ships than he would lying in his bed of snowy dirt. He thought of his fishing boat, seeing lightning strike it like an attack from Thenor himself. He was meant to be here, he knew, yet he'd let Magnus walk into that fort on his own, and now he was leaving Jonas behind.

His chest tightened as he turned, eyes up on the guard towers that were dark now, the men watching from the ramparts just silhouettes, hoping they hadn't been fools to trust Ollo Narp.

***

Alys felt panic shutting her down, unable to think.

She needed to warn her grandfather. She was too far away, but she needed to do something. And fumbling to open her cloak, she dug into her pouch with frozen fingers, pulling out his arm ring.

***

'You're coming with me,' growled the deep voice of the bald-headed guard. There may have been no hair left on top of his shiny head, but he had an enormous bush of a beard, and as he leaned over, it tickled Magnus' face. He had ice-cold hands, rough too, and he grabbed Magnus quickly, yanking him to his feet, away from Leonid.

Leonid scrambled to his feet, skidding in the dirt. 'Wait! What are you doing to him? Where are you taking him?'

'My friend, my friend!' Magnus pleaded. 'What about my friend?' But the guard wasn't listening as he dragged Magnus out of the hole, slamming the door shut after him.

'Be quiet, you blathering arse!' came a grumbling voice in the darkness, quickly joined by a chorus of other miserable men, all demanding that Leonid sit down and leave them in peace.

Magnus could hear them as he was dragged into the dark corridor that ran from the prison entrance to the stairs. And that handful of stairs led up to the square, he remembered, eyes darting around, unfazed by the guard's strong grip on his arm. He peered into the darkness, looking for signs of Jonas and Vik, wondering what was happening.

And then another man emerged from the shadows, looking him over. 'Well, now, so you're what all the fuss is about. Seems to me we'd better get going. Don't want to be left behind when those gates shut, do you, boy?'

***

Jonas' eyes slid right to the guards at the gates, who were impatiently ushering the last few traders out now, and then to the left, where he saw Ollo emerge from the prison hole stairs, a small cloaked figure beside him.

Shoulders tensing further, Jonas watched as Ollo handed Magnus off to another man, this one a trader he recognised from earlier, and that man quickly wrapped an arm around Magnus' shoulder and started heading across the square.

Holding his breath, Jonas caught Ollo's eye, nodding to him.

Ollo nodded back, almost imperceptibly and turned, arms out, trying to shepherd everyone out of the square. 'Be on your way! More snow's coming, can't you feel it? Be on your way now! It's time to go!' He watched as the trader ushered the boy towards the gates, gripping his pouch, knowing how much heavier it would soon be.

And taking a deep breath, Jonas slipped out of the alley, joining the exodus. He'd seen many of the traders over the two days they'd been in the fort, and he smiled at a few, bobbing his head, before lifting it as a man rode through the gates astride a dirty-white horse, a little girl sitting in front of him.

A little girl with a heart-shaped face and ice-blonde hair.

CHAPTER TWENTY ONE

Vik had seen Ulrick Dyre riding into the fort with Lotta, but there was nothing he could do. His mind skipped through every possible outcome, seeing none that were good. They just had to get Magnus out of the fort, and then they could go back inside for Lotta.

He stood to one side of the gates, deep in shadow, waiting for Magnus and Jonas to come out.

***

Magnus stumbled, mouth dropping open, staring up at his sister as she rode towards him on Ulrick's horse. He lifted his eyes, hood falling back, and Ulrick felt Lotta's head snap up, her body rigid.

'What is it?' he wondered, eyes drifting, seeing Magnus. Confusion then. Shock. And he shouted. 'Hey!'

The trader next to Magnus froze.

Jonas, some way back from Magnus froze.

Ollo, who'd had one eye on the tavern froze, and turning around with a grumble, he headed back into the square.

'What are you doing with that boy?' Ulrick growled, glancing around, wondering if the farmer was there. Wondering how Magnus was there.

In Slussfall?

'That's the boy who killed Malik Valborg!' someone called.

Everyone held their ground then, turning to Magnus, who could feel the trader slink away, leaving him all alone.

Jonas was caught. He had to do something.

Eyes on Lotta, who sat astride Ulrick's horse, terror in her eyes, he pushed through the crowd, heart thumping.

Things accelerated quickly.

The crowd, many of whom had been friends with and loyal to the dead silversmith, rounded on Magnus.

Hounds were barking in the distance, chasing a fox, who was tearing through the square with a chicken in its mouth.

'He didn't kill Malick!' someone called, impatient to get through the gates. 'Leave the boy alone! That fool Leonid knocked him down. It was an accident!'

'He was dragged off to the hole!' another shouted. 'How's he out here? He's escaping! Where's Ollo? Where's Baldur? He's escaping!'

Ollo puffed out a furious breath, thumbs tucked into his belt, seeing his plans unravel with speed, and pushing his way through the crowd, he started shouting himself. 'What's going on here? What's all this noise? Make way! Move!' And eyes up on Ulrick Dyre, who had caused all the trouble, he glanced around. 'What's your complaint with this boy?'

'He was in the hole, Ollo. You put him there!'

That was true, and Ollo had no power to release him either, which he knew most people knew, and he took one look at Magnus, as though surprised. 'You trying to escape, boy? Maybe you bribed one of my guards?' He knew Jonas would be nearby, and he only hoped that he would make himself scarce. If he wanted his grandson out, he couldn't afford to insert himself into the melee now. Ollo yanked Magnus' shoulder. 'You're coming with me. Back to your friends, the rats!'

A few cheers then, though some felt sorry for the miserable-looking boy, knowing Malick Valborg's death had been nothing to do with him.

Magnus panicked. The prison hole terrified him. The smell, the darkness, the fear of rats gnawing on him while he slept. 'No, please! Help me, please! Grandfather!'

Lotta's head was moving then, scanning the crowd, her eyes meeting Jonas'. He looked away, and so did Lotta, but not quickly enough. And Ulrick swung down from his horse with a creak, squaring his shoulders, eyes on Jonas, every sense on high alert. He twisted his head, seeing the wailing boy pleading with the old man, and he scowled. He was not about to let anyone stand in the way of his escape with Bergit and Lotta.

The hounds charged through the crowd, looking for the fox, knocking a man off his feet. And that man fell onto Jonas, who slipped on the icy surface, hitting the ground with a crack, hood falling back.

Some who had seen the old man fall, rushed to help him back to his feet. And as he struggled up, Jonas tried to bat them away, desperate to grab his hood to cover his face.

But it was too late.

'That's Jonas Bergstrom!'

'Can't be, he's long since dead! Jesper killed him!'

'It's him, look!'

And the crowd surged towards Jonas, who straightened up, hood over his face, hearing Alys' urgent warning in his ears.

Knowing that she was too late.

***

'You'll be pleased to escape from here,' Falla suggested, staring at Alys. It was almost entirely dark now, though the flames from the fire lit her face and Falla frowned, sensing again that she looked familiar. 'For we are certainly cursed now.' She saw Lief with Hakon and Ivan and their men in the distance, feeling free to talk of her fears. And she felt them acutely. With a child in Slussfall and another on the way, she felt terror closing in around her, fearing what would come in the night.

Eddeth sat opposite her, lifting a leg up to the flames as she pruned her toenails. 'Well, I'd say that's true. The Hunter said as much, didn't he?'

'Did he?'

Alys could tell that Eddeth was distracted and it worried her. It required a lot of focus for Eddeth to keep her thoughts under control, and when not under control, those thoughts had a habit of popping out of her mouth.

'Of course!' Eddeth dropped her left leg back to the ground, rolling down her trouser, and picking up her right. Her toenails were viciously thick and long, and walking had become painful. She needed to trim them before they started their journey in the morning. And thinking of their journey had Eddeth's mind buzzing. But seeing Alys and Stina watching her across the flames, she blinked, trying to focus. Dropping her right leg, Eddeth smiled, turning to Falla. 'Your lord has work ahead of him, yes indeed, but he can redeem himself, I'm sure. Unless, of course...' And Eddeth sneezed over the flames, making them hiss.

'Unless what?' Falla whispered.

Eddeth's eyes were wide as she remembered that dark figure with the enormous antlers. Never in her life had she imagined meeting a creature from her nightmares, and now she had met two. She shivered all over. 'Unless Thenor has already made up his mind. To have sent The Hunter after Hakon like that? Well, who knows what he's thinking, but if he bears the mark it's surely only a matter of –'

'Eddeth!' Stina muttered. 'I'm sure Falla doesn't want to hear that.'

'But I do,' Falla whispered. 'I do. I'm carrying a child. My boy is in Slussfall.' Her eyes blurred with tears, her body curling forward. 'I don't want to be doomed by a cursed lord. I must survive for my children.'

Alys understood how she felt. She glanced around. 'But what can you do? Your husband is loyal to the lord, is he not?'

Stina's eyes opened wide, staring at Alys, wondering what she was doing.

But Alys could feel what was in Falla's heart, and she continued. 'Your husband...'

'Lief is loyal to the Vettels,' Falla said with some resentment. 'His family was in Stornas with the old king. He believes they're the gods' choice to rule Alekka.'

'Perhaps they are,' Eddeth mused, eyes lost in the mesmerising flames. She felt sleepy, forgetting all about her toenails, thoughts meandering again. 'Or perhaps the gods have simply changed their minds?'

And then an explosion of noise, birds launching themselves out of the trees, flying away into the night sky. They could feel the air from their flapping wings like an icy wind.

Eddeth yelped, biting her tongue.

Stina grabbed Alys' arm, shuddering. 'What was that?'

Heads back, the four women stared up at the trees as the birds disappeared, the echo of their screeching cries reverberating around them like laughter.

***

Ulrick threw back his hood, eyes on the old man. 'Strange place to find one of Ake's old hands. In the market for a new fur, were you? A few spices?' He stepped towards Jonas, breath smoking in the near darkness. The hounds had run through the gates, barking ecstatically in the distance, and now silence descended upon the fort. 'And what sort of master of the square are you, Ollo Narp? Letting a spy make himself at home? I doubt Hakon will be pleased to hear about this.'

Ollo was reminded of what a stingy young lord Hakon Vettel was. And he knew Jonas to be an honest man. And if Jonas had promised him silver, then he was determined to see him deliver on that promise.

But to do so would require some careful maneuvering.

'Ahhh, Ulrick, what brings you back so soon? Did the lord not require your services for the big battle with the Vilanders? Perhaps he has other, younger men to call upon now?' Ollo pushed out his girth, feeling slippery ice beneath his boots. And then he caught a glimpse of another familiar figure lurking by the gates. Just a hint of a face, but he knew that face well, and ignoring any discomfort, his hopes rose.

Jonas saw a hint of that face too, and he willed Vik away, wanting him out of it. If he was going to get himself thrown into the hole or killed, Vik needed to stay safe. He had to get the children. 'Ulrick Dyre, you appear to have my great-granddaughter! And that there is her brother. I came for them. Heard someone had stolen them, and now I know who!' He felt enraged, temper exploding, ready to make a fuss.

The crowd grew mostly silent, some muttering to each other, quickly taking sides.

Not everyone liked Ulrick Dyre. Or, at least, they didn't like his busy-body wife. And Jonas Bergstrom was a famed warrior, his feats carved into the old saga stones that marked the road to Slussfall. Others had family members and friends whose lives had been taken by Jonas and his brotherhood of warriors loyal to Ake Bluefinn. They looked on with sharp eyes, not noticing the snow that was falling now.

Ollo did, though, and he thought of the warm tavern and his frozen feet. He needed to move things along quickly. 'Why do you have his grandchildren, Ulrick?'

Lotta remained silent, trying to find a path in the darkness, worried that one wrong word would doom them all. She closed her eyes, hoping to hear her mother's voice, but all she heard was the beat of her heart.

Ulrick stepped even closer to Ollo, not appreciating the man calling him out. 'That's the question on your lips? You've one of Hakon Vettel's enemies standing right behind you, and *that's* your question? Why is the old man not in the hole already? Or on the block, your sword at his neck?'

Ollo frowned, nibbling his moustache. He turned back to Jonas with annoyance in his eyes, realising that he was going to have to twist himself into knots to get out of this mess. 'I don't dispense justice in Slussfall, Ulrick Dyre, and nor do you. I'll have a word with Baldur, see what he wants to do about the old man.'

'He's our enemy!' Ulrick insisted loudly, his cries echoed by more than one voice in the crowd.

'I'm not your enemy!' Jonas spat. 'We fought on opposite sides once, but I haven't seen a shield wall in many a year. Look at me! Do I look like I came here spying? I came here for my grandchildren. I came to take them home!'

Murmurs of sympathy then. A few grumbles too.

'A good story, Jonas. I'm sure Hakon will enjoy hearing it when he returns. I'm sure he'd love to hear what one of the men who killed his grandfather has to say about everything.'

Murmurs rose into mutters, dark scowls and angry growls now, and Ollo realised that he was squeezed into a corner. 'Elmar! Rolf! Take him to the hole! The boy too!' And sniffing, he eyed the long-bearded Ulrick Dyre, wheeling around and heading past Jonas, who, surrounded by traders and merchants and curious onlookers, was quickly overwhelmed.

'No! No!' Magnus screamed, eyes bulging in terror, looking from Jonas to Lotta, who hadn't said a word, and finally to Ulrick, who turned away from them all, gathering his horse's reins, eager to see his wife.

***

Hakon wanted another cup of ale, though he could barely form a word. He doubted he could even stand, though it would hardly encourage confidence to stumble about like a drunk, so he pushed away his cup with a sigh, turning to his cousin. 'We heard that noise last night,' he slurred, the loud echoes of the scattering birds ringing in his ears, bleary eyes on Ivan, who sat awkwardly before him.

Ivan remembered.

He remembered what came after it too.

'We're in the forest, my lord,' Lief said calmly, not having touched a drop of ale. 'We'll always hear such noises. Likely a storm's coming. Winter's already here, I'd say. Things will only get worse.'

Ivan's shoulders were so tight it was painful. He couldn't think, couldn't see his way out of the maze of worries crowding his mind. 'Won't be long till we're home, though. No more forests. No more strange noises then.' He didn't believe that. Whatever was out there felt as though it wasn't going away anytime soon.

'We should talk about that!' Hakon decided. 'Talk about how to attack Ottby again. Or not Ottby. Forget Ottby. Let's sail straight to Stornas!' He leaned forward, the ale dulling his senses, making him forget his wound, and yelping, he jerked backwards.

'Cousin?'

Hakon felt cross, remembering the arrogant look on Reinar Vilander's face as he'd stabbed him. Anger simmered, and Hakon clenched his hand around his cup, lost in the memories of Ottby; the smoke and the noise and the pain and the panic.

'Hakon?' Ivan glanced at Lief, who looked just as concerned.

Hakon shook his head, eyes sharpening. 'We need ships! We have enough gold to buy them. As you said, Cousin, why let Ottby get in the way of what we seek. We'll wait out winter, make our plans. Build ships. Send men to buy more, steal them if necessary. We'll gather a fleet together ready for the Thaw, and then we'll begin.' His belly burned, the pain intensifying, and he had to clench his jaw to keep it at bay.

'That sounds the most sensible plan, my lord,' Lief agreed, though there was no enthusiasm in his voice. He felt on edge. The sounds in the forest were disturbing, unsettling. He was worried about Falla. He had to be strong for her, but his concerns were multiplying, and he didn't feel confident that Hakon was the right man to get them back to Slussfall alive.

He could almost feel the gods watching them, waiting to strike.

'It does,' Ivan agreed. 'Ships is the answer. I've always thought so. And once we command Stornas, we can finish the Vilanders. They'll be surrounded by then!' The thought of it made him smile, which was a nice change.

Hakon smiled too, mostly for show. 'Agreed. We'll hunker down in Slussfall, build ourselves a new fleet over winter. Attack Stornas come spring.'

'And if they come for us in the meantime, my lord?' Lief hated to say it, not wanting to unbalance Hakon again, but he needed to know. 'Ake returned to save Ottby. It may be that he's already on his way to Slussfall.'

No one wanted to think about that, but Hakon couldn't ignore it. Ake Bluefinn had an army bigger than any he could mount now. 'Then he'll find out how impenetrable Slussfall can be. Unlike Ottby, we won't have a problem holding our walls.' He thought of Mother, knowing how much she'd helped them get into that old fort; wondering where they would have been without her. 'We'll find a dreamer too. A dreamer will help. I'll send you out when we return home, Ivan. You can buy me a dreamer!'

***

Alys had left Stina and Falla behind, heading into the trees with Eddeth.

'Something's happened,' Eddeth decided. 'You look worried.'

Alys had seen flashes of trouble while she sat around the fire, a smile on her face and fear in her heart. 'My grandfather is captured. I heard Magnus screaming. I think they're in even more danger now.'

'In Slussfall?' Eddeth wondered, blinking rapidly. 'Are they in Slussfall?'

Alys nodded. 'Yes, I think so.' She glanced around. 'We just have to leave quickly in the morning. Not have any more trouble tonight.'

'And if we do?'

'Trouble is coming for Hakon. The gods have sent that trouble, and we can't get in the way. If something happens tonight, we have to try and escape.' It felt wrong to say because they would be turning their backs on those who needed help, but she had to think of the children. Of Jonas and Vik. They were all in trouble, Alys could feel it.

They couldn't delay getting to Slussfall.

'Agreed!' Eddeth wheeled around, shivering all over. 'Let's get back to the fire. I'm going to knock out a tooth if I don't warm up soon!' And one hand on Alys' elbow, she urged her back through the trees.

***

Vik returned to the campsite, cold and worried.

Angry too.

Ulrick Dyre.

That old prick.

Ulrick Dyre had captured the children, sold Magnus and kept Lotta. And now, thanks to him, both Jonas and Magnus were back in the prison hole.

He felt relieved that Lotta was alive. Magnus and Jonas too.

But for how long?

He barely cared about the flames he was trying to bring to life, though he wouldn't be able to help anyone if he froze to death in the night. So, leaning over, he tried to keep the wind away from the flames as they struggled near the wet moss and tinder.

It was no surprise that Jonas had been recognised, though Vik knew that his chances of slipping back into the fort and getting them all out had greatly diminished. Especially now that Ulrick would be on the look out for more trouble.

Wafting the smoke with his hands, Vik's frown deepened, his stomach rumbling, though he had no appetite. He just needed an idea.

And thinking of Ollo Narp, he realised that more than anything, he needed some help.

CHAPTER TWENTY TWO

'Things are going well, then,' Jonas grinned, trying to cheer Magnus up, though the smell of the prison hole was eye-watering, and he wasn't surprised that his great-grandson looked ready to cry.

Leonid was there, blinking rapidly, full of questions. 'What happened? Why are you back?' He felt guilty for being glad, but no one else would even speak to him. A few of the shadowy figures had yelled at him. One kept threatening to saw off his tongue. He felt relieved to have company, and almost happy to see Jonas.

It gave him a lift.

'Well, things didn't unfold quite as I'd hoped,' Jonas admitted wryly. 'Though, there's always tomorrow!' He glanced around, trying not to inhale, eyes on the iron door that had slammed shut behind him. He'd caught a glimpse of Ollo's face before he closed the door, and nothing about that face had encouraged him.

But there was Vik, and Vik was more resourceful than anyone he knew.

'So when do they bring supper?' Jonas wondered, pulling Magnus close. 'I quite fancy a nice leg of pork. A few beans. Dumplings and gravy.'

Magnus wrapped his arms around Jonas' waist. 'What about Lotta? Why didn't she say anything? What was wrong with her?'

It was a good question, and Jonas feared the answer, though he didn't want to say a word about Lotta being a dreamer. He'd seen her with her eyes closed. In the midst of all that panic and confusion, he'd caught a glimpse of his little great-granddaughter, and he knew that she was trying to find answers.

***

Bergit was almost angry to see her husband.

She'd been planning to make the cottage up nicely before his return, imagining she had weeks to go. She had wanted to buy a few barrels of ale to go with her new cask of wine, hoping to tidy herself up too. But here she was, at the door, hair tangled by the wind, wearing her oldest, least flattering dress, socks on her feet.

She didn't notice the girl.

Not at first.

'I... Ulrick!'

He almost collapsed into the cottage, eyes on his beautiful wife and her generous lips. Hands quickly around her waist, dropping to her rump, he pulled her to him, kissing her, feeling the sweet softness of the body he'd missed so desperately. He smiled, happy to touch her again. Relieved to be home.

Bergit pulled back, desperate for a breath. 'You're frozen solid!' She looked him up and down, feeling the familiar scratch of his beard on her lips. And then her eyes drifted past her husband to the little girl who lingered by the door. 'Who's that?'

Ulrick's lips wobbled. He'd waited for this moment for longer than he could remember and tears pricked his eyes. 'This is Lotta.' And turning back, he encouraged Lotta to come forward. She looked frightened and tired, and she hesitated.

Bergit did not look pleased to see her at all.

'What is she...' Bergit couldn't even force a smile. 'I don't understand.'

Ulrick barely noticed her irritation as he grabbed Lotta's hand, gently tugging her into the cottage. 'Let's get you by the fire. What a cold day we've had, Lotta and I.' He shut the door, locking it, shaking snow from his hair, flapping his beard. 'It's bitter out there!' And seeing that Bergit had remained staring at the door, not moving, he let go of Lotta and embraced his wife again. 'I brought her for you, my love. For us. So we can be a family again. At long last, we can be a family again!' And kissing her, he watched her eyes.

Which remained dead.

Lotta's eyes went to the flames, which beckoned, orange and bright, and holding out her hands, she walked towards them. The cottage was pleasant enough. A generous supply of lamps around the various tables of the small main room created a warm glow, and Lotta could see a door which likely led to the bedchamber Ulrick was always talking about. It was closed. She saw the kitchen area, shelves replete with jars and bowls; the small table with two chairs; a long bed nearby, layered with furs and pillows. And shuddering suddenly, Lotta was back in Ullaberg, listening to her father.

'But where are they?' Arnon de Sant screamed at the old woman.

Ria the hunchback, Lotta saw. The healer.

'Those raiders took the women! But where are my fucking children?'

Ria was crying. She was old and scared, and Arnon de Sant was almost shaking her.

Lotta felt sorry for her, embarrassed that she shared the blood of a man as cruel as her father. And then horrified.

What *was* she seeing?

'Lotta, come here. Come and see your new bed.'

'Ulrick!' Bergit moved quickly as her husband aimed for that shut door. 'Ulrick, we didn't talk about this! I thought it was time!'

'Time for what?' And pushing open the door, Ulrick froze, seeing the changes Bergit had made to their daughter's chamber. All her things were gone, replaced by a new double bed, furs on the floors, tapestries he didn't recognise on the walls.

Bergit's shoulders slumped as he spun back to her, pain in his eyes. 'It's been years. Nearly twenty years! We couldn't keep a chamber for a dead girl, or for one who would never come. I couldn't have any more children. You know that! I thought it was time. Time for a new life. We're going to Stornas, you said. A new beginning.' She felt irritated, her plans for that new life not involving a small girl with big eyes and long blonde hair.

Lotta peered into the chamber as Bergit shut the door.

'I've been buying what we need for the journey. For our new home. Our new life down south. We talked about it!' Her husband had frozen before her, and grabbing his hand, she squeezed it tightly. 'We talked about it!' she insisted, elbowing the girl out of the way.

Ulrick noticed, and taking Lotta's hand, he drew her back to the fire. 'You sit there. I'll find you a cup of milk. You'll be thirsty after our long day.' He was angry and disappointed, and most of all, hurt. He couldn't even look at Bergit as he placed Lotta on a stool and headed for the kitchen area.

Lotta stared up at Bergit, surprised to see the venom in her eyes.

She didn't appear to be a woman who wanted a new daughter. Not at all.

***

'You're not coming to bed?' Elin wondered, slipping her hand into Reinar's. He'd been at the map table for hours, and she'd finally lost patience, too tired to wait any longer. 'Ever?'

'No, I need to keep thinking. It's better now everyone's gone. I can almost see things clearly.' He noticed Sigurd out of the corner of his eye, wishing Ludo goodnight as he left the hall.

There was no sign of Ilene, who'd disappeared earlier with Berger Eivin.

Reinar smiled, pleased about that, though he didn't blame his brother for seeking a way to numb the pain. He thought about what he'd done with Alys, though a few harmless kisses wasn't something to worry about, he decided, flashes of guilt making him uncomfortable enough to doubt that statement.

'Well, don't be long. You need sleep.'

'I do.' And bending down, Reinar kissed his wife. 'I need sleep and training and a fort with gates that lock and men with weapons, fully armoured, and water-tight ships with competent helmsmen and –'

Elin held a finger to his lips. 'And sleep. Most of all sleep.' And taking away her finger, she kissed him again.

Reinar held her close, losing the desire to remain at the map table at all. Things were slowly becoming more familiar, and he felt an urge to make up for lost time, but hearing Sigurd's footsteps behind him, he let Elin go. 'Well, I'm sure sleep will be in short supply tonight,' he grinned, listening to a hungry cry in the distance.

'I shall have a pillow over my head!' Elin laughed, turning away. 'Goodnight, Sigurd.'

'Goodnight,' Sigurd muttered, stopping beside Reinar. The crying baby didn't bother him, but seeing Elin did. She had the same eyes as her brother, and it was becoming difficult to see them as two different people now. In all the years he'd known Elin, she'd given him no reason for concern. She could be a little up and down, but she'd always been kind, and his brother had been happy with her. Though now, after Torvig had killed Tulia, and Elin had run away from Reinar, he saw her through different eyes.

'You alright?' Reinar had noticed his scowling.

Sigurd shrugged. 'I want to kill something or hump someone or cry.'

'Well...' Reinar shook his head. 'I'd go with crying. Makes the most sense. You need to do some of that, I'd say. Likely the other two would just get you in trouble one way or the other.'

Sigurd nodded, agreeing. 'What are you looking at?' He inclined his head to the map.

Reinar turned back to it, happy to be tinkering. 'Slussfall. We need a way into the fort. A way to kill Hakon Vettel.'

Sigurd grabbed the ale jug, pouring himself a cup. 'And his

cousin.'

Reinar smiled. 'That's what Ake wants. No more Vettels.'

'Which means we have to kill the baby too.'

Reinar grabbed Sigurd's arm. 'Ssshhh! What are you saying that for?' He glanced around, but there was no one in the hall now. Not even a servant.

'Alright, calm down,' Sigurd grumbled, elbowing his brother away. 'You think Ake wants to leave any threads of that family dangling? I imagine he wants us to cut them all, even if he hasn't asked outright.'

'Oh no, he's asked outright.'

'Has he?'

Reinar sighed, still unsettled by Ake's words. 'I... I can't even imagine what we're going to do about that.' His voice was low, not wanting anyone to know. Not wanting to even think about it himself.

'Well, he's right. Alekka can't suffer through more of the same. Every twenty years another Vettel rising up, wanting to claim the throne? They have to be ended, Reinar. All of them. Every last one, child or not.'

His brother sounded oddly cold, Reinar thought. Sigurd had always been cynical, barely believing in gods or dreamers, but even so, he sounded so harsh. 'Well, let's get to Slussfall first. It's going to be difficult enough to get inside that fort. We don't need to worry about... that.'

Sigurd agreed. He didn't like the sound of it either, but if the Vettels hadn't been determined to take back the throne, Tulia would still be alive. She would be waiting in bed for him.

Naked Tulia. Sleeping Tulia. Peaceful and content Tulia.

Sigurd closed his eyes, not wanting tears to dilute his rage.

He would fix his attention on Slussfall, on the Vettels, and revenge.

***

Leonid had cried himself to sleep.

After explaining to Jonas what had happened, and how Magnus had ended up in the prison hole with him, he had cried out of fear and regret, worried that Jonas would want to kill him.

Jonas hadn't known what to say. Leonid was barely a man, and not a confident one at that. Having discovered who Jonas was, he'd become so nervous that when he wasn't crying, he was apologising profusely, shaking all over.

They were both grateful for the peace and quiet.

'I'm sorry for sending you in here, Magnus.' Jonas felt even more regretful than Leonid, if that were possible. 'It wasn't the best decision I've ever made.'

'But you were right,' Magnus insisted, not wanting his great-grandfather to blame himself. 'You were seen. Recognised quickly. You were right.'

'I'd rather not have been right about anything. But at least we know the lay of the land now. We've all the information we need, haven't we?' He leaned in, pulling Magnus to him until his hairy lips were almost touching Magnus' ear. 'And Vik's out there.'

Magnus felt a lift. 'Outside the fort?' he whispered back, feeling Jonas nod.

'And then there's Ollo Narp. He tried to get you out, I saw that. The man wants his silver rather bad. Always has.' Jonas' shoulders tightened as he considered their chances of getting out of the hole before someone decided what to do about him.

He peered into the shadows, though most of the men hidden by the darkness appeared defeated and not at all interested in their newest companion. But Jonas knew from experience that danger was always lurking, and he didn't intend to leave Magnus unguarded while he slept. He would nudge Leonid awake after a while and get him to take a turn watching the boy.

Though, he thought, shaking his head, that hadn't worked out so well the last time.

***

Hakon's steward was a clumsy boy who irritated him with his fussing. Hakon could hear him mumbling as he banked the fire, stumbling around the tent. 'Go!' he grumbled from his bed, stomach aching. 'Sleep elsewhere tonight, Rikkard, I wish to be alone.'

Rikkard was surprised, though not displeased, and straightening up, he nodded, heading quickly for the tent flap. 'Yes, my lord.'

Hakon wasn't listening. His mind had quickly returned to Slussfall. He felt the great relief of having captured the fort. It was a foothold in the South, and despite what had befallen them recently, that foothold remained strong. Ake Bluefinn didn't appear to be chasing them, and that gave them a chance to start again.

He shivered, dragging the fur up over his shoulder, groaning. The pain had dulled now, but it still throbbed like a heartbeat, keeping him from sleep. Though he would need to find sleep, for he had to wake up tomorrow like a lord worthy of a crown. Confidence could be as brittle as newly formed ice; one tiny crack could be devastating.

Hakon's belly ached, and his guts griped, and his head swirled with ale-soaked fears that had him panicking and angry and anxious. He held the fur tightly around his face, wanting to disappear.

***

Ulrick had disappeared into the bedchamber with Bergit, closing the door after them, leaving Lotta tucked up in bed in the main room, watching the glowing embers darken, wondering what she was going to do.

It was the first time in so long that she hadn't slept on the ground, that she'd almost forgotten the joy of a mattress and the pleasure of a pillow, though strange voices echoed in her head. Some she recognised; others terrified her.

She saw Bergit's face, and she felt worried.

Ulrick had promised her a new home with a woman who had long been desperate for a child, yet Bergit appeared anything but. She had looked at her with horror and distaste. Ulrick appeared not to see what Lotta could. He had tried to pacify his wife while they ate a tasteless soup and sat around a spitting fire together. Ulrick had smiled at Lotta, and offered her more soup, concerned by her listlessness, eyes on his wife, hoping to encourage some concern in her. But Bergit Dyre had stared at Lotta as though she couldn't see her at all.

It worried her.

Their whispering worried her too.

'You have ears like a hawk,' her mother would say with a smile, holding her close.

Lotta wanted to sob, but fear was blocking her tears. Fear was like a great damn holding them back. She couldn't cry. She couldn't feel.

Answers lay hidden in the darkness.

And Lotta feared that the way back to her mother was becoming more complicated than any of them had ever imagined.

***

'Thenor has turned away from you, taken his allies with him, thrown you to the wolves!' Mother cackled, creaking in the chair.

Hakon woke in a fright, bounding out of his bed of furs, staring at her.

Dreaming.

'Of course you are dreaming!' Mother laughed, enjoying his distress. 'I haven't risen from my grave, nor my pyre, which I cannot, you having left me to the birds and the beasts. A frozen corpse in a frozen forest. A meal for many!'

Hakon panted before her, eyes peeled open.

'Thenor has abandoned you, The Hunter has marked you. And what will you do about that?'

'Marked me?'

'He pointed his sabre at you. You saw that. You feel it too. You are marked, Hakon! The promise of death is carved into you now. See for yourself!' And lurching up from the chair, she bustled towards him, grabbing his tunic, pulling it up. 'There!'

Hakon couldn't feel his stomach wound. He felt no pain at all.

But he could see the dark symbol almost glowing in the centre of his chest.

'Over your heart,' Mother purred, touching it. 'For hearts are what The Hunter feeds on. Thenor's gift to him for all his hard work!' And smiling, she let Hakon's tunic drop, turning away. 'Though there are things you can do. Help you can find. If you weren't so blind...'

Placing a hand over his heart, Hakon shuddered. He could feel the heat of the mark throbbing beneath his palm. 'Help?' Looking up, he swallowed. 'But you're dead. What help can you be to me, Mother?'

'Me?' And the old woman laughed, returning to the chair, but she didn't sit down. She walked around it, muttering to herself, running a finger over the back of it, eyes low. 'I may be dead, though I have ambitions still. I can show you where hope lies... if... if you swear an oath to me.' And looking up, she grinned, teeth bared.

'But you're dead. This is just a dream.'

'Oh yes, and as a dreamer, I know how powerful dreams can be.' Mother stepped forward, voice rumbling. 'Give me your oath, Hakon. Give it to me, and I will show you the answer.'

CHAPTER TWENTY THREE

Alys woke with a start, immediately disappointed, Eddeth tugging her cloak.

She hadn't had a dream. Not even a hint of one.

'Come on,' Eddeth hissed. 'You can sleep tonight, for now, we must leave!'

Glancing around, Alys frowned. 'Where's Stina?'

The shelter was full of sleeping servants, a few of them snoring. It was still mostly dark, though Alys saw a faint blush of light on the ground. She shivered, frozen solid, wanting a fire. And then, blinking, waking herself up, she knew that she wanted to be away from the camp and Hakon Vettel more.

'She's with the horses, so come on, my sleeping dre–' And stopping herself before the rest of that word tumbled from her tired tongue, Eddeth shook her head, trying to wake up.

Nodding, Alys scrambled to her feet, shivering some more.

'I need a piss!' Eddeth declared, loudly enough to elicit a grumble from the corner. 'I'll meet you at the horses. Everything we need is there, waiting. Only thing missing is us!'

Alys was looking forward to riding, and resettling her long cloak about herself, she followed Eddeth out of the tent. Yawning, rubbing her aching eyes, she was relieved to see the welcome glow of purplish light building in the east. They were in the mountains, and it would help to be able to see the path. Eddeth was not the most confident horsewoman, Alys thought, smiling to herself, seeing Ivan staggering towards her.

In fact, it wasn't only Ivan. She saw Lief too, with Falla yawning behind him.

The camp was quickly coming to life, everyone eager to be on the road early.

Ducking her head in annoyance, Alys tried to avoid them all.

To no avail.

'Looks like a fine day ahead!' Ivan boomed with a sleepy grin, though he did not feel happy.

'I hope so,' Alys said. She saw Falla watching her and Lief staring at her, and feeling self-conscious, Alys ran a hand over her hair, thinking about Lotta. 'I wish us all a productive day on the road.'

'And where will you be heading?' Lief wondered, ushering Falla to the fire one of the servants had expertly brought to life. His wife was shaking as she hurried to the flames, unhappy to have been dragged out of bed so early.

'South, then east. To Ullaberg.' Alys didn't enjoy lying, though she was skilled at it, having spent years making excuses for what Arnon was doing to her.

Ivan tried to encourage Alys to the fire beside Falla. 'You'll need a good breakfast before you go.'

'We have food for the journey, thank you.'

'Well, you've been a great help, and one day, when Lord Hakon becomes the king, I'm sure he would welcome you to Stornas to thank you again for saving his life.' It was something to say, and Lief felt foolish for saying it, certain that few believed that Hakon would become the King of Alekka now.

Nodding, Alys stepped around the stone circle, eyeing the flames.

As much as she wanted to leave, she couldn't stop shivering.

'Run! Now!'

Alys spun around, hearing a voice.

'What is it?' Falla asked, staring up at her. 'Did you hear something?'

Alys looked at her blankly, mouth open. 'I...' She turned again, hairs on the back of her neck rising. 'I thought I heard Eddeth,' she croaked. 'I must go and find her before she wanders off! Goodbye!' It was a mumbled rush, and Alys found herself panicking, urged on by that loud warning.

Eddeth hurried up to her, stumbling into a hole, falling onto her forearms, yelping in pain.

'Eddeth!' Alys bent down to help her up. 'Are you alright?'

Eddeth pushed herself up with a groan. 'I'll be fine, just fine!' she insisted, worrying that she most certainly wouldn't be fine. Something had twisted, and she doubted she could put all her weight down on her right ankle, which she'd already strained. Wanting to test out that theory, she tried. 'Ouch! Soon! I will be fine soon! No need to worry!'

Ivan didn't look convinced. 'Here, I'll help you to your horse.' And he held out a hand, but Eddeth pushed him away.

'No, no, don't trouble yourself, Ivan Vettel!' And leaning on Alys, she urged her on, aiming for the horses. She saw a glimpse of Stina in the distance, already mounted. Haski and Wilf were still tied along the length of rope strung between the trees, saddlebags packed, waiting for their riders.

'Well, goodbye!' Ivan called after the women, feeling an odd sense of loss. Hakon had insisted they leave, and they certainly seemed eager to go, but he would miss Alys' company. She was nothing like Falla, he thought, eyes on the scowling woman who hunched over the fire, hands to the flames, grumbling at her fussing husband.

'Wait!' came a bellow from behind him.

And Ivan turned to see Hakon stumbling out of his tent, Rikkard following him, breath smoke swirling around them both.

'Ivan! Hurry! Stop those women!'

***

Ulrick was surprised to be awake so early after the exertions of his long journey. It was barely dawn, he realised with a yawn, and reaching a hand out to his wife, he was surprised to find Bergit just as awake.

'We need to talk about the girl,' she grumbled, pushing his hand away from the breast it was trying to fondle.

'We need to talk about more than that,' Ulrick said, hearing the displeasure in her voice. 'I have to find a ship, for we are leaving, my love. It is time to go north again.'

'What?' Horrified, Bergit propped herself up, glaring at her husband. 'But we're going to Stornas! We're going to the city! I've been preparing. Preparing to be a lady. To have a house! To be *your* lady!' Her voice was shrill; loud in the silence.

Ulrick frowned, turning his head to the door, knowing that Lotta would be awake, listening. He pulled Bergit to him, annoyed that she was letting the cold air into the bed. 'Stop it, woman,' he grumbled, resettling the furs around them both. 'You *will* be a lady. You *will* have a grand house. I promised you that, and I won't let you down. There are other lords. Other ways to achieve our goals.'

'Other lords?' Bergit spat. 'Other lords?' She was horrified. 'Are you that disloyal? You were Jesper's man before you were ever Hakon's, and now you speak of other lords?'

Ulrick sighed. 'The Vettels won't be happy with me. Hakon at least. I...' He didn't want to explain further. 'We must leave. Once they return, we won't be welcome. In fact, it might become dangerous to be here.' He thought of the old witch dreamer who would certainly want to get her hands on Lotta. 'I'll find passage on a ship today. We must act quickly, my love. The Freeze will come early this year, it's what everyone's saying. We must leave before we're stuck here, for if we are, we won't be able to remain in Slussfall. We'll have to find a tiny village somewhere and hide out till spring.'

Bergit's frown deepened. 'What did you do, Ulrick?' She grabbed his arm, squeezing, her voice rising again, her ambitions shattering. 'What have you *done*?'

***

Hakon's dream lingered like storm clouds as he strode around the firepit, ignoring Falla, ignoring Lief, ignoring Ivan, Rikkard trailing after him, his lord's cloak draped over his arms.

'You!'

Alys froze, swallowing, hands tightening on Eddeth's arm.

Stina, hearing Hakon's bellow, wrapped her hands around the reins, watching from the trees.

Eddeth sneezed, feeling Alys' tension. 'We must be on our way, my lord!' she insisted loudly, not turning around. She tried to limp ahead, but Alys released her, hearing the fury in Hakon's voice.

Trying to think.

She glimpsed Stina, willing her to ride, wanting her to escape. And then she turned around. 'Yes, my lord?'

Hakon snatched Alys' arm, yanking her to him, his breath snaking around them both.

Ivan hurried forward. 'Cousin! What's happening? What's wrong?'

'Wrong? Nothing, nothing at all. Isn't that right, *dreamer*?' Hakon grinned, watching terror spark in Alys' pretty eyes, hearing Eddeth's sharp intake of breath.

'What?' Ivan looked shocked.

Falla sat up straight, hand out to Lief, who helped her to her feet, eyes sharp with interest.

Everyone turned to look at Alys, whose mouth hung open, certain she could hear Hakon's dead dreamer laughing hysterically.

***

Reinar woke with a sense of purpose, and he was already down at the piers with Bjarni before Sigurd had even crawled out of bed. But, sent on his way by a grumpy Gerda, who had endured another sleepless night thanks to Liara Sansgard, he hurried down to join his brother.

Reinar barely noticed he was there, hopping out of *Dagger* and striding down the pier towards one of their newest ships, *Hawk Eye*.

'What's the hurry?' Sigurd croaked, realising that he'd left the hall without any breakfast. 'Are we leaving today?' He smiled sympathetically at Bjarni, who looked as exhausted as Gerda.

'I had a dream!' Reinar called, head down, running his eyes over the ship. Most of their fleet was old, though after thoroughly inspecting every ship over the past few days, Bolli felt confident that they were mostly watertight. 'I want spears. More rope. Braziers. We'll need to secure them. Somewhere to keep wood and tinder dry too.' He was muttering, almost to himself, as Bjarni stood beside him nodding.

'You had a dream?' Sigurd laughed, jumping on board. 'And now we're leaving?'

'I saw us trapped in ice, Brother,' Reinar said. 'It made me think. This winter's come at us so early. Surely The Freeze will arrive early too? We have to leave as soon as we can. Not delay a day more than we need to.' His shoulders were tight with tension, knowing that the king had tasked them with defeating the Vettels.

They couldn't keep him waiting.

'Makes sense,' Sigurd agreed with a yawn. 'But will we be ready?'

'Ake's left us enough men. We've got the ships. The fletchers are working on more arrows. Bows. Shields. I've had Gerda and Agnette organising food and ale too.'

Sigurd frowned, looking back up at the fort, rising out of the cliffs. 'And you're sure the Vettels aren't just licking their wounds, hiding deeper in the forest? Biding their time before attacking again?'

Reinar shook his head. 'Not likely. They've been weakened.

Would you try again? I certainly wouldn't. I'd head home and regroup, care for my injured men, restock my weapons, think of how to begin again. And they will. They'll be doing nothing but thinking about what to do next. Though now they know Ake's back from Ennor, they'll have to decide whether to wait for spring or build a fleet, press further South.' Reinar found himself getting impatient, wanting to leave now. 'All we can do is work on our own plans. Head for Slussfall as soon as we can. I think we can be ready in four.' He decided quickly, eyes on the snow clouds thickening around them, already blocking out the rising sun; conscious of how much shorter the days would soon become. 'Four days and we'll head for Slussfall.'

***

Hakon dragged Alys towards his tent, ordering his cousin to watch Eddeth. Eddeth, who was trembling and shaking and trying her very best not to look over to where Stina had been waiting with their horses.

Alys glanced over her shoulder at Eddeth as Hakon dropped the tent flap behind him, stepping towards her.

'Sit.'

He seemed angry, alert, and in great discomfort, Alys thought as she stumbled down onto a tree stump.

'You're Reinar Vilander's dreamer.'

Alys blinked into those strange eyes. She remembered seeing them before she ever met Hakon Vettel. She remembered telling Reinar about the man who was so hungry for the throne. And now, here he was, spitting at her, his anger boiling over. 'I... no.' She shook her head. 'I'm not, no.'

Hakon dragged a stump towards her, sitting down with a grunt. 'You're not?' He narrowed his eyes. 'You're sure that's the game you want to play, Alys? The lie you want to tell?'

'I am a dreamer,' Alys admitted quietly, warm all over. 'I'm not his, though. No.'

'But you were?' Once Hakon had sworn an oath to Mother, promising he would attack the Slave Islands and defeat Jael Furyck, she'd gleefully told him all about Alys and her secret.

Alys sighed, sensing that the only way out now was to reveal everything.

Almost everything.

'The Vilanders came to my village. They captured us. Took all the women onto their ships.' She saw her children running from her, and sadness filled her eyes.

Worry too.

Hakon listened, encouraging her to continue. She was so lovely and helpless. He couldn't stop staring.

'They were taking us to Goslund, they said, but your ships were there, waiting to ambush us.'

Sitting up straighter, Hakon peered at her. '*You* saw my ships? *You* saw that they'd attack?'

Alys nodded. 'I was never a dreamer. I'd never been one before. I had dreams since I was a child, though I was forbidden from revealing them. My mother... she was killed for it, you see, for being a dreamer.' She felt uncomfortable revealing so much, but she needed Hakon to trust her.

She needed Hakon to free her.

'So you saw the ships coming, and you spoke out?'

'I did. I had no choice. I told the Vilanders. They stopped your ships, took us back to their fort. Made us fight for them.'

'*Fight* for them?' Hakon was intrigued.

'Yes, they trained some of the women to use bows. They put them on the walls. And me?' Alys swallowed. 'Reinar Vilander stuck me in a cottage, told me to dream for him.' She tried to look miserable about that, though she wasn't. She looked back on Ottby fondly. She thought of her cat and her cottage and Agnette. Ludo and Stellan too. She saw the hall with its enormous fires and tables. The muddy square.

The shed. Torvig.

Tulia's dead body.

And shuddering, Alys waited, not sure what else to say.

Hakon chewed it over, staring at her. She was timid, trembling, and terrified, though he couldn't detect any lies in what she was saying. 'You killed my dreamer. That's what she says.'

Alys almost bit her tongue, realising how Hakon had discovered the truth. 'She came to you?'

Hakon nodded. 'She did. Most annoyed she was, you killing her like that. I imagine she wanted a helping of revenge, and I can hardly blame her. Who knew a dreamer could be useful even after death?'

Alys shivered, hoping the old witch hadn't told him about Lotta. 'I had no choice but to try and stop her. We were on opposite sides. Reinar Vilander promised us our freedom if we helped him defend his fort. Your dreamer was trying to hurt us. To hurt me. I did what I could, what I was ordered to do.'

'And how?' Hakon wondered, staring closely. Something about Alys was familiar, though he didn't know what. 'How did you kill her?'

Alys hesitated, knowing that if the old woman had been telling tales, she could hardly lie now. 'I asked the gods for help.' She almost whispered it, anticipating what would come next.

Hakon lurched off the stump, pain searing through his belly, glaring down at her. 'You spoke to the gods? Which gods?'

'Valera.'

'And she listened to you? Helped you?'

Alys nodded.

Hakon's eyes darted around the tent, his stomach rumbling. The heat from the mark was noticeable now too; a burning sensation over his heart. He touched it absentmindedly, trying to focus on what Alys had said, before dragging his hand away, suddenly self-conscious around the dreamer. 'Why would she help you?'

Alys couldn't speak; she didn't know what to say.

'*And*? Why would she help you?' Hakon spat angrily, grabbing Alys' chin, roughly tilting it towards his face, feeling her soft skin, enjoying the fear in her eyes.

'I... I don't know, my lord.' Alys' thoughts were scrambled. She couldn't find a way to safety. 'I... there are many gods. They don't all want the same thing. We are favoured by some but not others. I... I have little knowledge of these things.'

Seeing how terrified Alys was, Hakon leaned over, wanting to make her even more so. 'But you will learn, won't you?'

Alys didn't even blink.

'You will learn for me, Alys, for now, you are my dreamer, and you will help make me the king I was born to be.'

***

Ivan paced outside Hakon's tent, wanting to go in. He could hear his cousin bellowing occasionally, Alys yelping often, and it worried him. Hakon was erratic normally, but after what had happened in the forest...

Eddeth twitched beside him, ankle throbbing. 'What is he doing?' she hissed anxiously, trying to get Ivan's attention. 'Hurting her?'

Ivan's loyalty had always been to Hakon, and he turned to Eddeth with anger in his usually cheerful eyes. 'Is she a dreamer?' he growled. 'Is my cousin right?'

Eddeth's eyes bulged, not wanting to reveal things they had sworn not to say. But it appeared that Hakon had found it out for himself, and there was little Eddeth could do about it now. 'So I... believe.' Her eyes darted past Ivan to where their horses remained tied up amongst the trees.

Blinking.

She could no longer see Stina.

PART THREE

Prisoners

CHAPTER TWENTY FOUR

Bergit was in a terrible state. Angry. Throwing things.

She'd already smashed two bowls as she stormed from one end of the tiny cottage to the other.

Lotta didn't know where to look as she sat on a stool by the fire, hands clasped in her lap, eyes on the flames. Her great-grandfather was in the fort, likely imprisoned. Magnus too. And Vik was out there somewhere.

She remembered Vik Lofgren. He had carried her on his shoulders when they'd visited Jonas once. He was Jonas' best friend; a famous warrior, she remembered Magnus telling her. He was a bear man. Lotta had wanted to know what that was, but Magnus didn't know.

So if Vik was still free, there was a chance he could rescue Jonas and Magnus.

But as for her?

Lotta tried to ignore the angry woman, closing her eyes, wanting to escape into the darkness of her mind, but suddenly, Bergit was at the door, swinging it open.

'Go!' she shouted, pointing at Lotta. 'You're not wanted here. Just leave. Go! Go on, leave!'

Lotta stumbled to her feet, eyes on the freedom that beckoned. She froze, though, certain that Ulrick would be unhappy with his wife. But Bergit wasn't waiting for the girl to make up her mind, and, in a heartbeat, she'd grabbed Lotta by the hand and thrown her outside.

***

Ulrick's frown was deep. Seeing Bergit had been nothing but disappointing; shockingly so. They'd talked about another child for years. She'd appeared broken-hearted and bereft when she spoke of their dead daughter, Gala. He thought the sight of Lotta would have been a joyful moment to share, making their family whole again.

Shoulders slumping, Ulrick tried to focus. He needed to find a man with a ship and for that, he was going to have to speak to Ollo Narp. Unsurprisingly, he was loitering outside the tavern, head together with Haegel Hedvik, who had the brain of an idiot donkey. 'And what are you going to do about your spy, Ollo? Your prisoner?' he wondered sharply, enjoying the spark of anger in the rotund man's eyes as he turned around. 'I've heard nothing but angry grumbles all morning. No one's happy about him being here. Doubt he'll be safe in that hole for long.'

Sending Haegel on his way with a nod, Ollo flicked his tongue over his teeth, trying to appear far more nonchalant than he felt. 'Why do you care so much, Ulrick? When did you ever care about anyone but yourself?' He wasn't about to be intimidated. Ulrick was an old hand of the Vettels, put to use like a pack-horse. He was no lord, no leader. Never had been. Never would be.

'You think Hakon wants to hear how you let that old man creep around his fort, picking up information for Ake?' It wasn't what Ulrick wanted to talk about, but the idea that Jonas Bergstrom was Lotta's great-grandfather had unsettled him almost as much as Bergit's reaction to the girl. He needed the old man seen to, removed as quickly as possible.

'Ha!' Ollo wasn't about to be moved. 'You're full of fanciful ideas, Ulrick. I would've thought you'd be too busy reuniting with your wife to be worried about what I do with my prisoners. Can't imagine why you're strutting around the square so early. Things can't have gone well...'

Ulrick scowled, quickly annoyed. 'What I do with my wife is

of no concern of yours.'

'No?' Ollo wanted Ulrick back on his heels, well away from him and any plans he was making for Jonas. 'She's been very busy in the market. Shopping daily. Buying all manner of fabrics and furnishings. I imagine she has her heart set on a big house in the big city.' He eyed Ulrick, watching his discomfort grow. 'You and I don't need to be enemies.' And opening out his ringed hands, Ollo smiled magnanimously. 'We can both get what we want, surely?'

Ulrick stepped back, taking the measure of the man. It surprised him to see a hint of a spine. 'Well, keep Jonas Bergstrom locked up tight till Hakon returns and I'll have no problem with you, Ollo. Though, I can't say the same for everyone else.'

'And why do you have it in for the old man, then?'

'Jonas Bergstrom?' And now Ulrick was snarling. 'He killed more of my friends than I can count, and Hakon will want him to pay for his crimes against his family. Know that. Whatever you're planning, know that.'

Ollo picked up his shoulders, straightening them with a frown, eyes shifting past Ulrick to the alley, where a cold-looking little girl had emerged, glancing around. 'And the girl? She doesn't belong to you. What do you want with her?'

Ulrick looked further incensed, and leaning forward, he grabbed Ollo's cloak. 'I saved her, worm. She's mine, so you needn't concern yourself with the girl. Bergit and I are looking after her now.' And he shoved Ollo away.

'Is that so?' Ollo smiled, adjusting his cloak. 'You're looking after *that* girl, are you? Poor thing looks a little cold to me. Make sure you find her something warm to wear if you're going to let her wander around the fort all day. Think we're in for more snow!' And with that, Ollo strode away, eyes on the prison bars, hoping Haegel could get his message to Vik Lofgren.

Ulrick spun around, hurrying towards Lotta, who was doing her best not to cry. She was too cold to do much more than shiver and shake and stare.

'What happened?' And bending down, Ulrick pulled her into his arms, trying to warm her up. 'How did you escape? Why?' He whispered in her ear, not wanting anyone to hear.

Lotta didn't mind his hug because his cloak was furry and warm. She almost felt safe as she leaned into him. 'Your w-w-wife...'

Ulrick pulled back, staring at her.

'She threw me out. Told me to g-go.'

Ulrick's shock was painful, but he quickly cleared his face. 'Well, I think you misheard her, little princess.' And standing, he took Lotta's hand in his, leading her back down the alley to the cottage, afraid of what he would find. 'You see, Bergit loves children, especially little girls with long blonde hair. I think, perhaps, she just doesn't like surprises. Don't worry, we'll smooth everything over. Don't worry now.'

But Lotta was worrying. She had seen so many frightening things in her dreams.

She was worrying very much indeed.

Magnus frowned, turning to his great-grandfather who stood next to him, eyes on the square, watching Lotta. 'She didn't even look our way.'

Jonas snorted to cover up his own concern. 'Why would she? She didn't spend a day surveying the fort like you. She doesn't know we're over here, does she?' It was odd, he thought, that Lotta hadn't looked around at all. She knew they were there, and yet she'd seemed comfortable with Ulrick Dyre, hugging him eagerly.

That was something, Jonas supposed, relieved to think that the man wasn't mistreating her. But still, he'd have expected her to look around.

His eyes moved to Ollo, who strode across the square as though it was his own personal domain. Jonas hoped it was. He hoped that Ollo Narp had enough power in his sweaty little hands to get them all out of the fort alive.

***

Dragging Alys out of his tent, Hakon peered at Ivan, thick eyebrows almost meeting in the middle of his frown. 'Why are you standing around? The sun is up! We must get on the road, Cousin! Get moving. Get everyone moving!' He glanced at Eddeth, who was peering at Alys with terrified eyes. 'And where's your other friend, then? The dark-haired woman?'

Eddeth jerked upright. 'I haven't seen her, my lord. Not a sign!'

Alys could hear Eddeth's screaming thoughts, worried that they would tumble out of her flapping mouth. 'She wasn't well this morning. It's been a hard time for her. They were not kind to us in Ottby.'

'No?' Both Ivan and Hakon were suddenly more curious to hear Ottby gossip than worrying about where Stina had gone.

'Stina was raped,' Alys whispered, working to keep their attention on her. 'Repeatedly. Another of the women threw herself into the sea. They were... not kind.'

Ivan was surprised.

So was Hakon, as Mother had implied almost the complete opposite. 'Even Reinar Vilander himself?'

Eddeth quickly glanced at her boots, noticing how muddy they were.

'He was... distracted,' Alys said carefully. 'His wife was missing. There were rumours that she'd killed herself. He was unhappy. Angry.'

Ivan eyed his cousin, who lifted an eyebrow, further intrigued. 'And is that true? *Did* she kill herself?'

'I don't know,' Alys lied. 'I'm not an experienced dreamer, as I told the Lord of Ottby, but I saw glimpses of his wife plotting her escape. She lost her babies, you see. They were stillborn. It weighed on her, and she blamed her husband's bad luck for causing it. She ran away from him.'

Eddeth was surprised to hear Alys blabber on, pleased not to be accused of revealing all their secrets herself. But she could sense how desperately she was trying to keep the Vettels' minds off Stina, hoping to give her enough time to escape. And nodding enthusiastically, she encouraged Alys to carry on, which she did.

'I saw that she'd left. Reinar Vilander's cousin had helped her escape. But what became of her after that, I don't know. He wanted to find her, though. That was all he cared about. Your army was a distraction he didn't need. He just wanted to find his wife.'

Hakon listened with open ears, pleased to have such insight. He had affection for his own wife, but to be so distracted by her disappearance? Shaking his head, he flicked a hand at Ivan. 'Get everyone moving, Cousin. Lief and Jerrick will help you.' He pulled Alys to him. 'I want to hear more. You will ride with me this morning. I want to hear all about Reinar Vilander and his weaknesses. This man captured you, killed your husband...' He stared into her eyes, squeezing her arm until he saw her flinch. 'Perhaps he did this to you?' And he ran a gloved finger over the faded bruises on Alys' face.

Ivan watched, fists clenched. 'I doubt Mother would have taken it well if you'd put your hands on her,' he muttered, risking his cousin's wrath. But realising that Hakon wouldn't listen to him even if he could hear him, he turned away, wanting to hurry everyone along, for if he could get them onto their horses quickly, he could ride with Hakon and Alys and try to keep her safe.

Alys watched Ivan go, feeling more vulnerable. 'The battle...' she tried. 'So many boulders hit the fort. I fell. More than once.'

Hakon smiled, remembering Ottby. He'd felt invincible as Mother worked her magic and Ivan led their men forward, arrows shooting ahead of them, boulders shattering the walls, gates crashing open. He could almost smell the strange smoke in his nostrils, and he sighed. 'Well, perhaps you will have your revenge, Alys? Would you like that? Like to see Reinar Vilander again? Watch him die by my hand?'

He was breathing on her, his face edging closer and closer, and there was nothing for Alys to do but nod. 'Yes. I... would.'

***

Neither Agnette nor Gerda looked pleased with the news that everyone would be leaving in four days.

'But, but...' Gerda spluttered, pushing her bowl of porridge away, eyes on Liara, who lay asleep in Agnette's arms. 'The fort isn't ready, and what about Odd Forsten? Can you still trust him with such a responsibility at his age?' She peered around the hall, hoping that Odd hadn't crept in, though there was no one but servants to see. 'If only Tulia were here.' She said that somewhat wistfully, surprising everyone.

'Well, if Tulia were here I imagine she'd be going with them, Aunty,' Agnette murmured, not wanting to wake her daughter. Or did she? She found herself fretting constantly, which was unlike her. Lack of sleep had her mind in a disorganised mess, and she couldn't decide on the right path to take. 'Wouldn't she?'

Reinar nodded, wishing Tulia was there too, blaming himself that she wasn't. More than anyone, Tulia had warned him about Torvig. He felt Elin still beside him, uncomfortable that her brother was the reason for all their distress.

'She would, of course,' Bjarni said with a yawn, barely making it through one bowl of porridge. He was almost too tired to eat. 'But she's not, which Sigurd knows only too well.' He glanced at Agnette, who nodded, yawning herself.

They were all silent then, thinking about Sigurd, who pushed open the hall doors with a groan, surprised by the silence that greeted him. He felt odd, surprised not to see Tulia there. He kept expecting to find her everywhere he went, long black braid swishing behind her, smug smile on her face; that look in her eye that said it was time to go back to their chamber. 'What?' He saw pity in most pairs of eyes, discomfort in Elin's. And guessing what they were talking about, he almost turned to leave. 'Are you still eating?' he asked instead, walking towards Reinar and Bjarni. 'Come on! The weather's closing in out there. If we want to gather up our weapons, we should make a move.'

'And what about the snow?' Gerda implored, on her feet now. 'You're going to war in the snow? Like those Vettels?' She turned to her husband, who was sound asleep in his wheelchair beside her. 'You know what your father would say about that!'

'I do, but Ake's ordered us to go, Mother,' Reinar said calmly, smiling at Elin as he stood, placing a hand on her shoulder, kissing the top of her head. 'He wants the Vettels ended before they become an even bigger problem for him. He's enough on his plate without Hakon and Ivan causing more trouble. They're ours to deal with, so we'll take our ships to war in the snow. Just like the Vettels.' He grinned at his father in passing. 'But unlike the Vettels, we won't be defeated.'

***

Stina had been forgotten.

Alys hoped that was true. She rode in between Ivan and Hakon, trying not to let her worries show on her face. From experience, she knew it was a problem she struggled with, which wasn't helpful for a dreamer who was always seeing and hearing things. Alys wished she could see or hear something useful now, but her mind was trapped in the present, where her hands were red with cold, and her legs ached, and Eddeth rode behind her with Falla, sneezing often.

And then there was Hakon, who hammered her with questions, interrogating her, giving her little chance to think. Ivan tried to shield her, though he was on the back foot when it came to his cousin, and he often retreated into an indistinguishable mumble.

'We'll be at Slussfall in two days.' That thought had Hakon forgetting every ache and pain in his belly; every odd burning sensation in his chest too. His mind was fixed on the fortress. His father hadn't managed to capture it in three attempts, but Hakon had, and remembering that gave him a lift. With Ivan and Lief by his side, he had taken that old fortress, and now, he would retreat inside its comforting walls and plan his next attack.

With a dreamer by his side.

They were riding beneath a sky of dull clouds which threatened snow, though so far only a handful of flurries had drifted down towards them. The tree cover was sparse now, and their column marched slowly up the incline. The mountains were Ivan's least favourite part of the journey, though at least they weren't lugging the siege towers and catapults back with them.

All of those had been abandoned.

Ivan glanced at Hakon, who appeared calm for the first time in days. 'And what about The Hunter?' he wondered. 'You may have stumbled upon a dreamer, Cousin, but surely that threat remains?' Ivan had been terrorised by nightmares that had him waking in a cold sweat. He had seen The Hunter, antlers reaching high into the sky like branches, his giant sabre, nocked at the tip, threatening him. 'What if he comes again?' His eyes drifted to Hakon's chest, and looking up, he caught a spark of anger in his cousin's eyes.

Hakon bit down on a sudden urge to punch his cousin. 'I have a dreamer now, Ivan, so Alys will help me deal with that problem. She knows the gods, just as Mother did. She spoke to them personally, didn't you?' He smiled, watching her squirm in the saddle, enjoying the power he had over her now.

'And yet the gods let Mother die,' Ivan muttered, unable to stop saying things he knew would irritate his cousin.

Hakon ignored him. 'Why don't you move ahead, Ivan? The path is narrowing there. I don't want Alys dropping off the cliff.' And nor did he. For his dreamer was more precious to him than all the gold he was hiding in Slussfall.

She was more precious than anything in the world.

***

Vik glowered at the man who stood quivering at the end of his sword tip. 'Ollo sent you? *You?*'

Haegel Hedvik was a familiar face, useless with every weapon known to man, Vik remembered. No use to him at all.

'I... he did, yes.' Vik Lofgren's reputation was mighty, and Haegel felt his bowed legs wobble. 'If you want to get Jonas and the boy out, you need to listen to me.'

'Hmmm, do I now?' Vik was irritable, annoyed at the mess they'd made of things, and eager to put it right. Ulrick Dyre was a problem, Jonas and Magnus stuck in the hole was a problem, the weather looked like it was about to become a problem, and then there was Ollo Narp and his useless idiot, Haegel. 'Maybe I should just kill you? You who betrayed Sirrus? You who once supported Ake? You and Ollo both! Why shouldn't I kill you? After all we fought for? All the blood spilled to put the kingdom in safe hands, and you two just cared about your silver!' he spat. 'Seems you still do.'

Haegel wanted to deny it was true, but it wasn't. 'We can help you, Vik. Ollo sent me to tell you that we can get the boy out.'

'Just the boy?'

'You think we can get Jonas out?' Haegel shook his head, eyes jumping around the clearing, hoping there weren't any other warriors lurking amongst the trees. He was a gaunt, middle-aged man, deaf in one ear, more nervous than most, always worried that he hadn't heard what was coming for him.

Vik lowered his blade. 'It's just me. You've nothing to fear from my sword if you're telling the truth.' He sighed. 'You think I want to leave Jonas there? In that hole? And it's not just the boy either. I need his sister too.'

Haegel's eyes widened, and he tugged on his coppery beard. 'Well, I...'

'The silver Jonas promised you? He's got a lot of it, I know. But I can't tell you where it is. He didn't tell me. You want it? You want to deliver it to Ollo? Then you need to deliver Jonas and the children to me first. All of them.'

'But how?' It seemed impossible. Everyone knew Jonas was in the hole. Jonas and the boy. They would see an escape.

Vik scratched a stubbly cheek. 'We'll need to do it under the cover of night. And you'll need to pay off a few guards, I'd say. Or get them drunk. Or both. You'll have to get me in.'

'No!' Haegel held up a hand, remembering what Ollo had said. Under no circumstances was he to let Vik into the fort.

Vik stepped forward, sword rising again. 'No?'

Haegel swallowed. 'Ollo said you can't come in. It's too much of a risk. There are enough of Sirrus' men around to recognise you. Enough of Jesper Vettel's men too. Even some of Jorek's. It's not safe.'

Vik's shoulders were tense. His body vibrated with the need to act, though Haegel was not wrong. 'And you want me to trust you to get them out? You and Ollo?' He snorted irritably.

Haegel nodded. 'You can trust us, Vik,' he insisted. 'We were all together once, weren't we? Remember? With Ake and Stellan. Herold Stari. Soren Olstein.'

He was a dimwit, Vik knew, conveniently skating over how they'd betrayed Sirrus, whose shrivelled up head still hung from the gates, pecked on by birds. 'I remember. I remember Arn and Keld and Isak Berg too. I heard how you betrayed them all. What's to say you won't do the same to me? To Jonas?'

Haegel looked embarrassed, pock-marked cheeks turning as red as his long, thin nose. 'We won't. We won't. It hasn't been easy. Not what we hoped for, at least.'

'Well, easier than it's been for poor Sirrus, I'd say!'

Haegel sighed. 'We don't feel good about it, I promise. And now we've a chance to do something. A way to make it right.'

Vik doubted that was true. 'Well, the gods will be watching, I'm sure. Interested to see if you can redeem your wretched souls, you and Ollo, both.' And shaking out his right leg which was aching with cold, he pointed Haegel towards the trees. 'Go back and figure it out. You and Ollo. You'll have your silver, maybe your redemption too, if you help us rescue those children.'

***

Stina wanted to slide off her horse, fall to the ground and cry, but she thought of the children, and she thought of Alys and Eddeth, and she kept going. After the panic of her escape had receded, and she'd stopped looking over her shoulder every few heartbeats, waiting to be caught, she'd been able to find her way back over the army's path. It was easy enough with the mess Hakon's men and beasts had made, though Stina was certain that soon it would become more difficult. Snow was threatening again, and when it fell, as she was sure it would, she wouldn't be able to find the path at all.

Shaking her head, she gripped the reins with gloved hands, feeling a sense of purpose urging her on. Hakon Vettel had been threatened by The Hunter, and he had Alys and Eddeth. And he knew that Alys was a dreamer.

She had to get to Ottby.

She had to find Reinar.

CHAPTER TWENTY FIVE

Bjarni cradled his daughter as though he was holding an armful of eggs.

Agnette laughed. 'You won't break her!' She'd come out onto the field where Reinar and Bjarni were talking to Ake's men, most of whom had been sleeping in tents since their arrival. They'd been relieved to hear that soon they would be boarding ships bound for Slussfall. For though the sea journey promised to be bitterly cold and wet, it was better than being frozen to the ground like a block of ice.

Bjarni lifted an eyebrow. 'Not sure that's true.' Still, he tried to hold Liara more firmly, keeping her close to his chest. The wind was gusting on the exposed field, though she seemed warm enough in her snug fur wrap. 'She's so tiny. Like a baby rabbit.'

'For now, but wait a few days, and it will be like carrying a sack of barley, I promise. She eats like her father!' Agnette laughed, her attention wandering to where Reinar stood with Elin.

'What?' Bjarni followed Agnette's gaze. 'What's wrong?'

'Wrong?' Agnette tried to sound as though nothing was wrong, though she wondered if something was. It felt like something was. 'Nothing.'

Bjarni snorted, eyes quickly back on his daughter, who appeared asleep. 'You've been acting very odd around Elin.'

'What?' It was Agnette's turn to snort. 'I don't think that's true. I've hardly spoken to her.'

'Agnette...'

Agnette sighed. 'She's not right, Bjarni. You can see that, can't you? She's different somehow. I can't put my finger on it, but it's there. Something new. Something that wasn't there before.'

'Maybe it's more about you than Elin? You've just gone through a lot, what with the fort being under attack. That's not easy for anyone, let alone a woman giving birth.' Bending forward, Bjarni kissed the red tip of her nose. 'Not to mention the lack of sleep! You've enough to think about without worrying about Elin. She just needs time to feel at home again. Leave Reinar to worry about her.'

Agnette nodded, wanting her husband to think that that was exactly what she was going to do, her eyes drifting back across the scarred field to where Elin had slipped her arms around Reinar's waist, holding him close.

Reinar rested his chin on top of his wife's head. Memories stirred of meeting her, and loving her, and marrying her, and he smiled. 'You're sure you want to come with us? Four days on a ship? A battle? Who knows what will happen after that. I can't guarantee anything except discomfort and terror. Likely wounds and sickness and being half-frozen every minute of the day.'

Elin stepped back, hands on his chest. 'You know me, surely, you do? I won't be troubled by whatever the gods throw at us. I want to help. To be with you. I don't want to be left behind.' She saw Agnette taking her baby back from Bjarni. 'Gerda seems to be enjoying herself as the Lady of Ottby, so let her do it a while longer. And Agnette can help her.' She turned her sweetest smile up to Reinar, grabbing his hand. 'After all that's happened, I want a chance to start again. Now the curse is lifted, we can, I feel it.'

Reinar nodded, hoping she was right. 'Everything will be better once we get rid of the Vettels. Everything,' he promised, 'and then we can start again.'

***

Hakon had let Alys slip back to ride with Eddeth and Falla, both of whom had questions for her.

'What did he want?' Eddeth wondered, eyes bursting open.

'To know about the Vilanders.' Alys could see how eagerly Falla was considering her now that her true identity had been revealed. She was reminded of her grandfather. Once she'd felt resentful of him for forcing her to hide her gifts. Now she wished more than anything that they were still hidden. She felt exposed; trapped in a world of deception; conscious of how many people she had to please to stay alive.

'And what will they do?' Falla wanted to know. 'The Vilanders? They didn't come after us. Nor did Ake. Why? Will they give up now, at least for the winter?' Falla was desperate for some insight. She missed Mother's reassurance that their future would unfold as she willed it to. Now there was nothing but uncertainty ahead. Uncertainty and storm clouds gathering above them all.

'No.' Alys had to tell the truth as much as possible. Lies were like threads of yarn, and if she pulled too many into her hands and tried to weave an elaborate cloth, she would end up in a tangled mess.

Honesty was the surest path forward.

'The Vilanders will come, as will the gods.' Now she was whispering, wanting Falla onside. Sensing her interest, Alys was keen to foster some support, and hopefully, when they reached Slussfall, some help.

Eddeth's eyes widened further, and reaching a hand up to her face, she scratched her nose. Her nerves were pinging like lyre strings, and she thought longingly of her herbs and her cauldron, and the promise of some relief from all the tension.

Falla nudged her horse closer to Haski. 'You mean because of The Hunter? Will he come again?' Waves of nausea had her glancing around, wondering where she could dismount in a hurry and run into the trees.

'I hope not, but I'm not sure. Perhaps there is no need?'

Falla watched Lief riding between Hakon and Ivan, and lowering her voice, she continued. 'No need?'

Eddeth's nodding had her hair trembling. 'Well, if Hakon has the mark, death will come. Vasa will come. He will not survive the winter. The Hunter's work will be done!'

'But where would the mark be? How would we know if he has it?'

Eddeth swung around, worried by how close the next rank of warriors was riding to them. Servants too. She could see the spotty-cheeked boy who was Hakon's nervous steward. His ears appeared very much open, waiting to hear his lord bellow for him. And easing her horse against Falla's, Eddeth dropped her voice to a whisper. 'On his chest.' She lifted an eyebrow in Alys' direction. 'Perhaps you can see it? In your mind?'

Alys frowned. 'I can try, but it wouldn't be proof. I wouldn't be certain.'

'No,' Falla agreed, 'but someone else could find it. Perhaps his wife? They'll be reunited when we get to Slussfall. Karolina will see his chest. She can tell us!'

All three women straightened up suddenly as Lief turned his horse around, moving away from Ivan and Hakon, who closed up, riding with their heads almost together now. Lief nodded at his wife as he passed, going to check on his men.

Falla nodded back, glancing over her shoulder before leaning towards Eddeth. 'I know Karolina well. She hates her husband. She'll help us.'

'Us?' Eddeth looked surprised.

But Falla had already made up her mind, determined to act before it was too late. 'The gods have spoken, and I would rather help them than a cursed lord like Hakon. Only a fool would go against Thenor.'

Alys found herself nodding, knowing there was little she could do now but ride the waves, for they were taking her somewhere. In all the noise and confusion, Alys could feel it.

She was being taken somewhere important.

Somewhere she needed to go.

***

Ulrick had taken Lotta down to the piers while he looked for a ship to take them to Orbo. Merchants and traders had sailed between Slussfall and Orbo with great frequency since Hakon Vettel had captured the fortress, and though winter was approaching with speed, the piers were full, helmsmen and crews untroubled by the snow flurries that were once again trickling down from ominous clouds.

Ulrick felt an urgency to leave, though he didn't know why. If Hakon had been victorious, he would not return to Slussfall. He would press on to Stornas and capture the throne. But still, he wanted to be away before there were any problems. Though thinking of Bergit, he knew there were nothing but problems.

Perhaps it was best to wait? Wait to hear word about what had happened in Ottby? He had the coins to pay for passage, but he knew how stubborn his wife could be, and if she had set her mind on going to Stornas, nothing in the world would make her get on a ship to Orbo.

He glanced down at a red-cheeked Lotta, who appeared to be shaking with cold, her hand on his arm. 'What is it, little princess? Are you hungry? I think we need something hot to eat, don't you?' Ulrick felt ill, irritated by the bitter wind flapping his long beard up into his face. Flattening it down with one hand, he clasped Lotta's hand in the other. 'Come on, let's head back to the fort. I'll see who I can find in the tavern. There's always business to be done in a tavern!' His heart wasn't in it, though. He could feel himself changing course. Perhaps Hakon would be understanding? Though the old witch dreamer wouldn't, and that would cause problems...

'They're coming.'

Ulrick almost hadn't heard Lotta, but he felt the shivers charging up his body, and stopping, he squatted down. 'Who?'

'The army. Hakon Vettel.'

'Coming here?'

Lotta nodded. She felt a sense of urgency herself. 'Those who are left. But not Mother. She's dead.'

Ulrick dropped to his knees, stunned. 'You saw this? In your dreams?'

Lotta knew it was dangerous, far too dangerous, to reveal the truth, but she saw dark omens. She felt scared. They needed to leave, and if Ulrick listened to his angry wife, they never would.

Glancing around, Ulrick lowered his voice. 'You're a dreamer?'

Lotta shrugged, eyes sweeping the slippery boards of the old pier. She didn't know what she was. 'I have dreams that come true... sometimes. I saw Mother in her tent. She was on the ground, dead.' Lotta shuddered, remembering the ghoulish image. 'Hakon Vettel stood over her, and he was bleeding. They talked about leaving. About it all going wrong.'

Ulrick pulled Lotta into his arms. 'Well, now,' he whispered into her hair. 'Well, now, what a find you are.' And pulling back, he peered at her. 'But you must never tell anyone, Lotta. Dreamers are like gold, especially around these parts, where desperate men are looking to become lords, and lords are fighting to become kings. You must never tell anyone who you are.' He held her close again, feeling her terror. 'You think we should leave? Slussfall?'

'Yes. They will be here soon.'

Ulrick was confused, worrying about Bergit and Hakon. Too confused and distracted to wonder why Lotta was so desperate to leave her brother and great-grandfather behind.

***

They whispered a lot, worrying about who was slouching in the shadows.

Desperate men, mostly. Men seeking a way out of the hole and the darkness, and most of all, an escape from the smell.

Jonas felt the responsibility of keeping both Magnus and Leonid optimistic about their chances of escape, while trying to mask his own fears that there was no escape at all. He'd seen no sign of Ollo. No sign of Lotta since the morning. No sign of Ulrick Dyre either.

And more importantly, no sign of Vik.

Vik would be pacing their campsite, trying to think of a way into the fort. And maybe there was? One where Vik could slip inside unseen. They'd tried it and almost been successful, once. But twice?

'Maybe Lotta will help us?' Magnus lifted his head, peering through the bars again. He gripped those bars as though he wanted to rip them out with his numb hands and crawl through the hole, though they were made of iron, and he was a ten-year-old boy and not a god. 'Maybe she's seen a way?'

Jonas hoped she had, though he would not want such a weight resting on Lotta's tiny shoulders.

'Or Mother?'

Jonas smiled, listening to the boy's rumbling stomach. 'I can promise you something, Magnus. Your mother will be doing everything in her power to get us out of here. Lotta too. As will Vik. They won't rest until we're free. They won't.'

Leonid sat slumped on the ground by their feet, listening to his own belly growling, wiping a hand over his dripping nose, hoping the old man was right.

***

Hakon kept staring at the dreamer. *His* dreamer.

So much more pleasant to look at than his last dreamer.

He smiled. Mother Arnesson had been a stinking old bitch. A failure. She had failed to defeat Alys, and now, Alys rode behind him.

His.

The heat of the mark was a growing distraction, but Hakon

forced himself to look ahead as the afternoon dragged on. He saw the welcoming gates of Slussfall in his mind, his pretty wife running towards him, concern in her eyes. The memory of her warmth and sweet softness lingered, and Hakon closed his eyes for a moment, trying to remember every detail of her face.

'If you fall asleep now, you'll never make it back to Slussfall, Cousin,' Ivan grinned from his left. 'Your horse looks just as sleepy as you. Likely the pair of you will wander off that cliff, never to be seen again.'

Hakon blinked, waking himself up, nudging his horse to the left, well aware of how high up they were now. 'Just daydreaming,' he insisted, turning to Ivan. 'Nearly home.'

'We are.' Ivan felt miserable at the thought of it, but thinking of Slussfall was better than looking at the neverending stretch of mountains that lay ahead. It would be another day before they crested them, though then it would be downhill until they reached Vallen. 'It's not going to be easy,' he sighed.

'Easy?'

'Facing everyone.'

Hakon snorted. 'The road to success is paved with failure, Cousin, you know that. We can't expect to stroll through Ottby and into Stornas without any trouble. What's coming will give us an opportunity to gain the upper hand.' His own hands twitched with impatience, wanting to get behind Slussfall's walls, for once he felt safe and protected, he could think of how to attack. 'Once we're home, we'll gather everyone together. Make a real plan.' Ivan looked so uncertain that Hakon burst out laughing. 'It's a good thing for us that I'm the one destined to be king. You look ready to roll over and have your belly scratched! Is that what you'd do? Let Ake scratch your belly before he slit your throat?'

Ivan felt insulted. 'I want Ake dead as much as you, Hakon. You think I want to head back to Slussfall?'

'I think we'll be in Slussfall the day after tomorrow, and everything will be different then.' Hakon bit his teeth together, refusing to speak the words he could hear being screamed in his ears. Refusing to see anything other than victory on the horizon. 'If you can't think of that, think of something else. Like women.' And checking over his shoulder, he saw Falla looking her usual lovely self, chatting with the dreamer and the healer. Frowning suddenly, he turned back to Ivan. 'Whatever happened to the other woman? Alys' friend. What was her name?'

Ivan turned, scanning the columns of horses plodding up the mountain behind them. 'Stina. There was no sign of her. I'll see if I can find her when we stop.'

'Well, if she's run away, where's she going to go? What's she going to do?' Hakon was dismissive, not wanting to waste any time on the woman. He had the one he wanted most of all. And glancing over his shoulder again at Alys, he smiled.

***

Sigurd had worked hard to avoid Ilene since their... encounter.

But stepping out of the hall, he almost banged straight into her. 'Sorry!'

Ilene was pleased to see him, and she smiled, not moving, studying him closely. 'You look better.'

Sigurd grunted, dropping his head, moving past her, hearing her turn after him.

'I haven't seen you since that night. You do remember that night, don't you, Sigurd?'

She had a voice like a cat, sometimes harsh and screeching, other times soft and deep, almost like she was purring. He blinked, remembering the feel of her body beneath his hands. She was rounder, softer, smaller than Tulia had been. His body stirred, making him feel odd. Disloyal. 'I do.' Head up, Sigurd saw his friends in the training ring, eager to get in some practice before they departed for Slussfall. It felt like a long time since he'd used his sword, and he'd missed it. 'I have to go, Ilene. I need to train.'

'Well, perhaps we can train together?' Ilene wasn't about to let him slip away from her that quickly. 'I need to learn all I can before we leave. I'm not experienced. I need someone to help me.'

Sigurd turned to her with a sigh, determined to send her on her way, but she was looking at him with fear in her eyes, and he felt sorry for her.

'Everyone's been too busy repairing the fort, preparing the ships. I haven't known who to ask.' She blinked rapidly, sadness in her voice. 'I don't want to let your brother down. He's asked me to come, but what if I'm not good enough? What if I'm no help at all?'

'Alright,' Sigurd muttered, mouth barely opening. 'I'll help you, Ilene. We can find some practice swords, do some work together, but then I need to train with someone else.' He glanced quickly around the ring, spying Torfinn Bellig, one of his oldest friends. 'I promised Torfinn. He's been waiting for me.'

Ilene saw Torfinn fighting Berger Eivin, both of them red-faced and snarling at each other. 'Is that so?'

'Well, likely he's just finishing with Berger,' Sigurd grumbled, heading for the shed where the practice weapons were stored. 'Come on, then. We'd better make a start. I haven't got all day.'

And trying not to smile, Ilene followed after Sigurd, almost skipping with delight.

CHAPTER TWENTY SIX

Bergit didn't return to the cottage until after dark, much to Ulrick's annoyance. He'd spent the day traipsing around the fort with Lotta, making plans. He found an old trader friend who was heading up to Orvala once he sold his load of pelts and antlers. Ulrick wished he had the coins to buy every last one of them so they could leave right away, but he didn't. Whatever he had was needed to start again up North; to keep them afloat, able to move and adapt; to find shelter and eat; horses and weapons too.

And then there was Bergit, who unpinned her cloak in silence, eyeing the girl as though she had crawled out of the midden pit, covered in slop. 'I didn't want her back.'

Ulrick sighed, wondering how things could have soured so quickly between them. He glanced at Lotta, who shrank away from the fire she'd been warming herself by, eyes on the door. And turning to his seething wife, whose cheeks were flushed a deep pink, he didn't blame her. 'I've found us a ship. Asger Horken's here, full of helpful information about what's been going on up North. He's happy to take us. Day after tomorrow, he said. We just need to pack our things before then.'

Bergit looked even more irate, hands digging into ample hips, coppery eyebrows sharpening. 'I won't go!'

Ulrick stepped around the fire to his wife, reaching a hand up to her face. She had the most beautiful skin, he thought – soft and pillowy – though there was not even a hint of softness about her now. 'We're not safe here. I've heard Hakon's on his way. They didn't take Ottby, which means no Stornas.'

'What? Heard it from who?'

'Scouts,' Ulrick lied. 'Overheard them in the tavern, drinking and talking. Hakon will be here soon, they said, and after I took the girl and abandoned him, he's not going to be happy with me. And if he has a mind to get rid of me, what will happen to you?'

Bergit smacked his hand away, smoothing thick strands of orange hair down over her chest. 'You think I need you, Ulrick Dyre? That I simply sit here while you're away, pining for your return? Helpless to even chop a log of wood or kill a rat? You think I can't light a fire or skin a rabbit?'

'I think there are other ways to need someone. Many more than we can say here.' Ulrick's eyes moved back to Lotta, which only served to further irritate his wife.

Bergit bit her lip, trying to get herself back under control. Screaming and throwing things would hardly improve the situation, or get her what she wanted, which was her husband in her bed and the girl out on the street. 'We can sell her! If we're going to Orbo, we'll need more coins to start again. Many more. We can sell her!'

Ulrick's hopes rose quickly and fell steeply. 'Bergit, you must give it time. And as for Orbo... Asger isn't going to Orbo. He's going to Orvala.'

'*What?*' Now Bergit forgot about the girl entirely. 'But why would you want to go there?'

Ulrick smiled. 'A new lord. And a new lord means new prospects.' Turning, he winked at a terrified-looking Lotta. 'For all of us.'

***

Alys wanted to see her children. It terrified her that she wasn't with them, able to protect them. Somehow, her grandfather and Magnus had ended up in a prison, and Lotta was nowhere to be seen. Flashes of images flickered occasionally, but nothing hung around for long, and Alys felt herself starting to panic as her problems mounted.

Hakon yanked her towards his tent, tearing her away from Ivan, who'd been trying to decide where Alys and Eddeth would sleep now that they were officially prisoners.

'Hakon!' he shouted, annoyed at how rough his cousin was being.

Eddeth looked just as cross, watching Hakon drag Alys into his tent as though she was a carcass he was about to butcher. She started twitching, wondering what they were going to do now. 'Your cousin,' she muttered irritably.

'My cousin?'

'Imprisoning a dreamer? Mistreating her? How does he think that will make the gods change their minds about him? Does he imagine Alys can save him from Thenor's judgement?'

Ivan blinked. 'Can she?'

Eddeth peered at him, conscious of Lief approaching with another man she'd forgotten the name of. 'Well, why would she want to? A brute like that?' And wheeling around, ignoring Ivan entirely, Eddeth peered at the tent, hoping Alys would be alright.

Alys had bitten her tongue as Hakon all but threw her inside his tent. And now she stood by the small fire, enjoying the warmth of the flames, terrified of what would happen next. She kept thinking of Torvig Aleksen, who had raped Stina repeatedly, and would likely have raped her too if she hadn't killed him. But she didn't know how to stop Hakon. She had no sword or knife now, both having been taken from her. She had no weapon at all. And reminded of Ilene, who had viciously punched her in the eye, Alys squeezed her hands into fists.

'Tell me what you've seen today. What you see coming tonight,' Hakon demanded, pulling her towards him. 'Tell me!'

Shouting, yelling, angry men made Alys shake with fear, all thoughts fleeing her mind. 'I... I saw nothing.' It was the truth, but she cringed, sensing Hakon's hand twitch. 'Not yet. I must sleep for dreams to come. I rarely see anything during the day.'

His experience with Mother told Hakon that that was likely true, but it enraged him nonetheless. And dropping Alys' arm, he spun around, eyes on the tent flap. 'Those men out there, my men, they need to see hope. A sign that we're still in the fight. Once you entertain the thought of defeat, you lose your grip on victory. It slips from your grasp.'

Hakon's back was to her, and Alys enjoyed a reprieve from those menacing eyes for a moment. She could hear the fear in his voice now, and it helped relax her.

Hakon turned around, eyes aflame again. 'And today they saw me leading them. I was not defeated or near death. They *saw* me, alive and in command. The Hunter may have sought me out, but they did not see me cower and hide. I still lead my army.' He narrowed his eyes, wanting Alys to read his thoughts. 'I still lead them!' he bellowed.

Alys nodded vigorously. 'You must keep talking,' she suggested. 'To your men. It would help. And...' She didn't want to say it, but gritting her teeth, she carried on. 'You should show them that you have a new dreamer.' Alys forced herself to hold his gaze. 'Show them that you have insight again. A way to see what's coming. It might put your men at ease.'

'Well, not if you can't see anything, Alys. Not if you don't have any dreams,' Hakon grumbled sulkily, eyeing his bed. Rikkard had done an admirable job of setting up his tent, and after a painful day in the saddle, the bed of furs beckoned like a drop of water in a desert. And thinking of deserts led Hakon to the Kalmeran wine waiting for him in Slussfall, and his desire to be home intensified.

As did the burning pain over his heart.

'Perhaps, but if you wish to command what your men are thinking, you must lead them. Not just their bodies, but their minds. You must convince them that you're in control. Assure them with words as well as deeds. Give them the confidence to sleep soundly.' Alys doubted any of that was possible, but Hakon was a desperate man, and a desperate man needed a rope to cling to.

She watched his eyes glisten as he stepped back to her.

'And if something comes for us in the night? Or tomorrow?'

Alys didn't know what to say to that. 'You need your men, and they need you whether something comes tonight or not. You must show them that you'll protect them, like a parent makes a child feel safe. You have to reassure them.'

It made sense to Hakon, and he felt a sense of calm descend upon him, easing his anxiety. The fire helped too, as he listened to the soothing crackle of flames. He took a breath, suddenly seeing Alys with different eyes. She was beautiful, and he felt an overwhelming urge to kiss her.

He took a step closer.

Alys gulped, stepping back. Hakon's eyes had narrowed to slits, the pain in his body seeming to recede enough for him to entertain other thoughts now. 'Your men need to see you, my lord! If they think you've retreated into your tent, perhaps they will start to wonder if you are ill, unwell. If you... have the mark.'

'What?' Hakon grabbed Alys' arms, pulling her close. 'What did you say?'

'The, the...' Alys' tongue tangled with fear. 'The mark. If your men think you're hiding in here, they'll wonder what you're keeping from them.' Now she was speaking quickly, thoughts running like horses. 'You need to be seen out in the camp, before night falls, so they can see that you're unharmed. That there is no mark to hide.'

'Of course there's no mark to hide!' Hakon snorted, worried that the dreamer could see it. He could certainly feel it burning beneath layers of mail and leather and wool like a hot sun. 'There's no mark at all!'

'But your men don't know that. They'll be out there talking and whispering and wondering. You must show them that there is nothing to fear.'

All thoughts of tearing Alys' clothes off were gone in a flash as Hakon straightened up, grabbing the dreamer's hand, leading her out of the tent, knowing that she was right.

***

It was snowing again, and Reinar felt worried as he finished off his fish stew, looking around for Martyn, who had slipped into the kitchen with Bjarni to bring in another barrel of ale. He didn't particularly feel like ale, but the meal had been so salty that he was desperate for something to wash away the taste.

'I think Rilda tipped a bucket of salt into that stew,' Sigurd grumbled beside him, unable to finish his own bowl. He pushed it away, turning to look for Martyn and Bjarni himself.

'It's not Rilda,' Gerda sighed, feeling just as displeased. 'She broke her ankle.'

'Oh.' Both Reinar and Sigurd looked worried, having loved Rilda's cooking since they were boys. 'Well, who made the stew, then?'

'Rilda's niece, Fenna. Though she's not the cook her aunt is, that's for sure. We'll have to bring in a chair so Rilda can cook sitting down.'

'Or perhaps we just take away the salt?' Reinar grinned. 'The stew's probably edible under all that salt.'

Sigurd doubted that was true, but his attention was drawn away from the subject of salty stews to the odd coupling of Ilene and Elin on the other side of the hall, where they sat together, occasionally looking their way. He turned to his brother with a frown. 'What do you think that's about, then?' And inclining his head to the two women, he was pleased to hear the cheer go up as Bjarni and Martyn came out of the kitchen bearing freshly topped up jugs of ale.

Reinar followed Sigurd's gaze. 'Ilene's been alone since the Ullaberg women left. Elin felt sorry for her. She wants to get to know her, make her feel comfortable. At home.'

Sigurd snorted, his time training Ilene not softening his feelings towards her at all. She was too eager for his company, always looking his way, a constant reminder of what he'd done. 'You're making a mistake bringing her along, Brother. We're not desperate anymore. We've Ake's men, the new Slussfall men, why do we need her?'

'I'm not bringing her along to irritate you, I promise,' Reinar smiled, patting his brother on the back. 'She's decided to stay in Ottby, and she's a promising warrior, so why would I leave her behind?'

'Because she's a scheming troublemaker. A husband stealer. That's what Alys said.'

The mention of Alys' name was enough to wipe the smile off Reinar's face. 'Well, that's one way to look at things, I suppose. But any man idiot enough to ruin things with his wife by humping Ilene was asking for trouble in the first place. They can't just blame Ilene for the mess they made.'

Sigurd felt the tip of that spear coming for him, and he ignored it, lifting his empty cup to Martyn, trying to avoid looking Ilene's way.

Ilene could tell, though after their training match, she was feeling confident, knowing that it wouldn't take much to bring Sigurd around. She eyed Berger Eivin, who hadn't stopped staring at her since she'd arrived. He was a handsome, powerful-looking man, but no lord's brother.

Still, perhaps he could help her capture one?

'And this woman, the dreamer?' Elin wondered from her right, voice low, eyes on her husband, who was banging cups with Bjarni. 'What do you know of her? The one who lived in the dreamer's cottage for a time? She left before I returned.'

Ilene's eyes were drawn back to the Lady of Ottby, hearing the interest in her voice, sensing her desperation. She smiled. 'Oh, I know many things about Alys de Sant. Many things indeed. I'd be happy to tell you all about her.'

***

337

Alys quickly regretted her suggestion that Hakon present her to his warriors as some sort of prize. She felt foolish standing next to him, face burning with embarrassment, listening to the stews sucking in blackened cauldrons, hanging over fires that smoked and spat. It was raining, a light pattering, but enough to have them all shivering, edging as close to the flames as possible. Hakon stood on a boulder, shoulders back, head high, announcing to all the world that she was his new dreamer.

Alys could see Eddeth picking her wart, Ivan glowering beside her. And growing more uncomfortable by the moment, she turned her head, eyes drifting towards the trees, listening. Not to the bellowing lord, whose voice sometimes tremored as though he was in pain. Alys could hear it. She could see glimpses of his chest and his mark in her mind, and then she saw something more; deeper, deep inside Hakon's memories.

'Mirella, this is Hakon. My son with Arina.'

The woman glared at the man, jealousy flaring in green eyes. She was attractive, young. Golden hair hung past her breasts, strands at the sides of her face twisted into braids, pulled away from high cheekbones. She looked at the man with both love and hate, as though she couldn't decide which she felt more acutely. 'Well, you always wanted a son, Jesper. And now you have one.'

The boy was not quite a year old, Alys thought. He squirmed in his father's arms, almost fighting to get away from him.

'I always wanted a son with you, you know that, but what choice did I have? When you left me, what choice did I have, Mirella, but to find someone else?'

Alys blinked as Hakon tugged her closer, wanting to show her off. She could hear him talking to her, though her mind was trapped in two places and she wanted to stay in the vision.

It was important, somehow.

'Alys, tell my men what you've seen! Tell them of the victory that awaits us all!'

But Alys couldn't speak as the vision slipped away from her.

Mirella.

It was her mother's name.

***

Jonas had turned their horrific supper into a fun game as they all tried to guess what it had been. Leonid was almost smiling as he decided it was rats. That the cooks had chopped up rats and flavoured them with mushrooms. Mushrooms and a little thyme, he added with a flourish.

Jonas laughed, which did nothing to distract him from the foul taste in his mouth, but he could see that Magnus appeared more alert, so he kept the game going. 'Perhaps a little piss too?'

Magnus gagged. 'Yuck! Don't say that, Grandfather. Now it's all I can think about!'

Leonid smiled. 'I wouldn't put it past them. And besides, there's worse things than piss to be flavouring that stew.'

All three faces screwed up then.

'Shut up!' came a growl from the corner. 'Or maybe I'll cut you up into little pieces, and they can add you to tomorrow's slop!'

Leonid and Magnus looked worried, but Jonas laughed again, not minding the grumblings of that angry lump in the corner. The man sounded like death was coming for him; he wouldn't trouble them for long.

'I think whatever it was, it's stuck in my throat,' Magnus croaked. 'I wish we had something to drink.'

'Mmmm, I couldn't agree more.' So struggling to his feet with a groan, Jonas headed to the door, banging on it. 'We need some water in here!' he called. 'You need to give us some water!'

He aimed to make a lot of noise, hoping to attract the attention of a guard, wanting to get a message to Ollo, who would hopefully get a message to Vik. He'd had an idea for how they could get out, though it would only work if he could get Ollo's help.

But it wasn't Ollo who came to the door, opening up the little flap, peering through the hole. It wasn't even Ollo's man, Elmar, who had tried to get Magnus out of the fort, but it was someone Jonas knew.

Haegel Hedvik.

Jonas didn't register any recognition in his voice at first. He knew Haegel was Ollo's errand boy. They'd betrayed Sirrus together, with plenty of help it seemed judging by the number of familiar faces he'd seen around the old fort. 'We need water. Preferably some ale. I'd take some milk for the boy, if you've got any? After the turds you served for supper, we need something to wash it away.'

Haegel's eyes darted about nervously as Jonas stepped closer to the bars, grabbing them.

'Get word to Ollo,' he hissed. 'I need to talk to him.'

'He won't come. He can't. Ulrick Dyre made a big fuss. Ruined everything. He has to stay clear now, but don't worry, he sent me to Vik. We've talked.'

Jonas looked surprised, and then hopeful. He raised his voice again, turning around. 'What do you mean I'm not in a tavern?' he joked loudly, before leaning forward, lowering his voice to barely a breath. 'I know how to get us out. Something an old dreamer showed me once.' And curling a frozen finger in Haegel's direction, he urged him to come closer.

***

Alys hadn't been able to stomach any supper, no matter how much Eddeth insisted that she needed to keep up her strength. Her mind was fixed on the vision of the woman and the memory of her name.

Jesper Vettel had called her Mirella.

Perhaps it was merely a coincidence? Nothing to do with her mother at all?

Having decided that Alys' problem with the stew was its bland taste, Eddeth had gone hunting through her saddlebags, watched closely by one of Hakon's men. And returning to the fire, she handed Alys an apple. 'I packed this away for our ride. For Wilf. But you can have it.'

Alys shook her head. 'I'm honestly not hungry, Eddeth. Give it to Wilf.'

'But how will you sleep if you're starving? And how will you dream if you can't sleep?'

Alys thought back to her vision. She shrugged. 'I see things sometimes without being asleep.'

Eddeth knew that. 'But still, you promised that angry lord some dreams. If you don't give him any, what will he do?'

That was a good question.

'I've found you somewhere to sleep!' Ivan announced with a grin, pleased to have convinced Hakon not to keep Alys in his tent, which he had been floating as an option. His cousin, feeling better, had become far too interested in the dreamer, and Ivan was growing concerned for her safety. 'Falla said you can sleep in her tent. She's sent Lief to sleep elsewhere.' Ivan couldn't help but smile, imagining how Lief felt about that.

Alys looked relieved, smiling at Eddeth. 'Both of us?'

Ivan nodded. 'I'll take you now, if you like? You should get settled early, I think, before there's any... trouble.'

'Trouble?'

'Well, the way things are going, I expect we'll be trampled on by ice giants tonight. Or burned alive by dragons! What do you think?' Ivan was grinning, but he felt ill, not having been so terrified of the dark since he was a boy. 'And besides, best you hide from Hakon. He's had a lot of ale. Don't know where Rikkard found it all. Though, I think we're all on edge, aren't we? It's one way to deal with things.'

'It is,' Eddeth agreed, remembering her second husband. 'But it's hardly going to convince Thenor to change his mind, is it? Becoming a drunk? Yelling at everyone?' She was tired, feeling oddly irritable. Eager to get to Falla's tent.

Ivan shivered, ushering Alys and Eddeth away from the fire, thinking of his chamber in Slussfall's hall; the tapestry draped walls and the comfortable bed and the pleasure of shutting the door and being alone. Alone, or with an accommodating woman, hungry for his attention because he was the lord's cousin.

Knowing that whatever was coming for his cousin next would likely come for him too.

CHAPTER TWENTY SEVEN

'Is something wrong?' Elin whispered, hand on Reinar's naked chest. 'You're very quiet.'

'I've a lot on my mind, I suppose,' Reinar sighed. 'I can't let Ake down. I have to see to the Vettels, but I don't want to leave Ottby weak. More enemies are lurking out there than just the Vettels now, and they all seem to want the same thing.'

'Which is?'

'Alekka's throne. The Vettels clung to it for four hundred years, and now they want it back, but if not them, it would be someone else. Ake's dreamer sees trouble coming. Everywhere we turn, trouble's waiting for us all.'

'That sounds worrying.'

'It does, but we can fight back, attack before we have to defend. We can keep them out of Ottby, don't worry. Stornas too.'

'Maybe you shouldn't have let your dreamer go?' Elin murmured, feeling Reinar freeze beneath her hand. 'Though, according to Ilene, she had somewhere to be.'

'Ilene? You don't want to be gossiping with Ilene. She doesn't have a good word to say about most people.'

'Gossiping?' Elin snorted. 'Why are women always gossiping, yet men are talking? Hmmm?'

There was a flicker of humour in her voice, and Reinar smiled, though his thoughts had quickly turned to Alys, and he couldn't shake the worry he felt, not knowing where she was or if she was safe.

Realising that her husband's attention had wandered far away from her, Elin sought to bring it back, running her hand over his chest, down his leg.

Reinar closed his eyes, enjoying her touch, trying to relax.

'What's wrong?' she soothed. 'Something is. Something I've done?'

'Done?' Reinar turned to her. 'I...' He couldn't find the right words. She was grieving, and he didn't want to make her feel even worse.

'I left you, so I don't expect you to be happy with me. Perhaps you didn't want me to come home? Perhaps you met someone new? Hoped I wouldn't return?' Elin shifted away from him, moving to the edge of the bed.

Reinar spluttered. 'No, it's not that. Nothing like that.' Guilt tormented him, but Reinar didn't want to hurt her with the truth. He wasn't sure he even knew what the truth was anymore. 'It was... I didn't know why you'd left. I thought you were dead. In my heart, I feared that was the truth. There were whispers about why you'd gone, and what you'd done to yourself, even from those who knew you best.'

'You mean Agnette?'

Her voice was sharp, and Reinar blinked, not wanting to get Agnette in trouble. 'She helped you leave, I know, but she was worried about what you might do if you didn't go. She loves you, Elin. We all do.'

Elin sank back against the pillow, squashing it into a more accommodating shape, angry at Agnette for being such a busy body. She'd been the same since they were children, always unable to keep her big mouth shut.

Reinar waited for Elin to say something, but she didn't, and eventually, he rolled onto his side with a sigh, listening to the sound of the rain hammering the window.

***

Ollo and Haegel crouched over a table that was barely wider than a man. The tavern was packed on account of the snow coming down like a blizzard. Within moments, no one had been able to see a thing, and giving up on the day's trading, they'd decided to spend their coins on ale, and a chance to enjoy a warm fire and some good company. Though Slussfall's tavern was such a small, narrow building that there wasn't enough space for every man and woman who wanted to get inside, and even now, Ollo could see the door jerk forward as another cold body tried to squeeze in.

'But where are we going to find the herbs? *How?*' Ollo certainly wanted the rest of Jonas' silver, but he wasn't convinced that his plan was worth the effort.

'Mora might know. Or Eldrid Vissel. There's a few women we can ask. There's many we can trust. You know that, Ollo.'

Ollo dug a filthy nail between his front teeth, trying to free a piece of mutton. 'I know many things, Haegel Hedvik, and what I know most of all is that you're far too trusting for your own good. You think we just ask around, get more people in on this, and then what do we have on our hands? A cauldron full of greedy sods, all with their hands out, wanting their share. I've already promised Elmar something for trying to get that boy out, and then there's you, and now you want to invite more?'

Haegel cradled his empty cup, wishing Ollo would buy another jug of ale. 'I just don't see how we find the herbs on our own.'

Ollo laughed. 'We ask! We don't need to say why, do we? We simply ask. Some woman will know.'

'But then how will we make it?' Haegel leaned forward. 'The drink?'

'I'll get the lovely Mora to do it. She might even know where to find the herbs herself, don't you worry. Then we'll make up a drink and serve it to those guards.' Ollo realised that he'd had too much ale and hadn't lowered his voice at all. He bent forward until his big forehead was almost touching Haegel's. 'And then they'll go to sleep, and you'll get those gates open.'

'Me?' Haegel wasn't sure that's how it should go.

'Of course you, you blithering fool. I need to stay out of it, don't I? Ulrick coming back's ruined all our plans. He'll spot something for sure. Got eyes like a hawk, that one. Always watching, waiting to strike.'

Haegel wasn't convinced that was Ollo's real reason, but he didn't argue further. 'And when the gates are open?'

'When the gates are open, that's when the fun begins!'

***

Alys had tried to find her way back into the vision of the woman called Mirella. And then she'd stopped, knowing that it wasn't something Hakon would care to hear about in the morning. She had to find something to tell him. She didn't want to help him, but if she didn't please him with some useful tidbit, she worried what he might do to her. He needed her, so he wouldn't kill her, but the fear of being raped loomed large, especially after what had happened to poor Stina. Stina, who hadn't looked like herself since. Perhaps she never would, Alys thought with a sigh, hoping her friend was safe, wherever she was.

'Still your mind now, dreamer,' Eddeth murmured beside her. 'No chance of any sleep while your thoughts are charging around like angry trolls. Even I can hear them!'

They were lying on the ground together, Falla further away, snoring lightly, mouth wide open. And though neither woman trusted her, they felt grateful to her for inviting them into her shelter, far away from Hakon and his men.

'Go to sleep now, Alys,' Eddeth yawned. 'Go and find a dream.'

***

Hakon lay on his mound of furs, comfortable and uncomfortable all at the same time. His belly wound was healing, he knew, because he could barely feel it. Or was that because the agony of the mark was so overwhelming that it was almost the only sensation Hakon could experience now?

He closed his eyes tighter, impatient to fall asleep.

Rikkard lay on the ground in the corner, muttering to himself. He was an irritating companion, at times, Hakon thought distractedly, remembering Njall, whose head had been hacked off by one of The Hunter's shadow riders. And just thinking about The Hunter had Hakon shaking.

He remembered being a child, his stepmother leaning over his bed, whispering a story in his ear, not wanting to wake up Ivan, who lay fast asleep beside him. She would tell him about Thenor, the mightiest god of all, and how much he wanted to see the Vettel family returned to the throne. Hakon had always heard doubt in her voice, perhaps sadness too. He thought it was because she worried. Because she hated to see Jesper always going off to war, and eventually, taking his son and nephew with him. But maybe it was more? Maybe she knew that Thenor had never favoured them at all?

And mind racing with worry now, Hakon placed a hand on his chest, feeling the throbbing heat beneath his palm.

***

Lotta looked sad.

She was humming to herself as she stood on the pier watching the men ready the ship. The harbour was misty, the men's breath streaming before them. Red hands worked quickly, wanting to be underway before the weather worsened. And by the grim look of the clouds crowding together in the distance, soon it would.

'Princess!'

Alys watched her daughter turn towards the voice, her shoulders slumping, though her boots remained in place, firmly pressed together on the boards of the pier, not moving.

Alys stood on the opposite pier, a tear rolling down her right cheek. It felt cold on her skin. She lifted her hand, reaching out to her daughter. 'Lotta! I'm here! Can you see me?' Her voice was reed-thin, whipped away by the wind. 'Lotta!' Lotta looked around, staring at her, and Alys shivered, seeing no light in her eyes at all.

'Don't come to Slussfall, Mama. Whatever you do, don't come to Slussfall.'

'Princess!'

Alys frowned, hearing that man's voice again, then seeing him as he approached, thick cloak billowing around him, long beard flapping.

'We're ready for you now.'

'Lotta, no!' Alys cried. 'I'm coming for you! Wait, please, wait for me!'

But clasping the man's hand, Lotta turned after him, not even looking her way. And though she was leaving, walking towards the ship, her little head turned down to her boots, Alys could hear her voice like a bell ringing inside her head. 'Don't come to Slussfall, Mama. Please!'

***

After a disturbed night of odd dreams, Reinar woke with a thumping headache and a silent wife, and he spent the morning barking at everyone, not feeling like himself at all. But seeing Sigurd, who was trying his best not to look as miserable as he felt, he took a deep breath, trying to calm down. 'What's that?' he asked, eyes on the enormous mound of cloth his brother had carried down to the piers. 'A new sail?'

Sigurd shook his head. 'Old sailcloth for shelter. I've got three. Agnette's organising more. Weather's only going to get worse. No point freezing to death before we have any fun!'

Reinar nodded, pleased to know that Agnette was busy fussing, despite the added distraction of her infant daughter. He grinned at Bolli, who stood between him and Bjarni, muttering away as they checked on the progress of one of their oldest ships, *Long Serpent*. Bolli had had a crew of five men caulking it, and they'd just slid her back into the water. 'Better?'

'Better, but she won't take much of a beating nonetheless. Those sides weren't built high enough. One big wave and she'll be foundering.'

'Well, I hope not, but we'll put Sigurd on her, just in case.'

'Ha, not likely. I'll be on *Dagger* as always. Ludo's coming with me.'

'And you?' Bjarni yawned, eyeing Reinar. 'Who will you take on *Fury*?'

'You, I suppose,' Reinar decided. 'For who else could put up with your snoring?'

Bjarni tried to look insulted, though, according to everyone who knew him, there was no louder snorer in Ottby.

'And Ilene?' Bolli wondered with a wink at Sigurd, who glowered at him.

'Best if Ilene sails on *Fury* with me so I can keep an eye on her. Unless you want her with you, Brother? I'm sure she wouldn't mind.' It wasn't nice to make fun of the bereaved, Reinar knew, but he wanted to see some life in Sigurd's eyes, and poking fun at each other was something that came without much thought.

'No thanks, you're welcome to her. Besides, I'm sure Elin would enjoy the company.'

That had Reinar frowning again, remembering their argument.

Not really an argument, he knew, but still, he'd have to make things right before they left for Slussfall.

'And you're sure we'll be ready?' Bjarni asked. 'That the fort will be ready?' He was feeling on edge, not imagining how he could leave Agnette and Liara behind; gripped by an overwhelming need to make sure they were safe.

'Gates are on now,' Reinar said, gnawing a toothpick. 'That's the main thing. The walls will take longer. But I can't think who else would want to attack us now. Our enemy's waiting for us in Slussfall. We'll get the place secure, don't worry. And then we'll go kill those Vettels.'

***

Vik stood at the back of the long train of traders and farmers waiting to get into the fort. He caught a glimpse of Haegel, winding his way through the half-frozen men and women, doing his best to blend in and failing miserably. Skittish and nervous, he kept glancing around, looking like a thief.

Rolling his eyes, and not wanting to draw any attention to himself, Vik turned and headed to the back of the line, knowing that the guards' attention was mainly on the front, where they were questioning the traders and inspecting their goods.

'You're keen for trouble.'

Haegel shuddered as a gust of wind blew his hood down over his face. Flustered, he pushed it back up, staring at Vik, who held his own hood low, not wanting to show his face. 'I'm not, not at all. Ollo sent me.' He stooped, squatting slightly, not wanting anyone to hear. 'We've got a plan.'

'Is that so? Ollo's plan, is it?'

'No, it's Jonas'.'

That had Vik alert and ready to learn more. He motioned for two young women to go ahead of them, then leaned into Haegel. 'Tell me.'

'We're going to put the guards to sleep, then I'll open the gates, let you in, and you'll head for the hole. Elmar will be there. He'll unlock the door, and you'll take Jonas and the boy and slip out through the gates. I'll come with you to collect the silver.'

Vik scowled. 'Won't work. The other prisoners will shout out. They won't want to be left behind. And we can't afford to let them out too. They'll make a noise, a fuss. I won't be able to sneak out.'

Haegel picked his nose.

'How will you put the guards to sleep?'

'Jonas told me about some herbs. Said his wife had used them once. He reckons they can knock you out for hours.'

'Oh?' Vik trusted Jonas, but he didn't trust Haegel or Ollo to execute the plan with any competence. 'And how will you find these herbs? Do they grow around here? In this weather?'

Haegel shrugged. 'I hope so. Ollo knows a woman who's friends with Hakon's cook. She knows the old healer too, though she's mostly blind and deaf, so I'm not sure what help she can be.'

The line was moving quickly now, and Vik once again hopped out of it, moving Haegel to the back. 'Doesn't sound very promising.'

'It does. Don't worry, it does. Be waiting here again tomorrow, and I'll let you know if we've had any luck.'

Vik sighed, feeling impatient. 'I don't like the idea of them being in that hole. Jonas can take it, I know, but Magnus, he's just a boy.'

'Well, I...' Haegel didn't know what to say. 'I... I'll check on them, see how they're faring. Don't worry, I'll see how they are.'

Vik narrowed his eyes, peering up at the nervous man. 'Suddenly very helpful, aren't you, Haegel Hedvik? Is that because of Ollo? The silver? Or are you really looking to redeem yourself?'

Haegel dropped his head. 'All of the above, I think, Vik,' he admitted with a sigh. 'We're not sure we want to stay in Slussfall anymore, if you want to know the truth. Hakon Vettel's a miserable lord. Treats us all like dogs or slaves. Both mostly. Sirrus was a far better lord, a better man, though we can't go back now. Can't undo what was done. But some silver will give me another chance.'

'If Ollo shares any with you.'

'Well, he'll just have to. I've always been loyal to him. He'll just have to.'

Vik sighed, not liking relying on fools and traitors, but knowing that if he wanted to get Jonas and Magnus out of that hole and find a way to free Lotta, he had little choice.

***

Lotta had seen her mother in her dreams. It upset her, and she couldn't face her breakfast, feeling worried and nauseous all at the same time.

Ulrick tried to get her to have a bite of a flatbread, but she didn't want anything. Sitting opposite Bergit didn't help. The woman kept glaring at her, and Lotta could hear her angry thoughts shouting at her. She disliked children so intensely that Lotta wondered how Ulrick had ever thought that she wanted another.

'I'll take Lotta to the market, see what we can find for our journey,' Ulrick decided, smiling at his wife, who glared at him.

'*You*? You think you're the best judge of what we need?' Bergit grouched, her eyes back on Lotta, cold and unfeeling.

'So you're offering to accompany us, then?'

Bergit tipped back a cup of watery ale, sniffing. 'I suppose I am. Only way I can think of to stop you wasting whatever coins we have left. Hakon Vettel owes you a chest full after all you've done to keep him safe! Him and his father both!'

Ulrick nodded to please his wife, biting his tongue, not wanting to remind her that Jesper Vettel had lost his head, and according to Lotta, Hakon had lost his battle to take Ottby. He'd hardly done much of a job keeping either of them safe. 'Well, don't worry, once we get up to Orvala, we'll start again with Tarl Brava. He's a man worth fighting for.'

Bergit didn't look so sure.

Lotta felt terrified by the thought of travelling that far north, so far away from her family. And though the memory of her mother's face tugged at her broken heart, and the thought of her brother and Jonas trapped in that prison hole made her sick with worry, she knew that she had to leave Slussfall before it was too late.

CHAPTER TWENTY EIGHT

Jonas tried to smile for Magnus and Leonid, who were becoming increasingly morbid, though he couldn't stop kicking himself for his foolish decision to let Magnus go into the fort on his own. He wondered what Alys thought if she saw them in her dreams. Or Eida. Gripping the frozen bars with frozen hands, he stared out into the square. Trade had slowed as the afternoon progressed, hampered by heavy snow, and there was nothing much to see, though he preferred to stare out into the snow rather than look back into the bleak, soul-crushing darkness inside the stinking hole.

He nudged Magnus, who stood on the bucket in between him and Leonid, who was sighing painfully, stomach growling. It was hard to be so hungry and cold, Jonas thought with a yawn.

'Lotta!' Magnus cried suddenly, pointing to the familiar figure walking towards them, holding Ulrick Dyre's hand.

Jonas froze, staring at the little girl, who looked so much like Alys as a child that he felt tears coming. Ulrick pulled her away, and she was quickly lost behind a huddle of cloaks. Jonas scowled, wondering how it was possible to have so much bad luck.

How had Lotta ended up with that old warrior?

Vicious, heartless, hard as nails Ulrick Dyre.

'Lotta!' Magnus shouted, pushing his head against the bars, hand extended. 'Lotta!'

Lotta could feel the pressure of Ulrick's hand squeezing hers, and she didn't even turn her head towards her brother's voice. She knew he was there. She'd seen him as she walked into the square, but she couldn't bring herself to feel anything. It wouldn't help.

'What about this?' Ulrick suggested, inclining his head to a furry hat. 'Looks warm!'

'That's a man's hat,' Bergit grumbled. 'Hardly the right size for a scrawny child.'

Ulrick kept smiling, ignoring his wife's snarl. She was already coming around, he knew. The fact that she was there, walking the market with them told him as much. And soon they'd be on Asger's ship, sailing far away from Slussfall, and that bracing sea breeze would clear her mind. She would feel differently once they were away from the old fort.

'Lotta!'

Lotta ducked her head, staring down at her snow-covered boots. The snow had been cleared earlier, but her tiny boots were already buried up to her ankles.

'Who's that screaming boy?' Bergit grumbled. 'How does he know the girl?'

Ulrick didn't want to say. He shrugged. 'Lotta's a common name. Probably calling for his mother.'

Bergit wasn't a fool. 'I've never heard that name before. And certainly not in Slussfall. Seems to me there's more to this story, *Husband*, and if you want me on that ship with you tomorrow, you'd better tell me all of it.'

Ulrick let go of Lotta's hand, watching as she approached the fur trader, who held the hat out to her. It was far too big, but she wanted to pull it over her frozen ears, so taking it, Lotta dropped her hood, slipping it over her head. She instantly felt warmer. The afternoon breeze was intensifying, her cloak fluttering around her legs, and the wind had her ears aching, but suddenly, with the thick hat on her head, she couldn't hear the wind at all. She couldn't hear Bergit and Ulrick arguing beside her.

But she could still hear her brother calling for her.

Magnus sighed, giving up. 'She won't even look my way. She can hear me, I know she can!'

Jonas frowned. Lotta didn't appear under any duress. She stood alone, trying on hats as though she was with her mother and father. Not two strangers, one of whom had kidnapped her.

It didn't make any sense.

'Silver Tooth said his wife was a witch.'

'What? A witch?'

'That's what he said. Maybe she's done something to Lotta? Bewitched her!'

Jonas shivered, brow furrowed. 'I don't think that can be true, Magnus.' Though there was doubt in his voice, and his memories were stirring, shaking off decades of dust. 'I don't think that can be true...'

***

Reinar grabbed Gerda, pulling her out of the way as Bjarni's two old hounds chased Winter across the square. He was on his way to find Elin and make everything right, but the sight of that white cat had him doubting himself once more. 'You should watch where you're going, Mother!'

Gerda was surprised by the anger in his voice. 'And you should get some more sleep, my son!' And readjusting her cloak, she strode away from him, on her way to find where Martyn had taken Stellan.

Reinar sighed, though it did not relieve any tension in his body as he headed for Elin and Agnette, who were walking across the square.

'Perhaps you should be in the training ring?' Agnette grinned at Elin. She was exhausted, convinced that her daughter had her day and night upside down, for she was sound asleep in her arms once again, looking for all the world as though nothing was going to wake her up. 'You might need to know how to use a sword soon.'

Elin glanced over to where Sigurd was fighting Berger Eivin, who was mud-covered and growling, with a thick lip where Sigurd had punched him. Ilene leaned over the rails watching them, cheering Sigurd on, though he didn't look enthused about it. 'Reinar showed me how to use a sword a few times, but I was mostly useless. You must remember that?'

'I do. And a bow. You were useless with that too.'

Elin laughed. 'So I think I'll be the bandage wrapper and the wound stitcher.'

Agnette looked worried. 'I hope there won't be many of those.'

'Many of what?' Reinar wondered, stopping before them.

'Wounds,' Agnette said, staring at her cousin, who was staring at Elin as though something was wrong. 'Well, I think it's time for this one to have another feed. If I can wake her up!' No one said anything, or even looked her way, so Agnette disappeared, leaving Reinar and Elin alone.

Reinar sighed. 'I don't want to fight. There's too much to do and no point to it anyway.' He reached out for Elin's hands.

She gave them to him reluctantly, looking up at her towering husband. 'Is that what we're doing? Fighting?'

'Depends, doesn't it? I hope not. I just want things to go back to the way they were. To before you left.'

'Well, I'm not sure that's possible, Reinar. Things change. People change. Time makes it so.'

It wasn't going as he'd hoped, and hearing a scream of pain from his brother behind him, Reinar felt the urge to get moving, though it was going to be impossible to focus on anything while Elin was mad at him. 'I agree. Time changes us, but why not think about it in a good way? That time apart showed us both what we had? What we missed?'

Elin could hear impatience in his voice, but gentleness too, and she squeezed his hands. 'I hope that's true. I missed this place. I missed you too.'

Reinar smiled as she stepped closer, tilting her chin in that way that invited him to kiss her, and leaning forward, he did.

***

They were getting closer to Slussfall, and Hakon felt a lift, despite the heavy snow slowing them down.

He'd sent Ivan to ride further back, ignoring the rest of his men, inviting only Alys' company. 'Tell me what you dreamed of last night. And today. Have you had any visions today?'

Alys was starting to feel like a chicken, required to lay eggs daily. The pressure was becoming intense, but she nodded. 'The Vilanders are coming to attack you. At Slussfall.' She saw Reinar's face and blinked it away.

Hakon shivered. 'Coming? You mean following us?'

Alys shook her head. 'No. They were down at the harbour, preparing their ships.'

Hakon ran a gloved hand over his face. 'And how many do they have?'

'Perhaps twenty? Or thirty? I'm not sure, but there were more than I remember seeing before. And more men. Ake's men.' Alys couldn't lie because she had to keep herself safe. She had to get to Slussfall and save Jonas and the children.

Hakon looked worried and pleased and irritated all at once. He welcomed an attack on Slussfall. It would be a chance to rewrite his story. A victory over the Vilanders would change everything. Thenor couldn't fail to be impressed by a crushing defeat of Ake Bluefinn's men. He felt his chest burning, and reminded of what was at stake, he pressed Alys further. 'And what do you see of our chances?'

The weather was disintegrating, her ears aching with cold, and Alys wanted to disappear under her hood. 'I only saw Ottby. I haven't seen anything of the battle yet.'

'But you will, won't you, Alys? You will think on it and dream on it, and tell me everything you see because I need to know. I need to know every way I can defend us from our enemy. Every way I can defeat them!' Hakon was frozen to the bone, and despite the heat of his mark, he shook as the snow pounded them both. He could just make out Alys' eyes beneath her billowing hood and her blowing hair, and he felt a lift, convinced that the gods were trying to help him.

They'd sent him a healer, who had saved his life, and a dreamer, who would keep him one step ahead of the Vilanders.

And smiling, he nudged his horse on.

Ivan watched them, trying to keep the snow out of his mouth.

Eddeth rode beside him, eyes alert, barely bothered by the weather.

'Do you think the gods sent the vatyr and The Hunter?' Ivan wondered. 'To kill us?'

Eddeth laughed. 'Of course! Of course they did! You think they just wanted to play? To have a little fun? No, they were evil spirits, trying to take our lives! Did you not see all the bodies, Ivan Vettel? The heads?'

Ivan peered at her. Eddeth looked almost cheerful. Her hair blew about like a grey bush on top of her head, though she'd felt no need to put up her hood. Her old horse appeared far more miserable in the conditions than his rider, almost curling over as he pushed on through the wind-swept trees. 'But you're not a dreamer?'

Eddeth grinned, showing her teeth. 'Well, I'm beginning to wonder, aren't you? Though I think your cousin seems to prefer having Alys for company.' She laughed, then frowned, worried for the dreamer. Hakon Vettel appeared to be unravelling, and she feared what he would do next. 'Your cousin is in danger, and because you're his blood, so are you.'

'Danger?'

'From the Vilanders, the gods, their creatures! You must be watchful, Ivan. Your cousin will keep Alys by his side, wanting her to help him, but you?' Hood flapping against the back of her head, cloak rising all around her, Eddeth appeared nonplussed, nudging Wilf closer to Ivan's horse. 'He wants to live, and he'll do anything to save himself, but would he care to save you?' Eddeth looked away, squinting into the snow.

Ivan sneezed, shivering so intensely that he wasn't sure he could stop.

***

Ulrick had bumped into his helmsman friend outside the tavern, and the two men now stood drinking around a brazier with a group of old warriors they all appeared to know. There wasn't enough room inside, though the taverner was happy to supply more ale to his customers, so he'd brought out a few braziers and empty barrels to use as tables, and despite the blizzard, business was booming.

Bergit had no intention of being stuck listening to those drunk old men telling stories she'd heard too many times, so she'd taken Lotta back to the cottage. Ulrick felt concerned about leaving Lotta with her, but Bergit had assured him that she no longer wanted to throw the girl out.

What she wanted was information.

'We have a lot of packing to do, and, typically, for my husband, little time in which to do it!' Bergit grumbled, eyes on Lotta, who stood by the bedchamber door, not knowing where to look.

'I can help,' she tried.

Bergit hated the sound of her whiny little voice. 'No need,' she smiled tightly. 'You just stay where you are. I'll get everything ready, and then I'll think of supper.'

Lotta nodded, though she felt awkward just standing there. Her mother had made her and Magnus help with the chores. There was always so much to do, and no time to sit around. Mostly, she hadn't minded helping, but sometimes she'd wanted to stay in bed or play with her friends. Lotta wrinkled her nose, knowing it was probably more than just sometimes.

'And who was that boy?' Bergit wondered lightly, on her hands and knees, wiping the inside of her wooden chest with a cloth. Ulrick had told her some tale that made no sense, and not one that revealed the truth, she was sure. 'The one calling out to you from the hole?'

Lotta tried to hide her face.

'Someone, I'd say. Someone who knows you.'

Lotta knew that lying would likely get her a slap. In fact, she could read Bergit's thoughts, and lying would most certainly get her a slap. 'My brother.'

Now Bergit's eyes were wide with surprise. 'Your brother's here? How is your brother here? Where did he come from? Where did you come from?' Cloth still in her hand, she motioned for Lotta to come closer. 'Sit here, take that stool.' And when Lotta had made herself comfortable, Bergit took a seat before her, quickly glancing at the door. 'Now, tell me, how did you really come to be with my husband? And how did your brother come to be here, locked in that hole?'

***

Karolina sat in Hakon's chair, perched upon a fur-covered dais, growing nervous. Her servant stood beside her with Anders in her arms, and Karolina was suddenly aware of how urgently Anders needed to be changed.

The smell was eye-watering.

'My lady?' Baldur was growing impatient, watching as Karolina's attention kept wandering. It was like talking to a child. He clenched his jaw, trying to smile.

'I'm not sure why it needs to be decided now,' Karolina sighed. 'Why not wait until my husband returns?' She felt indecisive, uncomfortable making such important decisions without knowing what Hakon would want her to do.

'But my lady, the hole is filling up fast. We've had two murders in the past three days. Ollo's caught another three thieves. There's been a rape, and Botil Skarby stole Ragna Boden's cow! The people are growing restless. I've had nothing but complaints about Jonas Bergstrom. There are many who want his head off now.'

Karolina squirmed. 'It's my husband's place to choose the punishment for those men,' she decided. 'Not mine. I will not put anyone to death. I will not decide their fate.' She felt ill at the thought of it.

'But the people, my lady,' Baldur pressed. He had small eyes, bags of pink skin protruding beneath them. He was a man who slept little, always alert to what was happening in the fort, and he could sense tension growing. The mumbled conversations in the tavern and around the metalworker's huts were bleeding out into the square now, and he was growing worried. 'The people want Jonas Bergstrom's blood. Him and his ilk are responsible for killing men they know. Fathers and brothers. Sons too. They'll only grow more restless if nothing's done. The longer that man sits in the hole, the more trouble those agitators will stir.'

Karolina had heard some disturbances herself, and glancing at her son, she grew worried. 'But what did he actually do? Why would you want to kill him?'

Baldur Skoggi didn't roll his eyes, though he very much wanted to. 'Jonas Bergstrom is one of Ake's men, my lady. He was in Stornas when Jorek Vettel was ripped from the throne. He's been killing Vettel men for decades. Isn't that enough?'

'But why is he here? Why did he come? To hurt us?'

Baldur sighed. 'It doesn't matter why he's here. Once an enemy, always an enemy. Even if he'd walked through our gates with a white banner, your husband would still put him to death. He's an enemy of the Vettels. Always has been. His head hanging from the gates when the lord returns? That will make his victory over Ake Bluefinn all the sweeter!'

Karolina couldn't think of anything more horrible, but she nodded. 'Well, if it's what my husband would do?'

'It is, it is, my lady. I'll kill the boy too.'

'What? *Boy*?' Karolina leaned forward, dark eyelashes fluttering with worry. 'What boy?'

'Jonas has a grandson. Just as murderous as him by the sound of it. Helped with a murder.'

'Oh?'

'Killed a popular silversmith. Malik Valborg. Nasty business.'

'Oh, well I...'

'Murder is punished by death, my lady. There's no escaping it, no matter how old you are.'

Karolina could feel her servant's discomfort, which mirrored her own. 'You may kill the man,' she said reluctantly. 'He sounds as though he is an enemy my husband would want dead, but do not kill the boy, Baldur. I will speak to Hakon when he returns. He can make that decision himself. I will not displease the gods by killing a child.'

Baldur wanted to spit. The Lady of Slussfall was a weak woman, though that was no surprise. 'As you wish, my lady. I will organise things for tomorrow.'

Karolina was about to say good, but it wasn't good, and she didn't feel good about condemning a man to death, no matter what he might have done. And the more she thought about it, the crime of helping Ake Bluefinn take the throne from the Vettels was no crime in her eyes. She knew Hakon. She'd met his father. They were not good men, and she doubted that Jorek Vettel would have been any better. But clutching her hands in her lap, she nodded, saliva flooding her mouth. 'Thank you.'

CHAPTER TWENTY NINE

Bjarni was anxious. 'I've got a bad feeling.'

'Have you?' Sigurd looked surprised, head up, glancing around. Ilene stood nearby, talking to a swollen-lipped Berger Eivin. Unsure how he felt about that, Sigurd shook his head, trying to concentrate. It pounded, though, making it almost impossible. 'What about?'

'Slussfall. It won't be easy.'

'Nothing's easy about going to war in winter.'

'And it does feel like winter now, don't you think?'

Drops of rain fell down the smoke holes, bothering the flames, which struggled under their assault, hissing and spitting.

'It does, but Reinar can hardly tell Ake that he'd rather wait till spring. Feels like we need to go now. Like it's important. Ake knows more than he's telling us, and maybe his dreamer knows more than she's telling him. We have to go now.'

Bjarni sighed, watching Agnette talking with Elin. She'd yawned so many times that she looked ready to fall asleep on her feet. He didn't blame her. And though Liara was sleeping peacefully in their chamber now, he knew that the moment they slid into bed, she would start that mournful cry again. His heart swelled, despite his sleep deprivation, and he couldn't wait to hold her in his arms. She was a joy, and he would do anything to keep her safe. And just the realisation of that cleared his frown. 'I think Elin going is a mistake.'

Sigurd thought the same.

'Though Reinar's never been able to say no to her.'

'Which she knows.' It was odd how quickly his feelings for Elin had soured, Sigurd realised. Everything had come into sharper focus since Tulia's death, and he found himself turning against her.

'What?' Bjarni had watched Sigurd's face darkening as he stared across the hall.

'I've got a bad feeling too, I suppose. As though it's all going to go wrong.' Sigurd was whispering, not wanting his brother to hear. 'That may just be me, of course. I'm not seeing anything clearly at the moment.' And rubbing his eyes, he realised that he needed some sleep. He'd been drinking too much, talking too much, remembering too much, with barely any sleep in between. His eye was throbbing where Berger had punched him, the other one grainy and tired.

'No one can blame you for that, but you're not wrong, Elin is different.'

'Is she?'

Bjarni nodded. 'Agnette thinks so.'

Sigurd finished his cup of ale, wiping his mouth. 'If only Alys were here. She could tell us what's happening. She'd see what's coming.'

Bjarni's eyebrows were up. 'You? *You're* wishing we had a dreamer!' He was too loud, and turning around with a frown, Reinar walked over to them.

'What's this about a dreamer?'

He looked flustered, Sigurd thought. Irritated too. 'Just thinking it would be good to know what was waiting up in Slussfall. Good to have Alys here.'

Reinar immediately glanced over his shoulder, though Elin was near the corridor with Agnette, who had heard Liara cry and was heading for her bedchamber. 'Well, she's not, so why worry about dreamers? We need to focus on ships and weapons, food and supplies. On the fort and whether we're leaving enough men behind. Not on dreamers we no longer have.' His voice was low and impatient, worrying that he hadn't left them enough time to prepare for their departure. Bolli and Holgar had been working on adding small catapults to the ships. They had some from a previous attack on Orbo, when Stellan was in command of Ottby's forces, but now they were taking more ships to fit Ake's men, so they could afford to add a few more.

Slussfall's fort sat perched above its harbour, and Reinar knew from experience how easily a ship could hit those walls. But if they were going to get into the fort, they had to keep the ramparts busy. 'Do you think Hakon's back in Slussfall yet?' he wondered.

'If he's alive. You did stick him with *Corpse Splitter*.'

Reinar smiled, remembering.

'Well, we'd know the answer to both, wouldn't we?' Sigurd decided. 'If Alys were here.'

***

Alys couldn't believe that they were one day from Slussfall.

'And not a whole day either!' Eddeth exclaimed, full of energy, despite the cold and the long day and the lack of sleep. 'According to Ivan, we'll be there before the sun hits its peak!'

They were lying on the ground in Falla's tent. Falla had slipped out to say goodnight to Lief and not returned, and though she'd become friendlier since discovering that Alys was a dreamer, they were still pleased to be alone.

'I feel worried.'

'You do?'

Alys edged closer to Eddeth, who was twitching beneath her fur, not sounding very sleepy. 'Lotta doesn't want me to come, but why? I can't see why. She was going on a ship. I'm worried that we'll be too late.'

Eddeth could hear the pain in Alys' voice. The pain and the worry.

And the fear.

'But what about your grandfather?'

'He's trapped. He can't help. Whatever's happening, he can't help at all.' Alys felt herself panicking, and then Eddeth's hand squeezing hers.

'Deep breath, there you go! Just breathe deeply and let everything about Slussfall float away. If we can make it through tonight that will be some achievement, and then we'll worry about tomorrow and Lotta.'

Eddeth was right, and Alys tried to breathe, though her heart was racing, her body tense. 'I need to dream for Hakon. He wants to know all about Reinar. About what he'll do.'

'And you?'

'Me?'

'Don't you want to dream about Reinar? See what he's up to? Whether he's pining for you?'

'Eddeth! He has a wife.'

'Didn't stop him kissing you, did it?'

Alys was shocked. 'How do you know that?'

'Oh, I see more than most, don't forget that!'

'Well, it was just the once. He wasn't thinking clearly.'

Silence.

'Maybe twice, I can't remember.'

More silence.

'Eddeth!'

'What? What is it?'

'Were you asleep?'

'Of course I was asleep! What's happening?' And sitting up, panting, Eddeth blinked in the darkness. 'Are the vatyr back?'

Alys shook her head, tugging her back down to the ground. 'Not yet they're not. Go to sleep, Eddeth.' All her life she'd wanted to fall asleep quickly, but even as a child, she would lie in bed, mind wandering for hours in the darkness, looking for answers.

Alys blinked.

Looking for answers?

Why had she been looking for answers?

It was curious, she realised, wide awake now, wondering what answers she'd been seeking as a child. Wondering if she was still seeking them now.

Mirella.

The man had whispered it breathlessly, accentuating it with feeling. He had loved her, Alys could tell. Jesper Vettel had loved a woman with long blonde hair and green eyes named Mirella.

***

Jonas stared at his cottage, heart almost bursting.

It was newly built. He could tell by the colour of the wood; by the absence of the gardens Eida had spent years cultivating around the steps, leading out past the house to the outbuildings, down to the stream.

Newly built, and therefore, they were newly married.

Jonas turned to Eida, gripping her hand as though she was his prisoner. He didn't want her to slip away. It was a dream he had often, but she always disappeared, leaving him to wake up alone.

'We should never have let her go.'

Eida's voice was gentle and soft, full of sadness.

Jonas knew who she was talking about. 'It was what she wanted. It was what you wanted for her. For a reason, Eida. You didn't know what had happened in Tuura. To the temple. It wasn't your fault.'

'But if we'd kept her with us. If Mirella had stayed...'

Jonas turned to his wife, but she wasn't there. No one was.

And sighing, he turned back to the cottage, now just a heap of ash.

***

Reinar smiled, shaking his head. 'Think I'll sleep with my pillow *over* my head tonight!'

Elin didn't reply. The crying baby was a loud distraction, and she was struggling to cope with it.

'What's wrong?' He reached beneath the furs for her hand.

'That noise. Liara. I... I can't stand it.'

Reinar was surprised, then he realised that Elin was crying. He touched her face, feeling tears on her cheeks.

The baby's crying upset him too, though he didn't want to say anything. He didn't even want to think it. Liara was a gift from the gods for two people who deserved it more than anyone he knew. He didn't resent Bjarni and Agnette's happiness, but sometimes, it was hard not to be reminded of his own aching grief. 'I'm sorry,' he breathed, cupping Elin's face in his hands. 'It's been such a terrible time for you.'

'For me?' Elin felt annoyed, rising up on her elbows. 'I didn't go through it alone, Reinar. Don't you feel anything yourself? For our dead sons?'

'I...'

'Why can't you ever talk about them? About what happened? Am I the only one grieving? Is it always only me?' She was sniffing and seething, and sensing that Reinar had frozen, Elin flopped back on the pillow, turning away.

'I've a lot to think about,' Reinar tried.

'What?' Elin flipped back over. 'More important things than our sons? Our poor boys?'

Reinar couldn't bring his feelings to the surface. He couldn't give her what she so desperately needed from him. The pain upon seeing those dead babies had shut him down. It had been impossible to feel much after that. Even now. 'No, of course not. I grieve, Elin, but I can't fall apart. I can't let those feelings come. If they do, what will happen? I'll never want to leave our chamber. Never want to do anything but sit in here and cry.' He'd kept the pain just out of reach from the moment it had happened, but it was there, Reinar knew; he touched the edges of it often. 'I've had so much to do. After what happened to my father, so much. I couldn't just fall apart. Not then, not now.'

Elin didn't care what he had to do. She didn't care about the fort or his father. She cared about what they'd lost together, and how empty and lonely she'd felt ever since, not being able to share the depth of that loss with her husband. 'And when will you?' she whispered, voice hissing through her teeth. 'I think never, Reinar. But my body is empty. I grew our babies inside my body, and now it's so empty. I have nothing! And Torvig, he's dead, and I have nothing. Nothing!' Her tears quickly became a flood, and she started to hyperventilate.

'Ssshhh,' Reinar soothed, stroking her hair. 'Ssshhh, Elin. I'm sorry. Sorry for us. For the... babies.' Everything hurt. He saw his father, lying on his chamber floor, his mother screaming over him, begging him to help. He saw his sons in the arms of Eddeth and Rienne, not screaming at all. 'I'm so sorry they died.' He dropped his head to his hands. 'For so long, it felt like my fault. All of it did. I didn't know how to say it. I worried that I'd done it. That I'd done it to them!'

Elin sat up. 'But now you know the truth. You know it was that curse. We both know the truth now.'

Reinar couldn't speak. He saw Alys flying through the air, hitting the tree. He saw the symbols, roughly scratched into bark. He heard the ravens screeching in his ears, the howl of the wolf. And Hakon's dreamer had done it all.

Sometimes it was hard to see the truth.

Hard to feel what was real, and what was just your imagination.

His heart ached, and he put a hand over it, pressing down, feeling Elin's arms around him.

Sometimes it was hard to see the truth.

***

Bergit had softened over the day, and Ulrick was once again lying in her arms, head resting on her ample bosom, arm tucked around her waist, holding her close. 'We need to be gone early.'

'Why? Why are you in such a hurry? You really think Hakon will care about the girl?'

'I don't know. If he'd been victorious, likely not, but a defeat to the Vilanders will have him in knots. He wasn't right, my love. He acted like a madman at Ottby. Like a child let loose in an armoury!' Ulrick still couldn't believe what he'd seen. He remembered the smoke. The old woman. His escape.

And he thought of Lotta lying in the main room, hoping she was warm.

'Well, if he's lost to the Vilanders, seems to me he'll be looking for the right kind of men to help him get back on his feet.'

Once Ulrick would have been tempted to care. But Asger had told him about the new Lord of Orvala, and he hadn't been able to stop thinking about him. They'd met once, years ago, when Ulrick was a young man, and Tarl Brava was just a boy, his father's youngest son. It amazed him to think that after all these years and all those older brothers, Brunn had been the one to rise. His reputation as a warrior had grown into legend, and now he was a man whose power was increasing; who many were talking about as a future king.

Besides, Lotta saw danger if they remained, and his instincts were to listen to her.

Ulrick leaned over his wife, lips hovering just above hers. 'Our destiny lies further north, my love. I know it, and tomorrow, we'll begin our new adventure!'

PART FOUR

Slussfall

CHAPTER THIRTY

It was a relief to wake up with the sun.

Hakon rolled onto the ground with a yelp of discomfort, though he felt elated. They had made it through another night. One step closer to home and safety.

He stood, stretching his neck, not looking forward to another day on his horse. He thought of Slussfall and his wife and son, knowing that the quicker he got into the saddle, the quicker he'd be sitting in his hall, a goblet of Kalmeran wine in his hand, the wind wailing somewhere far in the distance.

The weather sounded horrific if the intense flapping of his tent was anything to go by, and Hakon yawned, eyes on the swirling flames of the fire. There was no sign of Rikkard, who had hopefully gone to organise some breakfast.

Yawning again, Hakon stood, pleased to see that the boy had laid out his armour. His boots sat on the ground, freshly polished. He saw a new tunic and an almost-clean pair of trousers, and desperate to change out of his sweat-soaked clothes, Hakon undressed. He kept his head up, refusing to catch even a glimpse of the mark, slipping off his damp tunic, throwing it to the ground. Hearing a noise, he spun around as Rikkard entered the tent carrying a bowl of porridge. Rikkard straightened up, eyes bursting open at the sight of the dark symbol carved into his master's pale chest. It was enormous, glowing like fiery embers.

'What?' Hakon snapped, body taut, panic exploding.

Rikkard stumbled, not knowing where to look. He quickly backed up to the tent flap. 'I...'

'Put the bowl on the table.' Hakon's voice was like a knife scraping across stone.

Rikkard, hands shaking now, moved further into the tent, aiming for the table as Hakon slipped his new tunic over his head.

'Now leave.'

Rikkard wanted to run. He'd seen the mark. He knew what it meant. His lord was doomed to die, and likely those around him would die too. He'd seen what The Hunter's men had done. He'd helped bury the bodies. 'I, I, I will go and find you something to drink, my lord,' he mumbled, legs trembling. 'I... you need something to drink.' He wanted to vomit. His entire body was shaking now as he turned around, reaching for the tent flap.

Hakon jammed his knife into Rikkard's back, pulling it out quickly, slamming his hand over the boy's throat, arm around his chest. And holding it there, as Rikkard stumbled, in shock, body jerking, Hakon drew his bloody blade across the boy's throat.

'Still in bed?' came the call as the tent flap rustled and Ivan stepped inside, mouth falling open in horror.

Knife in hand, Hakon dragged Rikkard's body to the other side of the tent, dropping it to the ground.

Ivan closed his mouth, vibrating all over. And spinning around, he tied the tent flap tightly, not wanting anyone else to come in. 'Hakon!' he hissed, turning back around. '*Hakon!*'

Hakon was bent over, wiping his knife on the wet grass. He stood, carefully drying the blade on his old tunic before slipping it back into its scabbard. 'You'd better have someone get rid of him.'

Ivan was speechless, spluttering, unable to even form words.

Hakon wanted him to go, and ignoring Ivan, and Rikkard's corpse, he continued dressing, which even after all these years, never came easily with no thumbs.

'But... but...'

'You think I should tolerate disrespect? That I should have suffered that boy's slovenly ways? Ha! What sort of lord would that make me?' Hakon snarled, lips curling, eyes sharp. 'Willing to be treated as though I'm no better than a stablehand! Is that what sort of lord you'd be?'

Ivan fumbled for an answer, not understanding why Hakon was turning on him. 'No, I –'

'You should have learned something from our fathers about how to treat those who don't show respect.' And now Hakon lunged at his cousin, finger pointing. 'We're on the same side, aren't we, Ivan? We still want the same thing?' He leaned in until their noses were almost touching. 'Still want to be in Stornas together?'

Ivan could only nod, stepping back, the stench of Rikkard's dead body in his nostrils. 'Of course, Hakon, I do. I'll...' He stopped, trying to think. 'I'll get Oskar to help Jerrick take Rikkard away. They're discreet.'

'*Discreet*? I could care less about discreet! The boy was useless. He insulted me, abused me, failed to do his job. Let everyone see how I reward such insolence!'

And flapping a thumbless hand at Ivan, he turned away, chest on fire.

***

Ulrick had been up before dawn, ensuring that their chests were as full as they could be. It wasn't in his nature to run away, but he tried to frame it as a fresh opportunity in his mind, knowing he would have to work hard to keep Bergit from sniping.

He smiled, eyes on Lotta, who was watching him silently from her bed.

Her hair was a knotted mess, and she looked hungry, he thought, as though she hadn't eaten properly in some time. He worried that that was true.

'Why don't you come here and I'll comb your hair?'

Lotta dragged herself up into a sitting position with a sigh. Her mother was close. She could almost feel her now. Magnus and

Jonas were in the prison hole. Vik was somewhere. And she had to leave them all behind.

It made her sad, and she shook her head.

'Go on,' Ulrick grinned. 'It's not so bad to have those knots taken out. If they get any worse, I'll have to take my knife to them!' He glanced at the bedchamber door, lowering his voice. 'Wrap that fur around you and come here. Sit on this stool.' It was impossible not to see his daughter when he looked at Lotta, and though it had been nearly twenty years since he'd lost Gala, the pain still echoed. Losing a child was like nothing he'd experienced in his life. He'd lost his parents, brothers, friends and lords, but his daughter? It was a nightmare from which he'd never awoken.

Realising that with Ulrick there was no point arguing, Lotta crept to the fire, sitting on the stool with a sigh.

Ulrick smiled. He'd retrieved his comb from his pouch, and he gently ran it through Lotta's hair, quickly catching it in a thick knot. He felt her flinch and he frowned, placing one hand on her head, so as not to pull her hair. 'I might regret starting this,' he laughed softly, not seeing Lotta anymore. 'So what story do you want to hear, then? Something about ghosts and spirits? About battles and warriors? Or maybe the gods?'

Lotta didn't speak.

'Or I can tell you about Orvala? I was there years ago, though I can still remember the place as though it was yesterday.'

'I would like to hear about the gods,' Lotta decided quietly, not wanting to think about Orvala. It was the last place she wanted to go, so far away from Magnus. He would be sad. He would blame himself. Though it wasn't his fault, she knew.

It was what the gods had been planning all along.

***

Alys felt odd as she tightened Haski's saddle. Though she was pleased to have slept soundly, she was surprised not to have had any dreams. And then panic started, knowing how many people would soon be staring at her with inquisitive faces, wanting to know what she'd seen.

'You look ready to fall down!' Ivan exclaimed behind her.

Alys yelped, biting her tongue as she turned around. 'What?'

'Sorry, I'm sorry.'

'It's fine. I...' Shaking her head, she tasted blood. 'I was in a dream.'

'Were you?'

'Well, no, not a real dream. I was just thinking. Wondering what will come next.'

'Just wondering?' Ivan's eyes moved past Alys to where Falla was snapping at the servants who were organising porridge for breakfast. Everyone was sick of porridge, wishing that bags of oats weren't the one ingredient the servants had been quick enough to take from their camp when they'd run away from Ottby.

Alys blinked. 'I didn't dream anything, if that's what you want to know.'

It was exactly what Ivan wanted to know. He felt on edge, constantly looking back at Hakon's tent, where he could see Jerrick and Oskar carrying out Rikkard's body, draped in a fur.

Alys' eyes burst open. 'What happened?'

All the noise and early morning energy was sucked out of the camp as everyone turned to stare at the body, wondering who it was.

Wondering what had happened.

'Hakon's steward, Rikkard.' Ivan felt sick, not believing anything his cousin had said. Rikkard was just a boy, the son of one of Jesper's men. He'd cared for Hakon with great diligence for nearly two years, always rushing around trying to anticipate his lord's needs in a quiet and respectful way. What Hakon had said made no sense, so why had he really killed him?

Alys saw flashes of the boy as Hakon stabbed him; the horror in his eyes.

'He was...' Ivan gave up quickly. There was nothing he could say. No lie that he could trot out, pretending it was the truth.

'Things will only get worse,' Eddeth whispered hoarsely from behind them, making Alys jump, biting her tongue again.

'Where did you come from?'

'I was here all along!' Eddeth grinned, though eyes on the body, she swallowed, lowering her voice. 'We'll all need to be on our toes around your cousin now. Especially you two.'

'Us?' Ivan glanced at Alys, who peered at Eddeth. The sun was rising higher, and she could see the worry in Eddeth's eyes.

'Of course!' Eddeth's worried eyes kept on jumping around, not wanting Hakon to sneak up on her. 'He'll blame you both for everything that goes wrong, and he'll most certainly not praise you for anything that goes right. In his mind, everything must work towards his survival now. Everything must be about beating back the curse of that mark!'

Alys shivered, turning to Ivan, who looked to be taking Eddeth's words seriously. As he should. Eddeth had good instincts about these things, and knowledge far greater than anyone she knew of. 'You must be careful, Ivan,' she warned. 'Listen to Eddeth, and stay away from Hakon until –' Alys stopped, not knowing what waited at the end of the sentence.

'Until?' Ivan was almost holding his breath.

'Until the gods have had their fun, of course! They will decide your cousin's fate now,' Eddeth said, watching Hakon striding out of his tent, heading straight for them. And wheeling around, cloak flapping, snow settling in her grey mop of hair, Eddeth bounded away.

***

Ollo Narp had a spring in his step.

The morning air was bitter, and snow was wet in his beard as he walked, though he barely noticed, for Elmar's wife, the lovely

Mora, had found Jonas' herbs. It had taken so long that he was growing worried that Jonas, being such an old man now, would just curl up and die before he could rescue him. Or perhaps his grandson, who was a skinny-looking boy, half-starved to begin with. He'd sent extra food to the hole, hoping to keep them going while he worked on finding the herbs. And now he would send Haegel out to tell Vik to be ready tonight.

And once they had their silver ...

Mind sparking with possibilities, Ollo rounded a corner, heading into the square, smacking straight into Baldur Skoggi, who strutted around the fort as though he was the lord himself. 'Watch it!' Ollo grumbled, stepping back.

Baldur turned on him. '*Me* watch it?' He didn't like Ollo Narp. Didn't trust him either. It made little sense for anyone to trust a man who would so easily break an oath for coins, especially a lord like Hakon Vettel, destined to be the king. He shook his head, eyeing the round man with disdain.

'You're barrelling around like you're running to put out a fire! Sun's barely up. What can be so important that you have to knock people over?'

'You appear to still be on your feet, Ollo.'

'True, though that's only because of my superior balance.' Ollo puffed out his chest, smoothing down his wet beard. 'So what's the hurry, then? What's got you in a flap?'

'Just wanting to get to the hole. Executions today!'

Ollo swallowed, his hopes sinking. 'Executions? Without the lord? Who's agreed to that?' He knew who it would be. There'd been grumbles ever since Jonas had been discovered and shoved into the hole. Many of Hakon's men were agitating, unhappy that the old warrior still had a head. Crowds had been gathering outside the hole, disturbing trade, getting in Ollo's way, making a noise and a fuss. It was becoming a real problem. 'Seems to me a man like Hakon Vettel would want to see his own executions. He won't be happy, you having all that fun on his behalf.'

It was something Baldur had considered too, though Ollo didn't need to know that. 'Hakon will understand the importance of keeping order. It's why he left me in charge. And if the sun goes down with Jonas Bergstrom's head still attached to his body, I can only guess what problems we'll have.'

Ollo shivered, watching the guards pulling open the gates in the distance. He could hear the squeal of hinges, the scrape of wood across ice. 'You're a braver man than me, Baldur. I remember how wild Hakon got when his cousin took off Sirrus' head. He didn't speak to Ivan for weeks!'

Baldur remembered, though it gave him little pause. 'So you say, but he'll thank me when he comes home to an orderly fort rather than roaring chaos and a pile of charred rubble littered with bodies.' And leaning in closer as more and more Slussfallers headed into the square, Baldur lowered his voice. 'You really want a riot, Ollo? In this weather, everyone's going a little mad. Impatient to know what happened in Ottby. On edge.' And straightening up, Baldur resettled his new woollen cloak, eyes on the sky, confident that the fog would clear soon. 'No, Hakon will thank me, I'm sure of it.' And nose in the air, he strode away.

***

They had been riding for some time, the sun finally emerging from behind a long bank of clouds, when Hakon ushered Alys forward, sending Lief and Ivan back to check on the men. He wanted some time alone with his dreamer, though Alys didn't want any time alone with him.

Eddeth smiled encouragingly at her, watching her go. 'It's a worry,' she muttered, more loudly than she'd realised. Her mind skipped to Stina, who'd always warned her about her blabbering mouth.

'What's a worry?' Falla wondered, eyes on Lief, who passed her with one of his almost-smiles. 'Eddeth?' Eddeth was busy chewing her lips, and she didn't appear to want to talk at all. 'You mean Hakon? Or Alys?'

Eddeth sighed. 'Well, I couldn't say, I'm no dreamer!'

'No, but you sense things, don't you?' Falla said, hoping to lead her on. 'It's obvious your gifts go far beyond healing. I can see that.'

'You can?' Eddeth was alert, eyes wide with interest. 'Well, I can't deny that's true. I won't! I surely won't, but as for what's wrong, well, I can't say for certain, but the lord is a worry. And what the lord might do to Alys is also a worry. She's a strong woman, I know. Oh yes, I know what she's capable of, believe me, but around a cursed lord going mad?'

'Mad?' Falla felt a wave of nausea rising, and she swallowed, willing it away. The mornings were the most unsettled time, and the constant rocking motion of the horse only made it worse. 'Hakon?'

Eddeth sneezed so explosively that Hakon twisted around, eyeing her sharply, and now it was her turn to swallow, deciding not to say another word. Though in the blink of an eye, her mouth was open again. 'Perhaps he's always been this way, but I sense a change. A descent down a dark staircase. Down to the very pit of evil which seeks to claim him. To Vasa's Cave itself!' She cocked her head to one side. 'Or perhaps Alari's? They are sisters, you know. Twins! One light, one dark, as vengeful as each other.'

Falla shivered, thinking of Mother, who had spoken of Alari with such reverence and awe. And yet now, without her, Falla felt afraid of those dark goddesses. 'But will they hurt us? If they wish to take Hakon, maybe Ivan, will they come for us all? For Lief?' She gripped her belly, worry in her eyes.

Eddeth frowned, annoyed that her thoughts had escaped out her mouth. Again. 'I wouldn't worry,' she tried, though there was little confidence in her voice. 'But I would encourage your husband not to stand in the way of the gods, especially Thenor. If his mind is made up, it's only a matter of time!'

Alys could hear Eddeth nattering away behind her, and she felt concerned. It always made her feel concerned to leave Eddeth alone with anyone, but Hakon was getting more incensed beside her, and her attention was quickly back on him.

'You don't *know*? How is that possible?'

'Your last dreamer was experienced,' Alys said, seeing a vision of Mother standing behind her daughter with hatred in her eyes. 'She knew how to be a dreamer. I've told you that I was never a dreamer, just a woman who tried to pretend she wasn't. I can't click my fingers and be changed. I wish I could.'

'Do you, though, Alys?' Hakon snapped, impatience and worry working away at him. 'I'm not sure that's true. I'm not sure you're trying to help me at all!'

'You made me a prisoner. What choice do I have?'

'And if I let you go? Freed you?'

'I would run away as fast as I could.'

Hakon laughed, further irritated, gloves clenching around the reins. She was a beautiful woman, though, and his feelings of anger quickly twisted into an ache of desire. 'Well, then I will have to keep you in my trap, won't I?' Hakon stared ahead, the sun bright before them, glaring into his eyes. 'Until I get what I want.'

'Which is?'

'To be the King of Alekka, of course. To return my family to Stornas. And once I claim it, perhaps I will think of letting you go? Though, by then, you may not wish to go anywhere. Whatever village you came from could never compare to Stornas.'

'No, but wealth and power don't appeal to everyone.'

Hakon looked surprised, doubting that was true.

'Some people seek a simpler life. They seek freedom.'

'And you?'

'Yes, I would like to be free again.' Alys saw Reinar. She felt Reinar's hand on her face, Reinar's lips kissing hers. And swallowing, she tried to will the image of him away. She had to help his enemy. In order to free herself and save her children, she had to help Reinar's enemy now.

There was no other way.

CHAPTER THIRTY ONE

Stina smiled wearily, pleased to think that after such a terrifying, bleak, hopeless time, she'd finally encountered some luck.

She had come across a family travelling to Ottby.

Ake's scouts had sent messengers across the South, demanding that all men who could wield a weapon head for Ottby, for the Vilanders were leaving to attack Slussfall. And this family of farmers: a father, his three giant-sized sons and their tiny mother, were answering the call.

Far from feeling anxious or worried, as Stina would have been, the farmer's wife beamed with pride. She was ruddy-faced and full of energy, urging her menfolk on, never lagging behind. All four of them were on horses, and they rode quickly, with skill and speed, wanting to make it to Ottby in time.

As did Stina.

'Should be there in three days, I'd say. Maybe two if we push harder,' the woman smiled at her. 'And my husband does like to push hard. With three sons chasing you, who wouldn't?'

'Three days? And what if they've left? What if they've gone to Slussfall when we arrive?' Stina had told them everything she could, and they were sympathetic to her plight, wanting to get her to Ottby quickly.

'We must try for two days, Gerold!' the woman called with a grin at Stina, wind tearing past her. 'Snow's holding off, the paths are clear. We should try for two!'

Her husband nodded, head bent against the wind. 'We can try, my dear. We can certainly try!'

Stina felt her hopes lift, but still... who knew how long they had before the Vilanders left for Slussfall.

***

Ulrick wanted to scream. They had made it down to the pier only to be told that there was no sign of half the crew, and certainly no sign of Asger, the helmsman.

'Weather's poor anyway,' yawned one of the crew, digging into his ear with a dirty finger. 'But those clouds will clear soon. Come back later.'

'*Later*?' Bergit stood beside Ulrick, two chests sitting on the pier at their feet, Lotta standing between them, yawning. 'But we're ready now!'

The man lifted a woolly eyebrow, surprised by her shrill voice. He straightened up. 'You're welcome to board, lady, though who knows if we'll even be at sea today.' He turned to Ulrick. 'You could always check in the tavern. Asger might still be there. He's got a thing for the taverner's wife, see. Every time we're here, can't get him away from her!'

Ulrick sighed. 'I will.' It was freezing, and the man was right, fog hugged the harbour like a thick blanket, and he couldn't even discern a hint of the headland in the distance. 'We'll go back to the fort. Bergit, you take Lotta to the cottage, warm up for a while. I'll leave these chests here, friend. We'll return shortly. Sooner than shortly if I can find Asger.'

'I wish you luck!' the man called, heading away from them, yawning uncontrollably, wishing he was one of the missing crew, still sound asleep.

Bergit clucked angrily next to Ulrick as they walked back down the pier, heading for the long path that led around to the main gates. She didn't want to leave at all, and now, after waking early to prepare for their journey, they had to hike back in the freezing fog.

She was livid.

Lotta could feel her tension bubbling beneath the surface, she could feel Ulrick's irritation, but most of all, she could feel her own fears rising that they would be too late.

***

Haegel scurried out of the fort looking for Vik, eyes jumping, long body twitching.

Vik frowned, heading to the back of the line of traders, trying to blend in, though surely someone was going to wonder what he was up to with that idiot drawing attention to them again.

'We've got problems,' Haegel muttered urgently, voice low.

'What sort of problems?'

'Baldur Skoggi's going to ruin everything. He's going to kill them today!'

'What? Jonas?'

Haegel nodded. 'Maybe the boy too. More besides!'

'*What?*' Vik's heart stuttered, eyes up on the wall. 'We have to do something. We have to get them out of there now!'

The woman in front of them glanced around, eyeing the men suspiciously, and Vik pulled Haegel away, tension gripping his body.

'Ollo doesn't know what to do. Baldur has the approval of the lady. She's given him permission. What can we do to stop him?'

'But the Vettel boy won't want his prize prisoner killed without him being there. Without making some sort of show. What's the hurry?'

'There's trouble inside the fort. A lot of Hakon's men don't like that Jonas is there. They're making noise, demanding his head.

Baldur wants to shut them up, restore order. So he says. I think he just likes being popular. Now everyone's yelling at him.'

'Well, Hakon Vettel will surely be yelling at him when he finds out what he's done.'

'Mmmm, but by then Jonas and the boy will be dead, won't they? We don't have time to think about what to do. Baldur's already in there sorting out the square. He wants to get all these people inside first. He wants an audience.'

'Ollo has to do something. Now!'

Haegel agreed. 'But what?'

***

Leonid was panicking, and though Jonas was working hard to keep him calm, the men around them were starting to stir now, making things worse. Leonid's panic quickly unsettled Magnus, who began to cry.

'We don't know what they're doing out there,' Jonas tried. 'Tidying up, maybe?' His voice was calm, hoping to soothe his great-grandson.

'They're bringing out the block. You can see that!' a man behind them grumbled.

Magnus wanted to be brave, but there was only so much bravery in a ten-year-old boy, and the sight of that old block of wood being dragged out into the square was enough to have him sobbing, knees knocking together.

'There's no sign of Hakon Vettel!' Jonas insisted, loud now, attempting to quell the rising terror. 'Why would they kill anyone when their lord isn't here?'

'Never stopped Baldur Skoggi before,' muttered one voice. 'He's a sick bastard!'

Jonas pulled Magnus close, wanting to turn the boy away from the bars where he was watching the fort, eyes peeled open in terror.

'Look, there's Lotta! Lotta, help us! They're going to kill us! Lotta, please! *Please!*'

Lotta froze, eyes darting to the hole where she could see her brother's petrified face. Tugging Ulrick's hand, she pointed to where men were clearing a patch of ground, dragging a wooden block into place; a wooden block stained with dark blood. 'What are they doing?'

Ulrick could hear the boy begging and wailing, and it made him further irritated. 'Getting ready to kill a few prisoners, I'd say.'

'But my brother!'

Bergit had stopped to talk to one of her friends, and they were alone. Ulrick bent down, finger to his lips. 'There's no need to let everyone know what we know.'

'But they know already, don't they? They heard Magnus when he saw me. My grandfather too. They've not tried to take me away, have they?'

It was true, but Ulrick didn't want to take the risk. 'Well, nothing we can do about the boy. We can't. Besides, we're leaving, never to return. What does it matter if he's dead?'

Lotta stared at Ulrick with such horror in her eyes that he felt an unfamiliar twinge of guilt, as though his long lost conscience was stirring.

'It matters to me,' Lotta whispered, tears falling down frozen cheeks. 'It matters to me, Ulrick.'

Ulrick ran a hand over his beard, feeling annoyed. He wanted to make her happy, but it was none of his concern whether the boy lived or died, and by trying to save him, he would likely put Lotta in danger.

But staring into those big, blue, tear-filled eyes, he sighed.

***

Alys was gripped by terror as she rode in between Ivan and Hakon, suddenly wanting to be back with Eddeth. She looked over her shoulder, trying to catch Eddeth's eye, but Eddeth appeared deep in conversation with Falla, which in itself was worrying.

'What's wrong?' Ivan wondered. 'Have you seen something?'

Alys didn't know what to reveal, but panic made her bold. 'I saw Slussfall.'

Hakon's ears pricked up, and drawing himself away from his brooding, he turned to her. 'What did you see?'

'Trouble. Unrest. Something's going on.'

'Are the Vilanders there? Are we under attack?'

Alys swallowed, fear assaulting her, fighting for control of her body. 'I don't think so. There are crowds of people. Angry people. Fighting. I don't know what's happening.'

'In Slussfall?' Hakon thought of his son and Karolina, panic surging through his own body. 'We must hurry, then.' He turned around, eyeing his men. 'Ivan, tell Lief to take charge. Grab twenty men on horses and let's get ahead.'

Alys nodded. 'I want to come.'

'You do?' Hakon didn't question why. He just had to get back to Slussfall as fast as he could.

***

Ollo was wondering if he needed to try and save Jonas at all.

It was the silver he wanted, and if Jonas was dead, then he could...

But Jonas swore that he hadn't told another soul where he'd buried it. Not even Vik. It was hard not to trust Jonas, whose reputation for honesty shone like a beacon. But that hoard must be buried close? Or was it?

He chomped through a warm flatbread, standing before a brazier, brow furrowed, eyes on Ulrick Dyre, who was approaching with speed. 'And what do you want?' he grumbled. 'You who caused all this trouble in the first place? Want to hand over the girl, do you? Have her killed with her brother and grandfather?'

Ulrick tore the flatbread out of Ollo's hand, pushing him away from the square, down the alley by the tavern, reminded of how he still needed to look for Asger. 'What are you letting them get killed for? *Today*? Hakon won't like it. You want to stay on the right side of our temperamental lord, you make it stop, Ollo Narp!'

'Oh, the hard man has a heart,' Ollo mocked, grinning, digging his thumbs into his swordbelt, not liking being shoved about like a slave. 'Who knew?'

Ulrick slammed him against the tavern wall, gnashing his teeth. 'You're the master of the square, as you're so fond of telling everyone. And the master of the square should be deciding who gets killed in his square, and when, don't you think? Or perhaps you have no power at all? Just a fancy title you made up yourself, hoping to attract a woman!'

Ollo waited for Ulrick to stop spitting all over him. 'Finished? You want to bark in my face anymore like the old dog you are?' He was furious, bumping his chest into Ulrick's. 'I want to stop it too, you arse. That old man owes me silver. You think I want his head off?' Ollo shook his own head. 'I don't, I promise you that, but Baldur? He's fixed on it. And now the lady's gone along with it. There's nothing I can do.'

Ulrick shrank back, realising that Ollo couldn't help him, so leaving him simmering in the alley, he turned away, heading for the hall.

***

Karolina was growing concerned by the shouting in the square. She had come out onto the steps, worried by the noise. Baldur had warned her that there was trouble, of course, and when he caught sight of the Lady of Slussfall, white fur wrapped around her shoulders, dark-blue dress whipping about in the wind, he left his men to finish their preparations and hurried to her side.

'Perhaps it's best if you don't watch, my lady?' he suggested. 'Though, if you'd like to, I can organise some seating.' He hated to pander, but he did like to be in favour, and pressing down his fur hat until it was firmly in place, Baldur smiled.

Karolina didn't like the man. He was ingratiating and heartless, but Hakon admired him greatly, so she didn't feel able to go against him, as much as she wanted to. 'The weather is closing in.'

Baldur glanced up at the sky. 'Fog seems to be easing, if you ask me. Those clouds are lighter now. I don't see snow coming either. Might even see the sun soon!'

Karolina sighed, shoulders tense, hearing her son wailing inside the hall. And attention drawn away from the noisy square, she turned her head.

'My lady!'

Spinning back around, Karolina smiled. She knew Ulrick Dyre, who was equally hard, but there had always been something charming about him. 'I didn't know you were back, Ulrick. I thought you'd be with my husband.'

Ulrick ignored the discomfort that statement stirred, convincing himself that he'd made the right choice. And now, once he'd settled this little problem and dragged Asger down to the ship, he would be on his way to find a better lord. 'You're looking well, my lady. Your husband will be eager to get back to you.'

Karolina tried not to shudder. 'And do you know when he'll return?'

Ulrick glanced at Baldur, who eyed him sharply, wondering what he wanted. 'Soon. I've heard he was defeated in Ottby, and is returning with haste. I expect you'll see him within days.' And smiling at Baldur, Ulrick leaned in close. 'Best you don't take off Jonas Bergstrom's head. Not with Hakon in a foul mood. Imagine if he comes home to find you took his one chance to defeat an enemy away from him?'

Despite his irritation at being told what to do by an old hack like Ulrick Dyre, Baldur looked worried.

As did Karolina. 'A defeat?'

Ulrick nodded, sensing her unease, knowing the Vettels' reputation for mistreating their wives. 'But never fear, that husband of yours will be on the front foot again quickly. Stornas belongs to the Vettels. He'll get you there soon.'

Karolina barely heard a word. Her husband would return as a defeated man. It terrified her. 'You will stop the execution, Baldur,' she said sharply. 'Ulrick is right, my husband deserves to have some satisfaction himself. Especially after his... unfortunate time.'

Baldur gnashed his teeth together, though he was not stupid enough to risk the wrath of the lord he was so eager to please. 'I will, of course, my lady.' He straightened up, eyes sweeping the fog-shrouded square, where crowds of angry men had gathered around the execution block, cups of ale in frozen hands. 'Though many won't be happy. There was a real change in the air this morning when I announced our plans.' He looked concerned, pulling on his short grey beard.

Ulrick slapped him on the back, eager to be gone. He could see Bergit in the distance, still talking to her friend, but there was no sign of Lotta. 'Well, if anyone can calm an angry crowd, it's you, Baldur,' he grinned. 'I wish you well, my lady. And don't worry, your husband will not dwell long on his defeat. He'll turn his attention to his next move. Any bad feelings won't linger.' His words were quickly spoken, though he felt bad for the lady, who was as nervous as a beaten dog. And bobbing his head, Ulrick turned away, cursing himself for his life-long weakness for females, young and old.

Lotta could see him coming. She waited in the middle of the square, behind the crowd of mostly men who were loud, and though it was morning, they appeared drunk. She saw them pushing each other, most with grins on red faces. Some were angry, but many just looked excited. She felt sick, not understanding how anyone could be excited to watch someone die.

Magnus called out to her repeatedly, his voice barely a murmur amongst the noise, but she turned to him, wanting to go to him, seeing Jonas almost pleading with her to come.

But she couldn't.

She had to leave.

'There you are!' Ulrick looked relieved as he scooped up her hand. 'We have to go. I sorted out your little problem. Found Asger tumbling out of the tavern too. He'll be on his way to the ship any moment now, just needs to round up the rest of the crew. Let's go tell Bergit.'

Lotta tried to hold her ground, not wanting to be pulled away just yet. 'But what happened? Those men are still there!' She had to shout up to Ulrick just to be heard.

Ulrick grinned, eyes on Baldur, who was approaching the execution block, hands out, trying to quell the crowd. 'See that man there? He's the bastard causing all this trouble, but I've had a word with the Lady of Slussfall herself.' Ulrick felt pleased with himself, forgetting how happy he would've been to see Jonas Bergstrom lose his head. 'He's putting a stop to it, see?'

But Lotta didn't feel comforted. The man was being shouted over, the crowd threatening him.

And then Bergit was there. 'Where is this helmsman?' she grumbled. 'We may as well forget it altogether, find someone else. If he can't even get to his ship on time, how can we trust him to get us all the way to Orvala?'

Ulrick glared at Bergit, not wanting anyone to hear where they were going. 'Well, he's coming now, so nothing to worry about, my love. Let's get down to the pier. We can hop on board, find ourselves a good spot.' And squeezing Lotta's hand, he turned her around, still smiling at the thought of besting Baldur Skoggi.

And then the first rock was thrown.

Baldur had mounted a stool to try and make himself heard, though nobody had liked what he had to say, and the first rock had been thrown at his head, shattering his right eye socket, knocking him off the stool, onto a flaming brazier, setting his cloak on fire.

Panic ensued, quickly spreading as Baldur's men hurried to drag their master out of the brazier, his cloak in flames, face drenched in blood.

Swords and knives were drawn, blades jabbing.

Bergit shrieked, knocked to the ground as men surged past her, wanting to join the fight.

One hand still gripping Lotta, Ulrick bent down to pick up his wife. He could hear the anger in the crowd, seething like wildfire, his senses finely honed. 'We have to go!' he cried, eyes meeting Lotta's. 'We have to get out now!'

CHAPTER THIRTY TWO

The crowd exploded at Baldur's guards, who were quickly trampled on, kicked and stabbed. Baldur had been dragged to the hall steps, deposited near the Lady of Slussfall, who stood there in shock.

'My lady!' Ollo called, hurrying to her side. 'Get inside, quick!' And pointing to one of the hall guards, who waited by the doors, frozen in place, he scowled. 'Can't you see what's coming? Get her inside now! Lock the doors!' And sword out, Ollo bounded down the steps, into the square.

Jonas watched him, hands on the bars, hearing voices outside the door, getting closer. Louder too. 'Leonid.' His voice was low. 'If they get in, you're going to run at them, head down. Run at them hard, then slip and slide past them. Run as fast as you can through the square into that crowd. Distract them, then lose them. I need to keep Magnus safe. I need to get him out of here.' He turned to his great-grandson, who was blinking furiously, ears open to what was happening outside the door. 'You will only do what I say. You won't think, just listen and do. Understood?'

Magnus nodded, terrified.

'Those men will likely come in, the ones who want me dead. Be ready for it, but don't worry, we have friends out there.' And head up now, looking through the bars, Jonas could see Ollo coming. He turned, eyes seeking the prisoners who'd emerged from the shadows. 'You want to live? You want your freedom? Then get on your feet! If they come in, we rush them. Grab their weapons! Knock them down. Then flee!' Jonas closed his eyes, listening, as the raised voices were joined by scraping blades and the odd shout of pain. And he prayed to Thenor to send his most loyal servant into the fray.

He needed Vik.

***

Vik threw caution to the wind.

There were worse ways to die, and few better than trying to save his oldest, dearest friend, and that friend's great-grandson. His thoughts drifted to Lotta, hoping he would find a way of saving her too.

Haegel stepped cautiously ahead of him into the fort, sword out, though he was no good with it, they both knew that. Vik had grabbed a helmet from an abandoned table. There was no sign of any traders now. Many had run out of the fort with their families. Others had joined the riot, which now appeared to be a full-throated battle, though it was becoming increasingly hard to see who was on whose side.

Shoving the helmet over his head, Vik closed its cheek pieces, immediately feeling more comfortable. The helmet was tight, squashing his ears, pinching his skin, but he didn't care as he followed Haegel, who pushed his way through the crowd to where Ollo was bellowing, jumping up and down, trying to see what was happening. He'd caught glimpses of men fighting to get into the prison hole, and that was certain to ruin all his plans.

'Ollo!' Haegel shouted, sword by his side, leading with his elbow.

'Haegel, you fool!' Vik grumbled, swinging for a man with a long knife who was aiming for Haegel's exposed midriff. Vik stabbed the man in the neck, watching him fall away, grabbing

Haegel and pulling him after Ollo. He caught a glimpse of blonde hair, and turning, he saw Ulrick Dyre with Lotta in his arms, heading for the gates.

'No!' he heard Ollo calling. 'Stop! Stop it!'

And spinning back to Haegel, Vik watched as he fell to the ground, stabbed through the belly.

'Aarrghh!'

Vik's heart pounded, his mind working quickly. 'Lotta!' he called after the girl, but she didn't even turn her head.

'No!'

He heard a creak of hinges as the prison hole door was yanked open.

'Shit.'

'Go!' Haegel gasped from the ground. 'Vik! Go!'

Head low, Vik barrelled through the tangled crowd, sun shining over the fort now, glinting off slashing blades and helmets. More men were arming themselves, grabbing everything they could find. He saw a spear gut a man, almost lifting him into the air, and sheathing his sword, Vik drew out two knives, running behind Ollo, who was fighting to get to the hole.

***

'Go! Go! Go!' Jonas pushed Leonid ahead of him, wishing he could feel a sword in his hand. 'Get behind them, Leonid!' he yelled, urging him on as the men burst into the hole, squinting in the darkness, searching for him. 'Go, Magnus, go!' And pushing them both towards the door, cramped with sword-wielding men, some covered in blood, Jonas held his ground.

Magnus didn't realise it until it was too late.

Jonas had made Leonid hold his hand, and now he was pulling him towards the door. Leonid pressed them back to one side, waiting as the angry crowd surged in through the door, and then he slipped outside as the other prisoners fought to distract and overwhelm the intruders. Magnus spun as Leonid tugged him away, realising that Jonas wasn't coming. He wanted to cry out, but he saw Jonas urging him on, and he thought of Lotta and his mother, and, tears in his eyes, lips quivering, hand squeezing Leonid's, Magnus turned his head to follow him.

**

They were at the gates.

Lotta couldn't go any further. Ulrick had been knocked down by a rock to the back of the head, and she'd tumbled down to the ground beside him.

Bergit was screaming, urging him to get up, worried by the blood oozing through his hair. Ulrick lifted his head, trying to wake up, but every part of his body was telling him to fall fast asleep.

Lotta grabbed his hand, sensing more danger coming. Men were running for the gates now, trying to escape, and the guards had decided to shut them, wanting to contain the rioters. 'We have to hurry! Ulrick! They're shutting the gates!'

Bergit suddenly wanted to leave Slussfall more than anything. 'Ulrick Dyre, you get up now or I'm leaving the pair of you behind. You think I want to be shut in with that lot?' And shrieking as more rocks were thrown their way, she yanked Ulrick's hand.

Head ringing like a bell, Ulrick staggered to his feet. 'Come on!' he rasped, swaying, eyes on Asger, who was hurrying some of his crew through the gates, eager to get to his ship before the trouble spread. 'Hurry!'

**

'Where's Haegel?'

'Stabbed.'

Ollo looked horrified. Haegel was like family.

'Alive,' Vik added, eyes on the prison hole, door open, men shouting, trying to fight their way both in and out.

'Vik!'

Vik was relieved to see Magnus, who ran up to him, eyes full of terror. 'Head for the gates, Magnus. Get out of here!' He saw him gripping Leonid's hand. 'Both of you. You know where the camp is. Head there!' And he vaulted past them, hearing Jonas scream, Ollo right behind him.

***

Alys couldn't stop trembling. She felt as though she was in Slussfall, as though she wasn't on her horse at all. She could almost smell the smoke in the square. She saw flashes of flames, heard angry voices roaring, blades clanging. Glimpses of Magnus rushed past her eyes. Of Jonas and Vik too.

And Lotta.

'Faster!' Alys called, urging them on. 'I see a riot!' She panted, panic stealing her breath. 'It's out of control!'

That had them all worried, especially Hakon. 'My wife? My son? Do you see them?'

Alys shook her head, dropping it low, spurring Haski on.

They were thundering through the forest now.

Getting closer.

***

The prisoners trying to escape the hole were weaker than those who had burst in, but far more desperate. Their lives were at stake, and they ducked blades and fists with more energy than their attackers, fighting their way towards the open door.

They didn't fear being cut or punched. They feared the executioner's block, and what would happen if they were still trapped in the hole when their lord returned. So they fought like their lives depended on it.

Which they did.

Jonas had been quickly knocked to the ground, overwhelmed by the men who'd caused all the trouble on his behalf. He felt the blade dig into his thigh. The pain of it barely bothered him as he jerked away, for he was too busy thinking of how to get a weapon. Freeing his right hand, he punched one spitting man in the eye, making sure to twist his fist so his knuckles hit him first. Then, head back, he wriggled, trying to free his hips.

Screams in the distance as men fell, scattering as Vik, working quickly with two knives, carved a path for Ollo to come in behind with his sword. Vik went low with one blow, hamstringing the man leaning over Jonas. Twisting his body, he backhanded his left knife high, tearing through the armpit of another.

As that man shouted, staggering, Vik cut his throat.

Ollo was grunting, swinging his sword, slipping on something he didn't want to imagine. The stink had his eyes watering. Someone had tipped over the bucket of shit, and they all started gagging, distracted by the foul smell.

'Get Jonas!' Vik called, trying to focus Ollo. 'I'll get us out of here!'

Ollo nodded, ducking a fist. 'What are you doing, Brand?' he growled at the man, who appeared so drunk he couldn't stand still. 'Get back to your alc! Don't get yourself killed for this!'

Jonas could hear Ollo, he could hear Vik, and then he could feel another blade digging into his arm. 'Aarrghh!' More men tumbled on top of him now. He headbutted one, wriggling some more. 'Vik!'

Ollo was there, stabbing his sword through a hairy neck,

dragging it out, spinning, slashing across an ale-soaked chest. None of their attackers wore armour. All of them were drunk. 'Roll!' Ollo shouted at Jonas, turning to check on Vik, who was surrounded by five men, two struggling, three looking almost sharp with intent.

Jonas rolled, staggering to his feet, pain in his eyes, blood soaking his trousers, dripping through his tunic. And bending over, he dragged a sword out of his dead attacker's hand. 'Let's get out of here!'

***

Something was on fire.

The sun was almost bright above them, rising to its peak, the fog clearing now, but smoke was drifting across the square as men fought all around them. Magnus saw women shouting too, some wielding bloody knives.

Everyone appeared to be fighting or running.

He glanced over his shoulder, trying to catch a glimpse of Jonas or Vik, though he couldn't see past two big men who were trying to knock each other out, both of them stinking of ale. He heard a man's voice, loud and sharp, trying to restore order. But looking around at the increasingly violent clashes, Magnus doubted there was any hope of that.

'Magnus!'

Head up, following Leonid's arm, Magnus saw that the gates were closing.

'No! We have to hurry!'

The guards were having a hard time getting them closed, though. There was a real push to get out, and they couldn't clear enough space to move them. Traders, women worried about their children, those sober enough to see that everything was about to explode, were desperate to get out before it was too late. Thatched roofs were catching light now, flames dancing from one shed to the next with speed.

'Lotta!' Magnus saw a flash of blonde hair, certain it was his sister, but he was knocked to the ground, hand slipping out of Leonid's, who had fallen ahead of him, both of them kicked and trampled as the rush to escape the burning fort intensified, the crowd surging forward in waves now.

Lotta heard her brother as Ulrick pushed his way through the gates, holding her in his arms, Bergit beside them. But in a heartbeat they had left the fort behind, and were on the path, heading for the piers.

***

It surprised Ivan how fast Alys could ride; how expertly she navigated her sprightly horse through the forest. She rode just behind Hakon, who, spurred on by the panic he could see in Alys' eyes, rode hard, knowing his way back to the fort better than any of them.

Alys seemed just as determined to get to Slussfall, and as Ivan drove his horse after them, jerking the reins quickly to avoid a hole, his mind started to wander, wondering what she could see.

***

Jonas helped himself to a blood-splattered helmet, shoving it over his head as he followed Vik through the square, dragging his hood up over it. They could see the main gates on an angle, hearing the fight to close them intensifying. Ollo pushed ahead of the two men, panicking. Men had seen him fighting to help Jonas and Vik, and those men, once sober, were likely to report his part in proceedings.

If there was anyone left alive by sundown.

The battle was still raging around him. He saw bloody tunics and cloaks, men with gaping wounds, smoke cascading across the spreading carnage, stinging his eyes. Overturned tables blocked their path, slush turning red, making everything slippery. An enormous dog ran past after a honking goose, nearly sending Ollo flying, and lookin pse of Leonid, and he slid through a gap in the crowd, determined to grab hold of him, one eye on the gates, which were moving   again. He turned, looking for Vik and Ollo, but the crowd had closed around him, and he couldn't see them any longer. But he could see Leonid and Magnus, and lunging forward, he grabbed Magnus' sleeve, pulling him close.

'Grandfather!' Magnus sobbed in relief, turning into his chest. 'I can't push through!   We can't get through!' He thought he'd broken a rib; it hurt to breathe. Leonid clung to Magnus' other hand, struggling to see a way out. 'Where's Vik?'

'Back there! Come on, let's keep going, he'll follow. We have to get out, Magnus. Through that hole, see! There!' And squeezing Magnus' hand, Jonas made for the gap between a man and a woman as the crowd writhed, threatening to knock them all off their feet.

'Open the gates!' came the cry from the wall, booming down into the square. 'Open the gates for the Lord of Slussfall!'

Jonas froze, trying to see Vik, but the men around him were tall, bigger than his friend, who was bigger than Ollo. He couldn't see either of them.

'No!' Magnus cried. 'What can we do?'

***

Ulrick heard the commotion, a horn moaning in the distance.

'What's that?' Bergit wondered, shuffling to the stern where Asger was barking orders at his men.

'We need to be gone,' Ulrick hissed in Asger's ear. 'You want your coins, you'll get this ship out in the harbour quickly. That horn means Hakon Vettel. We don't want any trouble now, do we?'

Asger certainly didn't. The Vettel boy was vengeful and likely to cast his net for blame far and wide. 'Oars in!' he barked at those men who were still milling around in shock, muttering to each other, many half asleep. 'Get your oars in!'

They could see smoke lifting from the fort now, and Lotta panicked, fearing for Jonas and Magnus. And then another feeling – that of heartbreak – for she could feel her mother.

***

'What's going on in there?' Hakon roared, standing in his stirrups, calling to the men on the wall. 'Get the gates open! I want my men inside. Now!'

His guards were panicking, hearing their notoriously intolerant lord's voice raised in displeasure, but there were still so many people in the way.

'Clear a path!' came a raised voice, and the head of the tower guards pushed his way through, long knife out, carving into anyone who didn't move. Yelps and shrieks. Screams of pain. He was oblivious, though, just wanting to get them away from the gates.

Jonas yanked Magnus towards him. Leonid too. They couldn't escape. He tried to see another path out of the melee, but bodies pressed closer together now, and Jonas curled himself around Magnus, trying to keep the men at arm's length. 'Watch it!' he barked, pushed in the back. The crowd was shifting, compressing further, and Jonas was lifted off his feet, just keeping hold of Magnus' hand.

'Grandfather!' Magnus yelped, dragged along after him, Leonid yanked in the opposite direction. 'Leonid!' And then the gates were shunted open, and Magnus' eyes darted about in fear, feeling his great-grandfather trying to pull him closer.

'Hold on, Magnus!' Jonas called, hearing a shout from behind as a burning roof collapsed, the fire spreading now, heading for the tavern.

'What is this madness?' Hakon screamed from his horse, eyes bulging in anger, sword drawn. 'Get this place in order! Put out those flames!' He turned to Ivan and the twenty men who'd accompanied them, all trying to get inside the fort. 'Kill those who have a weapon! Anyone who stands in your way! And close the gates! I don't want anyone escaping!' Eyes on the hall, he kicked his horse forward, into and over the close press of bodies, who all suddenly tried to turn out of his path, many of them tumbling, stumbling, falling onto each other, desperate to save themselves.

Some were too late.

Jonas threw away his sword, but kept the knife he'd picked up, tucking it down his trousers. He wanted to get rid of his helmet too, not wanting to stand out, but then someone would likely recognise him.

If he could just get around the horses, he could get them all through the gates before they closed. Head swivelling, he tried to find Vik.

Hakon turned to Alys. 'Follow me!' And he urged his horse on.

Alys felt a deep reluctance to move her horse, not wanting to hurt anyone, though Haski was quickly unsettled by the noise and the smoke and he started to panic. She felt as though she was being pulled in so many different directions. It was as though someone had hold of each limb and she couldn't move.

There were people everywhere.

Hakon turned back, irritated that she hadn't followed him. 'Alys!' he barked.

Jonas' head went up, and seeing his granddaughter, his mouth dropped open.

Sensing it, Alys turned to him before quickly looking away. She didn't want to draw any attention to her grandfather. Magnus was close – she could feel him – but Lotta... where was Lotta?

Nodding at Hakon, wanting to give her grandfather a chance to escape, she nudged Haski on, looking straight ahead, heart pounding.

Magnus saw her, eyes popping open. And then a hand clamped over his mouth, Jonas bending to his ear.

'Say nothing, my boy. She saw me. Say nothing now, Magnus.'

Magnus nodded, tears in his eyes, waiting as the hand was taken away. 'But what can we do?'

It was a good question, and only one answer came to mind. One he hoped Vik was thinking as well.

Run.

CHAPTER THIRTY THREE

Alys sat astride Haski like a statue, body stiff, shoulders frozen. She barely even blinked as she nudged him after Hakon.

Realising who had arrived started to turn the tide.

Hakon's slashing sword had an impact as well.

Men previously trying to kill each other, fell away, trying to protect themselves. Hakon showed no mercy, sword slamming down on every man within reach. He barely stopped himself from stabbing a crying woman.

'Hakon!' Ivan called, desperate to curb his cousin's violence. The skirmishes were being put down quickly now that the lord had returned, although the fires were another problem altogether.

'I need to see Karolina!' Hakon called back, not wanting to be stopped by his cousin.

Frustrated, Ivan spurred his horse forward, grabbing hold of Alys' arm. 'It's not safe!' he growled, letting Hakon go ahead. 'Stay with me till it all dies down!'

Alys nodded, head held high, not wanting to see her grandfather again; knowing that her son was in the crowd; worrying why her daughter wasn't. 'Ivan, you must open the gates! People are getting crushed! The rest of the men won't be able to get through when they arrive!' Ivan was a pliable man, eager to please her, but she saw reluctance in his eyes, not wanting to go against his cousin. She could hear his doubts as he debated whether it was the right thing to do.

Blinking suddenly, Ivan twisted in the saddle, spying one of his men. 'Jiri! Get the gates open quickly! Let the people out! The fire could get out of control, so let's ease the pressure in here! Where's Baldur?' He looked around, wanting to find the head of the garrison, or, at least, the master of the square. There had to be someone in charge.

'He's burned. Badly injured!' came the cry.

'Alys, come with me!' Ivan ordered, grabbing hold of Haski's bridle. The horse was becoming skittish, increasingly bothered by the noise and the sparking flames, trying to skip sideways.

'But Hakon...'

'He needs to make sure his wife is safe. His son too.'

Alys nodded as Ivan motioned for her to stay close, heading for the gates, conscious of the mess on the ground. Bodies of the dead and injured lay in their path; weapons, broken furniture, rocks, food, bloody slush. Even a dead dog.

'Get those gates open!'

Jonas watched his granddaughter, trying not to become distracted. He felt dizzy, ears ringing, remembering that he too was injured, though he felt little pain.

And then Alys' voice in his head, urging him to escape.

The gates were opening now, slowly, but to leave her?

'Go!' came her booming voice, and blinking, Jonas hunched over, making himself smaller, Magnus beside him, Leonid on his other side.

Where was Vik?

He couldn't risk looking around.

Vik and Ollo were trapped near the back of the crowd, looking after Haegel. Once the gates had been closed, they'd searched for somewhere to hide, but now they could see the gates creaking open again, and they saw a chance to escape.

Ollo laid his hand on Vik's arm. 'I can't. The guards will see me.'

There was fear in Ollo's eyes when Vik turned to him. 'Course you can. Change your cloak, cover your hair. We can help Haegel between us. Come on!'

Ollo looked uncertain. His instinct for self-preservation was sharply honed, and he was debating how best to save his hide. Swinging around, he saw the dead bodies of some of his friends, and he sighed. 'Well, I may as well go out in glory!'

Vik grinned, feeling worried himself. They had to hurry. Once Hakon caught wind of what his cousin was doing, he'd slam those gates shut. 'Hurry, then! We have to hurry!'

***

Karolina wasn't happy to see her husband, though she smiled as if she was.

She'd grown increasingly panicked by the violence in the square, worried by the fires and the unrest, but she felt little comfort in Hakon's return.

He was relieved to see her, though, and almost running across the hall, he flung his arms around her trembling body, pulling her close. 'Karolina!' He squeezed her, his chest burning, wanting to pull away, but the relief that she was safe overwhelmed him. The journey to Ottby and back had been horrific. His wound, the nightmares in the forest, the threat of The Hunter.

The mark.

Karolina squirmed, feeling crushed by his powerful arms.

'Anders? Where is he?' Hakon glanced around the hall, seeing no one, not even a slave.

'With Britta.'

'I need to see him.' Hakon felt an urgency to surround himself with his family. Deep in his heart, he feared what the mark meant. He feared what the gods would do to him.

He needed the reassurance of those he loved.

Hakon sounded strange, Karolina thought, following him through the hall, heading for the curtain. He was almost dragging her, his hand holding hers in a vice-like grip. She felt even more terrified, smelling the smoke.

Afraid of what would come next.

***

After a murky start, it was now the finest day in weeks, the wind barely a breeze.

Ivan glanced up at the sky, willing a cloud to appear. The buildings inside the fort were a mix of stone, wattle-and-daub, and timber; most with thatched roofs. Packed in tightly as they were, surrounding the square, it only took a hint of wind for one building to set its neighbour alight.

The violence in the square had quietened down with the arrival of their lord, and Ivan's presence on his horse, pointing his sword at everyone, threatening punishment for those who didn't disperse. Most slipped away, some back to their cottages, worried about the fire; others looked to head through the gates before someone pointed a finger in their direction.

Ivan glanced back at the hall, seeing no sign of his cousin, and sighing in frustration, he started bellowing orders. 'Water! We need more water!' Seeing that the open gates had released the pressure inside the square, he turned to Alys. 'Stay with me! I have to try and stop the fire before it spreads!'

Alys had thought about riding through the gates, seeing her grandfather edging closer to them, knowing that Magnus was with him, but she couldn't leave her daughter. Her sense of Lotta was blurry, though, and she glanced around, trying to see her. Surely she was here somewhere? But if she was, why didn't Jonas have her?

'Alys!' Ivan grabbed her arm, drawing her attention away from the open gates and the throng of people trying to escape the smoking fort.

Vik's head was up, hearing that name, and seeing the familiar figure sitting astride a grey horse, he blinked in surprise, stopping, Ollo banging into him. He was wearing a different cloak now, old and torn, making him look less like the master of the square and more like a beggar. Haegel was slumped against him, barely able to hold up his own weight. Vik had taken a quick look at his belly wound as he bandaged it, and experience told him that there was little hope for the man. But still, they couldn't leave him behind.

'We should leave Haegel behind!' Ollo decided, eyes on the guards who were shepherding them through the gates, feeling his friend become even heavier. 'He won't make it.'

'Shut up. He wouldn't leave you.'

That was true, Ollo knew. 'But what are we going to say?'

'Hopefully, nothing!'

Eyes on Jonas in the distance, Vik held his breath as they edged forward.

'Come on!' Magnus called, seeing the people moving ahead of them.

Jonas stumbled, almost toppling over his great-grandson, who had stopped right in front of him. He knocked into a man, who turned around with an angry glare. The man narrowed his eyes, first on Magnus, then on Jonas, and his mouth opened, readying a shout. Pushing Magnus aside, Jonas stepped forward, stabbing his knife into the man's belly. The shock rendered his victim silent, and holding the man close, Jonas stabbed him again, easing him down to the ground, leaving him there, lost amongst the crowd. And grabbing Magnus' hand, they moved quickly through the gates, heads low, Leonid beside them, leaving the fortress behind.

***

Karolina kept glancing at the open door as Hakon held his son to his chest. Anders had been growing restless, disturbed by the noise and the smoke, and his father's return had him red-faced and sobbing.

'He's missed me,' Hakon smiled, turning to Karolina. 'I think he's missed me!'

Karolina's dark eyelashes fluttered with speed. 'Yes, he has, but, Hakon, the fire. You must go. The smoke!' Eyes darting back and forth, she checked on her son, watching her nervous servant, who appeared ready to run through the door. 'What if we can't escape?'

Hakon ignored Karolina's worries as he handed the baby back to her. 'He's so much bigger. So strong already!' He could see his son wriggling, trying to climb out of his mother's arms, and it made Hakon more determined to fight, for his life, for his future, for the throne. 'Ivan is out there. He'll have it all under control, don't worry.' And arms out, he urged Karolina to come to him, holding his family close.

***

Clouds swept in from out of nowhere, buffeted by a strengthening breeze, and the fire spread.

Panic intensified as those who weren't looking to escape ran about trying to save their homes.

Ivan was swinging his horse around, pointing his sword in every direction, ordering his men to save the cottages, to protect the hall, to put the fire out. Hakon's household guards were battered and bruised after the riot, but weapons down now, they ran across the scarred square, carrying buckets of water. 'More water!' Ivan shouted, coughing, checking on Alys, who remained by his side.

They both heard a horn, and Ivan scowled, knowing that Lief was close. 'Oskar!' he called. 'Take the horses out of the fort.' And dismounting, he slid to the ground, reaching for Alys' hand. 'Come on, we need to move quickly.'

Alys glanced at the man in the red tunic, hoping she could

trust him with her horse. And slipping her boots out of Haski's stirrups, she threw her leg over his back, dropping down to the ground. 'Please tie him securely,' she pleaded as Ivan drew her away.

The man nodded, relieved to be given a task that took him out of the burning fort. And grabbing both sets of reins, he headed across the square, towards the gates, where Lief was riding in astride his giant black horse, mouth hanging open in horror as he took in the smoky carnage.

Falla panicked, following after her husband. 'Lief! You must get Borg. Hurry!' She could see flames dancing across the roofs of the cottages nearest the hall, yet there was no sign of Eggi and her son. 'Lief!'

'Wait there!' And Lief nudged his horse around the injured, and the dead bodies, leaving him in front of the hall steps. 'Karl!' he bellowed, dropping to the ground, eyes on the man who was following him. 'Take my horse! Wait here!' He couldn't see Hakon anywhere, but he saw Ivan with Alys, ordering their men to put out the fire. And eyes stinging with smoke, Lief slipped down the alley that led to his cottage.

***

Karolina needed Hakon to do something, but he wasn't moving, wasn't speaking. He wouldn't let them go. Anders was getting so upset now that she worried he would start vomiting. 'The smoke,' she tried again, wanting to escape Hakon's arms, but he held them both so tightly. 'We need to leave!'

The sharpness of his wife's voice cut through the haze in Hakon's mind, and he could feel the heat of the mark again, reminding him of how much he needed to prove to the gods. So grabbing her hand, he pulled her out of the bedchamber, into the hall, suddenly aware of just how intense the smoke was.

Ivan burst in through the doors. 'Fire's spreading! You need to get them out!'

Hakon could hear the panic in his cousin's voice. It woke him up further. Karolina's servant had hurried after them, and he turned to her. 'Britta, take my wife and son outside the fort. Wait there for me. Understood?'

The woman nodded, relieved to be leaving, and quickly following Karolina to the doors, they all disappeared outside.

Hakon hurried to Ivan. 'We're not going to lose the fort!'

Ivan nodded. 'The army's here now. We can put the fire out, don't worry, we just need to work quickly.' He started coughing again, smoke trapped in his throat, and glancing around the hall, spying a jug, he tipped wine into his mouth, swilling it around, swallowing it down.

Looking up, he started to say something to Hakon, only to discover that his cousin had gone.

***

People were milling outside the gates.

Warriors, servants, and traders and those who had been fighting in the fort, mingled with the returning army, merging together into one big mass of people.

Jonas moved through them slowly, trying not to attract any attention, worried that he'd be recognised before he could get Magnus and Leonid safely into the forest.

He hoped Alys would keep herself safe.

He'd no idea what had happened to Lotta.

'Keep moving,' he whispered to Magnus. 'Hands to yourself, eyes low, keep moving.'

And they slipped through the coughing crowd like snakes, curling right, then left, letting Jonas take the lead. He was tall enough to see where they were going; conscious of how many warriors flanked them now; worried by how far away the trees were.

Eddeth sat on Wilf, who did not like the crowd or the smoke. And hearing a bang from the fort as the fire caught something, he jerked in fright, rearing up, throwing Eddeth to the ground with a thump. She landed on Ollo, who dropped Haegel, who fell onto Vik, who lost his balance entirely, sprawling on the ground, one hand on his tight-fitting helmet which remained firmly wedged on his head.

Vik jumped back to his feet quickly, hand out to the strange-looking woman.

Eddeth shook her head, which clanged loudly, shocked to be down on the ground, immediately worried for Wilf, who had charged away. 'My horse! My horse!' And struggling back to her feet, she tried to see where Wilf had gone.

Vik saw an opportunity to get away quickly, and touching Eddeth's arm, he ushered her forward. 'We'll help you find your horse.'

Eddeth peered at the man, whose face she could barely see, hidden beneath the helmet. Her eyes skipped past him to the big-bellied man with the thick braids and his ashen-faced friend. 'That man is badly wounded. You can't carry him around like a sack of grain. Lay him down. I can tend to him once we find my horse.'

Vik froze. 'We can't. We can't stay here. We need to get into the forest.' He eyed the woman closely, hoping he could trust her.

Eddeth twitched all over, sensing danger and intrigue. 'Well, then, what are we waiting for?' And spinning around, ensuring that no one was looking her way, Eddeth hurried after Vik.

CHAPTER THIRTY FOUR

Having caught up with Wilf, who had quickly run out of steam and wandered into the forest looking for something to eat, Vik and Ollo stopped, laying Haegel on the ground, shocked to discover that he was dead.

Not really shocked, Vik supposed, surprised that Haegel had lasted as long as he had.

'Well, that's unfortunate,' Eddeth frowned, wishing she'd told the men to stop sooner, though, with a belly wound like that, the poor man had stood little chance.

Ollo bent over, hacking cough wracking his body, eyes full of tears. He didn't quite believe anything that had happened.

'What are your plans?' Eddeth wondered quickly, keeping a firm hold on Wilf, who looked as placid as a sleeping baby now that he was far from all the noise. 'You're escaping, yes? Running away?'

Ollo eyed the woman suspiciously. 'And you?'

'I'm a prisoner, I am. Taken by the Lord of Slussfall himself!' Eddeth glanced back through the trees, seeing the mass of people still gathered outside the fort. 'I'm looking to escape for sure, though I won't. Not yet.'

Vik felt just as suspicious as Ollo. 'Why not?'

'My friend's in there. Alys. I have to find her, help her. She's a dreamer, you know, a powerful woman indeed, but without me by her side... well, I'd hate to think what will happen!'

Vik grabbed her arm. 'You know Alys?'

Eddeth blinked. '*You* know Alys?'

'Who the fuck is Alys?' Ollo snapped, wanting to keep moving. 'They'll be looking for us before long.'

'Why?' Eddeth wondered. 'Who are you?'

'Friends of Alys',' Vik said. 'Jonas, her grandfather, is here. He was with Magnus. I'm Vik, his friend.'

Eddeth's eyes bulged in surprise. 'Well, aren't the gods full of mischief! Imagine that? With all those people out there, somehow, we found each other!' Eddeth felt a lift, some hope for the first time since they'd been captured. 'But we can't leave, not without Alys. And her daughter? Have you seen her?'

Ollo was getting more irritated by the moment. 'Vik, we have to go and find Jonas. They'll come after him.'

'But you can't leave!' Eddeth implored, grabbing the sleeve of the man named Vik. A handsome man, she thought as he tugged off his helmet. A strong-looking, handsome man, unlike the one who was blustering and bloviating next to her, beady eyes nearly popping out of his round head. 'Alys is still in there.'

Vik shared Ollo's urgency, but there was so much he wanted to know. 'What's your name?'

'Eddeth. Eddeth Nagel. Pleased to meet you, and this is Wilf,' she grinned, patting her horse.

Ollo didn't care, and with one look at his dead friend, he headed into the trees. 'We need to find Jonas!'

Vik eyed Eddeth. 'What will you do?'

Eddeth could feel her right foot twitching, wanting to go with the handsome warrior, but her left foot twitched more intensely, and she blinked. 'I must go back to my dreamer. She needs me! And if Reinar Vilander is coming, we need to be in that fort, doing what we can to help!'

Vik grabbed her arm. 'Reinar Vilander? Coming here?'

'Oh yes, after what the Vettels did, attacking Ottby like that, Reinar is coming for vengeance!' The thought of that made Eddeth giddy with excitement.

'You know this how?'

'Alys saw it. She sees a lot about Reinar, you know. Though that's hardly surprising!' And chuckling knowingly, Eddeth started picking her wart.

'I don't understand.' Vik was conscious of Ollo leaving, of Haegel dead at his feet, of needing to find Jonas. 'Reinar Vilander?'

'He kidnapped Alys! Yes indeed, best thing he ever did! He planned to sell her as a slave, but once he discovered how valuable she was, he kept her, made her his dreamer. And she helped him save Ottby from the Vettels and their old witch.'

Vik couldn't get his head around it.

'But once Reinar found out about Alys' children, he let her go. Of course he did! He loves her, I think. I can tell. But then, he loves his wife too. What a mess that is! Though hardly the most pressing concern for now, not with Hakon Vettel discovering that she's a dreamer, despite everything we did to try and keep that quiet. Cursed he is! Marked by The Hunter himself! He came for us in the forest, sliced off so many heads with that giant sabre of his. Pointed it at Hakon's chest, and we all know what that means!'

Vik could barely keep up.

'Vik!'

'Cursed by The Hunter? You mean he's been marked?'

'I would say so, though I'm not privy to Hakon Vettel's naked chest, no, I'm not! The gods don't appear to like the Vettels anymore, though, that's for certain. Oh, the adventure we've had, and now this. A flaming fort and men on the loose!' Eddeth was exhausted, shocked by how much had happened in such a short space of time. 'But I must go. I can't leave my dreamer, I can't!'

Vik nodded. 'We won't leave.'

'We won't?' Ollo grumbled, poking his head around a tree, unhappy about that.

'We'll hide,' Vik said quickly. 'We'll find a way to rescue you both, don't worry.'

'Well, either you or the Vilanders will! They're coming, you know. Coming to save us all!' And wheeling around with a grin, Eddeth hurried away, tugging Wilf after her. She stopped suddenly, glancing over her shoulder. 'And who are you, again? I will come back if I can, bring you some food, tell you more news!'

Vik smiled. 'I'm Vik Lofgren. Tell Alys I'm here. That Jonas and Magnus are here too.' He thought about Lotta, wondering where she had gotten to. 'Tell her we'll stay safe, but we won't leave. Not without her. Not without Lotta!'

Eddeth nodded, liking the sound of Vik's voice. It was as powerful and certain as a hammer, and shivering, she turned around, dragging Wilf through the forest, heading for the smoking fort.

***

Hakon's men, exhausted by two long marches and one disappointing battle, worked until they were at a standstill, heads drooping, spirits low. Their lord barely noticed as he strode from one end of the fort to the other, assessing the damage, demanding that the square be put back together quickly, conscious of how many people, horses, and livestock were being kept outside, needing to get back in. He was concerned by the gathering clouds which were now darkening with intent, wind swirling around them too. And though they all felt relieved that rain was on the way, Hakon wanted everything secure before the storm hit.

'My lord!' Lief came to a coughing stop beside him. 'It's out. It's all out.'

Ivan almost collapsed to the ground beside him. It was hardly the homecoming they'd wished for, and his mood was as dark as the clouds. The gods had most definitely taken up against them, he realised, spirits sinking as he tried to catch his breath. It wasn't just Hakon they despised, but him as well, and Slussfall. All of them. What else could explain what had just happened?

No one seemed to know.

Baldur was unconscious, likely dying. No one could find Ollo Narp.

There were bodies everywhere.

'We arrived back just in time,' Lief said, body aching. He slumped down to the steps, hands shaking, throat raw.

Hakon joined him, eyes on his dreamer who had crossed the square to see a returning Eddeth. 'Thanks to my dreamer.' He stared at his morose cousin, feeling a lift. 'You think we're cursed? But look at Alys! The gods brought her to us, her and Eddeth, and she got us back to the fort just in time!' He straightened his shoulders, the mark on his chest stinging like a burn, though no discomfort appeared on his face, which was beaming.

Falla had not returned to the fort, and Eddeth and Alys were enjoying a moment alone as they walked around the square, keeping their voices low.

Eddeth was speaking so quickly that Alys was struggling to keep up. 'But you didn't see my grandfather? Or Magnus?'

'No, no, not a sign of them, though Vik...' she grinned, 'Vik said they'd escaped too. He said he would try and find them.'

'And Lotta?' Alys pulled the hem of her black cloak out of a puddle of blood, grimacing. She could hear the cries of the wounded, some of whom were still lying in the square, and she felt the urge to help the servants and slaves tending to them, but she knew they wouldn't have long to talk privately. 'What about Lotta? I haven't seen her anywhere. I can't even feel that she's here.'

'But she was?'

Alys nodded. 'I saw her here, in my dreams.' Then she remembered the pier and the ship and Lotta telling her not to come to Slussfall, and she shuddered. 'She's gone.'

'Gone? Where?'

'On a ship.' Alys closed her eyes, trying to see anything, but all she saw was darkness. Darkness and a woman's voice. And opening her eyes, Alys felt the certainty of that voice pull her down like a stone dropping into the sea. 'North. Lotta's gone north.'

***

425

Lotta didn't feel anything.

The wind had numbed every part of her, and she had closed down her heart all by herself. It was a decision she'd made without thinking. Survival was all that mattered. Finding her family again. Keeping safe until then.

It was all that mattered now.

Ulrick's arm was around her, though it did not warm or comfort her. It could have been anyone's arm, and she could have been anywhere.

The ship rode the waves with a crash and a bang, sea spray flinging over the gunwales, white-capped waves swelling around her. She tried not to look at them; the constant motion of those waves was making her sick.

The crew hunkered down, wet backs against the gunwales. The faded blue sail was taut above their heads, puffing out proudly, filled by a strong wind.

And Lotta felt nothing at all.

***

Eventually, someone would put the pieces of the puzzle together and realise what had happened, Jonas knew, and they had to be far enough away from the fort when they did. But his worry for Vik and Alys and Lotta kept him dithering, trying to decide on the right course of action. Perhaps it was his wounds, he realised, needing to stop walking long enough to wrap some cloth around them. It wouldn't help Magnus and Leonid if he collapsed now. 'Wait,' he groaned, stumbling down onto a boulder. 'Just a moment. I..' Ears buzzing, Jonas reached for the bottom of his filthy tunic, looking to tear off some cloth.

'I can help,' Leonid said, wanting to be on their way quickly. His eyes never stopped moving, his ears open to every noise as he bent down, both hands on Jonas' tunic, tearing off a long strip.

'Where are you injured?' But he quickly saw the spreading patches of blood on Jonas' arm and thigh.

Magnus heard twigs snapping. Mumbled voices too. 'Someone's coming.'

Batting Leonid away, Jonas stood, missing his swordbelt, lost in the fort. 'Get behind me,' he hissed, shaking some urgency into his body. It had been a long few days without much sleep or sustenance, and he felt like collapsing, but straightening his aching shoulders, he started stepping backwards, wanting to feel the security of a tree trunk behind his back. Arms out, he shepherded Magnus and Leonid behind him, backing up until the three of them were almost pressed against the tree.

The snapping sounds stopped. The voices too.

No one spoke.

Leonid grabbed Magnus' hand, hoping that the boy would stay quiet.

Hoping he would too.

And then a voice.

'Jonas?'

Jonas' arms relaxed by his sides as Vik slipped through the trees looking as relieved as Jonas felt, Ollo grumbling after him. 'You took your time.' He glanced at Ollo. Behind Ollo. 'Where's Haegel?'

'Dead.' Ollo was miserable, wondering what he'd done, but thinking of the silver, he perked up. 'So we need to get going.'

'But Alys is in the fort.' Jonas turned to Vik. 'Did you see her?'

Vik nodded. 'I did, but we can't help her if we're captured. You don't want to end up back in that hole again. Or worse. Now that the Vettels are back, you probably wouldn't even make it to the hole. Not if Hakon finds out you're the reason his fort caught fire!'

It was a good point, and Jonas thought quickly. 'Help me wrap up these wounds and then we'll go. I know a place.'

***

Hakon sat at the high table as though nothing was amiss, his men filling the tables arranged in rows before him.

Everyone appeared stunned, confused, tired.

Hakon acted as though they were returning heroes, his smile bright, his eyes bursting with enthusiasm.

'We'll have to pull off some of the thatch. Start again. More snow's on the way for sure,' Lief said solemnly, wanting to head back to his cottage with Falla. He longed to lie next to her, holding her close in the silence of their chamber. He wasn't hungry. He didn't even care for the wine.

He needed to think.

Ivan looked just as thoughtful, sitting beside Karolina, whose eyes were on the dreamer and her sneezing friend.

She was pretty, Karolina thought, seeing Hakon's interest in her. Ivan's too. Ivan's she expected, but Hakon's? It did not displease her, though. She hoped and prayed nightly for her husband to find another woman; someone to occupy his time and his bed. And now he had a new dreamer.

Karolina smiled at Alys, hoping to find a moment alone with her, eager to see where her own destiny lay.

Alys dropped her eyes to the table. The food was plentiful and hot, steam rising from a bowl of pea and bacon soup. She ate without pleasure, though, just wanting the evening to hurry along. It was early, but dark, and a storm had swept in, battering the charred, ruined fort with vigour.

Eddeth sat next to her, eating like a horse. She was ravenous, enjoying the meal, already onto her second plate. 'They have some cooks here! What do you think?'

'I suppose so, Eddeth.' Alys was heartsick. They had travelled all this way, and Lotta had gone.

Eddeth stopped, mutton bone in hand, eyes searching Alys' face. Fires bloomed down the middle of the stone hall, flames tossed about by an icy wind that swept under doors and down smoke holes. 'We'll find a way out of this,' she whispered. 'We will.'

Alys tried to smile. 'I'm glad you came back.'

'Of course you are!' Eddeth grinned, 'for I'm a valuable assistant, am I not? And now that we're here, in this fort, we can start making things happen.' Her voice was a low rasp now, her lips near Alys' ear.

'Making things happen?'

'Oh yes, indeed. We're exactly where the gods want us to be. We are here, in Slussfall, where destiny will be decided!'

CHAPTER THIRTY FIVE

They were supposed to be leaving.

Now.

They were supposed to be leaving *now*!

Reinar turned around, annoyed that no one appeared as ready as he was. Even Sigurd was fussing about, making last-minute adjustments to *Dagger*. Elin stood on the pier, saying goodbye to Gerda. Ludo had disappeared back to the fort to get his gloves. Bjarni's two old dogs had followed him down the stairs, barking loudly, wanting to hop on board *Fury* with him.

Bjarni looked annoyed, barking back at them to keep quiet. He felt odd about leaving, worried that he was doing the wrong thing.

Agnette could tell, and she squeezed his hand firmly, not wanting him to see how scared she was, how worried that she'd never see any of them again. 'Look after Sigurd,' she said to Reinar, who'd joined them. 'He doesn't need any more injuries.'

Reinar smiled for the first time all morning. 'You think I can stop the gods? They've set their sights on Sigurd for sure. They're just using him for target practice now!'

Agnette leaned in, lowering her voice. 'And keep him away from that Ilene. She wants to be a lady, you can see it in her eyes. Alys said as much, didn't she? Poor Sigurd, the way he is, it wouldn't take much for her to get what she wants.'

'Bjarni!' came a voice, and Bjarni turned away, leaving Agnette alone with Reinar. The ships were busy as chests were scraped into place, oars slotted into holes, weapons secured under planks, ropes coiled and moved out of the way. *Fury* was stocked full of food, ale, and a crew of warriors as impatient to get underway as their lord.

'Keep an eye on Elin too,' Agnette warned, almost losing her balance. The harbour was generally calm, sitting in an estuary, but there was so much movement on the ships that the water rolled like waves, and Agnette couldn't stand still.

Reinar peered at her sharply. 'Meaning?'

Agnette glanced back at the stairs. 'I can't explain it. Elin was always my closest friend, and I forgave those little things she did when we were girls. But after the babies died, and now, with Torvig... I just have a bad feeling. Something's not right.'

Reinar brushed off her concern, eyes on Elin, who wore her favourite golden cloak, a blue dress peeking out beneath it. He frowned at Agnette. 'Grief makes everyone not right, Agnette. You've lost enough people to know that.'

Agnette could feel the wall Reinar had put up around his feelings for Elin, and she nodded. 'Well, I'll keep you in my thoughts. All of you. Come back safely.' And she wrapped her arms around Reinar's waist, feeling her milk leaking, anxious about getting back to Liara, who was surely ready for another feed.

'We will, don't worry. And you take care of yourself, and that baby. Hopefully, Gerda won't be too much trouble.'

'Ha! I've a feeling she'll be moving out of the fort entirely if she has to endure any more sleepless nights.'

Bjarni was back, frowning, fretting. 'We'd better get going.' He glanced around, seeing Ludo and Berger jumping on board their ships, his attention snapping to Sigurd, who was hurrying down the stairs carrying a tray of warm flatbreads. 'Looks like everyone's here.' He peered at Agnette, seeing tears in her eyes, neither of them wanting to say goodbye.

Reinar nodded, thinking of Ake. Knowing what the king wanted him to do.

They had sacrificed to Thenor, and he could still taste blood in his mouth. He hoped the Father of the Gods was with them. That he approved of Ake's need to kill Hakon's boy.

Reinar had kissed his mother and father goodbye. That made him feel odd too. Stellan's chair couldn't be carried down to the piers, so he remained back in the hall with Martyn, Rienne, and Liara for company. Reinar shook his head, still not believing that was true. For all the things that curse had wrought, the death of his sons and the loss of his father had cut him the most deeply. 'Come on!' he bellowed, voice carrying across the harbour where his fleet rocked and jostled against the piers. 'Time to go end those Vettels!' And reaching down, he grabbed Elin, hoisting her over the gunwale, into the ship.

Familiar faces were missing, Reinar knew. Some injured. Some dead.

He thought of Torvig and Tulia, nodding at Sigurd, who smiled, misery lingering in his blue eyes. It would feel even stranger for him, though hopefully, his brother would soon have a sword in his hand, a Vettel skewered on the tip of it.

Elin slipped an arm around his waist, smiling. She'd woken with an urgency to be gone, wanting to head for Slussfall. The old dreamer in Lundvik had warned that her husband's heart had been stolen by another, and she was determined to do everything in her power to get it back.

Reinar squeezed her, nodding at Holgar to get them underway. He saw his mother digging a cloth out of her purse, blowing her nose, and he smiled sadly, hoping he would see her again. He felt like a ship wrecked by a storm, but the sight of those cliffs and that old bridge gave him a renewed sense of purpose, and bending down, he kissed the top of Elin's head. 'Wind's fair,' he grinned, watching her hair blow around her face. 'You should have brought a hat!'

Elin laughed. 'I like the wind, you know that.'

And Reinar did. He felt certain about taking her along now, though as he stared at Agnette, his cousin's words rang in his ears and the worry on her face unsettled him anew. Turning away, he held up a hand to the men and women lining the piers, listening as the oarsmen slapped their long wooden blades down, slicing through the cold water, bringing them up again.

'My lord!' came a cry from the wall. 'My lord!'

Sigurd, whose attention was on his new cloak pin which had come undone already, unhappy with being forced through so much thick wool, looked up at the ramparts, sensing Ludo still beside him. He squinted, eyes narrowed against the sun, hand shielding his eyes. 'Who's that?'

But Ludo had seen perfectly, and he was running the length of the ship as a young boy slipped the mooring line, hopping out onto the pier with a giant leap, heading for the stairs.

***

Their bedchamber was grand, Eddeth thought, with a high ceiling and a wide stone hearth, and she felt pleased that Hakon had agreed to keep them together. He was becoming increasingly angry. Strange, extreme outbursts could be heard out in the square, down the corridor, and Eddeth was relieved that they were locked in their chamber all alone.

Once he'd discovered the reason for the riot and the fire, Hakon had become enraged, wanting to root out the men who had started it all, wishing he could kill Baldur Skoggi for making a mess of everything, though the useless man had succumbed to his head wound, and there was no path to vengeance there.

He'd sent scouts hunting through the forest, but those men had come back with nothing to report, which only infuriated Hakon further.

So it was a relief to be locked in their chamber, away from all the drama.

'What have you seen?' Eddeth asked as Alys joined her by the fire, enjoying the comfort of the fur-lined armchair. 'Anything?'

Alys shook her head. Lotta was at sea – she'd seen that immediately – but there had been no sign of her daughter since.

Magnus, Jonas, Vik, and another two men Alys didn't know were hiding in a cave. She hoped they were far enough away from the fort to stay safe, though, at the same time, she wondered how they were going to help them escape Slussfall from such a distance.

It was snowing heavily, flakes pattering the window, and though it was morning, the sky was dark with clouds.

'What about Reinar?' Eddeth wondered coyly, dragging her chair closer to Alys, who was holding her hands to the flames. 'Do you see him?'

'Sometimes.'

Eddeth nudged her. 'Why so sad?'

'There's no point thinking about Reinar. His wife is back in Ottby. There's no point thinking about him anymore.'

Eddeth nodded. It was better that they focused on getting out of Slussfall and finding Lotta. 'We need a ship.'

Alys looked up. 'We do. Vik's a good sailor, I know that. I've never liked the sea. It always made me sick as a child.'

Eddeth laughed, never having been on a sea journey in her life. 'Oh, I think it sounds like another adventure to me! Imagine what we might encounter up North!'

Alys didn't have a good feeling about any of it, but she nodded, jumping as the fire popped, remembering her last sea journey from Ullaberg to Ottby.

She could still smell the harbour, hear the gulls crying.

Feel Reinar's arms as he lifted her onto the pier.

***

'Holgar! Turn us around!' Reinar boomed. 'Get me back to that pier!'

Elin didn't understand. She saw Sigurd leaping out of *Dagger*, following after Ludo. She saw Agnette turn towards the stairs, Gerda too. She couldn't hear anything over Holgar's shouts and the crew's confusion, but she kept her eyes fixed on the stairway, waiting to see if Ludo would return. He'd disappeared up it quickly, Sigurd running after him.

And finally, backing up to the pier they had only just left behind, Reinar jumped out of *Fury*, charging after his brother to find out what had happened.

Eventually, Ludo brought a panting Stina down the stairs, Sigurd stumbling after him. 'They've taken Alys and Eddeth!'

'What?' Reinar's heart thumped, his body vibrating as he came closer. 'Who?'

'Hakon Vettel and his cousin. They took us!' Stina wanted to cry. She'd ridden into the fort only to hear that everyone had just left for Slussfall, but thankfully, one man had called out, recognising her, insisting that she'd still be able to catch the lord before he left.

Stina's companions were just as relieved after their long, fast journey, hurrying down the stairs after her.

'Where?' Reinar's guilt grew. 'What happened?'

'We were a few days into the journey when we were caught. Taken to a camp, where Hakon Vettel was injured. They made us care for him, save his life. They didn't know who we were, at first, and they were going to set us free.' Stina shivered, remembering the moment she'd seen Hakon snatch Alys' arm, yelling at her. She had drawn her horse into the trees with speed, remembering what she'd planned with Eddeth if something were to go wrong. 'I don't know how he discovered who she was. But he knew, I heard that. I had to leave. Eddeth stayed. We'd planned it that way.' And now tears came. All that pent up worry that she wouldn't get back in time. All the worry about Alys and Eddeth and what Hakon would do to them too. 'He was angry, so angry.'

'At Alys?' Agnette was there now, Bjarni beside her.

Reinar looked angry himself, trying not to imagine what Hakon Vettel had done to Alys. And then Elin joined them, and he tried to clear his face.

'The gods have cursed him,' Stina said, not recognising the woman who had slipped her hand into Reinar's, but frowning at her nonetheless. 'The Hunter came for him, pointed his sabre at him. And more. The gods have surely turned away from him now.'

Bjarni's eyes bulged open. 'The Hunter?'

The wind tore around them, a sudden gust, and they all had to hold down swirling cloaks and flapping hoods.

No one spoke.

Even Sigurd looked uncertain.

'Were they heading back to Slussfall?' Reinar wanted to know.

Stina nodded, shivering. 'Likely they'd be there now, if nothing else went wrong.'

'Alys will have told him about us, don't you think?' Ludo wondered, eyes on Reinar. 'He would have given her no choice.'

'I imagine so,' Reinar said, peering at Stina. 'Will you come with us? There's more I need to know, but we can't delay.'

'Yes. Please. I need to see Alys, and poor Eddeth. She tried so hard not to blurt out our secrets, though likely Hakon knows all of them now. And if they're in Slussfall, he's probably found out about the children.'

Elin's ears perked up.

'Children?' Reinar looked shocked, reality sinking in. 'Are you saying Alys' children were at Slussfall?'

Stina nodded.

'But what was she thinking, going to Slussfall? *Slussfall?*' Reinar was wild. 'Why didn't she tell me? That was never going to end well. Hakon Vettel was going to Slussfall!'

Reinar's voice banged off the cliffs, his anger echoing around them.

'Well, likely you had other things on your mind at the time, Cousin,' Agnette said gently, inclining her head to where Reinar's wife stood, looking on with curious eyes.

Taking a deep breath, Reinar tried to calm himself down. 'Of course. Well, come with me, Stina. You can sail with us. I want to hear everything you know about...' His eyes met Elin's. 'Hakon Vettel. I want to hear all about what games the gods have been playing with him.'

***

Karolina had barely spoken since she'd left the hall with Falla, desperate to find somewhere to be alone. The fort was almost orderly again. The broken tables and stools had been taken away, and wild storms had torn through the square, washing it clean of blood. Charred pieces of wood had been replaced; thatch brought in to shore up collapsed roofs. The traders were back, farmers and craftsmen too, though there was a general sense of unease, an unspoken mistrust now. Guards eyed the men with black eyes and broken noses, wondering if they'd been the instigators. Wondering if they'd helped Jonas Bergstrom escape.

No one had found Ollo Narp, but Haegel Hedvik's body had been located in the forest, and there was an assumption that both men had betrayed their lord to rescue the old warrior.

It made sense of what had happened, and settling upon that as an explanation, the urgent hunt for traitors slowed. Nobody had any information to impart. In the clamour to escape the burning fort, the focus had been on saving lives, not on escaping prisoners. Though some of those had been caught, and a few of them named Ollo as a traitor. It did them no good.

They were still thrown into the hole.

Karolina's attention drifted to those men who gripped the prison bars, reminded of how Baldur had wanted her permission to kill a boy, and she sighed, knowing that if her husband had been there, he would have done it in a heartbeat. 'I'm glad you've returned,' she smiled, squeezing Falla's arm.

'You are? But not Hakon?'

Karolina's eyes swept the square. Snow was falling heavily, and both women had their hoods up, gloves on. The morning air was bracing, the stench of smoke still strong, despite the wind's best efforts to clear it out of the fort. 'Not Hakon.' Karolina started to cry. She leaned closer, whispering in Falla's ear. They hadn't been alone since the army's return, and she hadn't been able to reveal her fears to anyone. Hakon's new dreamer had been confined to her chamber, and Karolina wasn't sure she could trust her or the strange healer either. 'Something's wrong with him.'

Falla tried to look surprised. 'Is it? How so?' She urged Karolina further away from the hall, skirting the market tables, heading for an alley, wanting to disappear amongst the houses where no one could see them.

'He has...' Karolina felt reluctant to reveal Hakon's secret, for it was certainly a secret he was keeping, even from her. 'He has a mark on his chest.'

Falla froze, dragging Karolina closer, eyes popping open. 'You've *seen* it?'

Karolina nodded. 'He's been keeping his tunic on all night. Not undressing. Not in front of me. He got up early this morning, no doubt thinking I was still asleep, but I watched him dress. I don't think he saw me looking. He was sitting down, turned the other way, but when he moved, I saw a mark on his chest. Like a tattoo. It was enormous. It was... almost glowing.'

Falla glanced over her shoulder, wanting to get back to the hall and find Alys and Eddeth. Looking back, she saw the fear in her friend's eyes. She was young, with a baby. Pregnant again. Falla understood how she felt. 'Do you want to stay married to your husband?'

'What?'

It wasn't safe to be talking of such things, both women knew, and their voices were breathless whispers.

'Do you love Hakon?'

'No. He scares me. I am... scared.'

'Well, then you must help me, dear Karolina, and I will help you.' And smiling, Falla slipped her arm through Karolina's, turning her back to the hall.

***

Reinar was conscious of his wife, who stood in the bow talking to Ilene.

Frowning, Reinar wondered at the wisdom of having Ilene on board *Fury*. The men were already grumbling to each other, most of them just wishing Ilene was giving her attention to them. Shaking his head, he turned to Stina. 'And Alys thought he had the mark?'

Stina nodded. She felt ill. They'd left Ottby in a rush, and the wind felt strong enough to blow them up to Slussfall in a day, though Reinar had told her it was likely to take four.

Four days.

Stina couldn't help wondering what Hakon would do to Alys in the meantime.

'And what did Eddeth say about it?'

They were standing by Holgar and Bjarni, though they appeared more interested in the pod of whales following them, skipping over the waves.

'She thinks the mark will slowly destroy him. Likely make him mad.'

That didn't sound good for Alys and Eddeth, but perhaps it was a boost for their chances of taking Slussfall? 'Will it kill him?'

'I don't know.'

Reinar shivered, shoulders up around his ears.

Four days.

Elin watched them, listening to Ilene.

'They're as tight as thieves, always have been.'

'And that's the woman who says my brother raped her? Stina?'

Ilene nodded. 'So she says, but who really knows the truth? The only other people who were in that shed are dead. Who knows what really happened?'

Ilene didn't hate Stina, though she'd never been particularly nice to her. But she hated Alys with a passion. Alys, who had twisted Arnon around her little finger, making him stay with her when he so clearly wanted to leave his family behind. Ilene had loved Arnon, she was sure. She had dreamed of becoming his wife for years, and she knew that he'd loved her too. It was Alys who had kept him from being happy. Alys who had forced him to remain with her. He wanted a divorce – he'd told Ilene that, many times – but Alys wouldn't let him go. She was selfish, thinking more of herself and her whining children than her husband.

A selfish, selfish wife.

A husband-stealing wife, she grinned, eyes back on Elin Vilander, realising that the accusation levelled at her for so many years, could now be turned back on Alys herself.

Alys, the husband thief.

'My brother never hurt a woman in his life,' Elin insisted. 'I never saw him mistreat anyone. It just doesn't make any sense.'

'Well, Alys is a known liar. She hid that she's a dreamer from everyone. Even her own husband! Perhaps she planned to kill your brother all along? Tulia hated him. I saw that. They were always arguing. Perhaps they trapped him in that shed? Cornered him? Tried to kill him? And when it all went wrong, they needed an excuse.'

Elin didn't know what to believe, but she'd always believed her brother.

Torvig could never be a rapist. He wasn't a murderer.

'And what are they planning now? That's what we should be thinking about, Elin. What are they planning now...'

CHAPTER THIRTY SIX

Night intensified Hakon's fears.

He sat in his bedchamber, fire blazing in the hearth, Lief silent opposite him, Ivan twitching on his right.

Hakon's chest felt as though a branding iron was being pressed down on it. He could almost feel his skin sizzling. Teeth gritted, he tried to will the image of that dark mark away. He didn't look at it. He never touched it. He didn't know the shape of it, the colour or texture. He didn't want to know anything about it, except how to get rid of it.

Alys was no help.

She'd dreamed that the Vilanders were at sea, but the mark?

How was he going to get rid of the mark?

'There are few places better to defend from, my lord,' Lief said, desperate to break the silence. 'We will be ready. They have ships, but we have walls.' He had spoken to Falla, who'd revealed Karolina's news about the mark, and Lief felt disturbed. Confused. He could sense that they all felt much the same, but for very different reasons.

'And what about Jonas Bergstrom?'

Ivan rolled his eyes, not wanting Hakon back on that track again. Clenching his jaw, he turned to his cousin. 'He's long gone now, and we've bigger problems than an old man who's got nothing to do with the enemy that's about to sail into our harbour!'

Lief was surprised by Ivan's outburst.

So was Hakon. 'How do you know they're not working together?'

'Everyone we spoke to said Jonas Bergstrom came to get his grandson. They said Ulrick had taken him as well as the girl. He'd come to get them back. That's nothing to do with you. Nothing to do with Slussfall. And it's certainly nothing to do with Reinar Vilander or Ake Bluefinn, both of whom want us dead!' Ivan almost jumped out of his chair. His frustration was boiling over, mingled with fear and terror and regret and tiredness. He blinked, grabbing a piece of cake from the low table before them, wondering when the servant would return with more wine.

Lief sensed that he needed to cool things down. 'We must turn our attention to what's coming, my lord,' he said, braving Hakon's intense eyes. 'Ivan's right. Jonas Bergstrom is a distraction we don't need right now. A path we shouldn't venture down.' The old man was no friend of his, but Hakon needed to stop obsessing over him. He was one man. One. And they had an army on the move, wanting to kill them all. He blinked, thinking of Falla, of Borg and the baby to come. They were his family now, and Lief felt conscious of making the right decisions to keep them safe. He tried not to look at Hakon's chest, though the call of that mark lurking beneath his gold-trimmed tunic was demanding.

Hakon wanted to scream. Everyone was against him, yet he needed Lief and Ivan on his side. He'd already lost Dagfinn, Njall, Ulrick, Rikkard, Baldur. Even Ollo Narp was gone. All men he'd leaned on in one way or another.

Not forgetting Mother.

He felt alone. Exposed. Afraid.

Dragging up his head, he growled. 'Fine, I accept that. Jonas Bergstrom is nothing. We'll turn our attention to the Vilanders now. All of it. I'll take Eddeth out of Alys' chamber. She needs to be alone so she can focus on dreaming. That Eddeth's always talking, always muttering. I doubt my dreamer gets much sleep with her blabbering all night long.'

Ivan froze, reading something else in his cousin's eyes. 'I imagine she'd feel more able to sleep with Eddeth's company. If you want her to dream, you need to make her feel comfortable.'

Hakon laughed. 'Are you offering to help? To take Eddeth's place? You have some ideas about how to make Alys feel comfortable, do you, Cousin?'

Ivan was quickly irritated. 'No.' Hakon was itching for a fight, and he was struggling not to give him one. 'Do what you wish. I was just trying to help.' He dropped his head, fiddling with his swordbelt.

They were like a pair of bickering children, Lief thought impatiently, wishing they would focus. 'We need to think about training the men, my lord. It's the men who will defend us from the Vilanders, not your dreamer. With the weather so bad I've hardly seen a soul in the training ring since we returned. We need to change that quickly. If our men aren't sharp, we stand no chance.'

'Are you sure about that, Lief?' Hakon laughed, running a finger around the rim of his silver goblet. 'You do remember Mother, don't you? Oh, but there are many ways a dreamer can hurt our enemies. I'll just have to have a little word with Alys. Impress upon her the importance of helping to defeat ours.'

***

'We need a plan. A way to help Reinar and Sigurd. If we help them get into the fort, they can free us!'

Their chamber had one bed, big enough to fit three people, but Eddeth still insisted on sleeping on the floor. Alys lay on her side, leaning over the bed, watching her. 'We're prisoners, Eddeth. What can we do to help them?'

Eddeth felt tense, longing for a tea to soothe her tension. Her saddlebags had been confiscated, Alys' swordbelt too, though Alys still had her cloak, and it lay over her, keeping her warm. A fire burned low in the hearth, but the stone walls were cold, drafty, and both women could feel the icy breeze attacking every exposed area of skin. 'Well, we have friends, like Falla. And Ivan. I imagine he's working away at his cousin. He won't keep us in here for long. He can't! If he wants a dreamer's help, he must treat that dreamer with respect.'

Alys smiled, listening to Eddeth grumble on her behalf. She lay back on the bed, eyes on the dark rafters, thinking about Magnus and Lotta. It had been so long since she'd stroked their hair, wiped their faces, held them in her arms. Lotta had such chubby cheeks. Alys loved the soft feel of them pressed against hers. And Magnus' hair had grown so long. She blinked, seeing a glimpse of him, tears flooding her eyes. His hair was short, she saw, hacked off roughly, wondering what that meant. He looked so thin. So tired.

She closed her eyes, listening to the wail of the wind, trying to think of what to do. And then, trying not to think at all. She needed a dream desperately.

Hakon would come to her in the morning, and she feared how angry he would become if she had nothing to tell him.

'What if Stina got to Ottby in time? That's what you should dream about,' Eddeth murmured, rolling over, missing the sound of Rigfuss' rhythmic purring. 'What if Stina got to Reinar before he left?'

***

Reinar had no plans to stop. They would remain on board until they arrived at Slussfall. It was no scenic adventure. Not a fishing expedition.

It was war.

They took turns relieving Holgar and those men who watched from the bow, alert to danger; whether it was from enemy ships, creatures from the deep, or fast-moving storms masked by darkness. It was always better to see what was coming before it arrived. To have some warning.

Leaning on the tiller, Reinar tried to keep alert, but the darkness and the constant motion of the ship had him feeling sleepy. He saw his wife, lying sound asleep next to Ilene, and he wanted to take Ilene's place. He was sure Ilene wouldn't mind. She'd spent the afternoon flirting with his men, when she wasn't gossiping with Elin.

Twisting his head to the right, he watched the waves glistening in the moonlight, remembering Alys' hair streaming behind her as she stood on board *Dagger*. She'd looked so sad and lost, though he could hardly blame her. Beaten by her husband, captured by him and Sigurd. What did he expect?

And now Hakon Vettel had her.

Alys the dreamer.

Reinar remembered what she'd done to Torvig, and it reassured him slightly.

Alys the warrior too.

***

Magnus, Leonid, and Ollo were asleep at the back of the small cave Jonas had led them to. Jonas sat in its mouth with Vik, watching the trees blow about before them, listening, waiting, expecting to be attacked at any moment.

'Still can't believe Reinar took Alys. A Vilander? When did those boys become slavers?' Jonas shook his head, running a hand through his hair. He felt impatient, frustrated with waiting, but they both knew that their best chance of getting into the fort rested on the Vilanders coming to attack the Vettels.

'Well, desperate times, I suppose,' Vik sighed, back aching from sitting around so much. He was growing just as frustrated as Jonas, but it wouldn't help anyone if they did something reckless now. 'Makes little sense, though. I doubt Stellan would have approved.'

'No, he wouldn't, and if I get my hands on either of them, I'll have something to say about it.'

'Well, according to that Eddeth, it goes a lot deeper than anything we know about. Don't imagine Alys will want you sticking your nose into her business.'

'She might not,' Jonas agreed, 'but this time, I won't be holding my tongue, I promise you that. Not after what her bastard husband did to her.' He glanced back at Magnus, listening to Ollo's deafening snores, thinking about Lotta. 'Why did Ulrick Dyre take those children in the first place? And why did he keep Lotta?'

'Magnus said she looked just like his own daughter. That's what the other man told him. The one with silver teeth.'

'Mmmm, that may be so, and I'm sorry for him if that's the case. I know how it feels to lose a daughter. But to take a child? And what about Lotta? Why was she so happy to go along with him?' Jonas poked the small fire at their feet with a stick. They were cold. So very cold. Snow lay on the ground before them, and though they hadn't wanted to attract any attention, dawn was on its way, and they were eager to cook the three small perch Vik had caught for breakfast. It was safer than burning a fire during the day when Hakon's men were likely to be out searching for them.

'Lotta has dreams, so who knows what she's seen? But the only person we can focus on now is Alys. And our best chance of getting her out of Slussfall is to wait for the Vilanders, and hope your friend Eddeth has the right of it.'

***

Unlike Ottby, Slussfall had only the two sets of gates to defend. Only the one set of walls. The fort perched up a steep rise, overlooking an open harbour, inviting enemies into the range of its archers, with no protection for them at all.

Though Lief did not feel confident. Not with Hakon in charge.

He didn't speak as he walked the ramparts with Ivan, squinting, the early morning sun glaring in his eyes. Hakon had left them to talk to the dreamer, and Lief didn't feel good about that either, worrying for Alys' safety.

He glanced around, not sure what he was thinking, but something pulsed in his veins, urging him to act. 'Karolina told Falla that she saw the mark on Hakon's chest.'

Ivan jerked to a halt, making Lief stop and turn back to him.

'The mark?' Ivan was horrified; the miserable-looking man had delivered those words as casually as if he was announcing what was for supper. He glanced around, seeing men coming out of the tower to his right, but no one within hearing distance. 'What?'

Lief came close enough to keep his voice low, though up on the ramparts, the wind was howling like a wild beast. 'Karolina is worried. Scared.'

Ivan liked Karolina. She was a good mother and a kind woman; far too gentle for Hakon. 'Scared of the mark?'

Lief nodded. 'Of the way your cousin is behaving too. He seems more and more... extreme.'

'He's been through a difficult time, you know that. Losing Mother. Losing Ottby. The wound. The Hunter.'

'He murdered Rikkard. We all know the boy did nothing wrong.'

Ivan's body tensed, feeling backed into a corner. 'And? How can I help you, Lief? What do you want from me? I'm not Hakon. What do you expect me to do?'

Lief felt disappointed.

In himself.

He had misread Ivan's face and his words. He was no more than his cousin's puppet, as he'd always suspected. They were joined by blood, by dependence on one another, and Lief doubted anything would separate them now. 'Forgive me.' His voice hardened as he stepped away. 'I felt concerned about the changes I was seeing. About how those changes would impact our chance of beating back the Vilanders. If the dreamer is right and they have the Stornas men, it won't be easy.'

'You forget that *I'm* the head of our army, Lief,' Ivan muttered. 'Hakon put *me* in charge. My cousin has been unwell, disturbed by what happened in the forest. Who wouldn't be? But he sees hope in this coming battle. An opportunity to turn our fortunes around. He's still the man destined to be king. You know it as well as I.' Ivan was working hard to convince himself that everything he said was true, barely thinking about Lief at all. 'And Hakon *will* change the gods' minds. He'll show Thenor that the Vettels are still the rightful rulers of this land, you'll see.'

He sounded like a child, Lief thought, nodding as though he believed everything Ivan was saying. And realising that there was nothing more to say, he turned away, heading for the guard tower.

***

Hakon had sent Eddeth out for a walk with Falla and Karolina, wanting Alys all to himself. And after they left, he locked the door.

Alys panicked, reading his thoughts. There was nowhere for her to go. No escape. Just one door. One shuttered window.

One marked lord with lust in his eyes.

He was a boy, Reinar had scoffed, just a boy, and Alys thought of Magnus, remembering how expertly she could distract him away from the one thing he wanted more than any other. Usually the rest of the meal she'd been saving for Arnon.

'And what did you dream of last night, Alys? Anything useful? Anything about our enemy?' Hakon smiled. The soft glow of the fire made Alys' hair glisten like gold, and he was transfixed, barely caring to hear what she said at all.

Alys thought quickly as he circled her, conscious of the bed beside her and the hooded look in Hakon's strange eyes. And she remembered her vision of the woman called Mirella. Distracted, eyes wandering to the fire, she hadn't realised how close Hakon was until he grabbed her arm, yanking her towards him. She froze, smelling wine on his breath. 'Yes, I did!' she exclaimed, trying to pull away. 'The Vilanders! I... saw things about them.' She tried to think of what those things might be, closing her eyes for effect. Or so she thought. An image of Karolina holding Anders Vettel came to mind, and when she opened her eyes, Hakon could see fear in them.

'What is it? What did you see? It was something. Definitely something.'

'I saw... your wife. Your son.'

'What?' Hakon hadn't been expecting that, and he straightened up, eyes full of worry.

'They're in danger. Your wife was screaming, clutching your son, trying to protect him. To shield him.'

All thoughts of Alys and the bed gone, Hakon turned away from her, staring at the fire. 'My son? What happened to him? What was happening?'

Alys could hear the anger in his voice now, and she panicked, squeezing her eyes shut again, trying to see something else. 'I hear a lot of screaming. Noise. Loud voices. Like an attack. I...' She opened her eyes. 'Your wife was screaming, your son was crying. I don't know why.' Alys shook her head. 'Sometimes, I only see fragments, and it's hard to know what they mean.' She remembered Tulia, regretting how much she sometimes only saw fragments.

Hakon strode back to Alys, grabbing her arm again. 'You must find out more.'

Alys nodded. 'I need some air. I need to breathe.' For though the chamber was drafty, Alys found the lack of freedom suffocating. She longed to feel the wind in her hair and sand between her toes.

Hakon peered at her. 'Air? Of course. I will take you for a walk. I will take you around the fort. Perhaps it will help to see things more clearly? And my wife! I will take you to my wife and son. Touching them might help. Holding something of theirs!' Hakon was desperate, squeezing Alys so tightly that pain contorted her face, and realising it, he backed away, eyes on the door. 'Grab your cloak. We'll go before the snow comes down again, for surely it will.' Hakon needed some air himself. His chest throbbed, and the thought of cold snow was welcome. He wanted to fall into it, soak his chest in it, take away the oppressive heat of it. And then he was stumbling, falling onto his knees, black patches flashing before his eyes, screeching noises in his ears.

'My lord?' Alys dropped down by his side, not sure what was happening.

Hakon couldn't hear her. Everything was dark, as though he was in the forest again with the giant shadow of The Hunter looming over him, lethal-looking sabre glinting in the moonlight. And then he heard a voice.

'I am coming, Hakon Vettel. I am coming for you!'

***

They had whispered about Hakon as they walked through the square, Karolina growing in confidence as Eddeth talked, amazed by how much knowledge the healer possessed of the gods. Knowledge of herbs and magic too.

'But what will they do to us?' Karolina fretted.

'Us?' Falla stared at Eddeth. 'The gods only care about the one who's marked, isn't that right, Eddeth?'

Eddeth shrugged. 'No idea! But if you want to avoid an angry Thenor, I wouldn't spend my time near the one he so desperately wants to destroy. Think of it like a frozen lake. The person standing near the crack is likely to fall in and drown, but those standing nearby have just as much chance of being sucked down to their deaths as well!'

That left Karolina speechless, shivering with worry.

Falla was determined to act. 'What can we do? Kill him?'

Karolina gasped. 'Falla!'

Eddeth laughed out loud. 'I don't think we need to get involved in that. The gods will take care of him, or perhaps the Vilanders?' And smiling now, Eddeth hoped more than anything that Reinar and Sigurd would arrive soon and put their swords to the vile Lord of Slussfall. 'But I'm sure you can work on his cousin, Falla. We need him on our side.'

Falla's eyes lit up. She thought of that fool Ivan with a smile, knowing how desperately he wanted to please her. 'I can get Ivan to kill him!'

'*Falla*!' Karolina felt ill.

Eddeth's attention wandered, watching three children tussling on the ground, fists flying. 'Not kill him. I doubt Ivan could be convinced to hurt his cousin, but perhaps he can help keep us safe? Protect us? A man as cursed as Hakon? He's a danger to us all. While he remains the lord here, no one is safe. No one at all!'

***

Hakon walked out of the hall, unsteady on his feet, Alys by his side. 'I can't see my wife anywhere, can you?'

Alys scanned the square, shaking her head. The market appeared busy, but she saw no sign of an elegant lady. 'No. Perhaps you should go back to the hall and sit down? I could go and find her for you?'

'You think I'm going to let you out of my sight?' Hakon snatched Alys' hand, pulling her close. He was still light-headed, ears buzzing, anger surging. 'You think I'll just let you leave?' Sweat dripped down from his hair, soaking through his tunic too. He felt like falling into a pool of cold water. And closing his eyes, he squeezed Alys' hand until she yelped. 'You will not leave my side, Alys. We will find my wife together, and then you'll see more. More of what is coming. I need you to see everything, do you understand me?'

He was shouting, and Alys felt afraid. He wouldn't kill her, he needed to keep her, but every shouting man with angry eyes was Arnon, and she flinched, watching his left hand twitch by his side.

'What's going on? Hakon?' Ivan emerged from the tavern, a deep frown carved between his eyebrows. 'Let her go!' And lunging forward, he yanked Hakon's right hand away.

Hakon swung around, left hand raised, incensed.

Ivan didn't care. He saw the terror in Alys' eyes, and he felt just as wild. 'You can't treat people this way, Hakon! Not boys. Not women. Not dreamers!' He was yelling, and sensing everyone freeze around him, he tried to stem his exploding rage. Pulling Alys closer, out of Hakon's grip, Ivan stepped back, staring at his wide-eyed cousin, seeing the sheen of sweat on his forehead. 'You're not yourself, Hakon. Perhaps you're ill again? Whatever the case, you need to leave Alys alone. Pull yourself together. If you want her to help you, you can't treat her like a dog.' And turning away from his cousin, he slipped an arm around Alys' back, heading for the gates, heart thumping.

Hakon watched them go, the voice in his head crashing around him like thunder.

CHAPTER THIRTY SEVEN

Sigurd and Ludo leaned over the shield rack, eyes on *Fury*. The weather had been helpful, the wind like a strong hand, pushing them up the coast towards Slussfall.

Ludo felt anxious, worrying about what they would face when they arrived.

The fort rose up from the harbour like a tower, he remembered. And those walls would be deep with archers assaulting them from the very first sight of their masts.

Sigurd nudged him. 'What do you think Alys is doing?'

'Telling him everything she can, I'd say. Wouldn't you? If you had children to protect, you'd tell him everything to stay alive.'

Sigurd nodded. 'So he'll know every secret, every plan?'

'If Alys dreams it, I expect so.'

'And will she try and hurt us?'

'Alys?'

'She is a dreamer.'

'She's not like that old witch, though. I don't think she'd know how to.' Ludo frowned, hoping that was true.

'But Alys killed the old witch, didn't she, so perhaps she knows more than she realises...'

***

Ivan walked Alys down to the harbour, wanting to give Hakon a chance to calm down.

She was grateful, certain that she was standing on the pier Lotta had stood on in her dream, warning her not to come to Slussfall. But why? What had her daughter seen?

Alys frowned, willing the answers to come, but she heard nothing.

Saw nothing.

'Did he hurt you?' Ivan asked, peering at Alys' face.

She tried to smile. 'No, not really.'

Ivan looked doubtful. 'I don't know what to do about him. I worry.'

'You should worry.' They walked down the pier, cloaks flapping in the fresh breeze, the sun lost behind dark clouds now. Alys' eyes drifted to the four merchant ships moored along the piers. She saw one warship too. Just the one. Further along the shore, she noticed sheds, hearing hammering and shouting as the shipbuilders worked on Hakon's long-desired fleet. 'What is coming for your cousin is dark, Ivan. You should feel worried.'

'Do you know that for certain, though?'

'No, but you can see what's happening to him with your own eyes. You don't need me to tell you what's coming.'

It was true, Ivan knew. Lief had seen it too. Soon everyone in the fort would see it for themselves. 'Will it get worse?'

'Yes.'

'But what can I do?' Ivan grabbed Alys' hand, turning her towards him. She was beautiful, desirable, but he blinked all thoughts of that away, only worry in his eyes now. 'I can't let something happen to him. We're like brothers. He's mine to care for, just as he's always cared for me. We're family.'

It was a strong bond, Alys knew, and that would likely become a problem for Ivan. 'You will come to a crossroads,' she said darkly, images tumbling before her eyes. 'In the darkness, you will not be able to see, only feel. You will need to choose quickly, which path you wish to turn down.' She shivered, seeing images of Ivan screaming now. 'You will be forced to choose.'

Ivan turned away, conscious of the gulls swooping down to the pier, stepping tentatively towards them, wondering if they had any food to share. Water lapped at the pilings, the ships butting against their mooring posts. He wanted to leave, to sail away from every one of his mounting problems.

But shoulders slumping, he knew that he couldn't.

For he was a Vettel, and the Vettels were destined to rule Alekka.

He couldn't give up now.

***

Magnus was angry.

Jonas was surprised by just how angry. 'Your mother won't want to escape only to find your head hanging from Slussfall's gates, will she?' he growled, snapping a twig in half, tossing it onto the pile of kindling he was making. 'You think you're a warrior now, at ten? Think you've got all the answers, do you?'

Magnus and Leonid had collected handfuls of moss, and they were laying it on the floor of the cave, drying it out. Magnus felt bored and irritated. Nothing was happening quickly enough. He didn't know where his sister was, but his mother was trapped inside the fort with the Vettels, and it was his responsibility to save her.

He wanted to save her!

Jonas grinned, watching Magnus seething beside him. 'Many times in my life, I've had to wait. Waiting is torture.' His smile faded quickly, and looking down at the twigs, he tried to drag his mind away from all the mistakes he'd made. 'But waiting gives you time to think.'

'Or waiting means you missed your chance.'

'True. It's the toss of a coin, isn't it? And when you're a man, making decisions is one of the hardest things you can do. Especially when it involves other people's lives.' Jonas glanced back to where Ollo and Vik were sharpening their weapons. 'When life and death hang in the balance, it's not easy to choose the right path.'

Magnus' face cleared, hearing the sadness in Jonas' voice. 'I don't want my mother to die.'

'Nor do I. I held your mother as a baby. I felt that tiny weight in my arms, and I knew I would lay down my life to protect her. And I didn't. I haven't.' He was angry and sad; disappointed in himself. 'I should never have listened to her about your father. I was a fool.'

'Sometimes, I wished you'd come.'

Jonas blinked in surprise. 'You did?'

Magnus nodded. 'When I heard Mother crying, when I saw her face, I...' He hung his head. 'I didn't know what to do. I couldn't save her.' Looking up, tears blurred his eyes. 'I didn't know what to do!'

Jonas pulled Magnus into his arms, tears rolling down his cold cheeks. 'We can't go back, can we? So we go forward, make everything different. Your father's dead, so we've all got another chance to make it right. We'll save your mother, Magnus. It just means biding our time here. Keeping alert. But we'll save her, I promise.'

***

Stina didn't know if they would make it to Slussfall in time to save Alys and Eddeth. She didn't want to imagine what Hakon might have done to them when he found out the truth. Especially Alys. She had killed his dreamer. He would blame her for his defeat in Ottby. Perhaps hurt her, if not kill her.

'But no man would kill a dreamer,' Reinar tried to convince them both. They stood by the mast, eyes on the murky horizon. The clouds were tumbling, dark grey and threatening a storm, and

Reinar was growing tense. 'Not unless he wants to die.'

'Or unless he's not in his right mind. Unless he can no longer make sound decisions anymore.'

Reinar watched Elin approach, and he tried to smile, though he felt worried, breath trapped in his chest. He wanted to stop, head ashore, light a fire and feel his fingers and toes again. Speak to his brother too.

And then Elin's arm was around his waist.

'Come and have something to eat,' she smiled, ignoring Stina.

Stina had been surprised by Elin Vilander's coldness towards her, and though she'd tried to smile and be friendly, Elin had barely met her eyes.

'Later,' Reinar said, 'but take Stina, she needs something to eat.'

Stina had little appetite, and she wanted to shake her head, but realising that she needed to keep up her strength, she nodded, following Elin to the stern, where Ilene was already helping herself to flatbreads and cheese. She sighed, knowing that the two women had had their heads together throughout the journey, no doubt talking about both her and Alys.

'Stina,' Ilene smirked, beady eyes bright with interest. 'I thought you'd never tear yourself away from the lord. You are as thick as thieves!'

Stina ignored her, taking a flatbread, using a wooden knife to dig into the small pot of soft cheese.

'I suspect my husband has a lot of questions,' Elin murmured, turning her eyes to Stina for the first time.

The wind roared, hair and cloaks flapping, sail snapping, strakes creaking, and Stina only just made out her words. 'He does. He wants to know what's coming. What danger we might face.'

'But you're no dreamer,' Ilene smiled. 'What could you possibly tell him?'

Stina would have happily pushed Ilene overboard, but she smiled back just as sweetly. 'Well, I can't share what I discussed with the lord, Ilene. He wouldn't want me to, I'm sure.'

Ilene clamped her lips together, looking at Elin.

'No,' Elin agreed, 'he wouldn't. My husband carries a great responsibility to keep us all safe. He'll do what is necessary to get us back to Ottby alive. He's a very loyal man.' She held a flatbread in her hand, though she didn't want it.

She didn't want food at all.

Stina shivered. Elin Vilander had a look in her hazel eyes that reminded her of Torvig, and she turned away.

'Your friend, the dreamer...' Elin began.

Stina turned back, fearing what was coming next.

'From what I hear, she did what she could to survive in Ottby. She helped Reinar defeat the Vettels. And now, what will she do to help the Vettels, I wonder? For if she is to survive in Slussfall, she'll have to help them, won't she?'

'Only what she must. As you said, she did what she could to survive. She has children, and to save their lives, she'll do whatever it takes.' This time Stina didn't take her eyes off Elin. There was something about the woman that made her uncomfortable, as though she was digging with a particular purpose in mind. No doubt Ilene had shared some gossip about Reinar and Alys, though what was there really to tell about Reinar and Alys?

'I imagine she will. When it comes to our families and the ones we love, we'll always do what we can to protect them. If only I'd returned to Ottby in time to save my brother, but sadly, I was too late.'

Elin's voice was as sharp as a blade, and Stina shuddered. She sensed Ilene smirking, and ignoring her, and leaving the cheese-covered flatbread on the chest, Stina stood, gathering her billowing cloak around herself, hurrying away from the women.

Stumbling down the deck with speed, she almost knocked into Reinar, who'd remained by the mast, lost in his thoughts. He watched her go, turning back to his wife, who was staring after Stina with an odd look in her eyes.

***

After returning Alys to her chamber, Ivan headed to the hall to confront Hakon. His cousin needed to understand the importance of keeping his dreamer safe. Having a dreamer gave them a better chance of surviving what was coming. It made no sense for Hakon to mistreat her.

When he found his cousin, though, his anger softened, for Hakon sat beside Karolina, cradling their son, tears in his eyes. 'What's happened?'

'Happened?' Hakon blinked up at him, confused. 'What makes you think something's happened?'

Ivan glanced at Karolina, who appeared to be pleading for help with her eyes.

'I'm just so pleased to be home, with Anders. Look how big he's grown!' And lifting the boy up, he turned him around to Ivan. Anders grunted, legs working hard, and Hakon lowered him, trying to make him stand on his lap.

'He has,' Ivan agreed dutifully.

'And Alys? You've returned her to me? Now that you've had your fun?'

'Fun?' Ivan took a cup of ale from the tray a slave was offering him. He smiled at the young woman, who bobbed her head shyly, disappearing back to the hall. 'Saving her from you, you mean? You were hurting her.'

'I was trying to get her to understand the seriousness of the situation, Ivan. That she needs to help us. I don't trust her, do you?'

Ivan didn't know. He wanted to. 'What choice does she have but to help us?'

Hakon handed Anders back to Karolina and stood. He felt better, the dark clouds receding now. He couldn't hear the voice anymore, but when he glanced at his wife, he remembered Alys' words, and he felt a jolt of fear. 'But the Vilanders? Can we trust her to go against them? She helped them defeat us, so why would she help us defeat them?'

Ivan sighed, finishing his ale quickly, wondering how long it had been since he'd had a woman in his bed. And realising that he didn't know, he decided the answer was far too long.

'Ivan?'

Ivan turned back to his cousin. 'Because she cares about living. She's been a prisoner twice over. I imagine she desires her freedom. If she helps us defeat the Vilanders, you will free her, won't you? She deserves as much.'

Hakon shrugged, though he had no intention of freeing Alys at all. He liked having a dreamer, especially one so beautiful. He glanced at his wife, who trembled beside him, fussing over Anders. 'Finish your wine, Karolina, and then I will take you to the dreamer, and she can tell us what she sees.'

***

'But what do you see?' Eddeth felt impatient for action, and though she knew that Alys was trying her best to find answers, it was hard to stay still and wait for something to happen.

'I see an end.'

Eddeth blinked, hopping back to the bed, where Alys sat quietly, eyes closed. She flopped down beside her, twitching. 'An end?'

Alys' eyes remained closed. 'Everything must end.' Her voice sounded far away, like an echo as she searched through the darkness, looking for answers. 'Life is a cycle, and the end of that cycle is death.'

Eddeth peered at her, sensing that Alys was elsewhere. 'What about the gods? Can they help you? Can Valera?'

Alys couldn't see the gods. She was in a dark forest now, trees like long-fingered spirits hanging over her, the moon glaring down a narrow path. 'I see no gods, only secrets, memories. Hidden away. Every answer is there, hidden away from me.'

Eddeth shivered beside her. 'The answers to what?' she whispered.

'The answers to who I really am.' And eyes springing open,

Alys turned to Eddeth, gripping her hands. 'We need to see more, Eddeth. To know more. We need the books. Your herbs. We have to get out of this chamber. Reinar and Sigurd will come.' That thought came like a clap of thunder, shaking Alys' limbs. 'And if I can't see what's going to happen, how will we help them?'

***

By dusk, their helpful westerly wind had become a wild storm, and Reinar found himself praying that Thenor would see them safely to shore.

The sail was packed away, the oars stored, and Holgar stood hunched over the tiller, jaw clenched, soaked to the bone, dragging on that old wooden stick until his shoulder wanted to snap right off. Reinar didn't envy him, but there was no one he'd rather have steering *Fury* through the storm. Apart from Bolli, who he knew would be cursing the weather gods on *Dagger*.

Reinar popped his head up often, though in the stormy darkness it had been hours since he'd seen another ship. He tried not to worry, knowing that they were in the hands of the gods now. And if the gods were with them, his fleet would survive to face the Vettels.

And if not...

Elin clung to him as they sat just behind Holgar, wet backs pressed up against the stern, swaying with the surging ship. He regretted that he'd brought her along, putting her in danger, though he couldn't deny it was comforting to feel her in his arms. Stina sat nearby, next to Bjarni, head down, and he thought of Torvig, and Alys who had killed Torvig, and he felt guilty for all of it.

He couldn't leave Alys with the Vettels. Whatever destiny the gods were weaving for him, he couldn't leave Alys in Slussfall. He heard Elin whimper as the mast creaked ominously, threatening to snap in half. Eyes up, squinting into the stormy darkness, Reinar wondered if Alys could see them. If she could help them somehow.

They would save her. *He* would save her.

But only if they made it to Slussfall.

***

Falla had retrieved Eddeth's saddlebags, tipping the contents into a basket which she carried through the hall and down to Eddeth and Alys' chamber, surprised to find that Alys wasn't there. 'Where's the dreamer?'

Eddeth was thrilled to see her, happier still to see what she'd brought in the basket. Falla had asked the cook for some herbs too, which she'd grudgingly harvested from her kitchen garden.

'Hakon took her,' Eddeth said distractedly, bustling about. 'I need a cauldron! Something to hang it on. A pestle and mortar too!'

'What? He *took* her?' Falla glanced over her shoulder, peering at the door. 'Why?'

Eddeth shrugged, choosing not to be worried. Worrying about things she had no power over sapped her energy, and Eddeth needed all her energy for what lay ahead.

She laid her grandmother's book on the table. Beside it, she placed a jar of honey, and a selection of mushrooms, willow bark, wormwood leaves and garlic.

She barely noticed that Falla had crept up beside her.

'I helped Mother, you know.'

Eddeth froze. 'The old witch?'

Falla nodded. 'She promised me vengeance. She wanted vengeance, and I helped her try and get it for both of us. For my son.'

'And now?'

'Now, I want to live. I want a future. The past can rot for all I care. It's now that matters. Now and what comes next. I have a son, a baby on the way. A husband I –' She stopped herself.

'Yes?'

Falla checked her enthusiasm. 'I want to live, Eddeth, so I will help you. You and Alys. Men are stubborn. Lief is too loyal. Ivan is worse. They live by some unspoken code. As though their honour, their reputation, their oath is more important than life. Than preserving life!' She shook her head, furious with Lief, who insisted there was nothing he could do to talk Ivan around; nothing he could do without Ivan's help. 'But we women, we know what it is to give life, so we do what we can to protect it, don't we?'

Eddeth's eyebrows were up, surprised to hear so much wisdom coming from Falla Gundersen, who'd seemed like such a shallow creature at first. 'You may help, then. Of course you may! We must work quickly, though. Alys needs to see what's coming, and we must help her!'

***

Hakon had taken Alys to his bedchamber, where she'd been relieved to see his wife waiting. And remembering Ivan's words about making the dreamer feel comfortable, he left the two women alone, Anders sleeping in his crib.

'I'm sorry,' Karolina whispered when she could no longer hear Hakon's footsteps in the corridor. 'I don't want to force you to see something about me.'

Alys didn't know whether it was possible to see anything, though she felt under pressure, knowing that Hakon would be furious if she didn't. 'I can try. Your husband wants me to try.'

'Why?' Karolina wondered, glancing at the crib. 'Have you seen something?'

Alys glanced at the crib too. 'Yes, I'm afraid I have.' Karolina Vettel almost curled away from her, not wanting to hear the truth, but she thought of Tulia, determined to do what she could to help Hakon's wife stay alive. 'I saw you with your son. You were screaming. There was a lot of noise, like a battle. I don't know what happened. Your husband was worried. He thought if he brought me here, I might see more. Perhaps by... touching you, or taking something of yours to dream with.' Alys thought of Salma's book, wishing she had it, but it was in her saddlebag with Haski, who she was worried about too.

'Oh.'

Alys smiled. 'I'm not an experienced dreamer, I'm afraid.' She took a seat beside Karolina, eyes on the flames swirling between them. The wind was strong, streaming down the smoke hole, whistling angrily. 'But I will try to help you.'

Karolina peered at her. 'My son. I only care about my son. About the one I'm carrying too.'

Alys nodded. 'You must keep them safe, I know, and I will help you. I can try.' She reached out, patting Karolina's hand. 'Don't worry.' And then she froze, more images coming to mind, and Alys quickly closed her eyes, seeing Karolina screaming, holding her baby to her chest.

And Reinar was there now, knife out, coming for her.

CHAPTER THIRTY EIGHT

The chamber smelled like Falla Gundersen, Alys thought as she crept back inside, not wanting to disturb Eddeth, who appeared sound asleep by the fire. But in the blink of an eye, Eddeth had bounded out of the chair, knife in hand.

'Where did you get that?' Alys wondered.

Eddeth was breathless. 'Falla. A surprisingly useful woman. Strong too. She helped me help you.'

'*Help* me?'

'You need to see!' Eddeth announced. 'And now, you can!' She stepped towards the table and chairs where she'd been working steadily since Falla had delivered her basket of supplies, sending a servant with the rest of the items Eddeth had requested. 'I have more flying powder! That will help, of course, and there's this.' She lifted a bowl, which stunk of blood.

'Chicken blood!' Eddeth said, reading her look. 'I also had Falla bring me Salma's book, which has just the spell we need.'

'For what?'

'Helping Reinar of course! With this spell, you can get the gates open. You can control the guard's minds. Make them do whatever you want!'

Alys looked doubtful, scratching her head.

'And then there's this!' Eddeth held up a tiny piece of blue cloth. 'It will help you dreamwalk.'

'To who?'

Eddeth smiled, taking Alys' hand.

***

Sigurd was having a nightmare.

Sigurd had had violent nightmares since he was a boy, so Ludo had remained mostly awake, not wanting his friend to launch himself off the ship.

The storm was terrifying; that was keeping him awake too. Ludo was not alone in that, he could see, peering out beneath his dripping hood. He wondered how Sigurd could sleep.

And then Sigurd lurched up with a yelp, panting.

Ludo grabbed him. 'Are you alright?'

Sigurd was quickly aware of the storm, the rain, and how cold he was. How wet too. He nodded, rubbing his eyes, feeling as though he hadn't slept at all. His hood flapped up over his head, dripping down his face. He brushed it back, rubbing a frozen hand over his hair.

'A nightmare?'

Sigurd nodded. 'I keep seeing Tulia.' Ludo couldn't hear him, so he shuffled closer. 'Tulia!'

'It must be hard.'

'It is. I keep seeing Torvig too. She's losing her balance, and I'm there. Stuck. I can't help her. I can hear her screaming, arms in the air, but I can't help her. I can't save her!'

Ludo felt terrible. It was hard to know what to say. Nothing could bring Tulia back. Nothing could bring Torvig back so Sigurd could kill him. There was no way to release his pain. He glanced down, seeing Sigurd's hands in white-knuckled fists. 'Tulia would want you to kill the Vettels, wouldn't she? To take Slussfall?'

Sigurd laughed. 'You really think that?' It made things easier when he thought of Tulia sitting with them, mocking their ambition and their oaths to Ake Bluefinn. She wouldn't be happy now. He could almost hear her grumbling in his ear, asking what he was doing, risking his life for a lord and a king. 'Tulia would tell us to go home. To fix the fort. To stay safe!'

'You don't think she'd like some vengeance? For Amir?'

Rubbing rain out of his eyes, Sigurd looked on in horror as *Dagger* rose up the wall of a wave, watching as the crew turned – those who were awake – gripping the shield rack, holding on for dear life.

'Hold!' Bolli roared, panic breaking his voice. 'We're going high! Wake up!'

Sigurd watched as the wave continued to rise, lost in the clouds now. He heard Tulia's scornful laugh, felt the warmth of her silky body draped over his. 'What are you doing, Sigurd Vilander?' she growled. 'Risking your life for your brother again? For what? What do you hope to gain? You want to please your gods?' He heard her laughing. 'But what have they ever thought about you?'

The wave rose even higher, Sigurd holding his breath now, clinging to a rope, Ludo slamming into him, both of them trying not to slide away.

'Hold on!' Bolli shouted, numb hands gripping the tiller like they were glued to it. '*Fuck*!'

The gods had saved him, Sigurd knew, seeing flashes of his father cradling a tiny bundle in his arms. The gods had saved him for a reason, and if they gave him another chance, he would prove himself worthy. Just one more chance and they wouldn't regret it, he prayed desperately, slippery hand losing hold of the rope he was clinging to.

'Sigurd!' Ludo could feel him sliding, and reaching out with his left hand, he grabbed Sigurd's tunic. 'Hold on!'

Squeezing one hand around the rope, Sigurd tried to. Teeth gritted, he snatched at Ludo, feeling his legs moving away from him, down the rising ship, watching as a hooded figure slid down the deck.

'Help!' came the shout, as Torfinn tumbled past them.

Whipping his hand away from Ludo, Sigurd lunged, grabbing Torfinn's arm, locking his hand around it, feeling the wet and heavy weight of his friend dragging him down.

He started to slide, shoulder wrenched in agony.

Bolli felt *Dagger* begin to crest the towering wave, knowing that they were going to come down hard. 'We're going down! Brace yourselves!'

And now *Dagger* tipped its prow over the wave, and Torfinn slid in the opposite direction, unable to find anything to grab hold of. Sigurd's left arm felt ready to pop out of its socket. 'Torfinn!' He tried to pull his friend back to him, but there was no strength in his arm at all.

Torfinn turned to Sigurd with terror in his eyes. Shards of lighting were slicing through the rolling clouds like golden blades, and screaming, arm straining, Sigurd yanked Torfinn towards him. Reaching up with his free hand, Torfinn snatched hold of Sigurd's tunic, trying to climb.

Sigurd could hear a raven's plaintive call.

Over the scream of the storm and Bolli's roaring voice, Sigurd could hear a raven, and he pulled Torfinn towards him, gripping him tightly as *Dagger* dove towards the sea. Breath pumping, he clung on, both men shaking and shivering. Ludo released his hold on Sigurd, helping Torfinn to squeeze in between them, showing him the rope they were gripping hold of. And turning, pushing in between his two friends, Torfinn tried to catch his breath, nodding at Sigurd, who closed his eyes, hoping to find the raven again.

***

Alys wasn't sure.

She didn't feel confident. She wasn't convinced that it made sense.

There were other people to find.

Eddeth glared at her in a very unlike Eddeth sort of way, and she sighed. 'Alright.'

'Read that chant before those herbs put me to sleep. Before someone smells the smoke and comes to find what we're doing!' Her voice boomed, and they both froze, staring at the door.

Alys turned to glare at her and Eddeth shrugged, embarrassed, silently pointing to the book. Nodding now, Alys ran a finger under each line of the chant, wanting to refresh her memory. She remembered dreamwalking with Agnette's help, wistful for the old cottage and Agnette's friendship. Her mind wandered to Stina, and she hoped that she was safe. She hadn't seen an image of her in days.

'Focus,' came the growl.

So taking one last look at the book, Alys pushed it to one side, wriggling about on her knees, trying to get comfortable. In order to slip into a trance, she needed to clear out any distractions, of which there were many. The steady beat of Eddeth's hands tapping the table started to calm Alys' mind, and the familiar scent of those herbs and the smoke wafting towards her loosened her tension.

And finally, closing her eyes, Alys saw where she needed to go, so taking a deep breath, she started her chant.

***

He followed the cat to the cottage.

It was dark.

Snow was on the ground.

The cat ran fast, bounding to the door, which was open.

And with a quick glance back at Reinar, Winter slipped inside.

Salma lay in the bed, face sallow, arms crossed over her chest, breathing ragged. He hurried inside, taking the stool that waited for him, gently placing one hand on hers.

'You came,' she smiled, though her eyes were closed, her voice just a whisper.

'Of course. Winter came for me.'

Salma opened her eyes as the cat jumped onto the bed, making himself at home by her waist, quickly padding out a spot, before curling into a white ball. 'He's always been a loyal friend. So loyal and wise.'

Reinar squeezed her hand. 'I can get Eddeth to come. Bring you something for the pain. Something to help.'

'No, Reinar. I have seen my end, and I have reached it. We must all reach our end one day, all of us. Even lords and kings. Even gods.' She paused, catching her breath. 'We can only hope that we arrive at that place having done all our work.'

'And you?' Reinar wondered, leaning closer. 'Have you done all your work, Salma?'

'Almost...' She smiled, tears in her eyes. 'Almost. But there is something I must tell you. Something you need to know...'

Alys watched them. She stood on the opposite side of the cottage, and though it was a small cottage, she couldn't hear them. She could hear Winter purring, though, and that sound made her smile.

Her attention drifted back to Reinar, seeing the familiar shape of him hunched over, far too big for the stool. She wasn't convinced that she should have come into his dream. She felt as though she was intruding.

And then he turned to her, standing quickly. 'Alys?'

Alys' mouth dropped open, her heart pounding. She thought about closing her eyes, and slipping out of the dream, but remembering her children, she took a deep breath. 'Hello, Reinar.'

He was standing over her in two paces, wanting to touch her, but he thought of Elin, and his hands remained by his sides.

'I'm in Slussfall, with Hakon Vettel. His prisoner.' Words tumbled from her lips in a panic. 'He knows that you're coming. I had to tell him.'

Reinar nodded. 'Stina told me. I know.'

'She's with you?' Alys stepped closer, wanting to grab his hands.

She didn't.

'She caught us just before we left. She's with us now, sailing to Slussfall.'

Alys felt relieved, happy that Stina was safe.

'Has he hurt you?'

'No.' She shook her head, not revealing her fears. 'No, but The Hunter has marked him. His wife saw it on his chest. It will send him mad. Perhaps it already has? I fear what he will do.'

'To you?'

'To everyone. Thenor is coming for him, so he must fight to survive.'

'Do you think he can? Survive?'

Alys saw a glimpse of Jesper Vettel holding Hakon in his arms. He was just a baby, as young as Hakon's own son. He'd looked so happy. So innocent. 'I don't know, but they have many weapons, so many men. Tall walls.'

Reinar smiled. 'I've been to Slussfall. Don't worry, we've made our plans.'

'But that's why I've come, to help you. My grandfather is here, with Magnus. His friend Vik, too.'

'Your grandfather?'

'He's... Jonas Bergstrom.'

The shock echoed through Reinar's body like a clap of thunder. 'Jonas? Your grandfather? And Vik, Vik Lofgren?' He shook his head, memories rushing past him of all the times Jonas and Vik had been at Ottby. They'd fought with Stellan. They'd fought with him and Sigurd when they were younger. His father had been in a brotherhood with them. 'But... I... I don't remember you. He didn't speak of you. You didn't speak of him. Why?'

Alys didn't know. She ignored the question, feeling unsteady, the sound of Eddeth's drumming pulsing like a heartbeat in her ears. 'They're hiding nearby, in a cave. Magnus is with them.'

'And your daughter? Lotta?'

He remembered her name. It surprised her. 'She's gone.'

'Where?'

'North. A man has her. He's taken her on a ship. I must find her, but first, I must get out of here.'

'And can you?'

Alys nodded. 'If you take the fort I can. I can show you how.'

Reinar reached up a hand, smoothing hair away from her face. 'No bruises,' he grinned. 'Makes a change, Alys de Sant.'

'Well, no one's punched me in a while, that's true.'

'I'm glad to hear it. You still have your sword?' He took his hand away, returning it to his side, embarrassed.

'No, they took it, but I've still got my cloak. Eddeth too. Don't worry.'

'Don't worry?' Reinar shook his head. 'I thought you knew me better than that.'

Alys felt muddled, feelings swirling around her. 'Your wife. She's with you now?'

Reinar nodded, dropping his eyes. 'Yes. She... came home.'

'I'm glad. You wanted her to.'

Reinar looked up, and they stared at each other for a moment, neither knowing what to say. And then Alys panicked, sensing that she was losing the trance. 'I... you must come to the main gates. Eddeth has a plan, a spell. We will let you in. Find the tunnel, Reinar! Take the tunnel and find my grandfather. They're in the caves. He will help you!'

Reinar was confused, barely listening. He didn't want her to go. 'I'll find Jonas. Whatever happens, I swear it to you, I'll find him. I'll find Magnus too.' He took Alys' hand, holding it to his heart. 'I promise.'

Alys stepped forward, wanting to feel his arms around her for just one moment.

And then everything went dark.

***

Ivan woke with a pain in his head and a woman in his bed.

He groaned, reaching out with mostly closed eyes, trying to grab the cup of ale he was sure he'd left on the bedside table, but feeling around, he realised there was nothing there, so bringing his hand back to the bed, he shoved it under the furs.

The woman didn't stir, and Ivan was pleased, enjoying the feel of her warm body pressed against his. Seara, he remembered, the sweet slave who always hurried him a cup of ale whenever he entered the hall. His mind skipped to Alys, wondering if Hakon had gone near her in the night. He remembered Rikkard, and what Lief had said. Guilt clawed at his conscience, trying to wake it up, but his loyalty to Hakon remained strong. Hakon had been the leader since they were boys, and Ivan had learned early on that a happy Hakon meant a happy life for all of them. He had no desire to sit upon a throne. No need to be a king. He wanted an endless supply of ale, beautiful women in his bed, coins in his chest, a reputation worthy of Thenor himself.

But he didn't want a crown. He hadn't been raised to seek the throne.

It was never his. It was always Hakon's.

And yet now?

What was Lief suggesting? And why didn't he want to listen?

***

The storm had swept away in the early hours of the morning, and Lief felt relieved. They had a lot to do to prepare the fort. If the dreamer was right about when the Vilanders had put to sea, they could arrive as early as tomorrow.

Lief froze, feeling his pregnant wife stir beside him. Falla was always in a better mood when she had a lot of sleep, so he kept still, arms by his sides, trying not to move.

And when the Vilanders arrived?

Lief knew the fort could hold out for weeks. Maybe months. They had an abundance of men, though that was perhaps not the asset Hakon thought it was, for those men needed feeding. Their stores were lower than ideal after a poor harvest, and having to take so much with them to Ottby. They were low on weapons too. Many had been abandoned in the mad dash home. Arrows, in particular, were a problem. They had taken an enormous supply to Ottby, leaving them scattered throughout the Vilanders' fort. The fletchers were working through the night, threatened with death if they didn't produce buckets of arrows in time.

Lief didn't doubt there would be death.

But whose?

The storm had passed, but he felt as though he was still caught up in the maelstrom, and without an ally, what could he possibly do?

Falla rolled over, frowning at him, one eye open, slipping an arm over his chest. And pulling her close, he sighed.

***

Eddeth hopped about with excitement. 'I need some basil for our spell. Some calendula too. Perhaps they'll let us out today?'

'I don't think so, Eddeth.' Alys felt odd. She felt reluctant to talk at all. After the dreamwalk, she'd barely mumbled at Eddeth before falling into bed. And now, her throat was painfully dry, her head aching. Memories of Reinar were swirling around her, and she felt unsettled.

'What did you dream of, then?' Eddeth felt impatient, eager to get on with the day. She'd been boiling water in the cauldron, and already had two cups of lavender and lemon balm tea steaming on the table.

Not even Alys' dark mood could taint her joy.

Alys blinked at her, trying to remember. 'A lot.' She was drained by it. Her dreams had come at her like frightened birds scattering across the sky. 'I saw Lotta. She was curled up on a ship with that man and his wife.' That didn't make her feel any better.

'His wife?'

Alys nodded. She hadn't liked the way the woman had been looking at Lotta. 'I saw Reinar's ships too. They were in a terrible storm.'

Eddeth sat down on the bed. 'Oh?'

'I saw Sigurd's blue eyes, full of terror, the storm crashing around them. Ludo was there looking after him.' She yawned, feeling worried. 'I saw Ilene.'

Eddeth screwed up her nose. 'I don't like that Ilene.' Then she saw something else in Alys' eyes. 'What?'

Alys looked away, towards the flames licking the blackened sides of Eddeth's new cauldron. 'I don't know.' She reached back under the pillow, pulling out the brooch Karolina Vettel had given her. 'It doesn't make any sense, but I think I saw Reinar trying to kill Hakon's wife. Her and her baby.'

Eddeth snorted. 'Reinar? Kill a woman and a baby? I doubt that! *Reinar?*'

It didn't make sense, and Alys decided to let it go.

The turning of the lock had them both jerking around. And within a heartbeat, the door had swung open, and Hakon stood there, eyes on the brooch in Alys' hand. 'Perfect! Just what I came to talk to you about. I want to know everything you dreamed about my wife!'

CHAPTER THIRTY NINE

Ivan pushed open the door with a sigh, wishing he was walking into Orbo's great hall; Orbo, where Jesper Vettel had ruled as lord, and he had been a boy with his cousin.

Where nothing was too serious. Where everything was fun.

Where the future shone before them like a glittering prize, not a black hole of doom waiting to swallow them whole.

He saw Lief's dour face, long and miserable, and he frowned, scooping up a boiled egg, popping it into his mouth. The hall was empty, apart from Lief. There was no one Hakon trusted to be around him and his family now. He'd shut them all out, keeping the hall doors permanently closed.

It wasn't the way to foster feelings of camaraderie before a battle, Ivan thought irritably. 'No sign of Hakon, then?' he wondered, not wanting to be drawn into another heavy conversation with Lief. Lief who harboured thoughts of overthrowing his cousin.

'He went to fetch the dreamer.'

'Oh?' Ivan straightened up, running a hand over his wild beard.

'It's wishful thinking, if you ask me,' Lief grumbled, 'expecting her to have the answers to all his problems.'

'Well, Mother always did.'

'Mother was experienced. An old woman who knew dark magic. What does Alys truly know? What can she help him with?' Lief stiffened as Hakon pulled back the curtain, leading Alys towards the map table. The tables behind them beckoned with an abundance of food, and his eyes drifted to a plate of pickled eel, which he always enjoyed, though he wondered at the wisdom of preparing such a banquet for breakfast. It was enough for twenty people.

'You're awake, Cousin!' Hakon beamed, eyes glassy. 'Just in time, for my dreamer has word of our attackers!' And almost pushing Alys over, he hurried her to the table, moving her so that she stood beside him, in front of Lief and Ivan.

Both men felt concerned, seeing the frantic look in Hakon's eyes. He was panting, sweat beading across his forehead as though he'd been running on a summer's day, yet not even the two roaring fires had taken the intense chill off the spacious hall.

'You do?' Ivan leaned forward. 'Where are they?'

'I saw them in a storm. They lost sight of each other, I think. They seemed far apart. More than one ship went under.'

Hakon beamed. 'The gods! The gods are coming to our aid, just as I knew they would! Certainly Thenor. And who better to have on our side than the Father of the Gods himself!' He took a goblet of ale from his new steward, a young man named Osmund, who looked nothing like Rikkard, he thought with a smile. Osmund was older, with a more confident air. Better to look at too. 'He's destroying our enemy for us!'

'One or two ships lost? That's not enough to threaten their assault,' Lief warned.

'Though perhaps they are slowed down? Blown off course? Needing to regroup?'

He was reaching, Lief saw. 'What else did you see?' he asked Alys.

Alys turned to Hakon, not sure if he wanted anyone to know.

'Alys saw Reinar Vilander trying to kill my son.'

Ivan looked surprised; Lief incredulous.

'That's the sort of man coming for us. A child killer!' Hakon snarled. 'Karolina was protecting Anders, wasn't she? And he was trying to kill her too!'

Ivan's mind skipped ahead. 'But that means he was inside the fort, Hakon. That he got in. And where were you? Where was I? Why was Karolina unprotected?'

Those were all good questions.

They turned to Alys, who swallowed. 'I saw only glimpses. I don't know what happened to the fort. They were in the bedchamber. The one you took me to last night,' Alys said. She saw Reinar, his hand on her face, smiling down at her. It didn't make any sense.

'We must protect our families!' Hakon growled, eyes on Lief. 'We must keep the Vilanders out of Slussfall! I want to see those fletchers. Have the men returned from the quarry? We need more rocks, boulders. We must crush them! Though not their ships,' he muttered, scratching his chin. 'Not their ships. We will draw them out of those ships, encourage them up the hill to the harbour gates. Trap them there. Slaughter them! We want a new fleet, don't we, Cousin?'

Ivan thought that a fleet of ships was the last thing they needed to worry about now.

'A fleet of ships to sail us straight to Stornas, where I will finally be crowned the King of Alekka!' Hakon's smile twisted suddenly, the pain in his chest crushing.

'Hakon?' Ivan stepped around the table as his cousin collapsed forward. 'Are you alright?'

Hakon straightened up quickly, lashing out at Ivan, hitting him in the jaw.

Ivan stumbled back, shock in his eyes.

'My lord?' Lief glanced at Ivan, not wanting to approach Hakon himself.

But Hakon was already shaking it off, chest pains receding, sweat pouring down his back. 'Stop fussing!' he growled, wanting everyone's attention back on the map.

Alys' eyes drifted away from the table towards the doors, which opened as Karolina and Falla came in with their children and servants.

'What's happened?' Falla wondered, glancing at Lief, who looked even paler than usual.

'Nothing! Nothing!' Hakon insisted, motioning for his wife to come closer. 'Have you had breakfast, my love? There's so much food. Alva's been busy, up before the birds!' The generous spread did not trouble Hakon at all. He barely glanced at it before drawing his eyes back to his wife, who was cradling his son. He felt a burst of rage, thinking of Reinar Vilander, wondering how he was going to keep his family safe. 'Ivan!' he announced suddenly, smiling at his cousin. 'When the time comes, Ivan will look after you!'

Everyone was surprised by that, especially Ivan, who was holding his jaw. 'What?'

'I will take charge of everything in the fort myself, Lief will assist me, and you, Cousin, will be in the hall, guarding my most precious possessions.' He saw Falla pick up her boy; Lief had revealed that she too was carrying a child. 'And you will watch Falla and her son!' Hakon glanced at Lief, whose wide mouth was slightly ajar, confusion in his eyes. 'There's no one I trust more.'

Ivan shook his head. 'But I...'

'Will be where you are needed most!' Hakon insisted. 'And if Alys' dream is to be believed, then you will face down Reinar Vilander himself!' Hakon thought about that, wondering if he should remain in the hall with his family, but Thenor needed to see him on the wall, bellowing orders from the ramparts, crushing his enemy. He didn't need to see Ivan and Lief.

He heard Ivan spluttering beside him, and ignoring him, Hakon kissed his wife on the lips and his son on the cheek. 'Now let's get to the armourer's and see if he's done as I've asked, for if not, I shall have to take off his head!'

No one spoke, and no one moved, but Hakon headed to the doors, oblivious. Glancing over his shoulder, he peered at Ivan. 'Take Alys back to her chamber, and make sure to lock her in! I don't want to lose my prize, do I?'

Ivan watched his cousin go, stunned.

Even Lief looked blind-sided, but smiling briefly at Falla, he strode after his lord.

The doors opened and closed behind them, and nobody spoke.

***

The seas had calmed overnight, the storm retreating, and despite a lingering worry over the rest of their fleet, most of them had managed a few hours sleep.

Even Reinar.

Elin smiled up at him, and he felt uneasy, remembering his dream.

'It's good to see Sigurd again,' she said, nodding towards *Dagger*, who was back beside them, cutting through the waves like a blade, red-and-white-striped sail billowing in the fresh breeze.

Reinar nodded, though he couldn't see the rest of the fleet. The storm had blown them asunder, and Holgar had spent most of the morning trying to tack back towards the coast, worrying about how much time they'd lost.

Elin's eyes drifted to Stina, who had sunk down to her haunches after spending most of the morning vomiting over the stern. 'And what do you think that dreamer is telling Hakon Vettel? Will she see everything you've got planned?'

'I hope not.' Reinar didn't look at Elin. 'She's not like other dreamers. And besides, she won't want to help him.'

'No? What makes you so sure?'

Reinar was still shocked by what Alys had revealed, wishing he'd had the time to ask her more. 'Because they're on different sides. Alys' grandfather fought with my father.'

Holgar, who was standing nearby, looked surprised. 'He did?'

Reinar nodded. 'Jonas Bergstrom.'

The old helmsman twisted around, shocked. 'We kidnapped Jonas' granddaughter?'

'That we did.'

'Well, lucky for us you didn't sell her. Don't think Jonas would have taken that well.'

'No, but I doubt he'll be happy either way,' Reinar muttered, remembering his promise to Alys. Elin looked at him quizzically. 'Alys won't betray us. She'll do what she can to help us because the Vettels are the enemy of everyone who believes in Ake. They're the enemy of everyone who wants freedom and safety for their family.' And stepping around his wife, and a still-stunned Holgar, Reinar headed back to the stern to check on Stina.

***

Ivan sat on the bed beside Alys.

She didn't move.

Nor did he.

'Do you really see Reinar Vilander trying to kill Anders? And Karolina?'

Alys nodded. 'It makes no sense, but I do.'

Eddeth was asleep in a chair by the fire, snoring like thunder.

They were whispering.

'And if he gets into the fort, what will he do?'

'What you would do in his place, I imagine. I can't read his mind. I don't know him.' That was almost true.

'Hakon is becoming... different.'

'The mark will do that.'

Ivan didn't want to hear that, yet what had he been expecting? 'He insists he doesn't have the mark. That it was simply a warning. That Thenor will return his favour once he proves himself worthy.'

Alys didn't know the gods well enough to be sure of anything. She glanced at Eddeth, realising that she needed to talk to her further. If they were the pawns Eddeth insisted they were, then they needed to know whose side the gods were truly on. 'Well, I wouldn't rely on it. You must watch him closely. You and Lief.' She saw Ivan flinch. 'Lief is loyal, isn't he?'

Ivan snorted. 'Not anymore. He wants me to betray my cousin, I'm sure of it.'

'His wife is pregnant.'

'I doubt he's doing it to protect her. He wants the throne

himself.'

'What throne?' Alys wondered. 'There is no throne.' She was annoyed, her voice rising. 'There is a king in Stornas, and he rules Alekka, trying to keep his people safe. He took the throne from your grandfather after ten years of war. And more. Not for glory, but because your grandfather was a cruel tyrant who slaked the land with the blood and sweat of his people, with little care for their lives. He valued nothing but himself and his throne and his line. What throne is there, Ivan? A chair cruel men occupy? That's not who Ake Bluefinn is. He's a leader, a man people care for, because he cares for them. Why try to remove him when he seeks to do the best for Alekka? The best for our people?'

Eddeth roused herself from her nap with a grunt, surprised to see Ivan and Alys sitting on the bed. 'When did you get here?' She rubbed her nose, stomach growling. 'I could do with another breakfast. That bowl of porridge wasn't enough for a mouse!'

Ivan hurried to his feet, staring down at Alys. 'Ake stole the throne. Whatever you say about him, Ake stole the throne given to us by the gods. Thenor himself chose the Vettels to lead Alekka. You must know that! Ake went against the gods. Ake and all those men who fought beside him. They took something from us, but also from Thenor, and I won't go against my cousin or the gods by giving up now. Is that what you think I should do? Throw up my hands and throw open the gates?'

'Why not?' Alys stood, ignoring Eddeth's raised eyebrows. 'You'd be free if you did.'

'Free? I'd be dead!'

'Not necessarily. I know Reinar. I could save you. You and Lief.'

Ivan glowered at Alys, confused. Running both hands over his head, he almost shouted in annoyance. 'I have to go. I need to get to the armoury!' And in three quick strides, he was at the door, yanking it open, disappearing down the corridor.

Alys turned to Eddeth, who was staring at her. 'I know.'

'Well, it was one approach, I suppose,' Eddeth grinned, 'though, perhaps not the best. They are blood. And more. Like twins, I think, those boys. Hakon is all the family Ivan has in the world. Hakon and his son. It would be hard for anyone to betray family.'

Alys saw the image of Jesper Vettel talking to the blonde-haired woman called Mirella, and she nodded, barely listening. 'I imagine so.'

***

Reinar led his fleet into a sheltered inlet, just big enough for their ships.

There were beacons along the shore, and he ordered Berger and ten of his men to head into the nearby village to threaten anyone who dared light them. It was a small village, stripped of its able menfolk, and no one argued with a growling Berger dressed in full battle gear.

They had arranged to meet at midday on the third day of their journey, wanting to regroup, refresh themselves, and go over their plan.

The ships trickled in, washed ashore, wet and weary men almost tumbling into the water, relieved to feel something solid beneath their feet. Some collapsed onto the golden sand, exhausted after the stormy night.

It took hours.

Eventually, Reinar counted twenty-eight ships. Two were missing, and he could only hope that they would find their way to Slussfall on their own, though he had a bad feeling after that violent storm.

'Pity we can't stay the night here,' Bjarni sighed as they shook by the hastily built fire. The villagers had helped the sodden men, bringing them dry twigs and logs, some tinder and food too. And though Reinar gratefully took the wood, he turned the women back with their food, knowing how tough times were.

'Well, the sand does look inviting,' Sigurd decided, remembering the stony beaches he'd slept on as they sailed from Goslund to Ottby. 'But I imagine our lord and leader will say no.'

'He will,' Reinar agreed, happy to see Elin and Stina cooking sausages over the neighbouring fire. Ilene stood nearby, scowling. 'We've got plans, plans disrupted by that storm, but they know we're coming. We don't want to give them even more time to prepare.'

Ludo brought a trencher of sausages over, barely reaching their small group before they were all gone. 'I...' And shoulders slumped, he turned back to Elin with the empty trencher.

Bjarni quickly gobbled down two sausages, eyes on Berger, who had trekked back to Ilene. 'There's trouble right there.'

Reinar followed his gaze, not liking the sound of more trouble, but turning his head, he shrugged. 'Berger's not like his brother.' And staring at Sigurd, who was about to open his mouth, he frowned. 'He's not.'

'Don't think Bjarni was talking about Berger.'

Reinar harrumphed, turning away. 'Let's talk about Slussfall.' He inclined his head for Sigurd, Bjarni, Holgar, and Bolli to follow him to where a row of boulders held back the sand, the village perched up behind the dunes. When they were far enough away from everyone else, Reinar started whispering. 'Alys came to me.'

No one knew what that meant.

Everyone turned to look at Elin, still crouched over the fire.

'Is that how you knew about Jonas?' Holgar wondered.

'What?' Sigurd wasn't following.

'Jonas. Jonas Bergstrom,' Holgar explained. 'He's the dreamer's grandfather.'

Bolli spat out his sausage. '*What?*'

Sigurd echoed his shock. 'Jonas? But...'

Reinar had no time for any of it. 'She said he's there, with Vik. They're trapped in the caves, trying to rescue her. With her son.'

Sigurd shook his head, eyes skipping past Bjarni to his brother. 'You had a dream. A *dream*! Why are you thinking any of this is real? I dreamed I was a raven, flying over the ocean, but I'm not about to take flight!'

Bolli snorted, regretting his lost sausage, now buried in the sand. He glanced at Ludo, wondering what was taking him so long.

Holgar was the quieter of the two helmsmen. 'You do know dreamers can come into your dreams, don't you, Sigurd? I remember Jonas telling us that. His wife would often visit him, he said.'

'Did he?' Bolli didn't remember that.

Holgar nodded. 'If Reinar thinks he had one of those sort of dreams, we may as well hear him out.' He lowered his voice. 'They were close, you know.'

Everyone turned to Reinar, who glared at Holgar.

Ludo trekked through the sand with another trencher, and their attention shifted back to the sausages.

'Elin said that's it. No more sausages.' And quickly grabbing one himself, Ludo stuffed it into his mouth, burning his tongue. 'Ow!'

'So what did Alys say, then?' Sigurd asked, wanting to get back to the dream he doubted was real at all.

'Alys? About what? Alys?' Ludo's eyes jumped back and forth. 'Did she come to you in a dream?'

'How do you know about that?' Bolli wondered. 'Idiot like you?'

Ludo ignored him. 'It's called dreamwalking. Agnette told me Alys did it to reach her grandfather.'

And the mention of Alys' grandfather rendered them all silent again.

'Jonas is going to kill us,' Bolli muttered. 'Vik too, if he finds out.'

'Alys said he's there. With Jonas.'

Bolli inhaled sharply, wanting some ale.

Ludo wasn't following. 'Jonas and Vik? Where are they? We haven't seen them in years.'

'In Slussfall, trying to rescue Alys.'

'Why?'

Reinar shook his head, getting impatient. 'It's a long story, but shut up for now and let me talk.'

Ludo clamped his lips together, gripping the empty trencher.

'I think we separate here.'

Confusion.

'We already know we're going to separate here,' Bolli grumped. 'We talked about it. Planned it. You're going to go around the headland, attack from the north, we'll take the harbour.'

'No, I mean separate even further.'

More confusion.

Reinar dropped to his knees, clearing the sand of shells and bits of driftwood. He drew a long shape resembling the coast, then making a mark for where they were now, he drew a looping line up to the harbour. 'Bolli, you and Sigurd head for the harbour as planned.' Taking the stick, he made a bigger loop, eyes on Ludo. 'Ludo, you hop on board with Falki, head further north where I was going. Come at the fort that way. Keep them busy while Sigurd tries to run them dry of arrows.'

Holgar peered at Reinar. 'And us?'

Reinar looked up at him before drawing another line. 'We follow Ludo, but when they stop, we carry on. Say four ships. Two hundred-odd men. We head through here, there's a tunnel, near the caves.'

'Tunnel?' Bjarni looked surprised. 'Caves?'

Bolli nodded. 'It's an old tunnel, built long before Sirrus' time. You have to climb a bit to get to it, but it's one way to approach the fort. Not everyone knows about it, though likely the Vettels do. The caves are nearby.'

'According to Alys, that's where Jonas and Vik are hiding. Alys' son too. We can get them, keep the boy safe, come at the fort from the front.'

'With two hundred men?' Sigurd looked doubtful.

'They won't be looking our way,' Reinar insisted. 'Because Alys is going to help us.'

CHAPTER FORTY

They needed to get out of their chamber.

Reinar and Sigurd would arrive soon, and they needed to get out of their chamber and gather supplies for the spell to help Alys open the gates.

Eddeth spun around, eyes bulging with urgency. 'We can ask Falla!'

'To get the herbs?'

'Of course! She organised the cauldron. She brought me my things. She'll come if you call her.'

'What?'

Eddeth grinned, nudging Alys, who sat on the bed beside her, both of them with books on their knees. 'Still your mind awhile. Stop worrying and fussing and thinking about Reinar and your grandfather and your children. Clear it all away with a giant broom!' Eddeth boomed, peering at her. 'Close your eyes!'

And realising there was no choice, Alys did.

'Now, think of Falla –'

Alys opened one eye. 'How do you know all of this, Eddeth?'

Eddeth frowned, ignoring her. 'Eyes closed! Now, think of Falla. Falla with those sashaying hips.'

'What?' Alys' eyes were open again.

'Don't say you haven't noticed! Have you ever seen anyone walk like that? Maybe she has hip trouble? I could certainly help her with that.'

Alys closed her eyes again, holding her hands over them. 'Go on.'

'Alright, think of Falla, see everything about her. Bring her into your mind. The colour of her hair, the sheen of it, like raven's wings it is! The dress she was wearing, the sound of her voice. And when you have a full picture of her, when you see all of her in your mind, start talking to her. Not out loud, though, just push your thoughts towards her. See her face, see her mind, and push your thoughts in her direction.'

Alys' mind skipped immediately from Falla, to Karolina, to her baby son, and right back to Reinar, who she saw holding a knife up to them both.

***

They didn't linger on the beach for long, and after kicking sand over the fires, Reinar and his men headed back to the ships.

Looking at his wife, he realised that he was running out of time to decide what to do with her. He caught a glimpse of Stina too, worrying about them both.

Elin turned back to him, sensing his eyes on her. 'What?'

'Just wondering what I'm going to do with you.'

'*Do?*'

'To keep you safe. I have to keep you safe.'

Elin walked back to him, boots sinking into the soft sand. 'And you will, don't worry, I trust you.'

Reinar inhaled sharply. 'You've got your knife, though. Still know how to use it?'

'Of course. Torvig taught me when we were children. You remember that?'

Reinar nodded, seeing her resemblance to Torvig and not liking it. 'Well, keep it on you. Be prepared to use it, Elin. Don't hesitate either. If someone's threatening you, someone you don't know, stab them.'

Elin grinned. 'I will, though I doubt I'll need to. Not with you by my side.'

She would argue about any plans he made for her, Reinar knew, but there was no way he was letting her anywhere near Hakon Vettel's archers. He would keep both her and Stina well away from the fort.

The afternoon air already felt cooler, the sun heading down, and though it felt like they'd only just arrived at the beach, it had been hours. Reinar scanned the horizon, searching for those missing ships, to no avail. He tried to remember who'd been on them, who was missing, but there were too many men under his command now and he couldn't.

'We head for Slussfall!' he cried, voice roaring over the wind. 'To end the Vettels for good! Every last one of them!' It was what Ake wanted, but Reinar still couldn't imagine how he was going to kill that child.

And yet, if he didn't?

He held up a hand to Sigurd, who was jogging across the sand after an impatient Bolli, big grin on his face. His eyes were sad, though, Reinar noticed, as he turned them on his brother.

'Maybe we can swap with Sigurd and Bolli?' Holgar grumbled behind him. 'Not sure I want to face Jonas and Vik.'

***

They'd been discovered by some of Ollo's men, all of them once loyal to Sirrus Ahlmann too. They knew Jonas and Vik. They'd suspected where they were hiding.

Eight of them.

Vik welcomed them into their cave, though he felt on edge. How many others knew of the caves, and who could they trust?

Ollo seemed happy for the company, and the help hunting,

fishing and finding firewood. The new men were more use than Leonid, who was nervous and clumsy, getting in everyone's way.

Magnus felt as anxious as Vik. 'But what if they tell someone?' They'd walked down to the stream, looking for supper. 'Do you trust them?'

Jonas shrugged. 'Nothing we can do about it now. But if they give us any trouble, they'll soon come to regret it. That's the thing about reputations, Magnus. People know who you are, what you're capable of. Makes them less likely to do something stupid.'

Vik laughed. 'You think we're still as good as our reputations?' He walked with a stick he'd fashioned into a spear, eyes on the stream rushing past them, high and cold-looking.

'I do. Why not? We're still here, aren't we, so why not?' Jonas was worried and impatient, doubts about waiting for the Vilanders growing by the day. They were trusting the word of a strange woman Vik had met in the forest. How did they know for sure if any of what she'd said was true?

He could almost see his wife then, smiling at him. And sighing, he turned to Magnus. 'They're in the forest because they've had enough of their lord.'

'So they say,' Vik grunted, slipping down into the stream, bracing himself for the cold water to come. 'But we still need to stay alert, Jonas.'

Jonas nodded, thinking the same. 'Sirrus' men made their own choices at the time. Ollo said he'd started forgetting things, making mistakes. They thought he'd gone a little mad, though it's no excuse for betraying him.'

'Course it's no excuse for betraying him!' Vik doubted that all his bellowing would get them any fish, and he closed his mouth, inclining his head for Jonas to take Magnus away.

Which he did.

'So we'll keep alert,' Jonas reassured his great-grandson as they walked further downstream. 'Wait it out.'

Magnus didn't feel reassured. 'But what will happen to my mother? What will they be doing to her? And what about Lotta?'

Jonas knew that in life, you had to be like a tree. He reached up, placing his hands on the trunk of the spreading oak watching over the banks of the stream. A tree this big could feel the wind, but not be knocked down by it. And taking a deep breath, Jonas smiled. 'We're not leaving your mother behind, Magnus. Not this time. We'll get Lotta, but only once we've saved your mother.'

***

Falla came to the door, once again convincing the guard to let her in. The young man was one of her many admirers, and he'd barely lifted an eyebrow as she'd bustled past him.

'The women need herbs,' she'd whispered. 'They need to prepare for what's coming. To help the lord.'

The guard had seen a cauldron, books and saddlebags pass through the door, and now there went Falla again with two overflowing baskets.

He shut the door with a sigh, eyes darting up and down the dark corridor, hoping Hakon wouldn't come along.

'You've done well!' Eddeth exclaimed as Falla stepped into the chamber, red-faced and ready to lie down. She saw the fire, and dropping her baskets to the flagstones, she hurried to it. Warming her hands before the flames, she turned with a sharp look in her eyes. 'I'm helping you to help myself,' she admitted. 'I wish for my husband to be a lord, and me to be his lady.'

Alys froze, seeing where this was leading.

'I was a lady once, wife of an old lord of a tiny island. But Lief is nothing like that blathering fool. Nothing like my second husband, either. He's a patient man. He's not cruel, though he's not soft either. He does what needs doing. He would make a good Lord of Slussfall.'

'And you think I can guarantee that?' Alys was puzzled.

'I think you will, or I'll tell Hakon about your plans.' Falla had thought it through. She wanted Hakon gone, but these women were loyal to the Vilanders. She was no fool. They would help the Vilanders get rid of Hakon and then what?

She didn't want Lief to die, or for him to become a prisoner, lost to her.

Eddeth was by Falla's side in two heartbeats, finger wagging. 'Don't threaten us, Falla Gundersen!' she growled. 'We're your friends! Here to help you! Maybe you don't know what it means to have friends, being the way you are. Maybe all you've done your whole life is play games, wanting to claw out some better existence for yourself? Likely you've never had a true friend. But friends don't threaten each other. And they don't turn on each other either!'

Falla stumbled, frowning. 'Friends?'

'Of course we're you're friends!' Eddeth was smiling now, all anger gone like the sun returning after a sudden downpour. 'And we'll help you. Willingly. We'll try to save you and your husband and your boy. Not because you're threatening us. Not because we're scared of you!' She snorted, then sneezed.

Falla blinked in surprise, never having been spoken to like that before, except by Mother, who'd been no friend of hers. She'd only wanted someone to do all those tasks she couldn't be bothered doing herself. The old woman would have happily killed her if it had helped her get what she wanted, Falla knew.

Alys nodded. 'I can't promise you anything, but you must convince Lief to help us. If he tries to kill the Vilanders, they can hardly reward him.'

'And Ivan?'

Alys felt sad about Ivan. 'He won't abandon Hakon. He can't. They're family. They need each other. But Lief... you can work on Lief.'

Falla nodded, smiling.

She could most certainly work on Lief.

***

Just a sliver of moon was visible in a sky scattered with stars as Hakon walked across the square with Karolina.

He had rushed around the fort all day, feeling as though he was being chased. It was an odd sensation he couldn't shake, unable to stay in one place long enough to achieve anything. He had run from the armoury to the fletcher's to the blacksmith's. He'd been down at the piers, ordering his men to pull their one remaining warship out of the water, storing it in the sheds, though he'd failed to order them all locked to protect those that were halfway through or nearing completion. He had checked the gates but forgotten to mention the idea for barricades he'd had in mind when he left the hall.

No wonder everyone was starting to look at him as though he was mad.

Was he going mad?

Hakon held Karolina close. She was wrapped from head to toe in fur, yet she shivered as they walked, trembling against him. Snow was on the ground, but not in the air, though it was achingly cold, breath smoke streaming from mouths and noses. 'You have nothing to fear from the Vilanders, Karolina,' Hakon insisted, twisting his head left and right, trying to determine what was masked by the shadows. 'Nothing at all.'

Karolina could only nod. She felt trapped and frightened, and not sure whose side she wanted to be on.

'Alys will help us,' Hakon assured her, squeezing her waist. 'And the gods will help Alys. That's what Mother said. The gods give dreamers the visions they need to help us, to show us the way. And you know how much Thenor wants to help the Vettels. He wants me on the throne! He sent me a dreamer!' Hakon kept saying words, as though the mere act of saying them would make them true. As though by saying them often enough, to enough people, he could convince everyone that they needn't fear what they saw with their own eyes, or heard with their own ears. They would believe him, because he was Hakon Vettel, Lord of Slussfall, their lord.

The man destined to become the next King of Alekka.

***

Alys stood in the shadow of the tree, watching her mother chase her grandfather's dog, who had stolen her boot. Digger. Alys remembered him. He liked to steal things and bury them. Usually bones or branches. Sometimes boots. Never food. When he stole that, he gobbled it down right away. Alys grinned, wondering how her grandfather had managed to choose such an appropriate name. Or perhaps it was her grandmother, she thought, glancing around.

Summer at the cottage was always beautiful. Flowers of every colour bloomed, a cornucopia of scents wafting through the air. The birds made homes in the rowan trees fencing the house, and the noise was cheerful and busy from dawn till dusk.

Digger ran into the bushes, disappearing, and Alys heard the splash as he launched himself off the bank, into the stream.

She heard a laugh from behind her, and turning, she saw Jonas with his shirt off, sweaty from chopping wood. He was going away, she guessed, wanting to have everything ready for her grandmother.

He'd always been preparing to go away.

As a child, it had terrified Alys, who never knew if she would see him again.

'I'll get him!' Jonas laughed, flinging his axe into the tree round he was chopping on.

Alys turned around, wondering where her grandmother was; there was only her mother and grandfather in the garden. And turning back, she saw her grandfather slip his arm around her mother's waist as she grumbled about how sweaty he was, protesting as he leaned in to kiss her.

On the lips.

Alys froze. Disturbed.

She squinted, stepping forward, wondering what was happening.

Jonas had forgotten all about Digger and the missing boot. He was too busy kissing her mother, who slapped him on the rump, sending him on his way.

'There'll be no cake for you if you don't get my boot back!' she laughed, cheeks flushed.

'My sweet Eida, light of my life, you can trust me!' Jonas grinned, disappearing into the bushes.

Eida?

Alys didn't understand, too stunned to move, ears buzzing like she was standing in a field of beehives.

And then the woman turned around, walking back to her, taking her hands. 'We wanted to keep you safe, Alys. For if anyone knew the truth, they would have taken you, used you, killed you. We wanted to keep you safe, my darling, here, at the cottage, with us.'

'But...' Alys shook her head, shivering. 'I don't understand. Who am I?'

***

Jonas ran a hand over Magnus' hair, settling the boy back to sleep. He'd had a nightmare, waking with a shout, on his feet, wandering around the cave. He was still mostly asleep, and it hadn't taken Jonas long to relax that shuddering body again.

'He'll want to come with us, you know,' Vik whispered beside him. He was poking the fire, hoping to keep the flames breathing, just enough to warm his toes. 'When the Vilanders come, he'll want to go to the fort.'

Jonas glanced at the boy, knowing Vik was right. 'I would, in his place. If they had my mother, I would.'

Vik nodded. 'Me too, though we can't let him come.'

'No, but he won't take it well,' Jonas grinned. 'He's as stubborn as me.'

'I agree. Must take after Alys' side of the family.'

'Thankfully.' Guilt nagged at Jonas, and he tried to turn away from it, but it lingered, memories flooding his mind like a stream. He saw Alys as a baby, his baby, for he had raised her from the moment Mirella had left her with him and Eida. She was six days old. They'd told Alys that she was six when she came to live with them, but she wasn't six years, she was six days...

He thought of Mirella often, and his heart broke, wondering what he could have done differently, knowing the answer was many things. With Alys too.

And Eida.

All the women in his life. All of them dreamers.

Each one suffering so much heartbreak.

Guilt weighed him down, making it hard to breathe. Guilt and grief.

But there was still Alys. Still a chance he could save his granddaughter and make everything right.

He would tell her the truth. All of it. Before it was too late.

It couldn't be too late...

CHAPTER FORTY ONE

Neither of them felt inclined to get out of bed, which was not like Lief, Falla thought. He seemed reluctant to begin the day, and listening to the thunderous downpour assaulting the roof of their cottage, she didn't blame him.

Borg was giggling in the next room, entertained by his nursemaid, and her cook was busy preparing what smelled like smoked fish and flatbreads for breakfast, so Falla didn't see the point of getting out of bed at all.

'But we should,' Lief yawned. He'd barely slept. Falla had talked to him at length as he'd tried to go to sleep, urging him to go against Hakon. She'd tried her best, insisting that the gods had turned their backs on the entire Vettel family, though Lief had held firm, knowing that without Ivan's support he would struggle to mount a serious challenge to Hakon's rule.

Falla sensed that he was about to get up, and eyelashes fluttering, she tugged his arm, pulling him back to her. 'Why not stay a little longer?'

Lief was used to her feeling ill in the mornings, so Falla's interest in his company was a pleasant surprise, and he felt his resolve crumble. But not entirely, and turning to her with a brief kiss on the cheek, he returned to his stretching, groaning morning routine.

Annoyed and surprised, Falla pursued him, wrapping one of the bed furs around her naked body, wriggling up to sit next to him. 'You're a good man,' she purred, leaning her head on his arm. 'And you may think you're doing what's right, but perhaps what is right has changed? You have your own child on the way. A wife. A stepson to think about. Keeping us safe is what you care about most, I know that, Lief. I see it in your eyes.' She lifted a hand to his stern face, turning it to hers. 'It's what you want most of all. Not the Vettels, but me, Borg, this child.' Falla slipped her other hand beneath the fur, resting it on her belly. 'I don't feel safe anymore. Karolina certainly doesn't.'

'What? From Hakon?'

'You've seen him. Sweating and twitching, eyes darting round. He can't hold your gaze for a moment. He is much changed. Can't you see what's happening to him?'

As much as he wanted to ignore the truth Falla was dragging into the light, Lief knew that Hakon was getting worse. 'It's been a difficult time.'

'Because of *him*!' Falla insisted. 'Because of what *he's* done. He took us to Ottby. He failed to take it. He displeased the gods. He's the one who's been cursed, and now, stuck here, imprisoned with him, *we* will suffer alongside him! Can't you see that? Don't you want to keep us safe?'

Lief felt under attack from Falla's rising voice and her fluttering eyelashes. 'Of course I want to keep you safe, but my oath...' He reached for his trousers, splattered in mud, not wanting to wear them, but in the rush to leave Ottby's forest, he'd left his clothes behind. Pulling them on, back aching, he tried to think. 'What man can go against a king?'

'He's not a *king*!' Falla sneered. 'Just a boy who wants to be one! Why should he, though? Simply by being born? Does that make a man worthy of being a king? Birth?'

Lief stood, cold feet on the furs Falla had draped around their bedchamber floor. It felt so soft that he almost smiled as he reached for his swordbelt. 'I think the gods choose the kings, Falla,' he said solemnly. 'So who am I to question their wisdom?'

Falla was growing impatient. 'Well, I'm sorry to hear that, for it appears that we have reached an impasse.'

Tying up his swordbelt, Lief turned back to her. 'What?'

'If you won't fight to protect your own family, why should we stay? I'm a mother, and my first responsibility is to keep my children safe. That's *my* oath. I won't stay here while you do nothing to protect us. While you choose loyalty to a madman and a god over us. I will *leave*!' And standing, throwing off the fur for effect, Falla strode towards the chair by the fire, grabbing her dress, letting Lief see her naked body. Hoping upon hope that something would pierce that impenetrable veil of stubbornness.

And staring at his wife's milky body, with its growing bump, Lief sighed.

***

Alys woke with a sneeze, surprised by that.

Surprised too that there was no sign of Eddeth leaning over her. She rolled onto her side, staring at the fire, which burned brightly, listening to the rain hammering down. She could see the sky, bleak and grey, through the small gaps in the shuttered window.

'I've had her removed. Taken to a cottage.'

Alys sat up quickly, pushing herself back against the wooden headboard, horrified to see Hakon sitting on a stool by the bed, watching her. 'What are you d-doing here?' she panted, breathless.

Hakon smiled. 'I wanted to know what you'd seen in your dreams before they slipped away from you. Before you spoke to another soul.' And leaving his stool behind, he came to sit on the bed, hand out, touching Alys' arm.

Alys swallowed, seeing his eyes full of desire, much like his thoughts. 'What about Eddeth? When will she return?'

'She won't. She's a useful woman, but so distracting. And for what we have coming, I want you entirely free of distractions, Alys, my sweet dreamer.'

'Then I should be alone!' Alys insisted quickly. 'I need to be alone, to think. To dream!'

'Though you have just woken, and surely you don't mind a little company? Just for a while.' Hakon ran his hand up Alys' arm, smiling.

Alys saw a glimpse of his mark in her mind, and she shivered. 'I dreamed about the gods!' It was the first thing that popped into her head, and it wasn't true, but it immediately distracted Hakon, who pulled his hand away, eyes popping open.

'What about them?'

'They were talking about... who they wanted to be Alekka's next king.'

Hakon didn't move. Didn't even blink.

Alys hurried on, weaving a story from flimsy threads, trying not to look as though she was making it all up. 'They were arguing.' She frowned, as though she was trying to recall more, edging further away from Hakon, who sat before her, mouth ajar. 'Fighting! There were two sides. Thenor on one. His brother, Eskvir, on the other. They disagreed.'

'About who should be king?'

Alys nodded. 'Eskvir wanted to abandon your family altogether, but Thenor convinced him to... give you a chance to prove yourself. So Thenor sent The Hunter to mark you... as a test. If you rose up and conquered the Vilanders, saved Slussfall, and took Stornas, you would be saved, your family's place in the gods' hearts restored. If not they would kill you, end your line. They agreed that this coming battle would be decisive.'

Hakon was stunned, hanging on every word. 'Decisive.'

'A way to settle things once and for all.'

'And Thenor did this to test me?'

Alys nodded, saliva flooding her mouth. One eye on the chamber door, she slipped out of bed. 'Yes. He wanted you to prove to Eskvir and the other gods how worthy you are.' She snatched her cloak from the bed, slipping it around her shoulders while Hakon was distracted. 'There is a lot to do. I saw the Vilanders and their ships too. They will be here today.'

That *was* true, and Hakon turned to Alys with surprise in his eyes. 'Today?'

'Possibly tonight. The sky was dark when their ships entered the harbour.'

The rain was loud, and Hakon stood, walking around the bed, wanting to hear every word. 'Today?' He was in a daze, desire, fear, and anger surging through his body. He peered at Alys, seeing how tired she looked, but so beautiful. Her hair was a touselled mess, hanging over her enormous black cloak, and he took a step forward, one hand out. 'Tell me something to help me. A way I can hurt Reinar Vilander. That's what Mother was so good at, knowing how to twist the knife. That's what I need now, Alys, a way to hurt him.'

Alys could sense the danger accelerating. He would rape her.

He would try to.

'Reinar's wife is with him!' She blurted it out, not sure what she was doing.

Hakon frowned, confused by that. 'You said she was missing. Lost to him.'

'She returned to Ottby. She's with him, on board his ship. I saw them together.' That much was true; Alys had seen images of them lying in each other's arms, sound asleep in *Fury's* stern.

She closed her eyes, feeling uncomfortable.

And opening them, she saw that Hakon had turned away from her, aiming for the door.

'What a gift you are, Alys,' he grinned, feeling the burn of the mark, but seeing it with new eyes now. 'A dreamer of such vision. Perhaps you don't know magic as Mother did, but Thenor would not wish to see me hide behind a dreamer. There's no glory in that.'

The rain was getting louder, and Alys held her breath, watching as Hakon gripped the door handle, willing him to leave.

'I'll send breakfast, but not Eddeth. I don't want anything else entering your head now. Just me, and the dreams you will have for me. I'll return after supper, and you can tell me what else you've seen.' And thoughts of tearing Alys' clothes off retreating now, he opened the door, slipping outside.

Alys shook all over, panting with relief.

But she was entirely alone, a prisoner, without even Eddeth to talk to.

So how were they going to help Reinar now?

***

The cottage had belonged to Hakon's old dreamer, and it stunk.

Eddeth pulled the hide off the window, wedging open the door. She thought of her fragrant cottage with her temperamental cat, and she felt emotional, wondering if she would ever see them again.

'It's not much,' Ivan said, one hand over his nose, not wanting to inhale. He wasn't happy about taking Eddeth out of Alys' chamber, sensing that his cousin had an ulterior motive for wanting her to be alone. 'But at least you'll be free. Free to come and go as you like.'

Eddeth eyed the door. 'I'd rather have stayed with Alys. She needs me.'

Ivan swallowed.

'Though I'm sure your cousin will be happy. Now he can do what he wants to her.' Eddeth saw the discomfort in Ivan's eyes, and she leaned on it hard. 'Alys has certainly seen his intentions.'

'She has?'

Eddeth nodded vigorously, turning back to the small kitchen area, running a finger over the multitude of jars stacked along one edge of the table. The odd item was familiar, but there were many things Eddeth had no idea about at all. She was intrigued and distracted, forgetting about Ivan entirely, knowing that she needed to come up with a new plan to get the gates open for Reinar, and quickly.

But without a dreamer?

'Eddeth?'

She turned around to where Ivan lingered in the doorway, just out of the teeming rain. 'Yes?'

'Alys? You said she saw things about my cousin?'

'Oh yes, I did! He wants to rape her, of course. Have her to himself, like a slave dreamer. Keep her locked up, dreaming for him, when he's not raping her. The poor woman. After what she's been through lately!'

Ivan looked down at his hands, fingernails almost black. He'd done little since they'd returned but sort out the mess of the fort, and prepare for the Vilanders' attack. He'd barely had any time to think, though that was mostly by design. He sighed, needing to leave. 'Can I get you anything else? '

Eddeth felt sorry for him, which surprised her, but Ivan was nothing like his cousin.

If only Ivan could see that.

'No! I shall give the place a scrub, get that horrible old hag's smell out of it! Then I'll get to work.'

'She *was* a horrible old hag,' Ivan agreed. 'Nothing like Alys.'

'No, well, Alys is young and inexperienced. If your cousin has his way, I'm sure it won't be long till she turns into an evil old crone just like that dead dreamer!' And pleased to see that she'd hammered home her point, Eddeth unpinned her cloak, glancing around the miserable cottage, wondering where to begin.

***

'But how much longer should we wait?' Ollo Narp had itchy feet. He stood outside the cave beside Vik, who was watching Jonas teach his great-grandson how to kill with a knife. He needed some ale, a woman, a bed; some certainty about the path he wanted to take next. So did his men.

'Eddeth said she'd come. We have to give her a chance.' Vik didn't know Eddeth, or whether he could trust her, but she'd talked in a way that gave Vik confidence that Alys did.

Ollo sighed, wondering if he should just slip away, though his men had been eagerly talking about supporting the Vilanders to end the Vettels, having had enough of their time on the wrong side of things.

Even Ollo could see that it was the wrong side now.

But still, it was hard to just sit in the cave and wait. He farted, edging away from Vik, who called on Magnus to watch his back.

Magnus looked up, distracted, not seeing the man approaching from behind, and in the blink of an eye that man had Magnus down on the ground, knife knocked out of his hand. The wiry old man grinned at Magnus, helping him back to his feet.

'You can't allow yourself to become distracted,' Jonas smiled. 'You need to know what's coming behind you as well as in front of you.' Heavy rain fell in front of the cave like a curtain, and no one felt like going outside. Magnus was growing so bored that Jonas was trying new ways to keep him busy. And besides, the boy needed to know how to defend himself, how to kill if necessary. He'd started teaching Alys when she was younger than Magnus. He wondered if she still remembered. He wondered why she'd never tried to kill her husband.

Perhaps she had?

Life could be complicated, Jonas knew, stomach rumbling. Sometimes people tangled themselves in knots they didn't think they could escape from. But there was always a way out, if you wanted to find one.

There was always a way out...

***

Reinar stood beside Bjarni and Holgar, not appreciating the weather.

'Don't think the gods want us to get to Slussfall!' Holgar cried over the furious roar of wind and rain.

'Well, possibly Ulfinnur doesn't!' Reinar agreed, eyes screwed up, rain running down his head, trickling down his back. He'd forgotten what it felt like to wear dry clothes. His were so stuck to his skin that he'd given up trying to peel them off. Shivering, his eyes drifted to Elin, who was talking to Stina under the sagging sailcloth. It was keeping off some of the rain, but enough of it was dripping through that all three women appeared to be shivering.

'And what are we going to do about them when we get there?' Holgar wondered, inclining his head to the women, unable to take his hands off the tiller. They were flying now, the sail as round as his belly after a three-day feast. He felt pleased, though they could have done without the freezing rain. Holgar shook his head, flinging drops of water over Bjarni and Reinar, who didn't notice, soaked through as they were.

'They'll stay on the ship, out of the way,' Reinar said. 'I'll leave someone to guard them.'

'Even Ilene?' Bjarni wondered.

Reinar shook his head. 'No, Ilene should get a chance to prove herself. I'll ask Nels to stay behind. He's been unwell since we left.'

'Not sure why you brought him!' Bjarni snorted. 'The boy would've been more use back in Ottby, mucking out the stables.'

'He's not that bad!'

'Never met a fight he couldn't run away from, that one.'

'He's good with a sword,' Reinar insisted.

'He is! In the training ring. But put him anywhere he might get hurt for real, and he'll find a reason not to fight. You know that.'

It was Nels Froder's reputation, and Reinar knew that he would likely leap at the chance to stay behind and look after Elin and Stina, though he imagined he would have a fight from Elin. She'd already indicated as much.

Elin knew that Reinar was talking about her, likely fretting and worrying, wishing he hadn't brought her along. 'Can you use a weapon?' she wondered, eyeing Stina, who was not enjoying being stuck under the sailcloth with the two women, both of them united in their obvious dislike of her.

'A weapon?' Stina shook her head, thinking of Ludo, who'd

been unable to teach her how to use a bow or a spear. She wished she'd confided in him about Torvig. Or Alys. Anyone. Tulia would still be alive.

Stina swallowed, knowing that was true.

Tulia would still be alive.

Ilene laughed. 'Stina couldn't hurt someone with a weapon if you tied them down! I saw her when they were training us. She's entirely useless.'

Stina sighed, staring out into the rain again. The men who hunkered down against the gunwales often looked their way with envy in their eyes, but Stina would have given anything to swap places with them. She didn't want to be sitting next to a snarling Ilene and a sharp-tongued Elin.

'Well, I suspect we'll be forced to keep each other company,' Elin decided, eyes on Reinar. 'My husband won't want us getting in his way.'

'But not me,' Ilene said gleefully, though her stomach was starting to gripe, nerves stirring. She smiled at Stina, who looked utterly miserable, wishing she was on *Dagger* with Ludo and Sigurd.

***

It was too wet to even play dice, and Sigurd peered up at the sky, wanting to see a hint of the weather changing. All he got was a ball of hail in the eye.

'Hail?' Ludo couldn't believe it. '*Hail?*'

Sigurd laughed, miserable and wet and wishing he was sitting under a sailcloth like Elin and Stina and Ilene. He'd seen them earlier, and as the rain filled up his boots, he felt envious, but at the same time, the discomfort was motivating. It kept him on edge, and he found his thoughts coalescing around the idea of killing the Vettels. Of taking back Slussfall for Ake. Of coming home to the cheers of his family and friends ringing in his ears.

And then leaving.

He wanted to go back to Varis, to Kalmera. Tulia had no family living that he knew of, but he'd saved some of hers and Amir's ashes, keeping them in two wooden boxes, and he wanted to return them to their homeland. It felt like the right thing to do. The thought that all he had left of Tulia now was a handful of ash in a tiny box made him mournful, and his attention drifted to his brother, whose heart had been broken when Elin left. Sigurd felt envious, wishing he had a second chance like Reinar. When Elin had disappeared, everyone assumed she'd run away to kill herself – everyone but Reinar, who'd held on to some hope. Yet now he had her back he looked far from happy, far from comfortable either, and Sigurd knew exactly what that was about.

Alys.

***

Alys felt relieved that Salma's book was still under the bed; surprised to find Eddeth's grandmother's book there too, though Hakon had obviously dragged Eddeth out of the chamber before she'd even had a chance to sneeze.

Alys hoped she was alright, wanting Eddeth to come and see her, for how were they going to get the gates open without her potion? Eddeth had found the spell in Salma's book, and though Alys could see the symbols to draw, she didn't know herbs, and she'd only be able to guess at half the ingredients required.

She needed to escape and find Eddeth.

To get away before Hakon hurt her. And he would.

Alys had seen it in his eyes. She'd seen flashes of it happening too.

Trying to distract herself, she took a seat by the fire, opening Eddeth's grandmother's book, hoping to find something she could do to help Reinar on her own, but her mind quickly wandered back to Hakon, and her eyes snapped to the door. Hakon was a danger to everyone around him, including her, and though she'd distracted him for a time with a tale of the gods, it was only a tale.

Or was it?

Alys peered down at the book. She hadn't studied it nearly as closely as Salma's, but now, stuck in her chamber, all alone, she could hopefully find out more. She smiled, wondering what Eddeth's grandmother had been like, getting a vision of a woman who looked just like Eddeth. And then Alys blinked, seeing her own grandmother, the woman she'd always thought was her mother. That voice, that face, she'd always believed they belonged to her mother.

And now?

Who was she really, and why had her grandparents kept so many secrets from her?

CHAPTER FORTY TWO

Slussfall's tall fortress was ringed by a single stone wall. It was as old as Ottby, with well-defended ramparts and four guard towers that gave a clear view over the harbour to the east, and the forest to the west. It had held strong for nearly twenty years against every threat from above The Rift until the Vettels had captured it.

Mother had helped, Lief knew. That old witch had been surprisingly useful against stubborn enemies, and now, without her, even he had begun to feel vulnerable.

Ivan stood to one side of him, Hakon on the other, all three of them staring down into the harbour from the ramparts.

'His wife?' Ivan felt uncomfortable. 'You want to kill his wife?'

'Of course!' Hakon rubbed his thumbless hands together, glee in his voice. 'Imagine how things will go after that?'

Lief, who had a wife he very much hoped would live through the Vilanders' attack, frowned. 'He'll be even more motivated, I would think, my lord.' His voice was a deep-throated rebuke, his eyes cold. 'I expect you'd feel the same. Just the thought of him hurting yours has you on edge, but if Reinar Vilander actually killed her?'

Hakon could certainly imagine it, though he dismissed Lief's worry. 'A man may try to hold himself together after a shocking heartbreak, but he'll not be the same. He won't think clearly, won't see clearly. He'll make mistakes, and we'll be ready to pounce.'

Ivan felt tense, every word tumbling out of his cousin's mouth putting him more on edge. 'Reinar Vilander isn't fool enough to keep his wife where she can be killed, Hakon. Why would he do that?'

Hakon didn't want to hear it, and turning to Lief, he sought a different opinion, though Lief didn't have one.

'Ivan's right, my lord. He'll keep his wife well out of range. She's not a warrior that I'm aware of. He won't risk getting her anywhere near trouble.'

Hakon felt irritated by both of them, his eyes wandering to the harbour. 'Well, he's risked her already, bringing her along! And he'll be too distracted by what's happening around him to keep her safe.' Thoughts of vengeance, temporarily held at bay by his life-threatening wound and the terrifying journey through the forest, came rushing back, and Hakon saw his father's headless body, lying in the snow. 'We'll do everything we can to target her. I'll ask Alys to find her, tell us exactly where she is.'

'If you keep going to see Alys, Cousin, you won't give her any chance to dream for you. And besides, it's distracting. We've more to worry about than Reinar Vilander's wife.' Ivan twitched irritably, thinking about Alys locked in that chamber. At Hakon's mercy. 'We haven't got enough arrows. The fletchers are doing all they can, but if you don't want us to damage the ships, we can't sling boulders or fire at them while they're on board.'

Hakon dismissed his cousin's fretting, chest burning now, mind skipping ahead. If he was to impress the gods, he had to make bold decisions, leading from the front with decisive strokes. And closing his eyes, he could almost see Thenor nodding his head in approval.

'Hakon?' Ivan wanted to scream. It was proving impossible to keep up with his cousin, though Ivan knew it was his job to try.

'We will end the Vilanders, and burn Ake's men to ash, *once* they're ashore. This can't be some neverending tug of rope, making incremental steps. We must crush our enemies with an iron fist! Every strength we have must be utilised. I demand it of you both! Keep thinking. Keep planning. The fort is secure, so that is not where our attention needs to be. It must be on how to make this the most one-sided victory in the history of Alekka!' And wheeling around, Hakon walked away from them both, heading for the guard tower, wanting to have a word with his fletchers.

Ivan and Lief watched him go, neither speaking.

Eventually, when Hakon had disappeared inside the tower, Lief turned to Ivan. 'Falla is worried,' he admitted. 'Without Mother here, guiding your cousin, she feels concerned.'

Ivan didn't speak. His attention remained on the harbour, watching a merchant ship unloading its goods. More furs, he thought absentmindedly. Antlers too. He'd been to The Murk many times over the years. It was such a mysterious, dark, dangerous place. Though, he realised, he felt no safer here, with the gods after them, and his cousin on the edge.

'I'll go down to the harbour, take a look around, see if there's anything else I can think of,' Lief suggested. 'We don't have the ships to attack them by sea. All we can do is wait for them to come to us.'

Ivan's silence continued, but he nodded, worrying about where his cousin had gone.

Hoping it was to the fletchers.

***

The rain had cleared, though the sky remained gloomy. Eddeth didn't notice as she bounded past the woodturner's hut with Falla and Karolina. They were both struggling to keep up with the healer, who had a habit of racing ahead, forgetting they were with her.

'We must be on our way before the rain comes down again! Wilf's a good horse, but he does hate bad weather!' It was a risk, Eddeth knew, trusting either of the women. Falla leaned towards being self-serving by nature, and though Karolina was desperate to get away from her husband, she was also afraid of what he might do to her if he discovered her disloyalty. And yet, Eddeth had taken them into her confidence, for she'd realised that the best way to help Reinar on her own was to put the guards to sleep. And now she needed to find some henbane and hemlock.

And besides, she'd promised to visit Vik.

'I won't come,' Karolina said, blinking at Eddeth, who had finally slowed down, dropping back, conscious of the weight of the saddlebags slung over her shoulders. Between Falla and Karolina, they'd found enough food to feed a small army, and Eddeth had stuffed her saddlebags full. 'It would create too much suspicion.'

Falla agreed. 'Well, as long as you don't reveal where we've gone. Or why.'

'I... I couldn't. I don't know.' That was true enough, though the small information Karolina did possess would be enough to get Falla and Eddeth in serious trouble. But both women were trying to help them all, and Karolina felt strongly about doing everything she could to keep them safe.

'That's the right answer!' Eddeth winked, turning into the stables after Falla. 'And your husband is no dreamer. He'll believe what you tell him if you flutter your eyelashes enough!'

Karolina nodded, wanting to cry. She'd seen Hakon's chest, more than once now, and she knew what that mark meant. Falla had told her that Hakon had murdered Rikkard, and in the back of Karolina's mind, she wondered if it was because Rikkard had seen the mark.

The thought of that terrified her.

'And besides,' Eddeth muttered. 'I've known Reinar Vilander since he was a boy. He's a good man. There's no chance he would try and kill you or your son. No chance at all!'

***

The day was running away from them, icy rain pouring down unabated, and Reinar was sure that soon they'd all be too cold to even hold a bow in their hands. He certainly couldn't stop shivering. And trying to take his mind off the rain and the cold, he attempted to focus on their plan.

Alys' plan.

And if it worked, and they got into the fortress, what would he do then?

With Hakon and Ivan Vettel dead, what would he do then?

Ake's words echoed constantly, like a warning he couldn't ignore.

Though he wanted to.

Elin left the sodden shelter behind and came to join him, slipping an arm around his waist. He looked down at her, smiling. He knew what it felt like to lose the ones you loved – the pain was indescribable – though Reinar was not concerned with breaking Hakon Vettel's heart.

Rain ran down his face, soaking his beard, and taking it in his hands, he wrung it like a cloth.

He wasn't concerned with breaking a dead man's heart.

But could he break his own?

Could he live with himself if he killed the baby?

Yet then there would be no more Vettels. No more Vettels to ever threaten Alekka again. Reinar closed his eyes, wanting the rain to numb him until nothing existed but Ake's words. 'Don't run from this, Reinar. I demand it of you, as I would demand it of your father if he still commanded this old fortress. I trusted him, put my faith in him, and now, I put it in you.'

**

Eddeth's grandmother's book was full of interesting stories, and once Alys had deciphered its odd ways and untangled its jumbled order, she began to enjoy reading it. Though, after a while, she started to see the gods differently, and instead of feeling comforted by the thought of them watching over and protecting her, she became increasingly disturbed. They appeared to be locked in the very battle she'd described to Hakon, which unsettled Alys even further.

Looking up suddenly, she wondered if the woman's voice she often heard was Alari. It was an evil, threatening sort of voice, taunting her, trying to scare her. And if Alari's goal was to thwart Thenor, it was likely that she would see Alys as her enemy, just as Hakon's dreamer had.

A knock on the door had Alys jumping out of the chair. Thoughts scattering, book clutched to her chest, she panicked as the door opened, Ivan walking in with a basket. He looked similar in so many ways to his cousin, though it was hard to dislike Ivan.

Alys smiled in relief.

'You were expecting someone else?'

'I was, but I'd much rather see you.'

Ivan was pleased, placing the basket on the small table by the window. 'Something to eat, from the kitchen. There's a jug of wine too. Thought it might help to pass the time.'

'What? Getting drunk?'

'Why not?' Ivan winked. 'A jug of wine for you, and the Vilanders to distract my cousin, so he doesn't come near your door.'

'And when he defeats them?' Alys didn't want to let Ivan off that lightly. 'Surely you don't think I can keep him distracted forever?' Memories of her dreams flickered, and she peered at Ivan. 'Do you know a woman called Mirella?'

'Mirella?' Ivan was surprised. 'Why?'

Alys shrugged, trying to appear nonchalant. 'Just something I dreamed last night. I saw Hakon as a baby, as young as his son is now. There was a woman with his father. Mirella, he called her, but I didn't understand who she was. Not his mother.'

'No, his stepmother.'

Alys froze. 'Stepmother?'

Ivan nodded, lifting the items out of the basket onto the table, annoyed that he'd managed to spill the wine. 'Jesper loved Mirella, almost more than himself, which is saying something!' He grinned, placing the wine jug on the table. 'They were together before Hakon was born, from what I've heard, but Mirella ran away, and Jesper married Hakon's mother, Arina. He didn't love her, he just wanted sons, though he ended up killing her and marrying Mirella after all. The Vettels have a way of getting what they want... in the end.'

Alys hadn't moved. Hadn't spoken. Her thoughts jammed together, not allowing her to make any sense of them, knowing that she didn't want to.

'How about a cup of wine?' Ivan asked, eager for one himself.

'So you knew this Mirella?' Alys turned to him, clearing her face.

'Of course.' Ivan picked up a fig, offering it to Alys, who shook her head. 'After Jesper killed my father, I went to live in Orbo with him and Mirella. She was like a mother to me.' He felt sad then, still not sure why she'd disappeared so suddenly, or whether she was still alive.

Alys felt displaced, as though the ground beneath her was crumbling away. She saw her grandmother's face, heard her grandmother's voice, and she tried to convince herself that she didn't know what any of it meant.

***

Eddeth had no idea where she was going.

Alys had tried to give her directions to the cave she'd seen in her dreams, though she'd struggled to explain the landscape in great detail, and Eddeth was lost in the forest, each tree and path looking just like every other. She hadn't imagined the cave would be that far away from where she'd bumped into Vik the first time. She smiled, remembering the handsome warrior.

'Not sure why you're smiling,' Falla grumbled. 'We're going around in circles! It will be dark soon, and we'll be lost in here.'

They'd stopped twice so she could vomit, and her mood was as sour as the taste in her mouth.

'I'm smiling because I'm thrilled to be away from that fort!' Eddeth said happily, and it was true. She hated feeling imprisoned, though guilt dulled her enthusiasm when she thought of poor Alys, who still was.

'Well, you won't be happy soon when we're trapped in this forest for days!'

Eddeth's smile brightened again, certain she could see a hint of stone in the distance. The trees were bunched tightly together, not indicating a path in that direction, but Eddeth's hunch strengthened in her mind, and she turned Wilf towards it. 'Come on! The quicker you stop grumbling, the more inclined the gods will be to help us. They don't like grumblers, you know, not at all!'

Falla frowned, grumbling some more, hoping Lief wouldn't send men out looking for them. Hoping that Eddeth would find those caves before she had to vomit again.

And then a man leaped out from behind a tree, brandishing a sword.

Falla bit her tongue, yelping in horror, her horse skittering about urgently beneath her.

Ollo grabbed the bridle, one of his men seizing Eddeth's horse before he could bolt, though, in the dense maze of trees, he wouldn't have gotten very far. 'And where are you ladies off to, then? Not the sort of place to forage for herbs.' He eyed Falla with a raised eyebrow, knowing whose wife she was.

'We're not hunting for herbs!' Eddeth declared loudly, scattering a couple of black woodpeckers into the air. 'Well, not any longer. We're hunting you and your friends, of course! We come with news!' She looked around eagerly. 'And where is Vik?' Eddeth had made Alys tell her all about Vik. 'Where is Vik Lofgren?'

And hearing the commotion, Vik came to see what was happening, smiling at the sight of Eddeth on her nervous old horse. 'So you finally came?'

'I did!' Eddeth chuckled, brushing hair out of her eyes which sparkled brightly. 'For I have news about our friends. Alys has seen them coming. Today!'

***

Low-lying clouds submerged the coast, but every now and then they caught glimpses of where they were, and it had them on edge.

The rain had stopped. Now their wet bodies were just slowly freezing, battered by an icy wind. Still, it kept them wide awake, thoughts rushing past them at speed, each one of them trying to remember what they needed to do. Reinar hoped he'd anticipated everything that could go wrong. He tried to think of anything he could do to make their success more likely, though Slussfall had been built to make everything hard. Shoulders aching with tension, his eyes drifted to the ships sailing along in *Fury's* wake. Everyone appeared alert now, men standing, weapons ready. The sun was somewhere, lost behind the thick clouds, heading for the sea.

'We can't come in close!' Reinar called to Holgar, who nodded, winking at his lord.

'Don't worry, they won't see us! Not in this soup!'

And it was true, Reinar realised with a smile. He'd cursed the gods for the weather, but it would help them slip around Slussfall without being seen. His good mood vanished, though, when he saw Stina standing by herself in the bow, staring out to sea. After all she'd been through, he hoped he could reunite her with Alys. Alys who was trapped with Hakon Vettel.

Reinar shook with fury as well as cold, trying not to imagine what he was doing to her, knowing that he had to stay calm.

If he was going to save Alys, he had to keep hold of his temper.

***

Alys didn't want Ivan to leave, though she needed to be alone. Soon Hakon would come back, wanting to know what she'd seen, and with Ivan sitting beside her talking incessantly, trying to distract them both, she stood no chance of seeing anything at all.

Sensing her discomfort, and realising that the afternoon was disappearing, Ivan stood, adding a log to the fire. 'I should be going. Hakon will probably be stalking the fort looking for me.'

Getting up, Alys followed him to the door. 'You're very close to your cousin, I know, yet you're not Hakon. He makes his own choices, and you must make yours, Ivan.' Alys wondered if she could get through to him, though, perhaps, like Sigurd, he did not value the insight of a dreamer? 'The gods will always give good men another chance.'

'To do what?'

'Become the hero you see in your dreams. The famed warrior you've always wanted to be.'

Ivan's eyes widened, staring at Alys.

'Jesper worried for his son. It made sense that he found someone to save Hakon from himself and all those bad choices he was likely to make. To fix his mistakes, take the blame for his failures.'

Now Ivan looked away, eyes back on the flames.

'But what about what *you* want? You can't give yourself so fully to another person and expect to get anything in return. You're young. Your life lies ahead of you, and Hakon...'

'Hakon?'

Alys stared at the door, knowing that soon Hakon would come through it. 'You're not your cousin, Ivan. It's never too late to take another path.'

Ivan grabbed the door handle, feeling flustered. 'You should drink the wine, Alys, it might make the night more bearable.' He spoke quickly, not wanting to give her another chance to speak.

Afraid of what she would say.

'The Vilanders will be here soon,' Alys said softly. 'You need to be ready.'

Ivan drew his hand away from the door, uncertainty in his

eyes, and blinking rapidly, he unsheathed a small knife from its scabbard, offering her the haft.

And turning back to the door, he disappeared outside.

PART FIVE

Judgement

CHAPTER FORTY THREE

The afternoon darkened as Eddeth sat before the flames beside Vik, Magnus watching her curiously. He was a handsome boy, Eddeth thought, though he didn't look like Alys, apart from the freckles.

He didn't smile.

'Alys told the Vilanders where you were. Reinar knows all about the tunnel.'

It felt odd to Jonas that his granddaughter had chosen to go into Reinar Vilander's dream; the man who had stolen her, separated her from her children, taken her away from her home. Though his arrival in Ullaberg had brought an end to her violent marriage, so perhaps she was grateful for that? 'Well, he'll know how to find it well enough. He's been in there with his father. His brother too. Likely he'll remember the caves, though perhaps we should go and meet him?'

'Not sure it's the best plan,' Vik grumbled. 'Attacking the fort during the day? We'll be too exposed. It's clear ground once you're out of the forest.'

Eddeth smiled at him, ignoring a muttering Falla, who was growing impatient to leave. 'Alys can't keep hopping into everyone's dreams, not without me there to help her anymore. And for now, she's locked away, so we must go forward. Do as we've planned!'

'And you think Reinar will?' Ollo put in. He knew the Vilanders too. They all did. Apart from Falla and Magnus and Leonid, all three of them silent. 'Follow the plan?'

'To save Alys?' Eddeth chuckled. 'He'd climb a wall of fire to save Alys, don't you worry about that!'

Magnus scowled. Jonas and Vik too.

'Well then, you'd better get back to the fort, Eddeth, before they come looking for you both,' Jonas said, standing. He was grateful for the saddlebags full of food that the women had smuggled out of the fort; grateful too for the two swordbelts Falla had found, and Eddeth had wrapped around her waist, replete with swords and knives. They'd been feeling vulnerable with only a few weapons between them, but now, thanks to the women, they had enough to cause a little trouble.

'And your husband?' Vik wondered, eyeing Falla. She reminded him of his first wife, who'd been a dark-haired beauty, and he felt oddly nostalgic for a time long gone. 'Does he know you're here?'

Falla took his hand, allowing Vik to help her back to her feet. 'No. He's a loyal man, an oath keeper, but despite that, I think he's seen enough. I feel he's ready to turn.'

'You do?' Ollo looked doubtful. '*Your* Lief? Lief Gundersen?'

Falla nodded, biting down on her irritation with Ollo Narp, who kept ogling her, sitting far too close. 'After what happened in Ottby? Our journey back to Slussfall? He's seen enough to know what lies ahead if he helps Hakon take the throne. My husband will not stand in your way, I'm sure of it.'

None of the men looked as sure as Falla, and Eddeth saw her trying desperately to convince them that she knew what she was talking about. 'Falla's right. There'll be many reconsidering their oath to their lord after what's happened. We just need to get you into the fort to kill him. Once he's dead, there'll be little appetite for battle.'

Knowing warriors as he did, Vik knew that was likely true, and he nodded at Eddeth, guiding her and Falla back to their horses as the fog intensified.

Magnus went with him.

He'd been a naive child when he left Ullaberg with Lotta, and so much had happened to change him in a short space of time. As desperate as he was to feel his mother's arms around him again, he was scared that he'd never return to being the boy she had left behind on that beach. Grabbing Eddeth's hand, he left Vik to walk ahead with Falla. 'Is my mother safe? Is she alright?' Tears came quickly as he stared up into Eddeth's blinking eyes.

She crouched down, grinning broadly. 'Your mother is a brave woman, Magnus. Braver than you could ever imagine.' They had not told the men and Magnus everything. There was simply not enough time. 'She's safe. In that fort, she's as safe as she can be. And don't worry, I won't let anything happen to her. I've some dreamer in me, you know. It's there!' And tapping her head, Eddeth stood with a groan. 'Oh, yes it is! I'll find a way to see what's coming next. You wait and see!' She thought of Alys, who would have given anything to be standing in her place, feeling a rush of emotion. 'You'll see her soon, Magnus, I promise.' And placing one hand on his shoulder, she lifted his chin with the other, staring into his eyes. 'I promise.'

***

Reinar was close. Alys saw flashes of him standing by Bjarni, black fur cloak billowing in the wind, face wet with rain. Sometimes, he was with his wife. She saw Stina too, with Ilene, who scowled at her. All of it made her frown.

All of it confused and worried her.

She sat in the chair by the fire, eyes closed, trying to shut every distraction away, wishing Winter was on her lap. Stroking his smooth white fur had always soothed her, and helped her too, she realised, knowing that there was something magical about the cat.

Some dreamers knew magic, but usually only those who chose a dark path employed it. Alys fingered Salma's book, desperate to find a way to open the gates for Reinar. She had little confidence, though, and opening her eyes, she sighed, sensing dusk approaching.

Looking over her shoulder, she glanced at the door.

She saw flashes of Hakon too, and that scared her.

He was a desperate man, and desperate men would do anything to cling to power. They needed to survive. Above all things, they needed to survive.

And that made Hakon a very dangerous problem indeed.

***

Falla stumbled into the hall with pink cheeks.

Lief strode to her side, scowling. 'Where have you been?'

Looking around in surprise, Falla noted the crowd of well-dressed men and women milling around as though they were enjoying a feast. The hall tables had been pulled out and decorated, extra candles brought in. Even Hakon's musicians had been put to work, entertaining his guests. She looked down at her muddy boots and her filthy cloak, feeling out of place. 'What's going on?'

Lief clenched his jaw. 'Hakon brought everyone together. He plans to sacrifice to Thenor later. He wants it to be a celebration.'

'Of what?'

'Of him.'

Falla saw Karolina out of the corner of her eye, trying to squirm away from her husband, who was roaring with laughter, slapping Ivan on the back. Even Ivan looked as though he didn't want to be there.

The hall was festive, Falla supposed, though, apart from whatever was amusing Hakon, the mood was somber.

'Where were you?' Lief asked again.

'Helping Eddeth,' Falla said, kissing him, hoping to distract him. 'I was showing her where Mother gathered mushrooms. We went into the forest.'

Lief looked angry, despite her eager kisses. 'You shouldn't

have left the fort, Falla, not in this weather. Jonas Bergstrom might still be out there. Others too. Men are missing. Hakon might not notice or care, but men are missing, maybe slipping away to join Ake?'

Falla blinked, looking bored. 'Well, no harm was done. We're both returned safe and sound, and now Eddeth has all the supplies she needs.'

'For what?' Lief wondered, slipping an arm around his wife's waist as he led her towards Hakon.

Falla smiled. 'No idea, mostly teas, I imagine. She can't stop talking about them.' She saw Lief's attention wander to his lord, barely listening now.

'And here's Falla!' Hakon announced loudly, drunkenly, pushing his wife towards the new arrival. 'I'm sure Karolina would like to escape the endless talk of arrows and gates and whether we're going to have enough pitch!'

Karolina eagerly left her husband behind, drawing Falla away from the men, heading for the nearest table, where she poured her a goblet of wine. 'What happened?' she whispered. 'Did you find the men?'

Falla didn't want to have that conversation. Not in the hall.

She simply nodded.

Ivan watched them. Karolina looked as though she was trembling, though it was particularly cold in the hall, he supposed. Candles burned in circular iron frames, hanging from the rafters, and in towering displays in the centre of each table. The flames in the long fire pits running side by side through the centre of the hall were bright and warm, but so many people were coming and going through the doors that there was a permanent chill in the air.

Or maybe it was him, Ivan realised, barely listening to Hakon, who was regaling some of Erlan Stari's remaining men with the tale of how they'd captured Slussfall from Sirrus Ahlmann. Though he failed to mention that they'd had Mother's help. That was the truth of it. The old witch had helped them get in when countless attempts by Jesper had failed.

But who did Reinar Vilander have helping him?

They had his dreamer.

So who was helping the Vilanders?

***

Despite the lingering odour of the cottage, Eddeth was making herself at home. She was enjoying the silence, letting her thoughts wander, often returning to Vik, or to Magnus, remembering her promise to him.

She had to work fast to get her potion ready, though there was the problem of how to get the guards to drink it. And when?

She suddenly felt muddled, oddly nervous.

And then a knock on the door had Eddeth biting her tongue, cursing the gods. 'What do you want?' she barked, finger in her mouth, tasting blood. No one answered, and cocking her head to one side, Eddeth wondered who it could be. She approached the door with caution, twisting her head from side to side, checking to see if she'd left out anything that might get her in trouble. Though, she realised with a shrug, it was unlikely that anyone would even know the names of the plants and mushrooms she'd collected with Falla. Still, she turned back to the table and picked up the bowl of potion, pushing it under the bed, before opening the door to a tall young man with a spotty face and a nervous look in his dull-blue eyes. He was familiar, Eddeth thought, with his slouched shoulders and his miserable face, shuffling his boots in the mud by the doorstep.

'What do you want?' Eddeth grumbled, tapping a foot.

'Mistress Falla sent me.'

'Oh? Why?'

'I work in the kitchen. I deliver food and drink to the guards.'

'Oh! I see!' Eddeth was delighted that Falla was so motivated by the thought of becoming the Lady of Slussfall. She was working quickly. Expertly. And, Eddeth hoped, discreetly. 'Come in, come in!'

The boy slumped inside, glancing around. It was the dreamer's cottage, and he swallowed nervously, eyes running to the table stacked with jars of things he didn't want to imagine, though he tried not to show any fear.

'What is your name, boy?'

'Aldo. Aldo Varnass.'

'And why do you look so familiar, Aldo Varnass? Have we met before?' Eddeth peered up at the boy, wondering if she could trust him, hoping that Falla hadn't made a mistake.

'Perhaps you met my brother? He was the lord's steward. Rikkard.'

Eddeth's eyes widened, and she could see the pain in Aldo's. 'Oh. Oh, dear. I'm very sorry about your brother. He was a kind boy, I remember. Such a shame, what happened to him.' Muttering to herself, she motioned for Aldo to take a stool. As well as grinding powders and potions, Eddeth was also cooking a mushroom soup for supper. She'd made far more than she could eat herself, but Aldo looked like the sort of boy with an enormous appetite, and she hesitated to offer him any.

'Mistress Falla said I could help, and I want to. The lord murdered my brother, and I want to help you kill him!'

Seeing the glint of hatred in Aldo's eyes, Eddeth clapped her hands in glee. This boy was set on revenge, and she felt confident that he would do everything in his power to help them. 'Well, then, Aldo,' she said, eyeing the cauldron with some reluctance. 'How about a bowl of soup?'

***

Ivan had no appetite. He saw how drunk Hakon was becoming, and it had him on edge. Suddenly everything his cousin did had him on edge. Their enemy was about to descend upon the fort, and

Ivan feared that the fort was about to descend into chaos.

They had barely put things back together since the riot, and now it was all about to be pulled asunder again.

'Why so miserable, Cousin?' Hakon laughed, patting Ivan on the back. He hadn't felt so relaxed in weeks; months, he was certain. The mark warmed his chest, and he smiled, realising that he'd been looking at it all wrong. Now, he saw it as an opportunity, a chance to prove himself worthy of the gods' favour.

And he would. Hakon could feel it.

He would.

Ivan tried to smile. He was sure he'd drunk just as much as his cousin, but instead of feeling giddy or gleeful, he'd grown increasingly morbid. 'Just trying to think through everything we still need to do. We got into their fort. Why can't they get into ours?'

Lief nodded, worried too.

'Because we had Mother. Oh, Mother, how I miss you!' Hakon slurred, slopping wine over Ivan. 'Never has there been a dreamer like Mother.' His mind skipped to his new dreamer, who was not skilled in the dark arts at all, and yet she'd managed to kill poor Mother.

He frowned, wondering what Alys could do. Voices ricocheted around his head: shouting voices, creeping voices, voices he didn't know. They warned that she was holding things back, not helping him as she could. She was a temptress, a teaser, a liar. A dreamer who knew so much more than she'd ever revealed to him.

A powerful, mysterious woman.

'Hakon?' Ivan looked concerned, grabbing his cousin's arm. Hakon had frozen, cup in mid-air, frowning as though he was listening.

And blinking, voices gone now, Hakon grinned. 'We may not have Mother, but we have Alys, and she will help us.'

'You can't expect much from her, Hakon,' Ivan warned. 'Alys barely has dreams.'

'Is that what she told you? And you believed her?' Hakon laughed, eyes on Lief. 'Well, no surprise there, I suppose. You're hopeless around women, Cousin. Always have been, always will be. Women, I'm sure, will be the death of you one day!' Leaning in close, he grabbed the neck of Ivan's dark-blue tunic, yanking him closer. 'You can stop thinking about Alys, though, for she's mine. My dreamer. My... mine.' And saying nothing more, Hakon strode away, ready for something to eat.

Lief tried to change the subject. 'The fletchers have done well. I've never seen them work so quickly.'

But Ivan wasn't listening. He was watching Hakon, trying to remember a time in his life when everything hadn't revolved around his cousin. Everything he thought or did, everything he said, all of it was designed to please Hakon. To help Hakon, to support Hakon.

And for what?

So he could unleash a monster on Alekka? A monster cursed by Thenor, interested in only what he could gain for himself?

'Alys isn't safe.' Ivan whispered it, not sure he even wanted Lief to hear him.

Lief frowned, edging closer. 'He won't hurt his dreamer. He needs her.'

'He does, so he won't kill her, but he will hurt her.' And tossing his empty ale cup onto the table, Ivan headed for the doors, wanting some fresh air.

***

Jonas was tense, distracted.

Vik could tell.

So leaving Magnus to finish his supper inside the cave, he headed outside to join Jonas, who had wandered down to the stream. 'You alright?'

Jonas nodded without turning around, enjoying the soothing sound of the babbling water. For some reason, it reminded him of Eida, and he felt both comforted and sad.

Then he felt Vik's hand on his back, jolting him out of his dream.

'It's confusing, I know. What's happened. What's coming.'

Jonas shrugged. 'It is, though Eddeth is confusing herself, so maybe she doesn't have the right of it all? She seems to think there's something between Alys and Reinar, but after he captured her? How can that be? And what were those boys doing trying to become slavers? Not in some foreign land either, but in Alekka!' Jonas felt irritable, and scratching his head, he peered at Vik. 'And what about Reinar's wife? Where's Elin?'

'We can't know any of it, not yet. But if Alys is going into Reinar's dreams, trying to help him, there's a good chance Eddeth's right about things.' She was an odd creature, Vik thought with a grin, and hopefully, a useful ally. 'But it's not that, is it? Something's been eating at you for days. Days and days, Jonas. I've spent too much time with you over the years to be fobbed off like some stranger. Secrets don't help anyone.'

Jonas froze, hairs rising on the back of his neck. 'Don't they?' He turned to Vik with sharp eyes. 'I'm not sure that's true. Secrets can keep you safe. Protect you from those who want to hurt you. Who seek to kill you.'

Vik shivered, seeing the odd look in Jonas' eyes. 'What do you mean? What secrets?'

***

Elin smiled at Reinar, enjoying the feel of his arms resting on her lower back, wishing they were lying in their bed, fire crackling, keeping them warm. 'When will we be there?' It was dark, and she had no idea where they even were. She hoped Holgar, who was leading their tiny fleet of ships, had some clue.

'Soon, I hope.'

They stood behind Holgar, who was barely blinking as he

squinted into the murk, looking for familiar shapes. He'd sailed to Slussfall many times over the years, in all sorts of conditions, including in the dead of night, though he was an older man now, his eyesight not what it once was, and he felt a tightness in his chest, hoping he wouldn't miss the mark he was aiming for. There was barely a hint of a star and no sign of the moon, and he had one man hanging from the prow, another leaning over the bow, eyes alert to any danger. Hopefully, they'd provide enough warning.

'And what will you do once we get there?' Elin wondered.

'Climb,' Reinar grinned. 'We will climb.'

CHAPTER FORTY FOUR

Men could be stubborn creatures, Falla knew, but she'd always possessed the skills to bend them to her will. It wasn't hard. They might be stubborn, but they were also predictable. It had never been hard to get what she wanted. Though Lief was proving far less pliable than she'd ever imagined. She knew he loved her, and he would love the child she was carrying, and perhaps one day, even his stepson. He would do anything for his family, she was sure, but break his oath to his lord?

Falla was beginning to realise that Lief might never do that.

But he was not her only hope, so slipping out of the hall, deep-red cloak swathed around her, she hurried towards Ivan. He hadn't gone far, so she found him quickly, slumped on a bench, eyes on his boots, head in his hands.

Sitting down beside him, she gave him a fright, and Ivan turned to her in surprise, never expecting Falla to seek his company. She'd always sneered at him and dismissed him and brushed away his every hint of interest in her.

But now?

'Your cousin is a problem, Ivan. *Your* problem.' Falla edged closer, her voice a deep murmur. 'You must do something about him before it's too late.'

Ivan was disappointed, and he moved away, bored with hearing the same thing from everyone he talked to. 'Lief sent you, did he?'

'No. Lief is as stubborn as you. As pigheaded a man as I've ever met. He wouldn't listen to me, but I hoped that... perhaps you might?'

Ivan had been obsessed with Falla Gundersen from the moment he'd first seen her, but now, even with her sitting beside him, the sweet smell of her freshly-washed hair seducing him, he felt oddly deadened to her charms. 'Because you want Lief to be the lord here? Is that your hope, Falla?'

His voice was mocking, and Falla felt insulted, though it was true. 'My hope is to save the life of my son and my unborn child. As is Karolina's. We both fear what Hakon will do. She's seen his mark. She sees him unravelling before her eyes, threatening and murdering people. Yet those in power do nothing. You see what a danger he's becoming, and you do nothing! We are helpless to make you both see the truth. We can't leave this fort, yet we fear the danger that's growing within it!' Falla took a breath, lowering her voice again. 'You do nothing,' she hissed. 'Nothing to keep us safe.'

'From Hakon?' Ivan bent to her. 'He's not our enemy.'

Falla heard a bird cawing from the ramparts. A raven, she guessed, thinking of Mother. 'Your enemy is often standing right in front of you, Ivan. Right in front of you, with everything you've ever wanted. Open your eyes before it's too late.' Falla was tempted to place a hand on his knee, but she thought of Lief waiting for her inside, and she stood. 'You're different than your cousin. I imagine you've always been different. And now is your chance to prove it.'

***

Sigurd hoped that their ships were completely hidden by the fog. He could barely see *Dagger's* mast, though often the moon would show itself, revealing where they were. He hoped it was where they wanted to be. Reinar was long gone, followed by Ludo, who would work on distracting the Vettels when dawn came.

If they waited that long.

Sigurd grinned, holding a cup of ale in his shaking hand. 'Cold enough for you?'

Bolli had taken a break from the tiller and was wobbling beside him, stretching out his back. 'You say something about the weather now, and that'll be that.'

'What do you mean?'

'I mean Ulfinnur is always listening to idiots predicting the weather. You say one word, and he'll decide to have a little fun with us, I guarantee it. Thunder, lightning, more rain!'

'Whose side do you think they're on, then?' Sigurd wondered, sipping his ale. 'The gods?'

'No idea!' Bolli snorted. Being a sailor, he was an overly superstitious man. Every cloud or drop of rain, every swell of wave or absence of wind was a sign from the gods, and he didn't want to presume what they were thinking.

Not out loud, at least.

'Hopefully ours,' Sigurd said, listening to the rhythmic slap of water against *Dagger's* hull. 'But we'll know soon enough if they are.'

Bolli mumbled, trying to take his mind off his griping belly.

They were nervous.

Sigurd heard whetstones scraping down blades, low chatter in the distance.

'They'll expect us. Alys will have told them we're here. They'll be ready for us,' he said darkly. 'Know that, Bolli. We're here to fight for Ake. To kill the Vettels. To take back Slussfall and avenge Sirrus' death.' He thought about Alys and Eddeth. 'And if the gods think what we're doing is worthy of their help, then they'll give it to us. But we'll do it either way. There's no choice. If Hakon defeats us, he'll move on to Ottby, then Stornas. He'll have our fleet, kill our families, take Alekka. There's no choice now.'

***

Hakon held his goblet aloft, flames glowing on his face, eyes glistening as he surveyed the packed hall. Slussfall was strong, so strong. He felt its stone walls enclosing him like a mother's embrace.

He couldn't remember his own mother, who had died when he was not much older than his son, but his stepmother had cared for him as though he was her own. She had been kind, he thought, missing her for the first time in months.

He saw Ivan slink back into the hall, quickly taking a cup from a table, filling it with wine, and Hakon smiled, remembering how close they'd always been. How rewarding it would be to defeat the Vilanders with Ivan by his side.

'We've been blessed by the gods!' Hakon began, quieting the murmuring hall with his booming voice. 'Ake has sent us the prize of a great fleet! We would take years to build so many ships, and yet they have come to us! They wait out there for us!' Hakon could almost feel his enemy's approach, though no bell had been rung in warning. In the murky night sky, he doubted any man could see what was lurking out in the harbour, though Lief had assured him that many were trying to.

The cheers were muted, despite the bountiful supply of food and ale his men and their wives had consumed. Hakon thought distractedly about a siege, and whether the Vilanders would be able to mount a sustained attack that would drain the fort of its resources. Though his thoughts felt contrary to everything he wanted to say and dismissing them with speed, he smiled. 'And once we have a fleet again, we'll be unstoppable!' Hakon frowned, seeking out Ivan and Lief, knowing that he had to remind them not to burn the ships. They needed every last one of them.

Just not the men sailing them.

'And once we dispatch the Vilanders, and hang their heads from the gates, we'll take to the sea, and be at Stornas before winter truly sets in!'

To most in the hall, it felt as though winter was already here. Snow had been falling on and off for days now, and no one felt particularly enthused by a winter attack on the great walled city of Stornas.

Ivan could sense the lack of enthusiasm in the hall, and feeling bad for his cousin and worried about what he might do, he lifted his own cup, raising his voice. 'And once we cut off Ake's head, we'll head for Ottby and capture that fort too! Alekka will be ours!' He tried so hard to reflect the hunger he saw in Hakon's eyes, but thinking of Alys and Falla and Karolina, it was a struggle. He peered at Hakon, who was frowning, searching for his wife.

She had gone to bed, he remembered.

And his thoughts turned to Alys.

***

Alys could feel the pull of her grandfather. He was unhappy. Worried. He walked beside Vik, both of them far ahead of her, but she knew him well enough to read his mind and body. He walked through the moonlit grove as though the weight of the world rested on his broad shoulders.

She followed them.

And suddenly Jonas stopped, turning with a heavy sigh. 'Mirella was a problem.'

Vik was confused, not expecting that. 'A problem? *Your* Mirella?'

Jonas nodded, shoulders tense. 'Eida wanted her to go to the temple in Tuura, to learn how to be a dreamer. It's what dreamers in her family did.' Jonas' voice became halting. He hadn't approached the subject in years. He'd rarely discussed Mirella with anyone but Eida. 'I didn't want her to go. She was our only child. The only one left.' There had been others, but none had lived past their first birthday.

Vik nodded. He remembered how reluctant Jonas had felt about sending Mirella away.

'But they both wanted it, and it made sense. She was a dreamer, and it made sense for her to learn how to use her gifts. So I took her. We both did. We left her there, in Tuura. She was only thirteen years old.' Jonas gripped his hands, looking up, staring straight through Alys, who watched with eyes peeled open, limbs tense. 'Something was wrong, though.'

'Wrong?'

'In Tuura. Eida hadn't seen it. She couldn't. They hid what they were doing there, even from dreamers. Tuura was being taken over by a sect who followed a dark god, and they turned my Mirella into one of them.' Jonas almost sobbed, still feeling that little body in his arms, her blonde head resting against his chest as she promised to see him soon. She'd been excited about going, but nervous, knowing how much she would miss them both. Jonas sensed Vik's confusion. 'She came back to Torborg, eventually, but she wasn't the same. We didn't recognise her. Eida couldn't see through her secrets and lies. Nor could I. She just wasn't there anymore. To this day, I don't know what they did to her, but the Mirella I knew was gone.'

Vik didn't know what to say.

He couldn't believe Jonas had kept so much from him.

'She did strange things. She stayed in her chamber and wouldn't talk to us. She was... casting spells,' Jonas admitted. 'We tried everything we could, but she locked Eida out of her mind, and me out of her heart. She wouldn't listen at all. And then she ran away.'

Vik remembered. He'd helped Jonas search for her. Eida had been beside herself, wasting away with worry, unable to find her daughter in her dreams.

'She was only seventeen.'

Alys froze, shocked to think that she too had run away from Jonas when she was seventeen, breaking his heart all over again.

'But she came back.'

Jonas nodded. 'Three years later, she came back. Three torturous years later, she turned up at the cottage. Just one afternoon. It was summer, late summer, and the heat was intense, I remember. Eida and I had been swimming in the stream with the dogs, all of us soaking in there for hours.' The dogs knew someone was there before we did. I remember them bounding out of the stream, charging for the house, so however successfully Mirella had hidden herself from her mother, she couldn't fool them.'

Vik glanced around, hearing a noise, but it was only a forest cat, slipping through the thorny bushes, twitching vole in its mouth. 'But she didn't stay long, did she?' It was so long ago now, and Vik was struggling to piece his memories together.

'No, just long enough to leave us her baby. Just long enough to give us Alys.'

Alys' mouth dropped open, wanting to hear everything, and then a noise, and a hand, and she was back in her chamber, Hakon Vettel standing over her.

***

Aldo had left Eddeth's cottage with his instructions, promising to return when the fort was under attack so they could get to work. Eddeth shivered with excitement, ignoring her fears, hoping she could find a way to get Alys out of her chamber before anything happened to her.

She laid everything out on the table, running a squinting eye over what she'd prepared, wringing her hands, stomach rumbling, regretting that she'd shared so much of her soup with that slouching boy.

Flying powder.

The bowl of potion.

A cup of licorice tea.

Her knife.

Eddeth picked it up, turning the blade, watching the flames catch the edge, pleased with how sharp it looked. And taking a deep breath, she slipped it into its scabbard.

***

Could it all be that simple, Reinar wondered, eyes on the cliffs?

They were slick and steep, not safe to climb in the dark, though to get to Slussfall's main gates in time they had little choice.

He turned back to Elin and Stina. 'You'll be safe with Nels.'

Elin was annoyed at being left behind. 'I was always better at climbing trees than you, Reinar Vilander,' she grumbled, but she stayed where she was as Holgar headed past them with a spluttering torch in one hand, hoping the wind wouldn't rob them of their only source of light.

Bjarni slipped over as he approached, falling onto his knees.

'You alright?' Reinar laughed, holding out a hand.

And jumping back to his feet as though nothing had happened, Bjarni nodded, ignoring a sharp pain in his right knee. 'Fine. Just fine.'

Berger followed after him with Ilene, who was hanging her shield over her back. 'Will they be waiting for us?'

'In the tunnel?' Reinar shrugged, wanting to take a moment alone with Elin. 'Hopefully not.' He tried to smile, feeling tense and impatient. He didn't like to put anyone in danger, though Alys had seen that this was the place to come.

He hoped she was right.

'You'll be careful, won't you?' Elin pleaded as Reinar took her in his arms. 'I don't want anything to happen to you.'

'I will, I promise. I'll send for you as soon as it's safe.' He didn't know what he was saying or thinking, he just felt the urge to leave, hearing the grunts and groans as his men started to climb. But feeling Elin's hand on his chest, he bent his head and kissed her. 'I love you, Elin. I always have, always will. I'll come back to you, I promise.' And kissing her again, he closed his eyes, seeing Alys' face.

***

Alys backed up quickly, smelling wine on Hakon's breath, sensing the tension in his body, and something else she wanted to ignore entirely. 'What is it? Has something happened?' She pulled the fur over her green dress, trying to cover herself.

'Happened?' Hakon grinned, teeth white and gleaming. 'Aren't you the dreamer, Alys? Is there something you want to tell me?' He moved quickly, crawling onto the bed towards her.

Alys shrieked, wide awake now. 'Stop! Hakon, stop! Don't do this!'

'This?' Trapping her between his powerful body and the headboard, Hakon smiled. 'You're a beautiful woman, Alys. A powerful, magical woman. Why wouldn't I want to have all of you? Claim you! Not just your dreams, but every part of you.'

'The attack!' Alys tried, twisting away from his pawing hands. 'I need to be dreaming about the Vilanders. The attack! I was in a dream, I...'

Hakon grabbed Alys, trying to pull her dress off her shoulders. It was torn at the seams, he could see, old and faded, and smiling, he tore it some more, ripping the green fabric.

Alys yelped, not needing to read his thoughts now. 'But I need to dream!' And then Hakon was yanking her down the bed, holding her flat with one hand, drunkenly pushing down his trousers with the other. 'Help!' she yelled, kicking her legs, trying to move. He was drunk but surprisingly strong. 'Help!'

Hakon slapped her, and Alys cried out, remembering Ivan's knife.

She had slipped it under the pillow.

Ignoring her terror, and resisting the urge to fight Hakon off, Alys went perfectly still, trying to conserve her breath. He was heavy, his hand pushing her down as though he wanted to push her straight through the bed.

Hakon was pleased by her submission, releasing the pressure of his hand, struggling to sort out his trousers, wishing he'd thought to take off his swordbelt. He was dizzy, thumbless hands fumbling. 'You needn't be afraid, Alys,' he slurred, fighting with his clothes.

'I'm only afraid for you, Hakon,' Alys panted. 'You won't see what's coming if you hurt me. I can't give you any warning about what's coming if you do this. The Vilanders are out there, in the harbour, I saw them!'

Ignoring her, Hakon finally pushed down his trousers, shoving a hand up Alys' dress, his other hand moving off her chest now. And freed to move, Alys slid away from him, one hand extended, slipping under the pillow, pulling out the knife. She rolled over, holding it to his face, quickly scrambling away from him. 'Get out!' she yelled. 'Go back to your wife, Hakon!' Body trembling, Alys almost fell off the bed, shouting loudly, hoping the guard would come in and help her.

Hakon smiled, excited by the challenge. 'You have a knife? To do what?'

'To stop you! To wake you up! The Vilanders are here! In your harbour!' she screamed, so loudly that her throat hurt, blinking eyes on an approaching Hakon. 'You must leave!' She saw her grandfather's face, saw him training her how to use a knife, a sword, a spear, and blinking him away, she tried to focus on Hakon's thoughts, listening as he stumbled through how he would disarm her.

'I'm glad to hear it, and I'll leave, don't worry, but first, I need something from you. For luck. With Thenor to impress, I'm going to need some luck.' And yanking up his trousers, Hakon circled her, hands out.

Alys tried to shut away her memories, which threatened to distract her.

She thought of Torvig and Stina, seeing the pain in her friend's eyes.

And she saw Reinar climbing in the dark, too far away to save her.

'My lord?' The guard knocked on the door. 'Is everything alright?'

Alys lifted her head, and Hakon lunged for her, knocking her back onto the chair. She grunted, swinging the knife up to his neck, horrified when he simply knocked it out of her hand, listening to it clatter across the floor.

Hakon was furious now, yanking Alys to her feet, off her feet, straight back to the bed, where he threw her down, rolling her onto her stomach, dragging down his trousers again.

Alys tried to move, but he had her pinned in place, hand on her back, pulling up her dress. 'Your father!' she screamed, images flashing before her terrified eyes. She saw Mirella. Beautiful Mirella.

And then Jonas, back in his cottage.

'Who is the father, Mirella? Who?'

'Jesper Vettel, but he can never know about her. Keep her safe for me. Whatever you do, Father, never tell anyone who she is. I have seen the future, and there are no Vettels in it. Keep her safe for me, I beg you. My daughter will always be in danger from those who know the truth.'

'Hakon!' Alys shrieked, trying to roll over. 'Your father is my father!'

Hakon's bleary mind was slow to react. Dropping Alys' dress, he rolled her over, lunging at her, hands on her shoulders, holding her down. 'What? What are you talking about?'

And then the door swung open, and in came Ivan, sword in hand.

'Get the fuck away from her!' Voice like stone, Ivan was quickly at the bed, poking his sword at his cousin's chest until he stepped away from Alys.

Hakon laughed, hands out. 'What are you doing, Cousin?' He was irritated, but drunk enough to find Ivan's anger amusing. 'Thought you were on the ramparts, watching for our enemy. According to Alys, they're already here.'

Ivan didn't want to talk. 'Leave,' he demanded, jaw clenching. 'Now!'

Hakon stepped back, still laughing, smile curling his lips, none in his eyes. 'Ivan, my cousin, my dearest friend, after all these years, you aren't going to let a woman come between us, are you?'

'A woman?' Ivan saw Alys sliding away from the bed, pulling down her torn dress, trembling as she backed up to the fire. 'It's nothing to do with her. You did this. *You*! We need to be focused on what's coming, not this! Get out! Go back to your wife!' As mad as he was at his cousin, Ivan didn't want to do anything either of them would regret. Hakon just needed to sober up, get some sleep and calm down. He would see more clearly in the morning.

Hakon sighed. 'Fine. Whatever you say. Whatever you want, Cousin. I understand. You couldn't have Falla, so you thought you'd have the dreamer. I understand.' He walked towards Ivan, hands by his sides now, chest aching, voices screaming inside his head like a flock of hungry birds. He heard Mother and Karolina. His crying son. And frowning, he dropped his head. 'I don't want anything to come between us, Ivan. Especially not a dreamer.'

Alys turned to the window, distracted, sensing something coming.

And when she turned back around, her eyes burst open, watching Hakon slip his hand behind his back, drawing out a long knife.

'Ivan! No!'

She remembered the voice, her mother's voice; she knew that now. 'I have seen the future, and there are no Vettels in it.'

'Ivan!'

But Ivan hadn't gotten his blade up before Hakon had jammed his knife into his cousin's belly, twisting it sharply, tearing it through his guts.

And then the first boulders smashed into the wall, signal bells quickly clanging.

CHAPTER FORTY FIVE

The sound of shattering stone made Sigurd smile. He nodded at Torfinn, who'd been given command of *Dagger's* catapult, and was working with his crew to hurry boulders into the wooden spoon in the dark.

'Won't take them long to find us now,' Bolli fretted at the tiller.

'No, but that's the straw we drew.'

'Hmmm, the short one again.'

Sigurd laughed, clapping him on the back. 'Or not. I don't mind the sound of that wall shattering. A little payback for what they did to Ottby.'

Bolli nodded, agreeing. 'Though as soon as dawn comes, they'll have eyes everywhere.' He worried about his ships, feeling vulnerable, stuck out in the harbour as they were, right under that old fort.

'Hopefully, not everywhere,' Sigurd grinned, thinking about Reinar, Ludo, and Bjarni, hoping they'd stay safe.

***

Ludo's throat was tight, fingers twitching, listening to the boulders crashing against Slussfall's walls. He wanted to launch his own catapults, but he had to preserve their firepower, for soon they'd be needed to draw the Vettels' attention away from the main gates, allowing Reinar and his men to slip inside.

If Alys and Eddeth could get them open in time.

***

Eddeth crept out of the cottage, hood over her head, Aldo beside her, carrying the bowl of potion. The night sky was heavy with clouds, the air thick with fog. She could barely see an arm's length in front of her. 'Well, well, well,' she chuckled as they walked, trying not to trip over anything. 'The gods have spoken!'

Aldo hoped the strange healer was right, jerking at the sound of something hitting the wall. Head twisting to the left, he wondered if they were safe.

'Come on! We're not going that way. We need to get to the main gates!' Eddeth's limbs trembled with excitement, but she saw Alys' face in her mind, and she felt a jolt of terror.

***

'Ivan!' Alys hurried to his side as he lay on the floor, Hakon slamming the door shut, disappearing down the corridor.

She heard the sound of the lock turning.

Ivan had one hand gripping his belly, the other reaching out, pain in his eyes. 'My... sword.'

'Ssshhh,' Alys breathed, wanting to keep him calm. She picked up the sword, moving it into his right hand.'

'I... I'm sorry,' he almost sobbed, trying to keep a tight hold on his sword, hearing Mother's premonition echoing around him, seeing her gleeful old face.

'I have to stop the bleeding.' Alys barely noticed the torn mess of her old dress as she ripped off thin strips of green cloth. 'I'll pad some of this into your wound, then I'll strap you up. Don't worry, I've done this before.' And seeing images of Sigurd, she felt a lift, knowing he was in the harbour; hoping that somehow, Eddeth would be able to get the gates open for Reinar without her.

'I...' Tears filled Ivan's eyes.

Alys leaned over him, smiling. 'I can read your thoughts, Ivan Vettel. Save your breath. I know your regrets, don't worry.' She *was* worrying, though, hands quickly slick with blood, feeling Ivan slipping away.

***

'My lord!' Lief had hurried into the hall, wide awake. He hadn't slept a wink, disturbed by dreams of his oath and his father, and his lord most of all.

'What have you seen?' Hakon demanded, all thoughts of Ivan and Alys gone, his voice authoritative and sober.

Lief was relieved to hear it. 'Nothing, my lord. It's impossible to see anything at the moment, though they're certainly in the harbour.' And right on cue, another crash shook the walls, the iron candelabras above their heads squeaking ominously.

'And Falla and the boy?' Hakon headed for the doors, wanting to get to the ramparts.

'They'll be here soon. They'll keep Karolina company.' Lief tried not to sound irritated as he ran down the steps beside Hakon, but Falla had insisted upon taking her time to dress, and he'd had to leave her with the servants, instructing them to hurry her along.

Hakon was pleased to hear it, suddenly remembering that he'd tasked Ivan with looking after his wife. He wheeled around, trying to find someone to take his place. And seeing a familiar figure emerge from the dark fog, he held up a hand. 'Erri! I want you inside, guarding my bedchamber. You'll remain there, ensuring that my wife and son stay safe until I come for you.'

Erri nodded, disappointed to be given such a tedious task, though his lord glowered at him sternly, and he was quickly heading up the steps.

Mind sharp and focused now, Hakon walked away from the hall with Lief, slipping down the street that led to the harbour gates, their journey slowed by the fog. Hakon didn't let it distract him, though, knowing that Thenor would litter his path to victory with traps, wanting him to prove how truly worthy of the throne he was. He could feel his chest thumping as he walked, the mark as hot as fire now.

'Where's Ivan?' Lief asked, hand out, already having tripped twice, the buildings seeming to lurch out of the fog, disorienting him. 'Surely he can't sleep through that?' Another crash had him thinking about Falla, wondering if the hall was the safest place for her to be.

'Ivan?' Hakon's voice was dismissive. 'No idea.'

***

Ivan gripped Alys' hand, knowing that he was going to die. Everything was darkening before his eyes. The chamber was already dark, he knew. It wasn't that. It was a darkness he could feel coming from within him.

An ending.

'What do you see?' he breathed, shivering suddenly, cold all over. 'Tell me.' Alys had draped a fur over him, slipping a pillow under his head. He couldn't feel any of it, but he did feel the cold creeping up his body, freezing every part of him. His teeth started chattering.

Leaning over, Alys smiled, trying to keep him warm. She

wished she could edge him closer to the fire, though she didn't dare move him now.

'I see the Vilanders. I see...' Alys saw her grandfather standing with Vik, and she remembered her dream. 'I see you.'

'D-d-dying?'

Running a hand over Ivan's hair, Alys closed her eyes, listening to the assault on the walls. 'You're going to live,' she lied, 'and become a famous warrior, with a wife and many sons. In a great hall. I see you sitting on a chair in a great hall.' A tear rolled down her cheek, and she brushed it away before it dripped onto Ivan.

'Sons?' Ivan didn't think Alys was telling the truth – she sounded so sad. 'And my w-w-wife?'

'Oh, she's a beautiful woman, with shining eyes, and a round, sweet face. A kind woman with a big heart.'

'And big tits?'

Alys laughed, wiping away more tears. 'I... couldn't say. Is it important?'

Ivan closed his eyes, feeling everything become so heavy. He couldn't keep them open at all. He tried to see the picture in his mind of the hall, and the chair, and the woman standing next to him.

She looked just like Alys...

Alys swallowed, glancing at the door, wanting to get some help. She needed to stitch Ivan up.

She needed Eddeth.

And then, lock squeaking, the door swung open, and Eddeth was there, basket in hand, a nervous-looking boy shuffling along behind her. 'My dreamer!' Eddeth bellowed, seeing a swollen-eyed Alys, who was clinging to a now-unconscious Ivan. 'Oh, that horrible man, what has he done?' She hurried to Alys, creaking down to the flagstones, hand on Ivan's chest.

Alys burst into tears, dropping her head. 'He's gone!'

Eddeth nodded sadly, seeing that Alys was right. 'He is, I'm afraid. Poor Ivan. Poor, poor Ivan.'

'He saved me from Hakon,' Alys cried, rubbing her eyes. 'He saved me from being raped. If only I'd...'

Aldo, still standing in the doorway, started jiggling nervously.

'You can't blame yourself, Alys. It was up to Ivan to do the right thing, to stand up to his cousin. And he did, in the end. For you.'

Another boulder smashed into the wall, and Eddeth jumped in fright. 'We need to move quickly now, before the guard returns. We can't stay here!' And struggling back to her feet, Eddeth swung around to Aldo. 'Any sign of him?'

Aldo shook his head, desperate to leave.

'Falla sweet-talked the guard, managed to send him away on an errand, but he'll be back before long. I could hear him grumbling as he went.'

Alys nodded, placing a hand on Ivan's head, hoping he would find his way to Thenor's great hall. 'We should go.' She looked up at Eddeth. 'But what about the spell to open the gates?'

Eddeth was already on her way to the door. 'No time for that now! But don't worry, I've got something else in mind. Should work just as well.' She turned back to Alys, who was staring at Ivan, tears in her eyes as she stood.

'I hope you're right, Eddeth. We need to get those gates open quickly!'

***

Karolina jumped every time a boulder crashed against the wall, Anders wailing in her arms.

Falla arrived with a crying Borg, leaving him to be soothed by his frazzled nursemaid, who looked ready to escape the chamber, eyes rarely leaving the door. Falla didn't blame her, but they were safer in here. Surely?

'I'm worried,' Karolina muttered. 'Hakon was so strange. So drunk.' She'd been relieved when he hadn't followed her to their bedchamber; pleased that he hadn't come to bed at all. 'How will he protect us? Keep us safe? I worry for his mind, now, when he needs to be in full command of it.'

Cringing at the ear-splitting sound her son was making, Falla drew Karolina away from the door, towards the hearth, where the fire was slowly dying. The chamber was freezing, and Falla realised that she was either going to have to take Borg from Eggi or make a fire herself, neither of which appealed. 'Hakon is cursed. You know that, Karolina,' she whispered. 'And by the end of this battle, with some luck, he'll be dead.'

Karolina gripped her son tightly, hand on his dark mop of hair, hoping to soothe him, desperate for the terrifying noises to stop.

***

'My lord, shouldn't someone go and wake Ivan?' Lief was unsettled by Hakon's disinterest in his cousin's absence; still confused that Hakon had asked someone else to watch his wife and son. 'He must be able to hear the attack? He didn't appear drunk when I last saw him.'

They were on the ramparts now, men busy on either side of them, moving braziers, dragging buckets of arrows into place. There was no hint of the moon, the fog creating a thick barrier between the fort and the harbour.

Between them and their enemy.

Hakon barely acknowledged him. 'You're saying that we *need* Ivan?' And quickly moving past Lief, he called to his head archer, a man named Olag. 'Spray the harbour, Olag! They're out there somewhere, so let's try and hit them. We can't wait for morning. We can't wait for this fog to clear. Hit them now!'

Olag nodded, almost falling over as a boulder smashed into the wall just beneath him.

'They're in range! There!' Hakon bellowed, pointing in the direction he'd heard the boulder coming from. 'There! Aim there!'

And leaving Olag to take charge of his men, Hakon turned back to Lief, unable to stay still. It felt as though spiders were crawling under his tunic, and he had a vision of the maggots in his belly. He tried to focus, eyes sharpening with intent. 'They're sitting in our harbour, laughing at us! Let's kill them all!' Catching sight of the brazier Lief was standing near, he twitched, eager to set fire to their enemy, but he couldn't risk damaging those precious ships. Ake had sent him a gift, and he had no intention of burning it.

Striding past Lief, Hakon made for the northern wall, wanting to check on his men.

***

They stood on *Dagger*, shields protecting their heads, peering into the fog, listening. Waiting. Some men held two shields, helping to protect those running the catapult. Torfinn had his own, for he was merely overseeing his men, not doing the hard work of loading the catapult in the darkness. They didn't dare light a brazier or a torch, not wanting to draw attention to themselves.

Not yet, anyway.

Sigurd jiggled in the stern with Bolli, impatient to feel his sword in his hand.

The first wave of arrows from the fort mostly hit the water, arrowheads piercing the dark sea, sinking to the harbour's frozen depths. A handful thudded into *Dagger's* deck; one hit a shield. There were a few muted cheers; some reassurance in the knowledge that their enemy was up there, bothered enough to attack blind.

Sigurd listened, thoughts of Tulia never far from his mind. He missed her voice, especially now, and grinning at Bolli, he realised that he needed to find his own. 'Again!' he roared. 'We hit them again! Keep them focused on us! Again!'

***

The sound of boulders assaulting the fort carried far and wide, every new crash resounding like thunder in the distance.

Reinar walked behind Holgar, crouching over, wondering if it was thunder?

'Keep going!' he urged, voice booming off the walls of the tunnel. It was dark, but Holgar carried a tiny torch in his hand; one he'd hastily constructed once they'd made it up the small climb, into the tunnel, and they were all grateful for its light.

Bjarni was breathless beside him, not needing to crouch at all. 'Longest tunnel I've ever been in. By the time we get there, I'm going to need a nap!' He thought of Agnette, hoping she was sound asleep, Liara lying peacefully beside her. His heart pounded as he squeezed his cold hand around the hilt of his sword, gripped by the urgent desire to keep himself alive.

'Not long now,' Reinar promised, certain he could see a smudge of light in the distance. He looked over his shoulder. 'Have your weapons secure. Shields in hand. They might be waiting for us!'

Berger grinned at Ilene. 'Stay by me. I'll keep you safe.'

'You think I came all this way to watch you?' she snorted, hoping she sounded braver than she felt, just wanting it to start.

Knowing that soon, it would.

***

Alys and Eddeth hurried down the hall steps, quickly immersed in fog. Aldo followed them, trying not to spill the potion; all three of them hooded and anxious. Alys could feel the sting of her bruised face, worried what Hakon would do if he found her gone.

'We must keep you safe from that man,' Eddeth insisted,

slipping a hand through Alys' arm. 'Reinar would never forgive me if I let anything happen to you!'

And thinking about Reinar, Alys jerked to a halt. 'I can't go with you.'

'What?' Eddeth wrinkled her nose in confusion. 'What?'

'*You* have to do it, Eddeth. If the guard finds me gone and tells Hakon, he'll send men around the fort looking for me. I can't come. I need you to get the gates open.'

Eddeth looked disappointed as Aldo stopped beside them, confused. 'No, you can't, but what will you do? Go back to the chamber?'

Alys shook her head. 'No, I'll go to Hakon. Keep him busy.'

'Oh no you won't!'

'Don't worry, I can distract him.'

Silence. Dark and foggy silence.

And then Eddeth sneezed.

'I'll be safe, I promise. Now go. I have to find Hakon!' And without waiting for any further arguments, Alys turned away from them, disappearing into the fog.

Eddeth shuddered, worried, nervous, and then quickly eager to get on. 'Well, don't stand about slouching, Aldo Varnass! Let's get to the gates!'

***

Hakon's mind skipped back to Alys, seeing her lying on her belly, confusing him. He'd hit her, he remembered. And then what? What else? Everything was so clouded in his mind, and he felt an urge to see her, to hear her advice. It was dark, but surely she'd be able to see. 'Lief!' he shouted. 'Go get the dreamer! Bring her up here. Let's see what she can find!'

Lief was already bleeding from shards of stone slicing across his face, and he didn't think it made sense to expose the dreamer to so much danger. 'Why don't we go and see her in the hall, my lord? It's safer.'

Hakon dismissed his concerns with speed. 'Bring her here! *Now!*'

There was nothing more to say, and Lief nodded, heading for the guard tower. Hakon watched him go, mind humming with loud voices, listening to the hiss of arrows flying from the walls.

Waiting for dawn.

CHAPTER FORTY SIX

The sound of the assault on the fort was a welcome development in what had been a tedious few days for the cave dwellers. They could hear the booms in the distance, and no one could sleep, though sleep would have been useful for all of them, Vik thought, yawning as he prodded the fire.

Ollo crouched beside him. 'And when it's all done?' His voice was a throaty whisper, not wanting anyone else to hear.

'Oh, you'll get your silver, Ollo. Jonas won't go back on his word.'

Ollo was pleased to hear it. He thought of poor Haegel, who'd been excitedly talking about what he would do with his share.

But that wasn't what was on his mind. Not the silver.

'The Vilanders, if they win, if we help them, they won't be happy with us.' Ollo inclined his head to where the rest of his men gathered around Jonas, preparing their weapons. They would leave soon, all of them, wanting to be ready.

'Nothing I can do about that, Ollo. You're the one who shat all over your reputation.'

'And you don't believe in redemption? A second chance?'

'It's not about what I believe. You're the oathbreaker. That's between you and the gods. Between you and Ake.' Vik was silent, memories of his conversation with Jonas still lingering, unsettling him. 'Though you help us take back that fort, put it in Southern hands again, and Ake will look more kindly on you, I'm sure.'

Ollo weighed Vik's words, hearing some doubt in them. Ake's reputation was one of fairness, though he could be a ruthless bastard at times. A stubborn, ruthless bastard, who valued loyalty above all things. He frowned, standing, eyes on Jonas, who was saying goodbye to his grandson. 'Well then, we'd better put Ake in a good mood, hadn't we?' And winking at Vik, he headed to the rear of the cave to check on his men.

'Everything alright?' Jonas felt out of sorts after his talk with Vik, wondering if he should have revealed any of it. Secrets were hard to keep, sometimes harder to share. He rubbed a hand over his face, wanting to head to the stream and splash some water on it, needing to wake himself up.

Vik nodded. 'Just Ollo, wondering if Ake will kill him.'

Jonas grinned. 'Who knows?'

Vik peered at Magnus, who was unhappy about being left behind. 'No point sulking. You don't want to get yourself killed before you get a glimpse of your mother again, do you? She'd never forgive us for that.' He saw the scowl on the boy's face, and he smiled. 'You think you can rescue your sister if you're lying dead out there somewhere, arrow through your stubborn little head?'

Magnus scowled some more.

Vik didn't blame him. Nor did Jonas. But Magnus wasn't coming with them.

'You'll be safe with Leonid,' Jonas tried, hoping that was true. 'Or he'll be safe with you. You know how to protect him now, so keep that knife with you in case you need to.' Magnus' shoulders straightened, and he smiled, seeing how eager the boy was to be useful.

'I do. We'll stay alert.'

'I hope so. You'll need to listen out for what's coming. In case someone is.' Leonid was there now, and though he was nine years older than Magnus, he acted much like his ten-year-old companion, and Vik was sure he could hear Leonid's teeth chattering with nerves. 'You'll need to hide. If you've got time, Magnus, hide.' He looked up, peering at Leonid, who nodded.

Vik's attention moved to Ollo, who was back with his men,

ready to leave, legs jiggling, hearing more thundering in the distance, leaving Jonas to take another moment with Magnus.

Jonas drew his great-grandson away from the men. 'We'll get your mother out of that fort, don't worry.'

Magnus nodded, feeling worried.

'And then we'll go and find Lotta. Stay here and stay safe, Magnus. A time will come in your life when you're the one running off with a sword trying to be a hero,' Jonas smiled. 'But this isn't it. The most helpful thing you can do is stay here. It's where your mother would want you to be.'

Magnus knew Jonas was right, but he wasn't convinced that any of those men would be able to save his mother. She was *his* mother. *He* wanted to keep her safe.

And then Jonas' arms were around him, and he almost cried, not wanting him to go, but in the next breath, Jonas had stepped away, smiling at him. 'We'll be back with your mother. Soon. Stay safe until then.'

***

There was no guard outside the chamber.

The door was open.

And death permeated the air.

Lief ran into Alys' chamber, horrified to find Ivan lying on the floor, draped in a fur, sword in hand. He dropped to the flagstones, lifting the fur, checking that Ivan was dead, and then, eyes sweeping the chamber, he saw the messy bed, furs on the ground, the overturned chair.

It didn't take long to determine what had happened.

But where was the dreamer?

***

Aldo was a useful assistant. A boy who knew his way around the hall kitchen, and while Eddeth had been putting the finishing touches to her potion, he'd helped himself to a cask of wine from Hakon Vettel's stores. Eddeth's potion had a strong scent, and she'd worried that it would disturb the flavour of ale.

Wine was a safer bet.

And now they hurried towards the alley by the main gates where Aldo had hidden the cask, jugs, tray and cups; everything he would need to deliver the potion-laced wine to the guards on the ramparts and those watching the gates beneath it.

The fog was oppressive, so thick that they were both struggling to navigate their way safely, afraid of what dangers were lurking in the square.

'Come on!' Eddeth called, looking over her shoulder, wanting to hurry the boy along. 'We need to get to the gates!' And turning back around, she tripped over, falling onto her hands and knees with a crash.

'Eddeth!'

'No, wait!' she shrieked as Aldo came hurrying towards her. He stopped abruptly, potion sloshing in the wooden bowl, tips of his boots just touching the body of a drunken man who had fallen asleep in the middle of the square.

'For the love of the gods, I think my heart stopped!' And back on her feet with a click of her hips and a wobbly smile, Eddeth slipped her arm through Aldo's, not wanting to fall over again. 'Slower, I think, don't you?'

***

Ludo paced the ship, unable to stay still. He was rarely left in command. He could usually turn to his left and see Sigurd, to his right and see Reinar. If not them, there was Bjarni. One of them had always stood near him, issuing orders, pointing him in this direction or that. There was usually even Bolli or Holgar. And once there'd been Stellan. But in the darkness, rocking on an unfamiliar ship, oddly named *Victory*, everyone was looking at him.

He knew the helmsman, Falki Grimsson, one of the youngest in Ottby. He had a nervous style, quieter than most. And though it was dark, and his hands remained on the tiller, Ludo could sense Falki constantly moving too. Twitching, wanting something to happen. Ready to begin.

Men waited in the bow by the catapult, rubbing cold hands together.

Ludo's mind drifted to Stina, and he felt a familiar twinge of guilt. He hoped she would stay safe with Reinar.

'Ludo!' called a man standing near the prow. 'Dawn! It's coming!'

And heart in his mouth, Ludo could see that he was right, the first sliver of light showing in the distance now. Turning to Falki, he took a deep breath. 'Alright. Let's go.'

***

Sigurd had so far managed to avoid getting hit, though arrows were now coming at them like hail.

'One way to use them all up!' Bolli cackled from his right, shield arm working hard. 'By the time that sun's in our eyes, they'll have nothing left to shoot at us!'

Sigurd hoped he was right. He heard more thuds, a yelp of pain, someone tumbling to the deck. He could see the first breaths of the new day, and lifting his head, praying to Thenor that Ludo was where he needed to be and that Reinar was safe, he heard the crash of boulders striking Slussfall's walls from the north.

Bolli grinned, slapping Sigurd on the back. 'The boy's there. He's there!'

They felt relieved, knowing how tricky it was to navigate the rocks around the headland in the dark. Bolli had wanted to swap places with Falki Grimsson, though he knew that Falki had the sharpest eyes of any helmsman in their fleet. And despite being light on years, his ability to see like a hawk made him the best man for the job.

'Well, let's hope he can keep the Vettels busy for a while. We don't have much left.' Sigurd had been up and down the ship with his shield, talking to Torfinn, working through their strategy. They'd decided to attack the fort all at once, wanting to swamp the Vettels' defenses like a cloud, giving their enemy little time to decide where to aim their reply. But now, with dawn coming, their boulders were almost depleted, and soon they would struggle to fling much more than a wet boot Hakon Vettel's way.

***

Lief had spent too long looking for Alys, disturbed by what he'd found in her chamber, reluctant to head back to the ramparts. He hadn't known what to do. If he went back to the wall without her, Hakon would go wild, ordering the fort searched, tearing it apart to find her, distracting everyone. And after seeing what Hakon had done to Ivan, Lief didn't want him near the dreamer. So, ducking his head, stomach churning, he headed for the guard tower, hoping the new day would bring an end to the thick fog. He could barely see a step in front of himself.

And then he banged into someone, knocking them to the ground with a yelp.

A woman.

'Are you alright?' Lief called out, bending down, surprised to see it was Alys. He held out a hand, pulling her to her feet. 'Where have you been? Hakon wanted to see you. I went to your chamber and –'

Alys squeezed Lief's hand. 'Let's get up to the ramparts. Come on!'

Lief pushed his feet down into his boots, not moving. 'Hakon did that? To Ivan?'

But Alys didn't have time for talking. She needed to keep Hakon up on the ramparts, far away from Eddeth and Aldo so they could get those gates open. 'We need to get to the wall!' And tugging Lief's hand, Alys moved him along.

***

Hakon's constant screaming had turned his voice into little more than a strained rasp.

Jerrick had managed to distract his lord for a time, but now Hakon couldn't be shifted from fixating on where Lief was with his dreamer. He was enraged, stomping up and down the rampart walk, barely aware of the boulders crashing into the wall.

Jerrick wondered where Lief was himself, wishing he would hurry, though the more pressing problem of the attack commanded most of his attention. No matter the trouble they had with their angry lord, it was nothing compared to the trouble they would face if the Vilanders took Slussfall.

'Jerrick!' Hakon turned towards him, arms flailing. 'Where's Edvin? I want him on the western wall!'

'You sent him away, my lord. He's taken his men to the north.'

Hakon growled. 'And why aren't our archers firing on the harbour? Why?' The mark was a searing pain in the middle of his chest now, and he kept blinking, trying to sharpen his vision, his skin crawling again.

'We must conserve our arrows, lord. The sun is rising, it's coming. We'll have more success when we can see.'

'You can't see, Jerrick? Are you too old? Do your eyes not work?'

Jerrick didn't think that insults were the answer to their problems. He clamped his lips together, swinging around as another boulder struck the northern wall, shuddering the ramparts.

And then Lief was there, emerging from the guard tower, leading a cloaked Alys towards his lord.

Hakon glowered at them both, suspicion in his eyes, Alys' words ringing in his ears. What she'd said made no sense. No sense at all. He didn't know what games she was playing, but he didn't have time for any of it. He needed to know what she could see. And reaching her, Hakon gripped her arm. 'Where have you been?' He blinked, seeing visions of Mirella now. Mirella and her freckled nose. 'I need to know what you can see, Alys. Where are my enemies? What are they planning?'

Lief, fighting the urge to pull Alys out of Hakon's hands, instead turned away to speak to Jerrick, knowing that waging war with the Vilanders was more important now than battling his lord. The sun was beginning to rise, and though dense bands of fog were still stretched across the harbour, he knew that the contours of their enemy would soon take shape.

Alys saw flashes of Hakon as a baby, and she felt odd. This man was her brother, they shared a father, yet he'd tried to rape her, he'd killed Ivan, and he wanted to kill everyone she cared about.

If she helped him, he would burn them all to ash, including her son.

'They've separated their fleet,' she started, trying to find a way to keep everyone safe, doubting it was possible, scattered all around Slussfall as they were.

'I know that!' Hakon snapped, squeezing her arm. 'I can *hear* that!' His archers were firing arrows at Reinar Vilander's ships – those anchored in the mouth of the harbour now – and he felt happier, though the ramparts were still under attack. He dragged Alys behind a protective wall. 'What are they planning next? Tell me!'

Alys didn't want to.

Hakon peered down at her. 'Tell me about Reinar Vilander.'

'What about him?'

'Are you trying to help him?'

'No! He captured me. Killed my husband!'

'Then why won't you tell me the truth, Alys? Why won't you tell me what you really see?' Hakon growled, lowering his lips to her ear. 'You think I can't see your lies? Can't hear them? Oh, you'd be surprised what I can hear, Alys!'

Alys blinked, Hakon's fingers digging into her arm, knowing that in order to save Reinar and help Eddeth, she had to put Sigurd in danger.

'They will move into the harbour. Those ships are coming closer. Now!'

CHAPTER FORTY SEVEN

The catapults stopped firing.

The fog still covered most of their fleet in a protective blanket, and Sigurd felt grateful for it. Still, arrows pierced the fog in whistling waves, his heart stuttering regularly, the shield above his head stabbed full of arrows. His body still stung from his last three arrow wounds, and he felt a deep dread of receiving another.

Torfinn had trekked back to him, nose dripping. 'Ready, then?' He held a shield in one hand, sword in the other. Hearing the whistle of arrows in the distance, he lifted his shield high, crouching slightly. The arrows shot over their heads, disappearing into their wake.

They were moving now, Bolli silent beside them.

He had no need to bellow orders. They had spoken quietly before dawn, gone over their plans. Everyone knew what would happen.

Everyone knew what was expected of them.

Sigurd grinned. 'To kill the Vettels? Always ready for that.' And he inclined his head for the men standing behind him to follow him into the bow. They had a burning brazier now, plenty of fire arrows too. The archers would remain behind with Bolli and the oarsmen when they landed.

Walking through his men, Sigurd spoke in a low growl. 'We land fast. Bolli has to drop and go.' It was a risk, but they'd all decided to bet their fortunes on the shipless Hakon Vettel not wanting to fire their fleet.

Sigurd, gripping his sword in his cold hand, hoped they were right.

Bolli was concentrating hard behind him, not wanting to send *Dagger* crashing into a pier. The fog was thinning, but still, it was a challenge for his old eyes, and his body tightened like a trap, barely a breath slipping through his lips. 'Stay where you are!' he grumbled loudly. 'Be nice to still be afloat when we hit the pier. He wished Sigurd and his men could have swum for it, but mail was heavy, and so were weapons. Best he dropped them off.

If only he could see the pier.

***

They climbed the roughly carved stone steps that led out of the tunnel, eager for a breath of fresh air. The tunnel had been longer than any of them had imagined. Only Reinar had been in it before. Most hadn't even known it existed, though they were grateful for its protection, and for the chance to sneak up on the fort unannounced.

Reinar hoped that remained true of everyone, but as he mounted the final step, head up, shoulders heaving, he was hit on the helmet by an arrow. Stumbling backwards, he knocked into Ilene, who was climbing behind him.

'Ilene!' Berger shouted as she tumbled down the stairs.

'Reinar!' Bjarni hurried to grab his friend before he fell after Ilene.

But Reinar held his ground, ears ringing, sensing the trouble that lay ahead of them now. 'Shields up!' he bellowed, all thoughts of exhaustion gone, his body suddenly thrumming with urgency. He twisted around, peering down the stairs. 'Bjarni, go to the back! Get those archers ready. Holgar! With me!'

***

'Aarrghh!' Bolli bellowed, arrow digging into his left arm. 'Pull!' he gasped, breath momentarily sucked away by a surge of shock and pain. 'Pull, you fuckers!' And leaning on the tiller until he thought he would snap in two, Bolli could feel *Dagger* slowly starting to turn away from the pier.

Sigurd was comforted by the sound of that familiar growl, lost in the fog behind him as he stood on the pier in the centre of his rapidly forming shield wall, iron rims clanging around him. There were four long piers, and the rest of his fleet had landed their crews on the other three. Soon every pier was full of Ottby and Stornas men, shields up, gripping swords and axes, some with spears, knowing how effective they could be in a shield wall. They needed to do everything they could to draw Hakon Vettel's attention away from his brother.

***

Hakon Vettel most certainly knew about the tunnel for Reinar guessed there were at least three hundred men waiting for them, shields up, archers in behind, firing a steady stream of arrows their way.

His shield was quickly busy, working left and right, his men filtering out of the tunnel entrance behind him. 'Shield! Wall!' Reinar roared, though he didn't imagine his men had anything else in mind as the arrows whistled towards them. 'Faster! Faster!' They had to get out of the tunnel quickly so their own archers could get to work.

Bjarni was bellowing, trying to push his men forward, but there was barely any room to stand, the Slussfall shield wall crowding them close to the tunnel entrance. 'Push forward!' he grunted, frown digging in deep. 'More room!'

Reinar heard him, and realising that he had to work quickly to clear some space, he turned to Berger, who stood on his right shoulder with Ilene, whispering in his ear. And nodding, Berger whispered to Ilene, who turned to the man beside her. They gripped their shields tighter, eyes on their lord.

'Charge!' Reinar screamed, shield protecting his shoulder as he barrelled forward, knocking into the wall of enemy shields. They were never going to survive if they waited, outnumbered, pushed back towards the tunnel.

They needed chaos.

The shields before him jerked apart, and Reinar pushed harder, Berger beside him, growling like a bear. They were running at them hard, more and more Ottby men emerging from the tunnel stairs, joining the charge, and there was nothing their enemy could do. Shields fell away as Hakon Vettel's men were knocked aside, losing any semblance of order.

Slicing his blade across one man's throat, Reinar forced his way forward. He looked over his shoulder, catching a glimpse of a snarling Ilene, cut over her eye already, blood streaming down her face, Berger taking off a head beside her with his giant two-handed sword. And then Bjarni. 'Bjarni!'

Bjarni turned, ducking a blade, stabbing his sword through the axeman's groin, leaving him to fall as he straightened up. 'Out of the tunnel!' he yelled, shield high as the Slussfall archers fired on them again. 'Move! Move!'

Reinar left him to it. They'd anticipated what might happen, deciding to divide their forces. Bjarni would work to clear the tunnel, and he would focus on killing their enemy, finding a way through.

Ilene was beside him now, screeching in anger, kicking a man in the balls as he lay on the ground, bleeding from his leg. Dropping to a knee, Reinar stabbed his blade through the man's throat, spinning around to slice a tattooed warrior across the back of his legs. The man jerked forward, tipping over, unable to stand.

Back on his feet, Reinar saw one of his friends stumble, a screaming man taking off his head with one clean strike of his sword. 'Ottmar!' he roared, rage burning, angry that he was here at all, throwing away the lives of his friends as though they were rotten meat.

Fog swirled around them like a whirlpool, the wind picking up, and Reinar could smell smoke and pitch in the air. He swung around, watching as one of Berger's men was felled by a knife to the back of the head, cursing that the man had been too stubborn to wear a helmet. He stumbled, shunted, unsteady on the frosty grass. It was icy, slippery, and Reinar sensed that Hakon Vettel's warriors were starting to regroup, surging forward in energetic waves.

He thought of Sigurd, knowing that his brother was relying on him.

They all were.

If they couldn't get through to the main gates, they stood no chance of getting into the fort.

***

Hakon ordered his men out of the rarely opened harbour gates. He felt hesitant about exposing them to an assault, but the Ottby men were on the piers; more were on ships, past the headland, assaulting the northern wall. It was a risk, but one he felt confident taking.

Alys held her breath next to him, eyes peeled open as the fog dispersed. She could hear the battle of shields, and men with spears and axes, the odd splash as someone was knocked into the harbour.

Lief stood beside her, thinking. Hakon was almost jumping out of his skin with confidence now, and it worried him. Everything Hakon did was worrying him, Falla's voice ringing in his ears. He leaned down to the dreamer as Hakon strode away. 'What do you see?' he whispered. 'Victory?'

'For you?' Alys whispered back, watching Hakon, who was shouting at his archers, thumbless hands flailing with urgency. 'What would victory look like for you?'

Lief ran his eyes over the harbour where the battling shield walls were fighting for control of the piers. He wanted to be down there, but Hakon had insisted he remain on the ramparts with him. 'Defeating the Vilanders, ending them all. Taking their fleet, sailing to Stornas, killing Ake Bluefinn, claiming the throne.'

Lief said it without feeling, as though he was reciting a recipe. They could both hear it.

'There is another way,' Alys promised him. 'If you listen to me, Lief, there's another way.' She smiled at him. 'I can help you, you and Falla, if you just listen to me.'

But turning his head after Hakon, Lief strode away.

***

Aldo Varnass thought he might vomit.

Eddeth's plan had sounded easy enough – something he did daily – and yet now, standing before the men, pouring wine into cups, Aldo saw that his hand was trembling. And not just his hand but his whole arm too.

One of the men laughed out loud, belly jiggling. 'You'll never make a warrior, boy, with nerves like that!'

The other guards who stood around the gates, eagerly taking the cups of wine Aldo was pouring, joined in.

'Imagine what he'd do if we were actually under attack!'

'We are, you idiot. Or they are. We're missing out on all the fun stuck down here.'

Tucked around the corner of the alley, Eddeth could hear them all. The guards were full of bravado, for none of them were facing any danger. She felt incensed on Aldo's behalf. He was a nice boy, if a little greedy, and she felt ready to stride out of her hiding place and give those men a piece of her mind. But jerking her head upright, boots firmly in place, she tried to remind herself of her job. And peering down again, she poured a good helping of potion into the next wine jug, stirring quickly, wanting Aldo to hurry back, for he had to get up to the ramparts before the guards on the gate fell asleep.

***

Reinar could see clearly as the fog dispersed, and what he could see was that they were more outnumbered than he'd realised. Hakon's men were now outflanking them, archers keeping them pinned in place. He couldn't catch his breath, bloody sword in hand, listening to the cries of pain from his wounded men as Hakon's archers picked them off.

He thought of Elin, back on *Fury* with Stina, and Alys in the fort, and he hoped with every strained breath that she'd found a way to open the gates.

Though how they were going to get there...

Berger was shouting at him. 'Reinar! We have to move! Forward!' Though it was more of a wish than a plan now, for they were surrounded.

Bjarni had everyone out of the tunnel, all his men under furious assault. He tried to make his way to Reinar, blocked by a long-haired warrior who was almost frothing at the mouth, swords twirling. Bjarni growled at him, banging his blade onto his shield, ready to teach him a lesson, but the man hadn't even raised his sword before he was tipping forward, knife in the back of his head.

Bjarni stood there, staring at him in surprise.

'Well, come on,' Ilene grinned beside him. 'Move!'

And then she was knocked off her feet, two men falling on top of her. 'Ilene!' Sheathing his sword, Bjarni hurried to help her up, elbowed in the eye, quickly losing his own footing.

A blade caught Reinar's forearm, just above his guard, and he stumbled into the path of an axeman. Holgar was quickly beside him, shunting Reinar out of the way of the hacking blade, which swung at Holgar instead, chopping down on his arm, taking it clean off.

'Holgar!' Reinar jumped back to his feet, rushing to his helmsman, horror in his eyes. 'Holgar!' And then he was ducking a vicious blow from the red-bearded axeman, who wanted a head this time.

Holgar didn't move. He lay beside his lost arm, in shock, body throbbing, clouds swirling above his head, the clash of swords ringing in his ears.

And then a shout in the distance.

Reinar parried red-beard's axe, dropping low, blade slicing across his thigh. The man stumbled forward, and Reinar stabbed up, into his eye, hearing him scream as he fell to the ground. Head up, conscious of Holgar whimpering on the ground, Reinar peered through the last vestiges of fog, his eyes on the approaching band of warriors.

***

Sigurd had one eye on the shunting shield wall in front of him, the other on the open gates. His wet boots slipped on the boards of the pier, Torfinn working hard beside him, stabbing with his spear. More and more Slussfall men were streaming through the harbour gates, bellowing as they rushed down to the piers to reinforce the shield walls. And then suddenly, the gates creaked closed, locked shut.

Sigurd's guts twisted, listening to someone scream as they tumbled off a pier, into the water, another man crying out as he was speared through the groin.

Hoping his brother was on his way into the fort.

***

It felt good.

Vik couldn't deny it as the battle joy sung in his limbs, urging him to deliver his enemies to Thenor. Every last one of them.

They came in behind Hakon's archers, who appeared to have Reinar's men pinned down.

And they tore them apart.

They'd crept stealthily for some time. At first, in the darkness, through the forest, winding their way through tangled trees, making their own path. Then, as dawn was ushered in, through the vanishing fog. And now they ran, blades glinting in shards of dull sunshine.

There were only eleven of them, but with the element of surprise, eleven men could do some damage.

'For Ake!' Jonas shouted. 'Kill them for Ake!'

It was their old cry. Simple. To the point. But it had always stirred the blood, and Vik winked at his best friend, two swords sweeping around, choosing his first victim: an archer, who stumbled around, eyes bursting open in shock.

Reinar almost smiled at the sound of that cry, shoulders tense, arm bleeding, head pounding as Jonas and his men slammed into the back of Hakon Vettel's archers. He bent to Holgar, who lay prone, face white with shock, armless shoulder pumping blood. And glancing around, Reinar saw one of his less experienced men knocked off his feet, punched in the nose, sitting there stunned. 'Gorm!' Reinar ran to him, pulling him up, slamming the rim of his shield into the chin of Gorm's attacker, sending him flying. 'Help Holgar! Bandage him up now! Stop that blood!' And shield up to his shoulder, he took one last look at his helmsman and headed back into the fray.

The sun was rising above the gloom now, and Alys and Eddeth would be at the gates, and if they couldn't get there in time, they would lose their only chance to get inside.

They had to hurry.

***

Eddeth didn't have any fingernails left.

The men guarding the gates had fallen down, slumping to the ground in sleepy heaps, clad in mail, snoring. The men on the ramparts hadn't noticed. They were too busy enjoying the wine Aldo had brought them from the kitchen. The boy delivered breakfast to them every morning, supper every evening, and though the wine in itself was unusual, they didn't think anything of it until their limbs started tingling, their heads spinning. And then their friends were collapsing before their eyes, and though they wanted to shout and sound the alarm, they too were quickly toppling over, falling down to the rampart walk.

Aldo and Eddeth glanced around.

The square was almost deserted.

Most of the army was now congregating on the eastern wall, archers attacking the ships still launching the occasional boulder at them. Others were down at the harbour where the Vilanders' shield walls were edging forward, fighting to move closer to land.

'We have to do it now, Eddeth,' Aldo urged, peering over his shoulder.

They remained in the dark alley to the right of the guard tower, waiting.

Eddeth shook her head, hesitating. She couldn't hear anyone outside the gates, but if they opened them too early? Picking her wart, her eyes bulged open. 'Wait! I've got an idea!'

***

'We have to get to the fort!' Reinar called to Jonas and Vik, who were back to back, fighting off the last dregs of Hakon's men as they scattered now, a few of them fleeing. 'Bjarni!' Reinar spun, eyes on his friend who stood with their archers. 'Get those men down!' And turning back around, panting, he parried a blade, shunting with his shield, jamming the boss into the nose of his opponent, hearing the snap of bone. 'We have to hurry!' He watched the running men taken down, one after the other, hands thrown in the air, bodies jerking, legs giving way as they fell to the ground.

Vik nodded, bringing his two swords across a bald man's throat, cutting it open. 'We go!'

Ollo was there, panting, red-faced, needing a drink. It had been a long night, and he hadn't expended this much energy since helping the Vettels take Slussfall. Not with his sword arm at least. Sweat beaded along his upper lip, soaking his back. He longed for a mail vest, his body stinging with cuts, and turning to his men, he shouted hoarsely. 'To the fort! Hurry!'

'Finish these men!' Reinar screamed at Bjarni, sensing that no one was interested in surrendering. 'Finish them, Ilene!' And leaving them behind, Reinar fell in beside Jonas and Vik, suddenly anxious, worried about Sigurd, exposed out in the harbour, doubting that Ludo could tear much of Hakon's attention away from what was likely happening on the piers. He felt anxious about Holgar too, who he'd known since he was a boy.

His wife, who waited on *Fury* with Stina.

And Alys.

He glanced at Jonas.

'We'll save that for later,' Jonas grunted, reading his look.

And nodding, Reinar lifted his head, hoping that Alys and Eddeth wouldn't let him down.

***

Hakon's attention was becoming more difficult to command, though Lief was trying his best to command it. His lord stood beside Jerrick barking orders, before running back to him, eyes on the battle unfolding on the piers.

'Why aren't you attacking them with arrows?' Hakon yelled at Lief, spittle flying. The sky was clearing now, cloaked in dull clouds, but the fog had gone, and they could see that the battle for the harbour was evenly matched.

'We're running low,' Lief said calmly, wiping his eye. Hakon was becoming as demanding as a toddler. And not for the first time. 'We must keep some in reserve, my lord.'

'For what?' Hakon barked. 'You want them to get in here? To wait until then?'

'I don't want to hit our men,' Lief tried.

'Good, don't, hit theirs!' And growling in anger, Hakon strode away, his thoughts turning to his wife for the first time in hours. If Reinar Vilander got into the fort, he would have to hurry to her side. He wouldn't let anything happen to his family.

And then he blinked, coming to a stop, looking to his left. Confused.

'Why are there no men to the west?' he growled, spinning back to Lief. 'Why have you no men guarding the main gates?'

Alys froze, needing to distract Hakon. 'My lord!'

But Hakon was not inclined to be distracted, and he continued to glare at Lief. 'This entire fort should be protected! What is wrong with you? Get men down there now!' His attention snapped to Alys, avoiding her eyes, not wanting a reminder of what he'd done to her. Of what she had said. 'What do you see?'

'More ships!' It was all that came to mind. 'More ships are coming!'

'From where?' Hakon's eyes popped open. 'Where?'

'I... the headland! They're coming into the harbour!' It was true, Alys realised, seeing glimpses of Ludo leading his tiny fleet towards the harbour to help Sigurd.

Hakon acted quickly, jaw clenching. 'Lief, take one hundred men! Take two hundred! Get down to the piers, through the harbour gates. Jerrick! Send thirty men into the square to secure the main gates! Thirty more on the wall!' He leaned over the ramparts, wanting to see some sign that his men had the upper hand down on the piers, though they were still shunting, edging back and forth, screaming insults, neither side giving way.

Hakon growled, thinking of all the catapults and siege towers they'd left behind in Ottby. Though, he reminded himself, he would not damage those precious ships.

He would not sink them.

And swinging around again, chest burning, he strode back to Alys.

CHAPTER FORTY EIGHT

After helping Aldo open the gates, Eddeth had been tempted to flee.

She felt afraid, but she would never abandon Alys.

And besides, body twitching as she waited beside Aldo in the alley near the gates, she was sure there was more work to be done.

Aldo trembled, listening to the pounding of boots overhead, hearing shouts in the distance. Eddeth dragged him further down the alley, away from the guard tower as more armed men came charging through the square, eyes on the open gates.

'Secure those gates!'

The men who had hurried down the ramparts saw the slumped bodies of the sleeping guards, some snoring loudly. And hearing a rumbling noise in the distance, they caught a glimpse of the band of warriors running for the fort.

'Ottby men are coming! Hurry! Get the gates shut!'

The men in the square abandoned shields, sheathing weapons, quickly pushing the creaking gates shut, suddenly aware that there was no beam to hold them in place.

'What's going on?' one man shouted, eyes sweeping the ground, looking around. 'Where's the beam?'

No one knew, and for a moment they were frozen, listening to the signal bell clanging above their heads.

'Just hold them shut!' came the panicked cries above. 'Form up behind them! Shield wall!'

'Archers!'

They didn't have archers. They were all down on the eastern wall.

It was too late for archers.

Reinar led his men, Jonas and Vik's too, running at the head of a wedge, shield up, sword in hand. The gates were closed, but he could hear the men on the wall. He heard shouts from behind the gates.

Panic.

And that panic told him to run harder.

***

It was hard to read minds when you weren't a dreamer, though knowing each other as well as they did, Sigurd hoped that Ludo could guess what he was thinking.

And what he was thinking was that he needed help.

He stabbed with his sword, knowing that it wasn't the most effective weapon in a shield wall – those tight spaces made it hard to move your arms – but his long knife had slipped out of his hand, lost underfoot. The old boards of the pier were slick with blood now, bodies lying at their feet, some still moving, getting in their way. And through gaps between their shields, they could see more men coming through the harbour gates.

He wondered where Reinar was.

Whether Alys had been able to help them.

Yelping as a blade scraped his leg, Sigurd jerked back. Torfinn popped up, slamming his axe down on the man's head. Torfinn's bearded axe was proving useful, hooking shields, dragging them down, but Hakon Vettel's men were doing damage to their walls. He could hear screams as the shield wall on the neighbouring pier started collapsing, men splashing into the harbour.

Blinking, trying to see through another splattering of blood,

Sigurd wondered if anyone was coming? Ludo? Reinar? Alys? Bolli?

He needed help.

They couldn't hold the harbour for long.

***

Reinar slammed into the main gates, shield first, hitting them in the centre, left shoulder jarring, wishing he'd thought to use his right. Pain exploded, memories of Ottby flashing before his eyes. The gates popped open, the force of his body dragging them apart, knocking those few men who were hurrying to form a shield wall down to the ground. 'Hold them here!' Reinar screamed at Jonas, quickly pulling his men away, knowing they didn't have long to get down to the harbour gates.

And then he saw scores of armed men charging through the square towards them.

Eddeth had dragged Aldo further down the alley at the sound of Reinar's voice, resisting the urge to announce their presence. 'We have to help them.' She nibbled her fingers, trying to see a path in her mind. 'We must help them!'

'How?'

'How about a little fire?' And catching a glimpse of a sword-twirling Vik Lofgren, fighting beside Jonas, she disappeared.

Jonas could sense that Alys was close, and it spurred him on. The sneering young warrior in front of him spurred him on too.

'Back again?' the young man grinned, feeling confident about his chances against this old has-been.

Then a blade pushed through his throat, pointing at Jonas, who leaned out, looking around the horrified man to find Ollo drawing out his bloody sword. And turning as the man collapsed to the ground, Jonas ducked a flying spear, which struck the gate behind him, quickly followed by another, clattering into the dust.

'Keep low!'

'Ollo Narp, you cheating bastard!' came the cry, though few were truly surprised to see that Ollo had turned on another lord. That slippery worm was always bound to follow the silver road, wherever it led.

Ollo didn't care what anyone thought. He cared about saving his arse, which was in danger of being strung up by Hakon Vettel if they didn't get to the harbour gates. More men were flooding out of the guard towers now, down the steps, into the square.

They were quickly surrounded.

Reinar heard Berger shouting Ilene's name, though he couldn't see either of them. He grunted, shield out, slamming its iron rim into a one-eyed man's cheekbone, knocking him sideways.

He had to get to Sigurd.

Eyes up on the ramparts in the distance, he thought he saw a glimpse of golden hair, and distracted for a moment, he was too slow to react, catching a blade on the cheek. 'Aarrghh!' Pulling away with a roar, Reinar saw Vik cut across his path, taking two blades to the man's face, not letting up until he was down on the ground, skin in bloody ribbons, throat slit.

'We have to get to the harbour!' Reinar panted, trying to see a way through.

And then he blinked, certain he could smell smoke.

***

'Fire at those men!' Lief bellowed as Ludo and his crews jumped down onto the piers, ready to support Sigurd.

Alys stood by Jerrick, whose head was swivelling as he tried to keep up with Hakon's orders. Hakon was stomping up and down behind them, and she feared what he would do next. He was talking loudly to himself, as though he was in the midst of an argument, seething with rage. She needed to keep his attention on the harbour, though Hakon kept staring back at the western wall, wanting to know what was happening.

'Is my wife safe?' he shouted suddenly, pulling Alys to him. 'What's happening? Is she safe?'

Alys looked surprised. 'I... don't know. Why wouldn't she be?'

'But your dreams?'

'She's safe while the fort is secure. You must only worry if there's a breach.'

The signal bell in the distance was a concern, though it had gone silent now, and Hakon knew that any trouble outside the gates would take time to become a problem. Still, the memory of Alys' vision stayed with him. 'Olag, you're in command of the wall! Jerrick! Get down to the harbour. Help Lief!' And yanking Alys after him, Hakon headed for the guard tower.

***

The smoke smelled like Eddeth, and Reinar almost smiled, certain that she was out there somewhere, trying to help them.

They had been in the fort many times over the years, helping Sirrus Ahlmann beat back attacks from the Vettels, and Reinar knew many of its secrets. So leaving Jonas and Vik and their men in the smoke, fighting off the onslaught of Slussfall warriors, Reinar motioned for Bjarni and Berger to bring their men, and, finger to his lips, he slipped away into the smoke.

Jonas sensed them go, knowing that soon they would be spotted, so he made a lot of noise, drawing attention to himself. 'You want to fight for Hakon Vettel?' he growled at the men surrounding him. 'A weak boy, cursed by the gods? Doomed to die by Thenor's hand?' He coughed, smoke clogging his dry throat. 'Are you mad? Mad enough to hold your oath when even the gods have broken with your lord? Thenor wants him dead, The Hunter has marked him, and you still want to hang on?'

Vik fought beside him as Jonas bellowed, trying to sow doubt in their enemies' minds. It never hurt to unsettle an enemy, though there wasn't even a hint that anyone was listening to him.

'What's going on?' came the furious roar in the distance. 'Kill them!'

Hakon was outraged that anyone had gotten inside the fort. He couldn't see more than shapes through the thick smoke, but he could certainly see that the gates were open, and drawing his sword, he pushed the dreamer behind him. 'Alys, go! Go to the hall! You must protect my wife! My son!' It was an odd thing to say, he realised, though Alys nodded, knowing that he was right. 'Drag open those gates!' Hakon screamed, lunging into the smoke. 'Wider! Get the breeze flowing!'

Jonas twisted around, hearing his granddaughter's name. Heart gripped in a cold hand of fear, he wanted to charge through the smoke and find her, but he heard Vik growling beside him, and he kept his stinging eyes on the task at hand.

'Let's go, before the smoke does.' And slipping away from Jonas, keeping his head low, Vik headed for the alley after Reinar, hearing Jonas turn after him.

***

Ludo's men pushed up to reinforce Sigurd's shield wall, and Ludo could hear the relief in his friend's voice.

'You took your time.'

'Thought you might like a chance to do something heroic. Give you something to talk about at the celebration feast!'

Sigurd grinned, then frowned, eyeing Torfinn, who had dropped to his knees. 'What is it? Torfinn?'

'Nothing!' Torfinn insisted, swaying as one of Ludo's men took his place. 'Nothing.' And he tipped sideways, legs cut to ribbons.

'Torfinn!' Ludo shouted as one of his men dropped down

to check Torfinn's wounds. An arrow thumping into his shield quickly drew Ludo away from his injured friend, straight back to where Lief Gundersen was commanding a new influx of Slussfall men.

Sigurd saw him. 'Bolli!' And turning to where their fleet waited in the harbour, he lifted up his sword, waving it like a banner. 'Now!'

Bolli, half deaf and grumbling away to himself, bellowed at his oarsmen. 'You hold water! Hold steady now! Archers! Let's help those boys out!' The wind was strengthening, though there was no fog in the harbour anymore and they could see exactly where they needed to aim. 'Steady now! Steady!' Bolli warned, head swinging left and right, turning his eyes up to the fort with a squint, hoping upon hope that the Vettels weren't going to try and sink their ships.

Lief could no longer hear Hakon shouting from the ramparts above him, though it gave him no confidence to think that Jerrick was in charge, knowing how easily Hakon could bully him. Still, at least he couldn't hear Hakon causing more problems, confusing everyone. Quickly dragging his attention back to his shield, Lief felt the man on his right stumble, though a shove with his shoulder had him upright again, stabbing through the gap between their shields.

He could see glimpses of Sigurd Vilander's smug face opposite him now, urging his men on, barracking insults, and he heard Falla's voice in his head demanding that he abandon Hakon. Alys' voice too.

But they didn't understand. They would never understand.

Surrender to the Vilanders?

Lief didn't think so.

***

Falla jumped off the bed as the door swung open, eyes on Alys, who rushed into the chamber. 'What's happened?'

Karolina had only just managed to get Anders to sleep, but he was quickly awake, crying again. 'Are they in the fort?'

Both women had heard the sounds of battle coming closer, growing increasingly worried.

'Yes, but it's alright, they're here to help us.'

Karolina wasn't convinced. 'But what if they hurt us?' She glanced at Falla, who'd sent Borg to sit near the fire with his nursemaid, who was trying to tempt the little boy with an apple.

Falla felt impatient, wanting to know if Lief was alright. 'They want to kill our husbands, Karolina, not us.'

'But Alys' dream!'

Falla ignored her, irritated by the crying baby, who had the lungs of a bellowing dragon. 'Don't you want to get away from Hakon? Don't you want your freedom?'

Karolina very much wanted her freedom, and she nodded.

'Then go and sit on the bed with your son, see if you can get him back to sleep. We must stay here and wait.' Falla eyed Alys, who knew she was right.

For soon, Reinar would come to kill Karolina's son.

***

Reinar heard a shout behind him, and ignoring it, he tried to keep his attention on what was before him, which would hopefully soon be the harbour gates.

Someone tripped behind him. He heard a yelp and a thump, thinking it was Bjarni, though he couldn't look around. He needed to get to those gates to let his brother and their men in.

Vik had almost caught up to him now, Jonas on his left shoulder. They knew how to get through the back alleys with their eyes closed, and with the amount of smoke swilling around them, they may as well have been running with their eyes closed.

Vik stumbled, jumping over a cat that had chosen the wrong moment to bound across the alley. Jonas nearly went over after him, but they both managed to hold their balance, charging after Reinar, who had reached the steps leading down to the harbour gates.

***

The archers on both sides enjoyed some success for a time, but as Bolli and his fellow helmsmen continued to pummel the Slussfallers from their ships, the men on the wall fell silent.

And though he couldn't turn around, that silence carved a hole of fear into Lief's heart. Their men had run out of arrows. He wasn't surprised, knowing how many they'd expended in Ottby. Likely the Vilanders had simply collected them all, doubling their own stores in the process.

And then Sigurd Vilander's shield wall started advancing, moving forward, one step at a time. The boards were slippery, but they were united, shields locked in place as they shunted forward.

'More men!' Lief cried, crouching behind his shield. 'Send more men!' Turning back, he wasn't fast enough to dodge a blade aimed at his lower leg, and it skewered him like a pig, blade digging in deep, scraping bone, before its owner yanked it out, preparing to stab him again. Lief quickly pulled out of the wall, shield at his chest, teeth gritted, unable to rest his weight on his right leg as his men closed up the gap. He heard splashes as some fell into the harbour, the cold water attacking their limbs, their heavy mail quickly pulling them under. 'More men!' he gasped, voice straining, hobbling now. 'Jerrick!'

And then another hiss of arrows and Lief threw up his shield, slipping on his own blood, falling to the ground with a crash.

***

Hakon quickly saw that they were mostly fighting smoke and each other, and puzzled by that as the smoke started to clear, he realised that his enemy must have headed for the harbour gates. So roaring and coughing, he ordered his men back through the square, needing to get ahead of them.

***

'Forward!' Ludo bellowed behind Sigurd. 'Move forward!'

The boards grew as slippery as ice, blood slick beneath their boots now, and they stepped with care, shields resting against turned shoulders and arms, aching bodies hunched over, bloody blades at their sides.

Edging closer.

Sigurd's eyes were on the gates, wanting to see his brother, worried why he hadn't. There wasn't even a hint that those gates were under attack yet. He saw Lief Gundersen, though, hobbling around, barely able to stand.

And eyes bursting open, he heard swords clashing, men shouting behind the gates now. 'Push! Knock them back!' he screamed, voice breaking. 'We move now!'

***

The passage before the harbour gates was narrow, for though the gates offered another exit, the lord who'd built the fortress hadn't wanted to make it easy for his enemies to get into the fort in a hurry.

The gates were blocked, guarded by Vettel men in red tunics, led by an older man Reinar recognised; a nothing sort of man, he thought, not on his list to kill, but in order to get through him and open up the gates for Sigurd, that man was going to have to die. So leaving his men to fan out around him, taking their blades to Hakon's guards, Reinar firmed up his sword grip, lunging forward, aiming for Jerrick's head.

Jerrick was on the back foot immediately, confidence low, doubting he stood any chance of defeating the bear-like Lord of Ottby. He parried the first blow, the power behind Reinar's strike jarring his arm. Teeth gritted, Jerrick brought his sword up quickly, deflecting Reinar's blade, aimed at his throat. And then he was moving his feet, trying to make room for himself in the narrow passage, ducking and weaving, working his sword with skill, trying to get through Reinar's guard.

Vik dragged his sword out of a big-bellied man, who fell backwards howling. He spun, pleased to see that Reinar appeared to have the better of his opponent, but in the next moment, he was cursing the gods as Hakon Vettel charged towards them from the opposite direction, leading an army of men into the crush before the gates.

'Jerrick!' Hakon could see him fighting Reinar Vilander. 'Stand down!' He wanted Jerrick out of the way, leaving Reinar for him. Chest on fire, the mark pulsing like a heartbeat now, he knew that this was Thenor's plan all along. He could almost hear that masterful god's voice in his ears, promising him the throne he'd been born to.

The Vettels of Alekka. Kings for all eternity.

And pale-blue eyes glinting like a sea under the sun, Hakon joined the fray, pushing his way towards Reinar.

CHAPTER FORTY NINE

Eddeth led Aldo through the lingering smoke.

As much as he wanted to charge after Hakon Vettel and stick his knife through that evil lord's heart, his first brush with screaming, dying, angry warriors trying to stab and slice each other to death was enough to convince him that following Eddeth was the right thing to do.

'Plenty of time for you!' she promised. 'Better you live now, or you'll never get your chance!' And they hurried up the hall steps, stopped by a giant man with a square-shaped face, who appeared as if carved out of stone.

'Where do you think you're going?' he boomed, recognising Eddeth and Aldo, but still, he'd been instructed not to let anyone into the hall.

'To tend to the Lady Karolina, of course!' Eddeth looked insulted, hair trembling in anger. 'I have herbs!' she said, patting the purse hanging from her belt which had barely more than a few stones and scraps of cloth inside it now. 'The lord sent me himself. Worried, he is. She is under great strain. Her and the boy both. I've been sent by the lord! The lord sent me!'

Eddeth was almost barking like a dog, and the guard, conscious of the rising sounds of battle in the distance, wanted her gone quickly. 'Get going, then! Get inside!' And leaping up the steps, he hammered on the door. 'Open the doors. Quick!'

Eddeth beamed at the guard, slipping her arm through Aldo's

as they raced inside, quickly trying to get her bearings. 'You know the lady's chamber? Have you been there before?'

Aldo nodded.

'Wonderful! Then we shall go, oh yes, indeed, for I sense that we are needed!' She looked around in surprise at Aldo, who had stopped, turning back to watch the doors close, locking them in, and she sneezed. 'Don't just stand there, my boy! Let's get to that chamber quickly. I hope they have a fire going!'

***

Reinar had both Hakon and Jerrick on him now, though he could tell that Hakon wanted his man gone. He was pleased, knowing that if he could draw everyone's attention away from the gates, Jonas and Vik could work on getting them open.

Jerrick, shunted out of the way by his angry lord, looked almost relieved, though he quickly came face to face with Berger Eivin.

Berger winked at him, motioning with his hand for Jerrick to come closer. 'I'm going to kill you!' he grinned, lifting up his sword until it was completely vertical, then grinning some more, Berger brought it crashing down towards Jerrick's skull. Jerrick skidded to the right, heart thundering now, unsettled by the laughing man, who came for him again, swinging wildly.

Reinar eyed Hakon, sensing that Vik was trying to carve a path towards the gates. 'You know Thenor sent me!' he smiled, ducking Hakon's sword, watching irritation spark in his mad eyes. 'He had The Hunter mark you, then he sent for me. He came to me in a dream, told me what to do. I'm to finish you off! Me and my army! Send you to Vasa's Cave, where you'll rot for all eternity!'

Hakon staggered to a stop, mouth open, sword in mid-air.

Reinar's voice had been a bellowing cry, and Hakon wasn't the only one who looked shocked.

Hakon's breath rushed from his mouth, his burning chest

painful now.

'You're surprised? What? You thought you could escape Thenor's judgement? That the gods still favoured you? For what? Your birth? Your grandfather? Your father? But what have you ever done, Hakon Vettel? What reputation do *you* have?'

Hakon was ice cold, shaking now.

From fear?

He didn't know.

Alys said that Thenor was giving him a test, a chance to prove himself to all the gods, and now he'd delivered his enemy to his door. It didn't matter what Reinar Vilander said, the voices in his head insisted. This was his chance to show everyone what he was capable of. 'You think Thenor wants you to kill me? A Vettel? But we are born of his blood. We are his line!'

'So you say,' Reinar growled, circling Hakon. 'Then why did he send me to end you? You and your cousin both!'

Vik had sliced his way through four men and now stood near the gates, eyeing the wooden beam that remained firmly in place. Ollo had worked industriously to get to his side. 'Help me get it off!' Vik rasped. He glanced at Ilene, her face red with blood, a wild look in her eyes. 'Cover him!'

Ollo nodded, knowing that he stood on the precipice of death if the Vettels and their men were to thwart them now. Jonas and Vik would put in a good word for him with Ake, but Hakon would be unforgiving, taking off his head, no questions asked. So sheathing his sword, he lifted his hands under the beam. 'Eadric!' he shouted to one of his men. 'Help us!'

Jerrick, still battling Berger, could hear him. 'No! Stop them!' Hakon didn't appear aware of anything but Reinar Vilander, and the noise reverberating around them was so intense that Jerrick shouted again. 'Stop!'

No one responded.

'Aarrghh!'

Berger jammed his blade into Jerrick's thigh, and he tipped sideways, unable to hold his balance, falling to the ground. Berger was over him quickly, shunting his blade through Jerrick's throat, pulling it out with a flourish, looking for his next victim.

'Move back!' Bjarni was bellowing, sensing that Ollo and Vik couldn't get the gates open. 'Move back!' He elbowed a bushy-bearded man in the nose, knocking him over, surging forward, sword swinging.

Jonas followed him, Berger too, both of them shunting men away from the gates, slipping on blood, ducking and sliding. And then the gates were freed, creaking open, beam dropping to the ground with a thud. Jonas was immediately pushed against Berger, losing his footing as a rush of warriors stormed inside.

Everyone was thrust together, some tumbling to the ground, crushed by bodies, kicked by bloody boots. Others couldn't move as they tried to free their arms, wanting to defend themselves. Jonas was trapped beneath a cheese-breathed warrior who spat in his face, trying to bring up his knife. Slamming his head forward, Jonas headbutted him, knocking the man away, needing to breathe. He groaned, pulling his legs out from under the dead body of one of Ollo's men, shuddering, seeing the man's guts exposed, his eyes fixed open. And dragging himself to his feet, Jonas saw Vik in the distance, Ollo beside him, fighting to hold the gates.

***

Sigurd's men were off the piers, pushing uphill now, scattering the Slussfall warriors into smaller and smaller groups. They clung together as Ludo led his men to join those on the right flank, leaving Sigurd to forge a path on the left.

The gates were open, blocked by those Slussfall warriors trying to get back inside the fort. Lief was limping, light-headed, losing blood. He needed to stop and wrap something around his leg. His ears were buzzing, which he knew was a warning of trouble to come. And then Sigurd Vilander was in his face, men surging past him, towards the open gates.

Sigurd grinned. 'I could blow you over, Lief Gundersen! By the look of your face and that leg, wouldn't take much!'

Lief growled, straightening up. 'You don't know what you're talking about.' His voice hissed through gritted teeth. He felt no pain, but he was losing so much blood that he was struggling to see. Lifting his left hand onto his sword grip, he tried to still his shaking arm, but everything was shaking now.

He thought of his wife. Borg. Their unborn child.

Weight shifting onto his left leg, Lief lunged low to parry Sigurd's strike. Sigurd stepped to one side, banging his shield into Lief's head, sending him flying. He wanted to get inside, to find Reinar and Alys.

He just had to end Lief Gundersen first.

And dropping down to the fallen man, who lay on his belly, knocked unconscious by the blow, Sigurd prepared to stab him in the back. It wasn't the noble thing to do, but some men had to die in order to save those who deserved to live. It was always the way, Sigurd thought with a sigh, lifting his sword up high.

***

Hakon and Reinar were back on their feet, some distance apart now, trying to make room as they sought to kill each other, but there were too many bodies lying around them, too many men clamouring for space.

No one could lift an arm.

'Thenor sent Reinar Vilander to kill your lord!' Jonas boomed, wanting to find Alys. His head was up, searching for a way out of the crush. There was no point to any of it if he couldn't save Alys. They had to get out of Slussfall quickly, find a ship and head north. 'Your lord is cursed! Marked by The Hunter! Stand back! Stand back and let Reinar Vilander deliver his fate!'

It made sense, Vik realised, seeing what Jonas was doing. He could barely swing a sword now, unable to do much more than headbutt and jostle. He didn't even have room to bring up his arms to sheath his swords and draw out a knife. 'Thenor is here!' he roared. 'He's watching! And so must we!'

Sigurd pushed into the fort, listening to the familiar rasping voice of Vik Lofgren; pleased to see him. Jonas too. He saw Ollo Narp, and frowned in surprise; a few other familiar faces pressed into the narrow space too.

Bjarni, Berger, Ilene.

And his brother, who everyone was quickly backing away from, leaving him to face Hakon Vettel.

Ludo stumbled in beside Sigurd, righting himself quickly, bleeding from the nose. He blinked. 'What?' And then his eyes snapped to where Reinar was rolling his shoulders, gripping his father's famous sword, *Corpse Splitter*. Ludo held his breath, hand on Sigurd's shoulder. 'No arrows sticking out of you yet. Tulia would be proud.'

Sigurd smiled, his attention on his brother, willing him to finish things. 'Reinar!' he shouted. 'Kill the prick!'

The crowd parted, moving in waves, Hakon's men gathering on one side of the passage, Reinar's men on the other. Jonas moved closer to Vik, sucking in a deep breath.

'You need a bench, old man?' Vik winked at him. 'A cup of milk?'

Jonas growled, lifting his head higher, wanting to find Alys, but first, they needed an end to things. After all these years, they needed an end to the Vettels.

***

The door was flung open by a panting Eddeth, who glanced around the chamber with mad eyes. 'Aldo, why don't you get that fire going. It's barely enough for a toddler to warm his toes by!' She hurried to Alys, who grabbed her hands.

'Did you see Reinar?'

Eddeth nodded, shivering all over, smoke in her throat. Slipping her hands out of Alys', she bent over coughing. And when she straightened up, she smiled. 'I did. For a time. Then he was lost in the smoke!' She rubbed her hands together, looking around. 'Is there anything to eat?'

'What about Lief?' Falla wondered, worry in her eyes. 'Did you see him?'

Eddeth shook her head. 'I've no idea what's going on out there. All I know is that we need to stay here. Whatever judgement the gods wish to bring down upon those men, best we stay out of it!'

***

Hakon circled Reinar Vilander like a wolf.

He thought of Mother, and his grin was predatory.

Confidence surged through his body now, the voices urging him on. There were so many: a woman, a man; old, young; he heard them all. He felt no pain in his belly anymore. His mark warmed him from the inside, and he felt convinced that he was stronger than he'd ever been in his life.

Powerful. Invincible. Worthy.

'I will kill you, Hakon,' Reinar warned. 'And then I'll hunt down your cousin, if he's not dead already, and I'll kill him too. And then...'

'What? You'll kill my son? A baby? You think I believe that? You think anyone here believes that you'll kill a baby?'

Reinar's face remained impassive. He barely blinked. It was as though his father was with him on one side, Ake on the other. They had tried and failed to end the Vettels themselves, and now that responsibility rested on his aching shoulders. He dropped them, lifting his head, shifting his legs, wanting to do both men justice.

And Hakon came for him, knowing that this was his chance.

They were all watching now, barely a noise in the passage. Just the odd moan and wail, the stink of death in the air, warning both men of what waited for them if they made a mistake.

And Thenor.

Thenor and his judgement about the lord who would one day rule Alekka.

Reinar blinked, not wanting to think about that. He parried Hakon's blade, knocking it to the side, shoulder throbbing. Hakon came at him again, eyes blazing, slashing aggressively, turning Reinar around. And seeing a glimpse of his brother looking on, Reinar was reminded of Tulia, and he kicked out at Hakon, slamming his boot into his knee. Tulia had always had the ability to kick high – she could take a man in the jaw – but Reinar had never managed it.

Hakon staggered, unbalanced, arm out to steady himself, keeping to his feet. His men roared, cheered by that, and Hakon whipped his sword towards Reinar's face as he skipped to the side, eyes full of intent.

Reinar swayed out of his reach, letting him skip.

He let Hakon grin and grunt and growl, and then he went for him again, shield leading now. His father had taught both him and Sigurd the value of a shield. They had railed against it as boys, only wanting to learn how to use their swords, their spears, their axes. But Stellan had shown them just how much damage they could do with a shield.

So feinting with his sword, Reinar drew Hakon towards his right side, watching his eyes following the blade. And then he swung up his shield, iron boss smashing into Hakon's jaw, breaking it.

Hakon roared, falling to the ground, rolling, struggling back to his feet, head clanging, face aching.

And Reinar let him.

He wanted to thrash the boy. His men needed to see a proper defeat.

Every man did. They needed to know that the gods had spoken.

That Thenor had made his choice. It would make whatever came next easier. More palatable.

Hakon's ears rang with laughter, though no one was laughing.

Not in the passage, but he could hear Mother, he could hear his father. And who else? Ivan? Where was Ivan?

He ignored the pain, shutting it away.

He didn't feel it. All he could feel was the mark, the heat becoming so intense now that sweat was pouring down his back. It was as though a hot poker was being jammed into his heart.

Blinking, Hakon firmed up his grip, trying to focus.

'Shall we start again?' Reinar taunted. 'Now that it's just you and me. Now that there's no old bitch sending wolves and ravens to get in the way.'

Reinar's taunting incensed Hakon, and he lunged forward, sword twisting, held like a spear, wanting to impale the Lord of Ottby. 'You don't think I have a dreamer, Reinar? But I do! I do! I have your dreamer! And she is a gift in so many ways.' His eyes were hooded now, and though he tried to smile, his broken jaw trapped his face in a ghoulish grimace, pain pounding him now.

Reinar's expression changed, body taut, anger flowing. 'What did you do to her?'

Jonas' head was up, trying to move forward, wanting an answer to that question himself. Vik grabbed his arm, keeping him back.

Hakon saw Reinar's anger flaring, sensing that he had him on the back foot now. '*Do* to her?' He laughed, jaw throbbing, struggling to speak. 'Nothing she didn't ask me to! Begged for it, she did! Over and over again!'

There was laughter, guttural and coarse.

Jonas was furious, wanting to kill the prick.

'You *touched* her?' Reinar's temper exploded. His father's voice was in his ears, warning him to calm down, but Reinar wasn't listening. He swung wildly now, throwing his shield away.

Hakon's confidence surged, and he skidded forward onto his knees, twisting his wrist, bringing his blade across Reinar's thigh.

'Reinar!' Sigurd shouted as his brother bellowed, staggering away. 'Focus!'

Ludo was beside him, struggling to keep still. He grabbed Sigurd's arm, teeth clenched.

Reinar tried to focus, but thoughts of Alys flooded his mind. He couldn't think at all. He fought his way forward, charging at Hakon now, not wanting to give him a moment. That broken-jawed bastard was going to die. And throwing his sword away too, ignoring the horrified gasps from his men, and trying not to imagine the look on his brother's face, he drew his knife. Charging with a roar, Reinar took Hakon full on the chest, barreling him over, slamming him onto the ground. Ducking Hakon's slashing blade, he stabbed him in the chest. 'You touched Alys!' he snarled through grinding teeth, spittle flying, bending to Hakon's face. 'Now you'll die!'

Hakon tried to move. Legs thrashing, he tried to move.

Thunder crashed overhead, clouds sweeping in like smoke, dark and threatening, and no one spoke. Eyes up, everyone wondered what was coming.

For surely something was.

It was suddenly so cold.

***

Alys could hear thunder, and feeling odd, she left the bedchamber, overheated by Aldo's blazing fire, wanting some air. Falla and Karolina talked constantly, Eddeth moved constantly, and the children cried constantly, and she needed to find some space to think. There was no one in the corridor now. She wondered where the guard had gone, feeling concerned. There was barely anyone in the hall at all. The slaves had hidden with the servants in the kitchen, none of them knowing who would be their master come the end of the day.

'Families,' came the voice as Alys walked, giant flagstones

cold beneath her boots, the fires having burned down to nothing in the central fire pits. 'Families love, and they hate. They come together, and they make war.'

Alys stopped. 'War?'

The man guarding the hall doors stared at her, wondering if she was talking to him.

She hurried forward, wanting to go outside, and suddenly seeing no reason to keep her locked in, the guard pulled up the beam and opened the door.

Alys stepped outside, surprised by how empty the square was. It was as though no one was there at all.

'Yes, war,' came the voice.

And Alys saw a man striding towards her.

He wore a black cloak, plain and long, sweeping the ground, much like her own. He was taller than most men, broad-shouldered, older, with white hair that fell past his shoulders, loose and wild. He wore a wide-brimmed hat that shaded his eyes, and Alys saw little of his face, though his perfectly groomed beard caught her attention: long and white, with a thick dark stripe straight down the middle.

'Families make war,' the man growled. 'And therefore, they must take sides.'

He stopped, watching her.

And Alys, frozen at the top of the hall steps, stopped, watching him.

'And I choose you, Alys, to be on my side.'

The man in the wide-brimmed hat smiled, teeth showing.

More thunder, and now rain.

Alys didn't notice. '*Your* side?'

'This land is mine, I command it, and for too many years, I sat back and watched as it was torn apart. Once I sought to keep the peace, to hold my family together, but I have come to see that as an impossible choice now. A path I am no longer able to continue down. So now is the time to choose, and I choose you. You and the Vilanders. We will go to war together, Alys de Sant.'

Alys hated that name. She didn't want it anymore.

Thenor, Father of the Gods, laughed. 'You wish to become someone else?'

'I wish to be who I was.'

'A Vettel?'

'I was never a Vettel. I never will be.'

Thenor smiled. 'Blood cannot be ignored, and you will not be able to ignore what stirs in your veins, Alys, as much as you might try. None of us can run from our ties. From who we are. Not even the gods.'

'And the Vilanders? '

'You must go back inside. Trust in me now, I ask that of you. Trust in me, for not every path leads where you hope, but eventually, with some luck, you will wind up exactly where you need to be. Go now, and protect that child, for he is your blood, and I have no wish for his to be spilled. Not today.'

Alys heard another crack of thunder, shattering the silence and she blinked, watching the square, unable to see Thenor anymore.

CHAPTER FIFTY

No one moved.

Reinar stood astride Hakon Vettel's body, bloody knife in hand, jaw clenched. 'Thenor is here!' He threw back his head, feeling the Father of the Gods all around them. 'Thenor is watching! He's sent me to take your life!'

The mark on Hakon's chest felt as though it was growing inside him now, setting him on fire. He couldn't breathe. Pain consumed him, fiery, hot pain, and he cried out, fear in his eyes. He shrank away from Reinar's blade, sobbing, and Reinar straightened up, watching him. 'No! Please!' Hakon begged, desperate to make the pain stop. It felt as though someone had their hands inside him, pulling him apart.

He felt his heart torn in two, his chest crushed, his limbs snapping.

Screaming, loud inside his head. Roaring laughter.

Hot flaming fire.

And then a voice.

'He's right, Hakon. You know he's right. I did send Reinar Vilander to kill you. And he has. You are dying, bleeding, ending. Though everything ends, eventually...'

Hakon blinked, seeing the man looming behind Reinar like a tree. He was so tall, so broad, his hat shielding his eyes, though if he were truly Thenor, Hakon knew that his eyes were pale blue. That's what his father had told him as he tucked him in at night.

Thenor, with his black-and-white beard and his pale-blue eyes. 'Just like you, my son. And one day, you will sit on the Alekkan throne in Stornas, and you will make Thenor proud.'

'Though that is not true, Hakon,' Thenor smiled, leaning closer now so Hakon saw nothing else. 'Your father was a cruel man, and I have had my fill of cruel, cowardly men who care nothing for their people. Who think that greed and self-interest is a worthwhile pursuit. I have had my fill of men like you.' And moving back, Thenor bent to Reinar's ear. 'Finish him.'

Reinar blinked, hearing that voice jolt through his body like a lightning strike, and he jammed his knife into Hakon's throat, pushing it down until he was certain the tip of the blade was scraping earth.

He stood there for a moment, seeing the image of his dead sons, knowing that Hakon's dreamer had cursed his family; seeing his father sitting in his chair, lifeless, a shell of the man he had once been. And nothing could bring them back.

Nothing could.

Nothing.

And dropping his head, watching the life leave Hakon's eyes, Reinar Vilander cried.

***

'What's happening?' Eddeth couldn't contain her impatience as Alys returned to the chamber. 'What have you seen?'

Alys felt odd. Upset. She'd seen everything.

'Hakon is dead.'

Karolina was stunned, eyes shifting to her son, who wailed in his nursemaid's arms.

'Oh!' That was more than Eddeth had been expecting.

'Reinar killed him.'

'And Lief?' Falla was beside her, panicking now.

Alys shrugged. 'I... don't know.'

That wasn't what Falla wanted to hear, and she rushed to the door, wanting to see where Lief was. 'You promised me!' she raged, turning back to Alys. 'You promised me!'

'Stop it, Falla Gundersen!' Eddeth grumbled. 'That won't help. Alys could never control all those hot-headed men out there. Fools, the lot of them!'

'Let me find Lief,' Alys said, knowing how much Falla had helped them. 'Let me sit quietly and see what I can find.'

Breath coming in panicked waves, Falla gripped her belly as Alys hurried to a chair, closing her eyes. Falla returned to a shellshocked Karolina, who wasn't sure what was going to happen to her and her son now that her husband was dead.

She blinked at the door, remembering Alys' dream.

***

'We don't want to go to war with you!' Reinar bellowed, stepping away from Hakon's dead body, eager to catch his breath. He was conscious of the tension simmering; the storm crashing down upon them, threatening a downpour. 'We don't want to kill you!'

It was true. The crowded passage reeked of death and bleeding wounds which needed tending to. Reinar thought of Holgar, lying by the tunnel, hoping he still lived. 'We need to help the wounded! We need a drink! A chance to stop and think! We don't need to be enemies! The South is Ake's kingdom! For twenty years he's ruled here as a good king! A good man! Throw down your weapons now, and he'll welcome you. Your lord is dead. Thenor took him! You saw that! The gods turned against Hakon! They wanted an end to him and his entire family!' And bending down, Reinar knew that he had to show them. Their faces were stunned, sceptical, and he needed to get through to them, so hoping that Alys had been right, Reinar took his knife to Hakon's mail shirt.

Sigurd and Ludo pushed through the crowd, helping him rip a hole in Hakon's mail and tunic, and eventually, they exposed the Lord of Slussfall's pale chest which revealed an enormous symbol, the tendrils of it spreading over his body like tree roots. Reinar gasped, almost stumbling away, surprised that he felt so surprised.

Sigurd turned to Ludo, who was too stunned to even blink.

And slowly, one by one, Hakon's men came to view the body, unnerved by the sight of that mark burned into their lord's chest, knowing that Reinar Vilander had spoken the truth; that the Father of the Gods had sent him to claim their lord.

And after that, there was no resistance.

How could there be?

But for Reinar there was no easing of tension. He felt displaced. Odd.

He needed to find Alys.

So did Jonas, and he was quickly moving through the crowd with Vik, trying to make his way back to the hall. Desperate to avoid them, Reinar slipped away, heading in the opposite direction, wanting to get to the hall before anyone could stop him.

***

Emerging from her trance, Alys blinked up at Falla. 'He's alive. Wounded. I think they've forgotten him. He's outside by the piers, on the ground.'

Falla looked ready to fall down, and she cupped her belly, thanking Valera, tears in her eyes. 'I need to see him! To help him!'

'Wait!' Alys stood, trying to bring herself back into the chamber. 'Eddeth, keep everyone in here, please.'

Eddeth jumped off the bed, weary with the drama of the day, but she nodded as Alys headed out of the chamber, closing the door behind her.

The guard had returned, Alys saw.

'You leaving?' he asked gruffly.

Alys shook her head, then nodded it. 'I suppose I am.'

It didn't take long. Her heart raced as she smoothed down her dress, brushing hair out of her eyes, feeling silly for doing both.

And then he was there.

'Alys!' Reinar ran to her, stopping just before her, hands on her arms.

He always had his hands on her arms, she thought with a sad smile, wanting to fall into his.

Reinar saw her swollen eye. 'What did he do?'

'Nothing, he did nothing. He tried, but nothing happened.' Alys felt relieved that that was true, wanting to cry. It was so good to see him.

And yet...

She tried to step back, but Reinar moved closer, not convinced. He held a hand to her face, gently touching around her eye. 'He did this to you? Hakon?'

Alys nodded.

A baby cried.

Reinar's eyes snapped to the door.

'You can't, Reinar. You can't.'

'I have to. You know I do. Ake ordered me to. I have no choice. I don't want to, but I've no choice. It's for the best.'

'The best? Killing a child? A baby?' Alys was horrified, missing her own children with a desperation she could barely contain. 'You're not that man. You'll never be that man.'

'No.' That was true enough. 'But to save a kingdom, a man must do things he can't stomach. To save a kingdom, a man must risk his soul. Ake told me I had to kill every last Vettel. I can't keep even one of them alive.'

'Then you must kill me.'

Reinar didn't understand. He heard footsteps, and he knew that he was running out of time. 'What do you mean, kill you?'

Alys didn't want to say it out loud, but it was the truth, and she couldn't run from it anymore. 'I saw... I dreamed... I discovered who I really was.'

'What do you mean?'

'I'm a Vettel, Reinar. My father was Jesper Vettel. If you want to kill every Vettel left in Alekka, you will have to kill me. My children too.'

'It's true.' Jonas' voice broke, and they both turned to him. He was staring at Alys, pain in his eyes. 'You saw it? After all these years, you saw the truth?'

Alys nodded, running into his arms, bursting into tears.

'Your grandmother tried to hide it from you,' Jonas cried, holding her close. 'I did too.' The feel of his granddaughter in his arms was a tonic for his weary body, and he felt a peace descend upon him, his aching limbs flooding with relief. 'We needed to keep you safe. If Jesper had found out, he would've tried to take you from us. Who knows what he would have done to you. For all that I could say about your mother, she never wanted that. She gave you to us when you were only six days old. Six days...' Jonas squeezed Alys, his eyes blurring now. 'Oh, my sweet girl, I've missed you!'

'I shouldn't have run away. All those years ago. I... I'm so sorry. For everything!'

Jonas held her close, feeling her shudder, and pulling back, he stared at her. 'I taught you how to kill, Alys Bergstrom. Taught you how to stay safe. To survive. You haven't forgotten, have you?'

She shook her head, eyes on Reinar. 'No.'

'Well, good.' And now Jonas' eyes were on Reinar too. 'I don't blame you for trying to follow Ake's orders. I don't blame Ake for wanting the boy dead. If he'd killed Hakon in the first place, none of us would be here now.'

Reinar looked uncomfortable, watching Alys as she slipped out of her grandfather's arms. 'Why didn't you say that you were Jonas' granddaughter?'

Alys almost laughed. 'When was I supposed to say something, Reinar? When you were dragging me away from my home? I didn't even know who you were. Not at first, and by then...'

Jonas felt awkward; in the wrong place. He thought of Magnus, wanting to get back to the cave to make sure that he was safe with

Leonid. 'I'll leave you to it,' he mumbled.

Alys stared at him, not wanting him to go, and yet...

Jonas smiled. 'Take your time.' He remembered what it felt like to be looked at the way Reinar Vilander was looking at his granddaughter, and though his feelings whipped around him in a maelstrom of confusion, he knew it was time to leave. 'I'll get Magnus, bring him to you.'

'Magnus?' Alys' face lit up, her heart lifting.

'He's nearby, in a cave. I'll get him, don't worry.' And turning away, Jonas headed out of the hall.

Leaving Reinar and Alys, and the crying baby behind the door.

'You won't kill him.'

'Won't I?'

'No. I know you. You won't.'

Reinar blinked.

'We're all Vettels, sad as it may be to say, but we aren't like Hakon or his father, or even his grandfather. And Anders' mother is a kind woman. A good woman. Give her a chance to raise the boy with love. Give her a chance.'

Reinar frowned.

'And me.'

'You?' He stepped closer, until he could smell her breath. It was sweet, like honey, and unable to stop himself, Reinar bent down, kissing Alys deeply, feeling her sink into his arms, head dropping back, kissing him with longing.

'Your wife,' Alys breathed, at last, leaning against his chest, her head under his chin.

Reinar gripped her arms, pushing away, staring down at her with pain in his eyes.

He didn't know how he felt.

And sensing it, Alys stepped out of his grasp.

'Hakon killed Ivan.'

Reinar was relieved to hear it.

'Ivan was a good man. He tried to save me from Hakon, to stop him... raping me. He protected and cared for Hakon all his life, and Hakon just killed him. Left him dying, didn't care about him at all.' Alys felt guilty, knowing that Ivan had given his life to try and protect hers. More than guilty. She felt sad.

'But he saved you?'

Alys nodded, relieved about that. 'He did.'

Reinar felt relieved too, shoulders releasing their tension at last. He stared at the door, hearing the baby's cry, softer now. 'There's a lot to do. Injuries, men to see to.' He turned away.

'I need you to find someone!' Alys said urgently, remembering Falla. 'Lief Gundersen. His wife helped us to open the gates. She helped Eddeth. I promised her things...'

Reinar lifted an eyebrow, but he nodded.

She smiled, not wanting him to go.

He started to leave anyway, but stopping, he turned back to her. 'Stina's waiting on *Fury*...' He thought of his wife and didn't say any more.

Alys shivered. 'I have to go north.'

'North? After your daughter?'

'Yes. I have to find her.'

'I have to go south.'

Alys nodded, wishing that wasn't true.

'I can send Sigurd with you?' Reinar suggested. 'Or Ludo? You need some help this time.' Now his voice deepened, determined not to let her go off on her own again.

'I'll have help, don't worry.' Alys thought of Jonas and Vik and Magnus. 'I'll have plenty of help.'

Reinar stared at her. 'Will I ever see you again?'

'You will,' Alys smiled. 'I'll have to bring Eddeth back to Ottby once we find Lotta.'

Reinar nodded, not knowing what else to say.

And reluctantly turning away from Alys, he headed down the corridor, walking away from everything Ake had tasked him to do.

Walking away from everything he wanted.

***

They picked through the bodies and pulled out the injured, carrying them into the square where market tables were used to care for those men who needed their limbs stitched up, wrapped up, or in some cases, sawn off.

Despite an overwhelming desire for ale, Reinar kept moving, wanting to ensure that everyone was taken care of, no matter whose side they'd fought on. He stopped by a table, peering down at an unconscious pale-faced man.

'Lief Gundersen,' Sigurd said behind him. 'I should've killed him.'

'Why didn't you?' Reinar turned around, eyeing his brother.

Sigurd looked puzzled. 'I heard Alys in my head, begging me to stop.'

'His wife helped her and Eddeth, apparently. She promised the woman she'd keep her husband safe.'

Sigurd was surprised, relieved that he hadn't followed through on his desperate need to stick his sword through the sullen prick's back. 'Dreamers.'

Reinar nodded, smiling wryly.

Sigurd turned to him. 'You alright?'

Shrugging, Reinar saw Vik coming towards him, Ollo Narp beside him. 'This should be interesting,' he smirked, nudging Sigurd.

'My lord!' Ollo exclaimed, hands open, eyes gleaming. 'I was delighted to help you reclaim Slussfall for Ake!'

'Is that so, Ollo?' Reinar narrowed his eyes. 'I'm sure Sirrus will be just as delighted to hear it. Sigurd, go get Sirrus' head down so Ollo can tell him how happy he is!'

Ollo frowned. 'We all make mistakes, Reinar.'

'Well, true, though most don't end up with our lord's head hanging from the gates, and his sworn enemy taking command of his fort, threatening the whole of Alekka. That's perhaps a little more than just a mistake, Ollo.'

Ollo looked embarrassed but slightly hopeful. Reinar didn't sound ready to kill him.

Yet.

Reinar bent his head, peering at him. 'You helped Jonas and Vik. Helped get Alys' boy out of the fort. I've heard what you've done. Keep on that path, and we all might view you more favourably one day, but don't expect miracles. No one will forget how you betrayed Sirrus. You'll carry that scar with you till the end. Like Hakon Vettel, you'll forever be marked by your betrayal.'

Ollo squirmed, unhappy to hear the truth delivered in such unpalatable terms. He dropped his head, though he felt a flutter of hope, for he was still alive.

'You saw that mark on Hakon's chest, so you know who stands behind me now. Betray our people again, Ollo, and I will come for you.' And threat ringing in Ollo's ears, Reinar turned away, inclining his head for Vik to walk with him. 'Is Jonas back?'

Vik shook his head. 'Not that I've seen. And Alys?' He noticed the twist of discomfort on Reinar's face.

'She's in the hall, with the women. We've taken the most seriously injured in there, by the fire. It's cold out here.'

That was true, Vik thought, thinking of his cottage for the first time in days, remembering his ruined old fishing boat, and his smokehouse. And glancing around at the gates as Jonas rode back into the fort, he thought of Lotta, knowing that it would be some time before he saw his home again.

Reinar turned back to the hall, watching as Alys stepped outside, torn green dress hanging off her, black cloak gone now. She'd been tending to the wounded, and it was too heavy, swamping her, making it hard to work carefully. She looked up, seeing the horses, unable to believe it was real.

After all this time?

And bursting into tears, Alys flew down the steps as Vik hurried to the horses, slipping his arms around Magnus' waist, helping him down to the ground. 'Magnus! Magnus!' Alys couldn't see. She was crying so much that she couldn't see a thing, and then there he was, her baby, Magnus, standing right before her, and she saw glimpses of him on the beach; that one last look as she urged him to leave, to take his sister and run.

'Mama!' Magnus couldn't breathe. He couldn't stop crying as

he fell into her arms, feeling her hands on his back, his shuddering, trembling back. And then she was pulling him close, enclosing him tightly, making him safe. 'Mama!'

He heard her sobbing, her heart beating.

And he knew that he was home.

CHAPTER FIFTY ONE

Eddeth was exhausted, back aching, but she took the saw from Aldo with a determination to get the job done. 'You've held that blade in the fire, then, Aldo Varnass? Kept it there, burning hot?' Eddeth didn't know if she had the energy or the fortitude to hack off another limb, though the gods were going to need every man for the battle ahead, even the one-armed ones.

Then blinking, Eddeth wondered how she knew that.

'The gods are a mystery!' she cried, grinning at Aldo as he crouched beside her, ready to help.

Falla frowned at Eddeth, who was making enough noise to wake the dead. She leaned over Lief, who was paler than she'd ever seen him, feeling worried. 'You need to sleep.'

'I need more ale.'

Sighing, Falla poured him another cup, feeling useless as a caregiver, already impatient with it too. 'I'll talk to that Reinar Vilander when I get a chance, don't worry. He just hasn't stopped. Hasn't stopped for a moment!'

'Talk to him about what?' Lief wondered sleepily, smiling at Borg, who sat on Falla's knee, playing with her hair, pleased when the boy smiled back.

'About you becoming the lord here,' Falla hissed, as though Lief should know what she was talking about.

He looked bemused. 'The lord? Here? Why? Why would he want that?'

'As a reward, of course! For all the help I provided. And you! You didn't kill them, did you?'

'Not as many as I'd have liked to.'

Falla slammed her hand over his mouth. 'Lief! That will hardly endear you to the Vilanders. And they'll have sway with Ake Bluefinn, won't they? They'll tell him who was heroic. Who deserved to be saved. Who deserves to be rewarded!' Looking down at her husband, who had nearly lost his leg, she worried that he hadn't been heroic enough. She hoped that wasn't true. Slussfall was an enormous fort, one she would gladly be the lady of. She didn't want to go back now, not when she'd come so far. Not when she'd suffered so much to help them both rise.

Lief gripped her hand. 'Stop,' he breathed, ready to pass out. 'Stop thinking.'

She glared at him, confused, his big hands reaching up to hold both sides of her face. 'What?'

'I love you, Falla. You're all I could think about today. Not Hakon. Not Slussfall. Not Stornas or my oath, just you. You and our family. And whether I'm a lord or a warrior or a farmer, I just want to protect you and love you and raise our children together and be happy.' He slumped back, exhausted, eyes closed.

And then he felt the most perfect lips in the world, soft and warm, kissing him tenderly, and he smiled.

Karolina turned away from them, Anders in her arms. Reinar walked towards her, and she trembled with fear. He was handsome and big, with a deep voice and a stern face.

'Do you have any family?' Reinar wondered, trying to get her to look at him, softening his voice. 'Somewhere to go? Someone to help you?'

Karolina shook her head, tears leaking from terrified eyes. 'No one. Nowhere.'

Reinar frowned. 'You're welcome to stay here, in Slussfall.' He saw Alys out of the corner of his eye, with her son, and he smiled. 'A new lord will be installed soon, though perhaps I'll talk to Ake, see what he thinks about Lief Gundersen remaining. The men here will respond to him, I think?' He was testing her out, seeing what she thought.

'They will, they will, my lord,' Karolina insisted. 'Lief has their respect.'

Reinar nodded. 'I'll talk to Ake, then, ask him to consider it. And in the meantime, you may stay here, raise your son. Raise him well, not like his father. It's important. I... it's important that he doesn't become like Hakon.'

'Yes, I will, my lord, I promise. I hated Hakon. I... had no choice!' Karolina felt relief and more tears came quickly.

Reinar watched her closely, seeing what Alys had been trying to tell him, hoping it would be enough for Ake. And then there was Alys and her son, Vettels themselves, and they were coming towards him, and there was nowhere to go.

Sigurd came up to him with two cups of ale. 'You might need something to drink, Brother,' he grinned, then frowned, confused by the look on Reinar's face. And turning around, he saw Alys with her son.

He was a tall boy, Sigurd thought, almost up to Alys' shoulder, and she was a taller than average woman. He looked worn out and dirty, a fierce look in his sea-green eyes as he considered the two big men.

And neither Vilander could blame him for that.

'Magnus, this is Sigurd and Reinar,' Alys said softly. 'My friends from Ottby.' She smiled at the men, who looked like they both wanted to run away from the ten-year-old boy.

Magnus scowled at them, feeling the warmth of his mother's hand on his shoulder. 'You stole my mother.'

That was true. They couldn't deny it.

'But you killed my father, and so you saved her too.'

Tears filled Alys' eyes, and she dropped her head, feeling embarrassed.

Magnus slipped his hand into hers, squeezing it. 'And when we find my sister, perhaps we will come to Ottby and visit you, see where you took our mother. She was happy there, I think.'

Reinar blinked, remembering Elin.

Heart torn in two.

Sigurd peered at Magnus de Sant, finding it hard not to like the scowling boy. 'You'd be welcome, Magnus. Ottby will forever be grateful to your mother. She saved us too. That might almost make us... even?'

Magnus frowned, and no one was convinced by that. He looked around, seeing a familiar face as Bjarni led Stina and Elin into the hall. 'Stina!' And running forward, he almost knocked into Ilene, who turned to glare at him, before smiling sweetly at Sigurd.

Alys lifted her eyebrows at Sigurd, who ducked his head, looking away.

'Magnus!' Stina burst into tears, relieved to see him, wrapping her arms around the boy. 'You're alright! I... I'm so relieved. But where's Lotta?'

Alys' smile faded. She shook her head, meeting Elin Vilander's eyes as she ran for Reinar, wrapping her arms around his waist. 'I don't know. Gone north in a ship. We have to leave and find her.'

'Tomorrow?' Stina wondered, letting go of Magnus and hugging Alys tightly, so happy to see her again.

Alys nodded, slipping out of her embrace, turning to face the woman who she could now feel staring at her.

Reinar didn't know where to look. 'This is my wife,' he croaked. Then clearing his throat, he tried again. 'This is Alys, the dreamer who helped us get into the fort. She helped us defeat the Vettels in Ottby too.'

Elin blinked slowly, staring at Alys as though she was an enemy she was ready to strike. She held Reinar's hand, her body pressed against his side. 'We're so very grateful to you... Alys. For all your help. I've heard so much about you, from everyone in Ottby. From Ilene. She told me so many things.'

Reinar frowned, hearing the edge in Elin's voice.

Stina frowned, seeing the venom in Elin's eyes.

Alys just blinked at Elin, tortured by the memory of kissing her husband. 'Well, I'm just happy to think it's over. That there are no more Vettels to threaten the peace of Alekka anymore.' She felt odd, knowing that she was a Vettel; that Magnus, who stood beside her, was one too.

No one knew what to say, and the silence quickly became uncomfortable.

Sigurd looked for an escape. 'I need to make sure everyone's got shelter for the night. Weather doesn't look too promising.' He nodded at Alys, smiled at Stina, and slipped away.

Reinar stared after him, feeling envious.

Inspired by Sigurd's abrupt departure, Alys sought to leave too. 'I need to find you a bed, Magnus. I'm not sure you've slept since I last saw you, or eaten. What have Jonas and Vik been feeding you?'

'Mother!' Magnus groaned, not wanting to go to bed yet, already forgetting how much he'd missed the sound of her voice. 'Just a while longer!'

'For what? To see more injured men and dead bodies? No, you need some sleep. Come on, we'll find somewhere quiet, hopefully with a fire burning.'

Magnus saw Jonas and Vik, and he disappeared with a wink.

Alys turned back to Reinar with a smile. 'We'll leave in the morning, if we can find a ship. Hopefully, we can find a ship.'

'You're sure you don't want more help? More men?' Reinar wondered.

Alys shook her head. 'I've got Jonas and Vik. That's enough.'

'And Eddeth.'

'Yes, and Eddeth. She's never been to sea, so she'd be unbearable if I left her behind,' Alys smiled as Stina turned her head, called away by Eddeth, who needed some help.

Leaving Alys alone with Reinar and Elin.

'I imagine she would,' Reinar said, cringing at the sound of Eddeth sawing off another limb.

'Well, it sounds as though there's a lot to do,' Elin murmured, eyes on Alys as she unpinned her cloak. 'I'll go and see how I can help.' And turning to Reinar, she pushed herself up onto her tiptoes, kissing him softly. 'I'm so glad you're alright.' And she was. Despite her discomfort around the dreamer and her annoyance at having been left down on *Fury* with Stina for company, Elin was happy to see Reinar again. It only reinforced how much she wanted him.

How determined she was to keep hold of him.

'I wish you a safe journey,' she said coldly, unable to smile at Alys as she stepped past her, heading for Eddeth.

Alys swallowed, not wanting to be left behind with Elin's husband.

She stared at her boots, the silence filled with all the things she couldn't say.

They stood close to a fire, and it was warm, and its glow was deep and comforting. Rain fell loudly, hammering the roof, and Alys yawned suddenly, ready to sleep for a year.

Hands by his sides, Reinar didn't move, though he knew he had to. 'I have to go. See what more there is to do.'

Alys nodded, stepping back. 'I'll see you in Ottby. Soon, I hope.' It was the worst thing to say, a pointless wish, for Reinar wasn't hers.

He would never be hers.

'I'll see you in Ottby, then, Alys de Sant.'

'Thank you for coming, Reinar,' Alys murmured. 'I knew you would.' And turning, holding her breath, she walked away, sensing Reinar's eyes following her, forcing herself not to turn around, gripping her hands tightly in front of her old green dress.

***

Eddeth yawned until her eyes watered. She couldn't remember when she'd last slept, and her body slumped against Stina's. 'I need a bed!'

They'd settled everyone down for the night, and Stina felt free to join Eddeth in yawning uncontrollably. There had been so many men milling around the square, coming in and out of the hall; those from Slussfall, Ottby, and Stornas; from Hovring and Vika too. They had tried to help as many as they could, not wanting to head off to sleep when even one man was suffering. But now, it was finally time to go. Though where to, Stina didn't know. 'Any ideas?'

Eddeth nodded. 'A stinking old cottage, but there's a bed. Just for one, though I don't mind sleeping on the floor!'

'Come on, then, Eddeth, before you have to carry me!'

They staggered past Jonas and Vik, who were debating their chances of finding a bed themselves.

'May as well sleep in a barn if they're going to leave that door open all night,' Vik grumbled.

Jonas' eyes lit up, thinking of the barn they'd slept in when they first arrived in Slussfall. 'That hay wasn't so bad.'

'No,' Vik agreed, heavy eyes almost closing. And too tired to wait another moment, he slapped Jonas on the back, urging him out of the hall.

Sigurd walked past them, back to his brother, who seemed reluctant to leave their injured men. Holgar had been carried into the fort, still unconscious, Bolli by his side. Torfinn had been stitched up and was now sound asleep and snoring. They both felt on edge, but Sigurd knew that they were going to struggle to even see in the morning if they didn't get some sleep. 'Come on,' he sighed, tugging his brother's sleeve. 'Go get Elin. I've found us all a cottage.'

'You have?'

'Mmmm, Falla Gundersen's offered us hers. She seems to think we have some sway with Ake, and who I am to tell her that he'd likely listen to his children before he listens to us!' His eyes met Ilene's, and she smiled smugly at him, arm through Berger Eivin's as they headed out of the hall together, cups of ale in their hands.

Sigurd muttered to himself, insisting that he didn't care.

Berger was welcome to her.

Reinar wasn't listening as his brother mumbled along beside him. Just the thought of bed had his body feeling heavy and lumberous. He stretched his hands above his head, trying to ignore battling feelings of guilt and desire, glancing around the hall, looking for Elin, though his mind was on Alys.

She would be gone in the morning, and yet he'd only just

found her again.

He rubbed his eyes, feeling annoyed.

Sleep would help, he tried to convince himself.

Sleep would help to set him right.

***

Alys was sure that she'd never been more tired in her life, though that wasn't true, she thought, remembering Ottby. And thoughts of Ottby whirled around her weary mind, trapping her in a state of exhaustion, unable to sleep at all. Magnus lay beside her, curled into a ball, and she couldn't quite believe it. She'd stroked his newly shorn hair as he fell asleep, head on her chest, and now he'd rolled away to the other side of the bed.

Leaning over, Alys pulled the furs up over his shoulder, wanting to keep him warm.

She hadn't wanted to sleep in the chamber Hakon had tried to rape her in – the one where Ivan had died, his blood still staining the floor – so Aldo had found them a tiny cottage tucked down past the hall, near the harbour gates. It reminded her of Lotta. She'd seen glimpses of her daughter sleeping in one of the cottages, frightened and cold. But where was she now?

Mind straining with weariness, Alys closed her eyes, one hand on Magnus' back, slipping into a dream.

***

Vik was snoring, which wasn't new, Jonas thought with a grumble, turning away from his noisy friend. The idea of the barn had sounded appealing to his weary mind, but in reality, it was freezing cold, and it stunk, and he thought of how many more comfortable alternatives there must have been.

Though it was better than the prison hole.

Eyes closed, Jonas felt relief loosen his tense muscles. Magnus was safe. Alys was safe. And now they just had to find a way north. Ollo had already given them the name of a man with a ship who regularly sailed from Orbo to Slussfall, having spotted him down on the pier. Jonas was grateful that Hakon Vettel had decided not to fire the ships. Grateful, and then, in a heartbeat, nearly asleep.

He saw Alys running towards him, and she was Lotta's age, long blonde hair in braids, decorated with ribbons; many ribbons, he remembered, with a smile. She had always been his to care for, to protect, from the very first moment Mirella had placed that tiny bundle into his arms.

He sighed, seeing the freckles on her nose as she lifted up a tiny white kitten, big eyes blinking, aiming to twist him around her little finger.

He was never going to let her go again.

***

'Magnus! Magnus!'

Alys was frantic. It was dark, and she didn't know where he was.

'He's gone!' Lotta was crying. 'Where's he gone?' She had crawled into her parent's bed after discovering that Magnus was missing.

She was five. Terrified.

Where was her brother?

Alys, eyes heavy with sleep, nightdress fluttering behind her, grabbed hold of Lotta's hand, not wanting to lose her too, and together they ran out of the cottage, into the night. 'Magnus!' Alys held a soapstone lamp in her other hand, the flame guttering, though the moon was full and bright, and she quickly located the dark lump of her seven-year-old son, lying curled up in front of the outbuilding, sound asleep.

Lotta was cross. 'He's sleepwalking again!' She looked up at her mother, whose face had relaxed.

'Here, take the lamp, Lotta, hold it there.' And bending down to Magnus, Alys tapped him gently on the shoulder. 'Magnus, wake up, come on now, we need to get you back to bed.' He didn't move, so she pulled more firmly, trying to turn him over, but when she did, she saw that it wasn't Magnus.

It was Arnon, and they were on the beach.

And there was no moon, just a stormy morning, and screaming women being rounded up like cattle in the distance, children running away, fleeing down the sand.

No Lotta anymore.

The arrow fluttered in Arnon's chest, shot through the mark of the hunter tattoo.

There was no blood.

And Arnon opened his eyes, reaching out to grab her arm. 'Hello, Alys.'

Alys' own eyes popped open.

She was wet through, panting. Her dream rushed back to her, and she shivered, seeing the first signs of dawn creeping under the cottage door. There was nothing new about the nightmare. She had it regularly, each time as terrifying as the last. Eyes closing again, wanting some more sleep, she wondered if she would ever be free of Arnon, hating that he had a hold over her, dead or alive.

And then she froze, remembering the rest of the dream.

Eyes open again, she reached out a hand.

But there was no Magnus.

***

It hadn't been hard to find them.

The voice had told him where to go.

The woman who came into his dreams had been so eager to help him. She had led him to Slussfall, where he'd slipped into the fort amidst all the chaos, hood low over his face, not wanting to be recognised.

The woman had been more than helpful.

She had shown him where to find a hoard of silver coins, buried in the forest, and with it, he'd commissioned a fisherman, who had a crew of six men looking to get back up north quickly, no friends of Ake Bluefinn or the Vilanders. They were Northerners, eager to be gone.

Arnon had paid them to stay on board, ready to leave at dawn's first light.

She had told him that too.

Now all he needed was his wife.

***

Though she felt worried, Alys wasn't surprised to find Magnus gone. He'd been sleepwalking since he was a little boy. Over the years, she'd often found him curled up with their livestock. Sometimes, he'd walked as far as Stina's front porch; even into the hall during summer when the doors would remain open all night. Ullaberg was small, and after so many years, Magnus could easily walk the entire village with his eyes closed, but Slussfall?

Alys lifted her hood over her hair, feeling the rain, cold on her face. It was a stormy morning, and she shivered as she walked, thunder booming overhead. The fort was a mess with so many men littered around, sleeping, most without shelter, now getting wet. They barely stirred, though, worn out, drunk.

Alys had no idea where her grandfather and Vik had slept, Reinar or Sigurd either, but suddenly, getting a sense of Magnus, she turned towards the harbour gates.

Panicking now, feeling Magnus' terror, she started running.

The gates were open, most of the bodies cleared away, and Alys slipped through them quickly, heading down to the piers, the strong smell of death in her nostrils.

Eyes jumping, fear gripping her heart, she saw Sigurd's ship, and many more, but no one appeared to be on board. The Ottby men were mostly inside the hall. There were a few merchant ships, trading ships, and...

Alys froze.

She was having a dream.

A nightmare.

Arnon stood on a pier, smiling at her, hand over Magnus' mouth, knife at his throat. 'Come along then, Wife, we have a daughter to find, don't we?'

She was having a dream.

Alys tried to wake up.

'Did you think I would let you get away with killing my dreamer? My dear Mother?' came the voice, and Alys spun around, seeing a dark-robed woman standing by the open gates, long white braid hanging down to her waist. 'That I was going to let you defeat me and ruin my plans for Alekka, Alys de Sant? That you would simply kill the Vettels, *my* Vettels, and go back to Ottby with the Vilanders? With your precious Reinar?' Alari laughed. 'As my father said, this is a war, and I am the Goddess of Magic. And with magic...' She clicked her fingers, pointing them at Arnon, '... anything is possible!'

Alys turned back to Arnon, who gripped Magnus like a man holding an enemy he was prepared to kill.

'Well, what are you waiting for, Alys? I will take you either way, but if you come quietly, I promise not to kill our son.'

Alys could read his thoughts. They were violent, screaming and loud, and she knew that he meant it. She had no weapon. Nothing but her cloak. So, hands by her sides, heart heavy with dread, she started moving towards the pier. Magnus wanted to kill his father, she could feel it. He wanted to save her, but he couldn't.

And the only way she could see to save them both was to go with Arnon.

'You'll see,' Arnon grinned as Alys approached, walking down the pier. 'You'll see, Alys. We're going to have the most wonderful adventure. Our family, together again!'

THE END

EPILOGUE

'I wasn't aware that we were enemies, Mirella. When did that become so?'

Mirella stood by the window, watching the snow fall.

It fell like a blanket, so heavy and cold. She shivered, turning around, forcing a smile. 'But we are not. I have never taken up against you, Alari. Why would you think that?'

'You know what happened to Hakon? To Ivan?'

Mirella blinked slowly. 'I saw, of course. It was a shame.'

'A shame? But you mothered those boys! Mothered them, then abandoned them! Just as you abandoned Jesper.' Alari was enraged, moving quickly across the flagstones, eye sparking with fury. 'You had such promise once, such a desire to serve, and now where are you?'

'You have come to me, Alari, so you know exactly where I am.'

Alari stopped, sensing more trouble than she'd anticipated. She cocked her head to one side. 'Eskvir trusts you.'

'Of course, we want the same thing, he and I. We all do.'

In two strides, Alari was breathing on her, skin crawling. 'You are different. Different than I remember. Why is that?' She looked Mirella over, though she appeared much the same as when she'd last seen her: shining blonde hair, delicate nose smattered with freckles, long, elegant neck. There were a few new lines now, a growing maturity about her, Alari saw, though nothing she wouldn't have expected.

But those green eyes... they were almost lifeless.

Devoid of feeling.

'I am happier,' Mirella insisted, smiling with some enthusiasm now. 'Being here, away from Jesper, it was the escape I needed. He was a cruel man, despite any love he may have had for me. Likely you're just seeing me as I was meant to be. At peace. Here. Away from everything.'

'You think Orvala is somewhere to hide? That you won't be found?'

'Oh no,' Mirella murmured, listening to the fire crackling behind her. 'I will be found, Alari. And soon.'

READ NEXT

BLOOD OF THE RAVEN
An Epic Fantasy Adventure
(The Lords of Alekka Book 3)

THE LORDS OF ALEKKA

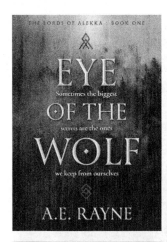

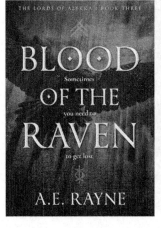

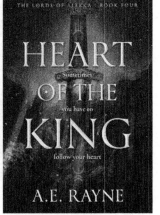

THE FURYCK SAGA

Sign up to my newsletter, so you don't miss out
on new release information!

http://www.aerayne.com/sign-up

ABOUT A.E. RAYNE

Some things about me, the author:

I live in Auckland, New Zealand, with my husband, three kids and three dogs. When I'm not writing, you can find me editing, designing my book covers, and trying to fit in some sleep (though mostly I'm dreaming of what's coming next!).

I have a deep love of history and all things Viking. Growing up with a Swedish grandmother, her heritage had a great influence on me, so my fantasy tales lean heavily on Viking lore and culture. And also winter. I love the cold!

I like to immerse myself in my stories, experiencing everything through my characters. I don't write with a plan; I take cues from my characters, and follow where they naturally decide to go. I like different points of view because I see the story visually, with many dimensions, like a tv show or a movie. My job is to stand at the loom and weave the many coloured threads together into an exciting story.

I promise you characters that will quickly feel like friends, and villains that will make you wild, with plots that twist and turn to leave you wondering what's coming around the corner. And, like me, hopefully, you'll always end up a little surprised by how I weave everything together in the end!

To find out more about A.E. Rayne and her writing
visit her website: www.aerayne.com